DYNASTY 14

The Campaigners

Also in the *Dynasty* series:

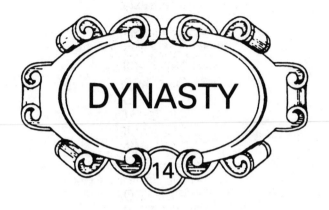

DYNASTY

14

The Campaigners

Cynthia Harrod-Eagles

Macdonald

A Macdonald Book

First published in Great Britain in 1991 by
Macdonald & Co (Publishers) Ltd
London & Sydney

British Library Cataloguing in Publication Data
Harrod – Eagles, Cynthia
The Campaigners
I. Title
823.914 [F]

ISBN 0-356-19535-X

Typeset by Leaper and Gard Limited, Bristol, Great Britain
Printed by Mackays of Chatham PLC, Chatham, Kent

Macdonald & Co (Publishers) Ltd
Orbit House
1 New Fetter Lane
London EC4A 1AR

A member of Maxwell Macmillan Pergamon Publishing Corporation

For my three lovely children, going out into the world:

> Ille potens sui
> Laetusque deget, cui licet in diem
> Dixisse 'Vixi'.

> Horace: *Odes*, III, xxix, 41

THE MORLANDS O

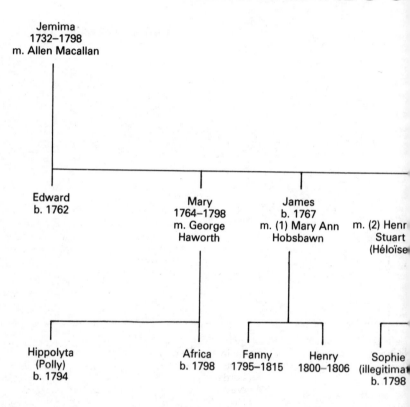

Jemima
1732–1798
m. Allen Macallan

Edward
b. 1762

Mary
1764–1798
m. George
Haworth

James
b. 1767
m. (1) Mary Ann
Hobsbawn

m. (2) Henr
Stuart
(Héloïse

Hippolyta
(Polly)
b. 1794

Africa
b. 1798

Fanny
1795–1815

Henry
1800–1806

Sophie
(illegitima
b. 1798

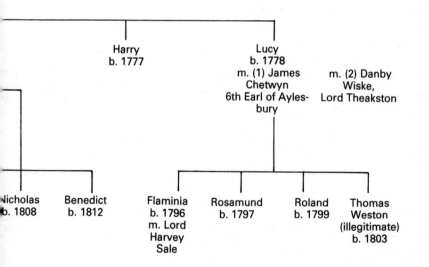

Harry
b. 1777

Lucy
b. 1778
m. (1) James
Chetwyn
6th Earl of Ayles-
bury

m. (2) Danby
Wiske,
Lord Theakston

Nicholas
b. 1808

Benedict
b. 1812

Flaminia
b. 1796
m. Lord
Harvey
Sale

Rosamund
b. 1797

Roland
b. 1799

Thomas
Weston
(illegitimate)
b. 1803

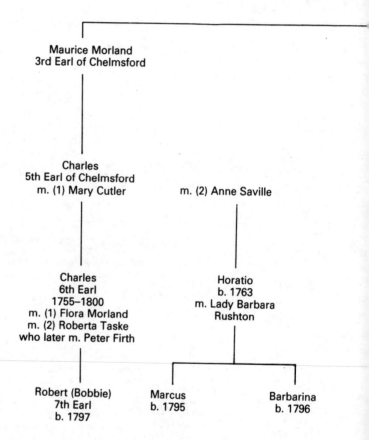

Maurice Morland
3rd Earl of Chelmsford

Charles
5th Earl of Chelmsford
m. (1) Mary Cutler

m. (2) Anne Saville

Charles
6th Earl
1755–1800
m. (1) Flora Morland
m. (2) Roberta Taske
who later m. Peter Firth

Horatio
b. 1763
m. Lady Barbara
Rushton

Robert (Bobbie)
7th Earl
b. 1797

Marcus
b. 1795

Barbarina
b. 1796

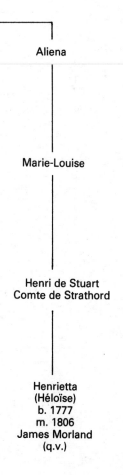

Aliena

Marie-Louise

Henri de Stuart
Comte de Strathord

Henrietta
(Héloïse)
b. 1777
m. 1806
James Morland
(q.v.)

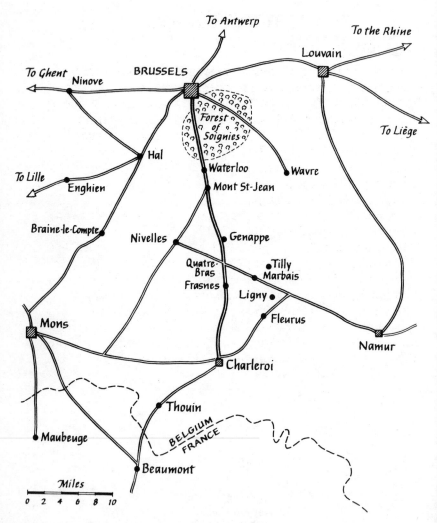

Area of the Waterloo Campaign

BIBLIOGRAPHY

Over the years the Waterloo campaign has been intensively examined and extensively described, and there is a wealth of excellent books for anyone wanting to read further. As one of the most readable and accessible, I can thoroughly recommend David Chandler's *Waterloo — The Hundred Days* for a general account of the affair. For a more detailed study, Sir John Fortescue's excellent *The Campaign of Waterloo* is now available as a separate volume from the rest of his massive *History of the British Army*.

In addition there are a great many personal diaries and memoirs written about the Waterloo campaign, many of which are available in published form. May I particularly recommend General Cavalie Mercer's *Journal of the Waterloo Campaign*; *A British Rifleman* by Major George Simmons; and for the French view, *The Notebooks of Captain Coignet*.

Finally I should like to recommend Sir Charles Oman's *Wellington's Army, 1809–1814*, which contains all the fascinating things he discovered about the army which didn't quite fit into the chronicle of events of his formal *History of the Peninsular War*.

BOOK ONE

The Exiles

Breathes there the man, with soul so dead,
Who never to himself hath said,
'This is my own, my native land!'
Whose heart hath ne'er within him burn'd,
As home his footsteps he hath turned
From wandering on a foreign strand!

Sir Walter Scott: Patriotism

CHAPTER ONE

March 1815

James Morland struggled to wakefulness from a heavy and unsatisfying sleep, and blinked for a moment in the grey light, unable to place himself in space or time.

Beside him his wife Héloïse pushed herself up onto one elbow and said sleepily, 'James? What is it?'

'I was dreaming,' he said. His voice sounded thick. 'I was riding over Marston Moor with Fanny. She was cantering ahead of me, and there was a deep ditch and I knew she hadn't seen it. I tried to call out to her, but I couldn't make any sound ...' Héloïse's hand rested on his arm as his voice trailed away. 'It was horrible.'

'It's still early,' she said. 'Go back to sleep, love.'

'Yes,' he said hopelessly. He was too wide awake now. He knew he wouldn't sleep again.

She must have heard the hopelessness, for the hand became hesitant, and she said tentatively, 'Can I get you anything?'

'No,' he said, and to break the contact with her turned over on his side away from her. He could feel her still looking at him, frowning; then after a few moments heard her sigh and felt her lie down again, close, but not touching him. He kept very still until her breathing grew steady — she was very tired these days, and sleep came easily to her — and then he relaxed.

It was three weeks since Fanny — his daughter, his first-born, his special delight — had died in childbirth, and yet still at waking he had that moment of blankness before he remembered it; a grey moment of formless apprehension that something was wrong, that it would have been better for him if he had not woken, ever again. Three weeks, only three weeks. For twenty years there had been Fanny, and now there was nothing. If he lived to be eighty, he would never see her again.

He felt bad about Héloïse, with one small, distant part of his mind. He knew that she worried about him and wanted to comfort him; but there was nothing he could take from her. He couldn't even bear her to touch him. Wrong — selfish, perhaps? But he felt, and couldn't help feeling, that the grief was all his, and that he was alone with it. No-one else had loved Fanny as he had.

Sleep was completely dissipated now: he was wide awake in the early light. They had taken to leaving the bed-curtains open, because he'd been having nightmares, and waking in the pitch-blackness had frightened him. This was the ancestral Butts Bed, its age-blackened oak panels carved with jolly mediaeval revellers roistering amongst gigantic bunches of grapes, vine-leaves and wine-butts: canting heraldry for the family of the long-ago bride for whom it had been made. In this bed generations of Masters and Mistresses of Morland Place had slept, had celebrated their nuptials, had been born and had died. James himself had been born in this bed; so had Fanny; and in this bed, too, she had died, struggling to give birth to a dead child, a boy, who would have been heir to the whole estate.

Lying on his side, he was facing the bedside table on which stood his candle in the silver candlestick with the dolphin curled round it which he had used since boyhood; and his book — a much-thumbed copy of *Rasselas* at the moment — with his place kept by a bookmarker Fanny had made for him long ago. The plaited silk string with the Turks-head and tassel was growing frayed now, but he had used no other since the day she gave it to him with a mixture of triumph, regal condescension, and narrow-eyed watchfulness which was so peculiarly hers.

She had been — twelve? thirteen? — at the time; it was the first thing her new governess, Miss Rosedale, had induced her to make for him. A hard task it must have been to keep Fanny to it, and probably she had only done it at all in the hope of winning some favour from him. Even so it was not well done — Fanny would never have put more effort into something she didn't enjoy than was absolutely unavoidable — and

4

James's extravagant praise had won him a frown from the governess, who knew how little it was deserved.

Well, he had known that too; but she was his little girl, his own, and he could not love her wisely when he loved her too well. His eyes filled inexorably with tears, and he turned his face down into his arm to try to press them back. The grief rose fresh and hot in him from some seemingly inexhaustible well.

There had been a black time, just after the funeral, when he had been seized by a kind of madness, had not been able to believe that she was dead. *They had shut her in her coffin still alive!* He had woken night after night sweating with horror. She was scrabbling at the lid! She was crying out, terrified, suffocating! Night after night he had struggled out of bed, caught between sleeping and waking, crying out to her, *I'm coming! Fanny, I'm coming!*; had gone running down the chapel stairs, stumbling over the hem of his nightshirt, his hair on end with the horror of it. The first time it happened, the family chaplain, Father Aislaby, had heard him and had come down to find him trying in vain to lever up the stone cover to the vault with his fingernails. He shuddered at the memory; but at least the madness had been a relief from the endless pain of loss. Sleep provided at best only a brief respite. Every morning he woke to the leaden realisation that she was gone, and he would never see her again. The tears seeped helplessly past his closed lids, and he pressed his face harder into the crook of his arm so that Héloïse should not hear him weeping.

Breakfast was a quiet meal. Edward, James's elder brother, sat at the head of the table and looked around the grave faces assembled there. Beside him sat James and Father Aislaby. Héloïse, Mistress of Morland Place, and owner of it too, now, sat at the foot, looking worn to the bone, and casting, evidently without knowing it, anxious glances at her husband between almost every mouthful.

Along the other side of the table were Miss Rosedale, the governess, and her two former charges — James and Héloïse's daughter Sophie, and Héloïse's ward Mathilde. The young women of the house had extra reason to regret Fanny's death, for it had caused the cancellation of Sophie's coming-out, and Mathilde's wedding to John Skelwith, Master Builder of York.

In Edward's view the latter was particularly unfortunate, not only because Mathilde, in whose happiness he had a deep and tender interest, was in love with her betrothed, but also because any delay to the wedding could only lead to Skelwith's hanging around Morland Place. Skelwith was a very decent young man, and Edward liked him enough almost to think he was good enough for Mathilde; but his antecedents were unfortunate. He was the result of an illicit liaison between his mother, Mary Skelwith, and James, and though no-one but Edward, James and Héloïse knew it, the more Skelwith was exposed to them, the more chance there was of the secret's coming out.

There was one other place at the table, but it was empty. Fanny's, of course! The sight of it made Edward feel irritable. There was no reason why the chair should not have been removed and the others moved up a little — Edward, for one, would have eaten better without that empty place mutely reproaching him at every meal — but James would not have it. If James had had his way, Edward thought, he'd have even had her covers laid for her. He seemed to want to turn the whole house into a mausoleum.

Edward looked now at his brother with a familiar mixture of pity and annoyance. James was not exactly unkempt — he had been shaved and dressed like an unresisting puppet by his man Durban, who would never let appearances slip — but he sat inside his clothes as if they had nothing to do with him, nor he with the world; shrunken somehow, his face drawn, his eyes blank. Today, Edward thought, like every other day, he would wander about the house like a lost spirit, seeking out anything that would remind him of Fanny. It had been the same when their mother died: Edward had flung himself into the work of the estate as a remedy, while James had mooned about all day and drunk himself stupid on brandy every night.

Edward had never loved Fanny, and had criticised James's handling of her from her infancy upwards; but he was genuinely shocked and grieved at her death. Poor Fanny had been married — to that reprobate Hawker — for only a few months, and had died most horribly in giving birth to a still-born child, and Edward would not have wished such a fate on anyone, least of all his own niece, his own brother's daughter.

Why, then, did the sight of James fill him with almost as much impatience as pity? He felt angry with himself that he should feel James's grief was as overstrung as his love had been. Good God, his brother had lost his eldest and favourite daughter: he had every right to be distraught with anguish! But Edward couldn't help seeing how worrying about him increased the burden both to Héloïse and to Sophie.

He shook the thoughts away and took his eyes off his brother's face and concentrated instead on the day ahead. His mind slipped into the familiar business of running the estate and filled it comfortably like a favourite shabby coat. He had to go out to North Fields to inspect the lambs — Shepherd had reported sickness amongst them, scours and staggers which sounded as though it might be serious. They were a special bunch, too, he thought with a frown, the fruits of his cross-breeding plan with a prize Merino ram, and the last he wanted to lose.

And this afternoon the Inspector-General was coming to look at half a dozen three-year-olds with a view to purchasing them as cavalry remounts. If he liked them, they'd probably go eventually to the Blues or the Life Guards, who still rode only black horses — the rest of the cavalry having gone over to a mixture of blacks, bays and browns. Edward hoped so: the Blues and the Life Guards were the only heavy dragoons who rode long-tailed horses, and Edward didn't approve of docking.

This latest business of Boney escaping from Elba and taking France again was shocking, of course, he thought; but a renewal of the war meant more Morland horses sold, which was good for the estate. And then there were the cereal crops — war kept corn prices high. Life had to go on, whatever your personal grief. If only James could understand that, and keep himself busy, instead of moping...

The butler, Ottershaw, came in with a letter, and everyone looked up. It was not the right time for the post to have been collected, so it must have been delivered by hand. Mathilde in particular looked at it with keen anticipation, which faded as

Ottershaw handed it to Edward, saying, 'It came by private courier, sir, so there was nothing to pay.'

Edward examined the outside, aware of all the eyes on him. It might be something important, even exciting; at least it was an interruption to the sad routine.

'It's addressed simply "Morland". Shall I open it?' Edward asked of the table at large. As the elder Morland brother, he had always been nominal head of the household, and since his mother's death had held the estate in trust for Fanny. But when Fanny died before reaching her majority, the Trust had terminated and a secret clause in her grandmother's Will had come into effect, by which everything had passed to Héloïse. It had been unexpected, and yet somehow not surprising: Héloïse seemed exactly the right person to perpetuate those standards and values which his mother had embodied, which were somehow the spirit of Morland Place. She would be a better guardian for the Morland family than Fanny could ever have been, and Edward accepted her gladly, as he never could have accepted his niece.

Well, Héloïse was now Mistress of Morland Place; but Edward still sat at the head of the table, and receiving a smile of acquiescence from her, he opened the letter himself and began to read it.

'I wonder who would use a private courier?' Sophie said into the waiting silence.

'John does sometimes,' said Mathilde, 'to take instructions to his employees in other towns. I suppose most business people do.' She was still at the stage where she introduced her beloved's name at every possible juncture in conversation.

'More likely to be an attorney's courier,' said Miss Rosedale, eating a kipper bones-and-all, as was her habit. 'Sophie, I think you should practise on the pianoforte today. You've hardly been at the instrument all week. And then we'll read some sermons together. If you'd like to join us, Mathilde, we can all get on with our sewing and read aloud in turn. There are shirts in the poor-basket, if you've nothing of your own.'

Héloïse gave her a grateful look, knowing that Miss Rosedale was trying to keep the young ones' minds occupied, and also to give her leisure to attend to her multifarious duties.

Edward had been reading the letter with a frown, and now looked up and said, 'Well, here's a go! Fanny's grandpa's dead — old Hobsbawn! I don't know who should properly have this — you, James, or Héloïse. What happens now, I wonder?'

He held out the letter, and as James made no move to take it, Father Aislaby passed it down to Héloïse.

Héloïse scanned the page and said, 'It is from Jasper Hobsbawn — old Mr Hobsbawn's cousin. It is very short. *"Sirs, I regret to inform you that Mr Joseph Hobsbawn died during the night of the 9th of March, of a seizure. By the terms of his Will, his entire estate passes to his grand-daughter Mrs Hawker. I await your instructions."* And that is all. What a very curious letter. But perhaps he is deeply grieved.'

'It sounds to me more resentful than grieved,' Edward said, 'and who can wonder? He must have been hoping at least to inherit the old man's spinning-mills, after all the work he's put into them. But he doesn't mention Fanny's death. Surely he must know about it? You did write to old Hobsbawn, didn't you, Héloïse?'

'Of course. I wrote to him at the same time as I wrote to Mr Hawker.' She sometimes felt that everyone forgot Fanny's husband, absent in Vienna at the Congress, rather too easily. He may have been unsuitable material for a husband, but he was Fanny's choice, and Héloïse at least believed that he had loved Fanny truly. 'Perhaps the letter might have gone astray.'

'More likely it's lying about Hobsbawn House somewhere, unopened,' Father Aislaby said wisely. 'It must have arrived shortly after the old gentleman died, and I don't suppose anyone would have been thinking about opening letters then. I expect it got put with a lot of other papers, and no-one's got around to dealing with it yet.'

'But what a queer thing,' Edward said, 'that the old man should have died on the same night as —' He stopped short as James gave him a bitter look; and then gave a slight shrug. It was unreasonable of James to suppose that they could go on without ever mentioning Fanny's death.

'But what will happen now?' Héloïse asked anxiously. 'If the mills were to come to Fanny, does that mean they now come to me? Or to the Mr Jasper of the terse letter? I must say that I do not at all want them, and he, poor man, must deserve them as much as anyone.'

James turned on her sharply. 'It's not a matter of deserving. Want them or not, if they were Fanny's, they will be yours. You will not give away anything that was hers.'

'But, James, I have so much,' Héloïse protested gently. 'What would I do with spinning-mills? I know nothing of such things.'

'That's nothing to the point. You can employ a manager, as others do. No-one would expect you to run them yourself. Fanny wanted them, and they were hers by right, and she shall have them, even if it is by proxy.'

Héloïse, seeing he was speaking not rationally, but from his deranged emotions, would have dropped the subject, but Father Aislaby had been struck by the legal aspects of the affair, and mused aloud, 'I imagine it will depend on which of the two demises actually took place first. It might be a very interesting case —'

'Interesting!' James glared.

Aislaby was not perturbed. 'Indeed. If Fanny predeceased Hobsbawn, even by only a few minutes, the estate will go to his residuary legatee – whoever that may be. But if the old gentleman died first, Fanny would have inherited, for however short a time, and the Hobsbawn estate would have been part of her estate when she died. A pretty tangle — and the stuff of which Chancery lawyers' fortunes are made.'

Edward took the letter back, and re-read it. 'It says he died *during* the night of the ninth. That could mean anything from sunset to sunrise. I suppose the first thing would be to find out exactly what time he died.'

'Why bother?' James said harshly. 'You see Jasper Hobsbawn believes the estate has gone to Fanny —'

'But he does not know she is dead,' Héloïse said, looking at him with unhappy eyes. This was not like the man she had loved and married.

'We don't know that. Most likely he's read your letter and everything is settled. Why stir up trouble? Hobsbawn meant Fanny to have the mills — well, she shall have them.'

'But, James, perhaps it is not right!'

He stood up abruptly. 'The letter says "during the night of

10

the ninth". Fanny died in the early hours of the tenth, didn't she? Then leave it be!' he snapped. 'She shall have what is hers by right!'

Héloïse looked stricken, and Miss Rosedale, with an appearance of calm, began gathering her charges up and ushering them from the table. Aislaby said, 'The truth will come out, sooner or later. The Will will have to be proved, and it will all come out. Someone had better write to Jasper Hobsbawn and ask him what time the old man died, and get the whole matter straightened out.'

'No-one's going to rob Fanny of her inheritance,' James growled, and pushing his chair back, stalked out of the room, leaving an uncomfortable silence behind him.

'Well, Héloïse?' Edward said after a moment. 'You're Mistress of Morland Place. What shall it be?'

She looked distressed, but there was no doubt in her mind. 'Whatever comes of it, it is only the truth that matters. I shall put the matter in the hands of good Mr Pobgee, the lawyer, and he will know what is best to do. I shall send this letter to him, and he can write to Mr Jasper Hobsbawn, if it is necessary.'

Aislaby nodded and stood up. 'Ten to one but that James is right, and young Hobsbawn knows all about it; but it's best to be sure.'

At Chelmsford House in Pall Mall, Robert St Vincent Morland, the eighteen-year-old Earl of Chelmsford, ran up the stairs two at a time and burst into the small saloon crying, 'Mama! Have you heard the news?'

He broke off abruptly when he discovered that his mother was not alone. Roberta, formerly Countess of Chelmsford and now Mrs Firth, was entertaining a morning visitor; seated on the sopha opposite her was the trim, severely fashionable figure of James Morland's sister Lucy, Lady Theakston.

'Oh, I beg your pardon, ma'am — I didn't know you were here,' said Bobbie. He was a tall, still a rather gangling young man, whose feet and hands seemed too big for him. He was very fair, with golden curls and round blue eyes just like his mother's, and that fine skin which shews every movement of the blood. His cheeks flushed now simply with consciousness

11

of being looked at. 'I didn't see your horses outside,' he said to Lucy to fill the brief silence.

'Probably because I sent Parslow home with them,' she replied, and indicated with an economical movement of the hand her daughter who was sitting beside her. Lady Rosamund Chetwyn, second of the three children Lucy had borne to her first husband, the Earl of Aylesbury, was aged seventeen; tall, freckled, sandy-haired, and to judge by her angular posture and restless hands, not yet accustomed to the dignities of a grown-up gown and coiffure. Both she and her mother were wearing black bands for Fanny. 'I mean to walk as far as the Admiralty afterwards and then back across the Park. If I don't exercise Rosamund,' Lucy said, as though her daughter were a horse, 'she gets restless.'

Rosamund didn't seem to mind this form of address at all, and grinned up at Bobbie as though she were still wearing plaits. 'Mama don't like it above half that she can't bring me out until we're out of black gloves. She hoped to get me married and off her hands by midsummer!'

'Hold your tongue, you abominable child,' Lucy said, without heat. 'To think that I came back from Vienna just to bring you out! It was the unluckiest thing, Fanny's dying like that,' she sighed to Roberta, who raised an eyebrow at the choice of adjective. 'Of course, strictly speaking we need to wear black gloves only for six weeks, but it might just as well be six months: there's nothing shabbier than a launch half-way through the Season! It looks so half-hearted — and I shall need all the help I can to get Rosamund off, despite everything her governess has done.'

'I don't mean to get married at all, Mama, so you may as well save your trouble,' Rosamund said, with a boldness which so disturbed Roberta that she intervened to change the subject.

'But what was it you wanted to say, Bobbie dear? Have you some news?'

Bobbie sat down on the edge of a chair and pushed a careless hand through his fair curls. 'Oh, Lord! Yes, Mama — I met Lord Anstey in the street outside Brookes's, and he said that Rothschild's courier arrived last night from Vienna.'

Lucy's expression sharpened with interest. 'Vienna? Hah!

Rothschild's are always first with the news. I always apply to them sooner than the Foreign Office — their messengers travel faster than Bathurst's. What is it, Bobbie? I haven't heard from Danby for over a week.' Her new husband was still in Vienna, one of the Duke of Wellington's aides at the Congress.

'Well, ma'am, it seems they have signed a new coalition treaty against Boney! Russia, Prussia and Austria are to provide seven hundred thousand men between them, all to be marched into Flanders as soon as they can be levied. And we are to provide five million pounds in gold —'

'Five million? But I haven't seen a single gold coin in years,' Roberta exclaimed. 'Nothing but this dreadful paper money. Where on earth will we get so much gold?'

'Rothschild's will provide the specie — isn't that right, Bobbie?' Lucy answered. 'I don't know what we'd do without them. Danby says they've practically financed the war single-handed. So we've signed a treaty? Well, this is famous news!' A quick frown drew her fair brows together. 'But the devil of it is that all our seasoned troops are across the Atlantic fighting that ridiculous American war.'

'Only the infantry, ma'am — we still have our cavalry,' Bobbie said eagerly.

'True enough — but what use is cavalry without infantry?' She shook her head, and Roberta, who had known her for a long time, smiled inwardly at how completely Lucy had become an army wife since marrying Danby Wiske, now Lord Theakston, where for so many years she had spoken of nothing but naval matters, the disposition of ships and the promotion prospects of captains and junior admirals.

'It was the unluckiest thing, to have shipped off the Penin-sula veterans just at the moment Boney chooses to escape. Apart from the 52nd and the 23rd, we've no-one who's seen any action,' Lucy went on.

'What about the Guards?' Roberta said.

Lucy wrinkled her nose. 'Hyde Park soldiers,' she said dismissively. 'Second battalions.'

'Yes, ma'am — but at any rate, under the treaty we are to provide as many men as possible,' Bobbie continued, im-patient to get to the heart of the subject, 'and the Army of

Occupation is to join with the Dutch and Belgian forces as soon as they can, and the Duke of Wellington is to go to Brussels to take overall command.'

'The Duke? Oh, famous!' Rosamund exclaimed. 'If anyone can beat Boney, he can!'

Lucy quelled her with a look. 'And how many men are we to raise?'

'Lord Anstey spoke of a hundred and fifty thousand men immediately and more later,' Bobbie went on, and turned a burning look on his mother. 'He said there's bound to be a flood of volunteers — everyone wants the chance to finish Boney off once and for all. And the militia are to be transformed into regulars; and as for officers, Lord Anstey says there are queues forming at the Horseguards already — men my age, and younger! Oh, Mama —!'

Here it was at last. Roberta looked alarmed. 'Now, Bobbie —' she began, but her son interrupted passionately before she could get to the inevitable negative.

'But, Mama, everyone will be going! It's the most tremendous thing that ever happened, and once the Duke has beaten Boney, the war will be over and I'll never have another chance! Oh please, mayn't I have my colours now? I want it above anything!'

'Lord! How splendid!' Rosamund cried, jumping to her feet. 'Oh, I wish I were a man! It isn't fair, really it isn't! To think of going to Flanders and marching with Old Hookey into France and fighting Boney — oh, Bobbie, you are lucky!'

Roberta found her voice. 'It's out of the question. No, really, Bobbie, how could you even ask?'

Despair filled the earl's pleasant young face. 'Oh Mama, please! You can't imagine how important it is to me!'

Lucy was fond of Roberta, and seeing her friend's distress, she interrupted on her behalf. 'Don't talk like a fool, Bobbie,' she said with her accustomed bluntness. 'You're the earl. Until you marry and provide yourself with an heir, you can't afford to risk your life.'

Bobbie reddened with embarrassment and distress. 'I beg your pardon, ma'am, but I already have an heir —'

'Yes,' Lucy said scornfully, 'your uncle Horatio, and his son, your cousin Marcus — both of them regular soldiers, and probably on their way to Flanders this very moment! If you go too, that will be all the eggs in the same basket. Off you'll all march into battle, and supposing you all three get killed? Use your wits, Bobbie. Don't you see you're upsetting your mother?'

Bobbie, still very red, turned towards his mother and stammered an apology.

'It's all right, darling,' Roberta said, distressed as much for him as for herself. 'I know how much you want to go and fight alongside Marcus, but really, it wouldn't do, you know. An earl has responsibilities.'

'Yes, of course, I understand,' he muttered, his eyes cast down in a vast effort at control. 'I'm sorry — I shouldn't have mentioned it. If you will excuse me now —' And with an awkward bow, he retired to nurse his *chagrin* in private.

'Oh dear,' said Roberta, looking at the door that had closed behind him. 'He does mind it so dreadfully.'

'He'll get over it,' Lucy said shortly. She was not normally noted for her tact, but seeing how the exchange had upset Roberta, she now firmly changed the subject. 'But we were talking of Rosamund's come-out. Of course Sophie was supposed to be coming out this Season as well, and we were going to launch them together, but now Héloïse talks of putting it off until the Little Season in October. I can't decide whether it would be better to bring Rosamund out then, or to wait until next year. What do you think, Rob? She'll be eighteen by then, but it isn't so very old, is it?'

Roberta tried to apply her mind to the subject. 'Eighteen is a very good age. Girls tended to be brought out much earlier when we were young, but I don't think it was necessarily better.'

Lucy pondered. 'On the other hand, I rather liked the idea of a joint ball, and I don't want to let Héloïse down.'

Rosamund looked hopeful. 'It would be better fun than coming out alone, Mama. Sophie's a dear creature! And there aren't near so many balls in the Little Season, so I wouldn't have so much opportunity to disgrace myself.'

Roberta looked shocked. 'I'm sure you wouldn't do any such thing.'

'Oh Lord, ma'am, you haven't seen me dance,' Rosamund

15

said cheerfully. 'A squadron of the Northern Dragoons is lighter on its feet.'

'You would dance very well if you would put yourself to the trouble of it,' Lucy said severely. 'I know what's in your mind: you hope to frighten off the men so that no-one will offer for you. But I tell you what, Rosamund — if I managed to get your sister Flaminia off, as dull as she was, I shan't be beaten by you, so resign yourself to it! You'll marry whoever I choose for you.'

Rosamund, with a wicked gleam in her eye, was plainly considering trying her mother's patience still further, when she caught a beseeching look from Roberta and changed her mind. A demure expression came over her face and she lowered her eyes and said meekly, 'Yes, Mama.'

Lucy narrowed her eyes suspiciously, and Rosamund, pleased with the effect she was creating, got up mincingly from her seat and walked across the room to a table by the window where some journals were laid out, and began leafing through them, with what she plainly imagined was a sweet, womanly expression on her face.

Seeing Lucy was about to expostulate, Roberta said hastily, 'Has a new date been set for Mathilde's wedding? What a sad thing for her! I know she was no blood-kin to Fanny, but they had been brought up under the same roof for many years, and she must feel it as much as anyone.'

'Mathilde had no love for Fanny,' Lucy said, 'nor Fanny for her. In fact, I don't think anyone really liked Fanny, except for her governess.'

'Oh, don't say so! You liked Fanny,' Roberta protested. 'After all, it was you who brought her out; and then when she spent her honeymoon in Vienna, you took great pains to introduce her and her husband to Society.'

Lucy shrugged. 'I had to do something. When Fanny needs must marry the most worthless reprobate in Christendom, someone must come to the rescue and restore her credit. Oh, that was like her! I'd come to think she was improved a little, when I had her for her come-out, but then to choose a gazetted fortune-hunter to marry! I can't understand why James gave in to her. It was a havey-cavey business — and dearly she paid for it, too, poor creature,' she added grimly.

'But you were asking about Mathilde's wedding: Héloïse writes to say that they've decided not to put it off any longer. There's going to be a very quiet ceremony on the 3rd of April, just the immediate family, no guests.'

'Such a pity for Mathilde. Every girl looks forward to her wedding.'

'Do they? I didn't,' Lucy said — unguardedly, considering that Rosamund was in the same room, though feigning not to listen. 'But I doubt whether either she or Skelwith has any ambition to go into Society, so it won't signify. Skelwith means to build an enormous house for them, with every modern convenience, as an advertisement to his trade: all fancy chimneys and wrought-iron balconies — you know the sort of thing —'

The door opened just then, and Roberta's face lit up as her husband, Peter Firth, came in. He had been Bobbie's tutor for many years, and as a young widow, Roberta had struggled for her son's sake against the deep attraction which developed between then, believing it would create a horrible scandal if they were to marry. But she had given in at last, and it had answered very well. Bobbie had been perfectly content to exchange a tutor for a father, and seeing his mother happy and blooming and wearing younger and frillier caps, he had shrugged off the gossip with the ease of the very young.

Now that his services were no longer required to teach Bobbie, Firth had begun a new and promising career as a secretary in the War Office under Lord Bathurst.

'Hullo!' he said. 'May I disturb you?'

'Oh, Peter,' Roberta said at once, 'Bobbie came in to tell us about the coalition treaty — have you heard?'

'Yes, our courier came in this morning with Wellington's report. It's splendid news, isn't it? We always used to say "The Congress dances but makes no progress", but they moved fast for once — Boney had only been in Paris for ten days! We're all in amazement at the miracle, that everyone is in agreement and everyone has sworn not to make any deals with Boney behind the others' backs. Let's hope it lasts!'

'But, Peter, Bobbie wants to go and volunteer. He wants me to buy him his colours.'

Firth looked at her cannily. 'You mustn't let it upset you,

love. Bobbie has a great deal of sense. He understands the situation.'

'Does he? He was so passionate.'

'Any young man would want to be in the thick of it — I do myself! But he knows it can't be.'

'But I hate to make him unhappy,' Roberta said mournfully.

'I tell you what, my love,' Firth said as though he had just thought of it, 'why don't we take him to Brussels, so that at least he can feel that he's a little closer to the hub of the universe?'

He got his effect. The two women stared at him, and Rosamund, her head bent over a ladies' journal, quivered.

'To Brussels? But Peter, how can we? How can you?'

He grinned. 'Easy enough for me. Bathurst wants a man on the spot, and owing to the intervention of a certain kind person —' he bowed in Lucy's direction — 'my name was put forward.'

'Oh, Peter, how wonderful!'

'Quite a promotion!' Lucy raised an eyebrow. 'Danby suggested you?'

'He did indeed — mentioned my name in despatches to Castlereagh, who passed it on to his lordship last night at the club.'

'I'm glad — and Bathurst couldn't do better, I'm sure.'

'Thank you, ma'am! So as I am to go to Brussels, my next concern is to secure myself some agreeable company. Should you like to come with me, Mrs Firth? And shall we ease Bobbie's pains and take him too?'

Roberta looked both eager and doubtful. 'Oh, I should love to go with you — but is it safe? I have just this minute told Bobbie he cannot risk himself —'

'Quite safe, my darling,' Firth laughed. 'Do you think I would suggest it otherwise? The army will be many weeks a-gathering, and when they are all assembled, they will march off to the French borders. Any fighting there is will take place on French soil, you may be sure of that.'

'But — surely — won't the Tyrant —?'

'Boney will have even more trouble getting an army together than we will. Don't believe all you hear about the

18

French being behind him to a man! What the French want most of all now is peace, and when Boney marched in, they did not so much welcome him as feel disinclined to fight him for the sake of the Bourbon! King Louis is not a man to inspire unquestioning devotion.'

'He ran like a rabbit as soon as Boney drew near Paris,' Lucy observed, 'and now he sits quivering in Ghent, making not the slightest push to get his kingdom back, as far as I've heard.'

'Very hard, ma'am, when you're his shape, to exert yourself,' Firth said with a smile. 'I think Boney's relying on the Allies' proverbial inability to agree about anything, and simply hoping we'll leave him alone. He doesn't realise that the reappearance of the Sheep-Worrier is the very thing to draw the Sheep together! I don't think he'll come flying out on the offensive — and even if he wanted to, I don't think he could raise a sufficient army before the autumn, by which time the Allies will be knocking on the door of the Tuileries again.' He looked at his wife again. 'So what do you say, love? Should you like to go to Brussels? Everyone will be there!'

'Everyone? Will they?'

'Oh yes. A great many people have gone already, for the investiture of the King of the Netherlands; and once Hookey and his staff arrive, it will be absolutely the place to be! Quite apart from the military and the diplomatic, there'll be half the *ton* there, to say nothing of all the mamas with unmarried daughters. I hear Mrs Fauncett has bespoken rooms for herself and Miss Lavinia in the Hôtel d'Angleterre; and Lady Tewkesbury is packing already. She never forgets the Duke has an eye for a pretty face!'

Roberta began to laugh, for Lady Tewkesury was her *bête noire*, a woman whose impertinent curiosity and sharp gossiping tongue had caused Roberta much distress in her time. 'Then we must certainly go. I should like to see her receive one of the Duke's famous set-downs!'

Firth turned to Lucy. 'I suppose Lord Theakston will be going to Brussels? He is sure to go with Wellington, is not he?'

'Yes, I suppose so. Since Castlereagh left him with the Duke when he came home, we must assume he means him to stay with him.'

Firth's eye travelled round the room to Rosamund, who had ceased to pretend not to listen, and he said, 'I wonder you do not come with us, and have Lady Rosamund's come-out in Brussels, ma'am.'

'Why, yes, it would be the very thing!' Roberta said. 'Oh, Lucy, what do you think? In Brussels it would not signify that it is late in the Season.'

Firth smiled. 'There will be handsome officers in plenty for her to dance with, to say nothing of princes and lords from all over Europe!'

Rosamund had almost stopped breathing, and was looking at her mother with an intensity which might have scorched a lesser mortal. Lucy deliberated without seeming to notice it. 'Launch her in Brussels? Yes, I suppose it might answer. It would certainly be agreeable to have Danby there to help me.' Her expression softened a little. She had expected to have to remain the rest of the year in England, and had been missing her husband a great deal more than she would ever have admitted.

Rosamund could hold her tongue no longer. 'Oh, Mama!' she cried, torn between ecstasy and fear, 'oh, please, please, do let's go! Oh, to be in Brussels where everything is happening! The Duke — the army! And *Marcus* will be there!'

Lucy looked at her askance. 'Marcus? You silly goose, you aren't still playing that childish game, are you? Depend upon it, Marcus hasn't had a thought to waste on you since he left these shores.'

With an heroic effort, Rosamund bit back her immediate response, and managed instead to say, 'Oh no, Mama, of course not. But it would be very agreeable to see him again.'

Lucy eyed her narrowly, and then shrugged. If Rosamund were going to be difficult, it would be as well to have her do it in a foreign country, where it could be more easily passed off. And if she didn't make a suitable attachment before the summer, there would be nothing lost, for she could bring her out again in London in the autumn without its seeming in any way untoward. That and the thought of being with Danby again were enough to persuade her.

'Very well,' she said at last, 'we'll go.'

'Oh, excellent!' said Roberta. 'I'm so glad, Lucy. It will be so agreeable to have your company while Peter is occupied.'

'And it occurs to me,' Lucy went on thoughtfully, 'that perhaps I should ask Héloïse if she would like me to take Sophie for her. If it answers for Rosamund, it will do so much more for Sophie. In Brussels she may put off her mourning without offending; and she is such a little, dark, foreign-looking girl that perhaps she might take better over there than in England.'

Firth was amused both at Lucy's reasoning and language. 'You might get an exiled French nobleman for her,' he said. 'Sixteen quarterings and pockets to let! Think how grateful your sister-in-law would be!'

Roberta gave him a stern look and said firmly, 'It must be very sad for the poor child, shut up there at Morland Place, with everyone grieving, and no companion of her own age. I think it would be a kindness to take her.'

'Very well — I'll write at once,' Lucy said with decision. 'We'll want to be off as soon as possible, of course.'

'Certainly. Time and the lure of matrimony wait for no man,' Firth murmured.

Morland Place was a house that seemed to engender routine; and certainly there was always so much for the Mistress to do that without routine she would not have been able to get by. Pleasure as well as work had its seasons and hours. Each day, when she had finished her early tasks, Héloïse liked to shake off all companions but her dogs — the old grey-muzzled hound Kithra, and the plumy-tailed spaniel Castor — and go upstairs to the nursery to visit her sons.

Today, the 1st of April, was chill and sunny, but there was a good fire in the day-nursery, and the children were sitting by it, engrossed in a game together. Their heads were bent over some toy soldiers that they were pushing about the floor, while Nicholas murmured a narrative for the action. Héloïse looked at them tenderly, glad that they were such good company for each other. They made their own world for themselves, and the troubles of the house touched them only obliquely.

Kithra pushed past her and padded straight over to

21

Nicholas, to jab his cold nose into the boy's ear. Nicholas laughed and put up his hands, and Kithra nudged under them, his yellow eyes shining with love. From the beginning he had regarded Nicholas as his own property, to care for and defend. It was by Kithra's tail that the boy had first pulled himself to his feet, and he had taken his first frail, tottering steps clinging to the hound's patient neck.

Nicholas was seven now, and still looking as though a breath might blow him away: thin, transparent-looking, his head too large on a neck too spindly, so that it seemed as though it might bend at any moment like a top-heavy flower. Above his broad, bony forehead, his hair was thin and soft and pale fawn in colour; below, his eyes were large and pale-blue and intense. Héloïse loved him consumingly, but Niocholas adored only his father, and accepted her love without comment or enthusiasm. Even now, as she entered, his first words as he scrambled to his feet were, 'Where's Papa? Is he coming up?'

'I don't think so, my darling,' she said, going to him to pass a loving hand over his brow: under the guise of pushing back his hair, she could feel if he had a fever. Nicholas pulled his head away from her, not irritably, but deliberately, under-standing the subterfuge.

'Why not? Where is he? He never comes now.'

'He is very busy at the moment, my love. I'm sure he will come later,' Héloïse said, trying to sound convinced.

Benedict meanwhile had not been waiting patiently for his turn for her attention. He was just three years old and still, in his petticoats and long curls, very much the baby. His face was heart-shaped and attractive, his eyes lustrous and dark with long lashes, his hair black and curly, his smile, when he wished it to be, ravishing. But no-one would ever have mistaken Benedict for a girl-child at any point in his life. He was as vigorous as a weed, and as healthy as Nicholas was sickly — except for a tendency to have dreadful nightmares. He was noisy, boisterous, devilish — also charming, beguiling, thoroughly manipulative. He was twining himself round his mother's legs, but if she had ignored him for Nicholas one moment longer, he would have pinched or bitten her for attention, and risked the consequences.

Benedict seemed to be his father's favourite, for he was easy to love and easy with his love, a child of casual wet kisses and happy crows of laughter. Before Fanny's death, James had liked to play with Benedict, hoist him shrieking on to his shoulders and run with him, wrestle him, toss him about, take him up before him on his saddle. Benedict accepted these as his due, while Nicholas watched with passionate, covetous eyes the embraces he would have valued and which Benedict took for granted.

James never wrestled with Nicholas — he was always too afraid of hurting him, or bringing on one of his asthma attacks. He spoke to Nicholas always gravely, and looked at him too little, for in James love and guilt were inextricably entangled. He blamed himself for his elder son's frailty, and didn't know how to give him the love they both needed; which he lavished, instead, on Benedict.

Yet in spite of this, the boys remained friends. Nicholas protected Benedict, bullied him as much as he was allowed to, and wrapped him round with a possessive love; while Benedict tormented his staid elder to distraction, but respected and minded him more than anyone else. They played together without quarrelling, and had invented a secret language and many elaborate, obsessive rituals to their play, as children will who are isolated from others of their own age.

They were 'Bendy' and 'Nicky' to each other; except sometimes when they were alone together with no grown-up near, when they would adopt strange personae invented by Nicholas, and become 'Captain Bean' and 'Mister Nister'; sinister characters who addressed each other in grave ritual exchanges which, to an outsider, would have made no sense at all.

Benedict, having claimed his mother's attention, could not now think of anything to say, but as he would not relinquish his hold on her, Héloïse sat down and took him into her lap, and thus pinned down by him, was allowed to continue to talk to Nicholas.

'Are you well this morning, my darling? Has the rash gone?'

'Yes Mama,' Nicholas said impatiently. He hated his frailty, hated to have his health mentioned, even though this very pent-up anger so often brought on his asthma. His breathing this morning was noisy, and he struggled to control it as his mother cocked her head attentively.

'Is your chest tight? I wonder if I should send for Dr Ross? Do you feel as though you might have one of your attacks?'

'I'm all right, Mama,' Nicholas said, feeling the old familiar choking sensation rising up as he fought with his anger. 'I don't want the doctor.' He must distract her attention. 'Have you seen what Bendy can do? Bendy, shew Mama — on the horse — you know! What — Cousin Africa did. Just like — you told us — Mama.'

He was clipping his sentences short to catch his breath, and Héloïse was looking increasingly worried; Benedict, understanding the urgency from his brother's look, scrambled off her lap. 'Watch, Mama. Watch me. See what I can do!' he shouted to catch her attention, and running across the nursery he climbed on to the rocking-horse. James had made it with his own hands for Fanny, long ago, carved and painted it, and given it a real horsehair mane and tail. It was shabby now, the paint chipped, the mane grown thin from the clutching of small hands; but still a nursery favourite.

'Darling, be careful!' Héloïse said in alarm as Benedict began to climb to his feet, to balance upright on the horse's back. 'No, it is dangerous — Benedict, do not!'

It was working, Nicholas thought with relief. The attention gone from him, the rage began to sink down, and after a moment he was able to swallow at last, gratefully, and the tight band around his ribs loosened.

'I'm Africa, I'm the Questring!' Benedict shouted, letting go of the mane and standing upright, his outspread arms rocking as he fought to balance. The story of the time their cousin Africa had run away and joined the circus as a bareback rider known as the Equestrienne was a favourite one, and though it had always been told as a Cautionary Tale, it was evidently a much-admired escapade. Héloïse was on her feet and crossing swiftly to snatch her child from danger, but it was too late. The rocking-horse rocked, Benedict's boots slipped on the shiny wooden back, and he tumbled off, hitting his head with a fearful smack on the polished boards of the nursery floor.

'Benedict!' Héloïse's cry was simultaneous with the child's

24

bellow, though nowhere near as loud. Castor barked shrilly; nursery-maids came running; Benedict was scooped up, his skull anxiously examined, his limbs felt over. Genuine tears rolled fat and freely from his eyes, and an interesting bump began to rise and redden on his forehead as his mother and the maids hugged, petted and soothed him, and decided amongst themselves with great relief that he was not much hurt after all. The tears and howls began to subside, and Héloïse decreed that there were to be no more of such dangerous tricks.

'To be sure, Nicholas, how could you be so foolish as to encourage him?' she said, quite sharply for her.

'I'm sorry, Mama,' Nicholas said meekly. His breathing was under control again, and everyone's concern was far removed from the state of his health: Benedict had done his job well.

Later, when Héloïse had departed and the maids were at the other end of the room, Nicholas expressed his thanks to his little brother in a laconic but heartfelt exchange.

'Mister Nister?'

'Yes, Captain Bean?'

'Story tonight?'

'Yes, *please*, Captain Bean!'

It was the greatest treat, doled out rarely, for Nicholas to tell him a story as they lay in bed in the dark after the maids had gone down to supper.

'Very well, then.' Nicholas nodded portentously, and a quiver ran through his younger brother.

'The Piepowder Man?' he said in an awed whisper.

'The Piepowder Man,' Nicholas said gravely. 'A new episode tonight.'

And Benedict's eyes grew round with anticipation, which was half delight and half terror.

The letter from Lucy arrived in the second collection of the day. It was brought to Héloïse in the drawing-room, where she was arranging the flowers Mathilde had picked that morning while out for a walk with her betrothed, John Skelwith. The walk had been encouraged by Héloïse, partly to allow Mathilde a little privacy with John, and partly to keep

John out of the house and out of James's way, for she knew that the sight of his unacknowledged son put an extra strain on James's already lacerated nerves.

As she arranged the cheerful yellow flowers in a blue vase, she listened critically to Sophie's performance of her new piece on the pianoforte. Sophie was careful and painstaking, and once she had mastered a piece, she struck the right notes with the right force at the right intervals, and the correct tune and accompaniment emerged; but you could not say she played well. There was no verve or zest or attempt at interpretation: it was merely the black dots on the page translated exactingly into sound. Héloïse caught Miss Rosedale's eye across the room and they both sighed, but silently. Sophie was the dearest girl, and it was not her fault if she was not musical.

Héloïse waited until Sophie had played the last chord before opening the letter, and read it to the background accompaniment of Miss Rosedale's low-murmured praise of Sophie's application.

'*Ciel!*' Héloïse exclaimed suddenly, drawing the attention of both her companions to her. 'But this is like her — this is like Cousin Lucy! *Toujours le dérangement!* And yet so kind! But I wonder — perhaps it may answer.' She looked up to meet the enquiring eyes. 'Miss Rosedale, I shall need your opinion. Sophie, my love, what would you think about going abroad for a few months?'

'Abroad, Maman?' Sophie's dark eyes, lifted from the keyboard, were bright with interest.

'Your aunt Lucy proposes to go at once to Brussels to join Lord Theakston, and means to take Rosamund with her and bring her out there instead of in London. There, she says, one may put off mourning without offence, and there will be young men in plenty to dance with. And she offers, like the kind creature she is, to take you, *chérie*, and bring you out at the same time. How should you like that, my Sophie?'

Sophie's cheeks were pink with excitement, but her eyes were doubtful. 'I — I don't know, Maman. I should like it very well, but — would it be proper? I mean, so soon after Fanny's death? I should not like to seem as though I did not care: I loved Fanny very much.'

Miss Rosedale placed a large, reassuring hand on her shoulder. 'No-one would think that, Sophie dear. If Lady Theakston thinks it will be acceptable, I'm sure it will.'

'*Bien sûr*,' Héloïse agreed. 'You will have been in deep mourning for six weeks, which is enough, in reason. Of course, here or in London, where one is known, it would not do, but abroad one may put aside half-mourning, I think. Would you like to go, *chérie*? Me, I think it would be an excellent opportunity, for one never knows when the chance may come again to travel and see another country.' She sighed faintly. 'It is twelve years since I was out of England. This war seems to have gone on for ever.'

'Oh, I should like to above anything, Maman,' Sophie assured her eagerly. 'I should be happy even just to go to Brussels, without being brought out as well.'

'But then, you know,' Héloïse said, briskly practical, 'Lucy can give you a much bigger ball than I, and introduce you to more people, and in all ways launch you better than if you wait until you come home. What do you think, Miss Rosedale?'

Miss Rosedale gave her opinion with decision. 'I think it would be an excellent opportunity for Sophie, not by any means to be missed. I have always been an advocate for foreign travel as a means of education — and with your languages, and Lady Theakston's connections, there is no knowing how far you may advance yourself.'

Sophie was glowing with pleased anticipation now, and Héloïse smiled too. 'Good. Then we have only to ask your Papa, my love, and it is decided. Cousin Lucy wishes to leave very soon, so we must write back to her today with the answer. She asks me to come too, and I wish very well that I might, but I have too much to do, besides leaving your poor Papa. But if he consents, Miss Rosedale shall take you to London, and hand you over to Lucy's care. I shall go and ask him now, and shew him the letter.'

It was easier said than done. Héloïse went first to the steward's room as being the most likely place to find her husband; but the steward, Compton, was there alone.

'I'm afraid I haven't seen him at all today, my lady. Mr Hoskins and I expected him this morning to go through the yearlings' list, but he didn't come at the hour he appointed, so

I took the liberty of sending Mr Hoskins back to Twelvetrees and got on with something else.'

Héloïse left him to his books and pursued her enquiries elsewhere. Ottershaw didn't think Mr James had ridden out, because his hat and gloves were still on the table. William the footman thought he had seen him in the orchard an hour ago, when he had gone for the letters. Then it emerged that Sally the housemaid had mentioned to Mrs Thomson the housekeeper that she had passed Mr James on the nursery stair a bit since, so perhaps he had gone to the nursery, m'lady. Héloïse thanked them all gravely, and went upstairs with a sad heart. She knew now where James had gone. She ought to have guessed before.

The Blue Room, as the West Bedroom was usually called, had been given over to Fanny's use when Héloïse married James. It had been a kind of bribe, to secure Fanny's acquiescence to the marriage; but Héloïse had been adamant that it ought in any case to be Fanny's, for it was the best and prettiest of the bedchambers, and Fanny would one day — so they thought — become Mistress of Morland Place.

She had slept there all the years of her growing up; from that room she had walked down the stairs to the chapel to be wed to Mr Hawker on the 15th of September; she had slept there on her return from Vienna until the night before her death. It was the place, probably, that one most associated with her in life.

It was a sunny room in the afternoon. The yellow light fell upon the priceless blue-and-white Chinese wallpaper, the white counterpane overspreading the plain, elegant lines of Eleanor's Bed — the oldest in the house — with its blue silk tester and curtains; upon the thick blue-and-white Chinese carpet in the middle of the floor; and on the grey-streaked, fox-brown hair of James Morland, who sat with his back to the window on Fanny's little boudoir chair, his head bent broodingly over something held in his lap.

He looked up as Héloïse came in, but his eyes rested on her for a moment only, and so completely without expression that it was as though there were no-one there behind them. Then he looked down again. Héloïse was frightened, not for the first time, by the degree of his withdrawal.

28

'James,' she said, remembering unbidden how he had always said her pronunciation of his name moved him indescribably. She wished it might so do now. She ached to touch him; was so lost and alone without him. 'James — I wish to speak to you.'

'Hmm,' he said — the merest acknowledgement of a sound, not even an interrogative. Héloïse clenched her hands, and the letter rustled stiffly between them.

'James, attend me, please! Here is a letter I wish you to read.'

'You read it to me,' he said without interest. He was merely humouring her.

'It's about Sophie,' she said. 'It's important. Please, James, attend! Sophie is your daughter too!'

She thought that might sting him, but he merely held out one hand for the letter without looking up from whatever it was he had in his lap. Defeated, she gave him the letter, and watched as he read it very slowly. At the end he stared blankly at the paper for a while, and then raised his head, not quite meeting her eye. She thought for a moment he would say no, that Fanny's mourning must be observed to the letter; but afterwards she concluded it had been foolish to think that. Just as he felt himself alone in his bereavement, so it mattered to him not at all how anyone else felt or behaved. They might all have worn scarlet and gone out dancing every night as far as he was concerned.

'Very well,' he said.

'You mean she may go?' Heloïse said.

'Why not?'

She waited, but it seemed that was all he was going to say. She felt she should go and leave him in peace; and then, angered by his cutting her off from him, she tried again to capture his interest, or even his attention. 'Lucy wishes to leave at once, as you see. If we can get everything ready, I should like Sophie to leave the day after tomorrow, straight after Mathilde's wedding. Miss Rosedale will take her to London. They can travel post —'

Now he looked up. 'Miss Rosedale? But Lucy asks *you* to go.'

Héloïse looked puzzled. 'I cannot leave. I am needed here — the estate — the house —'

'There are servants to deal with them.'

'The children — and Mathilde's wedding. There is so much to do. I could never get ready in time.'

He shrugged. 'Of course you could. And the children have the nursery maids and Miss Rosedale — they don't need you as well. You should go. You need the change of air.'

For a moment her heart was touched, thinking he was worried for her. Then she saw that his expression was reserved, almost watchful. *He wants to be rid of me*, she thought with faint shock.

'*You* need me,' she said; and even to herself, it was like the defiance of a frightened child. It was not a statement, but an appeal: love me, need me; come back from wherever it is you have gone!

James looked at her in silence for a long time, and she waited in dread, not knowing what he would say next, how she would survive, how their love would survive, if he were to say the wrong thing. At last he sighed — she didn't hear it, but she saw his shoulders rise and fall — and he said, 'I'm sorry. I'm no use to you just now.'

It was the tone of his voice that made her angry, though she hardly knew why. 'I don't want you to be useful, James. I want to be useful to you. Don't you understand that? I want to comfort you, but you shut me out, and I can't bear it!'

It wasn't what she meant to say, and she cursed her unready tongue, but he answered the words as they had fallen. 'I'm sorry, Marmoset,' he said, and the use of the old love-name was an appeal, but, oh, from a cold place! It chilled her more than his indifference. 'I can't take anything from you, not comfort, not anything. Sophie needs you. You should go with Sophie, make it a success for her, try to enjoy yourself. If you stay, it — it won't make any difference to me. I'm sorry.' He seemed to know at least that these were wounding words, for he looked up properly, meeting her eyes at last, and then lifted the hand in his lap to show her what it was he had been holding.

It was a little gold-and-enamel box, with a golden bird on the lid; when the lid was opened, the bird's beak opened and closed, and a little tinkling tune played, as though the bird were singing. Fanny had seen it in London on her way back

30

from Vienna, taken a fancy to it, bought it for the baby, thinking it would amuse it; for the baby who had killed her in trying to be born.

'She's dead, you see,' James said flatly. 'I can't get any further than that. It's all I can feel or think.'

He looked down again at the little box and turned it round and round in his hands. Héloïse stared at him, and felt resentment rising. *Fanny*, she thought, *always Fanny!*

But what about Sophie, dear, good Sophie who had every virtue Fanny so signally lacked, and a loving, generous heart as well? What about the little boys, longing for a look, a single word from their Papa? What about her, his wife, lover, companion, suffering for him, miserable without him? Did they all count for nothing? He was selfish, selfish! her heart cried angrily; and then she was shocked with herself for the thought. For a moment she had almost hated him. But the anger dissolved as rapidly as it had come, and she felt only the terrible helpless pity and longing again.

Her legs were trembling, she discovered. She needed very badly to go away somewhere quietly to recover herself.

'Very well,' she said at last, and her voice sounded quite calm. 'If you don't need me here, I will go with Sophie. I should like it very much.' James said nothing. 'We will leave immediately after Mathilde's wedding,' she added.

Still James vouchsafed no response, and she turned and went away; quickly, so that she would not be able to hear that he had not called her back at the last moment, to beg her to stay.

CHAPTER TWO

A frenzy of packing enveloped Morland Place. Boxes were brought down from attics, maids disappeared under clouds of muslin, cambric and silk, armchairs overflowed with bonnets and gloves and stockings, and every available surface was decked with trimmings, ribbons, feathers, beads and fringes like some fantastic indoor bazaar.

Sophie, faced with the entire grown-up contents of her wardrobe spread across her bed, realised in one searing glance its inadequacy to cope with even a week of social intercourse. 'I haven't anything fit to wear!' she cried despairingly, in unconscious imitation of every young woman since time began.

Héloïse, her capacity for worry severely stretched, what with James, the boys, Mathilde's wedding, Edward, and the household to fret about, still managed to crease her brow considerably over Sophie's plight.

'If only there had been more time, Marie and I could have made up one or two gowns for you, but as it is ...' She surveyed the heap doubtfully, and then squared her shoulders. '*Eh bien,* your mouse-ear cambric is very nice, and will do for a carriage-dress. I have some little jet buttons somewhere which would look pretty down the front. And there is plenty of wear still in these muslins —'

'But, Maman, they're little-girl's dresses,' Sophie said. 'And everyone is wearing flounces this year; and we shall be in such grand company.'

Héloïse smiled, wishing her own anguish were so easily remedied; but she took her daughter's problem seriously. 'Well, love, there are a dozen women in this house who can hold a needle, and it would be a shame if between us we could not sew a few flounces onto your muslins. And what a blessing it is that you are much of a size with me, my Sophie!

For you know my yellow persian will look very well on you, with some new ribbon trimming, for evening wear. And then there is my dark-red travelling-dress with the velvet bands: if we only take it in at the waist, it will do for you to wear on the ship. And my olive-brown pelisse I have only ever worn twice, and it will become you much better than me.'

Sophie, remembering all her early teaching about being humble and grateful, swallowed down her disappointment at the thought of going abroad for the very first time, and in such exalted company, in made-over clothes. Cousin Rosamund was bound to have everything new and smart — and London-made — and Sophie would appear in front of everyone as a dowdy country mouse. But she was lucky to be going at all, and she knew she ought to be grateful, and not think of finery, which was next door to the sin of vanity.

'Thank you, Maman,' she said bravely. 'I'm sure they will do very well indeed.' Héloïse, chin resting on her forefinger as she surveyed the simple frocks and sashes which so far had served Sophie's needs, merely grunted an acknowledgement; and for all her resolution, Sophie could not keep a slight quaver out of her voice as she asked, 'Shall I wear your yellow persian for my come-out?'

Héloïse looked up, frowning, as she returned from the contemplation of the problem to register what it was Sophie had said. And then her brow cleared, and she laughed and enfolded her daughter in a warm embrace.

'My yellow persian? Oh Sophie! My poor little love, did you think I meant to bring you out in rags? When we get to Brussels, *chérie*, you shall have all the new gowns you need, and the most beautiful ball-gown that ever was for your come-out! We're only making over these old gowns for the journey, until we get to Brussels and find out what is being worn. You shan't be Cinderella at your own ball, I promise you!'

Sophie returned her mother's hug with a lighter heart, and then had nothing more to do but be happy. She was seventeen, and going away from home for the first time, *and* going to have her coming-out ball in the most exciting city in Europe, *and* going to have a whole wardrobe of new clothes. She had to spend her tears on the consideration of how much she would miss Papa, and Mathilde, and dear Rosy, and the boys, and Monsieur Barnard, and all the other servants, and the dogs, and the horses...

Héloïse had no sartorial fears on her own behalf. She was not an inch wider in any dimension from the day she had married James, and all the smart clothes she had had as a bride still fitted her. Since they had been designed and cut in a plain and classical style, and since she was now a matron of thirty-eight with no pretensions to being dashing, she declared that she would need nothing more than a few simple muslins for warm days, which she could very well obtain in Brussels.

Marie, her maid, was shocked by this declaration, but had the sense not to argue about it then. The idea of her lady going to a formal ball, perhaps before kings and princes, in that old blue crape, seared her with shame, and when Héloïse was out of the room she took the precaution of taking it, and one or two other elderly creations, out of the box where they had just been packed and concealing them in her room. When the time came she would look pained and innocent, and there would be nothing for it but to call in a mantuamaker for her mistress, she thought happily.

Fortunately Héloïse was forced by the imminence of Mathilde's wedding to leave the packing almost entirely to Marie and her helpers. It was not that it was going to be a lavish occasion, but Mathilde must not feel that it had been shuffled off without due attention. Quite apart from the material arrangements which had to be made, Héloïse felt it her duty to her ward to have some very serious talks with Mathilde about Marriage and What to Expect, and also about Husbands and How To Manage Them.

Mathilde, though she had just had her twenty-sixth birthday, was completely innocent and had retained a very maidenly modesty which, coupled with a red-head's propensity for painful blushes, would have daunted a lesser woman than Héloïse. But Héloïse had been brought up by old-fashioned French nuns and prepared by them for marriage at fourteen, and what her education lacked in intellectual scope, it made up in practical common-sense. Over the two days, Mathilde received a wealth of useful information, in which marital congress was so well mixed with the management of servants, the cleaning of carpets, the dosing of common ailments and the best method of rearing domestic fowl that it slipped into her mind quite comfortably and almost unnoticed.

The upheavals to the household were observed from a safe distance by Edward with his usual air of patient bewilderment. While trying to attend to a hundred things at once, Héloïse still managed to spare a thought for his plight, realising that her absence from home would leave him comfortless and lonely. She directed her own footman, Stephen, to appoint himself Edward's manservant.

'He will probably not notice directly if you brush and mend his clothes and lay them out for him, but he will feel the better for it. And see that you serve him at meals as you usually serve me; and make sure he wears a hat if it is raining, and — oh, I leave it to your common sense, Stephen! You will know what to do.'

'Of course, my lady,' Stephen nodded. 'I shall make sure Mr Edward is comfortable.'

Héloïse then went to the kitchen to have a stern word with Monsieur Barnard, the cook, on the necessity of two courses at dinner every day, whatever Mr Edward said. 'He and Mr James will be like invalids,' she advised him in their native tongue. 'Their appetites will need to be coaxed.'

Barnard nodded and said he understood; standards would be maintained, and delicacies suitable to the bachelor palate sent in to tempt them. Then he wished her ladyship rather wistfully a delightful trip, and asked when she would be home again.

Miss Rosedale was also enlisted in the campaign for Edward's comfort. 'There will be no Mathilde to play chess with him in the evenings,' Héloïse said. 'And neither James nor Father Aislaby will take the trouble to talk to him, I know.'

'Chess I cannot offer; but I will undertake to play backgammon with him, and bring the boys down before dinner to cheer him up,' said Miss Rosedale comfortably.

Héloïse smiled, and took her hand impulsively. 'Dear Rosy! What should we all do without you? I must say that I could not for any consideration have accepted this invitation, if I did not know you were here to take care of everything, and keep the house running smoothly, and look after my boys —'

'Don't worry about anything,' Miss Rosedale said, observing the tears rising closer to the surface. 'You must put your mind to enjoying yourself, and bringing out dear Sophie to the best advantage. Leave the rest to me.'

Héloïse pressed her hand. 'And Mr James most of all I must leave to you,' she said anxiously. 'He is not himself. Dear Rosy, I wish I had not said I would go. But he will not let me — I mean, he is so —'

Miss Rosedale produced a large, clean, lavender-scented square of sensible linen, and patted Héloïse's shoulder while she employed it. 'Give him time, ma'am. Deep wounds take longer to heal. He'll come out of it in time.'

Héloïse looked up, red-eyed, red-nosed, looking, at that moment, much younger than Miss Rosedale, and infinitely more vulnerable. 'Do you think so? Truly?'

'Truly,' Miss Rosedale smiled.

'Because I have been so afraid that — that he will go away completely, and not come back.'

'Give him time,' the governess said again, sounding surer than she was. 'It's only a month since Fanny died.'

Miss Rosedale, who perhaps of all people in the world, had known and loved Fanny best, had not shed a single tear since her death. The truth was that she simply couldn't yet manage to think of Fanny as dead. She just went on feeling, quite illogically, that it was all a mistake, and that at any moment the door would open and Fanny would come storming in again to take up where she had left off, making everyone's life more difficult, but certainly more interesting. Someone as vibrant as Fanny simply couldn't stop existing, not just like that; so she offered comfort perhaps a little deceitfully, having no grief of her own from which to make judgement.

Héloïse accepted the comfort willingly, however, dried her eyes, and then sighed. 'I shall try to enjoy it — for Sophie's sake, if not my own. But I wish he did not want me to go.'

That was the heart of it, of course, as Miss Rosedale very well know. But she had no comfort to offer for that sadness.

★

Mathilde was married to her John in the chapel at Morland Place on the morning of the 3rd of April. It was a quiet, private occasion, the only outsider being John's best man, Tom Keating, who was the brother of John's first wife. John's mother had steadfastly refused to attend, and he had no other relatives that he knew of.

'We must be your family now,' Héloïse said to him warmly, as they waited in the drawing-room for Mathilde to appear. She felt desperately sorry for him. Whether he believed his mother to be being wholly irrational, or whether he knew or had guessed the real reason for her hatred of Morland Place and all its inhabitants, it must be equally uncomfortable and worrying for him. And she couldn't help being fond of him, both because he was such a fine, good young man, and because of his fleeting, haunting resemblance to James.

The great marble clock on the chimney-piece struck ten, and as if it had been a signal, the door opened and Mathilde came in, fresh from Marie's hands, and followed by Sophie, who had been keeping her company while she was dressed. There was a brief and flattering silence as Mathilde paused in the doorway. There was nothing of the fashionable Society wedding about her appearance, no satin, lace or pearls. Her gown was of fine white muslin, and over it she wore a soft silk shawl — white shot with primrose, and embossed white flowers. She wore neither hat nor veil, but her coppery hair was simply dressed with white ribbon and marguerite daisies.

She was no girl in the first flush of youth; but as her eyes sought those of her love, a smile of luminous radiance overspread her face, and she looked so lovely that more than one throat found itself unexpectedly constricted. Héloïse hurried forward to embrace her ward, and to whisper that she looked perfectly lovely, and then John came to take her hand on his arm, and they walked to the chapel with the family following behind. When they had taken their places, the whole household crowded in and filled the chapel: John might have only one person to invite, but there were no empty seats at his wedding.

Father Aislaby conducted the service, and the choir-boys sang an anthem; Sophie stood by to receive Mathilde's gloves and prayer-book, and Tom Keating, perfectly sober for once, produced the ring; the female servants cried just as they ought, and Mathilde spoke the words of her vow with a look of such love and trust for her John that Edward had to clear his throat and look away, and Héloïse reached out to pat his arm comfortingly.

What James felt about the whole thing was impossible to guess. Héloïse and Edward glanced at him uncomfortably from time to time. Had matters been ordered only a little differently, John Skelwith might at this moment be heir to Morland Place; and James couldn't but be aware that Mathilde's children would by blood be his grandchildren. But he sat impassive through the whole ceremony, his eyes fixed on the middle distance, frowning slightly as though he were working out mathematical problems in his head; and when the ceremony was over and everyone crowded forward with congratulations, he managed somehow to slip away unobserved.

In the drawing-room a collation had been spread by way of a wedding-breakfast, and champagne was poured to toast the happy couple. James did not appear, and Héloïse had to restrain her desire to go and look for him, and tried to prevent anyone else from noticing his absence. Father Aislaby brought the choir-boys in for cakes and lemonade, which filled the room and any possible silences nicely; and since the chaplain very soon got into a deep discussion with Tom Keating about hunting, it was left to Héloïse and Miss Rosedale to prevent the two eldest choristers from fighting with Nicholas, and the youngest from being persuaded by Benedict to exchange his lemonade for champagne.

Edward, feeling rather shaken by the whole experience, had to drink three glasses straight off before he was able to go up to Mathilde and take her hand to press it warmly.

'You look lovely,' he said. 'I hope you will be very happy.'

Their eyes met, Mathilde's a little shyly, Edward's filled with tenderness and sadness, love and regret. I was a fool, he thought: I should have married her when I had the chance, and to hell with the consequences! But he had also to be aware that John Skelwith had far more to offer a young woman and that, unselfishly, he ought to have no regrets for her.

'I hope you will, too,' Mathilde said hesitantly. 'I'll come and visit very often. We shan't be far away. And you must visit us, whenever you like.'

'Yes,' Edward said comprehensively. He couldn't imagine himself intruding upon their married bliss, nor imagine either of them wanting him to, but at times like this it was not what was said that mattered, but what was meant. He would miss her, and nothing would ever be the same; but because he loved her, he was glad she had what she wanted. He lifted her hand to his lips and kissed it. 'God bless you,' he said. 'The house will seem empty without you.'

A little while later, Mathilde slipped upstairs with Marie to change into her travelling-dress, and half an hour after that, she and her new husband climbed into the waiting post-chaise, their boxes already strapped on behind, for the journey to Scarborough where they were to spend their honeymoon. Héloïse and Sophie were to leave for London within the hour, and when James did not appear to wave goodbye to Mathilde, Héloïse began to wonder if he meant to let her go, too, without farewell.

Mathilde was kissed and hugged into a state of dishevelment, John's hand was heartily shaken, and then they were off. Héloïse waved them out of sight, and then dispatched Sophie to her room to put on her travelling-gown, and with a sigh went up to the great bedchamber to change her own clothes.

When she entered the room, however, she found James there, sitting on the edge of the bed, his hands in his pockets, staring at his feet. He looked up as she entered.

'Hullo,' he said, as if faintly surprised to see her.

'They are gone,' Héloïse said, a little accusingly.

'Thank God for that,' he said; and laughed harshly. 'Scarborough! Good God, what a hideous irony! I used to meet his mother there, God help us all!'

'I know,' Héloïse said quietly. 'You don't need to remind me. I don't suppose he knew it, however. Scarborough is near, and a fashionable place. Mathilde looked for you to say goodbye. She was disappointed.'

For once James looked at her, but it was not a loving look.

'Unscrupulous, love! Mathilde didn't care a penny-piece that I was not there to wave her off. You want to make me feel guilty; but you will not. There is nothing about her marriage to Skelwith which interests me at all — except to contemplate how happy she is likely to be with a man who takes her to the same place for a honeymoon as he took his first wife. Still, you promoted the match; I suppose you believe it will serve.'

Héloïse stood still in the centre of the room, her hands down at her side, defeated.

'James, why are you being so hateful to me?'

He jerked his gaze away from her. 'I am not being hateful to you. *Au contraire*, wife, I am being very patient.'

'But what have I done?'

He got up with a restless surge of movement and walked past her to the window. 'That's what you do — have you heard yourself? It's always you, you. You don't think about my feelings at all — only how they concern you!' His fists balled up, as if with frustration. 'It's my daughter who is dead, you know, not yours! You are not the principal sufferer in this particular tragedy — but to hear you talk, anyone would think you were the only person concerned!'

There was nothing she could say in reply to so monstrous an accusation. It ought not to hurt her, irrational as it was, but she stood, her head a little bent, and felt the barbs sink in, able to do nothing but endure them. Then she took a deep breath, and walked over to the end of the bed where her travelling-dress was laid out, and began to unbutton her gown; conscious of his eyes on her, trying to ignore them. After the top three buttons, she could reach no more, and struggled, frustrated, feeling the tears rising again, keeping her back turned on him so that he should not see them. Damn the buttons! Stupid things! Where was Marie? Oh, it was monstrous! In the old days he would have come and helped her but not now — she didn't even want him to.

'And now you are crying, in order to make me feel guilty,' James's hard voice came from across the room. She struggled harder to repress the tears, but they surged upwards despite her. 'Really, women are so unscrupulous!' A single sob escaped her, and she felt for her handkerchief, couldn't find it, and turned to face him, pressing her fingers to her eyes to hold back the tears. 'Not true!' she cried out angrily. 'Unfair! I tried not to! You know — I would not let you see me cry for — for anything!'

And she turned again and put her hands over her face and swallowed and swallowed to make the tears go down. She thought he had left the room, but suddenly he was behind her, quietly undoing the buttons she couldn't reach. She stiffened, unwilling to be helped by him, but knowing she could not manage alone. The fingers came to the bottom; there was a pause, and then the breath of a touch on the back of her neck, a touch of lips.

All her anger left her on the instant; all offences were forgotten, all her love surged upwards, restored and ready for him again. She turned eagerly to put her arms round him, to share a healing embrace with him; but he had moved away just out of reach, and stood looking at her with an enigmatic expression she could not interpret. The love and longing sank back down, thwarted.

'James,' she said, and tried once more, knowing that it was true that he was the principal sufferer, and that it behoved her to be the generous, the giving, the forgiving. 'James, I love you so. Don't shut me out.'

He looked at her a long time. Then, 'I'm sorry,' he said, and for a moment she knew he meant it. 'I treat you cruelly. I don't mean to. You mustn't think ... I'm half mad at the moment, you see. I don't know what I'm doing. It's nothing to do with you, really. I just want to hit out at anyone within reach.'

'I wouldn't mind if you hit out at me,' she said helplessly. 'But when you don't even know it *is* me —' But these were the wrong words — they sounded accusing. He looked weary at them, and turned away.

'I'm sorry,' he said again, and now it was a stranger talking. 'I don't mean to hurt you. It's just that I haven't anything for you at the moment. For anyone.'

He walked to the window again. Marie came in, looking hesitantly from one to the other. Héloïse nodded. There was nothing to be gained from continuing the conversation. Marie helped her to dress, but James did not go away, only stood at

41

the window, staring out at nothing, slowly rubbing at his left temple with his left forefinger — a habit he had begun since the funeral, which he was clearly unaware of. When Marie had finished dressing her, Héloïse bid her in a low murmur to go and see that Sophie was ready. The sound of her voice seemed to penetrate James's reverie, and he turned as Marie went out, and looked at Héloïse, and gave a painful smile.

'Well,' he said awkwardly. 'Well, well. So you're ready, then? You look very smart. I like that colour.'

Now, she thought. One last chance to reach him. She took a step forward. 'James,' she began.

But he lifted his hands, as if he meant to ward her off. 'I hope you have a wonderful time. Brussels in the spring! How exotic!' He tried to make it a joke, and failed. She heard the desolation behind the words.

'I don't care about Brussels,' she said steadily. 'I only care about you.'

'I know. I know.' His voice was defeated. 'I can't help it. It's better this way, Marmoset. I'm only hurting you. By the time you come back — things may be better. I really do hope you have a wonderful time. You deserve it.' He put his hands down, but she did not feel licensed to go forward and touch him. One corner of his mouth lifted in a wry smile. 'I do love you,' he said with difficulty.

'I love you too, my James,' she replied, and then there seemed to be nothing to do but to turn and leave.

A cheerful smile, a positive mien, for Sophie's sake. The post-chaise was in the yard, with four horses — *four!* Sophie was ecstatic — and the boxes tied on behind, and two postboys in blue drab coats and black hats, each with his whip and gleaming horn.

There was an orgy of hugging, kisses and tears and incoherent sentences. Barnard, who had already put a hamper of food for the journey into the carriage, pressed a paper of toffees into Sophie's hand, and then, when she flung her arms round his neck, actually kissed her — *smack!* — on her peach-like cheek, and then had to step back and trumpet briskly into a large blue handkerchief.

Miss Rosedale gave Sophie a beautiful little blank book,

with cream-laid paper and marbled end-papers, in which to keep a diary of the whole trip. 'You will enjoy reading it for the rest of your life,' she promised. 'Best handwriting, mind!'

Edward promised yet again to keep Sophie's horse properly exercised, and to look after Kithra and Castor for Héloïse; and then looked very bleak and managed with an effort not to bid them hurry back.

Héloïse went back to hug the little boys for a third time, and kissed Miss Rosedale again and gave her a burning look which said *look after everything for me!* and then went into a last-minute flurry of instructions to everyone, which did no good at all as they came out in French.

And then they were climbing into the carriage, and Sophie looked around and cried suddenly. 'But where's Papa?'

Héloïse's heart misgave on her daughter's behalf. And then James appeared mysteriously beside the coach and leaned in and enfolded Sophie quite naturally in his arms. She hugged him back, and then looked at him, and made a sound between a laugh and a sob and kissed him, and he kissed her too, and pressed her cheek tenderly against his.

And when he released her, he looked across at Héloïse, a long look of apology and supplication, and she leaned across Sophie to give him her hands. He took them and kissed them both.

'Have a wonderful time,' he said. 'I love you, Marmoset.'

She smiled, unable to speak. He stepped back, the postboy cracked his whip, the carriage lurched, and everyone broke into renewed goodbyes and frantic waving. Nicholas pounded along beside the carriage waving and wheezing, the dogs barked madly in near-unison, and then they were rushing under the barbican, and home and family were whisked away out of sight.

'We're off!' Sophie cried in a mixture of elation and apprehension. 'Oh, Maman, I'm so excited.'

Héloïse smiled at her and leaned back against the squabs, her own feelings so turbulent that it would take the whole journey to London, she thought, to get them back in order. The image of James's last look lingered on her memory's eye, healing much, making it possible for her both to leave and to come back.

But he didn't ask me not to go, she thought; and then thrust the thought determinedly away.

For Sophie, the holiday began immediately: everything was new and exciting. She had never been further than twenty miles from home, and was soon beyond her knowledge, so that even the scenery was a novelty to her. She gazed out of the window, noting every turn of the road, admiring every neat cottage or handsome view, exclaiming at every vehicle that passed them on the busy road.

The business of travelling intrigued her. When the tooting of the postboy's horn warned her that they were approaching a tollgate, she would lean out of the window at some peril to her bonnet to see the keeper hurry out and open the gate, and she had plenty of questions to ask her mother and Marie about charges and exemptions and how many pikes were covered by the one ticket.

Then there was the changing of the horses at the post-houses: the speed with which the grooms unpoled the team and led out fresh horses was remarkable, she thought. At the first change, at Knottingly, she was fascinated to see the postboys all seated along a bench against the wall at the side of the yard, with smocks over their coats to keep them clean until they were wanted. She heard the name 'Morland' passed from mouth to mouth, and felt proud that it mattered on this road to be a Morland. She was even more thrilled when the head ostler came hurrying up to the window and knuckled his forehead to them, grinning delightedly.

'Good day, m'lady! And miss! Honoured to see you in my yard, m'lady. And a fine team I've ordered out for you — Morland-bred 'osses, all four of 'em, and the best 'osses in Yorkshire, m'lady, as I'm sure I don't need to tell you.'

Héloïse merely smiled, but Sophie opened her eyes wide. 'Do you mean they come from our stables?'

'To be sure, Sophie. You must know that we sell our carriage horses to the post-houses all along the road,' Héloïse said.

'That's right, miss — m'lady. You can't do better than Morland 'osses, and so I tell everyone! Good doers, every one; and sweeter-tempered you couldn't want, which is a great

44

thing, m'lady, in man or beast. There now, all ready for you, m'lady! Stand away, Jem! Good day, m'lady. Pleasant journey, miss!'

There was no time for more: there was a cracking of whips, and the carriage shot forward again, through the archway and out onto the road. Sophie settled back in her seat, and said, 'Fancy being taken to London by our own horses! And what good things he said about them, too.'

She was much gratified by the compliment and the agreeable consequence it conferred: it added another dimension to her pleasure in the journey. For Héloïse it was simply an irony that her own horses were carrying her mile by mile further from the one place in the world she really wanted to be. What was she doing posting off to London, to Brussels, leaving her home and family, her little boys, her husband? A passionate desire rose in her to stop the chaise, to bid the post-boys turn round and take her back. France, her native land, had driven her from its shores more than twenty years ago: everything she valued was now English.

But he had wanted her to go. He did not want her near him. Yet Fanny's death was so recent. He needed time — give him time! Miss Rosedale was right. She was foolish, selfish, to expect anything from him yet. It was best that she go away and leave him alone, and then when she came back everything would be all right. He would have had time to get over the shock, and he would have missed her.

So she argued with herself; but underneath was the unspoken certainty that whatever had happened to her, it was to James that she would have turned for comfort. Trouble, sorrow, tragedy, ought to have brought them closer together; she should have been his one sure place, as he would have been hers. *He has turned away from me,* her grieving heart whispered; and quieter still, the unspeakable fear, *He has tired of me.*

And then Sophie cried, 'Oh look, Maman! The lady at the gate, and the dear little baby waving!' and Héloïse was forced to put aside her musings so as not to spoil her daughter's pleasure.

After Doncaster they opened Monsieur Barnard's basket, and refreshed themselves with some of the delicacies he had

45

provided. Héloïse looked into the basket and laughed.

'Dear Barnard! Judging by the amount he has packed, he must have supposed his *boîte* was going to have to last all the way to Brussels!'

'Oh, Maman, these patties! And curd tarts, and cold chicken!' Sophied cried, her healthy schoolroom appetite ousting any possibility of being elegantly indifferent to food. 'I do think picnics are the nicest thing! Things always taste better when you don't eat them at a table, with knives and forks.'

'*Tiens!* There is no water for mixing the wine. Well, my Sophie, you will have to have it unmixed for once. I hope you shall like it.'

'Of course I will!' Sophie said with a smile of self-mockery. 'After all, Maman, I'm a young lady now.'

The day wore on. The landscape grew flatter and less interesting, and the monotonous aspect of travelling communicated itself even to Sophie. She chattered less, and began to feel the carriage to be cramped and stuffy, and was almost as glad as her elders when they rattled over the cobbles of Grantham at last, past the massive red-brick façade of the George, and under the archway into its yard. They had made good time; but still it was six o'clock and it had been a very long day.

An inn-servant, given the nod by the post-boys, came hurrying across to open the door and put down the step.

'I am Lady Henrietta Morland,' Héloïse told him as she stepped out. 'I have rooms bespoken here.'

'Oh yes, m'lady, we were expecting you, m'lady. This way, *hif* you please!' The servant doubled himself obsequiously, beckoned to others more lowly to 'fitch oop her ladyship's loogidge', and conducted them into the inn, where the landlord met them with a wreath of smiles and several more bows each. All the fuss was gratifying to Sophie, who had never felt so important in her life as when the innkeeper revealed that he knew her name.

'My lady, welcome, welcome — and Miss Morland, honoured to receive you, I'm sure! Your rooms are ready, just as you ordered — a bedchamber *and* a private parlour, and a room for your maid, my lady — just so! And was you wanting to dine, my lady?'

'To be sure, in half an hour. Send up whatever you think suitable. But first we will have hot water — and my maid will direct your man which bags to send up.'

Sophie, though reviving rapidly with all the excitement of the inn — the first she had ever stayed in — thought she could not possibly be interested in eating again until the next morning at the earliest. When, however, they had been conducted to their apartments, and she had pattered about examining everything, and leaned out of the window to watch a chaise arriving and a gentleman in a curricle departing; and when the water had come and they had washed the dust of the journey away and dressed their hair and straightened their crumpled gowns, she began to think she might manage a morsel of something so as not to upset her mother. And when a rap on the door heralded the arrival of the landlord and two servants bearing trays of dishes to be set out on the table of their own private parlour, and the excitement of eating strange food in a strange place began to work on her, she found herself unaccountably hungry.

There was a heavenly pea soup with bits of crisp bacon floating in it, and a fat duck with dried cherries, and a date pudding with bitter sauce, and the handsomest cold ham with sallets, and a basket of pastries, and even a *blancmanger*. Héloïse might notice that the food did not come up to Barnard's exacting standards, but Sophie tasted everything and found it good.

After dinner, Sophie resumed her post at the window, which overlooked the yard, watching in fascination all the comings and goings, until the tea-tray arrived; and then, as they were to rise very early the next day, it seemed wise to be going early to bed. A day which had begun with a wedding and ended with dinner in an inn half-way to London contained enough excitement to put Sophie to sleep as though she had been struck on the head, to dream of galloping horses, post-horns, picnics and muslin dresses.

Héloïse lay awake for some time, listening to the sounds of voices and laughter from the coffee-room which was just below the bedchamber. The smell of cigar smoke drifted up through the cracks in the floorboards, and male voices conversed tantalisingly just beyond understanding. She thought of James, and wondered if he were at that same moment smoking a last cigar before the fire; wondered if, in spite of everything, he were missing her as she already missed him. Would the bed seem empty to him without her?

She drifted, waking at every sound. Every now and then the light of torches in the coachyard brightened the thin bed-curtains, and there were shouts and clattering and all the other noises of the changing of horses to disturb her. At last she fell into a restless sleep, her body twitching as it relived the miles of travelling, while her mind offered her images of parting and loss in sad dreams.

The following day was long and very tiring, for they travelled more than twelve hours with only brief stops. They were all very tired by the time they reached London, and even Sophie could manage no more than a perfunctory disappointment that, arriving after dark, they got no view of the great city other than an amazing spread of pinprick lights, seen from the top of Highgate Hill. It was eight o'clock when they finally drew up outside Lucy's house in Upper Grosvenor Street, descended stiff and chilled from the carriage, and almost staggered up the steps.

In the hall, all was light and warmth, welcome and smiles. Sophie stood bemused, like a rabbit mesmerised by lights. Butler, liveried footman, uniformed maids swam across her vision; and then there was the brisk figure of Aunt Lucy, in a twilled muslin gown and a beautiful shawl of Norwich silk, her fair curly crop disordered and threaded with a lilac ribbon, descending on them from the stairs to give them each a brief hard hug and bid them welcome.

'You must be exhausted! And hungry, too. Hicks, is there hot water in their rooms? You shall have supper as soon as you have made yourselves comfortable. Héloïse, my dear, Docwra will look after you. I'm sure your maid is in as bad a way as you are! And Sophie — good Lord, how you've grown since I last saw you! — this is Moss, Lady Rosamund's maid. She'll take care of you. Go along now, and I'll see you in the saloon when you're ready.'

All was arranged with great speed, and without the need for any words or decisions on the part of the travellers — a kindness they all appreciated. Sophie followed the trim, plump figure of Moss up the stairs, and was too weary to feel more than a slight apprehension about being attended by a real lady's maid. Since she had grown too old to be dressed by the nursery-maid, she had always dressed herself; and she wondered whether a London maid would sneer at her made-over clothes.

There seemed a great many stairs and a great many doors, and more candles than Sophie could believe necessary, and her spirits sank a little further. At Morland Place they lived, though comfortably, in a very simple way. She was not used to such grandness and luxury — she would certainly do something wrong and disgrace herself. At the very least, she would never be able to find her way around. Then at last Moss opened a door and stood back, saying, 'In here, miss.'

Sophie went in, and found herself in a smallish, neat room, with a dimity bed, a red plush armchair, a neat mahogany washing-stand and lowboy, and no signs of fabulous luxury other than the superabundance of candles, and a very large cheval-glass. There was a cheerful fire burning in the grate and steam rising from the ewer; and, as if by magic, her small trunk was standing in the middle of the floor, conducted up from the coach to arrive before her by some backstairs alchemy, which was intended to impress her as much as it did.

'Oh!' she exclaimed involuntarily, 'how nice this is!'

Moss turned to her, and revealed not only a round, pleasant face, but a ready smile. 'Yes, miss,' she said, without a hint of anything other than kindness in her voice, 'her ladyship thought you'd like it better than one of the grander rooms. Now just you let me help you off with your gown, and you can have a nice wash while I lay something out for you.'

Sophie's spirits wavered again. What would Moss think of her mouse-ear cambric, which still, to her, looked like a child's frock made over? Or her plain linen underclothes, with not a scrap of lace about them? But it was very agreeable to have someone to undo her buttons for her, and lift off her gown, and take off her shoes and stockings, just as if she were a child again; and the hot water was comforting and

49

refreshing, and the soap in the green china soapdish smelled deliciously of Otto of Roses.

When she turned again, she saw that Moss had laid out the butterfly muslin with the rickrack braid trimming, her second-best gown after the yellow persian, and she could not help looking an enquiry. If a mere supper after a long journey were to merit her second-best gown, what on earth would she wear if there were a dinner to come?

'Do you think that's the right gown?' Sophie asked in a small voice.

Moss smiled reassuringly and said, 'Oh certainly, miss. Her ladyship wouldn't expect you to be too fine, after you've been travelling all day.' Sophie could only swallow and submit. It only made it worse that Moss was being genuinely kind.

'And now I'll just dress your hair for you, miss,' said Moss when the gown was hooked up and settled. 'There's no doubt that travelling do make a sad bird's-nest of one.'

Crushed again, Sophie sat before the glass; but watched intrigued as Moss's fingers flew about and transformed the sad bird's-nest into a glossy crown, held in place with the minimum of pins, and making Sophie look — and feel — more elegant that ever in her life before. 'There, does that feel secure? Shake your head a little, miss — not too hard!'

'It's lovely, Moss. Thank you! You are clever!'

Moss looked pleased. 'There now, miss, I'm sure,' she said. 'You should see Mrs Docwra work — her ladyship's maid. It's her what taught me. But I'm glad you like it. Her ladyship has said as how in Brussels I might look after you as well as my lady — Lady Rosamund — so I hope I shall give satisfaction.'

'Oh yes, indeed, I'm sure you will. Thank you,' Sophie said fervently. 'But tell me, how —'

At that instant the door burst open as if it had been kicked, and a tall figure bounded in.

'Cousin Sophie! How splendid! Has Moss finished with you? Do come down to supper — I'm longing to talk to you!'

It was Cousin Rosamund — grown taller than ever, but with a womanly figure which filled the tallness out. A smiling freckled face, bright blue eyes, sandy-gold hair dressed high around her head like a burnished and slightly blurred halo; a

50

muslin gown which, though simple and maidenly, spoke elegance and expense in its every line, a gold filagree necklace about her throat, and a gold bangle on her arm. Cousin Rosamund was only a year older than Sophie, and not out yet, but she looked confident, elegant, fashionable — every inch a lady of the *ton*. Beside her, Sophie felt dowdy and bedraggled and, most of all, childish and unsophisticated.

'How do you do, Cousin?' was all Sophie managed, in a small voice.

Rosamund considered her with her head on one side. 'Lord! What has Moss been doing to you? You look like a fashion plate — and I was hoping for an ally, to stand with me against all this coming-out nonsense!'

'Now, my lady, don't tease poor Miss Sophie. Can't you see she's tired?' Moss reproved.

'Oh, go away, Judy,' Rosamound replied with complete good humour. 'No-one can be tired just travelling in a chariot all day. Dear Sophie, you aren't going to turn out to be mimsy and missish and think of nothing but clothes all day long, are you? I made sure you'd be more interested in dogs and horses and larks than dancing and —' she made an indescribable face at her maid — '*officers*!'

There was such spirit in the voice, and such good humour in the look she bent on her cousin, and such wickedness in the glance she gave her maid, that Sophie's spirits began to revive. There was nothing languid and superior in Rosamund's attitude. Perhaps it would be all right after all.

'I love horses and dogs, of course —' she began. But larks? It seemed odd to single out just one of the bird species of the world, though they sang very prettily of course.

'Good!' Rosamund seized her hand and tucked it under her arm and walked with her towards the door. 'I knew you were all right as soon as I saw you. We shall have some larks together, I promise you, and I shan't mind half so much being brought out if you are there to share it with me. They won't be on at me all the time to be ladylike with you to take the attention away from me! We'll share a room in Brussels, and have a famous time.' She glanced over her shoulder. 'Don't mind Moss — she's a trump, and never fusses about things!'

'I like her very much,' Sophie said, now that they were at

the top of the stairs and presumably out of earshot. She couldn't help thinking that Rosamund spoke rather loudly — though perhaps it was only because everything she said was so emphatic. 'But aren't you looking forward to going to Brussels?'

'Oh Lord! Yes — more than anything. Because, you see —' Rosamund halted and looked down at her abruptly. 'Can you keep a secret?'

'Well — yes,' Sophie said a little doubtfully. 'If it's not improper. I mean —'

Rosamund looked surprised. 'You strange thing! Of course it's not improper!'

Sophie felt herself blushing. 'No, no, what I meant was — well, as long as it's something there's no harm in keeping secret.' She felt she wasn't doing very well at explaining herself, and she very definitely didn't want to alienate this glorious creature, who had come to her hand so trustingly, like a beautiful wild deer.

'Oh, I understand you! You're good — I'd forgotten. But there's no harm to my secret, only Mama has funny ideas, and don't understand what it is to be young. You know what grown-ups are like.'

Sophie nodded, more pleased than ever that this elegant creature did not consider herself to be grown up.

Rosamund suddenly smiled and drew Sophie's hand through her arm again. 'My *good* cousin Sophie! I like that! I'm so wicked, I need a good person to right the balance! You can keep me straight when we are in Brussels. And, when we are in Brussels — here's my secret now, and be sure you keep it *absolutely* — I am going to be married! What do you think of that?'

Sophie was plainly bewildered. 'Married?' But how could a marriage be a secret from the grown-ups? Surely it must be Aunt Lucy who had arranged it? That was how marriages happened. 'How — to whom?'

'To my cousin Marcus — there now!' Rosamund looked at Sophie's bemused face, and flung back her head and laughed. 'Oh, Lord, you look so dumb-struck! But don't worry, no-one will try and get it out of you. No-one knows about it but you.',

'And — surely — your cousin Marcus?'

52

'No,' Rosamund said cheerfully. 'He doesn't know either, yet. But I shall tell him when the time comes. Hush! No more of it now — here's the saloon. They'll bring up supper as soon as your mother comes down. It will be a good one, too! No dreary cold cuts tonight — he promised me lobster patties and ratafia cream!'

'He? Who is he?'

'Jacques, Mama's cook. I went down to the kitchen after she'd interviewed him this morning and had a long talk with him. Oh, don't worry, he won't get into trouble. Mama won't remember what she ordered. She never cares about food. Can you imagine, not caring about food? Lord! I hope I'm never that old!'

Sophie couldn't help laughing, and followed her enterprising cousin into the lighted saloon, feeling that life from now on was going to be a great deal more interesting even than she had anticipated.

CHAPTER THREE

The house which Lucy had taken in Brussels for the Season was on the Rue Ducale, facing the Park and backing onto the ramparts of the city walls. It was an imposing building, the pale green façade ornamented by Ionic pilasters and stone copings picked out in contrasting white. All the houses in the row were painted in these pastel colours, which to English eyes gave them a cheerful but false air, as though they were only theatre scenery made of pasteboard.

The Park, which was the centre of much of fashionable life, was one of the wonders of the city. It was laid out with rolling lawns landscaped into interesting rises and hollows, secluded walks winding in and out amongst well-planted shrubberies and handsome trees. In the centre was a long, narrow lake, curving with the contours of the land, complete with water-fowl, and a tongue-in-cheek neo-Classical pavilion where refreshments were sold, which made a pleasant objective for a walk.

The Park was surrounded on three sides by houses, the Rue Ducale facing the Rue Royale across its green spaces, and the two together containing the smartest houses in the city. On the fourth side the square was completed by the sheer height of the grey ramparts, on top of which was a promenade shaded by tall elm trees. This was another fashionable lounge, from which magnificent views could be had of the whole city and of the surrounding countryside, the River Senne, and the dark mass of the Forest of Soignies.

Belgium itself, as the visitors had had ample chance to remark on their journey from Ostend, was very fertile and prosperous, with lush green meadows, unbelievably tall crops, fat cattle and glossy horses. Héloïse remarked that it was good to see a country where even the peasants and their beasts were so well-fed; but Lucy said that when the lower orders

54

were that prosperous, it made it impossible to get good, reliable servants.

The Firths had gone on ahead, and Peter Firth had kindly taken it on himself to hire the house for them. For himself and Roberta and Bobbie he had taken a more modest establishment in the quiet Place Capucines, and all three were on hand to welcome Lucy's party when it arrived.

'I hope you find it comfortable,' Peter said with the faintest doubt just evident in his voice as he looked at the huge barn of an entry hall, and the shabbiness of the wallpaper. 'It was the only house available that had a ballroom. I hope it isn't too big for you — but at least with summer coming, you won't have to worry too much about heating it.'

Héloïse and Sophie were staring about them with a rather bemused air, Sophie wondering at the size of the oak staircase, which looked as though each tread had been fashioned from a whole tree, while Héloïse was noticing the dust everywhere and the dullness of the mirrors, and mentally resolving to have conversation with the butler as soon as possible.

Lucy, however, merely glanced, and nodded. 'I'm sure it will do very well,' she pronounced. 'And these are the servants you engaged for us, I suppose?'

They were all local people — butler, cook, footmen and housemaids — and they came forward to be inspected with pleasant, welcoming smiles. Though it may have been true, as the visitors had heard, that there were a great many Bonapartists amongst the population of Belgium who had been quite happy under French rule, there had not been the slightest evidence of hostility towards them so far. Indeed, everyone seemed to welcome the English visitors, flocking over with heavy purses, and the holiday desire to empty them into Belgian hands.

Lucy's party had brought with them from England only their personal servants — Lucy's Docwra, Judy Moss for the young women, and Héloïse's Marie. Lucy, however, could no more have gone away for the Season without her groom, Parslow, and her horses, than she could fly. He had been sent on ahead with her riding horse, Hotspur, and a pair of her black carriage horses, and the first thing she wanted to do when she arrived was to go with him to inspect the stables he had secured, and to examine every inch of her precious beasts to see that no harm had come to them on the journey.

'You might just as easily have hired horses when we arrived,' Peter Firth said with an amused look. 'You must have seen what fine brutes the Flanders horses are — glossy, strong and well-fed.'

'Draught horses,' Lucy dismissed them contemptuously. 'Yes, strong, I grant you, but I couldn't drive behind a pair of them. And as for riding horses — why, even the Belgians themselves buy their hunters from England. You can't really think —'

'He's teasing you,' Roberta advised as Lucy grew agitated.

'Indeed I was,' Firth said wickedly. 'I wouldn't expect you to hire horses locally, but to buy them, of course.'

'Now, Peter —' Roberta warned, but Lucy only nodded agreement.

'It wouldn't surprise me in the least, with so many young officers on the spree in a fashionable city, if there weren't some excellent bargains to be had,' she said. 'When a young gentleman finds himself badly dipped, what can he do but sell his second hunter? I shall certainly have Parslow keep his eyes open for me ... Now why is everybody laughing?'

When Lucy had departed for the stables, Firth also made his excuses. 'If you will forgive me, I must walk up to Headquarters and see if there are any instructions for me. It's just across the Park, in the Rue Royale,' he added, and then, intercepting a burning look from Bobbie, added, 'Would you like to come with me?'

'Yes, do go, darling,' Roberta said. 'I shall stay and help Héloïse settle in. I'm sure there'll be plenty to do.'

'Including changing the position of every piece of furniture in the house,' Firth said genially, interpreting Héloïse's thoughtful frown with an accuracy that made her start, and Roberta laugh.

'Take your mocking step-papa away, Bobbie, before someone murders him. But come back and tell us everything, won't you?'

Rosamund would rather have liked to go with the male division, but contented herself with the other important business of the moment, that of securing a pleasant room for her and Sophie, on the second floor with a window overlooking the Park. The view commanded one of the main entrance gates, and they could also see down into every carriage which passed along the road.

'So we shall always know what's going on,' she said to her cousin. 'If we hadn't made a push for it, we'd have found ourselves with a room at the back of the house, and nothing to look at but gardens and blank walls.'

Moss and a very young Belgian housemaid unpacked the young ladies' boxes, while they knelt on the window-seat and kept up a running commentary for Moss's diversion on the scene below. Such dresses — such smart pelisses and bonnets — not a dowdy in sight! Such grand carriages filled with the *monde* — everyone so animated and gay! It was true what they had been told — Brussels this Season was as smart as London!

And above and beyond all, *so many officers!* Walking — or, well, swaggering might be the better word — lounging in groups chatting, riding by on the most elegant horses the Continent had ever seen — even Rosamund, determined not to be transmogrified into a débutante, couldn't help exclaiming at the sight. Oh, the uniforms — of Dutch blue and Rifleman green — the fur caps, the cocked hats, the kepis and shakoes — the cross belts and gorgets and epaulettes — the gold lace, the glossy Hessian boots — and everywhere the glorious, brave scarlet of the British! It would be a determined head that would not be turned by the sight; an unfeeling heart that was not in danger of being lost in Brussels that April!

The one officer of all others that she longed to see did not appear, but Rosamund felt confident that as soon as he learned she was in Brussels, he would come visiting. She had not seen him for more than two years, but when he went away he had sworn he would come back from the war still unwed, which to her mind was as good a promise as she needed.

With so much to do, time sped by, and it was after two o'clock when everyone broke off to gather in the morning-room to eat a cold collation, which Héloïse had had the forethought to order before they began unpacking. They had

57

hardly begun when Firth walked in with Bobbie, and surveyed the table cheerfully.

'Ah, that looks tempting! Breakfast is but a dim and distant memory. I must say there seems to be no shortage of food here! Are those duck eggs? I'm extremely partial to hard-boiled duck eggs. And cold beef, by Jove!'

'Never mind cold beef,' Lucy broke in impatiently. 'Did you see the Duke? Is Danby there? What's the news?'

Firth shook his head as he helped himself to meat and fruit. 'Wellington isn't there. Headquarters is all but deserted.' He grinned suddenly at the memory. 'You'd never know it for a military establishment: two ordinary houses thrown together, the doors guarded by nothing more imposing than a pair of Belgian gendarmes, and inside a couple of aides-de-camp, lounging in armchairs talking about horses!'

'They weren't even in uniform,' Bobbie said with evident disappointment, even disapproval. 'And Colonel Gordon had his feet up on the desk.'

Lucy grunted. 'Oh, the Duke's "family" was always like that. Even in Vienna they behaved as though they were at a house-party. But where is everybody?'

'Wellington's gone to Ghent to make his leg to the King of France. He only arrived from Vienna on the fifth, so this is the first chance he's had. He's taken most of his staff with him — including Lord Theakston, I'm afraid,' Firth added to Lucy. 'There was only Fremantle and Lennox there with Gordon, holding the fort. I made my report to them and had a chat and came away again. The Duke's due back on the eleventh, so I'm at liberty until then, unless the Prince asks for me — but I don't anticipate it, since we saw each other so recently in London.'

'The Prince of Orange? He's here, then?'

'Oh, yes — didn't I tell you he was coming out? He arrived a few days ago. All the Dutch royal family is here, of course. There's to be a grand reception for King William at the end of the month, probably a dinner and a ball — so you'll need to get your new gowns made up before then, ladies.'

The Belgian butler came in at that moment with a footman bringing the coffee, and conversation ceased while Héloïse

58

spoke to him rather sharply in French about the need to polish the silver before using it. When they had departed, Lucy resumed rather impatiently.

'Time enough later to talk about balls and receptions — what's the military situation? What of the Allied army?'

Firth made a comical face. 'What indeed! Sir Charles Stuart wrote to Bathurst last week calling it a "heterogeneous force", and that was too mild for the truth! Fremantle was very graphic — and disparaging. A large part of it consists of Dutch-Belgic troops of extremely doubtful reliability. When I tell you that half of them are veterans who fought under the Eagles — and you know what can happen when Boney comes face to face with his old sweats!'

'Yes, you only have to think of that dreadful Marshal Ney going over to Bonaparte at Auxerre, and taking all his men with him,' said Roberta. 'And after he'd made a solemn vow to the King of France.'

'Ney was rather a special case,' Firth said, 'but the Duke will have to keep his eye on the Dutch–Belgics all the same. Then there's a contingent of Nassauers apparently on its way, and another from Brunswick —'

'The Black Brunswickers? They're good soldiers — fiercely loyal to their Duke, and very well disciplined,' Lucy said.

Firth nodded. 'And Gordon says the Hanoverians are good soldiers too.'

'Yes, but Danby said that in the Peninsula the Germans were always deserting,' Lucy frowned. 'They were more trouble than they were worth.'

'Not the King's German Legion, ma'am,' Bobbie broke in eagerly. 'They're splendid fellows!'

'Oh quite,' Firth murmured mischievously. 'But then they're as good as British, aren't they?'

'And what British troops are there? Lucy asked.

'No veterans, except the Fighting 52nd, of course, and the 95th Rifles; and the Foot Guards will always put up a good show. For the rest, the infantry is untried, young soldiers and second battalions, with no field experience except for that short campaign under Gordon in Holland.'

'Cavalry?' Lucy asked shortly.

'Some Peninsula veterans — though as you know we used

very little cavalry there. Everything we've got at home is being sent over, but though they're the best-mounted cavalry in the world, and probably the best horsemen, they've only been used to parades and civilian duties. No-one knows how they'll behave in battle.'

'Tin soldiers, Colonel Gordon called them,' Bobbie said with evident disapproval.

Firth shook his head. 'I don't envy the Duke his task of pulling all the elements together and making an army of them — especially as Fremantle says King William is as jealous as a wife, and wants to keep everything under his own command, and argues with the Duke over every appointment. And the Duke's got old Hudson Lowe as Quartermaster-General, who's driving him mad, so Lennox says; and half the staff appointments were made by the Horseguards to pay off social debts —'

He stopped abruptly, looking round the circle of his audience, and realising that he had been speaking too freely. Lucy and Bobbie might be listening with intelligent interest, and Rosamund with fervour, but Roberta and Héloïse were looking distinctly alarmed. He smiled and changed the subject.

'Ah well, the English soldiers might be untried in battle, but their officers are very experienced in the ballroom! From what Gordon was telling us, there are balls and parties every night, to say nothing of the theatre and the opera, and the new exhibition of paintings that's just opened. That's proving very popular, though I suspect it may be because more than half the pictures, Gordon says, are portraits of British officers.'

'I imagine the country is very good for riding?' Lucy said.

'Yes, and there are plenty of pretty châteaux to go and visit. The Belgians are very hospitable if there's a profit to be made! Oh, and the famous Catalani is said to be coming to Brussels later this month. I've heard her fees for a single performance are so enormous that no-one who has engaged her has ever admitted to being disappointed with her voice! It's a great thing to put a high price on yourself!'

Roberta laughed. 'Oh, you do talk nonsense. Everyone knows she is a wonderful singer, and that's why her fees are high.'

'It may just as well be *vice versa*, my love,' Firth smiled.

Héloïse was frowning in thought. 'I suppose we had better have Sophie and Rosamund's ball as soon as possible, if there are all these entertainments. For one cannot take them about until they are out, *ça se voit.*'

'Quite right,' Lucy said. 'We might as well fix a date now for — how long will it take to arrange? — a week ahead? What about the sixteenth?'

Héloïse considered. 'Yes, I should think it could be managed. Of course, we don't yet know what the servants here can do, and then there are the gowns to have made — and the invitations —'

'We'll manage,' Roberta said comfortably. 'I'll help you with everything, don't worry. And Peter shall find out for us who is here, and who the best tradespeople are.'

Firth bowed. 'Certainly, mesdames — command me! I have nothing else to do until the Duke returns to Headquarters.'

The following morning Lucy declared she could not exist another day without being on horseback, and went off with her groom to exercise Hotspur in the Allée Verte — a charming grassy ride just outside the city walls. This left Héloïse with the two girls — Sophie eagerly and Rosamund most unwillingly — to the attentions of the mantuamaker and her assistants, who had been summoned up to the house with their patterns and fashion-plates and samples to discuss the all-important question of the Coming-out Gowns.

'Trust Mama to rub off when there's anything disagreeable on the go,' Rosamund grumbled. 'And on a day like this, to be skulking indoors talking of clothes!'

Héloïse smiled sympathetically, and tried reason. 'But you know, my dear, your mother has a whole trunkful of gowns, and it is not she who is to be the centre of attention. You and Sophie must appear to advantage. It is your most important engagement of the Season — of your lives, perhaps.'

'The only engagements I'm interested in are military ones,' Rosamund growled, and then was rather pleased with herself for the *double-entendre*, which made her say in a more equable voice, 'Besides, if Mama thought it was that important, she'd have stayed to see it done right, wouldn't she? Instead of dashing off and enjoying herself.'

'Perhaps she thought I might be of some help in guiding your taste,' Héloïse said gently. 'Come, the sooner we set our minds to it, the sooner it will be done. Don't you want to look well at your ball?'

Rosamund grinned. 'Well, ma'am, as to that, it don't matter a bit what I wear, I shall still appear to be exactly what I am — an intolerable little gypsy, so Marcus always used to call me!'

'But it isn't true,' Sophie protested. 'You are so tall and handsome, Cousin, and you always look so elegant! I wish I had half your advantages,' she added a little wistfully.

Rosamund looked rueful. 'There, now you have subdued me. Dear Sophie, I said you would be good for me! Come then, Aunt, I surrender. Bring on the patterns and samples! You may do with me as you please — I am so meek and good, you may even dress me in pink muslin, with frills, and I shall only purr like a kitten.'

Héloïse laughed. 'You are absurd! But you need not be afraid of pink muslin — I hope I have better sense than that!'

Having made her protest, Rosamund put all her energies into choosing her gown for the coming-out ball, and Héloïse was amused at how determinedly she chose this and rejected that, having a great deal of innate taste, and very strong opinions already about what she could and could not wear. Sophie plainly admired her, and felt that, by contrast, her own country upbringing and entire lack of experience prevented her from having any thoughts on the subject. It was only after steady encouragement from her mother that she could be brought hesitantly to express any preference at all.

Seeing her cousin's timidity, Rosamund good-naturedly threw herself into the business, and though once her ball-gown was chosen she might have excused herself from the rest, she remained to encourage and advise Sophie on the choice of several more morning-gowns, walking-gowns and evening-gowns, and even offered to accompany her when she went shopping with her mother for bonnets and gloves.

'It can be done in half the time,' she advised firmly, 'if only you are decisive.'

The mantuamaker, Madame Berce, was a small but handsome Bruxelloise with bright dark eyes, who wore the traditional black dress and black lace mantilla crossed on her breast, which made her look very Spanish. She spoke English haltingly, until she realised that Héloïse was French by origin, after which she relapsed into fluent but strangely-accented French. Sophie understood her well enough, but Rosamund, with a blank look, demanded translation.

This brought to the front of Sophie's mind something which had been worrying her on and off ever since they set foot on foreign soil, and when the mantuamaker was engaged in taking Héloïse's measurements, Sophie drew Rosamund aside to consult with her.

'Can I ask your advice, Cousin?' she said in an anxious undertone. 'You see, I've been wondering whether it's quite *proper* of Maman to speak to the servants and Madame Berce in French. I don't like to ask her, for you know she is the dearest person in the world, but she hasn't lived in London or anywhere fashionable; and my particular friends, Miss Laxton and Miss Greaves, told me that no *real* lady would ever admit to understanding French. And although I understood Madame Berce, I noticed that you pretended not to, so I wondered ...'

Rosamund was embarrassed. Under her governess, Miss Trotton, she had learned French and Italian, and could read both languages well enough when she put her mind to it. But from disinclination she had never practised speaking them, and far from pretending not to understand, she had found Madame Berce's strange accent made her French impenetrable. She did not want to give up her position as Sophie's idol and mentor, which she found rather flattering; but on the other hand, how could she criticise Aunt Héloïse, who was so kind and good?

'Well,' she extemporised, 'I think the rule is that it's all right to speak a little French, but it doesn't do to speak it well, and not like a French person. But of course,' she added with a burst of inspiration, 'it's quite different for your Mama, for everyone knows she is French. That's *quite* all right.'

Sophie looked anxious. 'But what about me, then? I'm not French, but I've spoken it since I was born, and of course I speak it to Maman and Marie and Monsieur Barnard all the time. But people wouldn't know that, would they? I shouldn't like anyone to think I'm not ladylike.'

Rosamund struggled. 'I think perhaps it would be best if in public — at balls and so on — you spoke English. But in private, and with close friends, there can be no harm ...' She saw with relief that Héloïse was looking towards them enquiringly. 'Oh, I think your Mama wants us! I'm glad I had most of my clothes made in London — think of the fittings you still have to come, and in this glorious weather, too!'

When the mantuamaker had gone, Héloïse decided that they had all been indoors for quite long enough, and invited her charges to put on their bonnets and go for a walk.

'Where shall we go? Shall we explore the Park?'

'Oh, ma'am, can't it be the ramparts?' Rosamund said at once. 'You can see from the trees that there's a wonderful breeze up there. And I dare say we shall be forever walking in the Park, until we are sick of it.'

Héloïse, looking from the window, saw that there were a great many splashes of red moving about on the ramparts, and smiled to herself. But she had no objection to a walk amongst the redcoats, and assumed that two girls plainly *not out* and wearing close bonnets and mittens would not attract any unwelcome attention.

In this she was quite correct, for while Rosamund's eager eyes scanned every officer's face, the officers were all much too well-bred to return the look, or even to appear to have seen the girls at all.

In the end it was Héloïse herself who attracted the notice. They were standing at one corner of the ramparts, looking out over the view towards the dark forest, when a gentleman passing behind them suddenly stopped, and then stepped to the side to get a better view of her profile.

'*Mon Dieu*, can it be true?' a French voice said fervently. Héloïse started and turned, to find herself looking up into a handsome face and shining hazel eyes. 'It is you! I knew I could not be mistaken, though I had only seen your back. I knew you at once, but I hardly dared to believe ... Héloïse! Dear Héloïse!' He took both her hands, smiling down at her tenderly. 'Let me look at you! It has been such an age — and

64

yet you haven't changed in the smallest degree.'

'Charles!' Héloïse exclaimed, in a mixture of surprise and pleasure and apprehension. 'But I am astonished. What are you doing here?'

'I might ask you the same thing,' he said, pressing her hands and laughing with pleasure. 'It is much more unexpected in your case! For myself, I am here with the Allied army — Perponcher's Division, you know — to fight for our King against the Ogre — if ever that fight shall happen! But what does it matter? We are both here at the same moment, by the most wonderful chance!'

He was speaking in French, and when he said 'our King' she knew he meant his and hers — he was thinking of her as French too. Everything about his words and gestures was claiming her as more than just a friend, as if no more than a few weeks had passed since that day amongst the trees of Sutton Bank when he had asked her to marry him and she had painfully refused. But that was nine years ago; she had changed more than he could imagine. She was very different inside, though he pretended, flatteringly, to think her unchanged externally.

The children were staring, though trying not to: she must make the introduction before he said something embarrassing.

'Sophie, *ma chère*, I don't know if you will remember Monsieur le Duc de Veslne-d'Estienne, for you were no more than seven or eight when you last saw him. Charles, you remember my daughter Sophie-Marie?'

'I do indeed,' Charles said, bowing gracefully, 'and I see she has grown into a very beautiful young woman. *Enchanté*, mademoiselle.'

Sophie curtseyed, glad that the form of the introduction relieved her from the necessity of saying how well she remembered him — which was hardly at all. She had a vague recollection of the Frenchman who was a friend of Maman's, who had visited sometimes when they all lived at Plaisir, but could not of her certainty have said that she recognised him. She glanced at Rosamund to see what she thought of it all, but Rosamund had on her blankest look.

Héloïse turned to Rosamund now. 'My dear, may I present

to you an old friend, the Duc de Veslne-d'Estienne? Charles, my niece, Lady Rosamund Chetwyn.'

'Your servant, mademoiselle.'

Rosamund curtseyed slightly, and the Duc was half-way through his bow when Héloïse added, 'Lady Rosamund is the daughter of my husband's sister.'

Those were the cruel words that had to be said. He stiffened, and straightened slowly, seeking Héloïse's eyes. 'How stupid of me,' he said under his breath. 'Of course you are married. I should have expected it.'

'I married my cousin James Morland,' she said steadily, holding his gaze.

He smiled a little crookedly. 'Then that explains everything,' he said, trying for lightness. 'You are here with your husband, who is, perhaps a soldier?'

Héloïse felt her face grow warm. 'No, I — he is not here, in fact. He remained at home in Yorkshire.' The Duc raised one eyebrow, and she stumbled on, 'I came with my sister-in-law, Lady Theakston — Rosamund's mother. We are bringing out our girls here.' She was making a poor hand of it, and pulled herself together with an effort. 'Roberta is here too — Lady Chelmsford as she was — with her new husband and her son.'

'Ah yes, I remember her kindness well. It was at her house that you had the coming-out of my friend Mathilde, wasn't it? And how is Miss Nordubois?'

'She is well, very happy. She was married this month to a very respectable young man. They are on their honeymoon at the moment.'

The Duc gave a rueful smile. 'So many nuptials! I feel a little out of step. But how is it you have come to Brussels on so important an occasion as a début?'

Héloïse hesitated. 'It is a complicated story, too long to be told here —' she began.

He looked contrite. 'Of course, how stupid of me. I am keeping you standing here in this breeze, which is surely too fresh for ladies. I am so sorry —'

'No, no,' Héloïse said hastily. 'We are enjoying it after a morning indoors. But perhaps we should be walking on.'

'Indeed, I must not detain you.'

Despite their words, neither moved. They hesitated,

looking at each other doubtfully. It was absurd to part thus, with nine years of things to say to each other. But what things? Héloïse thought despairingly. What had she to tell him, but about her marriage? She held out her hand to him.

'Well, goodbye,' she said, and there was the hint of a question mark at the end of the sentence that she was not aware of.

The Duc's spirits rose a little. 'May I call on you?' he asked, taking her hand. 'Would your sister-in-law think it an intrusion?'

Héloïse's eyes kindled. 'Oh no — please do! We are staying in the Rue Ducale — I cannot recall the number, but —'

'I shall find it,' he said, smiling with relief. 'And I am staying at the Hôtel d'Angleterre. If you should need me — if I can be of any service to you ...' He bowed. 'Your servant, madame — masdemoiselles!'

Then he was walking away like a man who could not trust himself further. Héloïse had sufficient presence of mind to turn and resume their walk in the opposite direction, and to be glad that Sophie and Rosamund saw nothing to interest them in a chance meeting between old acquaintances, and were now chattering together about governesses and what lessons they least liked. It left Héloïse free to resemble her thoughts, and to wonder why she had found the meeting so disturbing.

That evening the Firths dined with them at the Rue Ducale. They had risen from dinner and were gathered in the drawing-room awaiting the arrival of the tea-tray, when there was the sound of someone knocking at the street door.

'A caller, at this time of night?' Roberta said, raising her brows in surprise.

Héloïse found herself unexpectedly short of breath and unable to make any comment, but Lucy, looking up from that day's *Gazette de Bruxelles* which Firth had procured from a fellow-diplomat and passed on, said, 'It isn't so very late — not for a town full of officers. Probably someone from Head-quarters with some news just arrived.'

They all listened for the sounds from below, but the walls were too thick to be able to recognise any voices. Then there were brisk footsteps outside, the door opened, and in came a tall, broad-shouldered young man in the plain blue frock-coat of a British staff-officer. His well-muscled legs were closely clad in white net pantaloons and rather dusty Hessian boots; a cocked hat was tucked under his arm; and his sword was carried on slings rather than a frog, revealing to those in the know that he had seen service in the Peninsula.

He paused in the doorway and looked about him with a smile of satisfaction. His complexion was clear and brown, his sun-whitened hair a smartly dishevelled crop, and his face was decorated by a military moustache and a magnificent pair of side-whiskers. He looked every inch an experienced and a fashionable officer.

'Well, well,' he said happily, 'so I find you all here! No, don't move! You can't think how handsome you all look to these eyes of mine, starved of company as they are!'

The company was returning his gaze in a rather bemused manner; it was Bobbie who first leapt up and ran forward crying, 'Marcus! Marcus, it's you!'

He was clasped in a friendly and very muscular embrace, while Firth stood up and came forward with his hand extended, saying, 'It was all the camouflage that bamboozled us! Those whiskers are most becoming, I must say. How are you, my boy?'

'Very well, sir,' said Marcus, freeing one arm to shake his former tutor's hand, while the other slipped with easy familiarity round Bobbie's shoulders.

'You look it,' Bobbie grinned at him and thumped a fist against his cousin's chest. 'They must be feeding you too well — you're like a side of beef!'

'No cheek from you, young 'un!' Marcus grinned. 'How do you do, ma'am? It's good to see you again,' he added to Roberta; and '"Servant, your ladyship!" to Lucy.

Lucy's sharp eyes were taking in every detail of his appearance. 'Have you just come from Ghent?' she asked abruptly.

'No, ma'am, nothing so exciting. I've been at Ninove, no more than four miles away, looking for suitable lodgings and billets for the cavalry when they arrive. Not all staff jobs are so glamorous!'

'You're a staff-officer now?' Roberta said. 'But Marcus, how splendid!'

'To be sure he is,' Lucy said shortly. 'Can't you tell by his uniform?'

'Not everyone has your experience, Lucy dear,' Héloïse said with a smile. 'How do you do, Marcus?'

'Glad to see you again, ma'am,' he replied, and to the two girls, 'Miss Sophie! And Rosy — how splendid!'

Rosamund had turned first white and then red at Marcus's entry. She had risen from her chair, and now stood very straight with her hands down at her sides, her face rigid with an excess of emotion, only her burning blue eyes revealing her inner turmoil as Marcus advanced across the room to shake hands. He was so changed in appearance, he seemed so much older and more soldierly, that he was almost a stranger to her. She placed her hand in his like an automaton, and found that she was hardly looking up to meet his eyes.

The same thing evidently struck him, for he smiled — a gleam of teeth through that surprising, somehow *alien* moustache — and said, 'Why, Rosy, how tall you've grown! When I last saw you, you were still a schoolroom miss in long plaits, and now you're an elegant young lady! I must remember to call you Lady Rosamund, lest I offend your dignity!'

'Oh fustian!' she said hotly, feeling her cheeks glow with distress, though she did not quite understand why. 'I'm just the same. But you look so different — so — changed, somehow.' It defeated her.

He released her hand and grinned round at the company. 'Well, I believe I am changed, especially now that Hookey has taken me into his family. You can't imagine how much drill we aides have to do, to keep us up to the mark!'

'Drill?' Bobbie questioned obediently.

'Why yes! We're obliged to fall in every morning at six o'clock for two hours to practise the waltz and the quadrille, until we have all the steps perfectly.' He pointed a toe and raised a hand, and looked down at himself with such a comical air of not knowing what he expected to see that everyone except Rosamund laughed.

'You can't mean you do nothing but dancing,' Bobbie

crowed. 'Look at the size you've grown! You've shoulders like a bullock!'

Marcus gave him a look of limpid innocence. 'That's all the weight of the silver lace, my boy. I can't tell you, Bob, what a terrible burden it is!' Bobbie gave his arm a friendly punch in protest, and Marcus gazed round the ring of faces again and said, 'Oh, it's good to see you all! What brings you out here? I couldn't believe it when I got in and Fremantle told me you had arrived. I understand you've come out officially, sir? Some kind of liaison job?'

Firth inclined his head. 'It seems there's a vacancy for someone who speaks tactful German as well as French, since you are all to join up with the Prussians sooner or later.'

'Later, we profoundly hope! King William hates the Prussians worse than the French, and it's going to be the deuce of a job to keep the peace between 'em. So does that mean you are ours, sir, or London's?'

'Is there a difference? No, don't answer me that — of course there is! Certainly Bathurst and Castlereagh think I'm theirs — but I dare say the Duke wouldn't have accepted me if he didn't think I was his.'

'You soon will be, sir,' Marcus nodded, his eyes shining with an admiration which made him look, for a moment, nearer his real age than his whiskers and broad shoulders had previously allowed. 'It's not possible to work with the Beau without being magicked by him. I don't know how it is ...'

'Why do you call him the Beau?' Sophie plucked up courage to ask. The whiskers had rather intimidated her at first, but once he had made her laugh, she had got past them to the eyes, which seemed kind. They turned on her now, pale blue under fair brows, with lots of little lines about them, from squinting against sun and dust.

'Oh, because he is so neat and spare, you know — as clean and fresh as a pin, whatever the hour of day or night. So in the Peninsula we called him Beau Douro, after the river Douro.'

'And Hookey because of his nose,' Bobbie burst in, anxious to shew his knowledge.

'I don't know that it isn't because of his tongue,' Marcus said. 'When he digs into you —' He shuddered.

70

'Is he an ill-tempered man, then?' Héloïse asked in surprise.

'Oh no, ma'am — only he can't bear nonsense or inefficiency, and he has a short way with fools, or those who cross him. But he is as kind to his family as if they really were his own flesh-and-blood. When he asked for me, I could hardly believe it!'

'It is a promotion, isn't it?' Roberta asked.

'Why yes, ma'am. Lennox is going back to his regiment, you see, so there was a vacancy, and since the Beau knows Papa — and I'd been with him in the Peninsula —'

'But Marcus, wouldn't you rather be with your regiment when the fighting starts?' Bobbie broke in anxiously, feeling his hero's reputation was at stake. 'Wouldn't you rather be in the thick of it? I mean, it may be very grand being a staff-officer —'

Marcus grinned at his cousin reassuringly. 'Oh, don't worry, Bob, I shall be in the thick all right! It ain't the Beau's way to direct from a safe distance. He'll be where the fighting's fiercest, and where he is, we aides must go too, you know! I shall have just as much chance of being honourably killed wearing a cocked hat as wearing a shako.'

Bobbie blushed a little and said, 'Oh, but I didn't mean —' and there was a brief, embarrassed silence.

Marcus didn't seem to notice it, however. He looked around with a smile and said, 'But you haven't told me yet why you're here. Was it just for the fun of it?'

'You think it's going to be fun, do you?' Firth said with a wry smile. 'What it is to be young! No, no, we are here on business. The prowess of the English officers at dancing has penetrated even to England, so we have brought Miss Sophie and Lady Rosamund here for their come-out, where they may get better dancing-partners than in London.'

'Really? Why, that's splendid!' Marcus said, and smiled at the two young women. 'When is it to be? You must be sure to save a dance for me, if you don't mind being seen standing up with a staff-officers. Most of the young ladies in Brussels want line officers or nothing! But I know Rosy will be kind to me, at least, for old times' sake.'

Rosamund looked at the cheery, stranger's, smile which

71

was bent on her, and with a strangled sound turned and almost ran from the room, leaving a puzzled silence behind her.

'Oh dear, did I say something wrong?' Marcus enquired.

'I shouldn't think so,' Lucy said indifferently. 'She's overexcited, I expect.'

Sophie got up, and with a murmured apology went after her cousin, hearing the cheerful conversation resume even before she had closed the door behind her.

In the bedroom they shared, Sophie found Rosamund, not crying as she had expected, but standing by the window staring out sightlessly into the blackness, her face dark with misery and anger. She didn't turn as Sophie came in, and, not knowing what to say, Sophie simply came and stood near her in sympathetic silence.

After a while, Rosamund said starkly, 'Why did he talk to me like that? As if I were an idiot. No, worse, as if I were a child — a little child he didn't even know! All that — *stuff* — about dancing, and calling me a young lady in that — that — *intolerable* way!'

Sophie looked at her, feeling her pain, having nothing to offer by way of comfort. Grown-ups, she knew, often did things like that, without meaning to; and it was worse in this case, because Rosamund hadn't been thinking of him as a grown-up, but as one of them.

'I expect,' she said at last, tentatively, 'being away at war changes people.'

'It wouldn't change me,' Rosamund said stormily. 'And I don't believe he was changed, underneath. He was just being — I don't know — just shewing off. Because of Bobbie and Mr Firth and — being in Brussels, I suppose. I *hate* that sort of thing! Pretending to be something you're not.'

Sophie put two tentative fingers on her arm, and when the touch was not rejected, slipped an arm round her tall cousin's waist. 'I expect it was the surprise of seeing us,' she said. 'He wasn't expecting us to be here. Next time ...' The words trailed off, helplessly; but Rosamund was comforted. She dropped an arm across Sophie's shoulders and they stood in silence for a while, until a carriage, passing below in a clatter

72

of hooves and a flickering of lights, broke the stillness.

'Yes, I expect you're right,' Rosamund said, and her voice was lighter, more cheerful. 'Next time it will be all right. He was expecting me to have plaits, still.'

'And you weren't expecting him to have whiskers.'

'No. They did startle me a bit. But I must say, they're very handsome, once you get used to them.'

'Yes,' said Sophie doubtfully. She couldn't imagine ever getting used to them — only learning to look past them.

Rosamund said no more. Her native cheerfulness and determination had reasserted themselves, and she was already busily planning the next manoeuvre in her campaign.

The next day, the 11th of April, Madame Berce came up to the house with the first of the new gowns for fitting — walking-dresses for both Héloïse and Sophie. Rosamund, with a look of sympathy which Sophie didn't need, accepted Roberta's invitation to go out with her and Bobbie to walk in the Park, and Sophie and Héloïse went up to their respective rooms to try the gowns on.

Sophie's fitted her snugly, and not even Moss's critical gaze could find it necessary to demand any alteration.

'I must say, miss, you've a marvellous slender waist! It's a pity in a way the fashions don't show it off. But there — you hold yourself so nicely, too, and the new gown makes you look quite tall.'

In Héloïse's room an oblique struggle was going on between her and Marie. Mistress had asked for a degree of comfort in the cut of her gown, but maid was all for fashion and elegance, and the mantuamaker stood between the two, now pulling the material in, now letting it out. Marie, growing more heated, rounded on Madame Berce at last to say that the buttons were not evenly placed and that the hem dipped and waved like the English Channel. Madame Berce remarked frigidly that if mademoiselle meant the sea beyond Ostend, she had never heard it called anything but La Manche, and that she had been sewing on buttons since she was four years old and had never had any complaints until now. Marie retorted that she supposed Belgian people weren't particular about their appearance, if they were accustomed to having their clothes made up by four-year-old children.

At this interesting point there was a scratching at the door, and Marie stalked off on her dignity to open it, and to receive a card on a reluctantly polished silver tray, and the information that a gentleman was below asking for her ladyship.

'As if her ladyship would be likely to receive callers when she's having a gown fitted!' Marie exclaimed in exasperation, but Héloïse, her heart unaccountably jumping, called her over.

'Who is it, Marie? Shew me the card.' She took it and stared at it, and then whirled on the spot, catching the loose material out of the mantuamaker's hands as she ran to the dressing-table to examine the state of her hair. 'I will see him. Thank you, Madame Berce, I do not wish it taken in. The gown is just right as it is. You have made it exactly as I like.' And she left so quickly that neither of the women had time to protest or argue.

In the morning-room the Duc was waiting, standing by the table in the window where the journals were laid out; but his eyes were fixed on the door, and his face lit as Héloïse came in.

'Ah, you are at home after all! The servant seemed so doubtful —'

'I was with my mantuamaker,' Héloïse explained.

He smiled. 'Then I am surprised indeed to see you! I know such consultations are sacred, and not to be disturbed by a mere man! If you will forgive the liberty —' He bent towards her, and for a startled instant Héloïse thought he was going to kiss her; but he plucked something from the shoulder of her gown and held it out. 'A stray pin. I was afraid it might scratch your neck, perhaps.'

'I — I thought as I had kept you waiting so long, I should not delay by changing my gown,' Héloïse said, growing pink.

'I had but just arrived. Did it seem long to you?' he asked innocently. 'But indeed, that colour becomes you very well.' He gazed at her face indulgently, so that she didn't know whether he meant the gown, or her blushes.

But this was dangerous — even wrong, perhaps. 'Charles,' she began anxiously, and he forestalled her.

'Forgive me. Did I speak too boldly? I did not mean to

offend; but I cannot feel that you are a stranger to me. I cannot feel anything but that we are old and dear friends. Must I be formal with you? It shall be as you wish.'

'Oh, I don't wish it,' she said at once, and then bit her lip. 'It is just that — I am a married woman, Charles. That must not be forgotten.'

'Is it likely to be? No, don't answer that. It was a piece of the grossest folly on my part, when I saw you on the ramparts yesterday and looking not a day older than when I had last seen you, to suppose that everything was unchanged. But a woman like you — all loveliness, all goodness — was bound to marry! And to marry a better man than me, I hope and trust.'

'I love James very much,' she said. 'He was my first love, and we were betrothed when first I came to England. But — circumstances — kept us apart. When you honoured me by asking me to marry you, Charles, I was still in love with him, although he was not free. That was why I refused you. I could not give you my whole heart, and I did not feel it to be fair to you —'

'Oh! Wretched scruples!' he said, only half joking. 'I'd have been happy with any part of you.'

'No, you wouldn't,' Héloïse said seriously. 'And you deserved better than that.' He did no reply. She went on, 'Shortly after that, James became free, and asked me to marry him. We have been together ever since, most happily —'

'But he let you come here, to a foreign country, alone.' The criticism was implicit in his voice.

'I am not alone. I am here with friends,' Héloïse said defensively. 'And it was convenient to have Sophie's come-out here, rather than to delay it, as we should have had to in England.'

'If I were your husband, I should not let you go away from me for an instant.'

'James was busy. He has a great many responsibilities at home. And he has much on his mind —' She knew she was making a poor hand of defending James, and stopped abruptly, equally aware that she should not find it necessary to do so.

'I'm sorry,' he said quickly. 'It is not for me to criticise. I would not have done so, had I not felt that *you* were unhappy to be here alone.'

'Oh — no — I — I do not mind it —' she began, but could not go on. They looked into each other's eyes, both seeing what might have happened. If she had married him when he asked her — no, it didn't do to think like that.

'And you,' she said as lightly as she could. 'Did you marry — afterwards?'

He held her gaze steadily. 'No,' he said. 'No, I never married. Like you, I didn't feel I could give my hand without my heart, and my heart was — irretrievably elsewhere.'

Tears came to her eyes. She held out her hand in a gesture part denial, part entreaty. 'Oh, Charles — !'

He took it and lifted it to his lips, and then released it; and smiled at her, a painful, loving smile full of understanding. 'No, no! Dear friend, I didn't come here to make you uncomfortable. I would be honoured and happy to be allowed to escort you while you are in Brussels, to place myself at your service purely as an old acquaintance and your fellow-countryman. I do not believe there could be anything in that which would offend either your husband or Society; but if you feel it would be wrong, if it makes you unhappy, then I have nothing more to say but to bid you *adieu*, and God bless you.'

His generosity, his honest, gentlemanly feelings made her ashamed of her own. She could not be less generous with him.

'No, Charles, do not go. It is I who am sorry. I should be honoured to have your company while I am here.'

He smiled and bowed over her hand. 'Then I am — most truly — *your servant, ma'am*, as the English say!'

Héloïse smiled, aware that a small voice deep in her still spoke of doubt. It would be pleasant to have a man's arm to lean on; to have a man's company, a man's conversation; best of all that it would be an old friend, with whom one could play that most comfortable game of *do you remember?*

Why should it trouble her, then? If it had been Lucy's husband, or Peter Firth, or John Anstey, for instance, she would have accepted the comfort gratefully and thought no more about it. Why was this different?

Because it *was* different, that was all, the small voice

76

replied. The kindness of any of those gentlemen would not have eased the soreness of heart that she had brought away with her from Morland Place. James had not asked her to stay; though she missed him dreadfully, she believed that at this moment, he was not missing her. She looked up into Charles's warm eyes, and the small voice retired, quelled. Rightly or wrongly, she allowed herself to be comforted.

CHAPTER FOUR

The absence of the mistress from Morland Place became noticeable within a few days of her departure. When Mr Pobgee, senior partner of Messrs Pobgee and Micklethwaite, Attorneys at Law, rode into the courtyard and was obliged to dismount from his horse without having anyone to hold its head or lead it away afterwards, he thought that some sudden emergency must have occurred. But when having hitched his horse to a ring in the wall, he entered the great hall through the open door and not only found it empty, but saw a film of dust over the surface of the side-table, he guessed what was amiss.

Blowing the dust away and putting down his hat, crop and gloves, he stepped forward into the centre of the hall and called a cheerful halloo. This had no more immediate effect than provoking a volley of barks from some distant depth of the house. Presently, however, a clicking of nails heralded the arrival of a grey-muzzled hound which Mr Pobgee recognised immediately as her ladyship's, and which came up to him with gently swinging tail to thrust a cold nose into his hand.

'Well, Kithra,' he said kindly, rubbing the rough head, 'and where's your mistress, my boy?'

Kithra smiled in the silent way of his kind; and then hasty footsteps from the same direction brought a footman with an apron over his livery and a polishing-cloth in his hand, who stopped abruptly at the sight of the visitor and reddened with embarrassment.

'Oh dear, Mr Pobgee, sir, I didn't know you was here. Oh Lor', sir, have you been waiting long?'

'No, William, not long. But what's to do? The place is like the *Marie Celeste.*'

'Like the — beg pardon, sir?'

'The *Marie Celeste* — you know, man, the ship,' Pobgee

78

said, though with the distinct feeling that it was a mistake to pursue it.

So it proved. William's face lit with understanding. 'Oh no, sir, Marie's gone with her ladyship, sir. Was you wanting to see her, then, sir? I could fetch Mrs Thomson to you, if you like.'

Refraining from enquiring what business he thought the family lawyer would have with a French lady's maid, or why the housekeeper would be a suitable substitute, Mr Pobgee smiled kindly and said, 'No, no, William, that's quite all right. I'll speak to Mr James instead, if you can find him for me.'

William's face clouded. 'Eh, sir, I know where Mr James is, but he doesn't see nobody these days. Last time I 'sturbed him, he nearly bit my head off, beggin' your pardon, sir. I durstn't go near him, sir, honest!'

So the rumours he had heard were true! Pobgee smiled ever more gently. 'Then I shan't ask you to. You just tell me where he is, and I'll go and announce myself.'

William's brow puckered even more, for he knew that Mr Ottershaw, the butler, would have something to say about guests not being announced, which was not proper, not in a gentleman's house, and Mr Ottershaw liked things done just so. When he stumblingly expressed something of this to the lawyer, Mr Pobgee asked where Ottershaw was.

'He's tooken his day off, sir, on account of his old mother's ill, over to Healaugh. He won't be back until this evening.'

Mistress away, and butler off, Pobgee thought, and the house gone all to ruin. 'Then there's nothing to worry about, is there? Mr Ottershaw will never know I wasn't announced, for I shan't tell him — and you won't either, will you, William? So now, you just tell me where Mr James is, and all will be well.'

'Well, sir,' William said, still a little doubtfully, 'I see Mr James sitting in the chapel gallery a bit since; but he never sees no-one now.'

'In the chapel gallery?' Pobgee couldn't help exclaiming.

'Aye, sir, he stops there a lot, just sittin' and thinkin'.' His eyes grew round. 'I wouldn't stop there for owt, sir, if it was me, on account that's where the ghost walks, the White Lady;

but Mr James don't seem to mind her at all. But he never sees nobody, like I said, sir.'

'He'll see me. Don't worry, William. He'll see me — and I won't see the White Lady.'

He made his escape, concealing his smile until he was out of sight of the footman. White Lady, indeed! The lower orders were wildly superstitious, and believed profoundly in ghosts and fairies and boggets and such other nonsenses, and even being devout Christians didn't seem to make any difference. They held the two sets of beliefs side by side, even mixing them in a way that distressed an orderly thinker. He personally knew of many of them who believed the parish priest had magical powers, and could ill-wish them if they didn't turn up to Sunday services.

And it was inevitable, he supposed, that there should be legends about a house as old as this one. As family lawyer in a long line of family lawyers, he imagined he must have heard most of them. There was the story that the statue of the Virgin in the Lady Chapel wept real tears when a disaster was about to befall the family. Then there was the vision once seen by a housemaid, long ago, of a hanging woman suspended from the old lamp-hook in the great bedchamber; and though she had never been seen since, the story persisted amongst the servants as though she made nightly visitations.

There was the treasured story that a fortune in jewels was hidden away somewhere, in a secret place in the house no-one knew about, including the legendary Black Pearls which featured in so many family portraits. But no doubt the current favourite was the story about the White Lady, a ghost who, clad in a long white robe like nothing so much as a nightgown, glided up and down the chapel stairs wringing her hands and wailing.

Her range, Pobgee reflected, seemed to be widening. He had heard of her on the stairs; he had even heard of her walking up and down the banks of the moat where legend said she had drowned; but now, plainly, her run had been extended to include the gallery of the chapel. No doubt it was merely coincidence that this was where the lower servants usually sat during Mass; and also no doubt, she would soon be seen in the main body of the chapel itself, preventing the more nervous of the upper servants from attending inconvenient services either.

Despite his scepticism, a cold touch on his hand made him jump, until he realised it was only Kithra, following him across the hall, lonely for his mistress. With the hound close beside him, Pobgee mounted the chapel stairs, crossed the short landing, and walked through the open door into the gallery, and there saw James Morland sitting in a corner, his back to the wall, staring down into the half-lit, shadowy vaults of the chapel. His shoulders were hunched, and his expression, his whole posture, eloquent of misery. Kithra clicked across to nudge him, tail swinging, but James didn't even seem to notice him.

Mr Pobgee was a spare, elderly man, neat and orderly in his ways, but this was not a result of his years. He had been a spare, neat, orderly young man, and before that a spare, neat, orderly child. His life had been quiet, ordered, contented. He had been a model student, had followed his father into the family business, and married a good, quiet girl who had made him a good, quiet wife, with whom he was very happy. She had duly presented him with a model son who had grown up to follow him into the family business in his turn.

Through all this he had taken care of the Morland family business as his father had done before him and his son would do after him; he had watched the surges of their affairs and the turmoil that came after them, and had made no judgements. In his own life he had never wanted anything he could not have, never craved forbidden fruit, never known discontent with his lot. But he had watched James Morland, a difficult and reserved child, grow into a wilful, thoughtless young man, bringing trouble and sorrow to his family. And he had watched him bring up his daughter Fanny to resemble him — a wilful, thoughtless young woman, who had, inevitably and in her turn, brought trouble and sorrow to James Morland.

Everything about Mr Pobgee's life and character was the antipathy of James Morland's; and yet Pobgee looked at that hunched, miserable figure, and felt nothing but sympathy for him. Pobgee was a man whom the follies and passions of his fellow creatures might puzzle, but never surprised; and he felt desperately sorry for this man who so little understood his own nature, and who punished himself again and again, far more severely than anyone else would ever punish him. James's daughter Fanny was dead, and that was shocking and tragic; but immoderate as his love for her had been, so his grief would be immoderate. Looking at him now, Pobgee wouldn't be surprised if it didn't lead him in the end to kill himself; and though it would be not only a crime, but a cardinal sin, Pobgee couldn't help feeling that it might be the best solution for everyone.

For now, however, there was business to be done. He called James's name quietly, and at the third attempt, James looked up blankly.

'You asked to see me,' Pobgee said steadily. 'You sent me a letter.'

Gradually the words sank in, the animation came back into the handsome, spoiled face — but it was not an animation Pobgee was glad to see. There was something unnatural, wilful about it — the glee of a man bent on mischief.

'Yes — yes, I wanted to see you. It's about this inheritance of Fanny's — her grandfather's fortune.' He stood up restlessly, and the old hound jumped aside as he almost trod on it. 'Old Hobsbawn wanted her to have it, you know — he told me so himself — and now they're trying to cheat her of it; but by God, she shall have it, by this hand! And you are going to help me, Pobgee, to see that it comes to her — what's hers by right.'

It was a warm day outside, and even the chapel was only pleasantly cool, but Pobgee felt a distinct desire to shiver which was nothing to do with any possible emanations of the White Lady. *He speaks of her as though she were still alive*, he thought. And then, worse, *he doesn't remember that she's dead.*

'Her ladyship did write to me,' he began cautiously. 'Her ladyship is away, I understand?'

'What? Oh — yes — gone to Brussels. Her and Sophie,' he said as if speaking of some distant and casual acquaintance. 'The thing is, Pobgee, that we got this letter from young Hobsbawn — now he's a shady character, if you like! I shouldn't be surprised if we didn't find he's been up to all sorts of havey-cavey business. I mean, the old man's death was pretty sudden, wasn't it?'

Pobgee shook his head, hardly believing what he was hearing. 'You surely cannot mean to be suggesting that Mr Hobsbawn's death was anything but natural?'

'Well, as to that, who can say? There's no knowing what we shall find out once we delve into it — or I should say, once *you* delve into it, for obviously it's best if the enquiries have an official air about them.'

'I don't think you understand, James,' Pobgee said carefully. 'Her ladyship sent me the letter announcing Mr Hobsbawn's death, and asking me to take any action I thought necessary. I have written to the younger Mr Hobsbawn, asking if there is any indication as to the precise time of the old gentleman's death; so far I have not had a reply. Beyond that there is nothing I can — or should — do.'

James frowned. 'What the devil are you talking about? They say Hobsbawn died during the night — that means they found him dead in the morning, doesn't it?'

'That is what I have written to ascertain. It seems likely — I cannot say more than that.'

'Then all that would be known was the last time he was seen alive, when he went to bed. It would have to be assumed that he died first, and the Will would be found in Fanny's favour, wouldn't it?'

Pobgee's orderly mind boggled at so many leaps of illogic. 'That might be one possible interpretation, one possible outcome. But there are many other possibilities. The area of probate is one of the most notorious quicksands in the whole —'

James cut him off. 'Damnit, Pobgee, what do you think we pay you for? That's the outcome you have to make certain of! It's the only reasonable interpretation, after all, and that's what you've got to throw yourself into. The courts are there to see justice done, aren't they? And Fanny and I will have justice!'

Very little ever disturbed the elder Pobgee, but his eyes bulged now as he understood what James was proposing. 'You aren't — you can't be thinking of taking the case to Chancery?'

'Of course,' James said impatiently. 'Haven't I just said so? That's what the courts are there for.'

'No, no, you are wrong, quite wrong! Chancery is not there to see justice done. Chancery is its own end. No-one ever makes any money out of it, except the lawyers employed there. The rules are so impenetrable, the processes so long-drawn-out, so expensive, so incomprehensible — my dear sir, there are cases going on there which have been in conduct for *twenty years*! Lord Eldon himself said —'

'Oh pooh! You men of law always exaggerate these things!'

Pobgee grew agitated. 'No, sir, I do not — if anything, I understate the case! Men have been broken, bankrupted, have been brought to despair, to suicide even, but no-one has ever come out of Chancery with profit. When Shakespeare talks of "the law's delay" it is Chancery he refers to! Why do you think, when the prize-fighter has another at his mercy, he talks of "having him in Chancery"? If you were to take this case before Chancery, the whole estate would be swallowed up — yes, and still leave you with bills to pay that would cripple you and bring you to debtors' prison.'

'You obviously have a bee in your bonnet about the whole thing,' James said coldly. 'But in any case, the risk is not yours, so there is nothing for you to worry about. The risk is mine, and I take it willingly.'

Pobgee looked grave. 'I beg your pardon, sir, but the risk is not yours. I take my instructions from her ladyship, and I shall certainly do nothing of this gravity without consulting her most fully, and advising her in person of the ill-advisability of the step.'

James's brow drew together sharply. 'What are you talking about? You're the Morland family lawyer. What has her ladyship to do with it?'

'Her ladyship is the sole mistress of the Morland estate.'

'Yes, but I'm talking about Fanny's money, and Fanny's my daughter, not hers.'

Pobgee looked at him with awful sympathy. 'James,' he said gently, 'Fanny is dead. She cannot inherit now. Under the terms of the agreements drawn up under the Will of her late ladyship, and at the time of Fanny's marriage, everything she died possessed of went to her ladyship. Even if you were, *quia impossibile*, to win this case, Fanny would not benefit one groat.'

James face had paled, seemed thinner and older. 'Don't you say that to me. Don't you ever say that she's —' He couldn't say the word.

Pobgee spoke ever more gently. 'I have to say it to you. James, I've known you all your life. I knew your mother well, and I know you loved her. You were always her favourite — don't you think it would break her heart to see you like this?'

'Leave my mother out of it. What has she to do with it?'

'Because the one thing your mother loved even more than you was Morland Place, the estate, the inheritance. That's why she left it to her ladyship. If you took this insane case to Chancery, who do you suppose would pay for it? It would eat up the whole Hobsbawn inheritance, and then it would eat up the Morland estate, too. Well, I won't let you do that, to her, to the Family, to your mother's blessed memory. I won't let you do it to yourself.'

James was glaring at him redly, still hardly seeing him, obsessed by the one insane idea, that Fanny should have what was hers. Pobgee took a step forward.

'James, Fanny's dead. You must let her go.'

For one moment he saw the black rage boil up in the younger man's face, and he thought he would strike him; was afraid that murderous as it was, it would lead him to seize Pobgee by the throat and choke him. But then Kithra whined and pawed James's leg, and the moment passed. The rage sank down a little, and a veiled look came over James's face. It was not clear sanity, however, as Pobgee saw with a further sinking of his heart; it was the cunning of madness.

'Well, well,' he said, turning away. 'Well, well, perhaps you're right. Perhaps Chancery is not the answer. Tell me, what can be done to clear the matter up? There must be something. You attorneys have your ways, your little systems and understandings. What do you recommend?'

Useless to recommend forgetting the whole matter — and indeed, his professional duty to her ladyship prevented his doing that. 'Firstly, to find out if there is any way of establishing the time of Mr Hobsbawn's death,' he said carefully. 'I have already written the letter —'

'You could go there, couldn't you?' James said, turning eagerly. 'Ask questions, put them on the spot?'

'I could, but —'

'Oh, you'll get your expenses,' James interrupted with a curl of the lip. 'I'm good for that much, even out of my own pocket.'

Pobgee let it pass. 'I doubt whether a personal visit would achieve more than a letter, but I am willing to go if it is required.'

'It is required. They might lie in a letter — you don't know these people! But if you turned up there — suddenly, without warning — catch them unawares — you'd soon see if they were lying or not. You can always tell, can't you? And there might be other people to question — servants, friends, passers by — the medical man in the case. Yes, yes, a personal visit is essential! And what then?'

'If by any means the time of death can be established, then there is nothing more to do but to send the Will to probate,' Pobgee said calmly. 'But if, as may be the case, it is not possible, then the best course would be to try to come to some arrangement, agreeable to both parties, of dividing the estate — between her ladyship, as Mrs Hawker's heir, and Mr Hobsbawn's residuary legatee.'

James stared. 'Dividing? The devil! Why should we?'

'Because the only alternative,' Pobgee said, allowing herself to speak a little sharply, 'would be that very course I have condemned — to go to court, and lose everything. Better, surely, to have part of a healthy estate, than to see everything sink into the quicksand of Chancery?'

James looked dissatisfied. 'I don't like it. Look here, Pobgee, suppose I instruct you personally as Fanny's father, and promise to pay out of my own pocket — not involving the estate — what then? It would be worth it — Hobsbawn was as rich as Nabob, you know, quite apart from the mills. You'd win all right, and then — think of the fees! Think of the glory! What do you say?'

'I say no,' Pobgee said with spare humour.

James frowned. 'I'll get another lawyer.'

'None that would act for you. Be advised by me, sir; let me

make enquiries under her ladyship's instructions, and see what develops.'

And in the meantime, he thought, stop brooding, put Fanny to rest, and get out in the fresh air as you used to; but he did not quite dare to say it out loud. James's black humours were unpredictable, and though not a tall man, he was stronger and heavier than Pobgee, and there were no servants within call.

But James suddenly seemed to lose interest. The animation drained from his face, he turned his head away, and his eyes resumed that blank, inward stare that Pobgee had seen sometimes in sick animals when pain and fear brought them near to death. Pobgee watched him a moment longer, but he did not speak, or even seem aware of the lawyer's presence. There seemed nothing more to say or do, and so he left him there with the old hound for company, and went down the chapel stairs, across the hall and out into the blessed sunlight with the sensation of escaping from some evil enchantment.

His loss had been great, Pobgee told himself, and it was still so recent. The shock had disordered his mind, but he would come out of it at last and be his old self again. He thought of Héloïse, gentle, loving, trusting, and his heart misgave. For her sake, he hoped James would recover, and soon; but he couldn't help thinking that it was as well she was far away now and out of reach.

Lucy, accustomed in London to exercising her horses early to avoid the crowds, had no wish to change her habits in Brussels, and was glad to find that the Allée Verte at seven in the morning was agreeably deserted. She took Hotspur out alone, without even Parslow to accompany her, and after an invigorating gallop the length of the Allée, pulled up at the bridge at the end of the ride. There she sat for a few minutes, watching the slow, painted barges drifting up the canal, and the country waggons passing over the bridge, loaded the provisions for the city, and drawn by fat Flemish horses in tasselled harness. But her thoughts were far away, pondering the prospect of renewed war, and wondering what it would mean to them all.

Hotspur soon grew tired of this and began tugging at the reins, to be allowed either to move on, or, if his mistress felt obliged to remain in this reverie, to eat the sweet green grass at his feet. Lucy came back to the present, blinked, patted his neck.

'Yes, all right,' she said aloud, 'we'll go; and tomorrow or the day after we'll have a longer ride, through the woods, perhaps.' It would be a slow business, she thought, merely to ride here every day. She must ask some of the young officers where the best gallops were. She had seen enough already to know that the wealthier sprigs had brought their high-fed English hunters with them, and high-fed English hunters needed a lot of exercise.

She turned Hotspur and started back the way she had come, along the line of the elm trees, concentrating on keeping the big horse on the bit and cantering collectedly, instead of fly-bucking and shaking his head about as he wanted to. It was only when she had gone some distance that she became aware of the figure of an English officer standing in the middle of the ride, watching her. The flicker of annoyance at having her solitude interrupted lasted only an instant, to be replaced by a warm and spreading smile. A moment later she was reining Hotspur by the officer's side, and looking down at him with an expression that would have melted a basilisk.

Colonel Lord Theakston, formerly plain Danby Wiske, was made of softer stuff, and adored his wife of less than a year. He reached up for her hand, wondering for the thousandth time how he had been able to capture such a prize; indeed, how he had ever plucked up the courage even to ask her.

'Well, Danby,' she said with enormous satisfaction. 'But when did you get back?'

'Late last night — slept at Meyer's lodgings. Didn't know until this morning you were here,' he added with palpable regret. 'I don't need to ask how you are — you look wonderful.'

'You look tired,' she said, eyeing him keenly. 'Too much debauchery at the French Court, I suppose?'

He smiled at the idea. 'Finding it difficult to sleep alone,' he suggested.

'Pho! You can't humbug me. Wait, let me get down. I can't talk to the top of your head.'

She swung her leg free of the pommel and would have jumped down unaided, but Danby stepped close and held up his hands, and with a small smile she allowed him to lift her down. As soon as her feet touched the ground, he enfolded her in a most satisfactory embrace, and kissed her thoroughly.

When he released her she said a little breathlessly, 'It's a good thing we're alone. I don't think it is quite proper to allow oneself to be kissed like that in the Allée Verte, you know.'

'*Tant pis*,' he said economically, and kissed her again. Then he took Hotspur's rein over one arm and his wife on the other and they began to stroll rather aimlessly along under the trees.

'So you're back!' said Lucy, foolish with pleasure. He squeezed her hand against his side. 'And what was it like in Ghent?'

'Depressing. King Louis must be the most lethargic man in Europe, and his courtiers are as glum as toothache. You heard about the Duc d'Angoulême?'

'His army of resistance, in the south of France?'

Danby nodded. 'Failed. It was in the *Moniteur* yesterday — beaten at Lyons by General Grouchy. Angoulême and his Duchess are on a ship by now, fleeing for their lives; and that's the last of it. All France is Boney's.'

Lucy looked grave. 'It must have been a blow to the French Court. How did King Louis take it?'

'Didn't turn a hair,' Danby said with a sad shake of the head. 'News of a failed batch of cakes would have moved him more.'

'And this is the man the Allies are fighting for!'

'Everyone in Ghent was deep in gloom — defeated before they begin! All except the Beau, God bless him! Talks about beatin' Boney as cool as a melon, and looks down his nose at the disaster-mongers — you know that way he has!'

'But he's never actually met Boney in battle. I suppose he will beat him, won't he?' Lucy asked. Danby stopped, his brow furrowed, and looked at her thoughtfully. His hesitation made her nervous. 'Danby?'

'It's not so easy to say. Boney will be beat sooner or later, of course. He's only one man, and he'll grow old and tired and make mistakes —'

'You mean we'll have to wait for him to grow old?' she said in alarm.

'He's an extraordinary man. Well, the Beau is too. If anyone can beat Boney, it's him. But the Allied army ...' He shook his head. 'It depends how much time we have. The Beau can knock 'em into shape all right, but it will take time.'

'But everyone says Boney can't move before the autumn.'

'It never does to underestimate him. When he moves, he moves fast, and he likes to take his enemies by surprise. Now Angoulême's finished, he's got nothing but us to think about.' He was silent a moment, his eyes far away; and then his attention returned to Lucy, and he saw he had alarmed her. 'Don't worry, love. If it takes another twenty-two years, we'll beat him in the end. And he'll never cross the Channel — England's safe.'

He squeezed her arm comfortingly and walked on with her. After a moment she said, 'Is the Duke back from Ghent, too?'

'Yes, we all are. Brought back Lord Fitzroy Somerset too, so that makes the Beau happy. He always said he was prepared to fight the war without men or supplies, but not without his military secretary.' He was rewarded with a faint smile. 'And Colin Campbell's coming back to manage the household, and if we only can get rid of Hudson Lowe, Hookey's digestion might be saved at last!'

'They say he's going to ask for Oliver de Lancey to replace Lowe.'

'He wanted Murray, of course, but he's in America. But de Lancey's a good man.'

'Yes, I've heard so.'

'Well, then,' he began next, 'tell me about yourselves. Are you comfortable in your house? What plans have you made for Rosamund's come-out?'

'Oh, the house is first-rate,' Lucy said, detaching her mind momentarily from the war. 'The ballroom looks as though it hasn't been used since before the war, but by candlelight and with plenty of flowers all around, it won't shew that it's a trifle shabby. We've arranged everything for the sixteenth —'

'Sent out the invitations yet?' he interrupted.

'No — we're going to do that today.'

'Good. Better change it to the fifteenth if you can. The Duke's going on a tour of inspection of the fortifications, and I shall have to go with him. I'd be sorry to miss the ball.'

Lucy shrugged. 'It's rather short notice, but I don't see any difficulty. Naturally I want you there; and I rather hoped the Duke would give us a look-in — give it his seal of approval. And no ball would be complete without the handsome young staff-officers, of course. The fifteenth it shall be. Oh, and Danby, you must know, of course, that Marcus has been transferred to the staff! We saw him in his new uniform when he got back from Ninove. It's splendid for him, though I think he might be a little sorry to be leaving the field — but Roberta's delighted because she thinks there'll be less chance of his getting killed when the fighting actually starts.'

He halted again, and turned to face her, an odd look on his face — wry, almost guilty. 'Yes, I know. In fact, it was I who suggested him to the Beau. Said he'd make a useful replacement.'

'Replacement? For Lennox, you mean?'

'Not for Lennox. For me.' He held her gaze steadily. 'I'm going back to my regiment.'

She said nothing for a long time, but there was dismay in her eyes, and when she spoke at last, she had to wet her dry lips. 'Why? Danby, why?'

'You know why: because the Allied army's in a bad way, and the Beau needs all the experienced field officers he can get. I'm more useful in the field than Marcus, good man though he is.' He looked at her seriously. 'It can't be helped, love. The Tenth is coming out in a couple of weeks, and that just gives me time to hand over the reins before joining them. Marcus is just the kind of young man the Beau likes — hard-working, obedient — and his knowing Firth so well will be an advantage, since he'll have to work alongside him so much.'

Lucy tried to smile, but her eyes were bleak. Whatever Marcus might say to please Bobby, officers in the line were more likely to be killed than the staff. She knew it was a wife's business to support her husband and not to beg him to keep himself out of danger for her sake; but she had lost one man to battle already, and she had only just discovered the deep, satisfying comfort of Danby's love.

'Well, I suppose you'll say it's your duty,' she managed at last. 'And after all, if the Duke asks you personally, you can't very well refuse. I know he's very —' Something in her husband's eye gave her pause. She looked at him quizzically, and the truth slowly dawned on her.

'He didn't ask you,' she said, almost in a whisper. 'He didn't ask you — you asked him!'

'Lucy —'

'You volunteered, didn't you? It was all your idea!'

'Yes,' he said.

She stared at him a moment, and then pulled her arm roughly out from his grasp and walked away from him up the greensward.

Danby watched her go for an instant before pursuing her, towing the reluctant Hotspur and feeling a mixture of foolishness, guilt and exasperation. 'Lucy!' She walked on, ignoring him. 'Lucy, stop. This is silly.'

She stopped abruptly but did not turn, and he caught up with her to discover to his horror that she was crying. He had never seen her cry before, and it unnerved and distressed him.

'Oh, love, please don't! I can't bear it. Be angry with me, black my eyes if you like, but don't cry!'

'I can't help it,' she gasped through gritted teeth. 'D'you think I want to?' She groped helplessly for her handkerchief, and couldn't find it, and Danby pulled out his own and pushed it into her fingers with silent sympathy. She began to dab her eyes. Hotspur, who had been watching her with interest, took offence at the white linen and pulled backwards, snorting, adding to Danby's problems.

'Why do you men love war?' Lucy said at last. 'You think it's glorious. Weston could have had a shore appointment, but he went back to sea — to his death. Thank God my boys are too young ...' The tears which had been coming under control got loose again. 'Oh, damn —'

'Dearest,' Danby said helplessly. 'It isn't so bad —'

'It is!' she cried angrily through the handkerchief. 'You're going to fight — in a battle — against Boney — and what if you're killed?'

Hampered by a horse, Danby couldn't do what he longed to, and take his rigid, weeping wife in his arms. He sought desperately for something to say to comfort her. 'What if I'm not?' he offered at last, hopefully.

She made a choking sound which was a snort of laughter forcing its way through her sobs. 'Oh, Danby!'

'I know. I'm not much of a hand at this, but truly, I don't mean to get killed, and I came through the Peninsula in one piece. And then, you know, it had to be done. The Beau needed me.'

But Lucy's moment of weakness was over. She had stopped crying, and was mopping her eyes and blowing her nose in her usual brisk way.

'As to that,' she said a moment later in an almost normal voice, 'you did it because you like campaigning, and that's all about it! If I'd known what a tiger you were, I don't know if I'd have married you; but I have, and so I must make the best of it.'

Danby raised an eyebrow at the notion of appearing to anyone as a tiger, and offered Lucy his arm again.

'Have you had breakfast yet? Because I don't have to be at Headquarters until ten, and if we took Hotspur back to the stables, we could have a bite together.'

She met his eyes, and a look of perfect understanding passed between them. It was almost four months since they had seen each other. Breakfast could wait.

'Tiger!' she murmured, pressing his arm.

'To hell with the regiment!' he responded, pleased.

Hobsbawn House in Manchester, home of the late Mr Joseph Hobsbawn of Hobsbawn Mills, had been for weeks in a state of controlled chaos. The old man had been a great collector, not only of paintings and furniture and objects d'art, but of anything that ever came into his hands. He hadn't liked to throw anything away, and so every drawer and cupboard and dresser was stuffed full of papers, letters, receipts, concert-programmes, handbills, newspapers, old ledgers and all the multifarious flotsam and jetsam of a long and active life.

A dance-card from a Grand Gala Ball of 1775, complete with gilded pencil, was a memento of his first meeting with his long-dead wife; it lay alongside a school report from his daughter Mary Ann's convent school, one of grand-daughter Fanny's baby-shoes, a book full of pressed flowers, and a pamphlet on the Catholic Relief reforms favoured by Mr Pitt in his first term of office.

Important legal documents nestled in the same drawer with a bundle of letters from Fanny, a sheaf of poems written by Mary Ann in her girlhood, the menu from one of the first dinner parties at which she acted as hostess, an invitation card to an anti-slavery debate, and a lock of his dead grandson, baby Henry's, hair tied with scarlet thread.

'He was just like a blessed squirrel, Mr Jasper,' said Bowles, the ancient butler, shaking his head sadly. 'If ever I went to throw anything away, he'd always say, "Hold up, there, Bowles — it might come in useful one day." Not so much as a stocking could I get rid of, God rest his soul. And memory? Every blessed thing that came into this house he'd remember, and know just where to put his hand to it, which was more than I could, and so I tell you freely, sir. I'd have to go to the master and ask.'

That had been when they were looking for Mr Hobsbawn's Will. Jasper had been aware of the main provisions of it, but there was the matter of servants' pensions and small legacies, though he undertook, from his knowledge of the old man, to tell the servants that he was sure they had been taken care of.

For himself he was not so sure. Everything had been left to Fanny with himself merely as residuary legatee, and he had no idea whether the old man had left him anything at all. Also, if Fanny took over the running of the mills, it was quite likely she would have him dismissed from his position as mill-manager, and that would leave him quite without means.

Oh, with his experience, he could certainly get another position somewhere, and though it might not be as good, it would be enough to put bread into his mouth. But he had worked all his life for old Hobsbawn, put his sweat and his tears and, yes, his blood into making the mills better and more efficient, and it would be a hard thing if all that work had been forgotten at the end.

He and Bowles had rummaged through drawers and bureaux and boxes with increasing bewilderment, without coming across the vital document.

'You'd 'a thought Master would've put it in the safe, seeing it's so important,' Bowles grumbled at last, kneeling in a flowing tide of sheet-music that had overwhelmed him when a cardboard box fell from a toppling pile.

Jasper stared at him. 'Safe? What safe? I didn't know he had one. Why the deuce didn't you mention it before, Bowles?'

Bowles raised the hurt old eyes of a kicked bloodhound. 'You never asked me, Mr Jasper. I made sure you'd 'a known about the safe, you being Master's right hand, so to speak.'

'Good God! Of course it'll be in the safe!' Jasper said, hauling himself up and dumping the pile of papers he was clutching in an armchair. 'We've been wasting our time here. Where is it? And where's the key, do you know?'

''Course I know,' Bowles said indignantly. He was the butler, wasn't he? 'The safe's in the wall, Mr Jasper, in the dining-room, behind the portrait of Mrs Hobsbawn, where it's always been. And the key's on my ring, which hangs in my pantry, as you very well know.'

Jasper frowned. 'That doesn't sound very sensible. Anyone could have taken it and opened the safe, and made off with the contents.'

Bowles looked at him pityingly. 'But no-one don't go into my pantry, Mr Jasper, barring myself. I'd a' thought you'd know that.'

Jasper didn't waste time arguing the point, but sped off to fetch the bunch of keys. Bowles took so much longer to get to his feet that he only managed to reach the dining-room as Jasper was struggling to lift the enormous painting single-handed off its hooks.

'God, what a monstrous thing it is!' he panted. 'Why the devil did they paint them so big? He must have bought it by the square foot!'

Bowles looked disapproving. 'Here, let me help you, Mr Jasper. That was said to be a very speaking likeness of my poor mistress, God rest her soul, and a very gentle, kind lady she was, and always considerate of servants, which many as are born with the silver spoon in their mouths, as the saying is, forgets to be.'

'Well, then, she deserved a better portrait than this,' Jasper panted, easing it towards the floor. Within the massive gilded frame a very flat, two-dimensional, lady balanced, apparently on the tips of her toes, on a quite unnecessarily rumpled carpet, one hand resting on the head of a dog who seemed to be sprouting mysteriously from half-way up the wall, and the other resting at a most unnatural angle on a Bible lying on a table at her side. It was the vilest piece of work Jasper had ever seen, but for Bowles it seemed invested with all the sitter's qualities, and could not be criticised with impugnity.

'Master was always powerful fond of it,' the butler gasped now. 'Which was why he had it hung here, Mr Jasper, where he could look at it every day while he took his dinner.'

'More likely he hung it here to hide the safe. I wonder it didn't give him indigestion. There! God, it's a weight! And there's the safe, just as you said, Which is the key, Bowles?'

The butler selected it from the ring and handed it over in a silence partly reproving, and partly breathless, and Jasper put it into the keyhole, turned it, pulled down the heavy handle, and the safe door creaked open.

'He didn't keep very much in here,' Jasper commented. There was a promising-looking bundle of stiff-folded documents of legal appearance, which turned out to be the title-deeds to the house and the factory buildings and Jasper's own home. Then there were a number of boxes which, opened, revealed a quantity of jewellery whose antiquated and heavy settings did not disguise the quality of the stones.

'Mrs Hobsbawn's jewels,' Bowles replied to the enquiring glance from Jasper. 'Eh, I didn't know they was there! I thought Miss Mary had everything when she come of age. These were the mistress's what she got from *her* mother, as died before she were wed.'

Jasper calculated quickly that they must have been designed and created in the 1750s, if not earlier. No wonder they had been left locked up in the safe — they were hideous! Still, those diamonds were very fine, and the gold melted down would be worth a bit. Even just this one parure, sold for its constituents, would leave a man set up for life.

The only other thing in the safe was, mysteriously, a stuffed bird on an ebony stand, which even Bowles could not explain. As it seemed likely to disintegrate on inspection, Jasper hastily put it back and relocked the safe, while Bowles shook his head and murmured in a wondering tone, 'Just like a blessed squirrel, God rest his soul!'

It still left the problem of the missing Will. For the rest of the day, Jasper and the butler searched the house, rendering it more and more like a street market after a whirlwind, as things before decently hidden in drawers and cupboards were spread over tables and across the floor. The hour for dinner came and went, but Jasper Hobsbawn did not dine. Finally at nine o'clock the housekeeper, Mrs Murray, came in to enquire acidly if he wanted a bed making up for the night, which shocked Bowles into a sense of his duty and prompted him to add an enquiry about supper.

Jasper wearily accepted both offers. Bowles shuffled off to give his share of the orders, but Mrs Murray lingered to stare with angry eyes at the mess he had made.

'I was always on at him to let me clear out those dirty old cupboards. Encouraged mice, that's all they did, armies of the little pests, chewing everything and leaving messes everywhere! But no, he wouldn't have it. He would have everything kept. Well, much good may it do him now! And I hope you're going to put everything back the way it was, Mr Hobsbawn, because it isn't *my* job to clean up after you. Throw the lot on the fire, that's my advice, for there'll be hard enough work for everyone when the infantry comes to be done.'

For a wild moment Jasper thought she was suggesting sending for the troops to tidy up after him, and then he reclaimed his wandering wits and asked, 'What inventory, Mrs Murray?'

'Why, there's always an infantry when there's a death, didn't you know that?' she said scornfully. 'And that Mrs Hawker will want to know about every last spoon and picture-hook, if I know her, for I suppose the house and contents will go to her, won't they?'

Jasper picked at his dust-blackened nails wearily. 'I suppose so, but I can't tell you for certain, for we can't find the Will. Perhaps your famous mice have eaten it, Mrs M.'

She stared. 'Don't tell me that's what you're messing up my clean house for? Well, of all the — ! What does it matter if you can't find it? Mr Whetlore has a copy of it, hasn't he, the master's man of business? Why, you and that Bowles are no better than a couple of gapeseeds! Look at the mess you've made! And who's going to clear it up?'

Jasper was too weary even to feel embarrassed.

'Leave it,' he said. 'It'll only get worse when we do your infantry.'

'Leave it I shall, don't you worry,' Mrs Murray said sharply. 'I wouldn't clean up for that Mrs Hawker, ungrateful little cat! Let her have the mess, if she's having the master's fortune.'

Jasper looked at her cannily. 'You don't know for certain that she'll dismiss you,' he said obliquely.

She returned the look. 'Nor you don't know for certain that she'll dismiss *you* — but she will all the same, you'll see! We're both in the same boat, Mr Hobsbawn — and after a lifetime of loyalty and devotion.'

That was rather an exaggeration in her case, since she had only been housekeeper for eight years, to Jasper's memory. Still, 'I'm sure Mr Hobsbawn won't have forgotten you completely,' he said kindly.

She eyed him askance. 'Aye, well, as to that — them as lives longest will learn most. But if it was *you* that was coming into all this, Mr Jasper, I'd be a good deal happier — and so would the rest of the servants, *and* the folk at the mill, and they won't scruple to tell you so.'

Mr Whetlore, the attorney, brought the Will round to the house the following day and was closeted a long time with Jasper in the master's business-room, which had such a massy oak door that no sound could be discerned from within by those hovering in the hallway, even with an assiduous ear pressed to the panels.

They were not kept long in suspense, however. As soon as the lawyer had departed, Jasper rang the bell; and despite his years and his creaking joints, Bowles beat Mrs Murray to the door-handle. He flung the door open just as Mrs Murray jostled him for position, so that they were jammed together in the doorway in a very undignified manner.

'Oh yes, come in, Bowles,' Jasper said, looking preoccupied.

'Mrs Murray there too? Good, I wanted to speak to you both.'
They came in and closed the door behind them, and waited
while Jasper stared at the desk-top in deep thought. Then at
last he looked up and said with a bleak smile, 'You were right
about the inventory, Mrs Murray. Mr Whetlore is sending one
of his clerks around tomorrow to supervise it, but he says that
all the servants who wish to stay will be kept on and paid out
of the estate while it's going on.'

'And then what?' Mrs Murray asked sharply. 'What did the
master's Will say?'

Jasper sighed faintly. 'As we expected, Miss Morland —
Mrs Hawker, I mean — is to inherit everything.'

'Everything? Not everything, sir?' Bowles quavered.

'Yes — the house and contents, the personal effects, the
mills, everything.' He took a moment to control his voice.
'But, as I predicted, Mrs Murray, the servants are not
forgotten. Each of you has been left a pension equivalent to
your annual wages. You will be quite comfortable, you see,
whether you find another position or not.'

Mrs Murray opened her mouth, and then shut it again in
baffled rage. This, then, was the end of all her schemes, all
the hard work she had put in on that stupid old man! She had
been working quietly — and, she reckoned, successfully — on
becoming Mrs Hobsbawn number two, a comfort to the old
man's declining years — until that little cat Fanny Morland
turned up and cut her out. The prize of a widow's portion —
half the estate, perhaps — had dwindled before her eyes; but
she had thought that at least she would get something
substantial when the time came. She was, after all, more than
just a servant.

A pension equal to her annual wages! But her annual wages
were only the beginning, less than half of what she made out
of the house every year! She had controlled the household
budget, and of recent years the master had simply given her
whatever sums of money she asked for, for housekeeping.
What she didn't use, she had put quietly aside. Then there
was the food she sold out of the kitchen, the percentage of the
servants' wages for getting them put on, or not getting them
turned off, the new linen she bought for the house and then
sold at the back door — oh, there were endless ways a clever

woman could make money in her position. And now — ! She set her mouth grimly. It wasn't right! She had been robbed, and that was all there was to it!

Bowles was grateful not to be forgotten, but away from the warmth and comfort of Hobsbawn House, he knew he would find it hard living. Miss Fanny would probably turn him off, and he was too old to get another billet, and with nothing but his pension he would have to forgo all the little luxuries that made life worthwhile. No nice big joints of pork or beef, no fat goose on a Sunday, no roaring fires, no drop of claret or port with his dinner, nor one of the master's nice Trichinopoli cigars after it. It would be black bread and boiled bacon and make-do, that's what it would be, and at his age, after a lifetime lived in gentlemen's houses, he was pretty sure it would soon fetch him off.

He fixed Jasper with a wavering eye of appeal. 'What about you, Mr Jasper, sir?' he begged. 'Sure Master didn't forget you?'

'That's right,' Mrs Murray chimed in. 'He must have left you something?' There was a faintly predatory glint in her eye as she surveyed him. He was, at least, more tender meat than his late cousin.

Jasper looked at them sardonically. 'Oh, Mr Hobsbawn didn't forget me. After all, blood is thicker than water, isn't it? So we've been told. He left me a little something: a thousand pounds in the five-per-cents, and a recommendation to the new owner to keep me on as manager.'

It gave them pause. The income from that sum would be less than the pension either of them was to receive.

'It's not right,' Mrs Murray said vehemently, though she might just as well have been referring to her own situation. Bowles joined in, and they offered a litany of complaint until Jasper had had enough, and raised a hand.

'Mr Whetlore has asked me to stay here and help with the inventory, as well as continuing to run the mills until we have the new owner's instructions, so I shall have a roof over my head for a few weeks at least. You may save the rest of your pity for yourselves. I don't want it.'

Thus matters stood when Mr Pobgee's letter arrived at Hobsbawn House. The earlier letter announcing Fanny's death had not reached its destination, as had been supposed, and this second communication was brought to Jasper one day in the business-room, where he sat in a small space he had created out of the chaos of papers all around him, sorting through receipts for factory machinery.

'Letter, Mr Hobsbawn,' said Whetlore's clerk cheerfully, poking his head round the door. 'Addressed to you personal. Catch!'

Jasper caught it as it spun through the air, and cursed the clerk, who withdrew his head circumspectly. Jasper opened the letter and read it, read it again, and then put it down on the desk, and stared at the wall in astonishment.

'Good God!' he said. 'What an extraordinary thing!'

A moment later he was bellowing for the clerk, who looked round the door cautiously, expecting to be cursed again.

'Is your principal in the office today?'

'Mr Whetlore? Yessir!'

'Then run there as quick as you can and ask him if he would kindly step round and see me at once, on a matter of great urgency.'

'Yessir!' the clerk said, and dashed away, causing a gratifying stir as he passed through the house.

'This is very intriguing, very intriguing indeed,' said Whetlore. 'I don't think I have ever come across anything like it in all my years as an attorney. What an extraordinary coincidence! For both parties to die in the course of the same night —'

'Yes, yes, it is extraordinary — but what's to be done?' Jasper said irritably. 'What is the position regarding the Will? How does it affect us all?'

'It could all come down to a matter of minutes — indeed, a precise moment in time, if it could be determined, would decide all!' He chuckled, and then pulled himself together as Japser seemed ready to burst. 'In simple terms, sir, that a layman can understand, if Mr Hobsbawn died before Mrs Hawker, even by a matter of minutes, then she would have inherited the estate in its entirety, and it would now belong to — well, whoever her heirs are, and that I cannot tell you.'

'Yes, very well — and —?'

'But if, on the other hand, Mrs Hawker's demise took place before Mr Hobsbawn's, then the alternative clause in his Will would have taken effect. His entire estate would have gone to the residuary legatee.'

'You mean —?'

'Yes indeed, you are quite right,' Mr Whetlore chortled. 'If Mrs Hawker died first, you would now be a very wealthy man, Mr Hobsbawn. Dear me, how very diverting! But the extraordinary thing is that of course we don't know exactly when Mr Hobsbawn died, do we?'

Jasper looked like a man who had been struck on the head. 'He was found dead in his bed by his valet when he went to wake him in the morning. That was at half-past six. The butler sent for the doctor, who said he had died of a seizure during the night, in his sleep. But as to the precise time of his death —'

'Quite! He was dead and cold at half-past six, but who knows if he were still alive at two in the morning? He might have died the moment he laid his head on the pillow. We don't know, and we can't prove it either way.'

A slight sound at that moment drew Jasper's attention to the door of the business-room, and he saw to his surprise that it was not quite shut. With a gesture to the lawyer to be silent, he walked across to it and pulled it quickly open, but the hallway outside was empty and innocent, mocking his suspicion. He closed the door properly and resumed his seat.

'Very well, what do we do now? What is your advice?'

'You are in a better position at least sir, than you were. Before, Mrs Hawker was the undoubted heir: now there is some doubt. We must work on that. We must try to persuade the medical man who attended that morning to estimate the time of death, and hope that his estimate proves him to have survived Mrs Hawker.'

'Estimate? Surely they won't accept an estimate?'

'It depends on how much stomach they have for the fight,' said Whetlore with relish. 'They might find their own medical expert to swear that ours is wrong, and prove conclusively that ninety-nine per cent of men who die in their sleep die before midnight! If they want to take the case to court, it could be a bonny fight indeed! But their man of business will advise them against that, as I would have to advise you. These Chancery cases, sir, are not the thing! In the end, the whole estate would be swallowed up in costs. No, he will try to wear us down — bully us, even — and then he will advise, as I would, that the parties should come to a settlement.'

'Share the estate, you mean?'

'Just so. Even that will cause a handsome legal wrangle, as to whose should be the larger share. Not so amusing as a Chancery case, of course,' he said regretfully, 'but plenty of fun for everyone, all the same.'

'Damn it, Whetlore, I don't like your attitude!' Jasper burst out irritably. 'It may be fun to you, but it certainly isn't to me!'

Whetlore raised his hands. 'Just trying to keep your spirits up, my dear sir. Of course, you can always instruct another attorney, if I don't suit you.'

'No, no, of course not. I'm sorry. It's just — this whole damn' business makes me nervous. It's monstrous!' He banged one fist into the other palm in frustrated fury.

'Quite intolerable,' Whetlore said smoothly, doing his best to conceal his smile. It was not a very good best.

Jasper sat up late in the business-room, going over and over the same things in his mind until he was exhausted. It was past midnight, and the fire had burned down to nothing, and he was beginning to feel chilly, when there was a scratching at the door, and it opened to reveal Mrs Murray, candle in hand, dressed in a voluminous bed-wrapper, her face composed into an expression of tender concern.

'I beg your pardon, Mr Hobsbawn. I saw the light under the door, and thought a candle must have been left burning. I thought you'd gone to bed long ago.'

'I'm just going. I'm sorry you were disturbed,' he said tersely. He didn't want to talk to her. He didn't really like her, though she had never been other than polite to him. There was just something about her, something too smooth, oily, even...

'Oh, you didn't disturb me, sir, I was awake anyway. I don't sleep very well, as a matter of fact, and when I have one of my wakeful nights, I usually get up and go downstairs to get myself a drop of hot milk or something of the sort.'

A drop of brandy, more like, Jasper thought. 'Don't let me keep you, then,' was all he said.

'No, sir. A funny thing, though,' she went on blandly, overriding him, 'I was wakeful the night the master died. It must have been something in the air, I suppose — perhaps the poor soul's struggle as it left his body and winged its way to Heaven. But whatever it was, not a wink could I sleep. Of course, if only I'd known —'

Jasper's mind was wrenched back to attend to her words. 'What's that you're saying? You were unable to sleep that night?'

'That's right, Mr Hobsbawn. Just as I said.'

'And did you go down stairs at any time?'

'Twice, sir — once just after midnight, and then again between one o'clock and two.'

'And did you — oh, but why should you?' He turned away, smacking his palm with his fist again. 'It would be beyond anything great if you had just happened —'

'Happened to what, Mr Hobsbawn?'

'Happened to notice if your master was still alive. But you'd have had to go into his room, and why should you do that?'

'Because he called out to me,' she said, giving him an utterly guileless look.

He stared. 'What are you telling me? He called out to you?'

'Poor Mr Hobsbawn must have seen my candle going past his door — I go that way at night, rather than by the back-stairs, for it doesn't disturb anyone, and those back-stairs are horrid dangerous in my opinion, steep and narrow as they are. So I went in —'

'What time was that?'

'I don't know precisely, but it must have been about a quarter to two, for two struck by the church clock while I was in the kitchen. Anyway, master asked me to fetch him up a drop of brandy when I came back, as he couldn't sleep. I said did he want me to wake Simon — his man — and he said, no, a drop of brandy would do the trick. So I went down to the kitchen and warmed myself a drop of milk, and went back upstairs, and took the master in his brandy —'

'He was still alive?'

'Of course he was! What kind of question is that? I gave him his brandy and he said thank you and I said goodnight and off I went back to my room. But the milk didn't do the trick for me, for I never slept a wink all night, not until five o'clock past, and then no sooner had I got off than there was all the rumpus in the house because Simon had gone in to wake the poor master and found him dead.' She sniffed a little and touched her handkerchief to the corners of her eyes.

Jasper took two steps towards her as though he meant to embrace her, and then away again, and back and forth before the fireplace. 'But this is all we need! This is exactly the evidence we need! Why on earth didn't you speak up before, woman?'

Mrs Murray, who didn't quite like being called 'woman', bristled a little. 'Nobody asked me, Mr Hobsbawn. I'm sure I didn't know before that it was important.'

'The exact time of Mr Hobsbawn's death is very important! It's of paramount importance! It —' He stopped abruptly and looked at her with narrowed eyes. 'Were you by any chance listening at the door when Mr Whetlore was here today?'

'Me, sir?' she replied in strong indignation. 'I am a house-keeper, Mr Hobsbawn, not some slut of a between-maid!'

'Yes, yes, I'm sorry. Of course. It was just that — Mrs Murray, would you be prepared to make a sworn statement to the effect of what you've just told me? That you saw your master alive, spoke to him, after two o'clock in the morning?'

She regarded him sweetly. 'Of course I would, Mr Hobsbawn, if you thought it was important.'

'It would be of the greatest possible help to me,' he said, holding her gaze steadily. 'I should be very grateful.'

'Why yes, sir,' she replied. 'Of course you would. You're a gentleman, Mr Hobsbawn, and gentlemen know how to shew their gratitude properly.'

Jasper's mind was already bounding on ahead over the next thing to do; but something deep within it registered an uneasiness, although he was far too excited and preoccupied just then to wonder what was causing it.

105

CHAPTER FIVE

In the house in the Rue Ducale, Lady Theakston's ball was in full swing. Under the four huge chandeliers, between the row of rather spotted mirrors and the curtained windows leading onto the terrace, a large and glittering crowd danced, strolled and chatted. The scene was a tumble of colour — the banks of flowers hiding the damp or scuffed patches on the wallpaper, the pale muslins of the ladies, the sober hues of the civilian gentlemen, and everywhere the brave colours and gold and silver lace of the officers. At one end an orchestra of local musicians did their best to combat the rising tide of conversation; in the supper interval, it was said, a military band from a Guards regiment was going to play while the guests consumed lobster patties, cold chicken, salmon baskets and any quantity of champagne.

Despite the short notice, the ball was well attended. Lady Theakston was a noted hostess, and knew everyone; Lord Theakston was a bosom-bow both of George Brummel and the Regent; and it was rumoured that the Duke was going to give a look-in during the evening. Besides, it was known that Lady Theakston had invited every eligible man within riding distance; and all those mamas who had brought their unwed daughters to Brussels in the hope of getting them off were not likely to miss the opportunity of snatching up the crumbs dropped from Lady Rosamund's plate. There were even those who believed, though privately, that their own Celia or Anthea or Georgiana had an excellent chance of cutting out Lady Rosamund altogether.

Lady Rosamund wouldn't have minded in the least. She danced obediently, but with manifest boredom, her eyes fixed on the doorway through which any new arrival must appear. The young men presented to her by her mother or step-papa led her onto the floor and set themselves to charming her, only to find themselves baffled. Every witty remark, every polite question, every conversational ploy fell into a pool of indifference, and sank like a stone into porrage. It was very unnerving. They would have been grateful to find Lady Rosamund intolerably high in the instep, or too well pleased with herself, or even uncomfortably shy, but they had to admit it was none of those things. She was neither bashful nor proud — she simply had no interest in them. She might as well have been dancing with broom-sticks.

'Look at her!' Lucy cried wrathfully to Roberta, as her daughter trod carelessly on the toe of a subaltern of the 95th Rifles, making them both stumble. 'She's making no effort at all! She boasts of being a bad dancer as though it were something to be proud of!'

'It's very shocking,' Roberta agreed, 'but I think she would sooner ride than dance.'

'Well so would I,' Lucy said crossly. 'But you can't ride at night. Besides, I always liked dancing as well. When I was her age I'd been three years married, and if I'd behaved as she does, my mother would have whipped me. We're too soft on our children these days. But I'll get her off,' she added with determination as the dance ended and the rifleman bowed to his partner with an expression of deep mortification, 'if it's the last thing I do.'

Sophie was dancing with a Captain Dietmar, who had been presented to her, with her mother's permission, by the Duc. He was a small, dark man, with such a look of a sad pet monkey that Sophie was ready at first to forgive him for seeming rather dull. He had been telling her at great length about the administrative structure of the Allied army, and she had been doing her best to follow; but he had only got half-way through the First Corps — the Prince of Orange's command — and it was heavy going.

'And then there's the second division,' he said as they crossed hands for the turn. 'That's ours, Monsieur le Duc's and mine, you now.'

'Oh, you are in command of it? How splendid,' Sophie said, grateful to have something positive to say at last. She had been alternating 'Really?' and 'Indeed?' but was afraid it was becoming obvious. Captain Dietmar blushed a little.

'Oh no — not at all — how could you think so, ma'am? I only meant that we serve in it — in a very humble capacity as far as I am concerned! The General Baron commands — Baron de Perponcher — and Monsieur le Duc is his aide. I am in the first brigade — that's Bylandt's, you know — and we are five battalions, all Netherlandish, of course.'

'Of course,' Sophie said from the depth of her bewilderment.

'Now, the first battalion —' Dietmar began, but at that moment the music ended, to Sophie's relief. She was sure he must have had a very sad life, but was glad to have finished her dance with him, and only hoped that he would not ask her again later in the evening. She performed her curtsey, and as she rose from it, another officer in the same uniform appeared at Dietmar's elbow and clapped a hard hand on his shoulder.

'Well, Ferdy, you fascinating dog! You have monopolised Mademoiselle's attention for long enough, and now I absolutely insist that you present me to her, so that I can try my luck at driving the memory of your perfections from her mind!'

'Oh, now, look here,' Captain Dietmar protested, looking as though he did not like this form of address at all. Sophie wondered at it a little, but the newcomer gave her such a gaze of shining innocence, in which a gleam of wickedness was somehow imperfectly concealed, that she couldn't help smiling.

'There, you see, I have begun! Ferdy, the introduction, if you please! For the music will begin again at any moment, and I would not for worlds miss one single measure.' He removed his gaze from Sophie and fixed it on Dietmar, and said with a pretence of menace, 'If necessary, I shall have to make it an order, and you will have to obey.'

Sulkily, Dietmar said, 'Miss Morland, may I present to you Major Larosse, of ours.'

The major bowed, and, concealed by the action, managed with a pout to mimic the captain's unwillingness, and at the same time gave Sophie a wicked glance that made her want to laugh. But she was doubtful of the propriety of accepting the introduction through this medium, and hesitated to return the curtsey; and as if he had read her mind, Larosse said quickly, 'I have, of course, asked for your Mama's permission to address you, mademoiselle. She and my commanding officer are acquainted, as you know.'

The music had struck up again, and Sophie was glad to curtsey and place her hand on the offered arm of Larosse. He led her to the set, and said, 'I trust now I've come so gallantly to your rescue, Miss Morland, that you will reward me by pretending that we have known each other for ever — or at least since the beginning of this evening, which I believe is much the same thing these days!'

She couldn't help laughing, and he gave her a warm glance and said, 'That's better! You can't imagine how it struck me to the core to see you drooping under Ferdy's barrage! He's a very dull dog, but you mustn't judge all of us by him. We call him Jawbreaker in our regiment: not because he uses long words, but because trying not to yawn in his presence is a serious problem.'

Sophie was still laughing, but her cheeks grew a little pink. 'You should not speak so to me, Major, indeed you should not,' she said.

He raised an eyebrow. 'But we are old friends, are we not? We have put aside all that tedious nonsense about "Are you enjoying Brussels?" and "What do you think of the orchestra?" long ago, and have got to the comfortable stage of pulling to pieces our common acquaintances.'

'I don't suppose we have any,' Sophie said, a little sadly.

He cocked his head at her. 'Now, why that tone of voice? Do you think we shall run out of things to say so soon?'

'Oh — no,' Sophie said in some confusion. 'But I don't suppose I know anyone that you know. I am so very — this is my first ball, you see.'

'That is very much to recommend you,' Larosse said warmly. 'You should never be ashamed of innocence — only of ignorance.'

'But I am very ignorant too,' Sophie said, wondering at herself a little now, for she had not expected to find any stranger so easy to talk to.

'Not at all. Ignorance is having the means of improving oneself, and refusing to do so. You, it is plain to see, are learning every minute.'

'What am I learning?' she asked unguardedly.

He met her eyes. 'Just at this minute? To trust me; and to look directly at me, without false modesty. No, no, don't lower your eyes yet! I wish to admire them. They are most remarkably fine ones.'

'Oh —' Sophie murmured, between embarrassment and excitement. 'Please, you must not — you should not —'

'Should not what? Flirt with you? You think me a flirt?'

It was too harsh a word for Sophie to think of using, but she could not help feeling that such boldness on first acquaintance was not proper. She said nothing, and after a moment Major Larosse said seriously, 'I am sorry if I have offended you. Perhaps I took too much for granted. But please believe that I really meant it when I said we are old friends. I felt it so from the first moment; and I don't mean to be forward — only comfortable.'

Sophie looked up fleetingly, and caught a glimpse of such a pleasant, unthreatening smile that she looked again less fleetingly. Yes, she thought, it was comfortable. It had no right to be, but it was.

His eyes crinkled, just as if he had read her thought. 'Very good. You have taken your first lesson in overcoming convention, and passed with flying colours! And now let me tell you that I was not, as you feared, making love to you when I said you had fine eyes. I was merely making a truthful observation; and a man should not be punished for telling the truth, should he?'

She laughed. 'Now you are talking nonsense,' she said.

'Ah, but I do it most engagingly, don't I? There, another little shadow passed through your eyes! Be careful, Miss Morland, what you think, for every thought is visible to me in them. What was it this time? What did you fear?'

Sophie felt unaccountably brave with this odd stranger. 'That you might think me fast,' she said truthfully.

Larosse laughed, not mockingly, but with pleasure, and pressing her hand slightly, said, 'Dear Miss Morland, I am not such a coxcomb as to mistake frankness for fastness! Look, look over there, by the door. Do you see the woman in the *bleu céleste* crape with the gold flowers?'

Sophie turned her head. In the doorway, looking around

her as though she had just arrived, stood a woman who seemed to embody every physical perfection that Sophie lacked. She was tall, dazzlingly fair, moulded like a Juno, with magnificent shoulders, a long, white neck, and a face of classical beauty. Her hair was golden, arranged in a crown of shining curls. Her gown was deeply *décolletée*, and of the sort of vivid, stunning colour that Sophie hadn't the complexion to wear, and encrusted with gold embroidery. In her hair she wore a wreath of roses made out of gold foil — a daring final touch that gave her the look of a goddess just stepped down from Olympus.

'Yes,' Sophie said, almost in awe. 'I see her.'

'Now that,' said Larosse, 'is Lady Annabel Robb, and she *is* fast.'

'Oh, but she looks so beautiful!'

'She is beautiful,' Larosse agreed, 'but the most hardened flirt in the world, and utterly heartless. And yes, Miss Morland, looking at me with those too-expressive eyes, I do have cause to know it! I was infatuated with her for a whole month in my green days, but I came out of it pretty well — for it's like the chicken-pox, you know: you never get it twice, provided you survive the first time! Others haven't been so lucky.'

'What can you mean?' Sophie asked, intrigued. Her education, she felt, was going forward by leaps and bounds.

Larosse looked down at her, and then smiled and shook his head. 'No, it is enough for now. I shall save something to tell you next time. I shall only say now that it is not a good thing to be Annabel Robb's latest flirt. She eats young men for breakfast.'

'Oh, but please —' Sophie protested; but the dance was ending, and Major Larosse wouldn't say any more. He made his bow to her, and escorted her back to her mother, and then disappeared into the crowd.

'Are you having an agreeable time, my Sophie?' Héloïse asked.

'Yes, Maman,' Sophie said emphatically enough to satisfy her mother.

'You are rather red in the face, love. You aren't getting too hot, are you?'

111

'No, Maman. I don't think so.'

Héloïse smiled at her and laid the back of a cool hand to her cheek. 'I expect it's just the exertion of dancing. It will be supper-time soon, and you shall rest and grow cool.'

At supper, Sophie and Rosamund were reunited, sitting at the table with Lucy, Danby and Héloïse, and the guests they had invited to join them: the Duc de Veslne-d'Estienne, and two respectable young men from Maitland's Brigade, the First Foot Guards. It might have been supposed that these two young gentlemen would find the presence of General Perponcher's second-in-command and one of Old Hookey's senior aides somewhat daunting; but Lord Ponsonby and Harry Pyne had weathered the beatings of a private tutor, the privations of Eton, the debaucheries of Balliol and the terrors of Presentation together, and a couple of senior officers were barely a challenge to their sophistication, even when accompanied by a brace of unwed daughters fresh from the schoolroom.

Danby had chosen them as supper-companions for this reason, rather than from any intention of match-making — though he had reflected that young Ponsonby would be no bad match for Rosamund, and Harry Pyne, who was Ponsonby's cousin, was independently wealthy by a collateral inheritance. For the moment, however, it was enough that they should keep the girls amused.

They were doing so now with horrifying tales of life at Eton, suitably embroidered.

'That was the time we threw old Brook's bed — the usher, you know — out of the window into the street,' Ponsonby was saying airily. 'It had castors on its legs, and the street there ain't quite flat, so it started to roll. Lord! I've never run so fast in my life! But Harry here passed me, goin' like a hare, and caught it at the cross-roads, otherwise we should have been done up! Sent down at the very least, I should think.'

'For throwing a bed out of a window?' Rosamund said. 'Was that so very bad, then?'

Ponsonby grinned. 'Well, Brook *was* still in it.'

'Didn't have the choice, you see,' Harry Pyne drawled, 'seein' as we'd tied him to it with a sheet.'

'Oh, but don't worry,' Ponsonby added, seeing that Sophie was looking alarmed, 'it was only the first floor. He didn't come to any harm.'

'That's more than you can say for us, ain't it, Pon? Old Ascot Heath — the Head Master — gave us twenty a-piece for that little lark. Jupiter! Did that old fellow like flogging! I feel it yet — war wounds, you know. Ache when there's a touch of frost in the air!' He put on the voice of an old soldier reminiscing, which even made Sophie laugh.

'He gave fifty-two boys a round dozen each, once,' said Ponsonby. 'Though that was after our time, wasn't it, Harry? When he'd got into practice and built up his stamina a bit.'

'It sounds quite dreadful,' Sophie said breathlessly. 'How could you bear it?'

'They're roasting you, Sophie,' Rosamund advised. 'Pay no attention. Depend upon it, they were never in trouble in their whole lives. You only have to look at them.'

'Never in — ! Well, I forgive you, ma'am, for it must be beyond the imagination of a gently-bred female, but you can't have any idea of the savagery we were exposed to,' Pyne said solemnly. 'We were beaten like dogs, ma'am, for the most trivial offences — just for driving a tandem, for instance, up and down the streets of Ascot.'

'Well, to be fair,' Ponsonby added, 'It wasn't so much the driving, as the racing.'

'And it wasn't so much the racing, as the knocking down of the old fellow with the scythe,' Harry agreed judiciously. 'And forcing the Bursar's gig into the ditch. Though really, when I think of it, it only served him right.'

'Why?' Rosamund asked.

'Oh, it was a perfectly villainous gig, with the most horrible yellow wheels! The fellow shouldn't have been allowed on the road with it: it was an offence to every gentlemanly feeling. Really it was quite a public service to smash it to kindling.'

Sophie laughed, but couldn't help asking, 'Were they hurt? Oh, I hope not!'

Pyne exchanged an amused glance with his cousin and said, 'Why, ma'am, you are too tender! No, no, they both fell into nice muddy ditches, and had a very soft landing, I promise you!'

113

'Who is falling into ditches?' Lucy asked, her attention drawn by the last sentence.

'Shouldn't be surprised to learn it was young Pyne,' Danby said, giving him a stern look. 'The way he drives that phaeton of his.'

'Oh, sir! You impugn my skill with the reins!' Pyne protested.

'Harry's a noted Corinthian, sir,' Ponsonby agreed. 'Won many a race in his time. When we were with Graham in Holland, he was known as Top of the Trees. And General Maitland won fifty guineas on him once.'

'I've heard he's a devil to go,' Danby said drily. 'What about that race last week, to Waterloo and back? Driving unicorn, too! You'll break your neck one of these days, young man. These randems are not the thing, you know!'

'Why, sir, as to that, didn't our beloved Regent once drive a three-horse rig to Brighton in record time?' Pyne said innocently. 'You being such a close friend of His Highness, sir, you can hardly blame us for wanting to emulate him.'

Rosamund interrupted proudly. 'But Mama beat the Prince's time — didn't you, Mama? By ten full minutes — that's what everyone says, anyway.'

'Fifteen,' Lucy said, and then shook her head ruefully. 'But you shouldn't bring that up in polite company, you abominable child! It was all long ago, and quite forgotten now.'

'Not by me,' Danby said. 'I shall never forget it. Rode in your dust the whole way, my heart in my mouth. Sure you were going to overturn and break your neck.'

Lucy raised an eyebrow. 'You didn't have much faith in me!'

'Trusted you, all right — it was everyone else on the road!'

'So it's true, ma'am?' Harry Pyne said delightedly. 'The story is still told, but we feared it might be just a hum.'

'That I beat the Prince's time? Yes, but I was driving four horses. I shouldn't care to try it with a random rig.'

Pyne exchanged another sly glance with Ponsonby, and said, 'I'll wager you could still do it, ma'am, and handsomely! How about a challenge, a race? Straight down the road, a nice easy drive just as far as, say, Genappe or Quatre-Bras — that's about twenty, twenty-five miles. Pon could lend you a rig, and I know you have your horses with you —'

Danby looked thoroughly alarmed at this, and said firmly, 'Pyne, you abominable young man, you're putting ideas in her ladyship's head. I forbid you to say another word!'

'Oh, Mama, do!' Rosamund cried. 'I never saw you race to Brighton!'

'Hardly surprising, since you weren't born.'

'Well, but this would be the next best thing. And three horses! No-one but you could do it,' she added cunningly. 'No female, that is!'

'Flatter away,' Lucy said grimly. 'I shan't rise to the bait. My racing days are over.' Pyne began to protest, but she said, 'How can you think a matron of my age and dignity would have anything to do with such wild scheme, you absurd boy?' But they could tell she was pleased, and when she looked at her husband, their eyes exchanged an amused and tender smile.

'Well, ma'am, if you change your mind,' Pyne said regretfully; and then, lifting his champagne to his lips, 'I must say, this is a first-rate ball. I should think everyone in Brussels must be here!'

At his words, the animation drained from Rosamund's face, but as the lively conversation was continuing amongst the adults, only Sophie noticed. When they rose from the supper-table, the two young women went upstairs to repair the ravages to their toilette before the dancing began again, and when Moss went away for a moment to fetch some more thread, Sophie took the opportunity to ask anxiously, 'Is something wrong? Aren't you having an agreeable time?'

'Are you?' Rosamund asked. 'It seems to me the most insipid, tedious business, having one's toe trodden on by empty-headed young men!'

'Well,' Sophie said judiciously, 'some of them are rather dull; but I'm sure I have more of the dull ones than you. Lord Ponsonby and Lieutenant Pyne aren't dull, and you've danced with both of them.'

'Conceited rattles,' she dismissed them petulantly. 'The only campaign they've seen was with Gordon in Holland, and that counts for nothing; and the rest are nothing but Hyde Park soldiers who've never seen action at all.'

Sophie couldn't quite see why this made them ineligible as dancing-partners. 'I suppose,' she said tentatively, 'the ones who have seen action would be too old for our come-out ball. Our mamas were bound to ask the young men of our own age, or near it. The older ones probably wouldn't want to come.'

'The Duke said he would look in,' Rosamund said passionately, 'and he hasn't.'

'He still may — it's only just past midnight. He wouldn't want to come for the whole evening — not to a ball like this.'

'And Marcus isn't here!' Rosamund cried, coming at last to the heart of it. 'It's too bad! How could he not come? He's — he's practically *family*!'

Sophie's heart was wrung, but she had no comfort to offer. She remembered the soldierly, sophisticated man she had met that once in the drawing-room, and she was unable to believe, even for Rosamund's sake, that he viewed her other than as a distant relative, and a mere schoolroom miss.

'Perhaps he was on duty,' she said tentatively. 'The Duke might keep him busy; and you know, even if he came, he might not want to dance with you.'

Rosamund turned bleak eyes on her. 'He's different from when he went away,' she admitted. 'It's the campaign that's changed him. But if he had come, he'd have danced with me. It's *my* ball, after all.'

Moss returned with the thread. 'Now, my lady, let me just put a stitch into that shoulder-flounce. Why, Miss Sophie, you're so red in the face! Are you over-heated? You be careful not to catch a chill. Take the powder-puff, there, and put a little on your shoulders, miss. It won't do to be shiny.'

The two girls said nothing more, while the maid tweaked and pinned them into place and then ushered them to the door, saying, 'You both look as fine as fivepence, just as you should. It's your evening, young ladies! I hope you enjoy every minute.'

Sophie, at least, smiled and thanked her; and as they walked down the stairs, she whispered to Rosamund, 'She's right. Oh do try, Cousin! You are the most important person here, and everyone wants you to be happy, and all the young men want to dance with you.'

Rosamund looked at her long and thoughtfully, and in the

116

end vouchsafed no more reply than, 'Yes.'

But when they reached the ballroom, they had hardly had time to look about them when there was a commotion over by the main door, and all heads were turning, and a sensation was passed back in whispers through the crowd.

'It's the Duke! The Duke's here! The Duke has arrived!'

It was Sophie's first sight of the Great Man, and she was not disappointed. Though he was not tall, or splendidly dressed, he had about him enough air and presence to satisfy her; and to see in the flesh those famous chilly blue eyes under beetling brows, that famous beak of a nose — and at a ball which was at least partly in her honour — was thrilling indeed. Lord Theakston, Aunt Lucy and Maman had gone over to greet him, and he was smiling in an affable way, and then Lord Theakston said something that made him laugh loudly. There seemed nothing stiff or formal about him.

They moved a little further into the room, allowing the party the Duke had brought with him to enter behind him, and Rosamund seized Sophie's arm and gripped it so tightly that it hurt.

'Oh, please — you're pinching me!' she gasped; but Rosamund's eyes were fixed, her face straining forward like a gundog pointing.

'It's him!' she hissed. 'There, behind the Duke! He's come after all! Oh, Sophie — !'

A small knot of staff-officers had attended the Duke into the ballroom, dressed, unlike him, in uniform; and to the fore there was no mistaking the broad shoulders and handsome moustaches of Captain Marcus Morland. Sophie had to admit that he looked splendid. His plain staff-officer's coat fitted smoothly across his shoulders; his skin-tight net pantaloons were creaseless, his tasselled Hessians gleamed, and his fringed sash added the final touch of glory.

'I knew he would come!' Rosamund cried, and her voice was so vibrant with joy that Sophie said anxiously, 'Oh, Rosamund, be careful!'

'Careful?' Rosamund cried in amazement, her luminous face still towards him.

'Don't shew too much,' Sophie begged softly. 'Don't let everyone see what you feel!'

117

Whether Rosamund heard her she didn't know, for at that moment the party looked round for Sophie and Rosamund, and a path opened as if by magic through the crowd, and they were being beckoned forward with encouraging smiles.

'They want us,' Rosamund said, going so quickly that Sophie had to run a step or two to catch up with her; praying as she hurried in her cousin's wake that she would not do anything improper, like ignoring the Duke in order to speak first to Marcus.

But when they reached the waiting group, it was plain that even Rosamund's passion was not proof against the presence of the Field-Marshal himself, and she stood quietly with properly downcast eyes as Lady Theakston made the introductions.

'My youngest daughter, Duke, Lady Rosamund, and my niece, Miss Sophie Morland.'

'How d'e do? Delighted to meet you.' The Duke shook hands affably with each of them in turn, and, daring to raise her eyes to the famous face above her, Sophie saw a reassuring twinkle in the deepest eyes, to which she responded instinctively with a shy smile. Why, she thought, there's nothing stiff or frightening about him at all. 'And how do you like Brussels, eh?' he asked her kindly.

'Very well indeed, your grace,' Sophie said.

'That's right! Well done! Splendid! Well, I have brought you some of my family to dance with, you see. They all dance like zephyrs — answer to me if they ever tread upon a toe, you know!'

Everyone laughed dutifully, except Rosamund, who, colour high in her cheeks, looked up at him boldly and said, 'Is it to be war, sir? Will it be soon?'

For a fraction of a second there was a tense silence, and when the Duke said cheerfully, 'Oh yes, we will have to fight old Jonathon Wilde sooner or later. But there's plenty of time for dancing yet. And the cavalry's on its way out, you know. The Life Guards and the Royals are under orders, so my boys will have competition in the ballroom at last.'

'What news of the Tenth, sir?' Danby asked.

'Anxious to leave me, eh, Theakston?' the Duke said, and

there was general laughter, and the party moved on into the ballroom, Lucy throwing a fierce, reproving glance at Rosamund as she passed. Rosamund did not heed it, however: she was ducking her head this way and that, trying to catch sight of Marcus, for the general movement had hidden him from her view. The music was starting up again, and everywhere young men were seeking out their partners, or looking for unattached young women to lead to the set.

This was Marcus's chance, Rosamund thought. 'Oh where is he?' she whispered anxiously to herself. At any minute someone else might approach her. A captain in the smart rifle-green of the 95th was looking at her with the air of one plucking up courage to ask, and she tried desperately to evade his eye, searching, searching for Marcus in the throng. The rifleman was approaching diffidently — what a sheep! Rosamund thought contemptuously. Marcus would never be so meek.

The rifleman's fair face was flushed with his own boldness. 'I beg your pardon, Lady Rosamund — might I have the honour of the next —'

'Oh! there he is!' Rosamund breathed, catching sight of Marcus's pale crop over the rifleman's shoulder; and she thrust past him without even answering, leaving Sophie and the captain trapped in each other's company and almost equally embarrassed.

Sophie felt her cheeks glow with distress. 'I — I'm afraid my cousin didn't hear you, sir. I'm so sorry,' Sophie said, feeling desperately sorry for him. To be shy, and to have plucked up courage, and then to be brushed off like a fly, must be mortifying.

The rifleman put his hands behind his back and cleared his throat once or twice, and then ran a finger round his collar, stared up at the ceiling, and then down at his boots. At the end of this process he managed to command his voice enough to say, 'It's nothing, ma'am. Pray don't heed it. I mean, I'm sure — that is —' He met Sophie's gaze at last, to find dark eyes filled with quiet sympathy.

'It was very unlucky,' she said gently. 'I'm sure Lady Rosamund would have loved to dance.'

He pulled himself together. 'Pray do not regard it, ma'am.

119

I am very fortunate in having the opportunity now to ask *you* for the honour of the dance.'

Well, thought Sophie, he did the best he could in the circumstances; and it happened she was not engaged, and he seemed a personable young man.

'Thank you,' she said; then hesitantly, 'I'm afraid we have not been introduced.'

He squared his shoulders, taking command of the situation with something more like the insouciance she had already come to expect from the officers in Brussels. 'On such an occasion as this, ma'am, I believe a degree of informality is permissible. Might I have the honour of presenting myself? Captain Philip Tantony of the 95th — my colonel is well acquainted with your aunt and uncle.'

She smiled and curtseyed, accepting his credentials and his hand in the same movement, and allowed him to lead her towards the nearest set. He seemed a pleasant, good-looking young man, and if she was only his second choice — well, what of that? She only wished she could see how Rosamund was getting on.

Rosamund had thrust her way heedlessly through the press toward that fair head, and coming within reach at last cried, 'Marcus! Marcus! It's me!'

Marcus turned, looked surprised, and then smiled down at her. 'Why, there you are, Rosy! And looking every inch the *débutante*, if I may say so. What a pretty dress. Are you having a nice time?'

The crowd was easing now as more people made their way onto the floor, revealing at Marcus's side a tall handsome woman in *bleu céleste* and a great deal of gold whose identity would not have been a mystery to Sophie. She looked at Rosamund from under her eyelids, and Rosamund looked a surprised enquiry at Marcus. He smiled. 'Ah, yes — let me present you, love. Bel, this is a distant cousin of mine, Lady Rosamund Chetwyn: I've known her since childhood. Rosy, Lady Annabel Robb.'

Lady Annabel was too well bred actually to say that she found it a dead bore to be forced to notice infants, but only an infatuated man would not have gathered it from her expression. She inclined her head a fraction from the vertical, and drawled. 'How do you do, Lady Rosamund? What a splendid ball this is.'

Rosamund frowned, returned the greeting with a slight nod, and then turned her attention back to Marcus as if they were quite alone.

'But why are you so late? I thought you were never coming.'

Marcus laughed a little nervously, glancing sideways at Lady Annabel in the hope that she would not take offence at this rudeness. 'Oh, the Beau kept us all hard at it until past nine o'clock, and then I had to put on my finery, you know. But I'm sure you have not missed me. You must be the belle of the ball tonight, Rosy-posy.'

Both women raised their eyebrows at his jollity. Rosamund said passionately, 'Of course I missed you! I made sure you'd be here from the beginning — after all, you are family — well, practically! And nine o'clock was plenty of time to get here for ten.'

Lady Annabel was looking studiously in another direction now. Marcus frowned. 'Well, we had to dine, you know, and I could hardly come away before the Duke, could I? But now, Rosy, love, I must —'

'Oh, well,' Rosamund interrupted, waving a hand, 'You're here now, and I saved his dance especially for you, hoping you'd get here in time. But we'll have to hurry — it's starting already.'

Marcus was dismayed. 'I'm sorry, love, but I'm already engaged to Lady Annabel.'

Rosamund looked as though she couldn't believe what she was hearing. 'But I saved this one for you! The first after supper! And it's my first ball!'

Marcus screwed up his eyes in social pain, looking from one to the other, and said doubtfully, 'But surely — it doesn't matter which dance does it? I can dance another with you later?' Rosamund looked mulish. 'Unless — perhaps you wouldn't mind, Bel, in the circumstances — ?'

Lady Annabel gave them both a kind smile. 'Of course, I quite understand. *Family* business must come first.' She began to turn away. 'I'm afraid, though, I shan't be able to spare you another dance later, Captain Morland; but I'm sure you have your priorities right.'

'Oh no, wait! Bel, don't go — I mean — I'm sure Rosy understands — don't you, Rosy? I'll come and dance with you later, love, only Lady Annabel is always engaged well in advance of every ball ...'

Lady Annabel was still walking away, a tight little smile on her perfect lips, and with a final shrug and a glance at Rosamund, Marcus hurried after her, leaving his cousin feeling as though the ground had just been shot out from under her. She felt the tears rising inexorably, and took her lower lip between her teeth in determination not to let them spill over. *I won't cry, I won't!* she thought. A moment later she saw her beloved Marcus join the set, holding the hand of the Olympian goddess and smiling at her as though — as though —

Rosamund turned away from the sight abruptly, anger battling with the pain in her heart. She was just his little cousin, in plaits, while that — that *creature* — that overdressed, vulgar, *fast* creature — ! But she'd shew him! She wasn't just going to stand here. It was her ball, after all, and everyone wanted to dance with her. Well, she'd dance every dance with a different man, and flirt with them all, and make Marcus notice her; and then when he was mad with jealousy he'd come creeping back, and *beg* her to dance with him!

She looked around her, desperate for a man to dance with — any man — someone in uniform — someone to make Marcus jealous. Nearby was a very young gentleman in the buff collar and silver lace of the 52nd — the Fighting 52nd, one of the best of the line regiments, which had been with the Duke in the Peninsula. He was only an ensign, but he would do for a start. Unaware that she was glaring like a fury, she fixed her eyes on the young subaltern, who swallowed nervously, tried to look away, and then obeyed the silent summons and came tremulously forward.

'Would — er — would you care to dance, ma'am?' he managed to say past the constriction of his collar.

Rosamund seized his arm and marched him to the set.

After an hour, the Duke made his excuses and left, taking with him the more senior of his aides. Colonel Lord

Theakston went too, with an apology to his wife and a promise to return to say goodbye before leaving for the tour of the fortifications. The ball continued, however, at full tilt despite these departures. Even some of the Duke's family who were to leave with him at dawn remained, long inured to dancing until three and being on parade again at six.

Later still, Sophie was standing at the side of the room, for once alone, fanning herself vigorously and watching Rosamund with an unhappy frown. Rosamund was a different creature from the one who had moped indifferently through the sets before supper. This one was gay, flirtatious, excited, dancing each dance with a different young officer, talking, laughing, gesturing with her fan, tossing her head, fluttering her eyelashes — aping every coquettish trick like a hardened flirt. Some of the older young men evidently found it amusing, and Sophie bit her lip to see them laugh, though ever so discreetly, at her cousin; but the younger ones were captivated, and vied with each other fiercely, each one dying to make himself her ladyship's servant.

'Well, Rosy's having a splendid time, isn't she?' said a voice at her elbow. Sophie turned to see Bobbie Chelmsford standing with his hands thrust inelegantly into his pockets, his shoulders hunched in discontent. 'Do you like this sort of thing, Sophie? I mean, don't you think it's damnably insipid?'

Sophie was wise enough to know that the question wasn't a question, and merely made an interrogative sound in her throat.

'Well, damn it, it's all very well for the officers, but a man in a civilian coat is nothing! It don't matter who you are, if you're not in scarlet, the females just look down their noses at you. Three girls I asked for this dance, and they all fobbed me off, and then a moment later went walking away on the arm of some damned Light Bob, and looking at him as though he'd just stepped down off a cloud!'

'It's a great shame,' Sophie said warmly. 'But the loss is theirs, not yours. A girl who is captivated by a uniform instead of the man who wears it isn't worth fretting over.'

'Well, it's all very well for you to talk, Cousin Sophie, but you've danced with nothing but officers all night — and just look at Rosamund!'

'I'd dance with you, and gladly,' Sophie said, a little wistfully, 'only I don't suppose that would be any help.'

Bobbie looked at her suddenly, drawn out of his selfish concerns to consider her position. 'Aren't you happy, Sophie? I thought you'd danced every dance.'

'Almost every one,' Sophie said. 'It's a splendid ball, and I'm most awfully grateful to Maman and Aunt Lucy for everything! And it's very silly of me even to think —'

'Think what?'

'Oh, that all the lively, interesting people want to dance with Rosamund, and only the dull young men choose me. Because, after all, I'm not at all pretty, and I haven't a title or a fortune, so why shouldn't they prefer Rosamund?'

Bobbie didn't quite know what to say to that. He looked at Rosamund too, and said, 'Well, she does seem to be making them laugh. That fellow she's with now — Dutch–Belgic by his uniform — seems to be pretty amused by her.'

'It's Major Larosse,' Sophie said. 'But I'm not sure — he has a strange sense of humour.'

'Oh, you know him, do you?'

'I danced with him before supper.'

Bobbie looked at her rather wistful face and the mournful dark eyes following the dancers' movements, and suddenly reached out and took her hand.

'I tell you what, Sophie — why don't we go and dance? It's half over, but — well, will you? I should like it, if you don't think it will be too dull.'

Sophie turned her gaze on him, and her smile banished the wistfulness at once.

'I should like it very much,' she said.

The ball was almost over. The crowd on the floor had thinned a little, but there were enough diehards still to keep the atmosphere alive. Sophie had been watching her mother and Aunt Lucy out of the corner of her eye, expecting any moment the signal for the last dance. It was to be a waltz — aunt Lucy having reassured Maman that it was perfectly *comme il faut* in Brussels, even for very young women — and it mattered rather with whom one danced it. Lord Ponsonby was standing nearby, chatting to a staff-officer and looking about him at the unattached females. Sophie had seen him notice her, and rather thought he might ask her for the last waltz, which would be pleasant. He was an amusing rattle, and very popular.

The signal was given; the music started, Ponsonby began to turn towards her; and suddenly her hand was taken and placed upon the braid of a uniform cuff, and Major Larosse was leading her onto the floor.

'You will forgive me, I hope, for having neglected you so long; but I know in England that it is utterly forbidden for young ladies to dance more than twice with the same gentleman, and I was determined to have this particular dance with you.'

'Why, sir?' Sophie asked, a little breathlessly.

The dark eyes looked down into hers, making her cheeks grow warm. 'The last waltz? How can you ask it? There, I have made you blush again! Dear mademoiselle, this won't do! You and I are old friends, and nothing I can say ought to overset you. Shall we be conventional until you have recovered yourself? Well then, how have you enjoyed your first ball?'

'Very much,' Sophie said.

'But?' Sophie looked up, and he smiled. 'There was a "but" in the tone of your voice. And now I see it also in your eyes. What is it that has disappointed you? Your very first ball is meant to be the pinnacle of happiness.'

'Oh, it is — it has been!' Sophie said hastily, and when he continued to smile disbelievingly at her, she added unwillingly, 'Only it did seem that it was only the dull young men who wanted to dance with me.'

The smile became sympathetic. 'But I told you why — because I may not dance with you more than twice. But I am glad you found everyone else dull after me — and how charmingly frank of you to say so!'

'Oh, but I didn't mean — !' Sophie began absurdly; and then saw the gleam in his eye and laughed instead. 'You are roasting me!'

'Well, only a little,' he smiled, turning to face her and sliding his arm about her waist. It was a palpitating moment: Sophie had waltzed only twice before in her life, and it still seemed daring — almost indecent — so to be embraced in public, and by a man of the slightest acquaintance. She remembered suddenly Moss's comment about her slender waist, and utterly confounded herself, colouring again as she wondered whether Larosse could read that thought, too, in her eyes.

He smiled down at her, but said only, 'And here we are at the end of a delightful evening. How many treaties have been made and broken tonight, I wonder? So many crises occur in ballrooms, it's a wonder to me that we go on thinking of balls as mere amusement! There's your cousin, for instance, the bold Lady Rosamund.'

'Oh — ' said Sophie unwarily as Rosamund whirled by.

'Yes — "Oh" is very much the *mot juste*! There she is, circling in the arms of Tantony of the 95th — a very respectable regiment, by the way, and a distinguished officer, though his fortune is comfortable rather than large. Tantony looks like a man in a dream, but alas, she has eyes only for another. Poor Philip!'

Sophie looked, and saw Rosamund's eyes fixed burningly over Tantony's shoulder on Marcus, waltzing with Lady Annabel Robb. It would have been funny if it had been anyone else, she thought.

'So that is Bel Robb's latest,' Larosse went on thoughtfully. 'Not good; not good at all. And your poor cousin, doing her all to make him notice her. Oh yes, do not try to deny it,' he added as Sophie made a sound of protest. 'The secret — as far as it is a secret — is safe with me! I speak to you as a privileged friend. And don't forget I danced with Lady Rosamund earlier this evening. She managed a fair imitation of a fascinating witch, but I could tell her heart wasn't in it. I did my best to help her in her campaign, but I fear she has little chance against Bel's formidable battery of charms. I speak as an old campaigner myself,' he added, smiling down at Sophie. 'Until Bel releases him, he may not depart, you know. Your cousin would do well to resign herself.'

'Rosamund would never do that. She decided years ago that she and Marcus would be wed one day.'

'Calf love can be painful,' Larosse said sympathetically. 'But perhaps they still may, once Bel has had her fill of him.

It probably won't last long,' he added. 'She tires of pretty young men very quickly — more quickly than ever these days. The last such, young Ireton, held his position for only a month.'

'What happened?' Sophie asked, and he gave her a slow smile which made her feel rather confused and weak.

'Never mind. We should be talking about you, Miss Morland, not about Bel Robb, nor about your cousin. Here you are, waltzing in the arms of the most fascinating man in Brussels, and all you can do is ask questions about other men. Shame on you!'

'Oh — oh please — don't say such things,' Sophie murmured, half shocked, half delighted.

'Why not? You don't yet understand me, do you?' he said, whirling her faster. 'You are afraid I may mean more than I say — or possibly less. You are afraid my attentions to you may not be quite proper, or that you may make yourself appear foolish, either by accepting or rejecting them. You see, I understand you very well!'

He looked down at her, holding her very tightly, and yet smiling at her in a way that made her feel secure and comfortable, as though they had known each other for ever. 'Don't be afraid,' he went on. 'You and I are old friends — let's enjoy that while we can. War is coming, Miss Morland, very soon — sooner than anyone thinks! This is a delightful interlude, a hiatus between one period of real life and another. In it everything is as delightful and fragile as April flowers, and nothing really matters. Do you understand me? No, I see you don't. Then you must make do with trusting me instead.'

Even Sophie in her innocence knew that it was outrageous for him to bid her trust him on so slight an acquaintance; but instead of drawing back gravely, reproving him with a look, being properly cool with him, she found herself leaning to his embrace with pleasure, and smiling up at him; and heard herself saying in a confident voice she hardly recognised, 'Oh, but I do trust you. And I do understand.'

And, in a strange way, it was true.

CHAPTER SIX

Lord Theakston returned a little after three to find Lucy waiting up for him, dressed in bed-gown and wrapper. She was sitting in front of the dressing-table, leaning forward to get the best light on some bloodstock papers she was studying.

'And a very proper, feminine occupation it is,' he said, watching her from the doorway. She turned at his voice, and smiled welcomingly, making his heart turn over. 'Other wives sit at the dressing-table to curl their hair or polish their nails,' he suggested.

'Pho!' was Lucy's reaction to that. 'It's the new horse Parslow found for me — a very promising sort of youngster that young Farringdon wants to sell. I think if I took it back far enough, I'd find it was some kind of relation to my Hotspur.' She studied his face. 'How long have we got?'

'I have to leave at five,' he said.

'You look tired.'

'Exhausting things, balls, when you're not dancing.' He unwound his sash and dropped it on a chair, and began to struggle with his jacket. Lucy got up and went to help him. 'Went well, don't you think?'

'Yes, very. I was pleased — and surprised — at how well Rosamund behaved. After supper, at least, she danced very nicely, and made herself agreeable.'

Danby sat down to let her get at his boots, and said, 'She certainly had 'em flocking round. Don't think she was a bit too — well, coming?'

Lucy crouched and grasped his left boot carefully by the heel. Danby's man, Deacon, had said bitter things last time about finger-marks, and how long it took to eradicate them. 'What do you mean?'

'Feverish gaiety and all that sort of thing. Struck me there was a marked difference before and after supper.'

128

Lucy removed the right boot before she answered. 'Yes, there was, but I thought it was just the champagne. What do you think, then?'

'Marcus and his *femme fatale*,' he said with his usual economy.

Lucy sat down opposite him and watched him unbuckling his stock. 'You don't really think there's anything in that schoolgirl crush of hers, do you? I mean, he doesn't know she exists; and if he's entangled with the Robb woman — who brought her, by the way? I certainly didn't invite her.'

'She was in the Duke's party,' Danby said. 'She and Marcus dined with him at her cousin's, Billy Cecil. Couldn't refuse her when she came with the Duke.'

'Oh. No, I suppose not. But why would the Beau have anything to do with a woman like her?'

'Billy Cecil's on his staff.' He began on his breeches-buttons. 'And he knew her Pa — old Wansbeck. Served in India together. The Beau sets a lot of store on bloodlines and family and so on.'

'And very little on the social conventions,' Lucy added.

'Yes; but she behaves better with him, of course — bold and witty, but not beyond what's pleasing.'

'I'm very sorry to see Marcus embroiled with someone like her. But I suppose it can't do him too much harm. He hasn't enough fortune to interest her beyond a flirtation.'

'It's the atmosphere,' Danby said, wriggling out of his small clothes. 'Eve of war — last grasp at happiness — that sort of thing. Breeds nonsense. There are several betrothals every week, and flirtations grow like cucumbers. But Marcus —' He sighed. 'These steady, level-headed ones are the worst when they do go off the scent and start cur-dog hunting. If it had been me, now ...'

Lucy stared in surprise, and then saw the glint in his eye and came to him, laughing, to be scooped onto his lap. 'You!' she said, giving up her lips for kissing. An interesting silence followed. 'I wish you weren't going away.'

'It'll be a quietish few days for you,' he said. 'So many of us out of town. And Firth's going today as well, though he don't know it yet.'

'Going where?'

'To the Prussian camp, to make contact with Papa Blücher. The Beau wants an official visit from him before the end of the month, and someone tactful has to go and arrange it.'

'So poor Roberta will be bereft as well.'

'She has a son to take her round,' Danby said, nibbling Lucy's neck.

'It's not the same,' Lucy said, intercepting his mouth again. 'How long will you be gone?' she asked after a while.

'Five days. Soon pass. Just make sure you don't get taken in while I'm gone. Not all officers are gentlemen.'

'Do you think I don't know the difference. No, let me get up — you have the boniest knees I ever sat on! Do you think young Ponsonby would do for Rosamund? He has a neatish fortune, and the family's good.'

'Nice boy — but getting him to offer's the problem. Don't think Rosamund's his cup of bouillon. Bed?'

'Is there time?'

'Just lie down with me for a while. Makes it easier to hold you.'

They lay down together on the top of the bed, and Lucy settled herself comfortably on Danby's shoulder. She felt wide awake now, which was just as well, since they had so little time left. Danby held her close, and stroked her head a little. She thought back over the ball again.

'It did go well,' she said. 'I lost track of all the officers Rosamund danced with. And Sophie was in her best looks — almost pretty, for her. Héloïse ought not to have let her dance so much with the Dutch–Belgic officers, though. It's a waste of opportunity, for none of them would do, and she doesn't want Sophie to get a reputation for being foreign.' Danby grunted, a sound which was half protest, half laughter. 'And then she wasted another two dances on Bobbie.'

Roberta had been worried about Bobbie, because he hadn't danced very much, while at home he couldn't get enough of it. And then later she had come over to Lucy looking tragic, to say that Bobbie had told her the girls wouldn't dance with him because he wasn't in uniform. Well, there was something in it, of course. From the girls' point of view, they wanted to be seen to captivate the men of the moment — and a man in

130

civilian garb just couldn't confer the same status. But after all, Bobbie was an earl, and unmarried — it was his own fault for moping in the background. If Sophie hadn't taken pity on him ...

'I wonder,' she said suddenly, 'whether Bobbie might not do for Sophie? They're only very distantly related, and Sophie will have Héloïse's fortune, one supposes. But,' with a sigh, 'I don't suppose Roberta would like it. She'll want a greater match than that for her one-and-only.'

Danby made a sound in reply which she could not mistake for anything but a snore. She pushed herself up from his shoulder to look at him, and a smile spread over her face which none of her children had ever seen directed at them. His firm, handsome face was naked in its vulnerability as he slept, and made her feel the most enormous desire both to possess and to cherish him. He looked tired, the worry-lines about his eyes shewing pale in his tan as they relaxed; his temples looked fragile, the fair hair springing from behind them threaded here and there with a single strand of silver.

He snored again and stopped in the middle of it, swallowed, turned his head a little towards her and settled again; and she continued to look down at him, content just to watch him sleep, loving him with a great and peaceful love. It was so different, she thought, from her love for Weston. She had never felt this contentment of equality, of companionship, of certainty. With Weston it had been all passion and urgency. She had been his, but there was a sense in which he had never been hers — not because he did not love her, but because she had been too young and ignorant and untried to be able fully to understand him. She had loved him like a dumb animal, and mourned him like one when he was gone, because she had lost the chance ever to know him.

She lay down again, nudging into Danby's side and feeling his arms tighten automatically round her, in his sleep. Well, it would not be like that with Danby: he was her friend and lover as well as her husband, and no moment of their lives together was wasted. However long it lasted — the thought stopped her in her tracks, made her turn and look at it. He was going back to his regiment. There was going to be, sooner or later, a battle. Supposing he was killed?

Supposing I'm not? he had said. Oh, that was like him! But how could she bear it? She could not now imagine life without him. If he were to die ... If he were to die ... She tightened her arms round him and pressed her face into his neck, and in a moment fell asleep like that, for she was more tired than she realised. They were still in that position at a quarter to five when Deacon came to wake his master and help him dress.

Docwra brought up breakfast on a tray at noon, and Lucy woke refreshed and ravenous, and ready to tackle fried ham and eggs, and field mushrooms, pink and tender and fried in butter, and slices of the peculiar local spiced sausage. She accompanied it with several cups of heavenly, fragrant coffee, and wheaten bread and fresh butter. Danby was already a long way off. She pushed her lingering thoughts of him aside, and concentrated on the day ahead and the question of Rosamund's future husband. In spite of what Danby had said, she had half a mind to make a push for Ponsonby. He was a likeable young man, the sort she'd be glad to have as a son-in-law.

'Mr Firth left the newspaper for you, my lady,' Docwra said, indicating the copy of the *Gazette de Bruxelles* lying on the counterpane. 'He's orders to go to Namur today, and doesn't know when he'll be back, and he left his compliments, seein' as how you weren't up, my lady.'

'Yes, I know — his lordship told me,' Lucy said, reaching for the paper. She thumbed through it, reading out bits to Docwra as the maid moved about the room tidying up and laying out things for the day.

'There's half a page about the ball,' Lucy said, reaching the Society pages.

'Yes, my lady. Very complimentary too, so Mr Firth said.'

'Fulsome is the word I'd use. There's a guest-list here. Hm — hm — hm. I haven't heard of half these people! Who on earth is the Comte de Vaux, for instance? It says here he was one of our most distinguished guests. And Baron Altenmeisser? And, good Lord! — it says that the Duke of Wellington entered with the lovely Lady Caroline Lamb on his arm! Who can it be who writes this nonsense?'

'There's a heap o' calling-cards, my lady,' Docwra said a

while later, when Lucy had reached the stage of bread and honey. 'The knocker's never had a moment to itself all morning.'

'Really? People do get up early in this town, don't they!'

''Twas mostly gentlemen, my lady. And Mrs Fauncett and the like — ladies who weren't up so late last night.'

Delicately put, Lucy thought, amused. 'I don't want to look at all of them,' she said, seeing there was indeed a heap. 'Tell me some. I expect you've read them all, haven't you?'

'I glanced through them, my lady,' Docwra said with dignity. 'There's a deal of officers called with compliments to Lady Rosamund, and two of 'em left flowers — that was an Ensign Lantrey of the 52nd, and a Captain Tantony of the 95th.' She shook her head sadly. 'He called twice, my lady, lookin' as dumb-struck as a landed codfish, left two lots of flowers an' three calling-cards.'

'Three?'

'Two stuck together,' Docwra admitted, reluctant to spoil a good story.

'Get rid of the flowers,' Lucy instructed. 'What else?'

'Lord Chelmsford looked in on his way to breakfast with Mr Enderby at the Hotel Dangle-terry, and said he'd call back later, and be at your service if you was wanting anything, my lady. And Lord Ponsonby and Mr Pyne called, and three other officers from the Foot Guards right behind 'em.'

'Very good,' Lucy nodded. 'I think at this rate I shall be rid of Lady Rosamund before the month's out. What else?'

'The French Duke called for Lady Henrietta, my lady, an' he's calling back later. And there was a card for Miss Sophie, from a very nice class of a gentleman — a major, my lady, though it was only one of them Netherish regiments, by his uniform.'

'Oh, that must be the one she danced the last with,' Lucy said. 'A major in Bylandt's, I think he was.'

'Major Larosse, my lady,' Docwra nodded approvingly. 'Sure, an' didn't he chat to me just as if I was anybody! As pleasant as you could wish, not a bit high, an' boots you could see your face in! If Miss Sophie could fix him, she'd be a happy young woman.'

133

Lucy looked at her askance. 'He certainly seems to have fixed you! How much did he slip you to sing his praises?'

'He never!' Docwra said indignantly. 'Sure, haven't I a mind of me own, my lady, to know a gentleman from the other sort?'

'Well, it's wasted on me. You'd better go and croon to Lady Henrietta; and even then, you'd have done better to find out what his fortune is, for a lot of these Dutch–Belgic officers have nothing but their army pay, you know, which is no good to us.'

'I doubt her ladyship doesn't think the same way as you, my lady,' Docwra said loftily. 'She'd want Miss Sophie to marry where her heart is.'

Lucy eyed her maid coldly. 'I see the eve-of-battle atmosphere's got to you as well. I've never heard you talk such sentimental poppycock before — and I hope I don't hear it again! Anything else I should know about?'

'Mr Farringdon called about the horse, my lady,' said Docwra, subdued.

'Already? He must be getting desperate, poor boy!' Lucy said with satisfaction. 'I'll have Parslow look the animal over today, and try it out tomorrow, perhaps. By then he'll be chewing his fingers.'

'Yes, my lady. What shall I put out for you? Will it be the blue habit this morning?'

Lucy grimaced. 'No, I shan't ride. I must take Lady Rosamund walking in the Park, and give some of last night's beaux the chance to approach. Duty before pleasure. Put out the rose-coloured cambric; and tell Moss to have Lady Rosamund ready in an hour. She'd better wear her new poplin with the emerald ribbon, and then she can wear the green velvet bonnet with the feathers. That should make her stand out in the crowd.'

'She'll do that all right, my lady,' Docwra said enigmatically, still smarting from being called sentimental.

'And you'd better send word to Lady Henrietta — my compliments, and would she and Miss Sophie like to come with us. Double the bait and double the catch, as they say.'

'Yes, my lady.'

★

It was a breezier day than yesterday, which helped to blow the cobwebs out of the minds of those who had danced too long, drunk too much champagne and gone to bed too late. Sophie had been feeling very jaded, dull-eyed and lethargic, when she woke; but out in the fresh air, with the prospect of seeing new faces, she soon revived. She was wearing her new walking-dress, which was of twilled cambric, raspberry-pink with a pattern of tiny white spots, which looked very smart and fresh and suited her colouring; and her Angoulême bonnet, finished with a ribbon of the same material, tied in a large butterfly bow.

'I'm glad it's warm enough just for shawls,' she said to Rosamund as they walked behind their mothers along the gravel path that wound through the shrubbery to join up with the main promenade along the lake. 'I should hate to have to cover up my new dress with a pelisse.'

Rosamund looked sideways at her with disapproval. 'Thinking about clothes again, Sophie?'

Sophie blushed a little. 'Oh — of other things as well, of course. But I like my new dress, and — well, it's all very well for you, Cousin, but you're tall and beautiful and you look striking whatever you wear, so you don't have to worry about clothes. Not that I worry about them, exactly, but — well, it's agreeable to know one looks one's best, in case one meets anyone — '

'Yes, I suppose so,' Rosamund said more kindly. 'I'd sooner be riding, but — ' She scanned all the figures in sight for a moment hopefully, and then as her eye alighted on her mother and discovered her to be doing the self-same thing, she scowled.

'Look at my mother!' she said abruptly. 'Looking over every young man who passes to see if they might do for me — so dull and respectable, you'd never believe how wild she was in her youth! A fine fuss she made when Cousin Africa ran away and joined a circus. And now all she seems to think about now is making good matches, and never mind people's feelings! She made my sister Flaminia marry Harvey Sale, though everyone knew he was Cousin Polly's beau. And she's mad to get me off on some eldest son, no matter whether I like him or not.'

'But she married Lord Theakston for love, didn't she?' Sophie asked hesitantly.

'Of course she did. That's the whole point. But no-one else must marry for love! You'd think she'd know better, since she was made to marry my father for family reasons, and they were as miserable together as wet dogs.'

'Oh no!' Sophie said, shocked. 'You mustn't say so! I'm sure it wasn't true.'

Rosamund shook her head. 'You're such an innocent, Sophie! Don't you know anything? It was a famous scandal that she took a lover, and drove my father out of the house. He lived apart in lodgings like a bachelor, even when they were both in London at the same time! It was thought very shocking — no-one talked about anything else for months.'

'But how can you know that? You could only have been a child.'

'Oh, Lord, you can find out anything if you keep your ears open! And the great thing about my mother's woman, Docwra, is that she loves to talk. She told Moss all about it one evening when they were sorting linen, and my bedroom was just next to the linen-room.'

Sophie found the idea of her cousin listening at doors as disturbing as the idea that Aunt Lucy had done such shocking things. 'But — well, it's our mothers' duty to take care of us and make sure we marry well, isn't it?' she said hopefully. 'And it's our duty to obey our parents.'

'Is it? Would you meekly marry anyone your mother chose for you?'

Sophie looked uncomfortable. 'Oh dear! Well, you see, I'm sure Maman wouldn't choose anyone I didn't like. She married when she was only fourteen to someone who turned out to be a very horrid man, so I'm sure —'

'You see! My point exactly! They know from their own experiences that these arranged marriages don't work, but still they want to interfere, and put us in the same position! Well, I think it's our duty to resist to the last breath in our bodies! It's a point of principle.'

Sophie thought, and put her finger on the weak spot. 'But, Cousin, even if we refuse to marry the men we don't like, that doesn't bring us any nearer marrying the ones we do like,

does it? I mean, they have to offer for us, and if they don't —
if they like someone else, for instance —'

As if on cue, Lady Annabel Robb appeared round a bend in
the path, coming towards them, walking briskly on the arm of
a willowy young man with a pale face and limp yellow hair,
like flax. She looked devastatingly smart. She was wearing a
cream holland spencer, with shoulder-capes just like a man's
driving-coat, over a dress of figured violet silk, and a high-
crowned bonnet with enough purple feathers, Rosamund
thought furiously, to have tricked out a team of funeral
horses.

Both walkers nodded civilly to Lucy, the officer raising a
hand to his hat; and as they passed, Lady Annabel looked at
Rosamund and, with what Rosamnd took to be a satirical curl
of the lip, just acknowledged her, too.

'He can't like her! I can't believe he really likes her,' Rosamund said fiercely when they had passed by. Sophie could
hear the tears close under the surface — tears of fear and
rage. 'He must be — I don't know — bewitched or something.'

'She may seem different to him from the way she seems to
us,' Sophie said gently. 'It's always hard to know what anyone
likes in other people, isn't it?'

It was true, Rosamund thought, but it was no help.

Héloïse meanwhile was saying to Lucy, 'But that was the
lady Marcus danced with, *n'est-ce pas*? Who is she, Cousin
Lucy? She is splendid!'

'That's Annabel Robb, walking with her cousin. Have you
never come across her?' Lucy said. 'Well, no, I suppose you
might not have, living retired as you do — but you must have
heard of her?'

'I don't think so. Should I have?'

'She was Lady Annabel Cecil, daughter of the Marquess of
Wansbeck,' Lucy said. 'She married Hugh Robb, the Scottish
mill-master. There was quite a scandal about it at the time,
don't you remember?'

'The name is just familiar,' Héloïse said doubtfully.

'It was a *mésalliance*,' Lucy explained, 'and there was talk
at the time that Wansbeck had forced it on her, and certainly
that wasn't beyond him; but the plain fact was that she

137

wanted to get away from home, and Robb was as rich as Croesus — and quite a handsome man, in his own way,' she added inconsequentially.

'But yes, I think I heard something of it. Did not Mr Robb die suddenly of a heart attack when they'd only been married a few months?'

'That's right. It happened at Lady Somerton's, at a dinner-party given in their honour. He went down like a stone, right in the middle of the first course.'

'It must have been very shocking for everyone.'

'Serves them all right, for accepting the invitation,' Lucy said impatiently. 'No good comes of encouraging mushrooms like that — I wouldn't even have received them. And everyone knows Lady Somerton's dinners are uneatable. She won't pay her servants enough, so of course they take it out on her. When Robb dropped dead with his head in her turtle soup, there was talk all over Town that he'd been poisoned — as well he might have been!'

Behind her, Rosamund snorted with laughter, and managed to change it into a cough. Lucy shot her a suspicious look, but went on, 'So Lady Annabel was left a wealthy widow, and everyone ever since has courted her for her portion.'

'Poor creature,' Héloïse said feelingly.

'Don't waste your pity on her,' Lucy said shortly. 'She's a hardened flirt, and a thoroughly bad lot. There was that business with young Ireton last year ...'

'What business?' Héloïse asked vaguely. Sophie strained her attention, remembering the name Ireton from her conversation with Larosse. This was the story he would not tell her, then. But Lucy only shook her head, remembering the presence of the young women behind her; and they reached the junction with the main path, and at once saw Ponsonby and Pyne, walking arm in arm, who changed course to come over to them.

'It was a perfectly splendid ball last night, ma'am,' cried Ponsonby. 'Wherever I go, I hear nothing but praise and envy. The suburbs are humming with your name! The best ball that ever was, so I hear!'

'You may stop gammoning me, Ponsonby,' Lucy said

138

pleasantly. 'I know enough about young gentlemen — and particularly young officers — to know they're perfectly happy as long as they've enough to drink and enough pretty young women to dance with.'

'Indeed, ma'am,' Pyne agreed. 'I've even known 'em settle for enough women, without the qualifier; but my cousin speaks no more than the truth, I assure you. And so his lordship has gone out of town? My commiserations, ma'am. It's a hard thing, and when you've only just arrived, too.'

'Know what I think, Harry?' Ponsonby said promptly. 'Ought to devote ourselves to Lady Theakston and her party. See they're properly taken care of. Put ourselves at her command.'

'You're right, Pon! The Duke would expect it.'

'Owe it to Lord Theakston — put his mind at rest. Wonder if he didn't mention something of the sort before he went away?'

'You're right. Blessed if I hadn't forgotten! "Young Pyne," he said — meanin' me, ma'am, you understand — "take care of her ladyship while I'm away."'

'His very words, Harry!'

'All right, you two young fools,' Lucy said, laughing. 'You can stop perjuring yourselves. I shall be happy to include you in our schemes. I was thinking, in fact, of organising a picnic party to drive somewhere out of town — into the forest, perhaps. Are there pleasant places to see?'

'Oh, without a doubt — the forest is very fine, ma'am, and the countryside is pretty. You couldn't do better. When did you think of going?'

'As soon as possible. The day after tomorrow, perhaps,' Lucy said. 'The weather seems settled enough — no sense in delaying. Consider yourselves as engaged, will you?'

'With the greatest of pleasure, ma'am.'

'I shall let you know what I arrange. These schemes are nothing without numbers, so I must see who else can be persuaded to join us.'

'You will have no difficulty in recruitment, ma'am,' Ponsonby said. 'The difficulty will be rather to keep the numbers down.'

They parted with the two young gentlemen and walked on

139

and shortly afterwards were overtaken by the Duc de Veslne-d'Estienne.

'I called at the house, and was told that you were walking here, so I followed, hoping to encounter you,' he said. 'I hope the exertions of last night have not left you too much fatigued?' The question was directed to the party as a whole, but his tender look was for Héloïse.

'Not at all,' Lucy answered drily. 'It would be a sad thing for the continuance of the human race if young people were to be fatigued by dancing.'

They walked on, Charles naturally taking the place by Héloïse's side, and since the other three were brisker walkers, they gradually fell a little behind.

'How pretty your daughter looked last night,' he said. 'You must have been very proud.'

'Yes, I was; though I hardly know what I have to be proud of. I had nothing to do but to help her choose her gown. All that Sophie is, comes from inside her. She is naturally modest and good.'

'And the next thing will be to find her the right husband,' Charles said, and added apologetically. 'So I believe one's mind runs naturally, from début to marriage — '

'— and from marriage to children,' Héloïse smiled. 'Yes, a natural progression! I was a grandmother, I think, five minutes after she was born.'

Some mental image her words conjured for him left him silent. After a moment, Héloïse said, 'Thank you for leaving your card this morning. You must have been abroad very early.'

'Yes. In fact, I have not been to bed. I was required to ride to Nivelles immediately after your ball with a message for Count Bylandt, and have just got back.'

The association of ideas led her to say, 'We had a card also from one of Sophie's partners of last night — a Major Larosse. I believe he is one of your officers?'

'Oh yes, René Larosse is in the first battalion of Bylandt's. A very witty man.'

'It was nice of him to leave his card — but I suppose Sophie must take the compliment to herself. What are his circumstances?'

He smiled at her suddenly. 'You are thinking that perhaps he may make a husband for your daughter?'

'I am not such a matchmaking mama as that! No, my mind had not run so far ahead. I thought him interesting, I wondered about him, *voilà tout!*'

'It's right and natural that you should. He's a respectable man, and a fine soldier, though his fortune is not large. He comes from an old family in decline, I believe.' He hesitated. 'You should know that he fought for Napoleon, until the invasion of Russia. After that, he was so disturbed by what the Corsican had done that he gave up his commission and became a private citizen for a few months. Then in the summer of 1813 he joined the Allied cause. He fought very bravely at Dresden and Leipzig, against Napoleon.'

Héloïse looked at him carefully. 'You think him unreliable?'

Charles looked uncomfortable. 'It is not that I mistrust his commitment to our cause now. But it is hard for any soldier to like a man who abandons his general, however good the reason. It is unfair, I know, and Larosse has done the right thing, and one ought to admire him for it. But somehow one would *like* him more if he had fought for Napoleon to the end.'

Héloïse shook her head. 'How can you say so? To fight for a bad cause cannot be good. Poor Major Larosse! I like him all the more, if he is to be blamed for doing what is right.'

'I told you it was unfair. I know it is illogical, but I had to tell you how I felt — and how others feel. It is, perhaps, a man's way of thinking rather than a woman's. He is admired and respected, but not much liked.'

'Well, I shall be kind to him, to make up for it,' Héloïse said, and the Duc laughed suddenly.

'How fierce you are — fierce and small, like a sparrow! Well, Larosse will have the best of it, after all! But I have to say I do not think he could mean anything serious towards your daughter. He is a man of large, and sad, experience — older than his years in consequence. He must be nine or ten years older than Miss Sophie, but older still in himself. I would expect him to be attracted to a more sophisticated sort of woman.'

'Like Annabel Robb, perhaps?' Héloïse said; but she wondered at the Duc's analysis. It was Marcus, young and gentle and relatively inexperienced, who was kissing Lady Annabel's sandal. It would not surprise her to discover that an older man, saddened by his dreadful experiences, had been attracted by youth and innocence, especially such absolute innocence as Sophie's.

But Charles himself, she considered, was curiously innocent for a man of his age and experience — perhaps because he had never been married, nor had children of his own.

As if his thoughts had been following hers, he said, 'How I should have loved to have a daughter like Sophie to bring out! It must be a father's proudest moment. I wonder that Sophie's father could bear to miss such an occasion.'

Héloïse made no reply, but looked away, biting her lip. It came too close to a criticism of James for her to hear it with complacency — especially as one part of her agreed with it. It angered her that James did not value Sophie as he should, even though she understood that it was only because of his obsession with Fanny. She longed, absurdly, to discuss the whole thing with Charles, and such a longing was dangerous, as well as disloyal.

Oh but she missed James! The touch and scent of him, the sound of his voice, simply the being with him, which nourished something in her that was fed by nothing else. She wanted, desperately and absurdly, to go home — but home was not home when her husband was absent from it, as he was now in spirit. If only he would write to her, say that he missed her, that life seemed cold and comfortless without her, as it was to her without him. She was doing her best for Sophie's sake — and lifelong practice made it possible for her to present a complaisant exterior — but still she felt like an exile. It was like those early weeks after she first came to England, fleeing the Terror — parted from her father and her homeland, and fearing she would never see either again.

The others had reached the edge of the lake and stopped there until Héloïse and Charles caught up. It was a pretty lake, curved and narrow and edged with clumps of willow and alder, and a great variety of waterfowl inhabited it. A pair of swans drifted by like snowy galleons, and as the party stood admiring the view, a flotilla of ducks tacked and paddled eagerly towards them in the manner of their kind.

'Oh dear! We should have brought some bread for them,' Sophie cried as the mallards crowded round them, jostling each other with anticipation.

'Oh, Sophie, you're so soft-hearted, you can't bear to disappoint even a duck!' Rosamund laughed at her, though not unkindly.

Sophie blushed a little. 'I was only thinking that they must be hungry, poor things,' she excused herself.

'I honour your sentiments, Miss Morland,' said a voice at her shoulder, making her start, 'but you need not fear. I can assure you they are probably the best-fed ducks in Europe.'

She turned and looked up into the face of Major Larosse, who smiled down at her in a way that made her feel strangely weak and breathless.

'Are they?' she said foolishly.

'*Bien sûr.* Only consider how many ladies take this walk every day.' He turned to make his bow to the rest of the party. 'Mesdames — monsieur le Duc — I am happy to meet you all on this splendid day. A fine breeze makes one feel fit for anything, don't you think?'

Héloïse offered her hand. 'Thank you for leaving your card this morning, Major. I'm ashamed to say we were all still in bed when you called.'

'Indeed, you were where you should have been, madame,' Larosse said, taking the hand gratefully. 'After such a strenuous evening — but a delightful one, I think!'

'We were walking toward the pavilion — will you join us?' Héloïse asked cordially, aware that everyone in the group was drawing his or her own conclusion from the exchange. Charles and Lucy, no doubt were disapproving — Rosamund frankly curious — and Sophie — ? Glancing towards Sophie, she saw her daughter gazing studiously at the ducks, and wondered for an instant if she had done the wrong thing. So grave a contemplation of waterfowl surely betokened more interest in Major Larosse than a prudent mother ought to encourage?

But it was too late to draw back now. Larosse had thanked her and was now one of their party. He offered his arm to

Sophie, but at once, and very properly, offered the other to Rosamund; Charles did the same by Lucy and Héloïse, and so in two groups the party walked on. Lucy, who thought little of the Dutch–Belgic officers as a whole, was probably reflecting on the irony of their being seen on this first, important, day to be escorted by two of them.

There was quite a crowd already at the pavilion, and Héloïse was glad that they had the two gentlemen to force a way through the crush, and secure a table in a corner by the window for them. Here they could sit without danger to their gowns and order coffee and cake, and watch both the new arrivals and the people walking by outside.

Almost immediately Lucy noticed that Annabel Robb and her cousin, walking by a different route, had arrived before them at the pavilion, and were standing on the far side talking to some acquaintance. Fortunately there were enough people standing in between for her to be able to look away without being obliged to acknowledge them again.

In spite of her prejudice against the 'Netherish' officers, she had soon to admit that Major Larosse was not only very personable, but was an amusing companion, and was welding the rather disparate party together in conversation with a great deal of expertise. He began by telling a mildly amusing anecdote about the old couple with whom he was staying in a village about ten miles from Brussels, extracted a story about a French hotel from the Duc, and then gracefully turned the talk to the idiosyncrasies of innkeepers and servants in general, on which subject everyone had something to say.

Lucy found herself relating how Docwra refused to countenance any foreign pronunciation and had referred only that morning to the Hotel Dangle-terry, and realised how cleverly it had been drawn out of her. She looked thoughtfully at Larosse, and found he was looking at her with amusement and understanding in his eyes, as though he had read her mind. *This is a dangerous man,* she thought, and then saw him smile as though he had read that, too.

They had not been seated for very long, however, before others began coming up to their table to greet them and talk about the ball and the news of the day. It seemed everyone in

Brussels was walking in the Park that morning: soon there was a ring of officers standing round their table, and an outer ring beyond that, too. Young Farringdon edged his way through to bow to Lucy and fix her a wistful eye as he asked if she had had time to study his horse's bloodline chart yet.

'I've glanced over it, no more,' Lucy said casually. 'Was there any hurry, Farringdon? I can send it back to you if you like.'

'Oh, Lord, no, your ladyship! Keep it as long as you like. I merely wondered, that's all. He's a fine horse, my Magnus Apollo, and just fit for your ladyship. I simply haven't time to ride him as he ought to be rid, what with all my military duties, and I don't like to leave him to a groom to exercise. You know how it is, ma'am. I hate to see a good horse wasted, when he might be giving your ladyship so much pleasure.'

'I quite understand,' Lucy said. 'A corned-up horse can kick a stable to bits. But I never buy in a hurry, you know, so if there's someone else eager for him, and you want to be rid of him — '

Farringdon laughed just a little too loud. 'Be rid of him? Lord, no! Magnus is the kind of horse — well, ma'am, if I couldn't be sure he was going to the right person, I wouldn't part with him at all. That's why I thought your ladyship would like him. But there's no hurry — no hurry at all. Good Lord, no!'

Lucy smiled serenely. 'Good. Then I'll certainly think about it, and let you know if I want to try him.' She regarded Farringdon with a mixture of affection and regret. He was an extremely handsome young man from an excellent family, but his estate was heavily encumbered through the gaming madness of his late father and elder brother, a strain Farringdon seemed also to have inherited. All Rosamund's fortune would hardly be enough to redeem the mortgage on Oakleigh, let alone repair the depredations. No, much as she liked him, Farringdon would not do — though there was no harm in having him around for Rosamund to dance with.

'Come and sit by me,' she said to him kindly, 'and tell me what I must see in Brussels. And you must join our picnic-party into the forest on the eighteenth ...'

Ponsonby and Pyne soon joined the party; and then Bobbie

145

Chelmsford, walking briskly along the path outside, saw them through the window and hastily changed course, towing his friend 'Tug' Enderby into the pavilion with him. Enderby was doubly welcome to him at the moment, as being one other Englishman in Brussels who was not in uniform.

'We just had a splendid breakfast at the Hôtel d'Angle-terre, ma'am,' Bobbie said to Lucy, 'and guess what we heard — that the Union Brigade embarked today, and should be here by the end of the week! So my uncle will be joining us at last.'

'And my uncle, too, Chelmsford, don't forget,' Lord Ponsonby added with a grin. 'Sir William Ponsonby is the officer commanding the second brigade.'

'Pon will soon be able to out-uncle you completely,' Harry Pyne said with an innocent look. 'He has Colonel Sir Frederick Ponsonby already on the table, to say nothing of Sir Frederick's sister.'

'No, no, we can't allow that,' Enderby put in, joining in the spirit of it. 'Lady Caroline Lamb don't count now she's changed her name! Bob will see your Sir Frederick, and raise you a Captain Marcus —'

'What is the Union Brigade?' Sophie asked, just in time.

'The Royals, the Greys and the Inniskillings, ma'am,' Enderby said promptly. 'The best of the heavy dragoons, in my humble opinion.'

Pyne grinned. 'Humble is the right word. You don't know anything about heavy cavalry, that's plain: the Householders knock your Union Brigaders into a cocked hat! Just because your family has land up near Carlisle, Tug Enderby —!'

'And just because your cousin's in the Life Guards, young Pyne —!'

'You'll have to forgive them, ladies,' Ponsonby said, shaking his head sadly. 'It's the heat, I fear. To be exercised over such a trifle ... Now I heard something this morning that is even more exciting.'

'More exciting?' Lucy said drily. 'I wonder if we shall be able to bear it.'

'I think even you may find it interesting, ma'am. I was speaking to Lennox this morning, and he told me that Horse-guards have just let it be known whom we are to have to command our cavalry. I wonder can you guess, ma'am?'

'Lord Combermere, to be sure,' Lucy said. 'There's no mystery about that. The Beau wouldn't have anyone else.'

'He asked for Lord Combermere, ma'am, I grant you — but he won't get him,' Ponsonby said, with the air of one with a magnificent secret under his belt. 'Lennox told me the Duke of York is sending us Lord Uxbridge!'

'No, nonsense! It can't be,' Lucy exclaimed.

'You're adrift there, for sure, Ponsonby,' Farringdon said. 'After that business with Lady Charlotte — !'

'Just what I said when I heard, but indeed, it's true! And Lennox told me that when the Duke opened the letter yesterday, Cecil was with him, and exclaimed much as you did, and said the appointment would give rise to a great deal of scandal. But the Duke just gave him a cold look and said "Why?" So Cecil reminded him that Uxbridge had run away with his sister-in-law and that his brother had been obliged to divorce her — '

'More than I'd have cared to do,' Enderby remarked grimly. 'But then I've no taste for having my head bitten off.'

'Nor I,' Ponsonby said with a grin. 'But the Duke simply said he remembered the incident, and went on looking at Cecil as though he'd just crawled out from under a stone. So Cecil — babbling, you know — blurted out that Uxbridge has a habit of running away with everybody — '

'Poor fish!' Pyne said. 'I warrant he wished he might just sink through the floor.'

'— and the Duke said, "I'll take damn good care he won't run away with me. I don't care about anyone else," and went on opening the rest of the letters, as cool as an ice-house pomegranate.'

'He's a complete hand, the Duke!' Bobbie said rapturously. 'He don't care about all that nonsense, provided a man's a good soldier.'

'Uxbridge is a good soldier, and a good cavalry general,' Lucy said.

'He is, ma'am — better than Lord Combermere,' Enderby said. 'I've heard it on good authority that he'd have been used in the Peninsula from the beginning except that he was senior to the Duke then, which made it awkward.'

147

'But still, one would have thought — I must say, I'm surprised,' Farringdon said.

'It just shews,' Rosamund said sweetly, looking at her mother, 'that the Duke doesn't set any store by marriage and the conventions.'

Lucy looked wrathful, but Larosse intervened smoothly. 'Not so, mademoiselle,' he said politely. 'It only shews that he places the national interest above his personal discomfiture.'

Rosamund looked ready to argue the point, but at that moment Marcus came in through the pavilion door and walked straight towards where Lady Annabel and her cousin were standing. Rosamund had half-risen from her seat, and now dropped down again, angry, disconcerted, not sure what to do next. Had he seen them? Surely he must have — but no, he would not ignore them all so rudely. But he had known That Woman would be there — he had gone straight to her, and from the way they had greeted each other, it was plain that the meeting was happening by agreement.

Her tortured imagination offered her the scene and the words. *When shall I see you again? Tomorrow, perhaps? I shall take a walk in the Park — I'll meet you at the pavilion at two o'clock.* All accompanied by languishing looks, pointed glances, perhaps the careless touch of fingers on the back of a hand, she thought bitterly. Though she was only just 'out', she had seen enough of dalliance in public places and private drawing-rooms to know how it was done. But how could Marcus be taken in by it? How could he care for a woman like that — false from the crown of her over-curled head to the tips of her too-pointed shoes?

While she was involved with these hurt and angry thoughts, Marcus had seen the Morland party, smiled and bowed, and having spoken a few words to Lady Annabel and her cousin, was now leading them over to join them.

He greeted them all warmly, evidently in high spirits, and said to Lucy, 'It was a splendid ball last night, ma'am. I don't know when I've been at a better. You know Lady Annabel, of course — and may I present to you her cousin, Lord William Cecil?'

'I am acquainted with Lord William,' Lucy said, returning his bow with a nod of the head slightly more civil than the one she gave Lady Annabel. She knew nothing against him, and if he were on the Beau's staff, he must be regarded as acceptable. 'How is it that you are not gone with the Duke to Mons?' she asked of both the young men.

'Oh, someone must mind the shop, you know, ma'am,' Marcus said with a grin. 'And, besides, the news is just come that the Union Brigade is on its way here — '

'Yes, so we've heard,' Lucy said.

'Have you, indeed? News travels fast in Brussels,' Marcus said with a lift of his brows. 'Well, ma'am, it means that my father may arrive at any moment, and the Beau thought I should like to give him the meeting at the earliest moment. So here I stay,' and he slid a sideways glance at Lady Annabel which Rosamund at least noticed, and which suggested he was content in the arrangement for quite other reasons.

'And do your mother and sister come too?' Lucy asked.

'Yes, ma'am, they travel with him.'

'How very nice for them — and for you,' Lucy said, just managing not to betray how little she welcomed this additional piece of news.

'We've just heard about Lord Uxbridge, too, Marcus,' Bobbie said eagerly. 'He was with Moore at Corunna, wasn't he?'

'Yes, distinguished himself there. He's been one of my heroes since my schooldays. I'm looking forward to meeting him.'

'What's he like?' Farringdon asked. 'You've met him, haven't you, Cecil?'

'Yaas,' his lordship drawled. 'Met him for ever in Town. Tall feller — bit of a dandy. Perfectly agreeable.'

'I've heard he's proud — a cold man,' Farringdon said.

'Never saw anythin' of it myself,' Lord William said, lifting one brow a fraction. 'Though he's got a short way with subalterns — but then, who hasn't?'

'Is he as handsome as they say?' Bobbie asked.

'I suppose so. Always popular with the ladies. But Bel could tell you more about that than me. She knows him better than me, anyway, don't you Bel?'

Lady Annabel glanced about the enquiring faces and said, 'He is extremely handsome: tall, as Billy said, a fine figure,

149

flashing dark eyes, and his mouth — ' She stopped and lowered her eyelids and directed a mischievous look in Marcus's direction. 'He's altogether charming. All the girls who came out in my Season were in love with him. I expect most of us are still. It will be delightful to see him here in Brussels, especially as I understand he doesn't bring his lady with him.'

There was an uneasy silence, no-one knowing quite how seriously all this was meant. Lucy, disapproving more than ever of this bold young woman, broke in briskly, addressing herself to Marcus.

'Well, since you are staying in Brussels, perhaps you would like to join the exploring-party I am arranging into the forest? We shall go, some on horseback and some in carriages, and take a picnic meal and eat *al fresco*. I think it is just warm enough.'

Rosamund's heart rose. On a long ride she would have the best chance to talk to Marcus, for it was likely that only she and her mother would be on horseback. All the other females would probably ride in carriages, so Marcus would be obliged to spend at least half the time talking to her. It would be like old times at Wolvercote, she thought. On horseback and in the open air, he would forget all this silliness and sophistication, and be her Marcus again.

'Oh yes,' she exclaimed, unable to prevent herself. 'Do come, Marcus! It will be the greatest fun!'

Marcus flashed a smile towards her, and for an instant everything seemed sunlit and promising fair. And then he turned back to Lucy and said, 'How very kind, ma'am! Indeed, we should love to join you! Lady Annabel and I will come on horseback — won't we, Bel? She has a grey hunter mare I think even you would not be ashamed to be seen on, ma'am, and I'm longing to see how she goes when she's given her head.'

Lucy could do nothing but accept the situation. 'I'm sure we shall all be interested to see that,' she said drily. 'And you, Lord William? May we expect you of the party?'

Lord William went into a long and fractured explanation of why he was forced to decline her ladyship's very obligin' invitation, but Rosamund had stopped listening. Everything was as black as could be. Instead of the glowing picture she had for an instant contemplated, there was the prospect of spending a whole day watching Marcus *tête à tête* with That Woman. Filled with misery, jealousy and frustration, she turned her head away, to be looking anywhere but at Marcus's adoring gaze at Lady Annabel. There were plenty of faces nearby, and as she glanced over them unseeingly, one caught her attention, because its eyes were fixed on her face with much the same expression as Marcus's. Frowning a little, Rosamund searched her memory. Who? — oh yes, it was the officer of the 95th Rifles with whom she had danced twice last night. What was his name? A captain — had seemed rather struck with her — sent in his card this morning ... Tantony, that was it!

Faced with her frown, his smile had begun to fade into anxiety. She suddenly had an idea. Flirting madly with every officer in sight would not make Marcus notice her — or if it did, it would only be with disapproval. No, she must make sure he saw her with one adoring officer always at her side, gazing at her like a moonling just as he gazed at Lady Annabel. *That* would make him think! And this Tantony, she thought consideringly, was very good-looking, if you liked that sort of thing, and the same rank as Marcus, and in one of the most respected regiments. He ought to do very well; and if Mama had invited him to the ball, he must be respectable enough for her to approve of.

She would get him along on the picnic, ride alongside him, give him all her attention, and ignore Marcus until he was mad with jealousy, she decided. Realising that she was still scowling at Tantony, she made a rapid adjustment of her features and smiled at him instead, making him blink with surprise and swallow nervously. She lowered her eyelashes and looked at him under them, and saw him begin to smile hesitantly back. Yes, she thought, it would be all right. Mama, mad to get her married off, would invite on the picnic any young man she thought her interested in, as long as it wasn't Marcus.

She looked away for a moment, and then turned back and let Tantony catch her eye again, and this time smiled her nicest, pleasantest smile, in response to which Captain

Tantony, drawn like a moth to a lamp, edged through the bodies between them and arrived at her side, and bowed to her with an eager light in his eyes.

'Good morning, Lady Rosamund! I hope you are not too much fatigued by the ball last night? It was a splendid ball, wasn't it?'

The campaign, Rosamund thought, with a sideways glance at Marcus, was opened.

CHAPTER SEVEN

Miss Rosedale sat at the round table in the drawing-room. A bar of sunlight falling from the south window across the carpet to her feet had attracted both Kithra and Castor, who were stretched out in it like cats, dozing. Castor twitched and raced his paws in youthful dreams, but Kithra lay quietly, looking up at Miss Rosedale every now and then from under his eyebrows as if he hoped she might have changed into Héloïse while he slept.

She was writing a letter to Héloïse, which at Morland Place was not only a duty, but a pleasure. There was the quality of the paper, for instance: Miss Rosedale, despite her sturdy and sensible exterior, was something of a sensualist, and the smooth, unblemished sheets of cream-laid paper were wholly delightful. The ink, too, was of the best quality, and never clogged or ran, and the silver standish on its rosewood base was handsome and elegant. And the pen she was using, though merely the common drawing-room pen for everyone's use, was from the left wing of a goose, a small but telling luxury which she had been forced to forgo in the days when she bought her own pens, and even pennies saved were important.

She folded back her cuffs, gave a little sigh of pleasure, dipped the pen, and resumed. Her handwriting was always neat, and now she was making it as small as the thickness of the nib would allow, in order to get as much on the page as possible. Her poor mistress, she thought, would want to know every detail, no matter how trivial, of what had been happening at Morland Place since she left.

'The kitchen chimney set itself on fire again on Tuesday, and this time Mr Edward insisted on sending for the sweep and interviewing him in person to find out what was

153

wrong. It was quite a rousing interview, the sweep defending himself in such ringing tones that everyone in the house heard the whole of it! It transpired that the kitchen chimney has not been swept for two years, because Monsieur Barnard tells the sweep every time he calls that it is not convenient for the fire to be put out that day. Mr Edward soothed everyone's ruffled feathers with great tact; the fire was doused, and the boy was put up, and such a quantity of soot was brought down that old Fox was in raptures for his kitchen garden, which owing to the warm weather has already displayed evidence of blackfly on the bean-flowers!

But from black to white: I must tell you we have had a great deal of trouble from the White Lady, who is being seen at all sorts of hours and in all sorts of places, so much so that some of the servants are refusing to go into the chapel at all, much to the dismay of Father Aislaby. He feels the dilemma cruelly. If he refuses to acknowledge the White lady, he loses his congregation; but if he exorcises her in the proper manner, he is giving into foolishness and superstition ...'

The fact of the matter was, Miss Rosedale thought, that some of the younger servants resented being obliged to attend chapel twice a day, and would do anything to get out of it, including inventing ghost stories and pretending to be frightened of them. One or two of the maids were genuinely frightened; but most of the older servants, while believing wholeheartedly in ghosts and fairies, did not regard the White Lady as a threat — she being their own special ghost, their property, so to speak. Even they, however, were not above using her as an excuse to have an extra hour in bed in the morning.

It was the new mood of irreligion that was sweeping through the country, Miss Rosedale thought, one of the effects of the long war and if some people were to be believed, the new machine age. Everyone was restless, mad for continual change and excitement, no longer content to stay at home, to sit still and do nothing. To be sure, Miss Rosedale found Father Aislaby's services rather long, especially the morning one, but then it was not her religion, and she attended only to set the example, and in a spirit of concealed disapproval...

'All the upsets have brought on another attack of nightmares for poor little Benedict, who woke us all with his screaming five nights running. He does not remember anything about it, fortunately, as soon as he wakes, but it is disconcerting for the rest of us. Nicholas takes it all very calmly, I'm glad to say, and comforts his little brother with a great deal of tenderness. It is very good to see them so fond of each other; and the trouble seems to have passed now, thank Heaven ...'

The words, she thought, gave no inkling of the feeling of dread engendered by a child screaming in the darkness, and the general turmoil that resulted. She remembered Benedict sobbing in her arms, still shaking with terror as he poured out incoherent words. Something about powder it had been — that was what is sounded like: over and over again, *white powder.* Miss Rosedale wondered if it had to do with all the talk about the White Lady, for in her experience, young children learned a great deal more from the servants' chatter than from those who were engaged to teach them.

She had made little of it in the letter, not to alarm Héloïse when she was too far away to do anything about it, but Benedict had been badly upset by the nightmares, so much so that for several days he had looked drawn and anxious, and had been afraid to go to bed at night. And even during the day — she frowned as she thought of that very odd incident over the cloth dog. Benedict had a toy, a stuffed cloth object in the shape of a dog, rather crudely made but, in the odd way of children, very dear to him. One day during the nightmare period he had been brought into the house by one of the grooms, his face blackened by soot, down which tears were making fresh white tracks. The groom, plainly upset and much perplexed, said he had found the young master in the old draw-yard behind the kennels, crouched over a fire of twigs and straw on which the cloth dog was blazing merrily. The groom had been attracted to the scene by the smoke,

155

but as much by the young master's howls. 'I thought he'd burnt hisself, miss, he were greetin' that loud,' the groom said, his brow puckered with anxiety. 'Whatever could have happened, miss? Poor little lad's in a sad state, and no mistake.'

He spoke no more than the truth. Benedict was howling with fright and misery, but could offer no explanation of the affair. How had the toy come to fall in the fire? And who had lit the fire in the first place? Miss Rosedale's mind had turned immediately to one of the choristers, but they were all safe in the schoolroom with Father Aislaby. And the stable-boys were all busy about their duties — and in any case, Benedict had been alone when the groom found him. It was a mystery indeed.

Throughout this time Nicholas had, as she said in her letter, been very assiduous in comforting his brother, even promising to tell him stories in bed, but though Benedict had thanked him, he had looked no less afraid as bedtime drew near. It was good, however, to see the love between them, for Miss Rosedale was aware of what good reason Nicholas had to be jealous of his younger brother. James had lately taken the fit upon him to teach Benedict to ride, something he had never offered to do for Nicholas. He had brought Fanny's old pony Tempest out of retirement, and spent an hour a day in the paddock leading Benedict about. It was after the first of these lessons that Benedict had begun the nightmares, but Miss Rosedale dismissed Sarah's idea, that it was too much excitement that was to blame. Benedict had been overjoyed at his father's attention, but it was not the sort of happiness that brought on nightmares.

It was all over now, however. The peace of the household had been restored, and Benedict had been sleeping quietly again. And what, now, could she put in her letter about James?

'Mr James has been interesting himself very much in the business of the Hobsbawn inheritance. For several days now he has been shut up in the steward's room with a great many books on the law which he has borrowed from the Shawes library.' The law books had taken the place of the brief interest in teaching Benedict to ride. 'Mr Pobgee has taken the matter in hand, but I don't believe there are any developments as yet ...'

Pobgee had come to the house one day and asked for the favour of an interview with her. Miss Rosedale had gone down to the steward's room a little puzzled, for there was no family business in which she would normally be involved. When Pobgee gave her a kindly, sympathetic smile and asked her to be seated, she became not only puzzled, but alarmed.

'I have to ask you, Miss Rosedale, if you would be willing to make a statement about the circumstances of Mrs Hawker's death, and sign it before witnesses. It is merely to establish evidence of the exact time of her demise,' he went on quickly as Miss Rosedale opened her mouth to protest. 'If you are willing, I should like to ask you questions, and write down your answers in the form of a statement, which I will then ask you to read and sign. Will you allow that?'

'I suppose it is necessary?' Miss Rosedale said reluctantly.

'I fear it is.' Miss Rosedale thought a moment, and then nodded. 'Thank you,' said Pobgee. 'Now, to begin with, would you cast your mind back to the evening before Mrs Hawker's death. Where were you, and who was with you?'

So it began, simply enough: relating the bare facts of the matter. But within the first few questions and answers, Miss Rosedale's imagination had taken her back to that time and that place, and she began to relive, as she had never yet done, the events of the terrible night that took her dear Fanny, fighting to the last breath of her body, out of the world, and lost to them for ever.

Very soon the tears began to rise, and her throat closed up, and her voice failed. She saw again, so clearly, that white and suffering face, heard her terrible cries, watched her die all over again. Miss Rosedale broke down at last, put her hands over her face, and sobbed.

The lawyer waited in sympathetic silence at first, and then, growing distressed, came over to offer his handkerchief and pat her shoulder helplessly. The kindness only made Miss Rosedale weep the louder, as all the grief she had suppressed for so long burst out of her in a great and agonising flood. She wept inconsolably for her lost child, while Mr Pobgee bit his lip, and knew there was nothing he could do or say to help.

Well, it was over at last, and it had done her good. The

157

catharsis had burned out the unbearable aspect of her grief, and now she had begun to be able to lay Fanny aside. Not forgotten — no, never! — but the memories could be folded gently and put away, and the real business of life taken up again; the past could take its proper place and resume its normal proportions.

If only, she thought grimly, it were possible for James to do the same! But he had made a monster of Fanny, and that monster now ruled him. Like a demon god invented by some primitive tribe and grown out of proportion, the monster he worshipped now demanded hideous ceremonies and insane sacrifices, ruled him by wordless threat, and by pain, made the more horrible because in some self-wounding way he enjoyed and welcomed it.

She couldn't say any of that to Héloïse either. Héloïse, she knew, loved James too much and was too intimately involved with him to be able to understand the quality of his present madness. Everything he said and did and suffered hurt Héloïse deeply, and even devoted love could bear only so much pain. Instead she searched around for the simple matters to write about, the normal things that went on in the sunlit part of Morland Place, beyond Monster-Fanny's shadow.

'We killed a goose for Sunday's dinner, and when the bird was drawn, in its crop was found — of all things! — the missing sapphire from Mr Edward's stock-pin. There was a sensation in the kitchen! It must have been loose and fallen out when he rode out one day, and the goose must have pecked it up while it was grazing, as they do sometimes with small pebbles. And there it has been ever since, while we all searched high and low for it!

We had such a rain-storm on Sunday night, and it once again revealed the mysterious patch of dampness on the wall of the night-nursery, which Compton now believes is caused by a leaking rain-pipe ...'

There was plenty to say that would feed a homesick woman's appetite, Miss Rosedale thought, turning the page and beginning to cross it. Morland Place missed its mistress, even if James didn't. She wished she could write that James longed for her to return, knowing that was what Héloïse wanted and needed, but in all honesty she couldn't. Deep in his books hour by hour, or prowling the house like a ghost, or sitting in Fanny's room slowly turning over her belongings in his hands as though they might speak to him, he didn't miss anyone. Miss Rosedale thought he did not even notice their existence.

Parslow spoke so highly of Farringdon's horse that Lucy decided not to wait as she had planned at first, but to try it out immediately. Farringdon's groom, Pinner, brought it to the Allée Verte early the next morning, where Lucy and Parslow were waiting.

It was certainly a magnificent beast. Magnus Apollo stood over sixteen hands high, but there was no hint of heaviness about him: he was every inch a thoroughbred, with a fine head, sloping shoulders, deep chest, clean legs, and powerful quarters. He was a beautiful rich bay with long black stockings and a small white star; and as Lucy looked him over, he revealed that he was as kind as he was beautiful, nuzzling her in a friendly way as she ran her hands over him, and lifting his feet obediently when she tugged at his fetlocks.

'Ah,' said Pinner with a nod as Magnus Apollo blew enquiringly into Lucy's ear, 'you won't find a better-tempered 'oss in all of Europe. As sweet and kind in the stable as a ewe-lamb, Mr Parslow, I give you my word, and quiet to groom, rug, clip or shoe, which is more than you can say for some of these blood 'osses, as well you know.'

'Indeed, Mr Pinner. But good stable practice breeds good nature, I always say,' said Parslow. 'All of her ladyship's horses are gentle. Quiet handling makes a quiet horse.'

'I agree with you there, Mr Parslow. But there's the matter of temperament to take into account, and Magnus here has always been sweet-tempered. It's in his blood — his father before him was the same way: as kind as milk, for all that he was a hentire.'

Lucy straightened up and looked round. 'Apollo Doro, you mean? This one's sire?'

'Yes, my lady, that's him — though we called him Polly-dolly in the stable, my lady, not being so fet in foreign

159

languages as your ladyship. But Magnus here is the spitten image of Pollydolly, right down to the star, and the little white mark on his near-fore hoof, my lady, which I beg leave to point out, some people thinking it a blemish.'

'Yes, I see it. Well, Parslow, what do you think of him so far?'

'Nicely put together, my lady,' Parslow said guardedly. 'And I've no objection to a bay, so long as it's a good, rich colour — '

'Which Magnus is, Mr Parslow, you will admit,' Pinner said eagerly. 'I'm like you — can't abide a wishy-washy bay for anything. But handsome is as handsome does — '

'Which brings us neatly to the point,' Lucy said. 'I should like to try him. He has been broken to side-saddle?'

Pinner buckled his brow earnestly. 'Well, my lady, I shouldn't like to deceive you. Broke to side-saddle he was, for her ladyship took a fancy to him when he was only a colt, and would ride him; but he grew too strong for her, and so she gave him to my lord. So he's not accustomed to it, as you might say. Nobody but my Lord Farringdon and myself has ridden him for two years, and he's not what I would call a lady's horse, if you understand me, my lady. Not that there's any vice in him — '

'Yes, I understand. Very well, Parslow, you may put my saddle on him. I'll hold Hotspur. Give him a hand, would you, Pinner?'

It was an exciting moment, being thrown up into the saddle a few minutes later, and feeling a totally unknown horse surging with energy beneath her.

'He is a big fellow,' Lucy said, settling her skirts and gathering the reins. 'I'm not used to having so much horse between me and the ground.'

Parslow looked up at her. He had ridden the horse the day before, and found it well-mannered and even-paced, but he knew how powerful it was. 'Be careful, my lady,' he said. 'Remember he's not Morland-bred.'

'Nor was Minstrel,' she said, smiling down at him.

'True, my lady, but — ' He could not actually say *you were younger then*, but she could read his mind after all these years. 'He's very strong,' he finished instead.

Lucy patted the bay neck. 'I'll wager he's fast, too. Come, then, big boy, let's see what you can do!'

She put her heel to his side and turned him and sent him off down the greensward walking a few steps and then breaking into a collected trot. The bay horse arched his neck and felt the bit, his ears flicking anxiously back and forth as he felt the rider's weight move in an unaccustomed way. It was strange, upsetting. Where was the other leg? The balance was wrong. Would she fall?

But Lucy spoke to him reassuringly, sitting his smooth pace easily, and sent him into a canter. He felt her confidence flowing through the reins to him, began to remember dimly his training long ago, felt that her movement, though strange, was balanced, ceased to fear that she would part company with him. He was an intelligent horse, and within ten minutes he was happy with her, had grown relaxed and supple, mouthing the bit, arching his tail, shewing off his gay paces as she cantered him in and out of the trees.

'By God, Mr Parslow, but your lady is a rider!' Pinner said with frank admiration. 'I'd heard it said, of course, but I thought she were just a bold one to go, over timber and such-like. But I see it's more than that — she understands 'osses, which is more than I could claim for many a gentleman I've knew. It must be a pleasure for you to work for her.'

'Aye,' said Parslow softly, his eyes on the distant flying figure, 'she's a fine rider — the best. And she doesn't know the meaning of fear.' All the same, he thought, that horse was too big and strong for her, and that was all about it. Oh, she could ride him as well as any man — but what about the unexpected? Horses were unpredictable creatures, when all was said, and when the flash of lightning or the sudden noise or the herd of pigs half-glimpsed behind a hedge threw the horse into a panic, what then? She would not be able to hold him, and that was the truth.

The big horse came cantering back to them, lifting his forelegs and flicking his ears, the picture of high-spirits and enjoyment. And his rider was smiling, her cheeks and eyes bright under her absurd and feathered hat, making Parslow's heart turn over in him once again. He loved her and worried about her almost like a father.

161

She halted before the two grooms and leaned forward to pat the bay neck enthusiastically. 'His paces are so smooth!' she said glowingly. 'And he covers so much ground — it's like flying!' She remembered abruptly that she was not supposed to enthuse before she had bought the horse, and then decided she didn't care, and leaned forward to caress him again. 'You're a beautiful, beautiful fellow!'

Parslow knew her well enough to read her every expression. As Pinner took the bit-rings, he went round to help her down, and looking up into her face, knew there was no point in advising her against buying. She would have Magnus Apollo, no matter what he said. She put her hands onto his raised arms and met his eyes with a smile of delight and mischief that made her look no more than sixteen. Parslow jumped her down, swearing privately there and then that she would never ride that horse unless he had exercised it first, to take the edge off it.

Though she had been up and about since half-past six, Lucy took breakfast with Héloïse and the girls at eleven o'clock. At half-past twelve Sophie and Rosamund had gone up to their room, but Lucy and Héloïse were still sitting in the breakfast-parlour reading letters and the papers, when a rapping at the front door announced the first of the morning visitors. A few moments later the Belgian butler entered, and announced in a mangling sort of accent Milor' Chelmissfor', Madame Firss, Colonel Morlan', Milady Barbara and Mees Morlan'.

Lucy caught Héloïse's eye and for a second looked like bolting, before she controlled herself and rose to receive the visitors. Roberta and Bobbie she could greet with genuine affection; Colonel the Honourable Horatio Morland of the 2nd North British Dragoons was afforded a handshake and a cordial 'Well, Horace!' as he kissed her on both cheeks; but for Lady Barbara she could not bring herself to part with more than a curtsey.

Lady Barbara had been a Rushton, daughter of the Duke of Watford, and with ten thousand pounds, which popular repute would always double, she was entitled to have looked higher than a mere Honourable to wed. But at the time she accepted Horatio, his elder brother the Earl of Chelmsford had been married for eleven years without issue, and all looked set fair for Horace to have the reversion. Two years later the earl's wife died, and Lady Barbara had looked forward with perfect justice to becoming a countess in the fullness of time, a position she considered just return for her name and her fortune.

Then, horror of horrors, the earl had remarried, with indecent haste she always thought, and the new wife had produced a son — Bobbie. Lady Barbara had never been able to forget that she had been cheated of her rightful place in society, and that her husband and, hereafter, her beloved son had been robbed of their title. Marcus should have been Earl of Chelmsford after his father; the Chelmsford fortune should have been hers to spend. It was not right that a Duke's daughter should be living in such a small way in a tiny house in Park Lane, while Roberta, a mere soldier's daughter, had the run of Chelmsford House and a huge widow's portion to spend.

She and Horatio had watched Bobbie eagerly through the usual babyhood ailments; but when it became obvious that he was not going to be carried off before he reached his majority, Horace had shrugged and put expectation aside, bought himself a commission and settled down to an agreeable life as a regular officer in the Greys. Lady Barbara had devoted herself bitterly to economy, and to promoting the interests of Marcus whenever the opportunity arose, and to making sure that as much of the Chelmsford fortune as possible migrated into Marcus's pocket.

She had managed to persuade Roberta to have Marcus to live at her expense, and to share Bobbie's tutor with him; and when Bobbie, out of love for his cousin, had proposed buying Marcus's colours for him, she scotched her son's plan to join his father's regiment, and made sure he went into the most fashionable and expensive regiment of all, and was kitted out in the first style with every luxury a tonnish officer could dream of.

But still Bobbie was Earl of Chelmsford, and the disappointment had taken its toll of her. She was a sharp-faced, sharp-voiced woman who looked older than her years, and her youthful beauty had been burned out by discontent and

163

parsimony. She hated Roberta and was forced to conceal it in order to make use of her. She despised her husband for not somehow having got to be earl in spite of everything. She disliked her daughter as an encumbrance, requiring a dowry if she were to be married off respectably. She loved only Marcus, and even that love gave her little comfort, for Marcus had no ambition that did not touch on the military. Marcus loved Bobbie, and was quite content for him to be the earl, and merely laughed when Lady Barbara said he had been robbed of his birthright.

'Don't be silly, Mama,' he would say. 'Bobbie is the best man for the job. He was born for it. I should make a very poor hand at it. I don't want to be Earl — which is just as well, as I never shall be.'

Lady Barbara disliked Lucy, too — partly because she was only a gentleman's daughter, and yet had married into the aristocracy, and partly because Lucy made no disguise of her feelings towards Lady Barbara. But Lucy was a popular hostess, and had a great deal of money, and Lady Barbara was always looking for ways to promote her children and save money, preferably simultaneously. She had hoped to be able to persuade Lucy to share Rosamund's coming-out ball with Barbarina, and was furious when Fanny's death apparently put paid to that scheme. She had had to bring Barbarina out herself in March at what she considered enormous expense — Barbarina was already over eighteen, and to delay the début another year would leave her practically upon the shelf — only to learn that Lady Theakston had slipped away abroad and brought Rosamund out in Brussels. It was infuriating! All she could do now was to scurry over there herself, and Horace's regiment's being transferred there was the luckiest thing, as giving her the excuse.

The greetings over, everyone took their seats around the fire. Bobbie stood near his uncle, devouring every detail of the smart grey overalls and the scarlet jacket with the blue facings and gold lace, and Horatio stood with his back to the fire and threw out his chest, rather pleased than not with this ardent admiration.

'Well, Horace, you've made good time,' Lucy said. 'We only heard yesterday that the Greys were embarked.'

'We came on ahead,' Horatio said. 'Couldn't travel with the men, when I had my lady and Barbarina with me. We came by the packet.'

'I hope that wasn't too expensive?' Lucy said unkindly, but Horatio didn't notice.

'Oh, I had a warrant, of course,' he said easily. 'But we took the public canal-boat as far as Ghent, and I must say I've never seen anything like it for accommodation and provision. Every comfort — every luxury — meals as good as anything in Watier's — the best beef I've tasted in years! And the Flemish beer is excellent. Sitting on the cabin-roof and watching the fields go by was as fine a sensation as anything I've known. I was sorry to disembark, I assure you.'

Even Lady Barbara had a good word to say about the canal-boats. 'Not at all expensive, when you come down to it,' she said. 'You compound for the trip, food and accommodation all included. And the travelling was so smooth you would have thought you weren't moving at all. I wasn't the least seasick.'

'Yes, we've heard good reports of them,' Lucy said blandly. 'There is one gentleman from England — a Mr Cramer — who liked the trip so much that when he got to Ghent he stayed on the boat and went back again. I think he means to sell his house and spend the rest of his life going back and forth. The cost is so very reasonable.'

Roberta thought the teasing had gone far enough. 'I'm sure you will find Brussels a very pleasant place,' she said hastily. 'So much going on — the theatre and the opera, and three picture-galleries — the Park — '

'And gaming every night in a multitude of houses and salons,' Lucy said blandly. It was a cause of annoyance to Lady Barbara that both her husband and her son regarded gaming as something every gentleman of fashion must indulge in to some degree. They did so only moderately, having neither the inclination nor the income to dip deeply, but Lady Barbara deplored any expenditure of money without return.

'And any number of balls,' Roberta intervened again, shooting a cross look at Lucy. 'There are private dances every night, and public assemblies three times a week.' She smiled

165

at Barbarina. 'All the young ladies are very well pleased with Brussels.'

'Yes, we are in hopes of giving our dear Barbarina a great deal of pleasure,' Lady Barbara said, regarding her daughter with a mixture of dislike and calculation. Barbarina sat on the edge of her seat, her hands folded in her lap, and her eyes cast down, as though she hoped by keeping still and quiet to avoid any notice. She had the misfortune to have inherited her father's looks with little modification from her mother. She had his receding chin and rather bulging eyes, his pale eyelashes and sharp nose, his transparent skin and fine, fair hair; and Lucy thought as she had thought many times before that Barbarina needed only whiskers to complete the resemblance to a white mouse.

She had been bullied by her mother since birth, and knew that her only function in life, and her only hope of redemption, was to marry an exceedingly wealthy man, preferably with a title. Since she knew quite well she was plain, timid, and had but a small fortune, she didn't know how this was to be achieved. She could only hope that her mother would first mesmerise some suitable man and then bully him into offering for her. For herself she didn't care who it was: nothing could be worse than spending the rest of her life at home with Mama.

'I understand you had Rosamund's coming-out ball here a few days ago?' Lady Barbara said, the resentment clear in her voice.

'Yes, a joint ball for Rosamund and Sophie,' Lucy said, enjoying the moment.

'How fortunate for Sophie. I hope it went well?' said Lady Barbara.

'Very well, thank you,' Lucy said. 'Everyone was there. I'm told it was the best-attended ball of the season so far. And Sophie was in such looks.'

'I was telling Lady Barbara about your picnic plan, Lucy,' Roberta said hastily. 'I thought perhaps it might be possible to invite Barbarina to share the carriage with Sophie and Héloïse? Lady Barbara and I thought of staying at home quietly,' she added hastily as Lucy raised an eyebrow at her.

'Of course. There will be plenty of room,' Lucy said with a

smile at the white mouse. She had nothing against Barbarina — felt sorry for her, in fact. 'The plans are not complete yet. I'll send word to your lodgings as to where and when we are to meet, Lady Barbara. Where do you stay?'

'We're at the Hôtel du Parc,' Horatio put in, with a defiant look at his wife which told a story. 'It's so central, you know.'

'It's very expensive, however,' Lady Barbara said repressively. 'We really want to find a comfortable house to rent, but all the best ones have been taken already.'

Lucy smiled privately and caught Roberta's eye. She was fairly sure that one of the reasons that Peter Firth had taken a small house for Roberta and Bobbie was so that there would be no room to invite Lady Barbara and her daughter to stay. Plainly Lady Barbara did not yet know that. She would be devastated when she found it out, for the Hôtel du Parc was one of the largest and most expensive hotels in Brussels. Well, she could hint all she liked — Lucy was proof against that. She would not be coming to stay at the Rue Ducale, that was sure!

'Have you seen Marcus yet?' she asked to change the subject. 'You must be very pleased with his promotion. He looks very well in a staff-officer's coat.'

'No, we haven't seen him yet,' Horatio said. 'That pleasure is still to come. He's done very well for himself — very well indeed. But I knew how it would be. The Duke took to him. He's just the sort of young man the Duke likes to have about him. Of course,' he added with a glance at his wife, 'there's less opportunity to distinguish himself than with his regiment, but the experience will be very good for him, and stand him in good stead after the war. He'll be able to get a position in one of the ministries — or even go into Parliament if he wants. The Duke looks after his own, you know, and he has plenty of influence at St James's. Yes, I have told Lady Barbara that it is a very fine thing for our boy, the best thing that could have happened.'

'And now,' Lady Barbara took up the thread smoothly, 'there remains only for him to form an eligible attachment — and by what I've heard, he is well on the way to doing that already.'

'What can you mean?' Lucy was surprised.

'I understand,' Lady Barbara said smugly, 'that he has been paying very particular attentions to Lady Annabel Robb — and that the lady has received them most willingly.'

Lucy stared. 'And that pleases you?'

'But of course. Lady Annabel is from one of our first families. Her connections are excellent. And her fortune is very large — very large indeed! It would be a great thing for Marcus if he were to fix her.'

'And for her, my dear,' Horatio said. 'My son is quite a good enough match for her, as far as family goes.'

'Oh indeed — he is her superior in every way,' Lady Barbara said hastily. 'She will be the gainer — but I believe she has more than ten thousand a year!'

'I have to tell you that I don't believe she means anything seriously by Marcus,' Lucy said, much diverted. 'She is merely amusing herself with him.'

Lady Barbara looked triumphant. 'He is seen *everywhere* with her,' she said. 'It is quite an *on dit*, I assure you! And they are to ride together on your picnic, I believe? So kind of you, dear lady Theakston, to invite them both! No, I think everyone — unless they have an interest there themselves — will be expecting an announcement before many days have passed.'

There was a brief silence, and then Horatio said politely, 'So Theakston is to go back to his regiment? And how do you like that, Lucy?' and the conversation turned to other matters, until shortly afterwards he and his family took their leave, and Bobbie went with them, to walk up with the colonel to Headquarters to see Marcus.

When they had gone, Lucy, with a mixture of amusement and exasperation, adverted to Lady Barbara's last remark about Marcus.

'What can that ridiculous woman mean? "Unless they have an interest there themselves"? Who does she suppose is angling for Annabel Robb?'

'I think she supposes you to be angling for Marcus to marry Rosamund,' Roberta said gravely, at which Lucy burst out laughing.

'The woman is quite infatuated! Marcus is a very nice boy, but he's nothing but his army pay and the allowance his father gives him. As if he could support Rosamund on that!'

Héloïse said hesitantly, 'But Rosamund would not care about money, perhaps? She might be happy even to follow the drum?'

Lucy shook her head, still laughing. 'Rosamund? The very last person to be able to live on a small income! She'd be lost without servants and horses. She can't even put on her clothes without assistance! No, of all my children, Rosamund is the one most cut out to be a fine lady. Apart from anything else, only a very wealthy woman can afford to flout the conventions, as I'm sure Rosamund means to all her life.'

Roberta smiled, 'Well, on that point at least, you should know best!'

The day of the picnic ride dawned fair, and since the breeze which for the past few days had been keeping the temperature down had dropped at last, it looked like being quite warm enough for an *al fresco* meal. With Lady Barbara's absence secured by Roberta, who had invited her to spend the day with her, nothing seemed to be in the way of a delightful outing.

'You're a saint,' Lucy had said, and 'Are you sure you don't mind, Mama?' Bobbie had said.

But Roberta smiled. 'Of course not. I have such a large acquaintance here that my door-knocker will be busy all day. And when the visiting hours are over, I shall take Lady Barbara into the Park, and we shall meet all my friends again. I shan't be left alone with her, I promise you. It's Lady Barbara you should pity, for all my friends are respectable soldiers' wives with no claims to distinction — just the sort of people she most despises!'

The cavalcade which set off from the Rue Ducale consisted in the end of two carriages: a barouche driven by Charles conveying Héloïse, Sophie and Barbarina; and two of the Lennox girls, Georgie and Jane, and their particular friend Miss Burnett, in a landau driven by Miss Burnett's brother, who was a lieutenant in the Foot Guards and an intimate friend of Lord Ponsonby.

The horseback contingent numbered seven gentlemen and three ladies. The gentlemen were Ponsonby and Pyne, Bobbie and his friend Enderby, Marcus, Philip Tantony and René Larosse. As Rosamund had anticipated, she and her mother would have been the only horsewomen if it had not been for Bel Robb, and there would have been nothing to prevent her shining before Marcus as the one woman in the world with whom he could enjoy a good gallop. But at the appointed hour, Lady Annabel rode up to the house mounted on a showy grey mare, and dressed in a sky-blue habit with gold Hussar frogging, large blue leather gauntlets, and a hat which resembled a shako, with a leather brim and three curled feathers, dyed to match her habit.

Marcus, who had been hanging around outside for ages, staring up and down the road hastened to catch hold of the grey's head and gaze at her adoringly as he engaged her in conversation. Watching from the window, Rosamund scowled and slapped her boot irritably with her whip.

'Good Heaven!' Héloïse said from the other window. 'What a very — a very *bright* outfit Lady Annabel is wearing.'

'She looks ridiculous,' Rosamund snapped. 'All that frogging — like a uniform!'

Héloïse took pity on her. 'It is not very becoming. Gentlemen prefer something a little more feminine, I think.'

Lucy gave her a robust glance as she gathered her party together. 'Don't worry, Rosamund — you will be the better mounted. That grey is straight-shouldered, and too long in the back. Is everyone ready? Come, then, we mustn't keep Lady Annabel waiting.'

The party moved off round the square and down the hill, threading through the town towards the Namur Gate, and then onto the main road that led through the suburbs of the forest. The horse-riders followed the carriages, gradually and naturally falling into groups. Pyne and Ponsonby rode close behind the barouche, keeping always one on either side of Lucy, and chatting to her animatedly about her new horse. There was no doubt that Magnus Apollo looked magnificent, curvetting under Lucy's light hand, lifting his feet high and flirting his tail.

'So you bought him, ma'am! I didn't think you'd be able to resist once you'd seen him,' Pyne said seriously. 'Poor Farringdon!'

'I paid him a pretty price,' Lucy said. 'And it was he that approached me — I didn't force him to sell!'

'No, ma'am, of course not, but he's breaking his heart all the same. It was only to you that he could bring himself to sell at all.'

'You seem to know a lot about it,' Lucy said with amusement. 'What have you had to do with the business, Mr Pyne?'

Pyne smiled deprecatingly. 'Oh, very little, I assure you! Farringdon told me he was all to pieces, and I suggested he sold Magnus to you. He said he didn't know you were looking for a horse, and I said you would be once you'd seen Magnus. Then he asked about your groom, ma'am, and I was able to reassure him on that — '

'The devil you were!'

'Oh, everyone knows Parslow by reputation, ma'am, I assure you! And Farringdon loves that horse like a child. If there were the least chance of his being beaten or given short commons or left with his feet not picked out, Farringdon would have cut off his own hand rather than sell him.'

'I'm glad we were not found wanting. But I'm sorry to cause Lord Farringdon so much pain.'

'Magnus is a beautiful animal. You do him more credit that Farringdon, ma'am, if you'll forgive me,' said Pyne. Lucy looked at him, frowning, wondering what was behind all this flattery, but his face was completely guileless.

Then Ponsonby joined in. 'You outshine Bell Robb, ma'am, that's the best of it! She don't above half like having her nose put out of joint. I wonder, Harry, if we might organise a race later today? Magnus could beat Lady Bel's Nimbus over any ground!'

'You might not,' Lucy said firmly. 'There's to be no nonsense like that today. I expect you both to be on your best behaviour!'

Behind them Rosamund rode her mother's Hotspur, and the awareness that she was the only woman in the world her mother would have allowed on Hotspur's back eased some of her wounded feelings. Philip Tantony rode close beside her on her right, so close that their stirrups kept clashing in a disagreeable way, and more than once she had been on the brink of snapping at him, when she remembered that she had

171

to make Marcus believe Tantony was her beau. He chatted to her pleasantly about various aspects of the social life of Brussels, and if she had taken the trouble to listen to him, she would have found him a very agreeable companion.

Larosse rode on her left, and though this excluded him a great deal from the conversation, he did not seem to mind, but was content just to listen, or to ride with his own thoughts, or sometimes to drop back and talk to the ladies in the landau.

Marcus and Lady Annabel rode side by side, sometimes behind the barouche and sometimes off to the side of the road, always *tête à tête*, hardly seeming aware of the rest of the party. The landau came behind, and Bobbie and his friend Enderby rode beside it: Bobbie had struck up a friendship since the ball with Lady Georgiana Lennox, which was convenient, as Enderby was hopelessly in love with Miss Burnett.

The forest was beautiful: the beech trees raised their smooth, silvery boles straight up towards the sky, like massive columns supporting the lacy canopy of leaves. Lucy left the road to ride through the edges of it, and Major Larosse, shaking his head at Pyne and Ponsonby, broke away to accompany her. She smiled her thanks for the courtesy, glad that it was him, and that he had the sense not to chat, but allowed her to enjoy the place in peace.

It was very quiet in the wood. The horses' hooves made almost no sound on the thick carpet of last year's leaves and crumbling beech-mast. The new leaves were yellow-green and translucent in the sunlight against the black tracery of twigs and branches, through which could be seen patches of the sky, the fragile April blue of a robin's egg. There was almost no undergrowth — just moss, a few ferns and starlike wood anemones — but now and then, when a vista opened up through the trees, Lucy could see in the distance the heavenly blue smudge of the first of what would plainly be a carpet of bluebells.

'Beautiful!' Lucy said at last. 'Almost as beautiful as home!'

Larosse smiled. 'Home is always best.'

'Where is yours?'

He shrugged lightly. 'The world is my home, now. But I was born not so very far from here, in the Ardennes.' He looked at her. 'You would have liked it there, I think. Fine woods, gentle hills, little streams and handsome prospects. Fine riding country. My family had an estate there.'

She returned his look levelly. 'You cannot go back?'

'No. It is all gone now.'

'You speak of it so calmly. Like Héloïse. I can't imagine what it would be like to know you can never go home. I think I should die without England. You and she are very brave.'

'She is brave,' he agreed. 'I honour her.' He seemed to want to change the subject. 'So this is the fine horse you bought from Lord Farringdon. But I think he will prove too strong for you.'

Lucy laughed. 'Don't you begin that same old song! I've been warned by everyone from my groom upwards, but I've always ridden big horses, and I haven't come to grief yet.'

'I think my Lord Theakston does not know about it,' Larosse said shrewdly.

'And what has that to say to anything?' Lucy said defiantly. 'Lord Theakston does not choose my horses, nor I his.'

Larosse grinned. 'You are an English lady, I see that! English ladies are very independent and stubborn. It would not do for French husbands — they like to be obeyed.'

'Oh, English husbands like to be obeyed, but they aren't often indulged in the liking,' Lucy said, laughing. A ride opened out between the trees in front of them. 'Come, Major, shall we canter? And you may see how no woman of spirit could have refused this lovely horse when once he was offered.'

The servants and grooms met them at one o'clock in the pre-arranged spot with the provisions and other impedimenta. The place they had chosen was off the road, a flat, grassy space like a natural lawn with the forest behind them, and ending in a short, steep drop down to a pretty, fast-running stream. On the other side of the stream, a smiling vista opened up over some pasture and arable fields to a further mass of woodland beyond, the pink–brown of it just beginning to be flushed with green.

The ladies descended from the carriages, the horses were

173

led away, and everyone stretched themselves and walked about, exclaiming over the situation and the view.

'I am astonished at the height of those crops,' Héloïse said, standing at the edge of the drop and gazing out. 'They must be five feet high at least.'

Bobbie, standing near her, said, 'More, ma'am, I'm assured! Marcus says the rye grows to eight feet high in these parts. He has ridden through it, and been completely hidden from view, all but his head.'

'It's no wonder the Flanders horses are so fat,' Enderby said. 'Ah, they're spreading the rugs. What a charming place this is! And what a delightful idea of Lady Theakston's. May I escort you to a place, ma'am?'

The ladies settled around the spread cloths, like butterflies in their delicate, pale muslins, and the gentlemen hovered about them to see them comfortable, before hastening to secure themselves their favoured place. Everyone had an appetite after the long drive in the fresh air. Soon there was a pleasant sound of mingled eating and chatting, and as the party was sufficiently made up of those who liked to talk and those who preferred to listen, everyone was suited.

The noisiest corner was where Lady Annabel sat, with Enderby, Pyne and Lord Burnett grouped about her. She had found the ride along the road tedious, and was in a mood for mischief, and she gathered the three young men around her and kept them there effortlessly with her witty remarks and her laughter and her flirting, ignoring Marcus and allowing him no better view of her adored face than her profile.

Marcus, sitting just outside the magic circle, looked embarrassed and disgruntled. Georgie Lennox was nearest to him on his other side, and he did his best to cover his chagrin by chatting to her brightly, but he made hard work of it. Lady Georgiana tried to extend the conversation to Barbarina, who was sitting on her other side, but it was like trying to run through thick mud. She rolled her eyes despairingly at Bobbie, who good-naturedly came to her rescue, and turned the conversation to the ever-absorbing topic of how the leading families of London Society were related to each other.

Rosamund and Sophie were observing Lady Annabel and

her effect on Marcus. Larosse, seated between them, followed the direction of their gaze and raised an eyebrow.

'Has it happened so soon? Is she tired of him already?' he murmured. 'But no, I fear not, Lady Rosamund, not yet. She is punishing him, you see, and she would not do that if she had finished caring for him.'

'Does she care for him?' Rosamund asked, turning to look at him, glad of his frankness. 'I thought she was just — '

'Collecting him? Yes, perhaps — but she collects only what she fancies. One thing of which Bel can be acquitted is avarice. You see, Captain Morland has no fame or fortune to attract her. He is, to her, a pretty boy,' he said with an apologetic bow. 'She will grow bored and pass on to the next But not today — nor tomorrow, I fear.'

'You seem to know a lot about it,' Rosamund said. 'Do you know her well?'

'Better than she knows me. And a great deal better than Captain Morland knows her. I have the advantage of him there,' Larosse said with a smile for Sophie, to whom he had already told the story.

The smile made her bold. A little breathlessly, she said, 'Monsieur, will you tell now about Ireton — the story you would not tell me at the ball?'

'Ireton?' Rosamund said quickly. 'Isn't that the name Mama mentioned the other day?' Sophie nodded.

Larosse looked from one to the other and said, 'Lord Ireton was Lady Annabel's fancy last year in Vienna. It is a sad story.'

'A cautionary tale,' said Ponsonby, appearing behind them. The young women looked up enquiringly. 'Did I hear Ireton mentioned? Yes, I thought so.' He folded up gracefully and sat on the grass behind them. 'I suppose, ma'am, your mother must have told you all about it,' he said to Rosamund. 'She was in Vienna when it happened.'

'No, she didn't — but Major Larosse is just going to,' she said firmly. 'Aren't you, Major?'

Larosse looked from one to another, then shrugged and began, 'Harry Ireton fell in love with Lady Annabel in Vienna last year. He was one of Sir Charles Stuart's young men, and very well thought of, I understand. Lady Annabel encouraged him for a while, and then dropped him quite suddenly in favour of a Russian Guards colonel.'

'The irony being,' Ponsonby said, 'that it was Ireton who had introduced her to him in the first place — one of the Russian Ambassador's staff. Anyway, Ireton wouldn't take his dismissal and kept following her around like a little dog, and at last she told him she'd marry him if he performed some ridiculous feat. I think the Russian put him up to it,' he added. 'They're always doing mad things.'

'What sort of mad things?' Rosamund asked.

'Things on horseback, usually, Cossack tricks,' Ponsonby said.

'Stupid, dangerous things, risking their horses' legs as well as their own necks,' Larosse said with disapproval. 'All very well on Cossack ponies, which are used to it — '

'But what did they make him do?' Rosamund interrupted.

Larosse exchanged a glance with Ponsonby, and answered. 'Ireton? They persuaded him to try to walk right round the roof-parapet of the Hotel Opera, which was only about six inches wide, and sixty or seventy feet up. And of course the young fool was three parts drunk on champagne, and lost his balance, and fell to his death.'

'He was Macclesfield's only son,' Ponsonby added soberly. 'It broke the old man's heart.'

Sophie shuddered. 'How dreadful! But was it ever proved that Lady Annabel had anything to do with it?'

'It didn't need to be proved: she admitted it quite openly. But the Embassy hushed it up as far as possible, because of the Congress.'

'I'm sorry to see Morland hanging on her sleeve,' Ponsonby said. 'He ought to know better. But since he doesn't — well, Harry and I thought we ought to try to get him out of it. Harry's doing his bit now, you see — ' He nodded to the lively group, where Pyne was vying noisily with Burnett for Lady Annabel's attention. 'I'll take my turn later.' He met the surprised looks of the two young women, and smirked a little. 'Oh well, Morland's a decent chap, and a fine soldier. And I've the greatest admiration for your Mama, Lady Rosamund. That new horse of hers! Superb! No other female could handle it.'

176

Rosamund could not quite let that pass, and was soon in a lively conversation with Ponsonby about various feats of horsemanship, both performed and projected. Left to each other, Larosse and Sophie continued for a while to watch the drama on the other side of the cloth; then Larosse, turning to look at Sophie and seeing how grave she was, smiled suddenly.

'We should not let them spoil the day for us. I would not have told you the story, except that your cousin insisted. But Lady Annabel is not our concern. There are, thank Heaven, few women like her.'

Sophie looked at him carefully. 'Thank Heaven? Don't you like her, then?'

'She is vulgar, immodest, unwomanly. Why should you think I like her?' he asked in surprise.

'I thought, perhaps,' Sophie said carefully, 'you might still be in love with her.'

He looked at her for a long time. 'You are observant, aren't you, mademoiselle? But no, I am not still in love with her. I don't think I was ever in love with her.' He smiled abruptly, the smile that made her feel curiously as though she hadn't eaten for two days. 'Love is entirely too precious to be wasted on such as her: it should be saved for those who deserve it.'

Sophie had no argument with that.

The members of the party moved about, changed partners and positions as though taking part in some slow, elaborate dance. Ponsonby went to relieve Harry Pyne at Lady Annabel's side, and Pyne, with a conspiratorial grin at his cousin, went straight to Lucy and drew her into a conversation about her new horse.

'He's by Apollo Doro, isn't he, ma'am? A famous few guineas I won on *those* four legs! If your new fellow is half as fast as his sire, I should very much like to see him go across country!'

'I haven't had a chance yet to see what he can do,' Lucy said, 'but I'm sure he'll be fast.' She laughed suddenly. 'My groom thinks he's too strong for me. He took him out for two hours this morning, so that he'd be quiet enough for me to ride! Had to get up at dawn to do it, too.'

'I *thought* I saw Magnus in the Allée Verte this morning,' Pyne said, slapping his knee. 'Everyone in Brussels knows those black stockings! But how did you know he'd taken him out? Did he tell you?'

'Lord, no, he thinks I don't know what he's up to. But he forgets I've known him as long as he's known me. And besides,' she added with charming frankness, 'my maid told me — heard it from some of the other servants. She thinks Magnus is too strong for me, but also that it's not Parslow's business to stop me breaking my own neck if I've a mind to. Lord, how they do smother one, these devoted servants.'

'But you don't let them, do you, ma'am?' Pyne said wickedly, a gleam of admiration in his eyes. 'You don't let anyone tell you what to do?'

Lucy thought suddenly of Danby, and missed him with a physical pang like the griping of hunger.

'Oh, my rebellious days are over,' she said lightly. 'I'm a respectable matron now. Don't you see my grown-up daughter over there?'

'No-one would know it, ma'am. You look more like Lady Rosamund's sister.'

She eyed him narrowly. 'Gammon! What are you up to, young Pyne?'

He spread his hands innocently. 'Nothing, nothing, I assure you, ma'am. It's just that I hate to see a splendid racehorse tied up, when it could be running free and winning races.'

'Magnus, you mean?' Lucy said, puzzled.

Pyne only smiled, but she had the oddest feeling that he didn't mean Magnus at all.

Larosse took advantage of the Duc's absence from Héloïse's side to go and sit beside her.

'I have been waiting my chance,' he said, 'but it has been a long time coming.'

'Could you not have come to speak to me before, then?' Héloïse asked.

Larosse shook his head, dropping naturally into French. 'I have too much respect for my senior officer to interrupt his *tête à têtes*. And he has shewn no inclination until now to stray from your side, madame.'

She smiled slightly. 'The Duc and I are very old friends. You should not blame him for displaying loyalty, I think.'

He looked at her quizzically. 'Does that sentence hold a message for me? A criticism, perhaps? Someone has been talking of me to you — warning you that I am not quite *comme il faut* because I changed allegiances?'

Héloïse was distressed. 'Oh no, I assure you — !' She stopped, aware that that was precisely what someone had done. 'I assure you,' she changed the sentence, 'that I do not blame you in the least. On the contrary.'

He drew up his knees and clasped them to him, staring at the ground reflectively. 'I know what they say of me. It is hard to be judged disloyal — hardest of all because I know I would feel the same about someone in my position. Men are not logical,' he smiled painfully at her half-uttered protest. 'Like animals, like dogs, we respond to the signals we have learnt. Some of us are intelligent enough to know that is what we are doing, but still we do it.'

Héloïse kept silent, willing him to go on. He felt her sympathy, and resumed in a soft, reflective voice.

'If you have never met the Emperor, madame, you cannot imagine how he affects one. It is a kind of magic. I believe all great men must have it, for, *voyons*, he is not tall or handsome or imposing — but somehow, when you are with him, when he looks at you, you lay down your life at his feet without question. I loved him. We all loved him. I would have followed him to the ends of the earth.'

'I think you did,' Héloïse said gently.

The corners of his mouth lifted slightly. 'Yes — true! It was the end of the earth. Moscow! When I first saw it, the fabulous city — ! But all I had seen before, the men dying, the hunger, the stinking corpses — they were more real to me. And afterwards — ' He shuddered. 'Nothing — nothing — can ever remove the images from my mind of the retreat. We came out from that frozen hell, madame, a poor remnant, like black ghosts. And the Emperor was not with us: he had left us, to go on to Paris in his carriage. It was a military necessity, one sees that. But it was hard not to blame him.'

Héloïse nodded in silent sympathy, and he went on.

'So many had died, and for what? For nothing but his

pride! I left him then. I could not give him my allegiance any more — my intelligence denied it. Ah, but the heart! The heart still loved him — still loves him!' He paused. 'Do not be afraid — I am to be trusted. I will fight to the death to destroy him. But it will not be with joy, not with joy.'

There was a silence, in which Heloïse became aware of the soft, light voices of the rest of the party, which had formed an unheeded background to his confession, like the murmur of a stream. After a while she said, 'I honour you, Major, for telling me this. I know it cannot have been easy for you.'

He looked at her for the first time. 'You and I, madame, know many of the same things. Love once given cannot be taken back, even when the object harms us to breaking-point.'

How can he know? she wondered. How can he know about me?

'And we are exiles, too, both of us exiles from our beloved France. Perhaps when Napoleon is dead, we shall have it back, our France.' He said the word Napoleon as she would have said James — with painful awareness. 'It is hard to be French just now,' he went on. 'There are many in the Allied army like me, who fought under the Eagles. Men watch us, wondering if we can be trusted. The good Duc watches. But how one can understand Maréchal Ney!' He paused. 'The bravest of the brave, we called him. He brought the rearguard out of Russia — no-one else could have done it! And he would not cross the river until the last of the men was safe over. If you had seen them, tattered scarecrows, hobbling on black-ened, toeless feet — ' He stopped again. 'But even he, meeting the Emperor face to face, could not help himself. Like a dog you see kicked, but still creeping to the master's feet. Well, I shall not. I am no-one's dog.'

Héloïse listened to his revelations, understanding instantly and almost instinctively what he was feeling, the terrible tug of conscience, the intellect's rebellion, the blind love. He was a finer man than she had expected; she would have been proud to welcome him as Sophie's suitor. But what chance was there now that he could feel anything for her innocent daughter, tortured man that he was? She must reluctantly

180

accept the Duc's judgement, that he could not mean anything serious by his attentions.

As if he had heard her thought, he looked across the group to where Sophie was talking to Bobbie and Barbarina, and regarded her steadily for a moment. Héloïse saw the lines of his face soften, the corners of his mouth curve upwards just a little.

'She is all loveliness,' he said quietly. 'As innocent and gentle as a roe-deer.'

'Yes,' said Héloïse.

He looked at her, and smiled suddenly, an open smile, without shadows. 'I believe it was through your intervention that I was invited today. I thank you with all my heart, madame. I have had more pleasure today than I had imagined possible.'

'I am very glad, Major,' Héloïse said. 'I hope you will often join our parties.' But from understanding him perfectly, she had passed to understanding nothing. He had covered his spoor most successfully.

Half-way home, Harry Pyne so successfully and with such bland good-humour placed himself at Lady Annabel's side and absorbed her attention that Marcus could hardly object. In any case, his *tête à tête* with his desired object had degenerated into veiled accusations from him and the threat of ill-temper from her, and it was probably as well that it should be interrupted. He swallowed down his feelings and took up station beside Rosamund instead.

'So, Rosy,' he said, with an approximation of his old cheerfulness, 'it was a prime outing, was it not? Have you enjoyed the day?'

'Have you?' she countered quickly. 'I thought you looked rather blue earlier on. Perhaps the company wasn't to your taste?'

He looked at her, a little puzzled. 'What a sharp tongue you've grown, little cousin. Are you cross because I didn't spend more time with you?'

'Oh, as to that, I was well entertained, I assure you,' she said airily. 'Captain Tantony was most attentive.'

'He's a capital fellow,' Marcus said seriously, 'but not good enough for you, Rosy, by a long way.'

Her heart lifted. 'Oh? How do you find him lacking?'

Marcus smiled, and looked for a moment like his old self. 'Dull! He couldn't keep up with you for half an hour! Mark you, I don't know the man who could. You were a devil to go when you were in the schoolroom — now you're grown up, I tremble to think what you will do next.'

She regarded him quizzically, wondering how far this was the old teasing. Was his heart in it? Abruptly she said, 'I tell you what, Marcus, I do not propose to ride tamely along this road, to begin with. I'm going to ride in the forest. Come on!'

'Oh no, wait, Rosy — you mustn't. We can't leave the party.'

'I'm going to — and if you don't follow, I shall be all alone, which will be most improper!' She turned Hotspur and tapped her heel to his side, and sent him scrambling up the grassy bank and into the trees. Marcus hesitated a moment, and then shrugged and followed. He didn't want to be out of Lady Annabel's sight, but Rosamund could not be allowed to go off alone, and only he or Bobbie, as cousins and school-room friends, could fittingly accompany her.

Under the tree canopy he found her waiting for him, and as soon as he reached her she turned Hotspur and rode deeper into the woods.

'That's better,' she said. 'It was too insipid, riding along with those mimsy girls and those cloddish young men.'

Marcus laughed. 'Cloddish? You can hardly call Harry Pyne cloddish, for one! He has the readiest tongue, and a great deal too much high-spirit. I've half a mind to call him out the way he's been cutting me out with Bel!'

Rosamund bit her lip. 'Marcus, you don't really like her, do you?'

'Like her? My dear Rosy, it's gone a great deal further than like! I should have thought you'd realised that. I'm glad, really, that my father has come — it is past time for me to make my move, for who knows what may happen next?'

'What can you mean? What has your father to do with it?'

'I have to ask his permission, of course.' He looked at her, and seeing her still frowning, continued, 'To marry Bel. I'm

182

not yet of age, and of course I depend on him for my allowance.'

Rosamund had paled. 'Marry her? Marcus, you can't, you *can't* mean it!'

'Why ever not? You must have seen how I feel about her. Even you must have observed it is a case between us. What can there to be stand in my way?'

Rosamund mentally rolled up her sleeves. 'Well, to begin with, she's too old for you.'

'Oh, Rosy!' he laughed. 'She's only a few years older than me, and what can that matter? It's what is inside you that counts, and she's just a girl under that sophisticated exterior.'

'She's an old *girl*, if you ask me,' Rosamund said shortly. 'And hard as nails — and a horrible flirt.'

He frowned. 'You mustn't say those things to me, love. Bel has had a terrible life — you can't know the half of it! And sometimes — I own — she says and does things that — well, I don't care for them either. But when she's married to me, she'll settle down. She won't have anything more to be afraid of. She needs to be loved and cared for, you see. Oh, you can't understand, Rosy — you're too young — but believe me — '

'I'm not so young that I can't see she's making a fool of you. Lord, don't you know everyone's talking about it? They call you *Bel Robb's latest.*'

He flushed. 'That's enough. You don't understand what you're saying, and I should be very sorry to fall out with you, when we've known each other all our lives. Bel and I love each other, and one day you'll understand how that feels. And you'll love her too, when you get to know her.'

Rosamund regarded him silently, pained, incredulous, angry, but most of all, and surprisingly, sad. He really means what he says, she thought. He really doesn't know what she's like. Sooner or later he would discover the true nature of the woman he was courting, and then he would be horribly hurt; and while the Rosamund of yesterday, or even of a few hours ago, would have been glad to have him punished, this present Rosamund felt only sorrow that he was going to be so disillusioned. Loving him, she wished she could spare him.

But the pain was part of the cure, of course, and there was no sense in bleating — he had to go through it. For now she said, almost gently, 'She seems to be very pleased with Lieutenant Pyne.'

'It's just her high spirits — she doesn't mean any harm by it,' Marcus said, sounding confident again. 'Which is more than I can say for Harry Pyne. He and his cousin are altogether too fond of teasing and practical jokes. The trouble is, of course, that they haven't enough to do to keep them occupied. I'm not sure they aren't up to some mischief with your mother, too, Rosy. Have you noticed how they're always hanging round her? I think they're plotting something.'

'I think they want Mama to take part in some kind of a race,' Rosamund said. 'They were very taken with the story of her race to Brighton years ago, and I think they want to persuade her to repeat it here. She won't, of course,' she sighed.

'I should think not, indeed! It would be very shocking!'

'Would it? But Mama likes to be shocking. Only I think my step-papa wouldn't like it, and Mama is awfully weak when it comes to his wishes.'

'That's the way wives are supposed to be with husbands,' he said amused.

'Well, but an agreeable husband wouldn't try to stop a wife doing what she wanted, would he?'

'If you think that, Rosy, I must advise you never to get married!'

'Nonsense! You only have to marry the right person. You, for instance — you wouldn't want me to sit at home and sew, would you? Or ride a terrible one-pace screw instead of a proper horse like Hotspur?'

'Hotspur is a grand sort,' Marcus said, thinking he was changing the subject. 'I'm very impressed that your mother allows you to ride him.'

'Mama don't like me very much, but she thinks I'm the best rider she knows, apart from herself.'

'She's probably right,' Marcus said. 'I will say of you, Rosy, that you can handle a horse better than any man I've ever seen.'

She beamed with pleasure. 'So you see?'

'See what? Oh, I understand you. Well I promise you, love,' he said, smiling indulgently, 'that if ever we marry, I shan't try to choose your horses for you!'

184

'Good,' she said. He thinks he is playing a game, she thought, but we shall see. She had great faith in what Larosse had told her; and when Bel Robb had dropped Marcus for another, he would turn to her for comfort. And then he would see her courted by Tantony — and others — and would realise that he had loved her all along. It would be all right. She would get her way in the end.

'Let's have a canter along here,' she said, 'and then I think we had better go back to the others. They will be wondering where we are. Some of them,' with a sidelong glance at him, 'will be *quite worried* about me.'

BOOK TWO

The Sybarites

Life (priest and poet say) is but a dream;
I wish no happier one than to be laid
Beneath a cool syringa's scented shade
Or wavy willow, by the running stream,
Brimful of moral, where the dragon-fly
Wanders as careless and content as I.

Walter Savage Landor: *The Dragon-fly*

CHAPTER EIGHT

James Morland rode into York for the first time since Fanny's death without noticing anything of his surroundings — he could not even afterwards have said what the weather was like. In Davygate he dismounted, flung the reins of his horse to Durban, and ran up the stairs and into the offices of Pobgee and Micklethwaite.

It was fortunate that Mr Pobgee senior was at liberty at that moment, for James would have stormed into his room just the same if he had been closeted with the Lord Lieutenant of the County.

'Look at that!' he said, flinging down a letter on Pobgee's desk.

'Good God, James! What is it? What's the matter?' Pobgee said, half-rising to his feet in alarm.

'Read that, and you'll see!' James said, and began pacing up and down the room, his hands behind his back, muttering angrily to himself.

Pobgee eyed him cautiously, measured the distance between himself and the door, and then picked up the letter and read it through. It was from Jasper Hobsbawn, saying that new evidence had come to light which indicated that Mr Joseph Hobsbawn had died at a quarter past two on the morning of the 10th of March, and had therefore survived his granddaughter by three quarters of an hour.

'I see,' Pobgee said, having finished the letter. He placed it on the desk and eyed James sympathetically. 'I'm very sorry, very sorry indeed — but at least it is better to have the thing settled, one way or the other. Uncertainty in such a matter is the worst of evils, I assure you, where there is no question of material want.'

James halted abruptly and turned on him. 'What the devil are you chumbling about, man?'

189

'This letter — the new evidence. If Fanny died before her grandfather, everything goes to the residuary legatee. She would not have inherited. I'm sorry, James, but there it is. I'm sure her ladyship won't be too disappointed — she had no burning desire to own the mills, I know.'

'Devil take it, man, are your wits abroad? You don't believe it, do you? You don't really think that letter is anything but a lie from beginning to end?'

'It says here that they have a witness prepared to swear to the time of death —'

'They have a witness! They've bought and paid for one, more like! *Manufactured* one — and from the whole cloth, too! Humbug!'

'But what reason can you possibly have for supposing such a thing? My dear James, it would be dreadful in the extreme — a very serious matter indeed. I assure you in matters concerning the disposition of property, the punishment under the law for misrepresentation is condign.'

'What?'

'Punishable by death or transportation,' Pobgee translated.

James leaned his fists on the desk and bent forward to glare at the lawyer. 'Listen to me, Pobgee — if they had any real evidence about the time of death, they'd have brought it forward long ago. This is the letter of a desperate man. Do you really think, with the mills and Hobsbawn's personal fortune at stake, this cousin Jasper would shrink from a lie or two? What if it is a serous crime — what has he to lose? He's penniless — dispossessed!'

Pobgee shook his head. 'I really cannot believe —'

'Oh, but I can! Everything points to it. First Jasper writes to say that Hobsbawn's dead and everything has gone to Fanny. Then he learns Fanny's dead and starts equivocating — they don't know the time of the old man's death and can't prove anything. And then suddenly — so conveniently! — a witness is found to prove the very thing they want proving! If you don't think that's damned suspicious, well, I'm sorry for you!'

Pobgee shook his head non-committally, and picked up the letter to read it again, marking time, wondering what James was going to do or say next. But James remained where he

190

was, leaning on his fists, staring at the top of Pobgee's head. In the end, the attorney felt obliged to speak.

'It could be as you say. I can put it no more strongly than that.'

'Well, then?' James prompted.

'What is it you want me to do?'

'I want you to go there — find out. Talk to people, watch their eyes, find out who's lying. Find out the truth.'

'The truth? Is that what you want?' Pobgee said quietly.

'Yes, the truth! The truth is that Hobsbawn wanted Fanny to have everything, and by God she shall! I won't let her be cheated by these — *manufacturers*! Will you go there, Pobgee, and ask questions? Because I tell you now if you won't, I'll find someone who will. If necessary, I'll go myself.'

Pobgee sighed. 'Very well. I'll go, and try to sift out the truth. But I warn you it may not be what you want to hear. Can I trust you to accept it, whatever it is?'

'Oh yes,' he said impatiently, turning away. 'Don't worry about that.' And he went out of the room without another word.

Not right, Pobgee thought, staring at the empty doorway. Definitely not right.

There was the usual clot of traffic on the corner of Davygate and Stonegate, so when he had remounted, James turned his horse the other way, meaning to cut through Feasegate to Market Street. But as he passed the end of New Street he glanced down it, and saw a shop-window display which caught his attention. Without a word to Durban, he turned his horse into the street and rode up to the shop and stopped.

It was a display of automata, and in the centre was a musical-box with a little bird on the top of the lid, much like the one Fanny had bought for her baby, except that it was made of commoner materials. He stared at it broodingly for a long time, until Durban, growing restless, murmured a prompting, 'Sir?'

James frowned. 'Wait,' he said harshly, and then dismounted and threw Durban the reins, and walked into the shop.

The shop was dim, and smelled agreeably of wood and

varnish and new paint. James looked about him curiously, at first seeing no-one. Everything had about it the hallmarks of a new venture. He tried and failed to remember what shop had been here before — he didn't think he could ever have been in it, for he didn't remember it at all. And then the shadows moved, making him start.

It was a young woman who came forward to serve him, a slender, small young woman with a mass of dark curls caught up out of the way with a bit of green ribbon. In her plain day-dress of soft brown cambric, and with her dark hair, she had blended into the dimness at the back of the shop. James stared at her. Her face was pale and rather pointed, like a fox-kitten, with large dark eyes that looked up at him timidly, but without evasion, like some creature too young and innocent to have any apprehension of danger.

Nevertheless, his silent staring had unnerved her a little. Her small pink mouth trembled, her hands moved uncertainly and then came to rest clasped together as though for reassurance. 'Sir?' she said at last.

James did not realise the effect he was having. 'Who are you?' he asked abruptly. 'This isn't your shop, surely? You're too young.'

A blush stained her cheeks — a blush of absolute innocence — and the clasped hands lifted a little, defensively. 'Oh — I — no, sir, of course not. It's my father's shop.'

'And where is he?'

'He's upstairs — he's not very well, so I'm minding things for him. Did you wish to speak to him? I — I could go and see if —'

'No, don't disturb him. It makes no matter,' James said hastily, unable to take his eyes from her. So innocent! So pretty! He was fascinated. He felt an urgent desire to touch her — not lasciviously, but simply as he would want to touch a kitten or a foal — to stroke her cheek, perhaps, or touch that soft curling hair. The parted pink lips — so tender! The eyes, gentle, dark, shy — yet looking at him so candidly, as though she wished to know what he was like! 'What's your name?' he asked at last.

'Angelica,' she said, hardly above a whisper. 'Angelica Hesketh.'

'Angelica?' He stared enraptured at the fragility of her wrists, delicate as bird's bones, as they emerged from the buttoned cuffs of her long sleeves. 'And so your father is —?'

'Josiah Hesketh, sir. It's on the door,' she added, watching him.

'So it is.' Oh, that skin — like cream velvet flushed with rose, utterly unblemished! And the little, white, even teeth — he had not seen such teeth in all his life! 'I am James Morland,' he said abruptly.

'Yes, sir, I know.'

'You know?'

She almost smiled. 'I've seen you outside the Minster sometimes. And riding by. Everyone in York knows the Morlands, sir.'

He felt absurdly pleased. 'Do they? Yes, I suppose they do. Well, Miss Hesketh, so this is your father's shop?'

'Yes, sir.' She looked down at her hands and then up, and there was an enchanting air of faint puzzlement about her. 'What was it that you wanted, sir? Can I shew you anything?'

What, indeed, had he come in for? Whatever it was, it had completely gone out of his head. He looked about him for inspiration. 'Oh — ah — that one there, on the shelf.' It was a toy soldier — a drummer, all scarlet and pipeclay, with a black shako above a bright pink face. 'It looks a remarkably fine object. What does it do?'

She smiled properly now, shewing all the dear little teeth, and he would have given half his possessions to keep her smiling like that. 'It's very cunning, sir — shall I shew you?'

She turned away to lift the thing down, and he watched with a kind of hunger as her slender arms reached up, stretching her body, tilting her fragile head back. The indirect light penetrating from the side window outlined her hair and gown so that she seemed blurred with glowing, as though she had a faint golden nimbus. Now she turned back to him, placed the toy on the counter, and turned the key at the back. The damned thing sprang to life in a horribly realistic way, turning its head from side to side and rattling a smart tattoo on the drum, its arms jerking up and down like a victim of St Vitus.

The little Angelica watched it, her face wreathed in simple

193

pleasure, and then looked up at him with the shy delight of one sharing some delicious secret. 'He's one of my favourites, sir. Isn't he fine?'

It made an infernal noise — just the thing to delight the heart of a small boy. Of course: a small boy! 'He is indeed! He shall be my favourite, too, from this moment onwards. I'll take him.'

'Oh — oh, thank you, sir!' she said as fervently as if he had bought it for her. 'Will you have it sent, or will you take it?'

'I'll take it now,' he said, thinking he would have longer to look at her if she had to parcel it up. She began to move about, finding box and paper and string, and he was at liberty to lean one elbow on the counter and watch her, thinking how gracefully she moved, how well her simple gown became her, how slender was her neck, and how charmingly the little soft curls nestled against its nape. Once or twice she glanced at him from under her lashes — not coquettishly, but shyly, from a genuine modesty. When the thing was done, and he had no more reason to linger, he was conscious of a sharp regret. He might never see her again — what reason could he have to come again to a shop like this?

'So you go to the Minster on Sundays, do you?' he asked to prolong the moment.

'Yes, sir — most Sundays. Father likes it better there than St Helen's. He says St Helen's is too dark, and that God made us all creatures of the sunlight.'

'He sounds a wise man.'

'Oh yes, sir, he is.' The smile shone out again.

'And will you be at the Minster this Sunday?' James asked desperately.

She looked down, her cheeks pink again. 'I don't know — I — I suppose so. Only Father hasn't been well, and he might not go —'

'But he would not wish you to miss your Sunday devotion, I am sure. And no harm could come to you just that short step away.'

'Well, no, sir, I suppose not —'

'If you are there, I shall see you, for I go to the Minster this Sunday,' he said casually. 'Perhaps afterwards I might walk

194

back with you, to make sure you get safely home. That should ease your father's anxiety.'

She answered — he knew she answered, for he saw her lips move — but he could not hear a sound, and her eyes were hidden from him under eyelids as perfect and smooth as white rose-petals.

The horses were waiting outside in the street. James emerged, blinking in the light, feeling that something momentous had happened, and wondering how it was the world hadn't noticed and produced some phenomenon to mark the occasion — a rainbow, a hail of frogs, a winged bull or something. But everything appeared supremely normal, and Durban was looking at him — damn his impudence — with barely concealed surprise.

James flourished the parcel. 'Just something I saw that took my fancy,' he said casually. 'An automaton — amusing trifle — just the thing for young Benedict.'

Durban tried not to stare, but James could not know, of course, that the fact of his speaking at all was astonishing to his manservant, and his condescending to explain himself, to say nothing of his sudden air of cheerfulness — something that hadn't been seen in months.

Mr Pobgee travelled to Manchester in his own carriage, and slowly, his thoughts a good deal confused. There was nothing untoward in his going there — it was perfectly consistent with his responsibilities to her ladyship as her man of business, to verify the claims made by Jasper Hobsbawn. And indeed, Jasper Hobsbawn would expect it, for his own attorney would advise him to that effect.

But he did not know what he was going to find, or what he wanted to find. The suspicion that James had uttered was, of course, preposterous, and the product of his fevered mind; and yet now that it had been planted in Pobgee's brain, he could not help wondering why it had taken so long for this very vital evidence to come to light. He resolved to move cautiously — not that he didn't always move cautiously — but very cautiously indeed. It was not his business to be partial, but he couldn't help hoping that the evidence would prove to be incontrovertible. He disliked the whole business of the Hobsbawn inheritance, and he would have been glad to know that everything was going to the residuary legatee, so that he need have nothing more to do with it.

Mr Jasper Hobsbawn received him at Hobsbawn House with great kindness and generosity, as Mr Pobgee had to admit. On learning that the attorney had bespoken himself a room at the George Hotel, Jasper insisted on sending a servant there to cancel the instruction.

'You must stay here, sir — I insist! All the late Mr Hobsbawn's servants are still in employment, and you will be much more comfortable here than at an inn. And you will find it easier to pursue your enquiries from here. No, please sir, I won't hear of it. It will be good for the servants to have something to do — and I shall be glad of your company at dinner, too.'

It all boded very well, Pobgee thought. Jasper did not behave like a man with a secret to hide; nothing could have been more frank and open than his manner. Pobgee accepted the invitation, and was shewn to a very comfortable room. When he had changed his travelling-clothes, he rang and was conducted into a spacious dining-parlour where covers were laid for two at a long and shining table which would easily have seated twenty. Jasper Hobsbawn was seated at one end under a huge and appallingly-executed portrait of lady in a blue dress.

'My late cousin's wife,' Jasper said, seeing the direction of his gaze. 'He was devoted to her, and therefore to her portrait. It performs a useful function, however, in concealing the safe. You do not object, I hope, to this early hour of dining?'

'No indeed, I prefer it,' Pobgee said, taking his seat facing the portrait. The servants came in and placed the dishes on the table, and when everything was arranged, Jasper waved them away.

'We'll serve ourselves,' he said. 'I'll ring if we need you. There is but the one course, sir,' he added to Pobgee with faint apology. 'Eating alone leads one to eat simply. "You see your dinner", as they say.'

Pobgee said what was appropriate: the dishes seemed to him ample, and well-dressed. When they were alone, Jasper resumed briskly. 'I imagine there are things you want to ask me. You will not wish to wait until tomorrow.'

Pobgee nodded in appreciation of his thoughtfulness. 'You have seen your late cousin's Will, I suppose?'

'Yes. I can shew it to you after dinner, if you wish. But it is quite simple. Except for a few small pensions to servants, everything was left to Fanny — Mrs Hawker.'

'Everything? There was no residuum?'

'No. The residuary legatee was mentioned only in case of Fanny's predeceasing her grandfather, which naturally he could not have anticipated.' An indefinable look spread across his face — of distaste, perhaps.

'And who is the residuary legatee?' Pobgee asked, but he had already guessed the answer.

Jasper met his eyes steadily. 'I am.'

'Ah!'

'Ah, indeed. You may imagine with what emotions I learned that Fanny had died during the same night as her grandfather! She was always a contrary creature, and even in dying she managed to cause the maximum of turmoil!'

'Sir, I must ask you —'

'Oh yes, I know — don't speak ill of the dead. I'm sorry. But there was no love lost between Fanny and me. If our situations were reversed, I assure you she would have nothing good to say about me.' Pobgee admitted the justice of that, but silently. Jasper went on, 'Things seemed very black at first. I don't shrink from telling you that I have always wanted the mills. I dedicated my life to them. They were everything to me — wife, children, almost my religion! If Fanny had inherited them, she'd have thrown me out — I'd have lost even my position as mill-manager. You may suppose me to have felt like a man whose only child was to be snatched from him. And then when I learned she was dead ...' He broke off, and looked down at his hands. 'God rest her soul!' he said quietly.

There was a moment's silence. Pobgee studied the face opposite him. It was a strange one, even to a man of Pobgee's experience. It was thin and pale, with the pallor of poverty, and yet there was nothing coarse or brutal about it, and he spoke with obvious gentility. It was an interesting face, full of

197

character, of no little suffering. The eyes spoke of intelligence, humour, fervour; the hard line of the mouth of self-discipline, endurance, self-denial. A man of passion, who had never yet given his passion rein — who perhaps was not even aware that it existed.

It was the face, Pobgee thought, indulging in a little fantasy, of a potential martyr — of a man capable of suffering for a cause, of dying for an ideal; and yet he might also make a loving and tender parent, if life ever dealt him that chance. Examining the features, Pobgee saw that he was a man whom a woman might justly find attractive.

But he could be a dangerous man, Pobgee thought. All things were possible in that face, except pettiness. Pobgee would not say that Jasper was incapable of lying — he was aware that it was impossible to say that about any human being — but if he dissembled, it would be for something he considered very important. Were the mills that important to him? Perhaps. Perhaps.

'Yes, sir,' Pobgee prompted gently. 'You learned that she was dead?'

Jasper looked up, his eyes unfathomable. 'May I help you to a little of this beef? Fat or lean? And rare or well-done? The claret, sir — is it to your liking? The late Mr Hobsbawn had a fine cellar, and an excellent taste in wine. Even in the darkest days of the war he contrived to add to his bins. He boasted of Fanny's sharing his taste. Few women, I suppose, have any palate for fine wine — but then Fanny was a very unusual woman.'

The eyes brooded. Pobgee drank a little of the claret and found it excellent, and said so.

'Well, then,' Jasper resumed abruptly. 'It was plain to me that the inheritance depended on the exact time of my cousin's death — I make no concealment. But all I knew was that he had been found dead by his manservant at about six o'clock in the morning.'

'So early?'

'Mr Hobsbawn was accustomed to rising early. The physician was sent for —'

'His name, sir?'

'McGregor — Charlotte Street. He came, and gave it as his

opinion that Mr Hobsbawn had died of a seizure during the night.'

'You have asked him, I suppose, to give a closer estimate of the time of death?'

Jasper smiled faintly. 'It has not been necessary. In the course of a conversation with me, the housekeeper, Mrs Murray, revealed that she had seen her master alive during the night.'

He described the circumstances, and Pobgee listened attentively. 'Why did she not reveal this before?' he asked.

'I wondered that myself,' Jasper said frankly, 'but I suppose she did not know that it was important. You know what servants are like — they answer only those questions they are asked.'

'Is she — pardon me, sir — is she reliable?'

'Is she lying, do you mean?' He shrugged. 'I see no reason why she should. She stands to gain nothing — her pension is secured whichever way the Will goes. And the matter arose naturally in conversation — I did not ask her, and she did not know until I told her how much hung on her testimony.' Pobgee made no comment, and Jasper regarded him with a kind of grim humour. 'You will, of course, like to interview Mrs Murray and satisfy yourself of her veracity. Tomorrow morning I shall arrange it for you.'

Pobgee smiled and bent his head. 'Thank you, sir. You are most generous.'

'I have nothing to hide from you. You are welcome to interview anyone — or even everyone. A little of the chicken, sir? Or may I cut you some of the cold pie? Those pickles are to go with it — Mrs Murray's own. She has many talents — a woman worthy of her calling.'

Pobgee was puzzled — the tone was faintly ironic. Was there something to be read in that? He had gained the impression Jasper didn't like Mrs Murray — was he perhaps embarrassed at disliking someone who was to do him such good service? Jasper, he was sure, was not lying — but was Mrs Murray? And if she was, was it with or without Jasper's knowledge?

He remained puzzled the next day after the interview with

199

the housekeeper. She came into the study which Jasper had put at his disposal, smoothing her apron and giving him an enquiring look as though she had come to discuss the day's housekeeping programme. Her bland, respectful mien did not waver when Pobgee told her why he was here, and she answered his questions without hesitation. He could not fault her as a witness; yet he felt there was something not right about it. It was nothing he could put his finger on — merely a lawyer's instinct — but he felt something was wrong.

Why had she not spoken before about her midnight interview with her employer? She shrugged it off — no-one had asked her, she had not thought it important. But Pobgee could not imagine any servant keeping such a conversational titbit to herself. When the house was seething with the news that the master had died in the night, surely anyone would have said, 'I saw him and spoke to him only a few hours ago.'

All the same, she said it and swore it and was prepared to sign an affidavit to the purpose, and when he warned her of the awful consequences of bearing false witness, she merely and quite naturally looked puzzled, as though the warnings had no relevance to her. Oh, it was well done!

Having thanked Jasper and made his excuses, Pobgee summoned his carriage and had himself driven into the centre of the town, to seek out Dr McGregor of Charlotte Street. He was not surprised to find that the physician was out visiting a client, but had come prepared to wait for his return. After something more than hour, McGregor returned and declared himself happy to receive Mr Pobgee. He was a thin, elderly Scotsman, whose long bony nose was tinted even on such a warm day with ominous shades of crimson and purple.

'Come in, come in, sir — into my little sanctum! *Sanctum sanctorum*, that's what I call it! We bachelors have our little ways, don't we? We make ourselves comfortable in our own fashion! And will you take a little something with me, sir? I usually have a wee glass of something at about this hour. I have some excellent port wine here in this decanter — a present from one of my grateful patients. Six dozen, he sent me, sir, for curing him of the stone — a nasty complaint if ever there was one! Worth every bottle to be relieved of it, so he assured me. No, sir? Come, let me press you to change your mind! A little sound wine, sir, clears the blood and strengthens the stomach. "Use a little wine, for thy stomach's sake", so says the poet Paul — ha! And a good physician he'd have made, too — that's what I tell my patients.'

Pobgee declined with gentle firmness, and turned the physician's attention to the matter in question.

'Ah yes! Queer business, that — grandfather and grand-daughter dying the same night! Almost as if he knew. Hobsbawn, you know, was devoted to the little girl — oh, well, not so little, I grant you, by that time. But he doted on her — lived for her, you might say. She used to come and visit him, and he'd take her around in the coach, looking as proud as if he were her father, sir. And a remarkably pretty, intelligent young woman she was, too.'

'Yes, indeed. I knew Mrs Hawker all her life.'

'Och, well, you know all about it then. But Hobsbawn doted on her, as I said, and it broke his heart when she married, for her husband was a most disappointing man, not at all the thing! That's what brought on the first attack. He suffered a seizure — a mild one, but worrying enough at his time of life. He was very poorly indeed for some months — I thought he might pop off then, you know. But then Mrs Hawker came and made her peace, and it quite brought him back to life. He was his old self again when he learned that she was increasing. And if he'd lived to know how she died —'

He shook his head. 'A tragic death! If only we knew more about these things. But childbirth is a mystery, sir, a mystery, and no man will ever understand it! And another mystery it is, that Hobsbawn died the same night! You may think me fanciful, but often I've wondered whether she didn't come and fetch him, you know! For if he'd known she was dead, he wouldn't have wanted to go on living.'

Pobgee's intellect protested at this, but he concealed his impatience and, regarding the level of the port in the decanter, thought he had better get his questions out while there was still some chance of their being answered coherently. 'You were called to the house in the morning, I understand? And that was the first you knew of Mr Hobsbawn's death?'

'Yes, yes, that's right. They sent a boy to fetch me, and I

went up there straight away, but there was nothing I could do — he was quite dead, you know. Went off in his sleep in the most natural way.'

'At what time did you examine the body?'

'It must have been at about eight, I suppose. I cannot tell you precisely.'

'But they told me at the house that Mr Hobsbawn's man found him at six o'clock.'

McGregor frowned. 'Perhaps he did, sir — I cannot offer an opinion on that. I dare say they might delay in sending for me — panicking, the way servants do, and doing all manner of useless things. The boy came at about seven to my house. I had my chocolate, and dressed, and so was at the house at about eight o'clock.'

'Did you carry out a post-mortem examination?'

The physician raised an eyebrow. 'Of course not. Why on earth should I do that? There was no mystery about the death. Mr Hobsbawn was my patient — had been for years. He'd had one seizure, and in these cases, as I dare say you must know, a second is always a possibility — I may say, a probability.'

'And can you estimate at what time Mr Hobsbawn died?'

McGregor now raised both eyebrows as far as they would go. 'My dear sir, what an extraordinary question! I am a physician, not a soothsayer! How in the world would you expect me to know the precise instant he died? He was dead when I saw him, that's all I can tell you. Dear me, do you really think I am a magician or — or — a fortune-teller? I observe, I diagnose — I do not hazard wild guesses or exotic surmises! I find a man cold and stiff in his bed in the morning, who got into it of his own accord the night before, and I feel licensed to assume that he died in his sleep.'

Pobgee cut through the indignation. 'Indeed, sir, I quite understand,' he said soothingly. 'He presented the appearance of having died in his sleep.'

'Indeed he did.'

'The body was composed and peaceful, I suppose — not, for instance, contorted? The bedclothes were not disordered?'

'You may ask Mr Hobsbawn's manservant about that, sir,' McGregor said coldly. 'It was he who found the body, not I.'

Seeing he had fatally annoyed the physician, Pobgee felt it best to take his leave. He thanked him courteously, and left him to his decanter and his mutterings about being supposed to be a sorcerer or an Eastern mystic, and the layman's muddled thinking about the science of medicine.

Pobgee returned to Hobsbawn House, feeling that he was not much further forward. Everything, it seemed, rested on the testimony of the housekeeper, and there was no concrete reason to doubt her. The only thing more he could think of was to interview the old man's servant who had actually found the body. On arriving at the house he learned that Jasper had gone out, but as he had said the previous evening that Pobgee might interview anyone he liked, he asked the butler to send the manservant to him, and took himself off to the study he had used before.

After a very long wait, there was a scratching at the door, and it opened to reveal the late Joseph Hobsbawn's valet. Pobgee's heart sank. The butler was elderly enough, but the manservant was sere and bent, with etiolated arms, and legs that seemed to bow outwards even under the weight of so skeletal a body. The head was bald, and thrust forward like a tortoise's by the curvature of the spine, and the old man shuffled in slowly with his hands hanging limply, all knuckles and veins, at his side.

'You sent for me, sir?' he asked.

'Yes, indeed. I wish to ask you some questions. What is your name, my man?'

'Simon, sir.'

'Well, Simon, sit down if you please.'

The old man looked shocked. 'Oh no, sir, I couldn't do that. T'wouldn't be right, sir.'

'As you please, as you please,' Pobgee said soothingly. 'Now, I understand that it was you who first found your late master was dead that morning?'

The old eyes were watery enough, but they grew perceptibly moister. 'Yes, sir, that I was. And a better master there never was! I was with him upwards of forty years, sir, and never a cross word, though he had a short way with him when he was vexed, and spoke sharp to them as displeased him. But he was kindness itself to me, sir, and I never wished a better place nor the one I had, sir, and that's the truth of it.'

It was a long and tedious business. The old man's whispery, wavering voice rambled back and forth through his recollections and seemingly endless sentences. But he had little to add to Pobgee's information. His master had gone to bed at half-past nine as was his custom, and Simon had undressed him and pottered about putting things away while Hobsbawn read from a book of sermons — 'Very devout, my master was, sir. A good Christian and a good Catholic.' Simon had drawn the bed-curtains and blown out the candle at a quarter to ten, again just as he always did, and took himself off to bed. He had heard and seen nothing untoward until the next morning when, pulling back Hobsbawn's bed-curtains at the appointed time, he had found his master dead.

'Did you know at once that he was dead?' Pobgee asked.

'Well, sir, it isn't a thing that springs to your mind all at once. But Master was always awake already when I went in in the morning, and that morning his eyes were shut and he didn't stir. I called him, and then I took the liberty of touching his shoulder, and then I knew he was gone, sir.' His mouth trembled and he reached into his sleeve for a handkerchief and wiped it slowly over his face.

'I'm sorry to distress you, my good man, but can you describe Mr Hobsbawn's appearance that morning?'

Simon pondered. 'Peaceful, sir, like as if he was asleep, I'd say, sir.'

'His eyes were closed?'

'Oh yes, sir. But his mouth was open. But then most gentlemen sleeps with their mouth open when they get to that age, sir. It wasn't untoward, sir, except I couldn't close it, which upset me that much I started to tremble all over, and had to sit down, if you believe me, sir, to collect myself before I could go for help.'

'The bedclothes weren't disordered?'

'No, sir. He lay just as I left him, sir, on his back with his hands folded on his chest. That was how he slept, sir.'

As if, Pobgee thought, he had died the instant he fell asleep. And yet there was the housekeeper's evidence.

'Was Mr Hobsbawn a light sleeper? Did he suffer from insomnia?'

'From — a what sir?'

'Did he have trouble sleeping? Did he have nights when he lay wakeful, unable to sleep?'

Simon looked bewildered. 'I don't know, sir. Not that he ever told me. But I sleep at the top of the house. I wouldn't hear him up there.'

'He never called or rang for you during the night?'

'No, sir. Most considerate he was — he wouldn't have done that, sir, not in the night. Not unless he was ill.'

'Then you must have been surprised when you saw the brandy glass beside the bed in the morning?'

'Brandy glass, sir?'

'The glass in which Mr Hobsbawn took a nip of brandy, to help him get back to sleep.' Simon shook his head slowly. 'You didn't see the glass?'

'Not to notice, sir. But I was that upset, sir, I wouldn't be looking for anything of that sort.'

'No, of course not. Well, thank you, Simon. You may go now. You've been most helpful.'

Simon hesitated. His thoughts moved slowly, but they were not to be deflected. 'All these questions, sir — Mr Hobsbawn — there wasn't nothing untoward, was there?'

'About his death? No, nothing at all. Rest your mind, my good man — your master died naturally and quietly in his sleep, the best way to go.'

For the first time Simon grew agitated. 'Oh no, sir, begging your pardon! You don't understand — not being a Catholic yourself, sir, I dare say — but it isn't the best way at all! A man ought to know he's dying, so that he can make his confession and receive absolution before he goes. My poor master, sir, died without even a priest at hand. It was terrible, terrible! I keep thinking over and over, as how he died without making his peace. Of course, we sent for the priest straight away, before the doctor, even, but it's not the same as having the last rites when you're awake and knowing, sir, and that's the truth of it.'

It took a while to calm the old man enough to send him away, but Pobgee reflected that at least the delay in sending for the physician was now accounted for. It was good to have even one question cleared up. His visit to Manchester so far

205

seemed to have furnished him with nothing but uncertainty.

Probably at no time in his life could James more easily have
absented himself on Sunday morning. In normal circumstances, he would have been expected to attend both masses
in the chapel, unless it was a special festival of the Church,
when the whole family would go to the eleven o'clock service
at the Minster. But since Fanny's death he had been unac-
countable, and his temper had been short, and when he went
into the stables at ten o'clock and ordered his horse to be
tacked-up, no-one thought of reminding him of chapel, or
dreamed of asking him where he was going.

The information that his master was intending to ride out
was conveyed to Durban via the backstairs, but even he,
though naturally concerned, dared do no more than to appear
at his master's elbow and ask quietly if James wished him to
accompany him.

'No,' was all James vouchsafed. 'Give me a leg-up, will
you?'

Durban complied, and though itching to ask where he was
going and when he would be back, was obliged to hold his
tongue. There was something odd going on, however, that
much he did know. His master's mood was different. He
seemed feverish — if Durban had not known better, he would
have said he seemed almost gay. Moreover, James had dressed
himself that morning, sending Durban away, whereas since
Miss Fanny's death, Durban had had to dress him, like a
child; and despite his mourning-bands, he had chosen a
waistcoat which — well, Durban would call it inappropriate,
to say the least. Plain white or buff under a coat with
mourning-bands, Durban would have decreed as proper: red-
and-white striped toilinette, in his view, was not at all the
thing!

It was upsetting, particularly since Durban had hoped over
the last couple of days that his master was beginning to
recover. There had been one or two signs: he had been eating
better, for one thing — and then there had been the business
of the toy soldier. He had not simply given the thing to Benedict, but had spent quite half an hour shewing him how it
worked and watching him play with it; and he had been up to

206

the nursery twice more since to sit on the floor with the little boys and wind the automaton up for them.

Durban had hoped that he was coming out of his black mood at last, but now this seemed like a set-back. He was afraid that it was unbalanced behaviour: to go off on a Sunday morning all alone was definitely odd. And the strange cheerfulness did nothing to allay his fears. In his youth Durban had lived on a large estate: the young master's fiancée had died of smallpox a week before the wedding, and the young master had whistled lightheartedly on the morning he went off to the lake and drowned himself.

With a thoughtful frown, he watched James ride out of the yard, and wished he dared follow him, but of course it was out of the question. He comforted himself with the hope that no real harm could come to him, on a Morland-bred horse, and in an area where every soul knew who he was and what his circumstances were.

James was unaware of the concern he was causing his servant. He rode towards the city, his eyes everywhere, seeing the signs of spring all around him for the first time this year. The breeze was soft from the north-west, promising rain later, but for the moment the sky was a watery blue and scudded with clouds, and the fitful sunshine came and went, touching treetops and fence-posts and bushes as if pointing them out at random for his notice.

The wind brought on its tender back the sound of sheep — the old, familiar music of Yorkshire, more truly the essence of spring here even than the mad chorusing of the birds, so that one heard it almost without noticing, until something drew one's attention to it. They were marking the new lambs up at Ten Thorn Gate, he thought: the bellowing of the ewes as their lambs were separated from them, and the high bleating of the lambs for their mothers, carried to him clearly on the breeze.

The earth was flushed with the bright improbable green of the new grass, scattered here and there with the cheerful hardy flowers that came first in the spring and stayed longest. In Low Field three brood mares lifted their heads from grazing to look with interest as he rode by; and their foals, born in the snows of January and February, kinked up their

207

absurd tails and galloped the length of the fence, snorting like small dragons, and then veered in a bunch and tore away up the slope, bucking in sheer delight at the breeze and the sunlight and the joy of their own swiftness.

James looked as though with new eyes, and wondered what had happened to him. He felt as though he had been groping his way through a dark tunnel, hardly knowing whether he was going forward or back — and suddenly he had seen the shaft of light that was the end of the tunnel, and was running towards it. But what had changed? It was something to do with Angelica, he supposed. Something about her had penetrated the darkness that hemmed him in, had reached him and led him towards the sunlight. He did not know what it was, but he knew he must see her again. He pushed his horse into a trot, and then a canter. He wanted to get to her quickly, in case the magic, whatever it was, dissipated before he could grasp at it; before anyone else had the chance to drag him back into the tunnel. He must avoid speaking to anyone, until he had spoken to her. He felt almost superstitious about it: if he met her again and spoke to her, he would be saved; otherwise he would perish.

He left his horse in the stables at the Bunch of Grapes, and then was obliged to skulk around the back streets until it was time for the service to begin, for he knew that if he arrived early at the church, people would come up to him and talk to him and ask him questions. He wanted to slip in at the last minute so as to avoid notice, and to be able to be by the door to watch everyone come out, so that he did not miss her.

The service seemed interminable — the hymns dragged their feet to the sawing and thumping of the musicians up in the gallery, the prayers and psalms droned monotonously, and the sermon was surely the longest and dullest in ecclesiastical history! And then at last it was over, the procession had made its way back to the Chapter House, and James was free to slip out and take up his position behind a tree where he could watch the people leaving.

But it was not possible for him to escape notice. He was too well known and had been too long absent, and all the goodwill that was directed towards the family in general was at his disposal now. People pitied him for his bereavement, and were surprised and glad to see him; and first one and then another gathered round him to say the needful.

James answered distractedly, hardly listening to the questions, looking always over the shoulders of his tormentors towards the door. Where was she? Why did she not appear? And then it came to him in a flush of panic — she would use the South Door, of course! It was an unwritten custom that while the great folk came out through the West Door and gathered in the open space there to pass the time of day with their friends and neighbours, the lesser folk left by the South Door, and she, in her humility, would think of herself as one of them.

He turned abruptly, thrusting through the people around him, and leaving those who had been talking to him suspended in mid-sentence and thinking, according to their natures, either that it was very rude, or very sad. He hurried around the side of the cathedral to where the crowd was streaming out of the South Door, many-headed, many-coloured, densely-packed, seemingly impenetrable. He could not see her anywhere. His heart sank with despair. He had missed her!

And then a flicker of movement caught his eye; his head jerked round, and in the narrow alley that led through to Low Petergate he saw her. Only a back view, in a plain grey pelisse and a close chip-straw bonnet, but he could not be mistaken — he would know her anywhere. And as if Fate wished to reassure him, the figure paused, and the little white face turned to glance back for an instant, as though she had felt his eyes on her.

He darted across the road, thrusting his way past the Sunday dawdlers, emerged into Low Petergate, looked right and left, and saw the grey pelisse just disappearing down Grape Lane. He ran, and though she was walking briskly, he caught up with her only a few yards down the lane. She turned with a startled look when she heard the running footsteps, and seeing him, stood still, her cheeks crimsoning as her lips made a soundless 'Oh!'

James looked down at her with gratification, and could think of nothing to say. 'Well,' he managed at last. 'Miss Hesketh.'

She looked up at him and then down.

'I thought I'd missed you,' he said next. 'I came out of the West Door, of course, and then suddenly realised ...'

'I thought you hadn't come,' she said, hardly above a whisper. 'I looked, but I didn't see you.'

His heart bounded. She had looked for him! The dear, sweet, gentle thing —! 'I didn't sit in the family pew. I arrived late, and sat at the back, so as not to disturb anyone. Shall we walk on? May I escort you home?'

She murmured something which was plainly not a refusal, and he took his place at her side as they walked on down Grape Lane.

'Your father didn't come with you this morning. I hope he is not worse?'

'Oh — no — thank you, sir. He's mending, I believe, but wants rest more than anything.' James was delighted with the motherly way this child spoke of her parent's health. 'I told him he should stop in bed while he has the chance.'

'Your father's shop is quite new, isn't it?' James asked next. 'I don't recollect seeing it before.'

'We've been here six months,' she said. 'We came from Sheffield. Father had a shop there, but after my mother died, he didn't like it any more. He wanted to move. I think everything reminded him of her.'

'Your mother is dead? I'm so sorry.'

She looked up at him frankly. 'It's all right. I don't mind. It was a long time ago — more than a year now. She'd been ill for a long time, so I suppose it was a kind release for her. I don't really remember her being well, to say the truth. I've been keeping house and everything for Father since I was about twelve.'

'And how old are you now?'

'Eighteen.'

'So much? I would have thought you younger.'

'Would you? I'm quite grown-up, really,' she said. There was not the least coquetry about her. She received his attention like a child, without looking for hidden meanings or overtones, looking at him with the simplicity of one who had no image of herself, no awareness of her beauty, no experience of femininity. James was enchanted.

'I suppose you are,' he said.

'Oh, yes, sir. My mother was married when she was two years younger than me. Lots of girls are. And I keep house for Father and help in the shop and make all our clothes, which is the same as being married, really, isn't it?'

'Yes — in many ways, yes.' They turned into Back Swinegate. this was familiar territory to him. How often had he walked this way, from the Bunch of Grapes where he left his horse to the Maccabbees Club on the corner of Little Stonegate! His feet remembered, carried him automatically, but the memory seemed today strangely distant and irrelevant. The seeking of oblivion in brandy seemed, today, the oddest thing to do. In these narrow back lanes the sunlight was an oblique thing, but in the gap between the roofs overhead was the blue and breezy sky, and there seemed nothing in the world to escape from.

'Do you have any brothers or sisters?' he asked, wanting to keep her talking, to know everything about her.

'Only one brother — well, half-brother really. Father was married before, you see. He's in the Rifles,' she added impressively. 'He's in Flanders now with the Duke of Wellington, fighting against Bonaparte. He was in the Peninsula, too. We haven't seen him for a long time.'

At the corner of Back Swinegate and Little Stonegate a very narrow and dark alley opened up, and she turned into it automatically. He turned with her, finding the space between the blank walls so narrow that he had to walk very close to her, so that their arms brushed against each other. She did not seem to notice.

'You must be very proud of him. And you have no sisters?'

'Not now. Mother had another baby after me, but it died. It was that made her so poorly, I think. At any rate, she never had another, and stayed in bed more and more.'

He was pierced with the sense of personal tragedy simply and bravely born. 'My daughter died in childbirth,' he said suddenly, and she stopped and looked at him.

'Yes, I know. I'm so sorry,' she said, and laid an artless hand on his wrist. 'It must have been awful for you.'

Without thinking, he placed his hand over hers. 'Thank you,' he said. He met her eyes, and saw in their unclouded depths a completely unselfconscious sympathy. Then two very dirty small children shot into the alley shrieking at the tops of their voices in some chasing game, and they were forced to flatten themselves against the wall to let the urchins past. Angelica laughed and called after them, and then turned to walk on as though nothing had happened.

The end of the alley was just ahead, and James, knowing it debouched into Davygate opposite the end of New Street, knew also that his moments of delightful converse were coming to an end.

'Do you ever go out of the house, apart from to church?' he asked abruptly.

'Sometimes,' she said. She had a child's way of answering questions without wondering why they were asked. 'Father likes me to get fresh air when I can. When we lived in Sheffield, I used to go walking on the moors, or by the river. I liked the moors best, though. I miss them, now we live in York.'

'And where do you walk here?'

'On Clifton Ings, mostly,' she said. 'There's plenty of space there, and sometimes when the wind's in the right quarter, you can smell the moors. It's the next best thing.' Her eyes were wistful, remembering, and there and then James swore that somehow or other he would take her to walk on the moors before many days had passed.

'Perhaps I shall see you there. When do you walk there again?'

'I don't know,' she said. 'Happen tomorrow. Father likes me to get out in the afternoon, after I've cooked him his dinner, if the weather's fine. But sometimes the shop's too busy, and I can't be spared.'

Across Davygate, into New Street, and here they were, all too soon, at the alley that ran down beside the closed and shuttered shop. She turned to him and smiled up into his face. 'Thank you for walking with me,' she said. 'It was right kind of you to take the trouble.'

'It was no trouble. It was my pleasure,' James said, with more truth than was usually in those phrases. He continued to look down at her, and she hesitated, wondering if there were anything more she ought to say, and then, with a shy little bob of the head she left him, and disappeared down the alley. James turned away too, and began walking back the way he came, as the quickest way back to the Grapes, where his horse waited for him. He walked briskly, head up, eyes distant, and mouth relaxed almost to smiling as he went over every stored image of her in his mind, and planned busily ahead for all manner of delightful outings and occasions to come.

When he arrived back at Morland Place, Durban was lurking in the yard waiting for him with an anxiety which only increased when he saw his master's euphoria. He thought at first that he had been to the Maccabbees, as in sorrowful days of yore, but a further glance told him that ardent spirits were not the cause.

The groom took Victor's head, and the air about him was stiff with unasked questions as James swung to the ground and began to walk away. Durban stared after him despairingly; James paused and looked back, meeting his man's eyes, and for an instant the urgency in them penetrated his delightfully cloudy thoughts so that he felt vaguely that there was something he ought to have said or done, something that was expected of him.

'Sir?' Durban murmured, gently prompting.

James frowned an instant in thought. 'Oh, yes — Victor's pecking slightly on the off-fore. I think he may have a loose shoe. Take a look at it, will you?'

'Yes, sir,' Durban said, watching baffled as his master walked away towards the house, tapping his boot with his whipstock in a maddeningly rhythmical way.

Once in the house, James realised that the one thing he wanted above all others was not to talk to anyone, and as Ottershaw came forward to relieve him of his hat and gloves, his eyes alight with the desire for communication, James took refuge in a scowl and bolted up the stairs and to his bedchamber. They would hardly follow him here, he thought.

Having reached sanctuary, he pulled off his boots, shrugged out of his coat, and flung himself down full-length on the bed. Staring up at the canopy, his arms under his head, he thought about her again, saw her before him, slender

213

as a reed, and as pliant, the cream-and-rose complexion, the soft, artless mouth, the shy eyes. How perfect she was, unspoilt, unsullied! *Chaste* — the word came into his head — but without the chilly overtones that word sometimes bore: chaste as a young animal is, knowing nothing of the world and its possibilities.

He wanted to give her things — flowers and jewels and horses — gold and silver, ivory and apes and peacocks. He wanted to shew her things, all the beauties of his world, and tell her things, speak poetry to her, and play her music. A fragment of a poem was in his mind:

Behold that bright unsullied smile,
And wisdom speaking in her mien:
Yet — she so artless all the while,
So little studious to be seen —
We naught but instant gladness know,
Nor think to whom the gift we owe.

Yes, there was wisdom in her as well as beauty — a natural wisdom. He wanted to take her from that dark shop and place her in her proper setting like a jewel; to give her all she deserved. She should not cook her father's meals and work in his shop: she would become the gowns and carriages of a fine lady better than most he knew. She should have wealth, and rank, and the power that came with it. She should run a great house, and preside over a great table, and ride beautiful horses through the green spaces of her own estate.

Abruptly he rolled over and stretched towards the bedside table on his side of the bed, pulled open the drawer, reached into it for something around which his fingers closed with the blind intimacy of custom. Rolling back, he held it up above him on a level with his eyes. From within the oval silver frame, Fanny's face looked back at him: a miniature of her he had painted himself when she was eighteen — and a hard time he had had of it, to get her to sit long enough. Not that she was unwilling to have her likeness taken — it pleased her vanity to be painted — but because she always had so many other things she wanted to be doing.

Painted on ivory, with the miniaturist's delicacy: a white

214

face, delicately tinted with rose, a little pointed face like a fox-kitten, surmounted by a halo of dark curls, like a blurred nimbus; a long white neck, the base of the throat encircled by a gold chain on which a single sapphire was suspended — a drop of Heaven's blue captured for her delight. Yes, she should have sapphires — they would become her beauty, and her beauty deserved them! Her beauty and her modesty. He gazed at the portrait, and the portrait gazed back, faintly smiling, enigmatical, keeping its secrets ...

It was Father Aislaby who disturbed him at last. James felt that he might have known no-one else would dare!

'Yes, what is it?' he asked, not troubling to conceal his irritability, for certainly the chaplain would not care about it.

'It's Benedict — he's very upset.'

'Oh?' James's voice dripped indifference. 'Correct me if I'm wrong, but I was under the impression I employed three nursery-maids and a governess to take care of upset children.'

Aislaby merely watched him with those level, unimpressed eyes. 'It's gone rather too far for the maids. And it was Miss Rosedale who thought the matter should be referred to you. The boy's quite beside himself, and seems to think you'll be angry with him, and what with one thing and another, Miss Rosedale feels you ought to reassure him, unless you want a repetition of the nightmare episode. For myself, I'd as lief avoid it.'

'Why on earth should I be angry with him?'

Aislaby gave a grim smile. 'Unlikely as it seems to any of us that you could feel any emotion towards him as strong as anger, the child is quite convinced of it. It seems he has broken the automaton you gave him.'

James sat up. 'Broken it?'

Aislaby frowned. 'It's rather odd, really. Circumstances suggest that he broke it deliberately — indeed, it's hard to see it any other way. He smashed it beyond repair by hitting it repeatedly with the poker from the day-nursery fireplace; and yet now it's spoiled he's heartbroken. I know of my own observation that he valued it quite absurdly, the more so because you gave it to him; and why he should have destroyed it is beyond any of us to discover. But he did so, and now he is not only grieving, but afraid. He says he doesn't want to go to

215

bed — grew quite hysterical about it. I suppose he must think you will send him to bed as a punishment.'

James stared, as though trying to assemble the facts into some kind of sense. Aislaby grew impatient.

'So will you come, James, and soothe the boy? I really think you must.'

'Smashed, you say? Beyond repair?'

'Yes,' said Aislaby. 'Quite destroyed.'

James smiled slowly. 'Oh, it doesn't matter — it doesn't matter in the least,' he said with private satisfaction. 'I can always go back to the shop and get another one.'

CHAPTER NINE

Charles-Auguste de Brouilly, Duc de Veslne-d'Estienne, entered the breakfast-parlour of the house in the Rue Ducale to find Héloïse alone there, sitting in the window-seat, staring blankly out of the window. Her hands were folded in her lap over what appeared to be a letter, and her dark face was quite plain with unhappiness.

'*Chère amie*, what is the matter?' Charles cried at once, hastening over to her, his hands outstretched in an unconscious gesture of wanting to enfold her in his arms and keep all troubles from her.

Héloïse was startled from her reverie, and looked so surprised to see him that he felt obliged to apologise. 'The butler told me you were alone, and I took the liberty of assuring him that you would see me, and that there was no need to announce me.'

Héloïse forced herself to concentrate on his words. 'Yes — yes of course. You were quite right. I am glad to see you, Charles. Won't you sit down?'

She gestured towards a chair, but he sat down beside her on the window-seat, saying, 'Something has happened to distress you, I can see. Won't you tell me what it is? Perhaps I can help. You know that I would give my life to serve you.'

'Yes, I know. Thank you, dear Charles. But I'm afraid no-one can help,' she said sadly, and seeing the expression on his face, was forced to smile a little. 'Oh, don't be alarmed! It is nothing that threatens my life, I assure you. I — I have had a letter, that's all.'

'I hope it does not contain bad news?'

'No, not at all. Everything is just as I expected.' She began the sentence cheerfully enough, for his sake, but her voice wavered treacherously towards the end, and she bit her lip and turned her head away from him while she regained control.

Charles continued to look at her thoughtfully, and after a moment he said, 'Nevertheless, you are unhappy, and it distresses me more than I can say. Perhaps you do not want to talk about it — if that is so, then I shall respect your wishes and say no more. But you know I am your friend, and have the warmest concern for your welfare and happiness. If you can tell me what is the matter, I beg that you will. Not knowing the cause only increases my anxiety.'

She turned her head back and met his eyes. 'Oh, Charles,' she said. He regarded her steadily, his eyes full of an uncomplicated and warm sympathy, and she longed to tell him everything and be comforted. Here was one person in the world with whom her concerns came first — who wished to make it his business to see that she was happy. It would be a luxury indeed to take advantage of that. She, who had never had a mother, had always been the comforter rather than the comforted. It was she who had cared, worried, loved, given thought, taken trouble; from her adoring father to her adored children, her happiness had been to see that they were happy.

He smiled and pressed her hand. '*Oh, Charles* is well enough,' he said, 'but a little more matter would help us along. Your letter is from home — from Morland Place?'

'Yes,' she said. 'From Miss Rosedale, Sophie's governess — former governess, I suppose I must say now.' She looked down at the letter, crushed under their hands. 'She is a good correspondent. She tells me all the small details that interest me.'

'But? There is a *but*, is there not?'

Héloïse yielded a little more. 'She cannot tell me what I want to hear, because it is not so.'

Charles felt the quality of her resistance and of her longing. Very carefully he said, 'It is the same thing that has been troubling you since I first met you up on the ramparts, is it not? The reason that you are here alone — without your husband?'

She nodded, and at the word 'husband' her eyes began to fill with tears, and her lip trembled. 'He is — I cannot — it would be —' Trying to speak undid her. She gasped, snatched for her handkerchief, and the next moment was in floods of tears. Charles gathered her into his arms and gave her the shoulder of his coat to cry into, and was wise enough to keep very still, merely holding her until the worst was over. There was more grief here than he had supposed, he thought, as the shoulder of his coat soaked through. She must have been concealing it, perhaps even from herself, for a long time.

As the sobs slowed and she began to recover, she would have pulled away, suddenly feeling guilty and embarrassed. But he resisted the movement and said calmly, 'No, don't — it is so comfortable.' She relaxed again, and when she was quiet, she remained as she was for some time, her cheek against his shoulder, her wet handkerchief screwed into a ball in her clenched fingers.

'Tell me, then,' he said gently.

'It is hard,' she said. 'James is — a difficult man. I don't understand why. Perhaps it is being an artist — there must be some payment for the great gift. He sees things differently from us — but he hurts himself. Always he hurts himself.'

'He hurts you,' Charles suggested.

'Because I love him — not intentionally.' She paused. That was not entirely true, she thought. Sometimes he did hurt her intentionally. 'It isn't that he doesn't love me,' she explained, mostly to herself. 'It is — I suppose a kind of testing.'

'To see if you love him enough?'

'Yes. I suppose — yes.' The warmth of Charles's arms and the comfort of resting against his shoulder had eased her so much that his words slipped into the train of her thoughts as though they were her own. She felt at that moment no separation between them.

'He was lonely as a child — the middle one of the family, always the one left out. Sometimes I imagine him as a little boy, playing alone ... His mother described him to me — sitting under a tree for hours together with two stones and a dead leaf, making some kind of story for himself — some separate world where he belonged. It makes me so sad — I want to go back in time and take that child in my arms and make things right for him. And still he feels he does not belong. Still he looks for love, and can't seem to find it.'

'But he has you — you love him.'

'Yes. Yes, I do, and he knows it, and sometimes it makes him happy. But even his happiness has a quality of —' She paused, seeking for words. 'You know how sometimes on a beautiful day in spring the sunshine and the flowers make you want to cry?'

'Yes, I know.'

'I love him, and I know that he loves me, but lately — lately it isn't enough. I can't reach him, and it —' Another pause. 'I feel as though I'm shrivelling up, like a plant that lacks water.'

'Lately?' he prompted gently.

'Since Fanny died. No, before then, really. There was always Fanny, and it used to make me angry, because he never saw Fanny as she really was: not the real flesh-and-blood Fanny, but something he'd made in his mind of her. I grew to love her at the end. She had many good qualities, but how can a high-spirited girl with a great deal of imagination — for she had that, you know — how can she grow up normal and good when all the time she is being made into a story by the person closest to her? He was turning her into a monster. But her own good sense came to her rescue in the end. She was learning to govern herself, and I came to admire her very much, and to love her. Her death was terrible, terrible.'

She pulled away from him and unscrewed her handkerchief, only to find it quite unserviceable. He pulled out his own and she took it without comment and blew her nose, and then resumed, hardly noticing, except vaguely and gladly.

'It was such a tragedy, when she was beginning to be a good and useful woman. And now James — of course he grieves for her, that's natural, and as it should be. But it's more than that. He is making it into a punishment for himself. He is creating a world where nothing exists except Fanny's death, and living in it, and if he once decides that he belongs there, he will never come back. Oh, I know I am not making sense —'

'Yes you are. I understand what you're saying.'

She looked at him, chewing her lip. 'But there's Sophie — dear Sophie — and the boys, and me. Why don't we matter to him? Why can't he turn to us for comfort? If I were unhappy, I should turn to him. And though I've grown used in the past

220

to his shutting himself away when he's unhappy, now I find I can't bear it any more. I need to know that I mean something to him, that I'm important in his life. I'm so afraid —' Her voice sank a little. 'I'm so afraid that I shall stop loving him.'

She stopped, and did not seem to want to go on. He was silent for a while, afraid to say anything, afraid to say nothing. She had confided in him far more than she could ever have intended to, and he must be careful not to make her feel that she had been wrong to do so. Her loyalty, he knew, was fierce, and if she came to feel she had betrayed a trust in speaking to him like this, he would lose even the little of her that he had.

At last he said, 'I wish I could tell you what to do; but I don't believe there is anything you can do. There are souls who seem all the time to punish themselves, to make unhappiness for themselves when none exists. Perhaps he is one of them.'

'Yes,' she said.

'But you must remember that you have other responsibilities, too — not least to yourself. You must not let his unhappiness shape your life. If you cannot alter it —'

She looked at him. 'What are you counselling? That I should leave him in the darkness — even if it is of his own making?'

'I cannot counsel you. I would not — you are so much wiser than I.'

'Charles, I could not abandon him. Even if he does not know I am there, I must *be* there. But —' She hesitated.

'It is not enough for you,' he offered. 'You need to receive as well as give love — and it's right and natural that you should. Perhaps,' he continued cautiously, feeling his way with the words as he went, 'perhaps you should consider what course would produce the greatest good to the greatest number of people. So many depend on you, and on your happiness. If you give all your care to one person, who cannot benefit from it, others may suffer.'

'Yes,' she said, but she sounded hopeless. It was not what he had wanted — he had hoped to strengthen her a little. He lifted her hand to his lips and kissed it.

'*Chère amie*, so many people love you. Let them give you

221

that love — let it nourish you.'

'Oh, Charles,' she said, looking at him sadly; and then she withdrew her hand. 'Thank you for being so kind — for letting me talk to you.'

'It was nothing — I would do far, far more for you.'

'I know. I am grateful. But I must find my own way.'

'Of course — as long as you know that you are not alone.'

Rosamund and Sophie were at that moment walking in the Park, with Moss accompanying them to preserve the decencies, or, as Rosamund put it, 'to make sure we don't rub off and get up a lark'. The weather had turned cool and cloudy, but there was enough breeze to keep off the rain, and in their pelisses and with their hands tucked into their muffs, the girls were quite comfortable.

They were not suffered to remain long alone. There were officers in plenty also taking their exercise at that hour, who paused to touch their hats and exchange a polite word or two. Rosamund had already established a court in Brussels: some paying her attention because she was handsome and a good match, others because she was cheerful and sensible and encouraged them to talk about themselves and their heroic deeds. These latter tended to call her a *trump card* or a *right 'un*, and were by far the most vociferous of her attendants. She plainly enjoyed their company more than that of the languid, elegant creatures who merely made their leg, murmured a few politenesses, and watched her and the opposition from under lowered eyelids.

Moss, under strict instructions from Docwra, who took Rosamund's situation even more seriously than did Lucy, was of the opinion that there was safety in numbers, and the larger the group of young men of good family hanging around her young lady, the better she liked it. She had already determined that the two most serious suitors were Captain Philip Tantony of the 95th Rifles and Lieutenant Sir John Wilmot of the 52nd — the former because he was in love with Lady Rosamund, and the latter ecause he had been told by his formidable mother to find himself a bride as soon as possible. To her young lady's credit, Moss thought with mingled pleasure and disappointment, she encouraged neither to believe his suit preferred, treating them both more like younger brothers than potential lovers.

Moss was also, of course, keeping her eye on Miss Sophie, though she had nothing to worry about as far as Miss's behaviour went. Miss Sophie was well liked, and Lady Rosamund's court was glad enough to talk to her when their idol was not disposed to notice them, but without birth, beauty or fortune, she could hardly hope to attract many suitors. There was Major Larosse, of course — he was the most faithful of the faithful, being sure to appear the instant Miss set foot in the Park or the ballroom or the salon, and to remain at her side for as long as he could. But Moss shook her head privately over him, and could not bring herself to think of him as a serious suitor: he was not the least bit lover-like, a foreigner, and too old for her besides.

He had been the first to touch his hat to the young ladies this afternoon, and Sophie had greeted him with a look and a blush which it was fortunate Moss didn't see. He was now walking at her side, an expression of amusement on his face, as he listened to the chatter of Wilmot, Lantrey and Lieutenant Frank Webster as they tried to impress Rosamund and edge Tantony out from the favoured place at her side — which in any case he was wasting, since he hardly ever spoke a word, and was too shy even to look at her very often.

Lantrey was reliving the battle of Bussaco, which had been his first as a newly-commissioned officer, and was therefore the best remembered.

'If you can imagine, Lady Rosamund, there was the sun blazing down, and the chaussée winding up the hill towards the convent, and there were old Ney's two divisions toiling upwards through the gorse and the heather, and the Light Bobs and the Portuguese contesting every inch of the way —'

'And Old Hookey, ma'am,' Wilmot added, carried away by the story, 'standing on the ridge watching through his telescope as cool as an ice-house pomegranate, just as if the bullets weren't cuttin' up the turf all around him.'

'But you never saw the Beau flinch, whatever the Frogs threw at him,' Webster joined in admiringly. 'He's a complete hand! He don't care about gunfire, any more than his horse does. You never saw such a beast, ma'am, for —'

'— and there was General Craufurd' Lantrey resumed loudly, glaring at his brother officers, and knowing that once Lady Rosamund's attention was captured by a horse, his story would be lost, '—standing a bit to the left, watching and waiting for the moment to be right. For you see, unknown to Monseer Frog, he had eighteen hundred of us — the 52nd and the 43rd — drawn up in the sunken lane, out of sight, waiting for 'em. And then, just as the French drums started to beat the final charge, and the French officers were capering up and down like madmen, waving their hats on their swords and shrieking to their men to capture our guns —'

'— then Craufurd turns to us,' Wilmot leapt heedlessly on the narrative, his eyes shining with excitement, 'and he shouts out, so loud you could hear him right through the din, he shouts, "Now, 52nd, revenge the death of Sir John Moore!" —'

'So out we charged with a roar like a torrent,' Lantrey cried, 'and poured such fire down on 'em that in a few minutes the whole lot of 'em were thrown back to the foot of the hill! You never saw such a complete thing, ma'am! And the look of astonishment on their faces as we came out! And ten thousand Frogs driven back by only eighteen hundred of ours —!'

'Six thousand,' Larosse said quietly. Lantrey stopped short, and all eyes turned on him, Sophie's and Rosamund's questioningly, Lantrey's resentfully. He smiled. 'It is such a good story, Ensign, that there is no need to make it better by exaggeration. But it was a splendid charge.'

'And a famous victory,' Tantony said, looking across at him. 'Our side was outnumbered two to one, and more than half our force were Portuguese fighting their first battle.'

Larosse bowed to him. 'I wish to take nothing from the glory — especially not from the courage and spirit of the 95th, Captain.'

Rosamund looked at her quiet suitor with new respect. 'Were you at Bussaco, Captain Tantony?'

Tantony blushed and bowed his head, quite overcome, and Webster had to answer for him. 'He was indeed, ma'am — was wounded, too, but held his ground like a right 'un, and was commended in the warmest terms in dispatches.'

Wilmot looked as though he thought his friend need not lay it on quite so thick, but Webster was enjoying Tantony's confusion, and continued. 'And afterwards the 95th kept the French off us for three days while we organised the evacuation of Coimbra and marched off for Lisbon. Our retreat wouldn't have been so orderly if it hadn't been for them, I can assure you. And then they had to stay between us and the French all the way to Torres Vedras — frightful job! Ain't that so, Tantony?'

'That was the hardest part,' Tantony admitted. He looked about him, but everyone — including Rosamund — seemed to be waiting for him to speak, so he went on, 'Our men couldn't understand why we were retreating after such a victory — no use trying to explain advanced military theory to *them* — and the Portuguese were convinced we were abandoning them, and the French grew bolder every day, thinking we were in flight and that they were going to capture Lisbon at last.'

'And of course stores were running short by then,' Wilmot reflected grimly, forgetting for a moment to be charming to his Object. 'It'd been a long campaign.'

'Our cheerful rosy-cheeked lads were transformed to scarecrows,' Tantony remembered. 'The only way I could get 'em along sometimes was by getting 'em to talk about food. It was a sort of game we played. They'd each imagine what they'd like best to be eating, and describe it to the rest of us.'

Absorbed in the memory, he had forgotten to be shy, and his voice gained strength and resolution with each syllable. 'There was one youngster, Peel his name was, who had such a way with words! His description of his mother's plum dumpling kept us going for almost an hour one rainy night. I can still hear his voice, coming out of the darkness, describing the way the raisins burst in the hot duff and went black and sticky — made our mouths water. And all to the background of the squelch-squelch of our feet in the mud, and the pattering of the rain on the leaves ...' He paused, and no-one broke the silence. His eyes were far away. 'He promised that when the war was over, he'd get his mother to make the biggest plum-pudding in the world, and invite us all to his home to share it.'

'Well, that's something to look forward to, at any rate,' Lantrey said.

Tantony shook his head. 'He didn't make it. He was shot in the stomach the following night by one of the French advance-guard.'

'Oh, mercy me,' Lantrey said, screwing up his face in genuine pain.

Tantony nodded grimly. 'It's a bad way to go. He died in my arms — eventually.'

There was a reflective silence which no-one liked to break, and Larosse saw that all four young soldiers had forgotten the ladies for the moment. Sophie was looking grave at the story, but Rosamund was regarding Tantony with a thoughtful interest which made Larosse smile inwardly. He had been witness from the first to her careless use of her suitor, and could now read her expression quite easily. She had suddenly seen him as a real person, and not a contemptible one, either.

A moment later he was proved right when Rosamund said, 'I find walking against this wind surprisingly tiring. Captain Tantony, may I make use of your arm for a short way?'

Tantony was shocked out of his reverie, reddened, offered his arm with a stammered muddle of thanks and deference, and the three line officers looked suitably chagrined. Tantony was one of those very English men, Larosse thought, who was perfectly sensible until his heart was captured by some pretty face, and then he went all to pieces — although he had to admit that Tantony's choice of Rosmaund was to his credit. She would bring him out of his shell, if anyone could, by talking to him sensibly, like a man, and not simpering or playing on her femininity.

Glad of the excuse, Larosse now offered his arm to Sophie, and she took it happily.

'Were you there, too?' she asked him. 'I believe you said you were in the Peninsula?'

'Yes, I was there,' Larosse said with grim amusement, 'but on the other side, of course, mademoiselle.' The English officers looked a little embarrassed; but he continued fluently, 'We were the pursuing army of Captain Tantony's story. Of course our General Masséna knew perfectly well what Wellington was about — winter was upon us, and he meant to sit it out comfortably in Lisbon, supplied from the sea by the British navy, while we had only the choice of staying where we were and starving, or marching back across the mountains through midwinter.'

'I believe the Beau thought you would retreat,' Tantony said. 'Why didn't you?'

Larosse shrugged. 'I was not in Masséna's confidence — nor the Emperor's. But having followed so far, it would have been tame to go away with nothing accomplished. If we stayed, there was always the chance Wellington might attack us, or make a mistake. And again, if you remember, that was the winter your King went mad, and the Prince of Wales became Regent, and it was hoped that a change of government would follow, which would recall your army.' He smiled at the surprised faces. 'Oh yes, we knew all about it. Nothing went on in England that Napoleon did not know about within days.'

'That's what Mama's always saying,' Rosamund said vigorously. 'She says Boney's spies are everywhere, and that we'd do well to apply to Paris for the London news — we'd get it quicker that way.'

Larosse laughed. 'Your mother, Lady Rosamund, is an original!'

Sophie was still thinking of that winter of 1810, and the starving of the French army, which she remembered having heard about at the time as distant news, with as much reality to her as a fairy-story. But now here was a man who had actually been there! It had really happened! 'It must have been dreadful,' she said, and Larosse turned at once to the sound of her voice. 'What did you find to eat? Did you really starve?'

Larosse shook his head, and smiled, to make light of it. 'God knows how we survived. It was a miracle on a par with the loaves and fishes! No-one but Masséna could have kept us there for three months, where there had been scant food for a month. We ate grass, I believe, and tree-bark and roots. I am not sure we didn't eat boulders.' The others laughed, and he turned the conversation to them. 'But equally, I might ask why Wellington did not attack us — at least when we were weak with hunger he might have felt sure of a victory.'

Tantony answered. 'He is always careful of his army. That's being a — a sort of employee, if you like, of the people, rather than a dictator. He did say once that winter, when Craufurd suggested we sortie, that although he was sure we could win, it would cost thousands of lives, and since ours was the last army England had left, he would be sure to take great care of it. It's one of the reasons the men like to serve him — they know he will never throw their lives away lightly.'

'He is indeed very different from the Emperor,' Larosse said neutrally. 'But then the whole philosophy of war is different between the two armies. The French are good soldiers — the best in the world, perhaps —'

'Oh, here, no, I say!' Webster protested.

'We can't allow that, you know,' Wilmot said sternly.

'Well, but look — they are sturdy, active, handy — tireless on the march, and fierce in battle. Cheerful, adaptable — able to make themselves comfortable in any terrain —'

'By plunder, you mean,' Wilmot said. 'We saw plenty of that in the Peninsula. The Beau hanged our men if he caught 'em plundering.'

'Yes, of course, by plundering,' Larosse said, unbashed. 'To the French soldier it is part of the art and science of soldiering — and therein lies your difference: they regard war as something glorious in its own right. They are the children,' he added sadly, 'of the Revolution. To them force is the natural way to assert right, and plunder and murder and torture are the inevitable lot of the conquered.'

'By God, yes!' said Webster fiercely. 'Some of the things we saw as we marched through —'

A warning cough from Moss behind them reminded him that this was not a topic to be pursued before the young ladies, and he stopped abruptly.

'I do not condone it,' Larosse concluded. 'I merely offer you an explanation.'

'Yes, but look here, you're French yourself,' Lantrey began, causing an intake of breath at his gaucherie.

'He is our ally,' Tantony said firmly, looking at Lantrey in a way that made the Ensign discover something on his cuff that required very urgently to be brushed off.

'*Bien sûr, mes braves,*' Larosse said cheerfully and provo-

228

catively. 'I am one of you now; and I place my experience at your disposal. It will be as well for all my new friends to be under no illusion about the kind of army we will have to face. I know it is fashionable to deride the Emperor and his troops, and to proclaim how easy it will be to beat them. But you who fought in the Peninsula at least know how the French soldier fights. And I can tell you something of how Napoleon leads. Between us we may educate the Johnny Raws, as you call them, *hein?*'

There was a brief silence, and then Wilmot cried, 'I say, ain't that Colborne over there — our colonel, you know! Must go and pay our respects — if you'll forgive us, Lady Rosamund, Miss Morland? So kind! Delightful! Servant, ladies!'

The three line officers made their escape, leaving Tantony and Larosse with Rosamund and Sophie. Tantony looked across at the older man.

'You shouldn't, you know,' he said quietly. 'Lantrey's a fool, but a harmless one.'

'No fool is harmless,' Larosse said. 'But you are right — I shouldn't. Will you forgive me, mademoiselle?' He bent over Sophie's hand, and then smiled at Rosamund. 'I have driven away your suitors — I am very sorry. It is that sometimes I cannot bear to hear so much nonsense talked.'

'I don't mind. I don't suffer fools gladly, either,' Rosamund said stoutly.

'Do you think that Napoleon will beat us?' Sophie asked abruptly. She could feel against the bare skin of her neck Moss's restlessness at the question, but ignored it. Larosse, at least, would never treat her like a child.

He regarded her steadily. 'I think Wellington is the better general; but Napoleon is a magician. He is a failing magician, but his magic may work one more time.'

'But what does that mean?'

The question was from Rosamund, impatiently, but his answer was still directed towards Sophie. 'All I can say for sure is that when I look into the future, I cannot imagine Wellington being finally beaten, for if he loses one battle, he will retrench for the next; and even if he falls, another general will come and take his place. But the Emperor must lose at last, because he is one man, and he has only one death to give.

229

He fights for himself, the Allies for a cause.'

'We must win, then, in the end?' Sophie said.

'All of us, yes; but individually – who knows?' He smiled suddenly, and pressed her hand against his ribs. 'So we must enjoy the sunshine while it lasts — like a cat on a window-ledge — and not think about the gathering clouds. *Cher Philippe,*' he turned to Tantony, 'did I not hear that there were ices at the Pavilion today?'

Tantony took his cue. 'I think you may have — there was a rumour abroad.'

'Could it have been — *strawberry* ices?'

'Ah, now that may just have been air-mongering. Strawberry, in April?'

'It's almost May,' Rosamund pointed out.

'And strawberry ices I would certainly die for,' Larosse said genially, 'so perhaps we should walk that way and see if it is true. Mesdemoiselles, will you entrust yourselves to the venture?'

'With the greatest pleasure,' Rosamund said, catching Sophie's eye. The two young women smiled at each other with, for once, equal pleasure in the company. Tantony, Rosamund had discovered, was a different person once he got over his shyness, and was very far from being the ninny she had taken him for. She turned her smile approvingly on him, and this time he was able to withstand the shock almost without flinching, and with no more than the faintest blush.

The great Catalani had arrived, and every Brussels hostess was longing to boast of her. Few, however, could afford her fees. The Duchess of Richmond had engaged her, and the Duke of Wellington was to hold a dinner, concert and ball for the King of the Netherlands, with Catalani heading the bill; while Lady Tewkesbury did her best by claiming to have intended to hold a musical party, only to discover that the Duke had fixed on the self and same date, which meant of course that hers had to be cancelled.

'That woman!' Lucy said contemptuously to Roberta at the Bickersteths' ball.

'I shouldn't worry. Everyone sees through her,' Roberta said.

'Yes, but they go on inviting her. It only encourages pretension.'

'She invites herself. But you were talking about Catalani. Are you going to engage her?'

'Well, the dukes, duchesses and countesses have had their say, so it comes down to me, I suppose. Danby likes the idea, but I can't help thinking whatever we do will seem very small beer after the Duke's royal evening.'

'Don't compete, then,' Roberta said. 'Have something very select and intimate instead.'

'Invite just a few people, and drive the others wild with jealousy,' said Peter Firth, who had been listening to the conversation.

Lucy laughed. 'Ah, yes! Wouldn't it be delightful so to offend all the great hostesses that I never have to speak to them again?'

'You know I didn't mean that,' Roberta said. 'All I meant was not to hold a grand formal concert like the Duke's.'

'Yes, I have you now. The musical items at one end of the great drawing-room, and people gathering to hear them as they please; a neat, tight supper; and then allow the young people to press for a little dancing, quite impromptu, with a few tables for whist or hazard to keep the chaperones amused.' She nodded. 'I think it might do very well — stylish, you know, and different.'

'Much more in the Duke's taste, at least,' said Firth. 'He likes everything plain and spare.'

'So it shall be, then. A string quartet and Catalani's two songs, and something else — a Mozart violin concerto, perhaps.'

'Young Harry Pyne sings very well,' Roberta said. 'You might ask him to sing something, and have Rosamund accompany him on the piano.'

'And finish with some glee-singing, no doubt? That would be different! Lady Tewkesbury would be green with envy to have missed it all,' Firth laughed.

'But I'm serious! He sings well enough for the opera — I've heard him in London. And Rosamund —'

'Would play well if she troubled to practise,' Lucy said. 'If it were Ponsonby, now, or Burnett — but Harry Pyne is not a match.'

231

'Do you think Ponsonby may offer?' Firth asked. 'He and Pyne both seem more interested in you.'

'Pho! Don't talk nonsense! But Ponsonby has to marry sooner or later — he knows that — and Rosamund is of his rank, and well dowered. It's the worst of these independent young peers: if Ponsonby's mother had still been alive, I should have had a visit from her long before now.'

They watched the dancers circling for a moment.

'Who's that she's dancing with now?' Firth asked, seeing Rosamund's distinctive head through a gap in the throng.

'Tantony,' Lucy said shortly.

'Ah, yes. He's quite come out of his shell lately, hasn't he? I met him in the street yesterday, and he was almost chatty.'

'Rosamund seems to favour him, doesn't she?' Roberta said tentatively.

'It does no harm,' Lucy answered the implied question. 'He's a well-conducted young man, and he knows there's no question of his marrying her.'

The music ended, and the sets broke up; everyone was on the move, and the level of the talk in the ballroom rose accordingly. Lucy glanced sideways at Roberta from under her eyelids, and then gestured her head towards an alcove a little way off, where Bobbie had sat out the last dance with Barbarina, chatting comfortably. 'That is something a little more surprising. What do you say to that preference, Rob?'

'He feels sorry for her — and indeed so do I, poor little thing,' Roberta said defensively. 'He has such a kind heart, and of course her being Marcus's sister — I dare say she is almost like a sister to him.'

'I think you're being roasted, love,' Firth said, and Roberta blushed a little.

'Very well — but it's true. I don't think Bobbie has any serious thoughts about anyone yet. Why, only last week it was Lady Georgiana Lennox, and next week — who knows?'

'Hmm. I suspect Lady Barbara would like it of all things, though,' Lucy said. 'Her daughter to be Countess of Chelmsford.'

'No, no, you must be wrong,' Firth laughed. 'If Bobbie married Barbarina and had children, Marcus would never get to be Earl. Look, you see? She is going over to them now.

232

Should you like to wager what she'll do next? I say she'll snatch Barbarina away ... Yes, you see! Look how she shakes the poor creature's arm. Miss B. will have a scolding as soon as they're out of sight.'

Roberta was indignant. 'How dare she? As if there were something improper in sitting with Bobbie, and in full public view! If Bobbie wants to sit with her — or dance with her — or marry her, even, then Lady Barbara shan't stand in his way!'

'Oh, Rob!' Lucy laughed.

'Ah, the new set is forming,' said Firth. 'Lady Barbara's looking about for a sacrificial lamb to lead to the slaughter. My God, she's hooked Lord Burnett! Hooked, but not landed yet — see how he wriggles —'

'Mixed metaphor,' Lucy said sternly.

'There, she's got him. He leads Barbarina to the set, and looks about him sheepishly — yes, Lucy, I know he was a lamb a moment ago — and hopes no-one has seen how he was bamboozled!'

'Oh, look,' Lucy said with pleasure, 'there's young Farringdon with Lady Annabel! Now that's a match that would gratify many a heart — his title and her money! And poor Marcus wearing his heart on his sleeve, looking most put out. Lady Barbara needs to be in two places at once.'

'These ballroom dramas!' Firth said with a sigh. 'The life of a chaperone is too exciting for me — must go and have a calming talk to Fitz about the Hanoverian subsidy, and the possibility of riots between the Prussians and the Saxons. Adieu, ladies.'

He walked off, and Roberta and Lucy stood in companionable silence, watching the sets form, the brightly-coloured uniforms and silks and muslins whirling like disturbed birds and butterflies, and falling into place in a new pattern, stilling gradually as the places were taken up and the young people waited for the music to begin. Lucy noticed on the far side of the ballroom that Sophie was standing in a set with Major Larosse, and she frowned slightly. They had already danced together twice to her knowledge, and though Larosse had his back to her, she could see Sophie's face, and the child was looking altogether too happy. Héloïse ought to discourage that association, Lucy thought disapprovingly — but Héloïse had been quiet and distracted for some days lately, and too often *tête à tête* with the Duc, instead of taking an interest in Sophie's progress.

The music began. Lucy looked around for Rosamund, but couldn't see her anywhere. Her daughter being tall and red-haired, she was usually easy to spot even in a crowded ballroom, and it was not like her to sit out a dance, especially since there were now so many young men always vying for her hand. And then there was a flurry of movement to her right, and a late couple scurried to join the nearest set. Lucy's frown relaxed. It was Rosamund, looking very handsome tonight, even her mother had to admit, in silver-spangled white gauze over a silk slip of the palest blue, and her hair dressed with silver ribbons. She was looking happy, smiling not in the loftily-amused way she employed towards most of her suitors, but with the fresh candour of a child enjoying a simple pleasure — the way she usually looked when she went out riding. It was good to see her looking happy, but still it made Lucy sigh a little, for the young man who had led her into the set was Marcus.

Sophie was aware that in having danced three times with Major Larosse she had already laid herself open to comment. Even though it was a private ball, where more latitude in such things was allowed, it was on such a grand scale as to be practically public; and though she was not important, her position as Lady Theakston's niece meant that many eyes were on her. So when the music ended and the major invited her with a smile and a gesture of the hand to remain in the set, she felt she must refuse.

She shook her head, but did so with such palpable regret that he laughed, and said, 'What is it, Miss Morland? Ah, the proprieties! Yes, deuce take them, I had forgotten. I remembered only that we were friends.'

Sophie thought this was unfair. 'We are friends,' she said, 'but *they* don't know that. And it is not you who will be talked about.'

'*Touché*. Spoken with spirit, mademoiselle — I am justly rebuked. Burdens do not rest equally on our two sexes — but

234

I think yours has the best of it, in the ballroom at least.'

'No, indeed!' Sophie protested at once.

He raised an eyebrow. 'But in what other way are females at a disadvantage? It seems to me it must be delightful to be a woman, to be always deferred to, to have doors opened for one, and ices fetched, and chairs drawn out.'

'It is not delightful always to be — passive,' Sophie said with decision. 'Never to have the right to choose or to decide. To have to wait to be asked to dance, for instance: a man can walk up to the woman he prefers and ask her directly, but a woman can only wait and hope that the man she likes will ask her.'

'Indeed, that is a grave disadvantage, I allow,' Larosse said. 'But between you and me it need not be a hindrance. You may ask me to dance whenever you like, and I shall only admire you for it.'

'Now you're laughing at me,' Sophie said doubtfully.

'No, indeed, you wrong me. I am perfectly serious — but perhaps I am not the man of your choice. Dear Miss Morland, I apologise! I have put you in a very embarrassing position.'

'Oh no! Do not — I mean —' She saw too late that now he was teasing her, and coloured; but laughed too, for it was not cruelly done. 'I cannot ask you to dance again — it is too soon.'

'But you can ask me to sit out with you,' he said. 'There is a delightful alcove over there, sufficiently in view for the proprieties.' He bowed and simpered. 'Miss Morland, thank you. I shall be delighted. How kind of you to ask.'

Sophie laughed, and took his arm, and walked with him away from the dancers, who were making up the new sets, to sit down on the sopha in the alcove. His teasing had pushed the worry about propriety to the back of her mind; and she was too happy to be with him to care for tomorrow or gossip. For a while they sat in companionable silence watching the sets form and the dancing begin. Then Sophie glanced at him, and saw that his face was set in lines of sadness, and her heart misgave.

'Dance, children, dance,' he said softly, feeling her eyes on him. 'Who knows how many evenings there will be, or how many tomorrows? How many of these pretty young men will

235

still be dancing six months from now, I wonder? You would think they did not know that there is a war to come.'

'I think some of them are looking forward to it.'

'Yes — most of them, perhaps. What astonishes me is that even those who were in the Peninsula are looking forward to a battle — they who know what it is really like. They tell me,' he went on in the same quiet, conversational tone, 'that women forget the pain of childbirth; perhaps men likewise forget the pain of battle.'

'But you have not,' Sophie said, watching his profile.

'No. I am the outsider, the detached observer. I have been on one side and now I am on the other. My illusions have been worn away, and I can see war for what it is — an unpleasant necessity. I believe the Duke sees it so — but it seems we are the only two in Brussels who do.'

She was encouraged to ask something that had been puzzling her. 'If you think now that Napoleon is so wrong, why did you not think so before? Why did you fight for him in the first place?'

'A home question, Miss Morland,' he said wryly. 'How you thrust the little dagger straight between my ribs! Well, you see, I was also a child of the Revolution. It was exciting at first, to see so much that was wrong being swept away, and new vistas opening up, of truth and beauty and justice. Ah, words are so heady! Don't you feel it? *Liberté!* How the heart thrills at the sound! Words are the sweetest cheat of all! And there was much, you know, that was wrong with the old régime, much that needed changing.'

He glanced at her, as if to be sure that she was following him, and continued. 'But here is the irony — here is the inescapable twist! The people who wished to change the old régime were themselves part of it. They were born into it and moulded by it, and the only way they knew to change things was by the old methods. Lies and oppressions were to be got rid of by lying and oppressing. Torture was to be abolished by torturing the torturers. There was to be no more murder, once the murderers themselves had been murdered.' His eyes were deep with pain. 'Ends do not justify means: ends are shaped by means. You cannot escape, you see: wherever you go, you recreate the place you have come from.'

236

Sophie nodded. 'Yes, I see.'

He smiled wryly. 'Napoleon was the new man, promising the new world — and it was so much needed, for the old one was bad, corrupt, wasteful. We longed for the new world as dying men long for water. And we believed it was possible — we followed gladly, with pure hearts, like crusaders! Death, we thought, was beautiful — ours or the enemy's. But Napoleon, who ousted kings from their thrones in the name of the people, then found he had to climb onto the throne himself, still in the name of the people. He knew no other way. Ruler and ruled, they were all children of the old régime; and stone by stone, what was swept away was rebuilt. And so the road led to Moscow.'

He stopped and stared down at his hands, and Sophie held her breath, afraid to disturb him, as she would have been afraid to disturb a wound.

'After Moscow, I couldn't pretend to myself any more. I had known long before what I must do, but I hid it from myself, because I didn't want to be the betrayer — the Judas. But it had to be. He has to be stopped. That's all I tell myself now — he has to be stopped.'

Sophie said, 'But then — was it all for nothing? Can nothing ever get better?'

He looked at her now, and his expression softened. 'No — no, not for nothing. My poor Sophie, have I frightened you? The picture is not so bleak. For you see, though he is a child of the old world, there are many now who were born in the new world, and they will be the leaders of tomorrow, and the inheritors. Change takes a long time, that's all. The change won't be complete until everyone who remembers the old ways — and everyone who remembers *them* — is dead. Oh, there are new ideas in the air — haven't you felt them? There are changes still to come that we can't even imagine. The new world will be born — but the labour will be long and hard.'

Sophie was still trembling inwardly at his use of her name for the first time, but she saw where his argument led. 'Then, do you mean you won't see it?'

'No. It is too late for me. I'm a stepping-stone, and others will spring lightly over my head to the far bank.' He smiled. 'What things to be talking about in a ballroom! You are very patient, Miss Morland. Have you understood it all?'

'I understood *everything*,' she said, looking into his eyes, wishing to reassure him that he had not exposed his innermost feelings in vain.

'Yes,' he said lightly, 'I rather think you did. Everything that I said, at least. You are like your mother, you know — so full of caring.'

She coloured, but continued to meet his eyes. 'I am glad you spoke to me as you did. I am glad you felt you could talk to me like that.'

'You prefer it to being made love to, I think,' he said, smiling. 'Ah, but don't you know that at this moment what I want most in the world is to kiss you?'

He hadn't meant to say it: it was both dangerous and unfair. But the words were out and he watched Sophie's face, saw the shock closely followed by delight, and then a kind of bewilderment. I can read your thoughts, my Sophie, he thought — for it was long since he had called her that in his mind. You wonder what I can mean by it, but also you wonder at yourself, what *you* can mean by not being offended or angry, or wishing to rebuke me. For you don't, my dear delightful Sophie, that I can see quite well! Your heart is singing with a very improper triumph, and an even more improper wish that I might suit my actions to my words!

Harry Pyne approached Lucy in the pause before the last dance, when she was talking to their host, Lord Bickersteth, a dashing young Guardsman whose father had fallen at Ciudad Rodrigo, making him another of those independent young peers whose situation she so deplored.

'Lady Theakston — ma'am!' Pyne caught her attention and bowed. 'May I solicit the honour of your hand for the last dance? It's to be a waltz, ain't it, Bicky?'

Lord Bickersteth opened his mouth to reply, but Lucy saved him the trouble.

'Dance? I? You nonsensical boy, do you want me to make a figure of myself?'

Pyne managed to look hurt. 'Oh, really, ma'am, that's unkind! Am I so very unworthy? Bicky, I appeal to you — tell her ladyship I'm quite personable.'

'Pyne's all right, ma'am, my word on it,' Bickersteth drawled. 'A very pretty fellow, so my sister says.'

'You both know perfectly well that isn't what I mean. It's not the thing for matrons to dance at balls. Would you have me trip alongside my own daughter?'

'But, ma'am, this is a private ball. It's quite all right at a private ball,' Pyne protested.

'If it were ten couples and a fiddler in my drawing-room, I might consider it,' Lucy said, smiling at his absurdity, 'but with all of Brussels looking on? However, I thank you for asking me, even if you did do it to put me out of countenance.'

Pyne smiled and shook his head. 'You wrong me there, ma'am. I have been thinking this hour past that it is a crime above all crimes that Society condemns a woman to inaction simply because she is a mother. Do fathers sit at home by the fire reading sermons? Do men give up riding off to war and doin' jolly things, just because they've been married ten years and taken to wearin' sober waistcoats?'

'Of course they don't,' Bickersteth answered obligingly.

'And there's her ladyship, looking as young and fresh as a nineteen-year-old, and longing to dance the soles out of her slippers —'

'What are you up, you unscrupulous creature?' Lucy interrupted him. 'There's some point to this rigmarole, I know —'

'Point! Yes, you've guessed it, ma'am!' Pyne said quickly. 'In fact, two of 'em.'

'Two points?'

'A point-to-point. From Enghien to Braine-le-Comte — about eight miles — a nothing of a run, really, but the country's interesting,' Pyne said casually.

'We're gettin' it up, you see,' Bickersteth added. 'Next week. Tuesday.'

'We?'

'The Gentlemen's Sons,' Pyne said with a deprecatory smile. It was the nickname given to the Foot Guards, many of whom were billeted out at Enghien, but most of whom rode into Brussels every night to dance until dawn. They were the gayest of the gay, and though Bobbie might stigmatise them as Hyde Park soldiers, they were as popular as the Hussars with the young ladies.

'I see. And you're riding in it, are you?' Lucy asked.

'We both are — and Pon, and Farringdon, and all your particular friends, ma'am,' Pyne said.

'Missing the racing, you see,' Bickersteth explained. 'Newmarket — second home, usually. This year, nothing. Point-to-point the next best thing. Mean to have one every week. The Prince is all for it — goin' to put up a prize for the next one.'

'And what is it to do with me? You want me to bring a party and stand at the finishing-line, do you? Or do you want me to present the trophy?'

Pyne fixed her with a limpid gaze. 'We want you to ride in it, ma'am.'

Lucy felt, to her shock and delight, the hot blood course through her veins at the thought of it. She loved to race — had raced Minstrel point-to-point only two years ago and won — and she knew that Magnus Apollo would be fast. To let him out — to push him to the limit, see how fast he could really fly — oh, it would be magnificent! In her imagination she heard the pounding hooves, felt the thunderous vibration of the big body under her, felt the whip of the wind and the flying mane in her face ...

But it was impossible. She shut the lid down firmly on the vision, and looked cooly at the two young men. She had raced Minstrel on her own land, a private challenge; and that was England; and she hadn't been married then. To race here, in Flanders, with the eyes of all the world on them, with the most voracious gossips in Society just waiting for something shocking to seize on, was a different matter entirely. And there was Danby to take into consideration — not only because he wouldn't like it, but because what she did reflected on him. At home she might have more latitude, but she was here because of him, as his consort.

'No,' she said firmly. 'Was that what all this was about? No, definitely not.'

'But, ma'am — !'

'Can't you see how improper it would be? This isn't England.'

'Your horse is the fastest in Belgium, I'd swear on it,' Pyne said beguilingly.

'No.'

'We've asked Lady Annabel. She's game for it,' Bickersteth said.

'Bel Robb agrees to ride in a point-to-point, against officers of the Foot Guards?' Lucy said slowly.

'Yes, ma'am. And she's persuaded her cousin to put money on her, too. She says she's the best rider in the country, male or female, and is willing to take on all comers to prove it. Cecil's put up five hundred guineas that she'll win.'

'Good God,' Lucy said. The arrogance of the woman! 'On that long-backed grey of hers?'

'Yes, ma'am. She says if she's hunted Nimbus in Leicestershire and taken the brush, Belgium will be nothing to him.'

Oh, Lucy thought, I should like to shew her! I could beat her by half the distance! I could race her over eight miles and meet her on the way back! And to style herself the best rider — better than me! I should like nothing better than to take that five hundred guineas off her and toss it down a well!

Pyne, watching her face closely, said, 'We thought you wouldn't agree to a driving-race after all, but a point-to-point — why, nothing could be more seemly, more gentlemanlike — and just the sort of thing your ladyship likes to get up at home.'

Lucy met his eyes and gave him a wry smile. 'Get thee behind me, Harry Pyne! As I've already pointed out, this is not England; and the answer is still no.'

Danby had been called away during the evening and did not return before the end of the ball. He arrived at last at the Rue Ducale, ran up the stairs two at a time, and burst into Lucy's chamber to find her sitting on the sopha at the foot of the bed with a letter in her hand. She looked up dazedly when he came in, but he did not notice the letter or her expression. For once in his life, he was angry.

'What's all this about a point-to-point?' he burst out without preamble.

'How do you know about that?' she asked vaguely.

'They were talking about it at Headquarters. I should think everyone in Brussels will know about it by breakfast-time! Billy Cecil was full of it — all the details, including his infamous wager, which he seems inordinately proud of, I may say!'

'Oh, yes — Bel Robb means to prove she's the best rider in Belgium,' Lucy said, rousing herself from her own thoughts. She regarded her husband with a frown. 'You seem upset.'

'Upset? I should think I am upset! Damn it, Lucy, what the devil can you mean by it? Don't you see what a position it puts me in?'

She stared, taken aback. 'I? What have I to do with it?'

'Those boys are making a fool of you, and you can't see it,' he went on.

'What boys?'

'Ponsonby and Pyne. I haven't liked the way they hang around you, but it would have made things worse for me to object. But this is beyond the line! Damn it, this isn't England!'

Her own words, thrown back at her, brought the blood to her cheeks. 'Am I to understand that you have been told I accepted Bel Robb's challenge? You think I have been persuaded by Harry Pyne to ride in his point-to-point?'

'You evidently know all about it,' Danby said, but less heatedly. His anger was subsiding, leaving him feeling uncertain.

'Oh, I know all about it. Pyne asked me at the ball tonight — was quite pressing, in fact. Pointed out that my new horse was probably the fastest in the country, and that I was a better rider than the Robb woman.'

'You've been talking about how fast Magnus is ever since you got him,' Danby pointed out. He sounded defensive now, and Lucy's anger began to rise.

'And so you assumed I knew no better than to ride him in a race — or did someone tell you that I had accepted?'

He shifted from one foot to the other, looked deeply embarrassed now. 'Well, no, I don't know that anyone actually said you had accepted. But it was talked of as a settled thing.'

Lucy stood up abruptly, crushing the letter in her hand. 'Very well. Now I know your opinion of me, I must make sure not to disappoint you.'

'Oh, now, Lucy — I say —'

'I am a heedless girl with no sense of propriety. A wild madcap creature without consideration. Very well.'

'I didn't say that. I was — well, I'm sorry. They were all talking — looking sorry for me — you know how damnably people can —'

'I think I'll go to bed now,' Lucy said coldly. 'If you will excuse me — I must get my sleep. I shall have to put in a great deal of practice between now and Tuesday.'

'Lucy, for God's sake — you aren't really going to do this, are you?'

'You have shewn me quite plainly what you expect of me.'

Now he grew angry again. 'I've done nothing of the sort. For God's sake, what's the matter with you? I've said I'm sorry, haven't I? It was stupid of me —'

'It was,' she said icily.'Good night, Danby.'

He stared at her a moment longer, and then turned on his heel and left, closing the door quietly behind him. Lucy sat down on the bed, sustained for a moment by her anger; then as it seeped away, she began to wish she had not said what she said. She would now have to spend the rest of the night alone in the big bed, and she longed desperately for the comfort of his warm body beside her and his arms round her.

Why had he come in like that and attacked her? She had been so badly in need of comfort after reading the letter which had been waiting for her when she returned from the ball. She had longed for him to come home and make things right for her, and he had simply thrown an outrageous accusation at her without even giving her the chance to refute it.

The letter, from her married daughter, Lady Harvey Sale, announced that she was with child, expecting to be delivered in August. She had delayed telling anyone because of her previous miscarriage, had wanted to be sure before raising anyone's hopes; but all was going well and there was every reason to expect a happy outcome.

Lucy would be a grandmother in August. The news, on top of what Pyne had said earlier that evening, had thrown her into deep gloom. She, a grandmother! She felt suddenly that life was passing her by, slipping through her fingers. She was growing old, being resigned by life and Society to the fireside and the chaperone's chair, while inside herself she was still

243

hardly more than a girl, and longing to have fun, to dance, to ride, to do all the exciting things she had done all her life. She didn't want to be a grandmother. It was horrible, horrible!

And then Danby had come in and shouted at her in that intolerable way, angry because he thought she had done what she longed to do, but had in fact refused because of that very propriety she had always scorned, and which was forcing her into a life of inaction and tedium! Well, she would shew him! She would shew them all! Harry Pyne admired her — he didn't think of her as a grey-haired old matron. She would ride in his race, and beat that vulgar Bel Robb, and let who wanted criticise her.

She made her triumphant decision; and then surprised herself by bursting into tears.

CHAPTER TEN

James spent all of Monday afternoon walking about Clifton Ings, but Miss Hesketh didn't appear. Tuesday was wet, but he went there again, and stood hunched under a tree, staring through the teeming rain, thinking at any moment to see her come tripping along the path in galoshed boots and under a neat umbrella. But the clouds only drew lower and wetter over the soaked watermeadows, and the river swirled past brown and swift, chuckling under the roots of an overhanging willow as though enjoying the joke. When the premature dusk set in, James gave up his vigil and tramped back into the city where he had left his horse.

On his way to the Bunch of Grapes, he passed the end of Stonegate, and decided to stop in at the Maccabbees to dry off a little, for he was wet to his skin, and beginning to shiver. Standing before the fire, steaming like a water-spaniel, he nodded to the waiter to bring him a glass of port-and-brandy; and when this comforting brew had gone down and was warming his insides in a pleasantly familiar manner, one of his former boon companions came in and greeted him like a long-lost brother, and there was nothing for it but to order another.

He had not been to the club for a long time, and as the members came in they naturally gathered round him to chat and remember old times. One by one they left the group round the fire to dine and return, but James never got to dinner at all, and at around eleven o'clock he reeled out into the night with sufficient fumes rising from his empty stomach to his head to have lifted him off the ground like a hydrogen balloon.

It had stopped raining, but clouds still obscured the moon, and the wet cobbles glimmered in the light of the street-lamps and echoed emptily to his uneven footsteps. He wambled

245

down Little Stonegate, came to the corner of Grape Lane, and seeing the alley down which he had walked with Miss Hesketh, turned into it, and retraced their steps. The damp air seemed to be mixing with the port-and-brandy fumes to make him more drunk than ever. He had forgotten what he was doing and why, until he reached New Street and found himself outside the shuttered shop; and then he remembered that he had to get a new automaton for Benedict, to replace the one he had broken.

But the shop was shut! He leaned against the door and tugged uselessly at the door-knob, and then tried to prise back the shutters with his fingers; and then, in a fit of pique, began hammering feebly at them with his fists. It was fortunate for him that the watchman came along at that moment. A large hand, as hard as pickled beef, landed on his shoulder and tugged him back into the open street.

'Alloa! What's to do, lad? None o' that now — it's after eleven — tha s'd be in bed!'

James was turned around to face his captor. 'Whozzat?' he said, goggling. 'Smawith, izzat you?'

The watchman looked first astonished and then embarrassed. 'Eh, Maister Morland! I'm sorry, sir, I didn't know it were you. Is soomat wrong? You're not ill, are you?'

James lurched and leaned on him, and as his breath whistled past the Smawith's nose, the watchman realised what was what, and a grin spread across his whiskered face.

'Now then, maister, I've got you. That's right — lean on me, sir, and I'll tek care of you. Is your servant here? How did you coom into town? Eh, it's right treacherous stuff, is night air — goes straight to a man's head.'

He was plainly enjoying himself. James drew himself up to his full five feet five and swayed sternly. 'That's quite enough from you, Smawith. I'll have you know I had a soaking earlier on —'

'Nay, maister, I can tell that!' Smawith chuckled delightedly. 'And why not? It's a man's own business if he likes to get bosky once in a way!'

'I didn't mean that,' James said. 'My horse is at the Grapes. P'raps you'd kindly light me there.'

'Certainly, maister. And — mum's the word, eh?' Smawith

tipped him a ghastly wink, levered his stout caped shoulder under James's, and held his lantern forward to light the way. 'Mind out for th' kennel, sir! That's the dandy. Hold on to me, sir, we'll soon have you safe.'

Once he was on his horse, James had no further worries, for Victor, like Nez Carré before him, knew his way home even in the dark. Durban was waiting up for him and came running out into the yard by the buttery door as soon as he rode in.

'Thank God you're back, sir! Are you all right?' Durban cried, thinking for a moment that James must be hurt, from the way he was slumped in the saddle. But like Smawith before him, he was soon disabused. 'You've been wet through, sir! Why didn't you shelter from the rain? Here, boy, take the horse. Rub him down well, if you value your job. Come, sir, come, you need a rubbing-down too.'

Up in the bedchamber, Durban stripped off the damp clothes. James began to shiver again, and now couldn't stop, though Durban chafed him mercilessly with a rough towel before pulling a thick nightgown over his head and bundling him into bed. Then he left him for a few minutes, to return with a hot brick wrapped in flannel which he thrust in under James's feet. Gradually the shivering stopped, and the fumes overcame him again, and he went off to sleep.

The soaking and the lack of food had done their work, however. The next morning he felt languid and heavy-eyed, and by the afternoon he was plainly sickening for a cold. His desire to put on his hat and gloves and go out riding was therefore a mystery to Durban, who began to fear that his master's mind had been turned, after all. He protested vigorously, and went on protesting, following his master downstairs and across the hall and out on to the steps down to the yard. There, however, a gust of chill, damp air met them and James shivered, and wavered in his purpose.

'Don't go, sir,' Durban said gently. 'Bed's the place for you. I'll shove a warming-pan between the sheets and make 'em all hot and toasty. Lots of pillows — a hot toddy — and a good book. See, it's coming on to rain again.'

James turned hot, bright eyes on him doubtfully. 'Rain? Are you sure?'

'Certain sure, sir. Look, here it comes now. Going to be a wet 'un again.'

The prickling in the air became a mizzle, and a moment later a swathe of fine soaking rain was sweeping across the yard. Durban touched James's elbow, turning him gently back towards the house. James shivered again, and swallowed, finding his throat tight and painful. Bed beckoned deliciously. Surely she would not go out in rain like this? He let himself be guided indoors.

By night-time he was feverish, and Durban had a bed made up for himself in the great bedchamber, to be on hand if his master woke in the night. James was restless, sleeping and waking, turning and muttering, sometimes not knowing where he was. In the middle of the night, when Durban had dozed off, James woke him by crying out. Durban got up at once and went to him, and found James sitting bolt upright, clutching the bedsheets.

'I must get up! Durban, get my clothes!'

Durban soothed him. 'Yes, sir, of course. Where did you want to go?'

'She'll be waiting,' James said. From the fixed look of his eyes, Durban guessed he was between waking and sleeping. His brow under Durban's fingers was stinging hot. 'I must go to her. She'll think I'm not coming.'

'I don't think so, sir. I don't think she'll be there now. Not tonight.'

'Yes, yes, she'll be waiting there. I must go to her. Help me get up.' His words were urgent, but he made no attempt to move, and when Durban gently pushed him he lay down again, though he looked up at his servant anxiously. 'We can't leave her there all alone,' he said pitifully.

'No, sir, we won't. I'll go and make sure she isn't waiting. Don't worry, she'll understand. It's all right, sir, you just go back to sleep. I'll take care of everything.'

James subsided, and though he moved about restlessly and muttered, he didn't try to sit up again, and after a while he was still, and breathed more regularly. Durban looked down at him with pity. He had hoped that stage was past, but here was the old delusion again, that Fanny had been buried alive. It was a terrible thing to have in your mind, he thought — a

248

terrible grim image to carry about with you.

With the tenderness of a woman he stroked the hot forehead and saw the lines about James's mouth relax a little. 'Nice,' he muttered.

'You go to sleep, sir,' Durban said. 'Miss Fanny's all right.'

'Fanny,' James murmured. And then he really was asleep.

Thursday was dry, but cold and blowy, and James lay in bed languidly, imagining the watermeadows under the grey scudding clouds, the trees bending their heads fretfully before the wind, the river flowing dark and uninviting under the shadow of the willows. The path would be wet underfoot from all the rain. Surely she wouldn't go and walk there today? He imagined the scene empty — no neat little figure in a grey pelisse — and it comforted him a little. She would stay home today for sure.

But Friday was another matter. The wind had gone round in the night — James had heard it creaking the old bones of the house when he woke in the darkness before dawn — and then dropped. The sun came up pale gold in a translucent sky bent over a world perfectly still and sparkling with a carpet of diamonds. By nine o'clock the sky had deepened to blue, the sun was hot, and the grass was dry. It was going to be a beautiful day. Today she would walk on Clifton Ings, without a doubt.

His head ached and his throat was still sore, but he was not to be mothered by Durban any more. Durban was both anxious and cross.

'If you make yourself ill, it'll be me who has the trouble of it,' he muttered, banging the drawers as he dragged out neckcloth and stockings to his master's orders.

'You're turning into an intolerable old woman,' James rebuked him. 'And stop making that infernal row with the drawers! My —' He was about to say 'my head's splitting open', but stopped himself in time.

Durban looked at him suspiciously. 'I don't see what's so important that you've got to go out today, that's all,' he said. 'Another day in bed would set you up. You're not well.'

'Another day in bed will finish me off. And if you say another word, I'll turn you off without a reference. I want a

249

walk in the fresh air, that's all. Alone,' he added hastily as Durban's eye betrayed an idea.

In the end he took Kithra and Castor, who were pining for a walk, and reached the Ings at about noon, the earliest he thought she might appear. He had no idea what time of day shopkeepers took their dinner, but he thought that after three wet days her father might send her out early, for she must be looking pale by now, from too much confinement.

The dogs ran up and down, sniffing all the glorious smells like gluttons swallowing down oysters. Castor frisked about with one ear turned back over his head, chased a bumble-bee, barked and looked foolish. Even Kithra made honourable pretence of wanting to have a stick thrown for him, though he didn't go quite so far as to run after it when it had been thrown.

The sun rose higher and the day grew hot, and the dogs slowed down. James found walking more tiring than he had expected, though the warmth of the sun on his shoulders was pleasant. He reached the old willow-tree, which grew horizontally out over the river for a few feet before turning a right-angle upwards. The trunk made a convenient seat, and James sat, and pulled off his hat, and felt the heat of the sun on his bare head. The dogs ran up to him enquiringly and then wandered off to make a thorough inventory of the area, and James watched the water running past under the trailing branches and let his thoughts wander.

This had always been a favourite place when they were young. Many an hour he had spent sitting astride this tree-trunk, his bare feet dangling over the water, fishing with a worm on a bent pin. Ned and his friend Chetwyn had pursued their endless conversations here. Lucy and Harry had dabbled their feet in the water or tried to catch fish with their bare hands, and gone home muddy and been scolded for their pains.

Fanny had come here, too, with the rapscallion boys she liked to roam the country with, had paddled, fished, even bathed from this tree. Barefooted and tangle-haired, she had frolicked through her childhood as heedless as a puppy. He thanked God, now, that she had had that happy time. He thought of the lambs out on the moor, frisking and gambolling in the delight of sunny spring days, with no fore-shadowing of the slaughter-house and the knife to come.

Kithra gave a whine — his warning — and James looked up and saw her standing there, a few yards off, watching him. He had not heard her approach; now he gazed at her, enchanted, but almost afraid. She had left off the grey pelisse, and was dressed today in a round gown of pale green — Fanny's favourite colour — with a shawl draped becom-ingly over her elbows, and a dear little villager of satin straw tied over her curls with long green ribbons. She was holding a spray of tender young lime-leaves — not as a woman holds a posy, but as if she had picked them idly, as a small boy picks up a stick, and then had forgotten they were there.

He looked at her in silence, almost apprehensively. There was something luminous and strong about her today, like the strength that is in new growth when the first hot day draws it up from the dark earth — the tender tip of the seedling that can push through the hardest ground to reach the air and sunlight. She was young and strong and beautiful — so beau-tiful! — and he was tired and old. He felt that he must be grey and unlovely to her. He was afraid that she would find him repulsive. He was afraid that he would love her more than he could bear.

He should have said something: the silence had gone on too long. But she did not seem embarrassed by it. Today she seemed different — not shy and hesitant, like before, but quietly confident, as though he were someone she had known a long time, and had no fear of. In the end it was she who spoke. She twirled the spray of leaves back and forth in her fingers, and the corners of her mouth were lifted in a faint smile.

'I didn't think you'd be here today,' she said. 'I thought when I didn't come all week ...'

'It's the first sunny day since Monday,' he said, and his voice sounded unused to him, like a rusty gate.

'I couldn't come on Monday. The shop was busy, and I had to help. Father wasn't well. But he's better now. He said I should get out today while the sun was shining.'

He nodded, but didn't get up, or speak. He was happy just to sit and look at her. He'd be happy to stay here like this

251

for the rest of his life.

She tilted her head at him a little, like a bird. 'You've not been well,' she said.

'How did you know?'

'I didn't know. But you look sort of — dowly.'

'I got caught in the rain on Tuesday,' he said, feeling foolish. She smiled suddenly, and his heart performed a sickening acrobatic inside him.

'I heard about that. Mr Gardiner came in on Wednesday and said you'd been into the Maccabbees soaked to the skin.'

This was one of the members who didn't like James, and he feared mischief. 'Does Gardiner buy your toys? But he doesn't have any children.'

'No, he came in about a clock. Father mends clocks, too. He's right clever about it,' she said proudly. Kithra came to sniff her hands, and she patted him enthusiastically. 'Are they your dogs? I always wanted a dog, but Father said not when Mother was ill. He said the noise would be too much. But yours aren't noisy, are they?'

'That one, the big one, never barks at all,' James said.

'Why not?'

'They don't. Wolf-hounds don't bark.' She waited, bright-eyed, for more. 'There's an old story in the family that they were originally bred from wild wolves. There used to be wolves on the moors hereabouts in the olden days. All our hounds are bred from one original stock, and wolves don't bark, so perhaps it's true.'

She seemed pleased with the story. 'I bet it is true. I think he's a lovely dog. I like big ones best.'

'Would you like a puppy?' James said suddenly. 'There's a bitch that whelped recently. The pups will be weaned in another week or so. You could have one, if you liked.'

She lowered her eyelids shyly. 'Oh!' she said softly, but that was all.

He took it for acceptance, and stood up, feeling better and stronger. 'Would you like to walk along a little way? The path seems to have dried out.'

She walked along by his side, not close, as if she might take his arm, but about a yard away, casually, as children walk together. He looked down at the leaves in her hand, and she

252

looked too, and then smiled up at him.

'Have you ever eaten them? They taste right nice when they're new like this. We used to call them bread-and-cheese when I was a child.'

James laughed, and the feeling of apprehension vanished. 'I shouldn't think there's anything that grows in Yorkshire that I haven't tried to eat at one time or another! I used to wander these fields as a child, eating as I went. I've tried grass and leaves and berries and toadstools — it's a wonder I didn't die ten times over!'

'It wasn't your time,' she said as one pronouncing an accepted truth. 'Have you eaten clover-flowers? They're full of honey.'

'Yes, and daisies are peppery — the yellow part, anyway. And cocksfoot tastes like mouldy bread —'

'Horse-chestnut buds are nice, too,' she said. 'Did you ever fish in this river? I bet there's some big fish in it.'

'There used to be. I haven't fished for years. I don't know how it comes about,' James said.

The dogs trotted ahead of them, and they strolled along the river-bank companionably. James told her about his fishing expeditions, and then about his brothers and sisters, and his home, and his mother and father. He told her about riding and tree-climbing and river-bathing, and sailing toy boats, and making whistles out of reeds; about playing truant from lessons to sit with the shepherd up on the moors and share his bread-and-onion dinner and learn about sheep; about scaling walls, and stealing apples, and roaming the fields all day and begging pie or cake from the women of outlying houses when he'd missed his dinner.

He told her about helping with the harvest — long, scorched-brown days of dust and sneezes and the smell of hot horses and the prickle of hay inside your collar; the glorious moment in the middle of the day when everyone would find a bit of shade and the food would be brought out — huge crisp-crusted loaves, and pies like golden cartwheels, and fragrant ham you could smell right through the cloth, and buttermilk brought out from the well, so cold it hurt your teeth; and going home at sunset, drunk with tiredness, when the sky was barred with flame and purple and gold, and the dusk came

253

creeping out from the hedges like smoke, and the cooling earth gave back the miracle of all its smells, hidden through the heat of the day. And then at last would come that magical moment when the sky turned luminous, and suddenly the air was flickering with bats.

He told her about threshing, when the geese grew so frantic at the smell of the bruised grain that they would knock you down to get at it; and cider-making, when the smell of apple-juice was strong enough to make you drunk. Afterwards when you took the used straw-and-apple mash to the pigs, they would know it was coming, and stand with their forefeet on the pigsty wall, barking like dogs in their excitement.

In October they used to take the pigs up to Harewood Whin to feed on the acorns, he told her: that was when he knew summer was really over. But winter had its own joys — skating on the frozen moat, and tobogganing; bonfires, and roasting chestnuts and turnips; the landscape suddenly bare and accessible, the ploughed fields looking so neat like made-up beds under brown counterpanes, and the tree-shapes cut out clearly against the low winter sky; and then the thrill of the first scintillating snow, and all the excitements of Christmas, and the New Year's gifts, and the Twelfth Night revels.

They walked along by the river, the incongruous pair, and he laid out before her all the treasures of his childhood, and all the wonders of his world; and in shewing them to her, he found them again for himself. She listened to him with shining eyes and a curved and innocent smile, and he looked at her as he talked, and was happy. She was part of the beauty he had lost — no, not lost, but mislaid for a while in his confusion and pain. She was the beauty, he thought, of humanity.

By the time the Theakstons had their musical evening party, everyone in Brussels was talking about the race and the fact that Lady Theakston had accepted Bel Robb's challenge; and though he never spoke about it or gave the gossips any reason to think there had been words between him and his lady, everyone knew also that Lord Theakston did not approve.

Opinion was divided between those who thought it was a

lark, and that Lady Theakston was a right 'un and would beat Lady Annabel to flinders, and that the latter must have been wandering in her wits to issue a challenge to a female Corinthian like Lady T; and those who thought the whole thing was unspeakably shocking, and an intolerable disgrace, and that poor Lord Theakston was the most tried man in Europe, and much to be pitied.

Since representatives of both schools of thought felt it incumbent on them to express as much to Lord Theakston, he spent the next few days longing for Napoleon to appear over the horizon with a large army in order to give Brussels something else to think about. He had not spoken again to Lucy about the matter, knowing that opposition would only harden her resolve, trusting to her own good sense and affection for him to guide her.

He didn't know, of course, about the letter from Minnie, or its effect on Lucy, and saw her consorting with Pyne and Ponsonby and Bickersteth and other charming young rogues without understanding why it was she so eagerly sought their company. If he had visited her in her bedchamber at night, everything might have been straightened out in a moment; but he had his pride, too. He adored her, and felt slighted by her preference for these untried youths. Since she did not seem to require his company, he would not press it on her. Lucy waited every night in her bedchamber, ready to forgive him the instant he appeared, and crying herself to sleep like a green girl when he did not. And so the breach widened.

The party, with its very exclusive guest-list, came at just the right moment to drive the gossips wild, and the names of those who had not been invited were canvassed even more eagerly than those who had. Family duty had compelled Lucy, albeit reluctantly, to invite Horatio, Lady Barbara and Barbarina as well as Marcus, but in spite of everything that Lady Barbara could do in the way of hinting, suggesting and even downright asking, Lucy had not invited Lady Annabel Robb.

Marcus was angry at what he saw as a slight to his beloved, and told his mother he thought of refusing, upon which Lady Barbara rounded on him in a cold fury and told him he was not to be making them all look even more ridiculous than

Lucy already had. The situation was getting rather too complicated for Lady Barbara. Her love of money and titles made her as eager for Marcus to marry Lady Annabel as even Marcus could be, and yet she disapproved entirely of this foolish race and the spectacle it was going to make of them all. She could not blame Lucy without blaming Bel Robb, and she could not blame Bel Robb without disapproving of her, and yet she wanted to shew the world she approved wholeheartedly of Marcus's choice. The best she could think of to do was to ignore the whole affair, which made it especially galling that Lucy drew attention to it by not inviting Lady Annabel to her *soirée*.

All the brightest young sprigs of nobility were to be there — Lord Ponsonby, Lord Bickersteth, Sir John Wilmot, Lord Burnett and even Lord Farringdon, along with Harry Pyne, Frank Webster, 'Tug' Enderby, 'Figgy' Lichfield, Freddie Wykeham and the like. Naturally, there were those vulgarians who nodded wisely and commented that 'Lady T. don't miss a trick', and 'She will have her daughter off her hands by midsummer or perish', but that was only to be expected.

For the rest, the Duke was coming, and the Richmonds with their daughters; Lord Uxbridge and Sir William Ponsonby, and Colonel Colbourne and his wife; Lady Frances Webster, because though Lucy didn't like her, she was the Duke's latest flirt; and a clutch of respectable young women like Miss Burnett and the Honourable Miss Bickersteth to make up the numbers. To be tactful to the Dutch-Belgian contingent, and for Héloïse's sake, she had invited the Duc, Count Bylandt and Major Larosse; and finally, after a certain amount of heart-searching, Captain Tantony, because it seemed so particular not to.

The folding doors between the two drawing-rooms on the first floor had been thrown back, and at one end a low dais had been constructed alongside the piano where the orchestra would play and Catalani perform her two songs — she would never give more than two at a private function. Inconspicuously behind it stood Miss Burnett's harp, which would be brought out later, Lucy having discovered through rigorous questioning that Miss Burnett played *really* well, not just the 'prettily' of the fond Mama's opinion.

In keeping with the informal idea of the evening, there was no auditorium of chairs. They were scattered around the two drawing-rooms in the usual manner, along with sophas and tables, handsome arrangements of flowers, and a battery of candles. The Theakstons greeted their guests at the top of the stairs, and within the drawing-rooms footmen waited with trays of glasses. Danby, in his mysterious manner, had discovered a vintner in an obscure part of the city who had a hitherto undisclosed stock of pink champagne, and the comments of the guests as they received their glasses rose like birds' cries: how delightful, how original, how charming, how exciting!

As soon as the Duke had arrived and exchanged bluff greetings, and before he could be beguiled into serious conversation with his senior cavalry officers, Lucy gave the nod to the performers, and the first musical item took the air. The quartet had expanded into a ten-piece orchestra — two fiddles, viola, cello and bass, two oboes, flute, horn and timpani — which launched at once into a Mozart symphony.

Leaving a respectful space in front of the dais, the guests grouped themselves according to enthusiasm, and those at the near end were as glad to be able to continue chatting as the music-lovers in the further sanctum to listen. The footmen circulated silently, replenishing glasses, and the host and hostess moved from group to group receiving compliments.

'Much nicer than a formal concert! How clever of you, Lady Theakston!' cried Lady Bickersteth, who was not musical; and, 'What a wonderful orchestra! How one adores Mozart,' gushed Miss Halford, who was.

After the symphony there was a pause for conversation, and then the leader of the orchestra played a concerto; and at a nod and a shrug from Lucy, followed it up with a Romance and half a gypsy song, since Catalani was late. She arrived at last, sweeping through the throng and looking magnificent in gold-coloured crape with tinsel ribbons in her hair, and the guests fell into a most respectfuly hush as she took her place on the dais and nodded to the leader.

All the Morlands of Lucy's generation had been brought up to appreciate music and to play a musical instrument, and Lucy stood beside the Duke in wrapt silence to listen to the lovely voice soaring above the orchestra's accompaniment. Tumultuous applause followed the second song, and then Danby led the cantatrice away while Lucy began ushering the guests towards the dining-saloon where the supper was to be served.

The 'neat, tight' supper was one, she flattered herself, that even Héloïse's Monsieur Barnard would have been proud of, and as it was laid out on buffets for the guests to help themselves, in the Russian style she had learnt in Vienna, she was satisfied that this part of the evening would be as talked-of as the rest. There were hot and cold dishes, sallets, tarts and pies, fruit, cheeses, creams, and pastries heaped in delicious and delicate array like edible palaces on the long table. The bird-cries rose again: how delicious, how different, how original, how informal!

'A splendid idea of yours, Lady Theakston,' said the darkly handsome Lord Uxbridge, plate in hand. 'So much better than a seated dinner, where one inevitably finds oneself between the two dullest women in Christendom. This way one can talk to whom one likes.'

'Or to no-one, eh, Paget?' Colonel Ponsonby added, throwing a glance towards Marcus, who was standing all alone and with a forbidding frown between his brows.

'Ah, yes, poor Morland!' said Uxbridge lightly, and Lucy wondered for a moment if he were going to be indiscreet, but he went on with a smile, 'He should have joined the Heavy Brigade, like his father.'

'Quite right! My young men don't get taken onto the staff,' Ponsonby agreed. 'He misses his regiment, you see!'

'Talking of regiments,' Uxbridge said, 'why didn't you take that young nephew of yours under your wing, Colonel, instead of letting him join the Foot Guards? Don't you have any family pride?'

Ponsonby shuddered. 'Have you ever seen him on horseback? We've got enough headstrong neck-or-nothing boys in the cavalry already, without adding mine to the total! No, no, let Maitland have the governing of him, I say — and I wish him joy of it! There's never any knowing what my nevvy'll do next, but it's always shocking, and usually dangerous.'

The conversation had taken a turn perilously close to the

question of the point-to-point, and both cavalry commanders were longing to ask Lucy if she really meant to race tomorrow but couldn't quite bring themselves to do it. Lucy was perfectly aware of what was on their minds, and smiling sweetly, asked if there were any truth in the rumours that Napoleon was on the move at last.

'Not the least, as far as I can tell,' Ponsonby said. 'There's been some sort of troop movement along the frontier in the last few days, but Boney's still in Paris, that's for sure.'

'Something came through today about trouble in the Vendée,' Uxbridge added. 'An uprising of some sort, it seems. Whether it will come to anything remains to be seen, but it all helps to keep Boney off balance. It's a damned pity we couldn't have kept Angoulême up to the mark, but he had Grouchy against him, of course. A funny little man, Grouchy — looks exactly like a monkey, but he's the ablest cavalry general the French have. Don't you agree, Sir William?'

'Oh, yes, now that Murat's blotted his book.' The conversation became technical.

After supper, the guests drifted back into the drawing-rooms. The dais had been removed, and Miss Burnett, with suitable surprise and modest deprecations, was prevailed upon to play her harp. Lucy found herself standing beside Major Larosse during this recital, and to make conversation mentioned the rumours of troop-movements and repeated the analysis of Uxbridge and Ponsonby.

'What's your opinion, Major? You know Napoleon's ways better than they, perhaps?'

He gave her a wry smile. 'I wish they thought so, madame. Then I could tell them that this is always the Emperor's way, to gather his troops quietly over a long front, so that no-one shall know what he is planning, or where he means to strike. It was like that in 1812 — the Moscow campaign. A little here, a little there, no-one thinking anything of it — and suddenly there was a whole army assembled and ready to invade.'

'But it seems that Boney is still in Paris. Ponsonby was quite sure of that.'

Larosse shrugged. 'What then? He will move, when he is ready, very quickly. That also is his way. When everything is in place, he will pounce like a hawk. And what an army he has this time — scarcely a new recruit in it! All veterans, and well-tried commanders, who know him.'

'Yes,' said Lucy, 'the Duke has said he doesn't expect any deserters. Nothing but a marshal or two, he said, and they're not worth a damn.'

Larosse smiled obediently, but was saved from having to reply by the end of Miss Burnett's recital. The next unrehearsed item was to have been Harry Pyne's song, accompanied by Rosamund on the pianoforte. Rosamund had kicked a little at that, and asked why couldn't Sophie play instead.

'She practises more than I do. She has a piece all ready.'

'Sophie doesn't play well enough,' Lucy had said firmly, with scant regard for anyone's feelings. 'I'm not having my musical evening degenerate into a schoolroom concert, or before you know where you are all the other mamas will be thrusting their daughters up to sing and trundle out their one piece.'

Rosamund, resigned to her fate, was moving towards the piano now, and Lucy excused herself from Larosse and went to supervise the business. When she reached the spot, however, she found Tantony in place, looking very red. Harry Pyne smiled sweetly at Lucy and said, 'I have inveigled Philip into giving us a song, ma'am, if you will permit it. He sings like an angel — a male Catalani, if you like — and is just as hard to persuade, so don't discourage him now, I implore!'

Lucy gave him a furious look, but could only consent, and be thankful that during the last harp item the majority of the older people had lost interest and were gathered in absorbed conversational groups. Rosamund, she thought, was looking handsome and competent seated at the piano, her slender hands and white arms shewn to their best advantage, the light of the three-branch candelabrum Pyne had placed on the piano-top gilding her red hair into copper fire. It was a sight to make any young man fall in love, and she played as well as she looked — but if Philip Tantony were to make a nonsense of his song, with a weak voice, uncertain notes and rustic phrasing, his performance would reflect on Rosamund.

But from the first notes she discovered to her relief that

Pyne had exaggerated no more than a social amount. Tantony's voice was strong, pleasant and true, and he sang with taste and expression. He had chosen a song — 'My Lady Fair' — which both of them knew, and Rosamund, not needing to look at the keyboard, watched him as she played. Lucy was aware that it was in order to be able to follow him more closely, as a good accompanist should; but after the first verse, Tantony turned a little away from his audience, and looked at her too. By the time he began the last verse, it was plain that he was singing to her, and was hardly aware of anyone else, while her eyes were fixed on his face in the most flattering manner. It made a very pretty picture.

Lucy was furious — it was not what she wanted at all, a complete waste of a very promising situation. She heard the slightest sound beside her, and whipped her head round to find Harry Pyne not looking at her, his face suspiciously straight. That young man's taste for practical jokes, she thought, was getting out of hand.

There was another in the room who agreed with her. Marcus had wandered down to the concert end of the drawing-room largely to avoid his mother, who was trying to persuade Lord Uxbridge to give a dinner-party solely for senior cavalry officers and their ladies. He had brooded all through Miss Burnett's performance, and had hardly been listening to the beginning of Tantony's song. When it came to an end, however, and Tantony bowed and thanked his accompanist, Rosamund smiled and gave him her hand to kiss, and Marcus suddenly became aware of them.

Tantony, he thought, was a very pretty fellow, with just the sort of fair, regular, Grecian looks that women admired, and he was evidently devoted to Rosamund. He watched them with a frown as Tantony offered his hand to raise her from the piano, and Rosamund took it with a murmured comment that made him smile. They seemed, Marcus thought, to be as thick as thieves together — but Tantony wasn't half good enough for her. Why, a man like that couldn't begin to understand her, besides having no title and barely any fortune. Then he thought how two of those charges could equally well be levelled at him, and shook his head wryly at himself.

Rosamund glanced at him as she passed a moment later, on her way with Tantony to see after some lemonade, and Marcus made an odd little gesture with his hands as though he had begun to applaud her and then stopped half-way.

'Very nice, Rosy,' he said. 'You perform very well together.' And Rosamund smiled to herself, thinking that he didn't sound as though he thought it nice at all.

According to plan, Lord Burnett and Miss Burnett respectfully begged Lucy, on behalf of all the young people, for some dancing, and two of the orchestra returned to play country dances on fiddle and piano. The older people moved into the other drawing-room to make up a few card-tables and to talk about clothes, scandal and the war, and the young people formed a set to dance and flirt discreetly until they were stopped.

Lucy had no wish for it to turn into a regular ball, and had need also of an early night, to be fit for the race the next day, and so shortly after midnight she dismissed the musicians, and the party began to break up. As the crowd thinned, Héloïse went in search of Sophie, and found her standing by the piano chatting to Bobbie and Barbarina, while Major Larosse sat in the vacated musician's seat idly picking out a tune, his eyes fixed unnoticed on Sophie's face.

Héloïse paused and observed. What was she to suppose from this? The look Larosse bent on Sophie was not precisely that of a lover; yet it was too particular not to arouse speculation. He had danced with her that evening a great deal more than twice. Well, it was a private and informal dance, and the rules were not so strictly adhered to — but Héloïse had seen him dance with no-one else. The time was coming, she thought sadly, when she would have to discover what, if anything, the major meant by it, and warn him gently not to arouse public expectations.

While she watched, Marcus joined the group and asked his sister a question; Sophie's attention was released and she turned towards Larosse as though she had been awaiting the moment.

'Do you play?' he asked her, his hands running through the keys.

'Yes, but not well,' Sophie said. 'I try, but my governess says I have no ear and no execution. I like to hear it done properly, though. My cousin played very well, don't you think?'

'Yes, surprisingly well for a young lady.'

'Why surprisingly?'

'Because young ladies usually like to shine, and accompanying is a modest and retiring business. Unless one accompanies oneself, of course.'

'Can you sing, too?'

He smiled the particular smile that made her tremble, and said softly, 'Only upon special request.'

'Will you sing for me?'

He glanced past her at the group of young people chatting. 'Gladly — but in French. There are too many ears.'

Héloïse moved imperceptibly nearer. The major began to play and to sing. It was not a song she knew. It sounded quite modern, and the words were about a soldier going off to war, and saying farewell to his love. Larosse sang with his eyes fixed on Sophie's face, but their expression was one of sadness rather than supplication. Sophie listened almost without drawing breath, her eyes wide, so vulnerable that Héloïse trembled for her.

'And if the word should come that I have fallen, I would not trouble you to remember anything that will make you grieve,' Larosse sang in French. 'Remember nothing, nothing, of this frightful war — remember only that it's I who love you best.'

The last words were by way of a refrain, repeated at the end of each stanza, and the tune that accompanied them was so sad and so haunting that Héloïse thought she could never forget it.

Rien, rien de cette guerre affreuse,
Seulement que c'est moi qui t'aime le mieux.

She didn't know how much the other young people understood of the French, but the song was plainly familiar to one other person, for as Larosse came to the end, the voice of the Duc joined in. Héloïse turned her head.

263

He was standing beside her, looking down at her as he sang softly, '*Seulement que c'est moi qui t'aime le mieux.*'

'Oh, don't!' she said. 'Please don't.'

He smiled a little crookedly. 'It is only a song — "La Bayadère",' he said. 'It's a great favourite at the moment in Nivelles. All the Belgians sing it. You hear it in every café. Haven't you ever heard it before?'

'No.' She struggled for composure. 'It's very sad.'

'All the best songs are sad. Particularly soldiers' songs. Larosse sings well, don't you think?'

Héloïse shook her head, not in negation, but in dismay. The song had ended in applause, and Marcus, Bobbie and Barbarina had gathered round Larosse, adding their compliments to Sophie's. Larosse said something joking about its being a good song for cleaning tack to, and Marcus said something amusing, and they all laughed. But Héloïse had seen Sophie's expression, and would not easily forget it. His attentions were growing too particular, and Sophie's affections were in danger of being engaged. She knew she must speak to him. She bit her lip. 'Oh, I wish James were here,' she said.

If the Duc felt the blow, he did not shew it. He touched her hand lightly, understanding where her thoughts lay, and said, 'I will speak to him, as his superior officer. You should not be troubled by this matter. Will you permit me, as a friend, to attend to it on your behalf?'

'As a friend,' she said doubtfully, and then reminded herself what it must cost him to say that. 'Thank you,' she said.

When the guests had gone and everyone was going up to bed, Héloïse called Sophie back to speak to her alone for a moment. Sophie faced her with such a look of innocence and affection that for a moment all her words of warning fled and she could only smile at her daughter, and say, 'You looked so pretty tonight, my Sophie. Did you have an agreeable time?'

'Oh yes, Maman!' Sophie said. 'I do like Brussels! And I'm so grateful to you and Aunt Lucy for doing all this for me.'

The subject must be broached. 'Sophie, *ma chère*, this Major Larosse —'

'Yes, Maman?'

Héloïse struggled. '*Chérie,* some gentlemen have the knack of making themselves agreeable. They are so easy to be in company with that one may begin to grow fond of them without realising it. But one must not be deceived by the pleasantness into — into giving more affection than is asked for.'

'But, Maman —'

'One may like agreeable gentlemen, but one must not imagine that they mean anything more than to be pleasant company.'

Sophie shook her head. 'If you mean to warn me about Major Larosse, there is no need. I know he can never think of me in — in *that* way.'

Now Héloïse looked enquiringly. 'Has he said anything to you to make you think —'

Sophie grew pink. 'No! Of course not. He is very kind, and I love to talk to him, but I am not so vain as to suppose I am his object. He is so clever, and has travelled and done so much, and I am so stupid and ignorant. And I'm not even pretty. I know he could never care for me.'

It was all said so simply, without resentment, purely as a matter of fact, that Héloïse's throat closed up. Her dear, good, lovely Sophie, who knew her own worth so little! She was too good for any man! 'How do you feel about him, *chérie?*' she asked with difficulty.

The dark eyes — like James's, but velvet black instead of heavenly blue — became luminous. 'I like him so much, Maman,' she confessed softly. 'More than anyone I've ever met! But don't be afraid — I am being very sensible. I do think he likes me, because he always chooses to come and talk to me. He calls himself my friend —' She remembered the Bickersteths' ball, and what he had said then about kissing her, and blushed; but he had been teasing, that was all. She resumed, the dark eyes shielded now by the droop of her long lashes. 'I know that I must not think — there is the question of my birth, you see. Though everyone is very kind to me ...'

'Oh, Sophie!'

Sophie flung her arms round her mother. 'Oh, now I have hurt you! I didn't mean to! And I don't mind, truly I don't,

Maman, but I can't help knowing that when it comes to marriage, I may not look too high.'

Héloïse pressed the dark head against her cheek. 'The man who wins you, my Sophie, will be the most fortunate man in the world,' she said. 'And he will feel himself to be so, too, I promise you. One day, the man will come along who knows how to value you.'

Lucy and Danby met, not entirely by accident, on the landing outside her bedchamber. Both paused, and they looked at each other cautiously, unsure as to how the other was feeling. Finally Danby said, 'I think it was a successful evening, don't you?'

'Yes — very,' Lucy said, and then, 'Uxbridge means to reorganise the brigade, to put the most experienced officers with the most inexperienced troops.'

'Yes, it's the Beau's plan,' Danby said, wondering how to reach her. 'Lucy,' he said desperately, 'you don't really mean to ride in this race tomorrow, do you?'

Lucy softened: it was the approach she had waited for, longed for — the way open for honourable retreat. 'Do you mind it very much?' she asked, trying to sound neutral, and sounding instead a little stiff.

'Yes, you know I do. I wish you won't.' He felt around cautiously for words, and chose the wrong ones. 'It's one thing for a wild young woman like Bel Robb, but quite another for you.'

Lucy cooled. 'You mean I'm too old?'

He saw his mistake. 'Not too old, no — of course not. But you're a respected member of Society, a matron with a grown daughter, and it wouldn't be seemly —'

'Seemly?'

'I mean — damnit, Lucy, you know what I mean! Why will you try to make it hard for me?'

'I know what you mean,' she said frigidly. 'You mean I'm too old. Well let me tell you, Danby Wiske, that I can beat anyone, *anyone*, over any ground —'

'It's not a matter of whether you can win,' he said heatedly. 'You shouldn't even want to win. Do you really want to make us both look ridiculous —?'

Very much the wrong word. 'Oh, if you are afraid of what people will think of you, you may make it plain that you have nothing to do with it. Bet against me if you like — but don't complain to me when you lose your stake.'

She turned abruptly away from him and went into her room, slamming the door behind her. For a moment he stared at the closed door, perplexed, wondering whether to follow her, and then shrugged, and turned away. She was being utterly unreasonable, and there was no point in trying to talk to someone when their mind was made up like that. Let her make a fool of herself. He washed his hands of the whole affair.

Docwra would have liked to forget to call Lucy in time the next morning, but there were some things even she didn't dare to do. It wouldn't have made any difference, anyway, for Lucy barely slept, and was not only awake but out of bed and vigorously scrubbing her teeth when her maid came in. Docwra didn't dare protest, either, beyond sniffing disapprovingly as she helped her lady dress, and even the sniffs drew forth black frowns. Lucy felt cross, miserable and depressed, misunderstood, lonely and confused. She almost wished for a torrential thunderstorm to decide the thing for her, but the day outside was shrouded in the white fog which clears to a beautiful early summer day.

In the breakfast-parlour there was the smell of coffee, which was welcome to her, and of fried food, which was not. Usually Lucy was a hearty eater, and in view of the forthcoming exertion a substantial breakfast of fried beefsteak had been provided for her, topped with fried eggs and flanked by a couple of kidneys. But this morning, for some reason, her throat closed up and her stomach lifted warningly at the smell of the food. With Docwra looking on, Lucy could not admit defeat, and was obliged to go through the motions of eating, but the little she managed to get down seemed to lie in her stomach in a solid indigestible lump. She thought that Danby might appear, to remonstrate with her, or perhaps, after a change of heart, to wish her luck, but when the door opened at last, it revealed only the footman to say that her carriage had arrived. Lucy nodded resignedly to Docwra to fetch her cloak.

It was a hired curricle that awaited her outside, with her own pair of blacks harnessed. Parslow had gone down to Enghien the night before, leading Magnus, so that he would be fresh for the race this morning, and Lucy was to meet them both at the inn where they had stayed overnight. The white world was strangely silent as Lucy stepped out into it, as if they were the only creatures left alive. One of the horses sneezed and tossed his head, making his curb-chain jingle. They were very black in the white fog, and at the limit of visibility, and for an eerie moment Lucy felt that what was beyond them was in fact nothing, non-creation, the Void. She shivered, and hurried down the steps with Docwra at her shoulder.

Outside the city, on the road to Enghien, the fog was worse, and Lucy had to drive slowly, keeping her eye fixed on the edge of the road and having to trust that no-one would be coming the other way so early in the morning. Familiar things took on strange shapes when seen half-shrouded, and the blacks were nervous, peeking and starting at every gate-post and overhanging branch. An unseen cow coughing behind a hedge made them shoot up into the air, and a creaking shutter on an invisible house just off the road had them jittering on the spot, their ears going in every direction, and it was all Lucy could do to hold them and make them walk on.

But at last the wall of mist to the east began to glow luminously, and a golden stain spread slowly through it as the sun came up. Soon afterwards it began to thin like magic, and things first black then dark green began to take shape — hedges and trees and fields — with the remains of the fog clinging to them in tatters like fragments of muslin. As the sun lifted clear of the hedgerows, the last of the mist was sucked up, and the world was revealed calm and sparkling and joyfully familiar under a sky of innocent blue. The blacks put down their feet with a will, and threw themselves into the collar so that the curricle bowled merrily along the highway that had so suddenly ceased to be menacing.

At the inn-stables, Parslow was in the final stages of grooming. Magnus Apollo was on pillar reins out in the yard, while Parslow crouched down oiling his hooves, and the horse whinnied loudly to the blacks as Lucy drove in, nodding his handsome gleaming head up and down. His mane was plaited, the gloss on his bay neck was like the patina on lovingly polished wood, and his quarters had been brushed into a chequerboard pattern.

'My God, he's a picture,' Lucy called out. Magnus snorted impetuously and dug with a fore-hoof, to the peril of the oil-bottle. 'It's a point-to-point, you know, Parslow, not the County Show. He'll be covered in dust before he's gone fifty yards.'

Parslow fielded the bottle neatly and stood up, nodding neutrally to his mistress and exchanging a single glance with Docwra, who pressed her lips together disapprovingly. A groom belonging to the inn came out and took the blacks' heads, and Lucy climbed down and flung off her cloak and came over to look at her horse.

'How is he this morning?' she asked, sliding a carrot under the soft enquiring lips which were exploring her hands. 'There, my beauty, is that what you want? No no, that's my finger! You can't eat that.'

'He's fresh, my lady, as you'd expect. He'll be hard to hold,' Parslow said.

'I don't want to hold him, so that's just as well,' Lucy said. 'He looks magnificent.'

'Thank you, my lady. If you'll excuse me, I'll be tacking him up now.'

Lucy glanced at her watch, and a little of the queasiness returned. 'Yes, very well. You've remembered the racing-surcingle?'

Parslow was too good a servant to say 'of course'. He said, 'Yes, my lady,' and went to pick up the saddle, which was lying ready on top of the stable door. Magnus flattened his ears as he felt it on his back, and when Parslow reached under his belly for the girth, he lifted a hind foot threateningly, and then cow-kicked vigorously as the groom buckled it and drew it tight.

'Does he always do that?' Lucy asked, watching the big horse waltz backwards against the restraining ropes at the touch of the surcingle on his ginger belly. 'I thought that groom, what's his name, said he was the kindest horse in the world, and an angel in stables?'

269

'He's a little over-excited today, my lady,' Parslow said evenly. 'He doesn't mean anything by it. He's fresh, that's all.'

Fresh, and strong, Lucy thought, watching him. Now the saddle was on, Magnus was resigned to it, and was staring about him, head up, ears flickering, nostrils flaring to catch every scent that came to him on the warm morning air. Parslow approached with the bridle. Magnus took the bit obligingly, but once the bridle was on, he was anxious to be off, and though Parslow held him apparently without effort, Lucy eyed the swinging quarters and the rippling crest with suspicion, wondering if Parslow had deliberately corned him up to make her call the race off. If that were his plan — and she wouldn't put it past him — he would be disappointed, she thought firmly.

Parslow led Magnus to the mounting-block. Lucy saw the point of that — he couldn't both hold the surging horse and throw her up, so she suffered the indignity for once, pulled her skirt clear of her boot, judged her moment, and was up. It was rather like transferring from a small boat to a ship in a choppy sea, she thought: you had to choose the instant when the space between was the narrowest, and then move like lightning.

'Well, what news is there of the opposition?' she asked abruptly as she settled herself and her skirts.

'They say there's going to be a large field, my lady,' Parslow said neutrally. 'As many as twelve or fifteen young gentlemen mean to start, though how many will cover the point is no more than a guess. You'll do well, if you'll forgive me, my lady, to get out in front and stay there. There'll be one or two fallers at the jumps, and you don't want anyone fouling you and bringing him down.'

'Hmm,' Lucy said. 'It's the strategy I'd favour anyway, with a bold horse like Magnus.' She met her groom's eye, and knew perfectly well that he didn't think she'd have any choice about being out in front, because she wouldn't be able to hold the excited gelding back. 'You'd better get mounted,' she said. 'I have him.'

Parslow let go obediently and Magnus snatched at the reins and tried to take off. Finding Lucy wouldn't let him, he

270

revolved on the spot, snorting like a dragon, and then took to digging up the cobbles with his forefeet. Lucy sat his antics with outward calm, knowing there was no vice in him, that he was just young and excited; but she felt the power of him all the same, and knew that, even with a curb, she would not be able to hold him against his will.

It suddenly came home to her what a foolhardy thing it was to enter this race. Twelve or fifteen hotheaded young men of varying ability were at this moment mounting fresh corned-up English hunters, each meaning to ride a neck-or-nothing race over unknown ground, and devil take the hindermost. It would only take one of them to barge Magnus, or foul his path, or cross him jumping a hedge, and he could be brought down, and Lucy with him. A fall from this big horse at full gallop, or over a jump — to say nothing of the possibility of coming down underneath him, or being dragged, or landing in a ditch ...

Parslow led his horse out into the yard, jerking Lucy back from the contemplation of disaster. *Whatever had come over her?* She rebuked herself sternly. She had never before in her life thought such puling, cowardly, ninnyish thoughts. Had her nerve gone? Had she become indeed what Society thought her, a lace-capped matron fit for nothing but a fireside chair? She straightened up in the saddle and took a firm grip on herself and Magnus. She had the best, fittest and fastest horse in Belgium, and she was out today to shew that she as worthy of him — and so she would, or die in the attempt!

She saw out of the corner of her eye that Parslow was up. 'Ready?' she said, turning Magnus towards the yard-gate. 'You had better leave for Braine-le-Comte straight away, Docwra. Wait for me with the curricle at the Cock Inn.'

Magnus sprang forward even as she spoke, almost knocking the maid over in his eagerness. Parslow was still feeling for his stirrups as his horse dashed after Magnus, and he had no time for anything but a brief and speaking glance at Docwra as he passed.

The point-to-point was due to start at eleven o'clock, and at a few minutes before the hour, an officer and a trooper of Hussars could be seen posting down the high road towards

271

Enghien as though life depended on it. An informed observer could have told from the fact that the trooper wore a queue that they were of the 10th Hussars — the Prince of Wales' Own. If the same observer knew about the point-to-point, he could have put two and two together and guessed that the officer with the anxious frown urging his horse to ever greater effort was Colonel Lord Theakston, and that he was going to miss the start.

In fact it was after ten past eleven when the two horses skidded, sweating, through the gate into the meadow behind the church where the race was to start, and were brought to a halt that almost threw them on their haunches. The turf had been sadly cut up by the hooves of thirty or so mettlesome horses, and a broken hunting-whip lay in a trampled patch as mute witness to at least one minor accident before the start, but of the field itself there was no sign. Even the grooms had gone.

'Damn, damn, damn,' Lord Theakston cursed himself under his breath. 'Why didn't I leave sooner? Why was I so damned pig-headed?' He had lingered in bed that morning, pulling the pillow over his head so that he would not hear any sounds of rising and departure. He was not going to compromise his dignity by begging. He had his pride.

But his pride had retreated slowly before a parade of images of the sort which had troubled Lucy herself briefly — except that Danby's were more explicit and more bloody. He saw Lucy being bolted with, being thrown, being rolled on; in some horrifying multiple-horse crash, involving a six-foot hedge, an unseen ditch on the landing-side, and an abandoned farm-implement covered in protruding spikes and blades; saw her being brought home, broken and bloody, lying across a hurdle carried by silent, bare-headed peasants ...

It was useless to dismiss these images and tell himself that she was the best rider, male or female, he had ever met. They simply multiplied silently like spiders in the corners of his mind, and finally drove him from his bed yelling for his servant and his trousers. But he had delayed too long, he had missed the start, he was too late; and now if she were killed he'd have only his own stupid pride to blame ...

'Colonel, sir,' said the trooper in an urgent undertone, and Danby, returning from his black thoughts, followed the direction of the trooper's gaze to a corner of the meadow where a blessedly familiar male figure was holding two grazing horses, one of which was undoubtedly Magnus Apollo.

'Parslow!' he breathed. He swung his startled horse round and kicked it into a canter. As he drew nearer, he saw with a mixture of relief and fear that Lucy was there too, sitting on a stile at the angle of the hedge, hatless, her elbows on her knees and her head in her hands. Had she fallen even before the start? Was she hurt? He halted his horse with two bounces and flung himself off recklessly, and was by her side before she had time to do more than rise to her feet at the sight of him.

'Lucy! Oh, Lucy! Are you all right? My darling, are you hurt? What happened?'

'Danby! What the devil are you doing here?' It was not precisely a welcoming question, but it spoke of surprise rather than pain or trouble. He scanned her anxiously. There was no sign of mud or blood or contusion. No torn clothing. She seemed, indeed, quite immaculate, apart from her hatlessness.

'Are you all right? You haven't had a fall?'

'No, of course not. Of course I'm all right,' she said, and to his surprise she reddened as though with shame or embarrassment. 'I didn't go, that's all.'

His heart and stomach resumed their accustomed places, and he regarded her with growing hope. 'Why not?' he asked at last.

Her eyes shifted away. 'Oh, well —' She bit her lip, and flicked at the hedge with her whip. 'Well, you see —' And then her eyes filled with tears, and she said, 'Oh damn!' and caught at the first two with the back of her hand as they slid over her eyelashes.

'Oh, Lucy,' he said. 'Oh, my darling. You thought better of it, didn't you? You decided not to do it?' She nodded, still struggling with the unwanted tears. 'I'm so glad. Darling, you did right. Oh, Lucy, don't cry.'

'I'm not crying, damn it,' she lied, and then turned bright wet eyes on him. 'But everyone will think — they'll think — I was *afraid*.'

Parslow and Trooper Bird had put themselves politely on the far side of the four horses, and had their backs turned as well. Danby took his wife into his arms and held her with a

273

great upsurge of joy as she wept onto the shoulder of his extremely expensive gold-laced pelisse.

'Tell me what happened, love. Why didn't you go?'

Her answer came out in pieces and blotted with tears. 'I was going to race — I was determined. I was going to shew everyone. But when I got here, and I saw all the young men — in uniform — just boys, really. And Bel Robb on that grey weed, laughing like a man, and talking and flirting — but just a girl, after all, and so it didn't seem to matter, not with her. And then I knew I couldn't do it. Oh, Danby —' and here the tears surged up in earnest — ''s-some of them — were young enough to be my — my *children!*'

Danby held her tighter, having the common sense then to say nothing until she was recovered enough to need his handkerchief. He provided it, and she blew her nose and sniffed dismally. 'Everyone will think I scratched because I was afraid.'

'No, they won't,' he said soothingly.

'Parslow thinks Magnus is too strong for me. Everyone will think I couldn't manage him — or I was afraid Bel Robb would beat me, after all. Everyone will think —'

'No, they won't,' he said again. 'Everyone will think you did the right thing, which you did. It was a foolish, unseemly race, and you wanted no part of it.'

'I would have won,' she said, looking up at him, her lower lip trembling.

'Of course you would. No-one ever doubted it. Not even Bel Robb,' he added, but provoked no answering smile.

'Oh, Danby,' she said miserably. 'I feel so old.'

'Darling,' he protested, riven to the heart. She met his eyes, looking as small and bedraggled and helpless as a kitten only just reprieved from drowning.

'Danby, I had a letter last week, from Flaminia.' She drew an uneven breath. 'She's pregnant. I'm going to be a grandmother.'

Her voice wavered on the hated word, and Danby took her into his arms again, partly because he simply had to hold her very close, and partly because he didn't want her to see his smile. He thought in her present state of mind she might misinterpret it.

274

CHAPTER ELEVEN

The cricket match between the Foot Guards and the 10th Hussars, which was to be held at the Château Ladon, was the next event to arouse excited anticipation and provoke a perfect frenzy of wagering. The château lay in very pretty country about ten miles from Brussels, on the road to Ninove — an ideal distance to make a pleasant day's outing for the *beau monde* in carriages or on horseback.

The Comte de Ladon, a strange little man of simian appearance, with a hunch-back and a head too big for his body, was obsessively sociable, and besides accommodating the cricket match, threw his palace open for the day, promising refreshments of no common order for players and spectators alike; the cool shade of his grandest salons for such ladies as preferred to shun the heat of midday; his paved terrace for a grandstand, his orangery for dalliance, his stables for the horses; and when the match was over, a delightful moonlit picnic by the lakeside, with a display of fireworks to round it all off.

On the day of the match the barouches and landaulettes, the phaetons, the curricles and tilburies, and the gentlemen a-horseback converged on the old château, and by eleven o'clock the grounds were thronged as never before in their history with silks and muslins, blue coats and pantaloons, and a dazzle of uniforms. Everyone declared it a charming place. The mellow old stone of the château, with its pepper-pot turrets and blue slate roofs, was delightfully set off by the ancient creeper which rambled over it. The broad stone terrace dropped steeply to an old-fashioned formal parterre of gravel paths and sculpted box, beyond which was a ha-ha dividing it from the meadow where the match was to be held.

The meadow had been freshly mown for the occasion, leaving an uncut fringe of cocksfoot and mouse-ear and moon daisies. Along one side of the field was a row of handsome shady trees, just coming into full leaf, and beyond them ran a deep and light-dappled stream which issued from the lake on the other side of the house. Other trees grew here and there in the hedgerow, offering shade to the spectators, and more meadows lay beyond the hedges for those who tired of cricket and wanted to walk and refresh their spirits with a contemplation of nature.

'It's all so pretty,' Sophie said, looking around with appreciation. She and Rosamund had arrived early in Lady Theakston's barouche. Larosse and Tantony had presented themselves almost before the wheels had stopped turning, and having made their bows, asked to be allowed to escort the young ladies on a perambulation of the immediate grounds.

'Yes,' Larosse agreed. 'I believe that Ladon is one of the prettiest places in Belgium. It's a pity the château should have gone so much to ruin, though.'

'Has it? It looks very nice from here.'

'The roof leaks, however, and there's a great deal of dampness inside, and everything needs painting. De Ladon neglects it.'

'He's an odd man, from all I hear,' Tantony said.

'Odd, indeed. The title is an old one, but de Ladon has it by collateral inheritance only, from his mother. His father was a very low sort of man — a groom, or something of the sort, so they say.'

'There was no fortune with the title, then?' Tantony said with the sympathy of one whose estate was greater than his rents.

Larosse shrugged. 'His mother left him an income which ought to have been adequate, but he squanders it on affairs such as this one.' He gestured around him. 'How much all this will cost him is beyond me to calculate. The fireworks alone may come to a thousand pounds.'

'But, then, how extremely kind of him,' Sophie exclaimed. 'To do this, just to give us pleasure —'

'Oh, Sophie!' Rosamund said. 'He doesn't do it to please us. He's trying to buy his way into Society — isn't that right, Major? I heard Harry Uxbridge telling Mama so. He's always giving dinners and balls, but the best people don't accept his

276

invitations. He's always on the fringes of Society, never at the centre, where he wants to be.'

'The poor man,' Sophie said. 'Why won't people accept? Just because his father was a groom?'

'Not entirely,' Tantony said. 'There's his appearance, too, and —'

'But that isn't his fault, any more than that his father was low,' Sophie objected.

'These are egalitarian sentiments, mademoiselle,' Larosse said. 'Perhaps you are a child of the Revolution also?'

Sophie blushed. 'Oh, no, I —'

'You take up for him,' Rosamund interrupted, 'but you've never even met him. He may be a thoroughly bad man — being a cripple doesn't automatically make a man a saint, you know.'

'It doesn't make him a villain,' Sophie said, 'and you've never met him either.'

'But I have,' Larosse intervened, 'and I can tell you that he is a man of no education and very low tastes.'

'Oh,' said Sophie, disconcerted.

'I heard that his father was a drunkard and a gamester,' Tantony offered.

'If it was so, I'm sorry to say de Ladon takes after him rather than his mother. He is not the sort of man you would wish to be acquainted with, mademoiselle,' Larosse said to Sophie. 'But it is a lovely day, after all, and one may be grateful to de Ladon at least for providing us with the setting. Whom do you favour to win the match, Captain Tantony?'

'The infantry, of course,' Tantony said promptly. 'They must always beat the cavalry.'

'Nonsense!' Rosamund said at once, as he knew she would. 'The cavalry will beat! Don't you know it's the Tenth you're speaking of? And they have Tansley — you must have heard of Tansley! They call him the Mighty Oak. He struck six sixes in a row in a match against the Fourteenth —'

Rosamund had only learnt these things herself the day before, but argued them now with the passion of a convinced sportswoman.

Tantony took her up delightedly. 'Oh, of course, against

277

another cavalry regiment he's well enough, but that's no challenge! Now the Guards' team hasn't a man under five-feet-ten —'

'Well, if you prefer brute power to subtlety and strategy —'

Having started them off, Larosse was free to offer Sophie his arm, and stroll along with her in companionable silence as the cheerful argument developed.

Lady Annabel Robb, still basking in the glory of her win over the Gentlemen's Sons, came on horseback, with Marcus Morland accompanying her. She was beginning to find her young swain tiresome. It always happened that way. Virtue and innocence attracted her strongly, but after a few weeks she began to find them a dead bore. So it had been with the little Ireton, she thought sadly. His tender blushes and utter devotion had been enchanting at first; but, as so often happened with the virtuous ones, he began to want to impose his strictures on her, and to disapprove of the very aspects of her which had attracted him in the first place.

So she had snubbed him when he began to lecture her, at first gently, then forcefully. Finally she had been obliged to tell him roundly that he had ceased to amuse her, and that he was being impertinent when he told her she should not flirt with darling Sviatoslav, or go riding with him in the Prater dressed in Cossack trousers. Ireton had retired covered in chagrin, but a few days later he was back, humble and repentant, begging to be taken back into favour. That, too, had soon ceased to amuse. Besides, the imbecile was always under her feet, and turning up uninvited to spoil her *tête à têtes* with Sviatka.

So between them she and Sviatka had thought up the Dare, thinking that Ireton, who hadn't enough red blood in him to feed a flea, would refuse and be too ashamed to shew his face thereafter. But he had surprised them all by accepting the challenge.

She sighed at the memory. In spite of what people said of her, she was not heartless, and she had been fond of the little Ireton, before he took to sermonising. His death had been horrible, a cruel blow. It had spelled the end, too, of her affair with Sviatoslav, for though he was a lovely and unscrupulous rogue, he was ambitious, and the scandal had threatened his career.

But Marcus Morland was made of sterner stuff, she thought, and would take his dismissal like a man when the time came. And the time would not be long in coming if he went on making himself disagreeable over the point-to-point. He had been subjecting her to a diatribe ever since they left Brussels.

When they arrived at the château they went straight into the stableyard. The yard was already full of officers, their horses being led away by de Ladon's servants, and several of them came over to greet Annabel in a way which Marcus found unnecessarily familiar.

'What ho, Lady Bel! Are you here, then, with your famous grey?'

'Don't tell me — you're to bat for the Gentlemen's Sons!'

'I wish I'd known! I've put my shirt on the Guards to win, but I'd have kept it back for a wager on you to make forty runs!'

'How about a race after the match — three times round the lake, for a hundred guineas?'

Marcus scowled frightfully, but Annabel only smiled, leaning down from the saddle to say lighty, 'Now, then, good people, give my poor Nimbus room to breathe! And if either side wishes me to bat, I am entirely at their service. I have no prejudices, you know!'

'Aye, that's a fact,' said someone, Marcus couldn't tell who, in a knowing voice, and there was some laughter.

Farringdon must also have heard and disliked it, for he stepped up to Nimbus and said loudly, 'May I help you down, Lady Annabel? Since none of these other oafs is gentleman enough to offer?'

'My good Farringdon, do you think I cannot get down by myself?' Bel laughed. 'But here, you may take my hands. I shall not refuse you, and make you look nohow in front of your peers.'

Farringdon jumped her down, and she remained a moment with her hands in his, smiling into his eyes. 'Thank you, my dear,' she said softly. 'That was well done.'

'You are no more than a feather,' he replied in kind.

279

'I believe it's a matter of rhythm. Only a clod would make heavy going of it.'

'And, like the Duke, I believe in getting over heavy ground as lightly as possible,' Farringdon smiled.

Marcus flung himself from the saddle and thrust his reins at a nearby servant. 'Here, don't stand gawping! And take her ladyship's horse as well, and make sure they're well rubbed-down!' He stepped up to Bel, glared at Farringdon, and offered her his arm as forcefully as possible. 'Come, Bel, I said we'd join my mother, and she'll be wondering where we are.'

Bel stared at him, but took his arm and allowed herself to be led, almost towed away from the group. When they were out of earshot, however, she snatched her arm back and snapped, 'Don't you ever do that again!'

'Do what?' Marcus snapped back, still frowning.

'Do what? Why, shew your jealousy like that, puppy!' Bel cried, her anger rising. 'Do you want to make us both objects of ridicule?'

Marcus blushed with anger. 'Puppy, is it?' he said.

'Yes — puppy, I said — for so you're behaving, snatching me away from Farringdon like an idiotic jealous boy! Placing me in a position where to resist you would have made me look even more foolish than —'

'If you won't rebuke Farringdon when he takes liberties with you, then I must!'

'Takes liberties? My God, you are positively Gothic! And how dare you presume to question anything I do?'

'I shall do so, when it seems questionable to me!' Marcus said heatedly, and then tried to moderate his anger. 'Oh, I know you don't mean it. I know it's just high spirits with you, but you don't seem to realise how it looks to other people. A lady's reputation is a fragile —'

'Don't lecture me about reputation, you curate! Do you think I was born yesterday? I know a great deal more about good society than you ever will, with your ridiculous rustic notions —'

'Ridiculous, are they? Well let me tell you it isn't me they're talking about after that point-to-point!'

She snapped her fingers. 'Pho! What do I care what the vulgar gossips say about me? Or the mossy-backed old dowagers? They're jealous, that's all, because they haven't enough blood in their veins to do anything a quarter as enterprising, and they know it.'

Marcus recognised that this was a jibe at his mother, and grew unwise in his jealous anger. 'It isn't only the dowagers, as you call them, who are talking about you. Or laughing at you.'

'Laughing?' Her brows drew down fearsomely. 'Who is laughing?'

'Those young men back there,' he said, jerking his chin over his shoulder. 'Those officers you like so much to flirt with and make jokes with as though you were one of them. Well, they don't think you are one of them, I can tell you! They don't like you the better for acting like a hoyden. You made a fool of yourself over that point-to-point, and you won't see it!'

She glared at him. 'I *won*, in case it has slipped your memory. I beat them all, and they admire me for it!'

'They *let* you win!' If he had not been beside himself with jealously, he would not have said it. As it was, even though he saw the instant of doubt replaced in Bel's eyes with naked fury, he went blundering on. 'You placed them in a damned awkward position, don't you see? When Lady Theakston withdrew and you didn't, they had to let you win, or appear ungentlemanly. It was damned embarrassing for them. You should never have gone in for it in the first place — it was bad form.'

'Ponsoby and Pyne begged me to, if you remember.'

'They're a pair of jokers. They did it to make a fool of you — and you let them!'

'Oh, then it was not bad form for your precious Lady Theakston to accept? They weren't trying to make a fool of her?' Annabel sneered.

'It's different with her,' Marcus said shortly, beginning to wish he had not started this. It was going further than he liked, now that his anger was cooling.

'How is it different?'

'Because they wouldn't have let her win. She probably would have won anyway, but it would have been a straight race —'

281

'They *didn't let me win!*' Bel hissed furiously, turning on him, her fingers hooked as though she longed to tear at his face.

Marcus stood his ground, pale now, appalled at what he had said and what she had revealed of herself. 'I'm sorry, Bel,' he said now, wanting only to placate her. 'I didn't mean it. Please let's not quarrel.'

She drew back into herself instantly, covering her rage with a mask of icy contempt. 'Quarrel? It isn't possible to quarrel with you, Marcus. You're just a boy. One doesn't quarrel with boys.'

It hurt, even though he tried not to let it hurt. Boy? Puppy? He told himself she didn't know what she was saying, but he was all too afraid that she did. There was a moment's silence, while he tried desperately to think of a way to recover the situation, and then they were disturbed. From the direction of the stableyard they had just quitted came de Ladon, hurrying towards them, his hands outstretched.

'Lady Annabel, Lady Annabel, how delightful!' They turned, and Annabel's expression became veiled. The count reached them, his face wreathed in obsequious smiles. 'How delightful I am, Lady Annabel, to honour you to my humble palace!' he cried. 'Such a joy! Oh, madame, I am overwhelm!'

Without waiting for invitation, he seized her hands and kissed first one and then the other. Her natural instinct was to snatch them back — there was something very disagreeable about the little man's effusion, and, indeed, their acquaintance was so slight as to make his kissing her hands an impertinence. But out of the corner of her eye she saw Marcus's indignant anger, saw that he was about to intervene on her behalf and warn de Ladon away, and the devil in her lifted its head. She would shew him, the impudent puppy! She would make him suffer for what he had dared to say to her!

'My dear Count,' she cooed, stitching a smile across her face, 'how very genial of you to invite us all here. What a delightful day we shall have of it. And how charming of you to come and greet me in person. I'm sure it was more than I looked for.'

De Ladon was first astonished, and then visibly writhed with gratification. 'Oh, my lady — so affable — such honour

282

— indeed, the pleasantness is all my own, I assure you! How gracious to see you here, at my abode! But the day is already hot, and you must be fatigued after your such a ride! Permission me, I beg, to escort you into the house to take some refreshment. A glass of wine for your ladyship — and a sit in the coolness, until you shall be good again.'

It was the last thing Annabel wanted at the moment, but Marcus looked as though he would burst, and so she bowed and accepted, placing her hand on the count's offered arm with a suppressed shudder. 'I shall be delighted,' she said. 'Excuse me, if you please, Captain Morland. I find the journey here has *fatigued* me more than I expected.'

Marcus could do no more than bow, though his face was grave and disapproving. Five minutes, Annabel told herself as she allowed the count to lead her away. Five minutes only, and then she would be out again in the fresh air. Nothing much could happen in that time. She would back herself against any man for five minutes, and de Ladon was only half her size, and lame into the bargain. And it would shew Marcus precisely what she thought of him.

The sun climbed the blue arch of the sky, the shadows under the trees grew shorter and deeper, and out in the meadow on the green grass young men in shirt-sleeves ran about in the heat of the day in pursuit of a ball. Their comrades encouraged them loudly from the side-lines in between draughts of cool ale or chilled champagne, and made increasingly wild wagers on the outcome of the match, the innings, or sometimes even a single ball. The occasional Dutch, Belgian or French eyes that were bent on the scene saw only that it was true what they had heard: the English were quite, quite mad.

Those not so dedicated to pure sport chatted, ate and drank, strolled about, and went from group to group around the meadow to gossip and flirt. There was always a lively group around Lady Theakston's barouche, and towards it Marcus in his misery gravitated to seek the comfort of old affections. After hanging about the fringes, chatting to various of his acquaintance, he drifted closer until he was lounging against a coachwheel immediately behind Rosamund, who was sitting on an upturned box watching the play and listening with half her attention to a genial argument between Tantony and her step-father about battle tactics.

The match had struck a plateau, where bowlers and batsmen had got the measure of each other and nothing much was happening. After a while, Marcus leaned forward and murmured to Rosamund, 'This is dull work. Should you like to take a turn along the river-bank with me, Rosy? I hear there are some enormous fish in this reach.'

'Yes, if you like.' Rosamund accepted the invitation as casually as it had been given, but could not help feeling inside a quiver of anticipation as Marcus gave her his hand to help her up. Lord Theakston nodded his permission, and Tantony flickered a look at Marcus which was balm to his bruised vanity. He tucked Rosamund's hand under his arm and they walked away through the trees.

'One of the nice things about an occasion like this,' he said, 'is that one doesn't have to be quite so stiff and formal about chaperones and so on. The occasion is itself the chaperone, so to speak.'

'Yes,' said Rosamund. 'I suppose a good deal of flirting will go on today.' Marcus bit his lip and didn't answer that. She noted it, and looked about her at the trees, dappled in sunlight and whispering slowly in the gentle air. 'It's a pretty place.'

'Yes. And how comfortable this is,' Marcus added a moment later, pressing her hand a little against his ribs. 'Just like old times. We were always good friends, weren't we, Rosy?'

Rosamund couldn't quite let that pass. 'Where's Lady Annabel?' she asked casually. 'I thought she came with you?'

'I escorted her on the journey,' Marcus said magnificently, 'but she has so many old friends here that she cannot need my continuous attendance. I believe she is in the Count de Ladon's party at the moment.'

Aha, Rosamund thought with one of Docwra's expressions, so that's how the milk got into the coconut! 'Well, that will be nice for him,' she said generously. They reached the river-bank, and stopped to look down into the clear water that ran swiftly over the gravel bed. The true Rosamund was not far beneath the veneer of *débutante*. 'I say,' she exclaimed suddenly, snatching her arm free to point, 'look at that fellow! Isn't he big? There, in the shadow of the weed. He must be three feet long at least!'

'I see him! That's a barbel — see his long whiskers? He digs in the gravel with them for food.'

'Oh yes. And there's a whole shoal of fish over there, look! How they keep in one place like that, against the current! What sort would they be?'

'I don't know. Some kind of carp, I suppose. There must be all sorts of fish in that lake of de Ladon's. I say, I wouldn't mind spending a day or two here with a line!'

Rosamund wrinkled her nose. 'Dull sport! I can't see what you see in fishing — sitting all day staring at the water with nothing to do.'

'No female ever can understand. It's a man's sport,' Marcus laughed.

'Pho! Men just like to make a mystery out of it, to be superior. Hunting, now — or shooting! Did I tell you I went out with Parslow last winter at Wolvercote — just after rabbits and pigeons, you know — and he taught me how to load. And my step-papa says he'll teach me to shoot this winter, and when I've learnt, I'm to have my own gun.'

Marcus laughed. 'You're a trump card, Rosy! I don't mind betting you'll be a capital shot — you always had a good eye with a catapult. Do you remember that time we hunted the squirrels in Berkeley Square? You wanted to catch enough to make yourself a muff!'

'And you hit that dog by mistake and it chased us nearly all the way home!'

'Ungenerous! Trust you to remember that,' Marcus laughed. 'Never mind, I'll challenge you to a return match when you've got your gun — only with pheasant instead of squirrels this time. Next winter —'

'Yes,' said Rosamund, her smile fading a little. 'Next winter — if the war's over by then.'

'It will be. It must be,' he said, but without conviction. 'You should rather say, if you're not married by then. For I don't suppose any normal husband would approve of that sort of thing.'

'No,' Rosamund said neutrally.

She met his eyes, and he chewed his lip a little before asking diffidently, 'That fellow Tantony, Ros — is he serious? Does he mean to make you an offer? You seem to see an awful lot of him.'

'He's in love with me,' she said bluntly.

'Oh,' said Marcus delicately. 'And you?'

'It doesn't matter what I feel about him,' she said with a humorous quirk of her mouth. 'Mother wouldn't consider him, anyway — he's not of my station in life, and that's all there is to it as far as she's concerned.'

'But he's a gentleman,' Marcus said, 'and an awfully decent fellow.'

'No title and no fortune,' Rosamund said economically.

'No, of course not,' Marcus said thoughtfully. After a moment he added, 'And of course you're not of age for another three years.'

Rosamund didn't think it necessary to reply to that. They strolled on along the river-bank, her hand comfortably under his arm, talking of this and that like old friends. After a while they saw Bobbie and Barbarina coming towards them from the other direction.

'Hello!' Bobbie cried. 'Isn't it a lovely day? Bab and I were trying to count how many birds we could hear, but there must be hundreds of them, and all singing fit to burst.'

'Oh, hang the birds!' Marcus said. 'Have you seen the fish? Ros and I just saw the biggest shoal of carp you've ever seen!'

Barbarina was smiling, and looking, in her pleasure, almost pretty. Rosamund stood beside her listening indulgently as the two cousins wrangled happily about the wildlife and fell to boasting jokingly about their prowess with rod and gun. In the back of her mind was a sound like the first distant fanfare of triumphant trumpets.

Héloïse and Charles walked up to the house to pay their respect to de Ladon, for whom Héloïse, like her daughter, felt a little sorry. Larosse took the opportunity of asking if he might shew Sophie the herb garden which lay beside the house.

'It's laid out in formal patterns — a little like the gardens at Villandry, only not on such a grand scale, of course,' he said, and Héloïse, who had been hesitating, for she knew she ought to have a firm word with Larosse, yielded.

'Oh, Villandry! When I was a child, before the Revolution, Paper took me to see the gardens there. So clever, all the shapes and knots and patterns! Yes, do go, my Sophie. You should see, since you can never see Villandry now. I shall come myself and look, later.'

The herb garden was surrounded on three sides by tall yew hedges, and on the fourth by the wall of the kitchen garden, so it was sheltered and very warm and quiet. The air was full of the scent of box and lavender used to edge the herb beds, and of hot gravel and hot brick; and apart from the scrunching of their footsteps, there was no sound but the drowsy drone of a thousand bees busy amongst the herbs, and the occasional distant cry from the cricket-match echoing on the summer air.

The herbs were laid out so that their colours — all the different greens, and sage-silver and purple and yellow — made patterns and shapes which were defined by the edging bushes and, according to sixteenth-century lore, had magical or astrological meanings. Larosse told Sophie what little he knew about them as they wound their way about the paths and finally reached the arbour in the centre. Here there was a sundial, and an iron trellis-arch over which pale old-fashioned roses rambled, shading an old iron bench beneath. They paused to look first at the sundial. There were words carved in the stone rim about the bronze centre-plate, but they had been worn away by age and rain, so that only the first and last were legible.

'*Tempus* — and *umbra*,' Sophie pronounced, tracing them with a finger. 'What does it mean?'

'It is all that is left of the motto *Time is only a shadow*.' Larosse said. 'It is a little of a joke, you see.'

'Yes, I see. Rather a sad joke, though.'

'Does it seem sad to you? I think it is meant to be reassuring,' he said, amused.

'But *shadow* — the word makes one shiver.'

'Ah, yes,' he said, looking down at her bent head. 'There are many things which cast a shadow over us, mademoiselle. Some are unwelcome. *Qui nunc it per ita tenebrioscum illuc, unde negant redire quenquam,*' he declaimed.

Sophie shook her head. 'I didn't learn Latin, though my cousin Rosamund did. What does it mean?'

'The poet Catullus. "And now he treads the path of shadows, whence, they say, no man returns",' he said. 'But some shadows are welcome, like the delicious shade of this rose-arbour. Will you sit with me for a little while? You should not stand long out in the sun at this hour of the day.'

She gave him a shy smile, and sat, and he took his place beside her. Around them the garden basked in the heat, giving up its aromatic scents, and bees and butterflies busied themselves in the sweetness of the sage and thyme and hyssop flowers.

'They are so insignificant, but the bees prefer them to anything, even roses,' Sophie remarked wonderingly.

'They are wise, then. Herbs may not have the flamboyant beauty of the rose, but they have a beauty of their own all the same, and they contain far, far more sweetness,' he said.

She looked up, and then quickly down again. He spoke the words as if he meant more by them than their obvious sense; and there was that in his eyes when he looked at her ... But she must not allow her wishes to run away with her imagination. She knew what she was, and that he could not think of her. The garden, the sunshine, the roses, the bees — it was all too beautiful to bear. She sought for some sobering thought to steady her.

'Maman speaks as though she does not believe the war will end,' she said. 'Did you notice how she said I would never be able to visit Villandry? I think she believes France is lost for ever.'

Larosse had been looking with enormous satisfaction at the tip of Sophie's ear and the wispy dark fronds of hair that curled round it. Now a shadow crossed his face and he looked away across the garden. 'Well, she is right in a way. The France she knew is gone for ever, and many of its treasures with it. If she went back, I don't know that she would recognise it.'

'And your France?' Sophie ventured.

'Mine, too.'

'Then — why —?'

'Why do I fight? Ah, my Sophie, sometimes I ask myself the same question. Because I have a task unfinished. Because I owe a duty. Because there is a debt unpaid.' He laughed cynically. 'My God, how men deceive themselves with words! How we dress up our weakness and folly in fine clothes and call it kingly names! Whereas women — you say nothing of your lives, but live them, knowing in yourselves that what you do is important.'

She looked at him, startled. 'But — all I shall ever do is perhaps to be married.' Perhaps not even that, she thought sadly, but did not say it aloud.

He smiled at her. 'I must tell you a story, *chère* Sophie. Can you listen?'

'Yes,' she said, a little breathlessly because he had used her name again.

'Well, then,' and he looked away across the garden, the focus of his eyes changing as the sunlit scene before him faded and he stared instead into the past of his memory. 'It was when we were in the Peninsula. The good Captain Tantony has told you of his march to Lisbon as part of the rearguard of Wellington's army, staying always one pace ahead of Masséna's advance guard. I was in that advance guard. And what a march it was!'

He reached out quite unconsciously and took Sophie's hand and carried it back to his lap, where he held it in both his, stroking it a little, absently, with his thumb. Sophie sat very still and quiet, afraid to disturb him and his line of thought.

'We were hungry and cold; we had been on campaign a long time without rest, had fought battles and marched, and fought again ,and marched again. We had believed all along that we could beat the British with one good battle, but it had not proved so: we crushed them, and they rose again; we advanced and they evaded. And now it was growing colder, and the land was bare and inhospitable, and it rained — Lord, how it rained! The tracks were mired deep by the feet and the wheels and the hooves of the army we followed, and the fields were picked bare. There was nothing to eat, nowhere to shelter, and no hope of going home. In the spring, at the beginning of the campaign, our men had sung as they marched along. But now they didn't sing. They just tramped, head down in the rain, step after step looking at the mud.'

Sophie saw it too — a scene fantastically different from the real one before them.

'Still we kept on, harrying the rearguard, picking off their sentries in the dark, keeping them from sleeping as we were kept by the fear of losing touch with them. I jollied the men along, shouted at them, joked with them; but my heart was sick.

'And then came the day —' He paused. 'No different from any other day, really. We were marching down a broad track over the emptiest country I had ever seen. It was so empty and bare that it wore down our spirits, and when the rain began the men didn't even curse it, just glanced up, resignedly, and then down again.

'We went past what was left of a village. The inhabitants had fled, and it looked as though it had been stripped, and probably looted as well. Two of the houses had burnt down. It was all dead and bare. And then suddenly there was a movement. A woman came to the door of one of the cottages and just stood there, watching us.

'She was young, no more than twenty, I suppose — a peasant girl with a kerchief tied round her head, and an apron of sacking tied over her skirt, and a baby in her arms. I don't know what she was doing there, or why she hadn't gone with the rest, or whether she was alone. But there she stood, watching us go by in the rain.

'Another time she would have been in some danger from my lads, but today they were too depressed by the rain and the hunger and the cold to give her even so much as a glance. They just trudged. But I looked at her. She wasn't beautiful or remarkable in any way — just a peasant girl with a baby. And then she hitched the baby over on to her hip to ease the weight, and suddenly everything changed.'

He stopped again, pressing her hand hard as though to ensure her attention. 'How can I make you understand? It was that movement — so natural, almost unconscious. She had done it a hundred times before. But suddenly I could feel her — her *self*, as though I were inside her body. I felt the

290

weight of the child heavy in my arms, and the weight of its life and its dependency heavy on my soul. I knew the dull daily worry of feeding it and caring for it and keeping it warm and safe. I felt the mud under my bare feet, and the cold in my bones, and the endless faint complaint of my stomach which had never had enough to eat, or known dainty fare, in all its life.

'And I saw through her eyes the scarecrow army marching past. She had seen the British pass the day before and now she watched us go by with the flatness of absolute indifference in her eyes, and I saw us insubstantial — grey, ragged men going by on their way to some unknown and unimportant destination. We were ghosts, a ghost army passing away into the shadows, and when we had gone, she would forget us as though we had never been.

'And I saw also that she was right to forget us. Because she was more real and more important and more alive than any of us — than all of us put together. The small thing she did — to conceive and bear that child, and to sustain it and protect it and bring it to adulthood — was more important than all the battles and victories of all the armies in the world.'

He stopped as though the narration had wearied him. They sat in silence a while, and the warmth and colour of the garden and the humming of the bees gradually seeped back into their minds.

'Before that day, I was heartsick, but still I believed. Since then, it has all been different. Oh, I have gone on doing my duty, but I have not been able entirely to believe that what we do is important, we men.'

'But still you do it?' she said, and her voice, though soft, sounded shockingly intrusive to her ears. She felt him turn his head, and turned hers, too, to meet his eyes.

'Still I do it,' he said. 'Because I don't know what else to do. There was never anyone who could teach me how to stop being a ghost.' He looked down at her captive hand, and stroked it once more, and lifted it to his lips before restoring it to her. 'You are real, my Sophie, and what you do matters. Remember that.'

'You could —' she paused, having confounded herself with her own thoughts, and then, because he was looking at her

291

with that secret smile in his eyes, forced herself to continue. 'You could leave the army — not go. You could do something else.'

'Become a peasant — live in a cottage and till the earth?' he suggested, smiling.

'Even that would be better, if it was what you believed was right,' she said bravely.

'How simply you see things. Well, I could, let's admit. I even hope that I will — in my own way. But first — first I have a promise to keep and a debt to pay. Ah, the fine words again! First, let us say, I must finish the ghostly work, for no better reason than that I have always had a dislike of things left unfinished.'

'I wish you need not,' Sophie said very quietly.

He looked at her seriously for a long while, as though following her thoughts. He seemed, she thought without resentment, to be able to walk in amongst them as easily as a man walks about his own house. 'I wish I need not, also. But it seems to be in my nature, and we are all what we are, *n'est-ce pas, mon amie?*'

She didn't answer, but he seemed satisfied. He looked out across the garden again, and whistled softly — it was the tune of the song he had sung to her at the musical evening, 'La Bayadère'. After a moment he said cheerfully, 'But here is your Mama, and Monsieur le Duc come to see the garden. I hope she won't be disappointed — it is not on the scale of Villandry. We should go and meet them, perhaps?'

As the long shadows fell over the meadows, and the violet dusk deepened under the trees, and the sun sank at last below the horizon with a final glimmering rim of molten gold, Lieutenant 'Figgy' Lichfield of the Foot Guards hit the ball clean over the hedge into the lane for six, and thus secured a completely unsurprising victory over the 10th Hussars by four wickets.

'I think we did very well, all told,' Lord Theakston said, contemplating a grass-stain on his overalls that his man Deacon was going to be very unhappy about. 'Thurrock stood to his wicket like a man, and Tansley did all we expected. I thought they'd beat us by twice as much!'

Lucy looked at him. 'You mean you knew we were going to lose?'

He grinned. 'Of course. Hadn't a chance against Lichfield's giants.'

'Well, I wish you'd told me! I lost fifty guineas on them.'

'That's all right,' Danby said cheerfully. 'I had two hundred on. One has to back one's boys, you know.'

'I wouldn't have,' Lucy said with stout practicality. 'No sentiment where money is concerned. You could buy a useful road-horse for two hundred and fifty guineas.'

'Talking of sentiment,' Danby said, 'have you noticed that Marcus and Bel Robb seem to be at outs? She hasn't spoken to him all day.'

'Well I saw him go for a walk with Rosamund. I just hope the silly child doesn't start that nonsense again about wanting to marry him.'

'You'd sooner she married Tantony?'

Lucy frowned. 'Tantony's a very decent young man, and there's more to him than first meets the eye, but he's still not a match. Oh, dear, what a nuisance it all is! Why couldn't she form an attachment for an eligible young man with a title and neat fortune, like any normal girl?'

Danby leaned close enough to nibble the rim of her ear under cover of her hat. 'Because she hasn't any normal mama,' he murmured. 'Is anyone taking you to the picnic, Lady Theakston? Would you care to share my rug?'

'I should be delighted, sir,' Lucy replied demurely. 'But you must beware of my husband — he's a very jealous man.'

The evening was warm and absolutely still, even the faint breeze having died away, and dusk blended so subtly into moonlight that there seemed no transition. The moon had risen even before the sun went down, and hung so huge and yellow, low in the eastern sky over the lake, that it looked improbable and false, like one of the globe-lanterns at the Vauxhall pleasure gardens.

'One almost expects to be able to see the string,' Marcus said.

'I like it,' Rosamund said. 'It makes me feel quite frivolous, as though nothing really matters.'

'Perhaps nothing does,' Marcus said moodily. 'Nothing is ever really quite what it seems.'

She eyed him understandingly. 'Nonsense! Lots of things are. Horses, for one thing.' He gave a faint smile. 'And my mother — she's as transparent as glass. She couldn't dissemble if she tried.'

'How wise you sound suddenly. You've grown up, Rosy.'

'I've been using my eyes, that's all. Trot always said I was a noticing one, but now I'm out of the schoolroom, there's more to notice.'

Marcus grunted. 'Why did your mother decide not to race?' he asked abruptly.

'Why, to please Papa Danby, of course. She's perfectly nutty on him, really, and she realised at the last minute how much he would hate it. It's rather pretty to see them together, sometimes,' she added reflectively. 'It gives one hope.'

He smiled unwillingly. 'You think such a happy union could be repeated? You don't think it's unique?'

'Lord, I hope not! That would be like believing you'd never find another horse you'd like as much as your first pony.'

He burst out laughing. 'Oh, Rosy! Does it all come down to horses with you?'

'Horses can teach you a lot,' she said firmly. 'That's why Papa Danby manages Mama so well. She has an odd kick in her gallop, and hates the curb; but he lets her go her length, and she comes back to hand of her own will. So it should always be, if two people are suited.'

'Ah, yes,' he said, his smile fading. 'Suited. But sometimes the heart can't be governed.'

Rosamund was about to say something quite rude and derisory, but was interrupted by the arrival of Bobbie and Barbarina with Captain Tantony, who had come to join them.

'The lake looks so very black,' Barbarina was saying, eager to be frightened.

'Sinister and dangerous,' Rosamund suggested wickedly.

'Dangerous? Is it very deep, then?' asked Barbarina, wide-eyed.

'It's quite deep in the middle, I believe — around the

island,' said Bobbie. 'A man could drown, easily.' Barbarina shuddered satisfactorily.

'How fantastic that Chinese pagoda looks in the moonlight, with all its curlicues cut out against the sky,' said Tantony. 'By daylight it simply looked shabby.'

'The magic of the theatre,' Marcus said.

'But where are all the ducks?' Rosamund asked. 'I thought you said there were lots of wildfowl on this lake?'

'They'll all have gone to bed in the rushes,' Tantony answered. 'And probably a lot of them roost on the island at night. How the poor old things will panic when the fireworks begin! De Ladon means to have them set off from the island, you know, so that they reflect in the water.'

'Oh, that will look pretty!' said Barbarina. 'He must be a kind man — though it makes me shiver to look at him. He looks so very —'

'He can't help it, Bab,' Bobbie said shortly, seeing Marcus's expression.

'Oh, no,' Barbarina said, remembering her brother's sensitivity on the subject. Lady Annabel had spent nearly the whole day in de Ladon's company, and to judge from her behaviour she didn't find him repulsive at all. Barbarina didn't like Lady Bel, but if she was her brother's choice, that was enough for her. 'Let's go down to the water's edge, and see if we can see where the ducks are sleeping,' she said with a valiant effort to change the subject.

'Don't go too near the edge and fall in,' Marcus said shortly, and turning away, walked off into the darkness without another word.

'There are usually glow-worms on the path round the lake, so they tell me,' Tantony said, watching Rosamund as thoughtfully as she was watching Marcus. 'Lady Rosamund?' He offered his arm, and she came back with a start, and remembered the campaign, and took it with a smile.

'Yes, gladly,' she said. 'I suppose you will tell me they aren't half the size of the glow-worms you saw in Portugal?'

'Well, it's strange you should say that,' he began with a grin, 'but at Coimbra they had glow-worms —'

'The size of tennis-balls,' Rosamund finished for him. They all laughed, and Tantony relaxed again. Lady Rosamund had known Marcus Morland all her life, he told himself firmly. They were childhood friends, that was all.

As the moon rose higher, it changed from yellow to white, and then to burning silver, and threw down a blue-white light so intense it seemed surprising that it was without heat. The picnic de Ladon had provided was superb: nothing had been stinted. His servants moved about the groups on the lakeside shore, offering delicacies and refilling glasses, and the warm night air rang with the clatter of eating and the sound of voices and laughter. The cold light and the abrupt shadows were strangely exciting, and everyone was more vivacious than they would have been in the normality of a candlelit drawing-room.

De Ladon was in ecstasies: not only had the *beau monde* accepted his invitation *and* stayed on for supper, but the lovely, vivacious Lady Annabel Robb had been in his company for most of the day, taking his arm with the most flattering smiles, listening to his stories, and now, at supper-time, gathering around him a group of the most handsome, dashing, well-born young English gentlemen in Brussels: mostly officers, in their gorgeous uniforms — the very high-nosed, elegant, drawling, sporting young men who usually most despised him.

De Ladon was already in love, and after a whole day of feeding his social hunger with improbable dreams, his sense of reality had retired defeated, and he was waiting for no more than the right opportunity to offer his heart and his hand to Lady Annabel — to invite her to become the next Comtesse de Ladon, and châtelaine of the palace she had graced all day with her glorious presence.

Annabel, though loathing the frightful little man very little less than when she had first set eyes on him, was enjoying the effect she was having. The more the dowagers had looked down their noses and hissed amongst themselves, and the more the young men had looked uneasy and embarrassed and put out, the more she smiled at Monsieur le Singe, as she called him in her mind, and listened as if fascinated to his tedious stories. Most of all she had enjoyed Marcus's misery, for though he had made a brave effort at paying attention to his red-headed cousin, he had spent a good deal of the day hanging about in the middle distance staring at her with a mixture of pique, fury and longing which was ambrosia to her.

Farringdon found Marcus standing in the shadows watching Bel's court and the ridiculous posturings of de Ladon, and stood beside him for a while in the silence of sympathetic suffering.

'What the devil is she playing at?' Farringdon said at last with a sigh. 'Is she just amusing herself, or has she a fancy to his title?'

Marcus glanced at him, before resuming his moody stare. 'If she had a fancy to a title, she might as well have had yours.'

'I haven't a penny to my name, and she knows it,' Farringdon said without resentment. 'I knew I never had a chance with her, but I just liked being her choice. It was flattering, you see.' He gave a little shrug. 'I know it was different for you. I'm sorry, Morland. I never meant to give you pain.'

'I thought she cared for me,' Marcus said. 'She *said* she cared for me.' He stopped abruptly with the memory that she had not actually said so, not directly. He had interpreted her words that way, because he wanted to.

Farringdon offered him all the comfort he could. 'She must have cared for you, to go to all this trouble to punish you. She can't *like* him.'

Marcus watched his goddess with new understanding. 'She was just toying with me, and I made a damn' fool of myself, thinking she —' He writhed inwardly with embarrassment. 'How you must all have laughed at me,' he said bleakly.

'Oh, no! Never. We were sorry for you —'

'Thanks. That's infinitely worse.'

'— and we were jealous of you. Everyone wants to be Bel Robb's latest beau, even if it only lasts a few months. I'd have given everything to swap places with you — only of course, I had nothing to give.'

Marcus gave him a glance of gratitude, and they watched in silence for a while. Knowing that she didn't love him, that probably she had never loved him, that she was shallow and vicious and vain, unfortunately didn't make any difference at all to loving her. He wanted his place back, and if she had beckoned to him, he would have gone. It was humiliating to have to acknowledge his folly and frailty. He wanted her. He remembered the kisses, and the touch of her long cool fingers on his face, the scent of her skin, and the exotic promise of her eyes; and most of all the glorious feeling of walking into a ballroom with her on his arm and knowing every man in the room was longing to take his place. He wanted it all back, and he hated himself for it; but no other woman was like Bel Robb.

'But what the devil is she *doing?*' he cried angrily as she allowed de Ladon to kiss her hand. He had thought, damn his stupid conceit, that he would be the man who could keep her, where so many others had failed. As it was, he hadn't lasted even as long as poor little Harry Ireton. 'What can she want with de Ladon?'

'God knows,' Farringdon said, and they lapsed again into gloomy silence.

Sophie and Larosse stood by the lakeside tossing small stones into the water and watching the ripples spread. In the moon-light the water looked almost solid, like oiled silk being shaken.

Larosse studied Sophie's profile against the shining pewter of the lake and wondered what it was about this grave child that so shook his senses. She was not beautiful in the accepted, social way. Her nose was too long and her mouth was too wide and her skin was too dark. She was small and slight and brown-haired and brown-eyed and, compared with someone like Annabel Robb, utterly nondescript. And yet, from the first he had been drawn to her by a feeling so profound that it devastated him. She had a way, he thought, of living in her face that was unlike any other female he had ever known. She was so absolutely *there*, he thought, undisguised, looking out from her eyes at the dangerous world with no defence but the courage of her frankness and her irreproachable innocence.

And it was an innocence, he thought, that was not born of ignorance, but was something innate, which would survive all experience. He saw something of it in her mother; and could

298

imagine Sophie twenty years on, or thirty, still regarding the world with that simplicity which would always expect the best and would therefore — a surprising number of times — elicit it. It was a rare quality, and precious, and would almost always be undervalued in a world which regarded appearance more highly than intrinsic worth.

From the very beginning, from the instant of first seeing her, he had felt that he could talk to her without disguise, and that she would understand whatever he told her. He would not have to play a part, to go through the acceptable social manoeuvres and employ the acceptable social codes: he could talk to her, naked soul to naked soul. And so it had proved; but they did not live in a vacuum — they lived in the world which was governed by the rules he so despised, and he knew that he was culpable in allowing himself to enjoy Sophie's company so much.

She was pensive now, and he knew why. He could follow her thoughts as easily as his own, for they passed quite undisguised through her eyes and across her features. He was angry with himself — and afraid — and longing — and doubtful. Why could not everything be simple? Why could he not whisk her away to some deserted island where they might live together out of reach of the trammelling world?

She came to the end of her train of thought, and sighed — he saw it rather than heard it — and then felt his eyes on her, and turned her face to him with a little enquiring lift of the brows.

'It's been a long day,' he said. 'I hope it has been a happy one?'

'Oh yes,' she said. Her eyes said, 'Any day spent with you would be happy,' and he smiled painfully.

'It has been happy for me, too. I wish it might last for ever — but all things pass. Tomorrow I go away.'

'Go away?'

How he longed to take her in his arms. 'Yes, to Ghent. I am required to be of service to my sovereign for a week or two. I suppose it shall not be less — I hope it will not be more.'

'Two weeks?' Sophie said, as though it were an expanse of time too vast to see the end of. 'And then — shall you come back here?'

He looked into her eyes. 'I don't know,' he said gently. 'I hope so — but it depends on events. It depends most of all on what the Corsican does.'

'Do you think —'

'That he will attack so soon? Perhaps. I don't know. But whatever happens, my Sophie, I want you to know —' No, damn it, he couldn't! Oh God, for a fresh start, for a clean slate, for a soul and a life like Sophie's, the history all unwritten! She looked up at him with dark eyes like clear water, and hope naked in them, and doubt. 'It has meant a great deal to me to have had your friendship these weeks past.'

Not enough! said her eyes, and he knew it. Don't you know, little friend, that I long unspeakably to hold you close to me, and kiss you and kiss you until those doubting eyes close with rapture?

'It has meant more to me than I can hope to explain to you. A friendship such as ours is a rare thing — how rare I think you will understand as you go through life.'

Go through life — without you, said those eyes, and he saw hope leave them, and saw her lips part in a little quivering sigh that for him was as sharp and barbed as any arrow. She looked down, and said so quietly that he barely heard it, 'I have been glad to be your friend.'

He looked down at her bent head, and felt like a murderer. 'Perhaps we had better go back,' he said.

She nodded, and when he offered his arm, she took it without hesitation. Any other woman would have refused, to prove her proud independence. Every time he thought he could not love her more, he was proved wrong.

De Ladon fluttered around from group to group, urging everyone to move towards the lake edge, to take up positions where they would be able to see the wonderful spectacle that he had devised for them. His broken English became more broken than ever, but for once he noticed nothing of the coolness and snubs with which so many people treated him, for his heart was full of Lady Annabel, and the proud fact that the best of Brussels Society — and the best of the English visitors — were *here*, in his grounds, drinking his champagne.

300

Lucy moved to a vantage-point, her good-humour revealed by the fact that she allowed herself to be first hustled by de Ladon and then jostled by others seeking the same advantage. She seemed to have got separated from her own particular party, and looked round for Danby, without whose arm she felt oddly exposed this evening. She looked round, and found herself confronted by Lady Barbara in a rage.

'Well, ma'am, and I hope you are satisfied with yourself!' Lady Barbara began explosively.

'Tolerably so,' Lucy said, raising her eyebrows. 'Should I not be?'

'Oh, there's no use in playing Madam Innocent with me! I know what you have been up to. From the beginning I saw it — but I did not think you would be so brassy-faced as to go about it openly!'

Lucy cared too little about Lady Barbara's opinion even to mind being called brassy-faced, and was intrigued to see how far this infatuated woman would go. She gave her a coolly polite stare, and said, 'I haven't the least idea what you are talking about, ma'am, and I must say I have even less interest. But no doubt you will enlighten me.'

Even in the moonlight it was possible to see Lady Barbara blush with anger. 'Oh, you know, all right! Don't trouble yourself to dissemble with me! You shewed quite plainly that you were jealous — yes, ma'am, jealous! — that my Marcus had formed so eligible an attachment. You couldn't bear it that he was going to marry Lady Annabel instead of your daughter, in spite of all your scheming and contriving —'

'Scheming?' Lucy laughed. 'Can you really believe that I wanted Rosamund to marry your son? Roberta said it was so, but I didn't believe her.'

'Yes, that would gall you, wouldn't it?' Lady Barbara sneered. 'That Marcus preferred Lady Annabel — that she was ten times as handsome and fifty times as rich as Lady Rosamund — that they were in love with each other —'

'And so I determined to spoil things,' Lucy said. 'I should like to know how I managed it?'

'You may laugh and mock all you please, but you shall not get your way, ma'am, I assure you. You may have detached Lady Annabel — God knows how — but it won't bring you any nearer to a match between my son and your daughter. I have better plans for him — and just remember that Lady Annabel is not wed yet. There's many a slip, ma'am, between cup and lip, and don't you forget it!'

She stalked off, leaving Lucy feeling half amused, half disgusted. When Danby joined her a moment later, she slid her hand gratefully under his arm.

'What did your favourite *grande dame* want?' he asked. 'She seemed a little agitated.'

'She came to tell me that my plot to make Marcus marry Rosamund instead of Bel Robb wouldn't work,' Lucy said wryly.

'Is that all?' Danby smiled. 'Well, you are such a scheming mama, you deserve to get your come-uppance.'

Lucy looked at him doubtfully. 'I am not what she thinks, but her ambition gives me a disgust of my own. What have I been doing and thinking and saying these weeks past? That Rosamund must marry well, a man of substance and title. I am too like her for my own comfort.'

'No, nonsense,' said Danby comfortably. 'You want Rosamund to make a good match, and that's right and natural. But you would not let worldly ambition push you into marrying Rosamund to a bad man for the sake of his money or position.'

'Wouldn't I? I'm not so sure. Just now I feel I have not been a very likeable person of late. I wonder Rosamund doesn't hate me.'

'Rosamund would never marry anyone she doesn't like — she's as strong-minded as you.'

'I want the best for her, that's all,' Lucy said, sounding puzzled.

'Of course you do. And I agree with you that she ought not to marry a man with no fortune at all, for she would never be happy without horses, and horses are devilish expensive to keep.'

'Yes,' she said, and looked a little happier. 'Marcus could never afford her. I'm right, there.'

Danby squeezed her arm. 'Quite right. You must have the courage of your convictions, love. Ah, look, the fireworks are beginning!'

When the first set-piece was finished, and there was a pause while the next was set up, Danby saw Sir Hussey Vivian at a little distance, and left Lucy for a moment to go and speak with him. While he was gone, Philip Tantony took the opportunity to approach her and ask her diffidently if he might have a word with her.

Lucy came back from her thoughts and eyed him sympathetically. It was fortunate for him, she thought, that he had come to her after Lady Barbara and not before.

'I think I can guess what you want to speak to me about,' she said.

'Can you, ma'am? Yes, I suppose it must be obvious, although you are probably astonished at my presumption,' Tantony said with a self-deprecating smile.

'Shall we say courage? And I'm not astonished. I have come to know you a little better, Captain, in the last week or so.'

Tantony bowed. 'It's kind of you to say so, ma'am. All the same, I know I am not what the world would consider a good match for your daughter, and it's only because of the depth of my feelings for her that I dare to approach you, to ask your permission to address her.'

She regarded him thoughtfully. 'Tell me, do you think Rosamund likes you?'

Tantony spread his hands. 'I — I wish I could be sure,' he said. 'Yes, I think she likes me. Whether it's more than that, I don't know. Sometimes she seems — fond of me. At other times —'

'Well, yes, I understand. It's a young woman's prerogative to conceal her hand a little. And she could hardly express more than liking for you until you had declared yourself, could she?'

'And I couldn't declare myself until I had spoken to you,' Tantony said, finding the interview much easier than he had expected. Lady Theakston seemed more genial, and certainly more receptive to his request than he had anticipated.

'Very well, Captain. You are doing just as you ought. You had better describe your circumstances to me.'

He looked down at his feet, suddenly shy. 'From the first moment I saw your daughter, Lady Theakston, I knew that —'

'Yes, yes,' Lucy said hastily. 'We'll take that as read. God knows why, but you fell in love with her. But your circumstances, Captain. Could you support my daughter?'

Tantony braced himself. 'I am independent, ma'am. My father was a gentleman — Sir Braine Tantomy, of Branksome Park — and I was his only child. My father died four years ago, leaving his entire estate to me. It is an old seat in Suffolk — good land, but much in need of improvement, and the rents are not what they should be. But I mean, when we have beaten Boney, to devote all my energies to it, and I believe it can be made to pay handsomely in a few years' time. I have seven thousand pounds in the three-per-cents which would be settled on my wife, and my income is about two thousand a year.'

Lucy was agreeably surprised. She had expected less. Still, she said, 'That is not a great deal, considering my daughter's rank and dowry.'

'No, ma'am,' Tantony said frankly, 'but I have taken expert advice, and I believe the estate could easily yield four or five times that amount, once it is improved. More, even, if there were a certain level of capital investment. There are neighbouring farms whose land runs along with mine which I should dearly like to buy —'

'Quite,' Lucy said, seeing the fervour of the true farmer in his eye. 'Well, Captain, I am pleased to know that your circumstances are better than I had supposed. To be equally frank with you, you are not the match I envisaged for my daughter, as I expect you must know, but you seem to me to be the kind of man who might well make her a better husband than someone of greater wealth or rank. I want my daughter to be happy as well as respectable, and so I give you permission to address her. But —' she stemmed his outburst of gratitude with a lift of the hand — 'I have to tell you that I don't think she will have you. You proceed entirely at your own risk — I would have you understand that.'

'I understand,' Tantony said, smiling at her in a way that made her hope for an instant that Rosamund would accept him. 'I am grateful, ma'am, for your permission and your warning. I shall proceed with caution. Your servant, ma'am!'

He bowed and moved away, and Lucy watched him go, thinking that this quiet, gentle, unassuming soldier might well be the one man who could bring her wilful, headstrong daughter to hand.

At almost the same moment, Larosse, who had gone to fetch Sophie some lemonade, came face to face with Monsieur le Duc. He would have bowed and passed, but Charles halted him by a hand on his cuff, and said, 'So, Major, you are leaving at dawn for Ghent. I wish you will call in to my lodgings on your way — I have a packet to be taken to His Majesty.'

'Sir,' Larosse said, and waited to be released. But the Duc continued to look at him a little quizzically.

'I hope, René,' Charles said at last, 'that you will use the time wisely, to reflect on your position. No man is an island — particularly not a serving officer. We are all in the public eye, you know.'

Larosse stared at him at first in bewilderment, and then in slowly-growing realisation. 'It was you who arranged this, wasn't it?' he said at last, anger following realisation. 'You asked to have me transferred.'

'Yes,' said Charles.

'May one ask why?'

'It was necessary, *ça se voit.*'

'I think, sir, you take too much on yourself —' Larosse drew himself up stiffly.

'Calm yourself, René. We are talking now man to man, but I am still your superior officer.' Larosse breathed hard, and Charles went on quietly, 'You have been paying very marked attentions to a young woman, and arousing expectations in certain quarters which I have a notion you cannot live up to.'

Larosse opened his mouth to protest, and closed it again.

'What the devil were you thinking about, man? You are an officer and a gentleman — you have no right to toy with the affections of a green girl in her first Season!'

'I didn't —' Larosse began; swallowed and tried again. 'I

never intended to toy with her affections. Good God, sir, can you believe that of me? You who — you are not without interest in that family yourself, sir, as I have seen. You know what — you know how one feels.'

'Yes. Yes, I know. I can guess. But the cases are not precisely similar. Her ladyship is in no danger.'

There was a brief silence, and Charles met Larosse's eye with sympathy. 'Use the time to think what you're doing, René, that's all I ask. If you want to marry the girl, then for God's sake go about the matter properly.'

'My circumstances —'

'I know your circumstances.'

Larosse stared. 'Have you —?'

'Told her ladyship? No. It's your own business — at the moment. There are things that can be done, however — ways around. There are always ways around.'

Larosse bowed his head, and Charles looked at him with great sympathy for a moment, and then patted his arm briskly and walked away.

A few moments later Larosse rejoined Sophie, gave her the lemonade, and received her grateful smile.

'They are just going to begin,' she said. An explosion made her jump, and the first sky-rocket burst into yellow stars in the velvet sky. 'Oh! Oh, look, how beautiful!'

'Yes,' said Larosse, looking only at her. She felt his gaze and turned to look up at him.

'I wish you weren't going away,' she said, emboldened by the excitement and the lateness of the hour.

'So do I,' he said. Every part of him seemed to hurt in sympathy with his mind.

'But you'll come back?'

He didn't answer immediately, but the innocent eyes continued to look up into his trustfully. 'Yes,' he said at last, painfully. 'Yes, I'll come back.'

CHAPTER TWELVE

After waiting in vain for two letters to be answered, Mr Pobgee called at Morland Place one day in June to see James, and met him in the stable-yard, where he was watching her ladyship's ponies being put to in the little park phaeton. Pobgee was surprised at the difference in James: he was still too thin, but was no longer bowed and marble-faced with his grief. He seemed cheerful — almost, indeed, hectic — and greeted Pobgee with off-handed haste, as though he were in a great hurry.

'Hulloa, Pobgee — you here? A fine day, isn't it?' James's eyes flickered towards him and away again. 'Look out for the crupper, boy — you've got it hooked up! Come along now, you ought to be able to pole up quicker than that.'

'May I have a few words with you?' Pobgee asked, when it became obvious that James was not going to ask him what he wanted.

'I'm just going out,' James said.

Pobgee was astonished — not so much by the rudeness, for it was obvious that James was not intending to be rude, but by his complete lack of interest in the matter of the inheritance, which had been an obsession with him for so long. This, Pobgee thought gravely, was some new stage in his madness.

'I shan't keep you long,' he said firmly, 'but I must have your instructions. Come, James, a few minutes — in private.'

'Oh, very well,' James said, almost sulkily, and turned back to the house, snatching off his hat with an irritable gesture. Pobgee saw that he had had his hair cut recently, and that it was brushed into the fashionable style which Pobgee believed was called The Windswept, or something of the sort. Now he came to notice it, Pobgee thought, James's neckcloth was tied with more than usual care, and he was sporting a fancy waist-coat. One might almost suppose —

'You'd better come through to the steward's room,' James

flung over his shoulder, striding across the hall. Pobgee hurried in his wake, passing James's man, Durban, who gave him a burning look of significance which, unfortunately, Pobgee could not interpret — was it warning, or supplication? Both, perhaps. In the steward's room, James turned and looked at him enquiringly, slapping his boot with his crop in a manner that suggested a sand-glass had been turned for this interview, and that Pobgee was going to have to speak quickly and to the point.

'Well, what is it?'

'I have written to you twice, James — have you read the letters?'

'Letters? I don't know. I don't remember. What were they about?'

'About the Hobsbawn inheritance, to be sure,' Pobgee said patiently. 'I wrote to tell you of my visit to Manchester and the progress I have made.'

'Well, well, to the point, man! What progress *have* you made?'

'I interviewed all the principals in the case, and I have doubts, the gravest doubts, about the evidence as to the time of Mr Hobsbawn's death. Unfortunately — 'he forestalled James quickly, 'I have nothing but my suspicions. The housekeeper has made and signed a statement before witnesses that she saw Mr Hobsbawn alive after the time of Mrs Hawker's death, and I fear that statement, in the absence of any evidence to the contrary, is likely to be accepted by the Office of Probate.'

'In a word, then, the inheritance will go to Jasper Hobsbawn?' James said impatiently.

'In a word, yes — unless we can uncover some further evidence, and frankly, I do not see —'

'Oh, well, it can't be helped,' James said. 'Anything else?'

Pobgee looked his astonishment. 'James, are you quite well?'

'Well? Yes, of course I am. Never better. I had a cold — nothing to speak of — all cleared up now. Was there anything else? Because I really must be on my way.'

'No — yes — I must have your instructions. What do you wish me to do?'

'Do? Why, whatever you think best. You know more than I about these matters. Use your own judgement. Anything else?'

'No — no, there was nothing else.'

'Good. Well, thank you for calling. Let me know if anything else comes up, won't you.' He strode to the door and bellowed, 'Ottershaw!' and turned back only to say, 'Ottershaw will shew you out. Forgive me if I run along now.'

And then he was gone, leaving the lawyer bemused and anxious. It was Durban who came to shew him out, not the butler. Pobgee said, 'Is your master well, my man? He seems a little — nervous.'

Durban glanced about to see that no-one was in earshot, and lowered his voice to say, 'I'm that worried about him, sir, and I don't know what to do. He goes out and never tells me where, and won't let me come with him, and he's not himself, as you see. I don't know if I ought to write to her ladyship about it. I'm afraid — it's his changes of mood, you see. He's cheerful now, but it's not a natural cheerfulness, if you take my meaning, sir — and who knows what might come next?'

'Yes, I see.' Pobgee pondered. 'Perhaps you could follow him, at a discreet distance —'

'I tried that, sir. He saw me and sent me back. Very angry he was, too. And it isn't my place, sir, to spy on him. Only —'

'Quite. Well, I don't think you ought to upset her ladyship just yet. But if you have more cause to worry, send me word, and if necessary I will write to her ladyship myself.'

'Yes, sir. Thank you, sir.' Durban stood aside with a bow of the head; and as Pobgee passed, he said, very quietly, his eyes still down, 'Only I worry about him, you see.'

Pobgee paused to lay a sympathetic hand on Durban's shoulder. 'Yes. He is lucky to have you, Durban. I'm sure in his heart he knows that.'

Out in the yard, James found the phaeton ready. He climbed up into the driving-seat and, looking about him, spotted the newest and youngest stable-boy peeping from behind the stable-door, where he should have been getting on with the mucking-out.

'You — Satterley! Yes, you — come here, boy!'

The boy came out, trailing his broom, looking terrified. It

309

was his first week in his first job, and here he was in trouble already! The groom holding the ponies' heads gave him a fearsome scowl and he inched forward, trembling.

'Put that broom down and get up here beside me. I shall need you to do something for me.'

Satterley's mouth dropped further open, and he looked down at himself with eloquent astonishment. He was not the sort of servant a gentleman took up beside him on his plush upholstery. The other grooms in the yard gawped, too; but the head lad knew better than to argue with Mr James the way he was these days, snatched the broom from Satterley's nerveless fingers, and shoved him hard in the small of the back. The child obeyed the thurst, climbed trembling up beside his master, and tried to make himself as small and clean as possible by perching on the very edge of the seat and hunching himself up with his fists between his knees.

James neither looked at him nor spoke to him. He nodded to the groom holding the ponies with a curt, 'Let 'em go!' and drove briskly out of the yard. Turning onto the track, he touched the ponies with the whip and put them into a fast trot, and Satterley clutched the seat as the phaeton bounced over the ruts and wondered — half terrified, half hopeful — what his master might want with him.

He had been lucky to get this position, he knew. Grooms — anyone to do with horses — were the élite of the serving classes, and Morland Place was the best billet in the whole of Yorkshire, everyone knew that. His Ma had been a sewing-maid up at Morland Place when she was a girl, and it was her what got him took on as stable-lad, a place any of his friends would have given an eye and all their teeth for. Mr Hoskins, the Head Horseman, had been doubtful about him, on account his Da was only a tapman, and usually only the sons of horsemen reckoned to get taken on in the stables. But his Ma knew Mrs Thomson, the Housekeeper, what had been girls together up at the Place, and Mrs Thomson had spoke up to Mr Hoskins. Mr Hoskins was sweet on Mrs Thomson, him not being wed and her making him pies and cakes and such, and so it had been fixed up.

Satterley remembered the fearsome warnings Ma had given him on his first day, about doing as he was told, and speaking only when he was spoken to, and calling everyone 'sir', and never presuming, because the upper servants at Morland Place were that particular, and everything had to be done just so. He'd to work hard and not lark about, and maybe one day years ahead he'd get to be a groom proper, and then he'd be Someone, and wear a spotted neckerchief.

But Satterley had an imagination, and he couldn't help wondering now, as some of his terror at being so close to a member of the Quality evaporated, whether the master had seem something special in him, and was singling him out for glory. Gentleman's Tiger? Personal groom, even? Satterley blithely eliminated Mr Durban from the landscape, doubled his own height and weight, and gave himself a luxuriant moustache no member of the gentry would have tolerated on a servant for an instant. First thing he'd do if he got to be groom would be to buy Ma a silk dress to wear to church of a Sunday. Purple silk, with flounces. And a hat with feathers ...

James drove at a fast trot for about a mile, and then pulled up beside the great chestnut tree that stood at the bend of the track.

'Jump down and hold 'em,' he commanded. Satterley jumped, eager to display his speed and skill, and took hold of the bit-rings smartly as he had seen it done in the yard of the Hare and Heather when he had been waiting for his Da to finish work, and a coach had come in. James wound the reins and climbed down, too, and under Satterley's astonished eyes, walked across to the tree and crouched down to grope under the tangle of bushes that grew behind it. A moment later he dragged out a wicker hamper which he hoisted up into his arms and brought across to load onto the floor of the phaeton.

Then he climbed up again, took up the reins, and nodded to the boy. 'All right, you can let 'em go now, I have 'em. You can walk back from here. Go straight back, mind, and no dawdling.'

'Yessir. Nosir,' said Satterley, more astonished than ever.

'And keep your mouth shut about this.'

'Yessir,' said Satterley, his jaw sagging as he realised his special task was completed, his chance for glory had come and gone. He jumped aside as the ponies went past him, and turned to watch the phaeton whirl away in a cloud of dust until it was out of sight. His dreams were shattered; that moustache might never now be grown.

Pride goeth before a fall, as Ma was fond of saying when Da started boasting about Old Steggs, his champion ratter — a twenty-three-er, and named after Da's Uncle Steggs on account he had big ginger eyebrows just like him. And true enough, the day after Da had been laying it on thick and rare about Old Steggs being the best ratter in the Ridings, he'd been bitten in the foot by a big brown 'un, and it'd gone bad on him, and he'd nearly died.

Satterley realised glumly that not only was he not being singled out for glory, but that his master's enjoining him to secrecy had put him in a very nasty position. When he got back, he'd be bound to be asked what Master had wanted him for. If he refused to say, he'd be in trouble with his superiors, who would certainly cuff his head and call him impudent; and if he told, he'd be in trouble with Master, and probably lose his job.

He was in half a mind to go straight home there and then, and never go back to Morland Place again. But then Ma would give him what-for, and tell Da into the bargain, and Da would take a rope's end to him. What a life, he thought. Who'd be a stable-lad? He stuffed his fists into his pockets, hunched his shoulders, and trudged back along the track towards Morland Place.

Angelica was waiting at the appointed place, the little bridge where the Poppleton road crossed Holgate Beck. She was standing looking down into the water like any idler, but turned quickly as soon as she heard the phaeton approaching. She was wearing a round gown of mouse-brown cambric, with a shawl across her elbows. The straw villager, of which James was growing rather fond, was dressed with two pink roses, and the green ribbon was tied in a becoming bow under one ear.

As he approached, he imagined fondly how she might look in white muslin. He would like to buy her a white muslin gown — one with raised glossy spots, like Fanny had had when she was brought out — and wondered when her

312

birthday was. It had not occurred to him before that girls of her station in Society did not, of course, wear white gowns: a white gown signified that you had nothing to do all day but keep it clean. But his Angelica would look more than ever like an angel in white: it would set off her complexion and her glorious dark curls. She ought to have one. She could wear it on Sundays when the shop was shut. Better still: with as free a hand in imagination as Satterley, he eliminated the shop and the widowed father, and set Angelica in a picturesque little cottage somewhere, with nothing to do but walk about the garden cutting roses. A basket on her arm ... the straw hat ... a lacy white parasol on her shoulder ...

He pulled up the ponies opposite the vision in brown. 'Hullo! Am I late?' he asked cheerfully.

She looked up at him anxiously. 'Oh — I — I don't know. I don't suppose so. Only — it's such a busy place. I was afraid —'

'Can you get up? Come round to the other side. I can't get down and help you, for they won't stand yet: they're too fresh. That's right — take my hand, and step.' Angelica came up nimbly and sat beside him, and he smiled at her approvingly. 'You're as light as a feather! How do you like the rig?'

'It's very handsome,' she said. 'And such fine horses.'

'You should have seen the first pair I bought for it! Cream-coloured Arabians, as like as peas in a pod, and they moved together like a dream!' he said. 'Hold on to the side now, and we'll be off.'

He gave the off, and the ponies sprang forward. He sent them into a trot and drove off up the Poppleton road. Angelica sat very still, tense and silent beside him, and had he not been so wrapped up in his own euphoria, he might have noticed that she didn't seem to be enjoying the outing as he intended she should. About a mile further on, he turned off onto the track that led eventually past Millfield Garth and out on to Scagglethorpe Moor, and it was only when they had left the public road and were driving along a high-hedged lane between empty fields that she relaxed at last and began to look about her with anything like pleasure.

A sound from the basket on the floor between their feet startled her, and she looked towards him enquiringly.

313

James laughed. 'A secret! You'll find out when the time is right.'

'Is it a picnic? I thought it was something moving in there,' she said, smiling for the first time.

James evaded the question. 'It isn't in your way, is it? Good. Well, I promised you a drive on the moors, and what a fine day we have for it! I wish I might take you to a place more worth seeing. I'd like you to see the North York Moors, but we'd need a whole day for that. The moors here are rather tame, I'm afraid.'

'But full of history,' she suggested. 'You said about the battle — Prince Rupert and the Cavaliers —?'

'Oh, yes, the battle of Marston Moor. We'll come back that way — past Wilstrop Wood and over Marston Moor and back through Hessay — make a circle of it.'

'And did your family really fight in the battle?'

'My ancestors, yes. And Prince Rupert, they say, slept the night after the battle at Shawes, which used to belong to my family in those days. That was the old house, of course, not the present one, but on the same site.'

'Eh, it must be grand to have so much history in your family,' she sighed. 'I don't suppose my ancestors did anything interesting at all.'

'You think it interesting to get yourself killed in a battle?' he said, amused.

'Of course! Better than dying in your bed, without ever having seen anything but the one village.' She looked about her. 'I'm glad I've known two towns, anyway. That's more than most folk get to see.'

He was enchanted by her view of the world. Fanny, he remembered, had been to London, Manchester and Vienna by Angelica's age.

'I suppose you've been to London, haven't you?' she asked, as though hearing his thoughts.

He nodded. 'I've been to France,' he confessed.

Her eyes grew round. 'What — Paris?'

'Paris,' he said, and laughed. 'I've seen Boney face to face, and taken tea with Madame Josephine in the Tuileries.'

'There!' she said, sighing with satisfaction. 'What I wouldn't give to see Abroad! That would be before the war, I suppose?'

314

He wondered briefly what age she imagined him to be, but assented. It was before the war, in a way, if you considered the two halves of the war separately. 'Perhaps you will go abroad one day. Would you like to see France?' He had a brief but satisfying vision of himself escorting her up the gangplank of a Channel packet; arriving in Calais — her wonder at being Abroad; sitting beside her in a box at the Paris Opéra, she in white satin, diamonds sparkling in her hair …

'Small chance,' she laughed, shattering the vision. 'Unless I marry a soldier and follow the drum!'

'A soldier! No, you shan't marry anything so low as a soldier. I don't know,' he added defiantly, 'but that you're too good to marry any man.'

'Oh, but I must marry, Mr Morland, else what'll become of me?'

'Call me James,' he said.

She looked at him doubtfully. 'I can't,' she said. 'It isn't right.'

'Not right?'

She began to blush. 'You're — you're a gentleman. My pa's only a shopkeeper. It wouldn't be right.' She hung her head, and her voice became almost inaudible. 'I don't even know if it's right for me to be here. I don't know —' Her voice disappeared altogether.

They were on the moor track now, the country opening up all around them, a smiling prospect, flushed with summer richness and full of larksong. He pulled up the ponies, wound the reins, and turned to her.

'Angelica! Oh, don't look like that — it's what I always call you in my mind! You don't think I could go on calling you Miss Hesketh all these weeks, do you?' She shook her head, her eyes still downcast. 'Angelica, I brought you here to see the moor. You told me so much about the moors at home — where you were a child — and you said you missed the openness and the sky. So I brought you here to give you pleasure. Is that wrong? Do you feel it's wrong?'

'I don't know,' she whispered.

'Don't you? But I do! It makes me happy to see you smile, to see you look about you like — like a horse let out into a field for the first time in spring. You can see how glad they are to be out of the stables and on to the green grass, and you look like that! Is it wrong to want to give you that pleasure?'

She looked up now, and seemed — he didn't understand why — almost ashamed of having been doubtful. 'Oh no! Of course not! I'm so grateful to you, Mr Morland —'

'James.'

She shook her head again. 'I don't know why you're so kind to me, and I'm sorry I was so ungrateful —'

'No, nonsense. Look, now we're here, shall we open the basket? The ponies are quiet now — they'll stand. Have you guessed what it is?' She shook her head, smiling shyly. 'It's a present for you. Something you've always wanted.'

Her cheeks grew pink. 'A present?' she said wonderingly.

He unbuckled the straps, and then watched her face as he lifted the lid in order to get the full value of her pleasure. Her eyes widened and her mouth made a soundless 'Oh' of astonishment as the puppy, which had been asleep, sat up and shook itself, yawned, and then stood uncertainly and waved its tail. Its rough coat was brindled like its sire's, but its ears were scraps of chestnut-coloured velvet.

'Oh — oh — he's so lovely!'

'You remember the old dog, Kithra? Well this is one of his children — one of his many children, I may say. He's a pure-bred Morland, so his blood goes all the way back to those wolves I told you about — assuming that story has any truth in it!'

She reached over to caress the rough head, and the puppy licked her hand extravagantly, and reared up to lock his paws over her wrist in an attempt to reach her face and wash it. He didn't bark, of course, but every other inch of his body was expressing eagerness to please and be pleased, and Angelica stroked and fondled him with both hands, her face enraptured.

'He's so lovely!' she said again. 'What's his name?'

'His kennel name is Kai — one of our traditional names — but you can call him anything you like, of course,' James said, watching her with keen pleasure, feeding on her unselfconscious smiles. But as he spoke, she looked up at him, and the smiles disappeared like spring sunshine, and her eyes clouded with doubt.

'Oh, but — Oh, Mr Morland, I can't! Really I can't! It's ever so kind of you, but —'

'Can't? Nonsense, what is all this?'

'I can't take him,' she said miserably. The eyes went down again, and the cheeks were very pink.

'But why not?' She shook her head silently. 'Don't you like him? Well, then, if you like him and I want to give him to you —'

'But what would Father say? He'd never let me. He'd say I shouldn't have — and it's too much — and — and — I just can't, that's all!' she finished in a burst.

'But this is nonsense,' James began, and then to his horror he saw tears shining under the fan of eyelashes.

'Please don't be angry with me!' she whimpered, fumbling in her sleeve for a handkerchief.

'Oh Lord! Now don't cry; please don't cry! Of course I'm not angry! My dear, I shan't press you, I thought you'd want to have him, but if you don't like it, there's no more to be said.'

'I'm sorry, really I am.' Her words were muffled by the handkerchief.

Though considerably puzzled, James said heartily, 'Nothing to be sorry about. We'll say no more about it. Come now, dry your eyes, and we'll drive on. I meant you to be happy today.'

'Oh, I am,' she whispered, wiping the tears from her eyes. 'It's so kind of you. I'm that grateful —'

'Well, you can shew how grateful you are by taking care of the puppy while I drive. I'm afraid he may try to jump out. Perhaps you could hold him on your lap — his paws are quite clean,' James said.

She finished wiping her eyes, blew her nose, sniffed a little, and then the clouds were gone and the sun came out again. James marvelled at the resilience of youth: five minutes later, her face shewed no mark of her recent tears.

'I don't mind if they are dirty,' she said, scooping the big pup on to her lap. 'I just think he's lovely.' The puppy lashed his tail and licked her chin and wriggled in an ecstasy of adoration, and she hugged him to her and fondled his ears and submitted to the licking with the greatest delight. James drove

317

on with a private smile of satisfaction. After that, he thought, she wouldn't be able to bear to part with the whelp.

Mr Pobgee was not a great club man. Although he was a member of York's three main establishments, he used them rarely, preferring the comfort of his own home, or the peace and quiet of his office, which itself was as solidly comfortable as any gentleman's club. On his way back to his office on this day, however, he made an exception. His patience, already tried by James's strangeness, was further frayed by the usual lengthy delay in getting across the Ouse Bridge, which was worse than ever these days, since the bridge was being rebuilt to make the river navigable to larger vessels. The work had been going on for five years already, and to judge by the progress so far, would not be finished in his lifetime!

On the right side of the river at last, Mr Pobgee passed Booker's in Coney Street, and on an impulse decided to go in and take a glass of something restoring, and perhaps look at the papers for half an hour. It would be pleasant, he thought, to step out of the stream of life for a few moments, and be where no clerk could find him.

Booker's was not fashionable like the Maccabbees. It was old and rather shabby, and the food tended towards huge smoking joints, monumental beefsteak pies and gigantic suet puddings rather than the daintier fare favoured by the modern diner. It was the haunt of the older breed of gentleman, whose coats were cut for comfort rather than style and who regarded the reading of books as a terrible waste of hunting or shooting time; but it was comfortable in its undemanding way, and many members of the professions used it to avoid having to rub shoulders with their rich and crotchety clients in the smarter clubs.

Pobgee stepped in, found himself a comfortable chair in a quiet corner, and sent for sherry and *The Times*, which owing to the miracle of modern transportation was actually yesterday's, galloped up the toll-road from London at a steady twelve miles per hour. There was no news from Brussels, however: all was rumour and counter-rumour. The Russians were approaching Frankfurt; they had not passed Dresden. There were troop movements on the road from

Paris to the frontier; Boney was in Laon — in Maubeuge — he was still in Paris.

Pobgee had just finished *The Times*, and was considering a second glass of sherry and the *Chronicle* when he was hailed by his old friend Havergill, one of York's leading physicians, president of the Dispensary, and director of the Board of the County Hospital.

'Hullo, Pobgee! It isn't often we see you here,' Havergill said cheerfully. 'Business poor today? Will you take something with me?'

Pobgee gestured towards the decanter at his elbow. 'Have a glass of sherry with me,' he said cordially. 'The redeeming feature of Booker's is the Founder's cellar: this sherry is excellent.'

Havergill sat with affable readiness, and glanced about him as Pobgee beckoned to the waiter to bring another glass. 'Your own sherry, as I remember, is quite drinkable. It can't be that which brings you here. Is there something I should know about in *The Times*? Or are you meeting a client here?

Pobgee smiled. 'It's nothing like that, old fellow. I've an intractable problem that's troubling me, and I thought I'd go to ground for a while to try to puzzle it out.'

The servant came with the glass, and Pobgee poured the sherry.

'Your health, old fellow,' Havergill said. 'So, what's this problem of yours? Anything you can talk about?'

Pobgee sighed. 'It's a matter of a Will.'

A wise nod. 'Ah! Tricky things, Wills.'

'It's a matter of establishing the time of death of one of the parties, but as he was an old man who died in his sleep —'

'Yes, I see. The best way to go, for the patient, but damned inconsiderate towards the grieving relatives, what? What does the physician attending say?'

Pobgee sighed. 'He's a damned superannuated drunken old fool of a Scotsman,' he said with unaccustomed heat, 'who took an hour to have his breakfast before going to see if deceased really was deceased.'

Havergill grinned unsympathetically. 'Ah, yes, I know the sort: qualified in the days of sorcery and spells and witches' brews! They bring our bright new profession into disrepute.

319

Fortunately there aren't so many of them as before, but they wreak God knows what havoc while they linger on. But did he not hazard a time of death?'

'He told me in no uncertain terms that he was a doctor, not a soothsayer, and that when a man went to bed of his own accord one night and was found cold and stiff the next morning —'

Havergrill sat up straight. 'What's that? Cold and stiff, did he say?'

'Yes — why?'

Havergill grinned. 'My dear old friend, cadaveric rigidity, of course! I shall begin to think you as witless as the drunken doctor! Surely it must have come in your way before now? The principle of *rigor mortis*.'

'Good God!'

'Indeed! And are you quite sure he said the deceased was stiff?'

Pobgee nodded. 'Cold and stiff, those were his words. And now I come to think of it, the old man's servant said that when he found his master in the morning, he couldn't close the mouth —'

Havergill snapped his fingers. 'There you are, then! It's all Lombard Street to a China orange that the old gentleman had been dead eight hours at least. What did he die of, may one ask?'

'A stroke — his second.'

Havergill nodded. 'Most likely died as soon as he put his head to his pillow. That's often the way it goes. Cadaveric rigidity comes on after about eight hours, beginning in the face and jaw —'

'Ah!'

'And developing over the rest of the body over a period of several hours. So all you have to do is to get a statement from your Silenus as to the extent of the *rigor* when he saw the corpse —'

Pobgee looked almost agitated. 'My dear Havergill, you are quite sure about this? That if a corpse is rigid in the jaw, it must have been dead at least eight hours?'

Havergill shrugged. 'It's no mystery. They've made extensive observations in all the major medical schools — Edinburgh included! The rate of development of rigidity is not absolutely constant, but in a general way, you can take it as eight hours to the onset.'

Pobgee sat back, smiling. 'I knew it! I knew she was lying! Now I have her!'

'Have whom?'

Pobgee shook his head. 'I may not say more. My dear friend, you have helped me more than I can tell you! I am extremely grateful. Armed with this knowledge, I believe I can uncover the truth — and that must be desirable in this case! Have another glass of sherry, Havergill.'

'Gladly,' Havergill said, extending his glass. 'I haven't the least idea what you're talking about, of course, but as a man of science I am always happy to drink a toast to Truth — the daughter of Time, so they say, though who her father may be is a mystery.'

Pobgee smiled. 'As a man of law, I have to confess that in Chancery she all too often ranks with the widows and orphans — dispensable, you know, and coming a long way behind the men of property in importance. But in this case —' he lifted his glass — 'she may just prevail!'

'*Fiat justitia!*' cried Havergill, and drank.

It was the quiet time between dinner and tea. Edward and Miss Rosedale were playing a lethargic game of backgammon. Father Aislaby was reading the paper, and James was at the piano, playing Bach rather badly, his mind elsewhere. The room was silent but for the tick of the clock on the chimney-piece, the muted click of the counters and the occasional rustle of a turning page; and over the quietness the notes tinkled, bright and uneven, like a summer stream trickling unemphatically over its stony bed.

Ottershaw came into the drawing-room with as much agitation in his face as he felt it proper to express. 'Sir — Mr James, sir!'

James looked up, his hands suspended. 'Well?'

'There's a — a person to see you, sir.'

'At this time of night?' Edward said, mildly surprised. 'Not bad news, I hope.'

'What sort of a person, Ottershaw? Won't it wait until tomorrow?' asked James.

'He was very insistent, sir,' said the butler, his eyes attempting to convey a warning. 'I took the liberty of shewing him into the steward's room, sir, as he wouldn't go away.'

'The devil he wouldn't,' James said, surprised.

'Would you like me to see him for you?' Aislaby offered. 'I was thinking of going up to my room anyway.'

The butler said hastily, 'He wishes to see Mr James, sir, on a private matter — confidential, he said.'

'Did he give his name, Ottershaw?' Aislaby asked.

Ottershaw gave an extraordinary squirm of unwillingness, but could not refuse to answer so direct a question. 'I believe it was — Hesketh, sir.'

The effect was varied. James went red and looked away, Miss Rosedale glanced up quickly and then down again at the board, Father Aislaby looked at James gravely and Edward was merely puzzled.

'Doesn't mean anything to me. Do we know a Hesketh, Jamie? Not one of ours, at any rate.'

'It's all right,' James said tersely, standing up and shutting the piano-lid with unintentional force. 'I'll go and see what he wants.' He glanced at the others, and now only Edward was looking at him. 'You'd better not wait tea for me. I don't know how long it will take.'

Ottershaw led him across the hall with an eloquent silence which James was too agitated to notice. In the steward's room, a strange man stood by the empty fireplace, waiting. James nodded to Ottershaw to go, and closed the door behind him.

'I'm James Morland,' he said briskly.

Angelica's father, he thought, was in no way fitted by nature to be progenitor of an angel. He was a small man, thin, pallid, and with the hollow cheeks and hollow chest of more illness, James reflected, than he had probably told Angelica about. His clothes were plain and decent, old, but of good cloth, though they seemed to have been made for a stouter man. His eyes were large and blue and mild in a bland face, and meshed around with fine lines, as if he had spent all his life screwing them up in the course of his work. He held his hat before him in his hands, and turned it round slowly by the brim — otherwise, he was quite still. James searched for any resemblance to Angelica, but could find none. Presumably,

322

he thought, she favoured the dead mother.

'What can I do for you?' James said at last, when it appeared that Hesketh wasn't ready to initiate conversation. 'It's a late hour to come calling. Couldn't it have waited until the morning?'

'I can't be abroad in the daytime — I have to attend my shop,' he said. He had only a slight South Riding accent — worn away, James supposed, by years of dealing with gentle-folk. His manner was carefully neutral — neither subservient nor challenging. He spoke not quite as equal to equal, but perhaps as one whose sphere of influence was so far removed as to make any comparison of status pointless. 'I'm sorry to disturb you at your fireside, but I have something which belongs to you.'

He put down his hat and stooped, and James saw that there was a basket on the floor at his feet, which before had been hidden by the angle of the desk. Hesketh reached inside the basket and brought out the puppy, holding it by the scruff and supporting it with the other hand. He held it out towards James unemphatically. The puppy looked sleepy and bewildered.

James didn't move. 'You are mistaken,' he said.

'I think not.' He made a little pushing movement. 'I wish you will take it, sir.'

'You are mistaken,' James said again. 'The animal is not mine. I gave it to someone as a present.'

Hesketh, seeing James did not mean to take the puppy, set it down gently on the floor. The pup wobbled, sat down, and lifted a hind foot to scratch behind one ear. In the middle of scratching it yawned hugely, forgot what it was doing, and lay down and dropped its head onto its paws.

Hesketh straightened and met James's eyes steadily. 'You gave it to my daughter,' he said.

'Yes,' said James defiantly. 'She said she wanted a dog, and one of our bitches had just whelped, so I —'

'For God's sake,' Hesketh cut across him quietly, 'what were you thinking about, sir? Don't you know what people have been saying? Don't you know what a scandal you have brewed up?'

James felt his face growing hot. 'Scandal? Nonsense! What

323

the devil is all this?'

'Walking with my daughter — talking to her — taking her out in a carriage alone — and now giving her presents! What can you be about? A man of your reputation —'

'You are impertinent, sir!'

Hesketh ignored the interruption. 'And my daughter — my good little girl, who has never in her life deserved even a cross word from me! Since her mother died, she has been my joy and my support — and you come along and ruin her reputation for your own selfish sport. Are you quite insensible? Don't you care about anyone but yourself? What has Angelica done to deserve such cruelty from you?'

'Cruelty? You're raving, man! Can you really suppose I would ever harm her? A girl young enough to be my daughter —?' His voice wavered, then strengthened. 'How dare you suggest that I would ever —'

'It's what people think that matters. Can't you see what you have done?' Hesketh never raised his voice, and somehow it made him seem more formidable — a small and insignificant man, who was not daunted by the roaring of lions. 'Oh, I don't think you meant her harm. I know about your daughter, Mr Morland, God rest her soul, and I'm right sorry for you. You wanted a little girl to pet and spoil, that's all, like you spoiled your own daughter, and you fixed on my Angelica — for what reason I don't know.'

James turned his face away. 'I forbid you to say another word! Leave this house immediately!'

'Nay, sir, when it comes to my daughter's welfare, I will speak as I feel I must, just as you would in the same circumstances. You fixed on my Angelica, and she being that innocent, bless her, she didn't know to refuse you. That's the irony of it, Mr Morland — if she'd been the girl the gossips are making of her now, she'd have known better than to have put herself in the position to be talked about.'

'I meant her no harm,' James said. 'I wanted only to give her pleasure.'

Hesketh tilted his head a little. 'I don't know,' he said slowly. 'I think at bottom you must have known it were wrong, or else why did you go about it so secretly? You never came to me like a man and asked my permission, did you?'

James said nothing, rigid with mortification. At last he muttered, 'What is it you want?'

'I want you to leave her alone, that's what. I want you never to come near her again, nor speak to her, nor think about her.'

'But I —'

Hesketh raised her voice a little for the first time. 'What's going to happen to her when I'm gone? She must make a good match, or she'll be destitute — and how is she to get wed, I ask you, if you ruin her reputation?'

James stirred at that. 'I can make it all right. I'll give you money for her, for a dowry,' he said eagerly. 'A good dowry will make her the most eligible match —'

'She was eligible before,' Hesketh said with quiet dignity, 'and she'll be so again, without your help. You just keep out of our lives from now on. We don't want your money, Mr Morland: we just want our peace of mind.'

He nodded calmly, picked up his hat and the empty basket, and walked past James and let himself out without another word or look. James found himself thinking that there was a resemblance between father and daughter after all. Then he was alone, and there was nothing any more to distract him from his hideous thoughts.

Shame — burning shame and dismay! He looked his own folly in the face without disguise, and for the first time in his life he could find no justification for an action of his of which the world disapproved. He had never cared before for the generality of opinion; he had held himself above it. He had disliked upsetting his mother because he loved her, but the things he had done which had upset her he had regarded without guilt or regret; and so it had been throughout his life.

But now he was racked with shame, and he could not turn his face away from what he had done, or pretend it did not exist or did not matter. Useless to say he had meant no harm: he had not — but Hesketh was right that he had known at the bottom of his heart that it was wrong. He had exposed that innocent girl to scandalous gossip and ruin, and there was nothing that he could even do to make things better. He had taken what he was not entitled to — sought comfort where he had no right. Now all was desolation and misery. He had lost her, and his self-respect.

The door opened and he turned to see Ottershaw standing there, and Durban hovering behind him. He looked at their anxious faces and sympathetic eyes, and remembered the scene in the drawing-room with a fresh access of shame, hot and indigestible as bile.

'What do you want?' They hesitated, glancing at each other, and, goaded, he suddenly cried out, 'Does everybody in Yorkshire know my business?'

Impossible to go back into the drawing-room. Impossible to stay here. He looked down at the sleeping puppy, and, hardly aware of what he did, scooped it up into his arms. 'Get out of my way,' he snarled at the servants, and thrusting past them, went out into the hall and up the stairs. He went blindly, seeking a safe place, and instinct led him like a pursued animal to go to ground in the nursery.

In the nursery there was peace. His two little boys slept innocently in their bed, Nicholas on his back, snoring slightly, Benedict curled up like a cat with his dark head cupped on his hand. James stood a while and regarded them. His sons — children of his lawful union with his lawful wife — no room for guilt there, no reason for shame, no cause for discomfort. All was as it should be. He could watch them and love them without reproach.

Nicholas gasped in his sleep and coughed, and James stirred uneasily. No, even here there was not perfect peace, after all. Nicholas was not quite right. He remembered the bitter winter when he had been born — Héloïse's pain, and the bloody struggle from which the boy had emerged misshapen and damaged. James felt uneasily that it was his fault, that he had not done the right things, that he should have fetched help sooner, or from a different source. He should have arranged things better: the ultimate responsibility had been his. Héloïse had suffered, had almost died, and Nicholas was the lasting proof of that. He was the silent, unending rebuke.

The boy had coughed himself awake, and was staring at his father with wide eyes, too preoccupied with his respiratory troubles to wonder what James was doing there in the middle of the night. Looking about, James saw water and glass on the

326

bedside table; he dumped the puppy, poured water and brought it to the boy. While he propped Nicholas's head and fed him sips of water, the nursery-maid appeared, sleepily, from behind her screen, drawing a shawl round her with an automatic movement. She stopped abruptly when she saw the master, shocked fully awake; but James shook his head at her, and gestured her away, and she retired, doubtful but obedient.

'Better?' James asked at last, and when Nicholas nodded, he eased him back onto the pillow. Benedict was awake now, too, sitting up, eager for adventure, intrigued by the novelty.

'What are we doing?' he asked his father chirpily. 'Is it a game?'

'No, love,' James said, smiling at the dark, handsome little boy, so different in his healthy vigour from his pale brother. 'Not a game. Your brother's not well, and I'm taking care of him.'

Nicholas scowled. He hated to have his infirmity always pointed out, separating him from the world inhabited by the rest of humankind, the normal world of good health. If he had no legs or no arms, he might have accepted his exile philosophically; but the barrier was so thin and transparent, like a single window between him and normality, that it frustrated him unbearably to be shut out.

'I'm all right,' he snapped angrily. 'I wish you wouldn't fuss so. I'd be all right if only you didn't fuss.' And he turned over on his side, away from his brother, hiding his face from his father, hunching his shoulder defensively.

Benedict had seen the puppy now, and whooped with excitement. 'A dog! A dog! Papa, is it for me? Is it Christmas? What's his name? Is he mine?'

James smiled indulgently. 'It's for both of you. His name's Kai. But you'll have to learn how to train him properly.'

Benedict was ecstatic. 'Nicky, look! A dog, for us! Oh, look!'

Nicholas scowled into the pillow, and put an arm over his head. 'I don't want a dog. I hate dogs. I wish you'd all be quiet and go away and let me sleep.'

James was wounded by the rejection. 'Then it shall be Benedict's dog,' he said stiffly. 'Here, my boy, he's yours.'

327

'Thank you, Papa! Can he sleep on the bed?'

It was too much! 'No, he can't,' Nicholas cried, near to tears. 'I won't have him on my bed. I hate him!'

'Well, just for tonight, perhaps,' James said. 'Tomorrow we'll make a bed for him, shall we, Benedict? And now you had better go back to sleep, both of you. It's late.'

Benedict lay down again, rather bouncingly, and dragged the pup into the curl of his arms, and after some writhing about, they got themselves comfortable.

'Goodnight, Papa,' Benedict said cheerfully. Nicholas lay rigidly, his face hidden, his eyes shut tightly against the tears. James looked at him for a moment, and then shrugged. Children could be odd when woken from their sleep, he thought.

'Goodnight,' he said lightly, and went away. Some of his pain had been eased. Tomorrow, he thought, he would shew the boys how to make a bed for the pup. He liked carpentry — it was so soothing. And he would help them train the dog properly, and spend more time with them generally, and be a good father to them. That was the way ahead. As to the other business — his mind shied away from naming it, even to himself. Well, he wouldn't think about it anymore. It was all over, all forgotten. Everything would be all right now.

The carriage brought Rosamund and Sophie back from Lady Conyngham's ball accompanied only by their maid, for the Theakstons, with Lady Strathord and the Duc had gone on to another reception at the Duke of Brunswick's. As the carriage pulled up outside the house in the Rue Ducale, the butler opened the door smoothly and the two young women came up the stairs in all the glory of satin evening cloaks, tall feathers, long gloves and fashionable bullion-fringed reticules in the style of sabretaches.

The butler looked at them critically as they came past him into the hall, for his bulletins on the progress of the young ladies' romances kept the servants' hall rapt. They didn't look tonight, either of them, as though they had much enjoyed themselves. Perhaps the June weather was growing too hot for dancing — and tonight was particularly sultry. Her ladyship was looking fagged, while Miss was plainly moped to death.

Moss, their maid, passed him with a roll of the eyes as she hurried in their wake, gathering gloves and scarves and cloaks from them as they walked across the hall and started up the stairs. In their room she helped them to undress, unhooking their buttons and catching up the delicate muslins as they stepped out of them. Lady Rosamund's was white over a pale pink slip, with a flounced hem and butterfly sleeves; Miss Morland's pale primrose over white, with bands of ruched satin at hem and sleeve, and a Russian bodice.

She unpinned their headdresses and brushed out their hair for them, unlaced their busks and collected up their jewellery, all in a silence which she longed to break by enquiring what it was that had happened that evening. But Lady Rosamund had grown up since they came to Brussels, and no longer chattered to her maid, or teased her, or asked her advice. When the young ladies were in their nightgowns and wrappers, there was nothing more for her to do but gather up the bits and pieces, bid them goodnight, and leave them to their supper and each other's confidence.

A tray had been set out on the low table with cold patties, fruit, wine and lemonade, and as Moss went out, Rosamund and Sophie sat down to either side of the table and settled themselves comfortably. Rosamund stretched her long legs out and yawned, and reached for the wine-jug.

'Lord! What a long evening! I thought Moss would never go. You could see she was just dying to ask us questions. What a good thing you didn't say anything, Sophie, or we'd never have got rid of her. Will you have some wine?'

'Hmm?' Sophie said vaguely, looking up from the contemplation of her empty plate.

'Oh dear, you are blue-devilled!' Rosamund said sympathetically. 'Here, have one of these patties, and when we've talked about my problem, we'll discuss yours for as long as you like.'

Sophie gave a wan smile. 'There's nothing to discuss,' she said.

'Oh yes there is,' Rosamund said briskly. 'You mustn't be so easily downcast. But first I need to consult — I don't know what to do, and though you haven't much experience, I trust your good sense. Besides, no-one else knows so much about it

329

all. Sophie, do you attend me?'

'Yes — yes, Cousin,' Sophie said, rousing herself. 'Go on.'

'Well, then — I have had a proposal of marriage.'

Sophie's reaction was gratifying. Her rather pale face grew pink with surprise and pleasure. 'A proposal? Oh, I'm so glad! Oh, Rosamund — he has spoken at last! And what did you say?'

Rosamund gave her a wry look. 'Of whom are we speaking, do you suppose?'

'Of Marcus, to be sure! Why?' Sophie was puzzled. 'Do you mean it was not him?'

'No, my dear, it was not. It was Tantony.'

'Oh.' Sophie paused, watching her cousin's face, trying to determine what her reaction should be. 'But Marcus has been so attentive lately,' she said at last. 'He rides with you, walks with you — dances with you. He is always at your side.'

'Tantony, too.'

'Well, yes, I confess I have wondered sometimes that they tolerate each other so well.'

'I can tell you why, dear Sophie — it's because Marcus is not a suitor, and Tantony knows it! Oh yes, he attends me, he seeks my company — but it is his little pigtailed cousin he sees when he looks at me! He is comfortable with me, because we were childhood friends, and because he feels he can talk to me without restraint. He confides in me, Sophie,' she finished on a note of disgust, 'because he doesn't regard me as a grown woman.'

'But — it is agreeable, at least, to be confided in, surely? I'm sure I should be glad if —' She stopped herself. 'What does he talk about?'

'Endlessly, of Annabel Robb.'

'Ah, yes. I see now,' Sophie said. 'How horrid for you!'

'Sometimes I could gladly hit him! I find myself wishing I were a man so that I could call him out and run him through,' Rosamund said vigorously. 'It's all that woman — her perfections, his unworthiness; her cruelty, his suffering! I hate the sound of her name! I wish she would marry her monkey, and have done with it! Except that it wouldn't stop Marcus talking — it would only give him a fresh field for speculation! I can hear it now — can she really love him? Has she done it only for ambition? And if so, why him and not another? Tcha!' She made a sound of exasperation.

'But do you really think she will marry the Comte de Ladon?' Sophie said wonderingly, unwittingly adding fuel to the fire. 'I made sure she was only doing it to torment the other officers, like poor Lord Farringdon and —'

'Sophie, *tais-toi*! I have to listen to speculation about Bel Robb in the Park and in the Allée Verte and on the ballroom floor, but if I have to have it in my bedroom too I shall grow demented!'

'Sorry, Cousin,' Sophie said with a faint smile. 'Well, then, what did you want to consult about?'

'Why, about Tantony's offer, of course. You see, he's a dear man, and I am very fond of him, but of course I have never considered him in the light of a husband. That was always Marcus's place, as you know, and no-one else was ever to have it. But now —'

'But now?'

'I begin to wonder if Marcus will ever stop talking about Bel Robb. And also —' She stopped and bit her lip.

'Yes, Cousin?' Sophie encouraged gently.

'Also I begin to wonder if I want him to.' She looked at Sophie anxiously, and Sophie, not knowing what to say, merely made an enquiring sound. 'You see,' Rosamund went on painfully, 'I can't help seeing that Marcus has made a great cake of himself over this affair. It was bad enough when he was "Bel Robb's latest" — oh yes, I know that's what they called him! — when he was her dupe, her spaniel; but now he's her nothing-at-all, and still he gazes at her like a moonling and starts when he hears her name mentioned — well, it isn't very glorious, is it? He doesn't appear in this business like a hero, Sophie. In fact —' she shook her head unhappily — 'he appears very much like an ass.'

'Oh, no, Ros!' Sophie protested. 'Not that! No, I'm sure people don't think —'

'I'm sure they do. I know they do. Oh, he'll get over it, I suppose, sooner or later — but will I?'

Sophie opened one hand in a helpless gesture. 'How can I say? Only you can know that. Don't you love him any more?'

Rosamund looked at the candle-flame for a few moments,

her face grave. Her hair was lit to dark gold by it, and the shadows carved her features in alabaster against the shadows behind her head. 'Yes, I still love him. I will always love him. But I think perhaps he will never want to marry me — and I wonder if he would be the right husband for me, even if he did.'

'And Captain Tantony? What of him?'

Rosamund's eyes softened. 'He is so kind, Sophie! So gentle! He bears with Marcus's nonsense with the greatest patience, and never shews any signs of exasperation at having our *tête à têtes* interrupted, which considering he has been courting me these weeks past is noble indeed! And he is very brave, and funny, and interesting now that he has stopped being so shy. And he does love me a very great deal.' Her lips curved into an unusually gentle smile, for her. 'It quite touches me to see how much.'

'Then what is your problem?' Sophie asked.

The smile faded. 'Do I love him enough? And if I accept him, and Marcus gets over Bel Robb at last, will I regret it, and start longing after Marcus again?'

Sophie looked helpless. 'Again, how can anyone but you know that? Do you think it's likely?'

Rosamund sighed. 'I don't know. I think Tantony is the better man. But he has a fortune — modest though it may be — while Marcus has nothing. And I have always loved Marcus and meant to marry him. If I take Tantony, shall I appear mercenary? Shall I appear inconstant?'

'Do you care about that? Do you mind what others think?' Sophie said in surprise.

Rosamund shrugged. 'Oh, not to others — to myself!'

There was a silence, and the candle-flame burned steadily, undisturbed by any breath on the still June evening. At last Sophie said, 'What did you tell Captain Tantony?'

'I said I would give him my answer at the Duchess's ball on the fifteenth and he accepted that. He was so sensible and considerate about it all. He told me that he approached Mama weeks ago for permission to address me,' she added wryly. 'What patience! If I were in love, I couldn't have waited all that time! But he said he wanted to give me time to get to know him. Well, I do, pretty thoroughly, I think. I enjoy his company. I miss him when he is not there — when duties keep him away. But is it enough?'

Sophie searched in her own experience for something that might help. 'Perhaps if you imagine how you might feel —' she began uncertainly. Rosamund waited. 'How would you feel if you were never to see him again?' she asked, with her eyes cast down.

Rosamund reached across the table impulsively for Sophie's hand, all contrition. 'Oh, Sophie, I am a selfish beast! Here I am talking on and on about my silly problem when you are breaking your poor, dear, *good* heart over Major Larosse! But you will see him again, dearest Sophie! I know you will! He did care for you. It must be duty that keeps him away. It can only be that.'

Sophie accepted the comfort, returned the pressure of the hand, but shook her head. 'I don't know. No, no, I mustn't think of him. Don't talk about it, Ros. Go on about Captain Tantony — do!'

'Very well.' Rosamund considered. 'I should dislike it extremely if I never saw him again,' she said at last. 'And yet —'

'Marcus again.'

'I'm so *used* to loving him, I don't want to give it up,' Rosamund confessed. She gave a rueful smile. 'Perhaps that's all it is — a sort of — nostalgia.'

Sophie shook her head. 'You don't have to choose between them, you know,' she said. 'I mean, there are other men in the world, and others will certainly offer for you. You don't have to take Captain Tantony just because Marcus does not make you an offer. You might refuse them both.'

Rosamund smiled. 'Dear Sophie, how clear-minded of you! Of course I might!' She stretched and yawned. 'I shall take that into consideration as well. And now, shall we go to bed? Tantony calls for me early tomorrow morning, so that we can ride in the Park before he goes on duty. I must say Harry Clinton plays on poor Tantony's good nature a great deal, for it always seems to be him who gets the disagreeable duties! I tell him to refuse, but he just laughs and says he is a soldier and must obey orders, even when they interfere with his pleasure!'

333

It was all said so naturally, and with such good humour and accustomed pleasure, that Sophie thought Rosamund was probably much closer to making up her mind about Captain Tantony than she realised.

CHAPTER THIRTEEN

Rumours proliferated, but there was no real news. Napoleon, it appeared, had sealed the border, and nothing was allowed across: no courier, no mail, no horse or cart, no boat, peasant or even ox might leave France to give any hint to the Allies in Belgium as to what was afoot.

Brussels looked to its military leaders for the tone of its behaviour, and found nothing to alarm. The Duke continued to give parties and attend balls; his staff-officers were the most languid of the languid, and were never heard to discuss anything more serious than horses, new boots or flirtations. Brussels Society stirred uneasily at each new rumour, and then settled again to the pursuit of pleasure.

Only amongst the wives of senior officers was there any hint of anxiety, and that was because their menfolk were increasingly absent from their hearths. Lord Theakston, now restored to the bosom of his regiment, was stationed out at Tournay, a disheartening forty miles from Brussels, though on a good road. Peter Firth was at Ziethen's headquarters at Ligny, travelling between there and Blücher at Namur, and occasionally back to Brussels. The Duc was the best off, out at Nivelles only sixteen miles away, and coming in almost every day to consult and report. Everyone looked forward to the Duchess of Richmond's grand ball on the fifteenth, to which all the most senior gold lace had been invited, for the opportunity it would give those at the outlying stations to taste the joys of civilisation once again.

Amongst the young people there was no apprehension that did not relate to their own private affairs: they walked, flirted, danced, rode, picnicked, attended reviews, cricket matches, horse-races and river-fêtes. The June weather was perfect: hot and sunny with occasional thundery showers which were welcomed as they cleared the air and laid the dust.

335

On the thirteenth, two topics of conversation were preeminent: the choice of gown and partner for the Duchess's ball, and whether Lady Annabel Robb would really marry the Comte de Ladon. Sophie and Rosamund, accompanied by Moss, were largely preoccupied by the first as they spent the morning shopping in the Rue des Anglais. They were taking advantage of the relative quietness of the fashionable shops, due to the absence of much of the *ton* at a cricket match which the Duke was attending with Jane Lennox, one of the Richmond girls.

Sophie had to have a last fitting for a new ballgown with Madame Berce, who had so many orders for the Duchess's ball that she could not spare time to come up to the house; and Rosamund, whose gown was already finished, had a number of small and satisfying matters such as gloves, stockings, spars and feathers to attend to. She had devised a new headdress for herself for the ball, and was being very secretive about it, insisting that she would make it herself, despite Moss's apprehensions that my lady was no needlewoman.

'If you would only let me know what you want, my lady, I'd make it just as you like,' she said persuasively. 'Only think how shocking if your stitches was to come undone in the middle of a cotillion!'

'Thank you, Judy,' Rosamund laughed, 'but my stitches will do well enough for what I want! You'll see it when you come to dress my hair, and not before. I want to surprise everyone.'

'So long as you don't end up surprising yourself, my lady,' Moss said, folding her lips disapprovingly.

Rosamund only laughed. She was very gay these last few days, Sophie thought, and wondered if it had to do with Philip Tantony. She had not spoken again about his offer, nor indicated to Sophie whether she meant to accept or reject it — indeed, it was impossible to tell even if she were still thinking about it. When her purchases were completed, she accompanied Sophie to the mantuamaker's, and kept her entertained while she had her fitting with stories of the officers, of daring deeds and jokes and flirtations and nonsenses.

Sophie listened gratefully, and if her smile was a little wan, only Rosamund noticed it. The fitting over, they stepped out into the sunshine of the street and idled along the flagway in the direction of home. They turned the corner into the Rue Ducale, and then both young women stopped so abruptly that Moss walked into them and dropped a parcel. The horseman coming along the street towards them was Major Larosse. His hand went up to his hat in a automatic gesture even before he had registered whom it was he was saluting.

Then his eyes met Sophie's, and he seemed to pale with some searing consciousness. Her lip trembled, she coloured, and the brief look of pain and reproach was veiled as she lowered her eyes. It all happened so fast that the major's momentum carried him past before he could even pull down from a trot to a walk. Moss had picked up the parcel and was murmuring, 'Walk on, miss, do! It don't do to stare,' as she administered a gentle nudge in the back with the handle of Lady Rosamund's parasol; but Rosamund, never one to stand upon ceremony, had turned to see what the major would do.

'He looks back — just a glance. Ah, but he's going on.' Her voice fell with disappointment; then rose again. 'No, wait, he's stopping! He's looking again — sees me watching. Common politeness should tell him he ought —'

'Please, Ros, walk on,' Sophie murmured, scarlet now with agitation and distress.

'Stay, Sophie. He's speaking to his servant. He means to come back and do the pretty by us.' Rosamund stood like a rock against all nudgings and tuggings watching the major dismount and pass the reins to his servant. The servant moved on, leading the major's horse, and Larosse was walking back towards them with a clinking of spurs on his dusty boots.

The meeting was on the corner of the flagway, opposite the Park railings, in the strong afternoon sunlight of a June day: an officer in Dutch-Belgian blue, pulling off his hat to two handsome young women in light-coloured muslins, accompanied by a maid weighted down with parcels. It was a *tableau vivant* repeated all over Brussels every day, so commonplace as to excite no interest from any observer; it could have been the illustration for a two-volume novel of the lighter sort, regularly condemned by governesses and consumed by them avidly in the privacy of their rooms. Only the principals knew how momentous it really was.

'Lady Rosamund — Miss Morland — how do you do?' said Larosse. His eyes were on Sophie's face, but hers were determinedly on the pavement, and it was left to Rosamund to observe the amenities.

'Well, Major Larosse, what a pleasant surprise! You've come up from Nivelles, I suppose?'

'Yes, ma'am. I came from Namur, in fact, though I passed through Nivelles. I have not been with my regiment for two weeks now.'

'Namur? You were with Old Papa Forwards? Then I suppose you have come to report to the Beau on the state of readiness?'

'Amongst other things,' Larosse said. He was finding it hard to keep his mind or his eyes from Sophie. 'Are you going home, or do you have more errands? May I walk with you?'

Rosamund smiled warmly. 'To be sure you may, if we are not keeping you from your duty. You may give us each an arm — it is always welcome when one has been shopping. I don't know how it is, but lounging about shops is the most exhausting business of all. I can dance all night and never feel tired, but half an hour in a draper's shop leaves me as limp as a dish-rag.'

Larosse almost smiled at that. 'You look very far from limp, ma'am. Positively vigorous, I would say. Do you go home?'

Rosamund looked innocently bland. 'Not immediately. We had but just decided to take a turn in the Park to refresh ourselves when you came riding past.' Sophie glanced at her in surprise, and Rosamund pinched her warningly. 'We shall be glad of your company, shan't we, Sophie?'

Sophie was unable to speak. All her feelings, with which she had battled these past weeks and which she thought to have conquered and controlled, were surging upwards in a wild fountain of joy at his presence, mingled with longing and despair and pain and frustration. He had looked at her with such a burning look — what did it mean? And yet he spoke to Rosamund in so normal a tone — and what did that mean? A moment later he had taken his place between them, and even with her eyes cast resolutely down, she could see his blue sleeve, the elbow crooked towards her, the cuff offered for her hand, and feel the closeness of him, the warmth of his presence, his undeniable physical self.

'Miss Morland?' he said quietly when she did not move to take his arm. Slowly she looked up, to meet his eyes. He was looking down at her with such an expression of tenderness and appeal that her heart turned over. Trembling she slipped her hand under his elbow and laid it on his cuff, and at once it was pressed briefly but warmly against his side.

They walked on, and Rosamund said pleasantly, 'Well, Major, what's the news? It's all rumour here. Are the French on the move?'

'I believe so,' he said a little absently, 'though there is nothing certain known. I have no news. But Napoleon has certainly left Paris, and that, to me, is ominous — he moves fast when the time comes.'

Rosamund shrugged slightly. 'The Beau has gone to a cricket match today. I'm sure he wouldn't have done that if there were anything to worry about.'

A little more animation crept into Larosse's voice. 'Perhaps not. But I came to warn the Duke that he must be ready at any moment. Our forces are widely scattered — it will take a dozen hours to bring them together, even after the orders have been given. And a dozen hours may be too many, especially given the way the two armies are disposed.'

He stopped abruptly, but Rosamund nodded to him encouragingly.

'Yes? Go on.' Larosse hesitated, and Rosamund smiled. 'Come, Major, my step-papa was one of the Beau's staff-officers, and I listen to tactical talk all day long. You needn't be afraid I shan't understand.'

Larosse bowed. 'Very well,' he said. 'The Prussian head-quarters are at Namur, as you know, and the Allied British at Brussels, leaving a space, a natural corridor, if you like, between them. Moreover, Wellington's supply lines run north-westward towards Ostend, while Blücher's run eastward through Liège towards Prussia. Now, an army in retreat naturally retires along its supply route, you can see that?' Rosamund nodded obediently. 'Therefore if there were any need for them to retire, they would move further away

339

from each other, rather than drawing closer together.'

'Yes, I see that — but surely the Duke must have thought of it, too?'

'He believes the French will attack by trying to cut his supply lines. But, you see, I know Napoleon! I have fought with him over many a campaign, and he has an invariable tactic when he is outnumbered.'

They reached the Park gates, and Larosse stepped back to allow them through.

'Is he outnumbered?' Rosamund asked when they had linked arms again.

'To the best of our knowledge he has about 130,000 men, whereas the Allied and the Prussian armies each number about 100,000.'

'So together they outnumber the French, while separately they are weaker,' Rosamund said thoughtfully.

Larosse looked impressed. '*Bien sûr,*' he said. 'You think like a general, mademoiselle! You think like Napoleon. In such a case, his strategy is always to attack one wing with all his force and destroy it before turning on the other wing, so that at any time he will only be engaging half the enemy's force — you understand?'

'Certainly. And in this case —'

'In this case the disposition of the armies means that he can position himself between them, drive a wedge between them, engage whichever attacks first, and destroy it before the other can come to its aid. Suppose it is the Prussians who attack first —'

'Very likely,' Rosamund agreed. 'The boys all say that Papa Blücher should have been a Hussar — he can't bear to sit still!'

'But if Napoleon beats the Prussians, they will retire eastwards, towards Liège, widening the distance between themselves and Wellington. And then the Emperor will turn on Wellington —' He stopped again, frowning.

'But you must not linger here,' Rosamund said firmly. 'Delightful though your company may be, had you not better be going to the Beau and telling him all this?'

'I have told him already,' Larosse said grimly. 'I was directed to the cricket match from Headquarters, and he

340

received me courteously and listened as I explained my thoughts. Then he asked me to go back to Headquarters and write out a report in detail for him to look at tonight.'

'Oh?' Rosamund said, considering the tone of his voice. 'Is that not good?'

'He didn't believe me,' Larosse said. 'He is convinced that Napoleon means to attack to the westward, to cut him off from Ostend. He is British, *voyons*, and thinks always of the sea! But I know the Emperor, as he does not. He will not do that; it is not his way.'

'But can't you convince him?' Sophie said. He turned towards her. For some time now she had forgotten her embarrassment in the flow of his words, and was looking at him anxiously, her small hand gripping his cuff tightly. 'You must go to him again and make him understand.'

He laid his hand over hers. 'Don't be afraid, mademoiselle,' he said. 'I did not mean to alarm you. After all, I may be wrong —'

'But you're sure you're not,' said Rosamund.

Larosse shrugged. 'All I can do is advise. But I shall write the report and leave it for him to read tonight, and tomorrow I will present myself again and see what I can do to persuade him.'

'So you will be staying in Brussels for a few days?' Rosamund asked.

He seemed flustered. 'I don't know — yes — I suppose so. But I don't know when I shall be recalled, or what further orders I might be given.'

'I was wondering if we would see you at the Duchess's ball?' Rosamund went on. 'Sophie and I will be there. There was such fun about it, you know, for the Beau meant to have a grand dress-ball about this time, and drew up his guest-list for the grandest affair of the Season. The King and Queen were invited, and the Prince, of course, and Prince Frederick; and the Duke of Brunswick and the Prince of Nassau; and your Prince Bernard, and the Duc de Berry and all his crowd. The Duchess said that there'd be so many royal people there'd be no room for commoners! And then she routed the Beau completely by sending out invitations for the fifteenth before he could get his written, so he's had to postpone!'

341

Larosse smiled. 'Yes, I heard the story from Count Bylandt
— but Wellington takes it in good part, I understand.'

'Lord, yes — they pretend to be great rivals, but he'll be
there just the same. He wouldn't spoil the Duchess's ball for
words — and he'll dance with all the Lennox girls in turn, just
to shew there's no hard feelings. So shall you go?'

'You do me too much honour, Lady Rosamund,' he smiled
without rancour. 'I'm afraid I'm one of the commoners for
whom there will be no room! A mere major, you know —!'

Just then Lord Burnett came strolling along the path
towards them, with Miss Burnett on his arm. Greetings were
exchanged, and then Burnett said cheerfully, 'Well, Larosse,
what news from Mons, eh? Have the French crossed yet?'

'There will be no news from Mons,' Larosse said. 'Charleroi will be the Emperor's object.'

Burnett gave a superior smile. 'Oh, stuff! He means to cut
us off from Ostend — the Beau says so.'

'From Charleroi to Brussels the road lies open,' Larosse
said stiffly. 'That is where he will cross.'

Burnett gave an unpleasant smile. 'Well, you should know,
I suppose, having been in his pocket for so many years! And
there's only Bylandt's brigade to guard the road, too — what
luck for Boney!'

Larosse was pale, except for two red spots of anger on his
cheek, but he controlled himself with an effort and kept
silent. Rosamund was startled to see revealed for the first
time the animosity against the Netherlanders who had served
under Napoleon, which she had heard about. She intervened
firmly.

'It's lucky for us that the major does know a little of the
way Boney thinks, and tells the Beau about it. It gives us the
advantage, for it's certain that Boney hasn't anyone who can
explain the Beau to him! Do you go to the Duchess's ball,
Miss Burnett? I heard Lord Hay saying it would be too hot —
can you imagine such nonsense? As if it could ever be too hot
for dancing! But we mustn't keep you — I can see you're in a
hurry. Goodbye — goodbye.'

The two groups parted and walked on. When they were out
of earshot, Larosse said quietly, 'That was kind of you, Lady
Rosamund. I'm sorry you should have been forced to witness

the esteem in which I am held by some of the Allied officers.'

'Freddy Burnett is a fool,' Rosamund said firmly, 'and you should not regard him. I would have told him so roundly, had not his sister been present, for she's a nice enough little thing — insipid, but harmless.'

Larosse smiled. 'Your opinions are always so vigorous,' he said. 'I admire your strength of mind.'

'I never was one to dress up a broom and call it a man,' Rosamund said blithely. 'Burnett is a venomous worm, and I'll tell him so when I next see him. Let him try asking me to dance on Thursday night, that's all!'

They reached a turn of the path, and Larosse stopped, and looked from Rosamund to Sophie and back. 'Lady Rosamund, I know you are kind, and I have the impertinence to think you do not entirely dislike me. May I ask a great favour of you? I should like to speak to Miss Morland in private — just a few words. Would you — could you —?'

'Of course,' Rosamund said quickly. 'Nothing could be easier. Now, Moss, don't flap so, like a dear old brown hen! All shall be decent and respectable, I promise you. The major and Sophie shall walk on ahead, and you and I can dawdle far enough behind not to overhear. They'll be in your sight all the time, and so nothing could be more proper. Will that suit?'

She had deliberately not consulted Sophie's face as she spoke, for she knew her retiring cousin might well shrink from such an interview. Yet Rosamund felt it essential that the major should be allowed to explain himself, if explanation were possible. Having singled Sophie out for the warmest attention, he had disappeared without word, leaving her miserable. *Something* must be said, and since from Sophie's point of view things could hardly be worse, Rosamund felt anything he said must be a help.

So she withdrew her hand from Larosse's arm, and stepped back, even making a little pushing gesture towards the couple in her eagerness to bring them together.

'Thank you — I am very grateful,' Larosse said, and wasted no more time. Keeping Sophie's hand trapped against his ribs, he turned away and walked off down the path, fitting his stride to hers, but walking as briskly as he could make her

343

in his eagerness to secure their privacy. Sophie's silence was due more to consciousness than unwillingness. Like Rosamund, she hoped Larosse had an excuse; and no-one could have been more ready to hear it. Her fear was that her feelings might escape her control again. Simply being with him was making her unruly senses sing; and she did not want to be trapped a second time into offering more than was wanted or welcomed.

'There — I think we are far enough ahead,' Larosse said after a while. He looked down at her pink cheeks with concern. 'I have hurried you too fast — you are quite breathless! I am sorry — let us walk more slowly now. Are you comfortable?'

Sophie made a small sound that might have been interpreted as assent.

'You did not say anything when I proposed — or your cousin proposed — for us to walk apart. You do not feel that you err in being alone with me?'

A brief flashing glance, quickly shielded. 'Oh, no!'

'Then, my dear Sophie, I may begin.' Having said so, he did not continue at once, but Sophie was comforted. He had spoken her name again, and in such a tone, that she felt at once at ease with him, as though these past weeks had never happened; as though she had spent her whole life walking thus with him, and waiting with confidence for his words.

At last he sighed and said, 'It is so much harder than I expected. Often and often these past weeks I have imagined myself with you — just like this — and in my imaginings I poured out my heart with such eloquence, sure of your approbation and understanding. Ah, but there's the rub! In real life, my Sophie, I am not so sure of my own deserving. You have every right to be angry with me. Indeed, I do not understand why you are not.'

'Oh, no!' she said quickly. 'Not angry. Only —' She stopped.

He looked down at her tenderly. 'Only? What then, bird of my heart? Tell me roundly. I have treated you infamously, have I not? I deserve no mercy.'

Now she looked up at him, a clear, frank look which seared him to the heart. He waited, feeling as though he had exposed his breast to a shining blade.

'You were away so long. Might you have not returned?' she said.

The blade went home. 'Yes, I might have come back to Brussels on several occasions,' he said frankly, 'but I did not. I avoided it. Out, words! I avoided you.'

Her lips made a silent 'Oh' of hurt, and he pressed her hand tightly.

'Ah, no, don't! Not because I didn't care for you, my heart, but because I cared for you too much. I was afraid of your influence over me. I knew myself in danger, and I fled.'

She looked bewildered. 'But how could I hurt you?' He didn't at once answer. 'I thought,' she said, very low, 'I thought you had only been amusing yourself with me.'

He smiled at that. 'Was I so very bad, then, at expressing myself? I thought I had been all too obvious.'

'But you did not — it was not like — what I saw other men doing and saying. And so I wasn't sure.'

'I did not flirt with you, you mean? Well, no — but you would not have cared for that. We were friends, were we not, my Sophie, from the first moment? I told you so, and you, with your dear, trusting nature, believed me.'

'Then — you meant me to — to —?'

'To love me? Yes, yes, of course! For I loved you from the first instant I saw you.'

He stopped to look down at her, covering her hand with his. She looked up with almost equal hope and doubt.

'I love you, Sophie. Believe it, for it is true. I shall love you until the drawing of my last breath — and probably beyond, if there is a forgiving God. But I had no right to do so —'

'Oh, no!' Sophie cried eagerly. 'It was I who — I thought you could not mean anything serious. I told myself I must not think of you. I know I am not of your station — not worthy of you —'

'My Sophie,' Larosse said unsteadily, 'if you say such tings I shall undoubtedly lose control of myself and strain you here and now to my heart. Not worthy? My dear, dear love, you are infinitely too good for me! You are lovely, and good, and innocent —'

He broke off abruptly and bit his lip at some recollection that troubled him. Sophie waited for him to resume, and

345

when he did not, she said quietly, 'But if you meant me to love you, why did you go away? Why did you not —' She couldn't quite be so bold as to say the words.

'Why did I not speak for you? Approach your excellent mother to ask for your hand in marriage?' She nodded mutely, and an expression of great bitterness crossed his face. 'Because, much as I want to, I cannot marry you.'

The words were like a sword. Sophie felt them almost as a physical blow, and involuntary tears sprang to her eyes, which she blinked away determinedly. 'Because I am — because I was not born in wedlock?' she asked in a small voice.

He looked blank, as though he had not understood her; and then said, 'Oh, my dear, was that what you thought? Am I such a fool that I would throw away the best and loveliest thing that ever came into my life for so trivial a reason? No, it was nothing to do with you, no reason connected with you. I want more than anything in the world to marry you, but I cannot, because I am married already.'

Oh, this was bitter! This was worse than anything Sophie could have imagined! She looked at him with a sickening sense of betrayal, of all hope dying there and then. She felt as though she were tumbling through the air from a great height, and the feeling of vertigo made her want to close her eyes; but she could not. She looked at his face, the face she loved and had learned to trust, and the only word that came into her mind was *why?* Why had he singled her out, made her love him — even now told her he loved her — when he was already married to another? She turned her face away at last and sighed, a small sigh of pain which hurt him worse than anything she might have said.

'Oh, don't, my heart, don't turn away from me! I am a blackguard, I know, and I deserve nothing from you. Curse me, rail at me, if you like, but don't turn your face from me, my Sophie! It isn't as you think. Let me explain to you. Will you listen to me?'

She nodded. They were walking slowly along a path in a public park, arm in arm, and she no more knew how to leave him than she knew how to fly in the air. She thought she would have liked to die just then; but such things were never arranged for one's convenience.

'Yes,' she said. 'I'll listen. Go on.'

'I believe I told you once,' Larosse began, 'that my family had an estate in the Ardennes, in the little spur of the hills which belonged to France. It had been in my family for generations, passed down from father to son, added to and improved by each generation. Not a large estate, but neat and compact, and beautiful — so beautiful! I wish you could have seen it, my Sophie — you would have loved it.'

She shook her head. She did not want him to talk like that. It was too painful.

'I grew up there, in an ancient world where nothing it seemed could ever change, except the seasons. We were far from Paris, and I was only seven when the Bastille was stormed: the Revolution was a distant thing that happened to other people. The first I really remember of it was when they killed the King.' He sighed. 'I was ten years old. I had been out with my dog, hunting rabbits on the hillside. I came home, dusty and tired and happy, and found my mother weeping. I remember it so clearly! I'd never seen her cry before, and it frightened me. My father was standing over her, looking stern. He said to me, "The King is dead. René, a new age has begun." He'd always been interested in new ideas, you see: but I saw only that my mother wept as though it were the end of the world. I put down the rabbit I had brought back on the table, and it was so soft and limp and brown; its eyes were half-closed, and there was blood on its nose and on its white paws. I had never thought about death before. I was frightened, and I began to cry, too.'

Sophie pressed his hand in sympathy, and he looked down at her bleakly. 'To my mother, it was the worst of sacrilege, and she could not resolve it in her mind. She died a few months later. I believe now that she simply couldn't live in a world where such things were possible. It was a terrible blow to me. My father was a stern, forbidding man, who believed that men must be strong and unyielding. He brought me up with harshness, tried to make me like himself. After my mother's death, I learnt not to shew love, for love was weakness, and was always punished. I thought I had learnt that lesson well; but early influence is hard to shake off — my

347

mother had loved me, and I her. It needed only to find the right person —'

His eyes had that soft shine she remembered, and now could not bear. 'Go on,' she said defensively.

'Well, then: there was another estate, on the other side of the hill, owned by the Beauvais family. Our lands ran together, we shared a boundary, and my father had always longed to unite the two estates. Purchase would not do it: they were an old family, and proud. But I was my father's only son, and the Beauvais had only a single daughter.'

Sophie flinched inwardly — they had come to the heart of it, then.

'We were betrothed almost in our cradles. I thought nothing of it — it was a fact I had grown up with. We were to have been married when I reached my majority, but in 1797 Beauvais *père* was dying, and the plans were brought forward. Laure and I were married in the autumn, by the new form of civil ceremony. I'm glad, now, that my mother did not live to see it. She was an ardent Catholic, and it would have broken her heart to see her son marry without the blessing of the Church.'

As before, his words had the power to take her away from the here and now, and project her into the place of his memories. She saw it all — the young people, very cowed and bewildered, the stern patriarch, the dying father doing his best for his only daughter. A joyless feast it must have been, she thought.

'It was a joyless marriage,' he said, as though he heard her thoughts. 'Laure was even more a child than I was, grieving for her father, of whom she had been very fond, terrified of my father, as indeed was I. He had firm ideas about a woman's duties. Laure was expected to run the household with rigid efficiency — she who had never done anything before more demanding than playing with her kitten! I helped her all I could — secretly, for my father would have beaten me if he discovered me doing a woman's work — but still she was always in error, always being rebuked, almost always in tears. My father was a virtuous man — he did what he did not from spite or cruelty, but because he believed it was right — but there was no warmth in him. He disapproved of Laure

348

because she did not run the house efficiently, and because she did not produce an heir; and where he disapproved, he knew it his duty to punish.'

They walked on slowly, neither of them aware of the least thing around them. Acquaintances passed and touched their hats, but Larosse did not see them. He was not even aware of Sophie as a separate entity: she was part of him just then. He felt as though his thoughts could pass to her without being spoken aloud.

'So things stood in 1799 when Napoleon came back to Paris to expel the corrupt Directory and establish the consulate, with himself as First Consul. My father didn't like that. He was a true Jacobin, and the idea of government by personality was as abhorrent to him as a return to the monarchy would have been. But I thought that Napoleon would usher in the new world we had been waiting for — the world which would justify the murder of the King. For the first time my father and I argued about something other than my personal failings! Then in 1800 Napoleon was declared virtual dictator and moved into the Tuileries, and slept in the bed of Louis VI himself! My father was incensed at his pretension; I said that it was a gesture of equality; we quarrelled fatally, and he ordered me from the house. I was eighteen, old enough for military service, and so I went to join the army, to prove my allegiance to the Consul.'

'And — Laure? Your wife?'

He shrugged. 'She remained. She belonged more to my father than to me. Of course I expected to go back — at eighteen, you don't think very far into the future. I didn't suppose I was leaving home permanently. But things changed. My father moved from disapproval of Napoleon to active resistance. He plotted with others first to remove, then to assassinate him. The plot was discovered; my father was arrested, tried, and executed.'

In the silence that followed, Sophie could think of nothing it was possible to say to such an appalling revelation. She saw from his face that, however little affection his father had inspired, Larosse had yet cared for him, and his death — especially the manner of his death — had affected him deeply.

349

'The estate, of course, was confiscated. Napoleon was merciful — it was known how things stood between my father and me, and I was exonerated, and the Beauvais estate — Laure's dowry — was awarded to her, and therefore, by association, to me. I think my own estate would have been given back, too, except that the man who had exposed my father's part in the plot had a desire to it himself, and demanded it as his reward. In later years the Emperor promised to restore it to me one day, but as things fell out ...' He shrugged.

'And so did you go back, after your father — died?'

'Not immediately. I wanted to prove my loyalty to Napoleon, you see — away from active service, at home in the hills, I might have come under suspicion. He was very suspicious in those days — there was more than one plot against him. But when the peace was declared, I went home — or rather, to Laure's home.'

He smiled reflectively. 'I hardly recognised her. She had grown up so much; she was like a different person. And there was a cousin of hers, Lucien, who had come to live in the house and help her to run the estate. They were kind to me, tried to make me welcome, but I could see that I was a stranger to them, too; and an awkward one. I was surrounded by ghosts — I made them uneasy, made them remember things they didn't want to remember. Laure was afraid also, I could see, that I should want her to be a wife to me. So I made it clear from the beginning I would sleep separately, at the other end of the house. We rubbed along pretty well; but when the war began again, and I spoke of going back to my regiment, they gazed at me so hopefully.' He smiled wryly. 'They waved goodbye with such relief when I left, and went in and shut the door before I was out of sight. I never went back after that. And now, of course, I am a proscribed person. While the Emperor lives, I may not return to France.'

He stopped, and after a few moments Sophie saw that he had come to the end, that his narrative was complete as far as he was concerned. But for her it was only the beginning of the story. The most important things had not been said.

'It is so very sad,' she said. 'I feel for you so much! But, Major —'

350

He looked startled. He had been far away in his thoughts, and came back with a jolt when she spoke, to say, 'René! You must call me René. "Major" is absurd, when I have just told you everything — you must see it so.'

She shook her head. The name was like dark honey on the mind's tongue, and she longed to use it, but she was too shy to say it aloud. 'What of Laure? Do you know what has become of her?' she said at last.

'She was still at the farm a year ago,' he said, 'and still living with her cousin. After we took Paris in March last year, I met an old acquaintance who gave me news of her. I thought that when things were settled I would go back and see how she did, and ask her if she would like me to divorce her so that she could marry her cousin. Ours had only been a civil marriage, you see. I was in no hurry, of course — I had not met you then, and had no intention of ever remarrying. But then the Emperor escaped from Elba, and so everything changed again.'

Sophie began to see the way forward. 'So you think it is possible —?'

He stopped and turned to face her. 'Yes, now we come to it, my Sophie! Provided the Emperor is beaten and France is liberated, I can go to Laure, arrange for a divorce, and be free to marry again. But you see that it is a great deal to ask of any woman, that she wait for me, and on such terms of uncertainty.'

'Uncertainty?'

He looked grave. 'We do not know how long this present war will continue. The Allies talk of being in Paris by the autumn, but the Emperor may not be so easy to defeat. The war might last a year — or five years — or ten; and while it lasts, I am helpless to pursue matters.'

'Do you think it will last so long?' she asked in a small voice.

'No. I think matters are drawing to their close. I think he will not last another year. The times are passing him by — the world has moved on. It is as I told you in the herb garden, my love — he is a child of the old order, and there is no place for him in the new world. I think by this time next year he will be gone — dead, perhaps; but even when he is gone,

351

matters will take time to arrange. It might be another year after that before I am free to marry. Two years, Sophie, two long years. Now you see why I did not feel able to ask you to love me — and why I went away.'

'But you came back.'

'You were always in my thoughts. I thought by staying away I was doing what was best for you; hurting myself, for your good. But then I remembered what you said at the ball, about women being able to choose only when they were asked, and it seemed to me that I was denying you that choice, your only choice. So I came back.' He studied her face carefully. 'It is a great deal to ask, *chère amie* — too much, perhaps. It will require careful thought, and much consultation. But if you are willing to wait for me, my Sophie, I wish more than anything in the world to marry you.'

She gave him both her hands with a gesture of such complete trust that it brought tears to his eyes. 'I will wait,' she said. 'I'll wait as long as necessary.'

'No, my love, you mustn't give me an answer now. You must take time to think about it.'

'I don't need to think. I love you — only you.'

He lifted her hand to his lips, and then to his cheek. 'Then we must go and see your mother, and I must tell my story again.' A movement caught his attention, and he glanced sideways, and then grinned at her. 'Your faithful Cerberus is coming! I have kissed your hand in public, which is a grave sin! Now we shall have to marry, or your reputation is ruined.'

Sophie laughed, and turned to face the rapidly approaching Moss and Rosamund. Rosamund smiled delightedly. 'So it is all settled!' she cried as she reached them. 'I knew how it would be. I am so glad, Sophie! My congratulations, Major!'

Larosse allowed his hand to be shaken, but said, 'No congratulations yet! There are many hurdles to be overcome before I can deserve them.'

Rosamund waved those away lightly. 'Pho! Fences were made to be got over. But tell me, Major, why did you stay away from Brussels for so long, and break poor Sophie's heart, if you loved her all along?'

352

René took in Moss's shocked indignation at the freedom of the talk, Rosamund's frank curiosity and Sophie's rather bewildered euphoria, and began to laugh. Everything seemed so incongruous — and most incongruous of all was his astonished happiness. War might renew itself at any moment, bloody and horrible war against his own countrymen, but he stood in the sunshine in a city park and laughed with exuberance.

'Because I didn't think she would have me,' was all he said.

Héloïse wandered about the room, hardly knowing where she was or what she was doing. Sometimes she sat down for a moment, only to get up and walk again restlessly. She seemed to be seeing things with minute and painful clarity: each dust-mote falling through the bar of sunlight from the window seemed individually etched on her memory; the pattern on the carpet was enormous and close, magnified in maddening detail; the individual petals that had fallen from the roses in the bowl on the table seemed preposterously significant. They lay scattered on the polished surface, in a way which seemed to her wounded mind plainly not random: she felt that if she could only understand their arrangement, everything would be all right again.

She walked round the table and back to the window, her hands twisting themselves together. On the window-seat the letter lay open, a bland white face crossed with black marks, so innocent, so innocuous. She picked it up again, and though she did not precisely read it, certain words and phrases jumped out of it and embedded themselves in her mind like shards of glass.

'... *need not believe me, if you don't wish to. It is common knowledge ... seen by a score of people ... young enough to be his daughter ... as soon as your back was turned ...*'

How could she have retained such bitterness for so many years? It was unreal, it was an absurdity! Héloïse put down the letter and slowly wiped her fingers on her handkerchief, as though the paper might have been envenomed. The twisted mind, the bitter, angry woman, the imagined crime — imagined? It was laid out in such detail, and witnesses referred to. Would she have invented a story which could so

353

easily be refuted? Would she have named witnesses if they had not, in fact, witnessed anything?

Her mind moved away, like someone shifting in an uncomfortable seat. John Skelwith — how did he feel? Did he know? Had his mother told him? Had she poured it out to him, about his 'real' father, and his real father's crime? John starting his new life with Mathilde — had Mary Skelwith poured the poison into Mathilde's ear, too? Well, why not? Why suppose she should have shewn any restraint? When you have a good story, don't you want to tell as many people as possible?

Story? But was it true? Was any part of it true? Was there any truth in it — which was a different question.

Very well, take it at its lowest and most provable level — if he had, for any reason, taken a young female out riding in the carriage, alone, unchaperoned, that in itself was a betrayal. To do what might be misinterpreted — must be so, indeed — was to expose her to gossip and pity, to the malice of those who would always think the worst. And her own carriage, which he had designed for her with such love, an age ago, in happier times!

Even if it were as innocent as that, it was crime enough. *But what if it were true, all of it?* The word *Scarborough* presented itself in her mind, and she flinched from it. She knew about Scarborough where James had carried on his guilty liaison with Mary; where perhaps John Skelwith had been conceived. Scarborough! It was a word which stood in her head for all the things she could not bring herself to name. But they say that a dog which has once bitten a human being can never be trusted again. When a taboo was once broken, every subsequent breach became easier to commit. He had betrayed his first wife: why should he not betray his second? He had been so insistent that she went away — why? He had not written to her since she left Morland Place — why? And now his most bitter enemy had taken the trouble to write to her with such a detailed account — the child's name, even ...

Child. Héloïse stopped somewhere near the door, and looked long and hard at the architrave, her eye following the grooves up, across, and down, and then back again. A child —

354

young enough to be his daughter. It was all part of his madness over losing Fanny, of course. He had tried to replace her with this — Miss Hesketh. God, how she wished she didn't know the name! But is was not a criminal liaison. Probably he only wanted to talk to her — *talk to her, when he would not talk to you. Tell her all the things he held back from you. Let her comfort him, when he would not let you near.*

Crime enough, even if there were nothing worse. She turned back towards the window, crossed the unploughed acres of the carpet, stared again at the letter, white-face-up on the worn red plush of the window-seat.

He has stopped loving you, her mind told her calmly, in a tiny voice, distant but ringingly clear, like something heard across empty snow fields on a crisp winter's day. He has turned away from you, as once he turned to you; and you always knew that one day it might happen. The dog that bites. Scarborough. Common knowledge. Mary Skelwith. Oh, not true, not true! *But what if it were . . .?*

The door opened, and there was Sophie, pink-cheeked and bright-eyed from her exercise, looking at her enquiringly. Back from her fitting. New ball-gown. Special occasion. She must not spoil Sophie's pleasure. A girl's first Season should be special. Dear Sophie, the comfort of so many years without James, her pride, their love — looking excited, and unexpectedly happy, she realised, dragging the scattered fragments of her thoughts together.

'May we come in, Maman? I have brought someone to see you.'

Héloïse assembled a smile, put her hands down to her sides and made them unclench. 'Of course, *chérie.* How did your fitting go? Do you like your new gown? Did Rosamund get her gloves?'

'Oh, the shopping was successful, and the gown is heavenly,' Sophie said with a laugh — actually a laugh — 'but now there is something much more important to think about. Maman, here is Major Larosse to see you.'

She stepped aside, and Larosse came in, hat in hand, his eyes going at once to Héloïse's, his expression happy and apologetic and hopeful and anxious all at once. What mother could have failed to understand? She looked from Larosse to

Sophie, and Sophie laughed, and ran to her and flung her arms about her mother's neck.

'He has something very particular to ask you, Maman,' Sophie said into Héloïse's ear, their cheeks pressed together. 'And, do *do* say yes, for it's what I want most of all in the world!' She planted a kiss on her mother's cheek, and then released her, and returned to her lover's side, to give him a look so confiding that Héloïse saw at once how far things had gone — too far easily to reverse them. 'Now I'll leave you together,' Sophie said happily. 'I shall be in my room with Rosamund if you want me.'

The door closed softly behind her, and Héloïse looked at Larosse with a defeated air. He had come to take her daughter away, she thought, and then dismissed the idea briskly. If he and Sophie were in love, what could be better?

'Come in, Major,' she said. 'Won't you sit down, and tell me all about it?'

'I shall tell you all,' he said with a pleasant, frank smile, 'but there is so much, and it is so difficult, that I think I must do it standing. And, if you will permit, in French.'

It took him half an hour. He told her far more than he would burden Sophie with just then, and she asked more questions, not having perfect trust to help her along. At the end she asked, as Sophie did, why he had gone away.

'I thought it best for her,' he said. 'I felt that it was unfair and wrong of me to ask her to commit herself to such an uncertain future. I am a good deal older than her, as you know, and I felt responsible. I thought if I went away, she would forget me and find someone else. But then when I saw her in the street she looked so pale and forlorn, and she gave me one searing look, Madame, of mingled reproach and forgiveness, and I knew I was being more unfair than I had been before. I had never given her the chance to speak her mind, to make her thoughts known: I had chosen for her, without consulting her wishes. In that instant, I made up my mind to present her with all the facts, and let her decide for herself.'

Héloïse didn't speak, and he went on, a little apprehensively, 'Was that wrong? Do you disapprove of my actions?'

'You do not think quite as other men,' Héloïse said slowly. 'Sophie is very young. At her age, older people make decisions for her, for her own good.'

'And was never anything decided for you, for your own good, which you disliked?' he asked with a smile.

She shook her head. 'I am her mother. You can't ask me to see things from your point of view.'

'It is just what I am doing. From mine, and from hers. Madame, if I did not believe I could make your daughter happy — *eh bien*, happier, let it be said roundly, than anyone else could! — I assure you I would have spurred my horse on and never looked back. I love her, and if I am allowed, I will cherish her, to my dying day.'

Héloïse thought for a while. 'One must be practical,' she said at last. 'This divorce? Can it be obtained?'

'Assuredly, it can be done,' he said. 'Actually it was only a civil marriage — the Church was not involved. And I did not tell Sophie, of course, but Laure has been living *en noces* with her cousin for many years. There are, I believe, several children. She will welcome the release as much as I. It is a matter only of opportunity — and time.'

'And then will you get your estate back?'

'No, that is gone for ever. But I am not destitute. Over the years I have had little inclination to spend what I earned or acquired. I have a considerable sum in gold, hidden away in various safe places, which will be enough to purchase a gentlemanly estate, and to furnish a portion for my wife — if I am to have a wife. I may as well tell you frankly that I never wanted one before, and if I cannot have the one I want, I shall never look elsewhere.'

Héloïse smiled at last. 'You really do love her.'

'I really do love her.'

'Then I am content.' The smile faded from her face so rapidly that he stepped forward, thinking she was about to faint. 'I shall write to her father,' she said bleakly. 'My permission you may have at once — his you must wait for. But I do not think he will withhold it. He has no — he will trust my judgement, I believe.'

'Thank you, madame, from my heart,' he said; and she looked so exhausted, he felt he should not detain her longer.

He would have shaken her hand, but she did not seem to know that he was there any longer.

'Shall I send for someone?' he asked gently. 'I fear you are not well. May I ring for your maid?'

'No — please — I am well. I wish only to be alone.'

He said goodbye, bowed, and let himself out; but, uneasy about her, looked round for some servant to despatch. The butler was at the street door, admitting another visitor. René walked towards him, and saw that the newcomer was the Duc. The two men eyed each other cautiously.

'Well, René — you are back from Namur?'

'Yes, sir — I arrived this morning.' He glanced at the butler, who retired a pace or two. 'I have just had an interview with Madame,' he went on in a low voice. 'I think you can guess my business.'

The Duc looked surprised. 'You have resolved matters?'

'I have laid everything before her, my hopes and my intentions, and she approves them. As soon as we have beaten the Emperor I shall put matters in train for a divorce.'

The Duc laid a hand on his shoulder. 'Excellent man! You have done as you ought. And if I can help in any way — I have His Majesty's ear, you know. I may be able to expedite matters, once we are back in Paris.'

'Thank you, sir. I shall be truly grateful for any help. But I fear my news was something of a shock to her ladyship. She seemed upset when I left her. I thought of advising the butler to send her maid to her.'

The Duc looked grave. 'I will go in to her at once. Leave it with me, René — I am one of her oldest friends. I shall know what to do. Come to my lodgings this evening, if you can, and we will talk further. For now — *adieu.*'

Charles found Héloïse sitting on the window-seat, her hands in her lap, rocking like a child in pain. He hurried to her.

'Heart of my heart, what is it?' He drew her against his shoulder and held her. After a while, he said, 'Can you tell me what is wrong? Is it something that Larosse said?'

She shook her head; and then the words burst from her, low and painful. 'He will take her away too! Well, that is good — but it hurts. Charles, what shall I do? How can I ever go home? I'm so afraid —'

'But what is it, darling? What has happened? Only tell me — I cannot help unless you tell me.'

'No-one can help,' she said, and pulled away from him, covering her face with her hands. He saw the letter lying on the window-seat beside her, and after a brief hesitation, picked it up and read it. His brow furrowed with distaste and anger as well as shock.

'It can't be true,' he said at once when he had finished it. 'This woman — she was your rival, perhaps? She says here "I suppose you will think I am telling you this to spite you." Surely you cannot rely on her word?'

'It's true,' she said. She dropped her hands and looked at him helplessly. 'How much of it, I don't know. But it doesn't matter how much — that he could do something so public, which would be bound to be talked of, is enough. But it isn't even that,' she went on when he would have interrupted. 'Gossip — scandal — I can ignore.'

'What, then?'

'It is that he doesn't love me any more. When he did this — whatever he did — he didn't think of me at all. I wasn't in his mind. I did not exist for him. If he can forget me so completely, he cannot love me. That is what I cannot bear.'

He said nothing. He was painfully torn — on the one hand, wanting to persuade her out of her suffering, on the other hand rejoicing that she might be free of her husband, to turn to him at last.

'And now I have to write to him to ask permission for Sophie to be betrothed to Larosse. But he does not care about Sophie either. Perhaps he might not even reply to the letter. If I never went home again, he would not care, or even notice.'

He was silent, struggling with himself. Finally he said, 'You don't have to go back. You might stay here — with me.' She said nothing, but he felt her resistance. 'I would take care of you — be everything to you. You have Sophie. When the war is over, we could all settle down together, in France! Even if I could not marry you in the eyes of the Church, I would be a husband to you in every other way, and never leave you. Think of it, Héloïse — France! The King on the throne again, and everything as it was. We could go home — home, after such a long exile!'

'Oh, Charles,' she said, and the negative was so strong in her voice, the hopelessness, that he could not let her speak.

'No, don't say anything now. Now you are unhappy, you must not make a decision now. But think about it, my dearest one. You know that I love you — that I have never loved anyone else. I believe, long ago, you were on the brink of marrying me. If it could work then, it could work now. We are old friends, we suit each other. We could go back to France, and be happy. Just think about it, that's all I ask.'

She nodded wearily, unable to fight any more, and he kissed her brow and stood up contritely. 'I have worn you out,' he said. 'You must go to your room and rest. Let me ring for your maid. It has been a tiring day for you.'

'Yes,' she said, to any or all of it. The thought of sleep was delicious, beckoned to her with its sweet seduction of oblivion. Charles rang for her maid, and waited with her in tactful silence until Marie appeared to escort her mistress upstairs.

CHAPTER FOURTEEN

The Earl of Chelmsford, walking briskly along under the trees of the Allée Verte on the morning of the fourteenth, saw Lady Theakston cantering towards him on Magnus Apollo, and stepped out into the early sunlight to accost her. The sun flashed from the brass buttons of his new blue coat and the dazzling whiteness of his neckcloth, and Magnus Apollo took exception to one or both and shied violently, actually managing to lift all four feet off the ground at once.

Any other rider, Bobbie thought with a mixture of admiration and guilt, would have been unseated, even thrown, but her ladyship merely gathered her horse up again, turned him, goggling and trembling, to face the sartorial menace, and apostrophised Bobbie roundly with a selection of epithets she must surely have learnt from her acquaintance in the Guards.

'I do beg your pardon, ma'am,' Bobbie said, when she had her dragon under control again. 'I made sure he would have seen me in time.'

'He had his eye on more distant horizons,' Lucy said. 'Stand, Magnus! Hold up, you fool!' Seeing she had him square, Bobbie went forward and offered his fingers. Magnus snuffed tremulously, then mumbled them apologetically with his lips.

Bobbie took hold of the rein, and squinted up at her ladyship. 'I say, ma'am, you are a regular Trojan! How do you find he goes now?'

'Like the beating of my own heart,' Lucy said, stroking the gleaming neck fondly. 'Unless some young fool in a fancy waistcoat startles him. What the deuce are you doing out so early, anyway? No-one comes here before ten o'clock but riders.'

'I came looking for Marcus. I called at Headquarters, but they said he's not on duty yet, and that he'd probably taken

361

Bab riding in the Allée. Have you seen them? I wanted to tell him the news.'

'Yes, they're fooling around up by the canal bridge. Barbarina's on the most knock-kneed, spavined brute of a job-horse I've ever seen. It'll have her down before she's an hour older. Marcus must have had his eyes shut when they led it out! Only a brother would be so careless as to let — what news?'

Bobbie smirked with pleasure at being the one to break it. 'Bel Robb is going to marry her count!'

'You'll have to do better than that!'

'No, no, I assure you, ma'am, it's the genuine specie this time! As solid as the Bank of England! I had it from Figgy Lichfield. He was riding in from Enghien this morning, and passed right by Château Ladon, and the count practically waylaid him in the road to tell him the good news. He don't mean to keep it to himself, ma'am, I assure you! As pleased as a cat in a butter-churn, so Lichfield says, and wants all the world to share his happiness. So Lichfield, being a conscientious fellow, rode straight in to town to find someone to tell, and happened upon me.'

'But do you believe it? It sounds like a hum to me,' Lucy said doubtfully, checking Magnus as he fidgeted.

'It's going to be announced in the *Gazette* today, so it must be true.'

'Well, I'm astonished. What can she be thinking about? There are plenty of titles she could marry if that was all she wanted. His fortune is nothing remarkable, and she can't have any liking for his person, surely?'

'I've been wondering about it myself, ma'am, and it occurs to me that perhaps she likes de Ladon because she can keep him under her thumb. And he hasn't any pa to disapprove of her — no relatives to all, in fact. Perhaps she means to settle here permanently and play the great lady.'

Lucy shook her head. 'Desperate dull she'll find that! However — it's her beef, so she may chew it as she likes. And this was what you wanted to tell Marcus, was it?'

Bobbie looked conscious. 'He'll read about it later anyway, but I thought — as things are — he'd be grateful for a chance to prepare himself. People are bound to — well, *look* at him.'

'Oh, yes! They'll come up and tell him the good news with the greatest of glee,' Lucy snorted, 'and watch his face for every twinge while they do it.'

'Just so, ma'am. So I thought I'd walk up here and catch him before he sees anyone else; and if he wants to go off on his own for a while — well, I can escort Bab home for him, too.'

'Oh, of course!' Lucy was not fooled by the insouciance. She eyed the elaborate necktie, and the starched shirt-points almost high enough to poke out his eyes. 'So it's a case between you two, is it? And what does her mother think about that?'

Bobbie grinned ruefully. 'You'd think she'd like it — me being an earl — but she don't. Looks as blue as megrim whenever I call, but can't quite bring herself to forbid me! However, Uncle Horace is all for it, so it don't signify. I just wish this dashed business with Boney was over so that I could make all fair and take Bab away. She and Mama get on so well, and I'm afraid her mother bullies her a good deal.'

'An understatement, I should say. Well, nobody could fail to get on with your mother. I shall call on her later today and talk to her about it. Meanwhile — to the rescue, Saint George! She's a good enough sort of girl, and the blood's sound — the Rushtons are an old family, even if the money's new.'

'Thank you, ma'am,' Bobbie said with a grin, and strode away on his philanthropic mission.

By mid-morning, the news of Bel Robb's engagement was all over Brussels, and by evening probably the only people not talking about it were Sophie, who was deeply *tête à tête* with her major in the morning-room, and Lucy, who had much more important things to think about: Danby had come in from Tournai. She had been expecting him anyway for the dress-ball, and had hoped he would come early so that they would have a little time together before Deacon started fussing about whether his dress-coat still fitted him properly and whether the lace on his hat was dull; but this was a whole day early — better than she could have hoped!

He had been sent by Sir Hussey Vivian to report to the

363

Beau about an alarming new development. The 10th Hussars had been detailed to keep an eye on a detachment of French cavalry which had been stationed on the border just south of Tournai. The previous day — the thirteenth — one of the Hussar pickets had suddenly realised that his opposite number, whom he had been idly regarding with the inattentiveness of boredom, was not a cavalry picket at all, but a member of the National Guard, whose normal duties were no more military than a customs officer's.

The man, when captured and questioned, had been perfectly happy to tell them that the cavalry company had been withdrawn to Maubeuge on the River Sambre to support the building of a bridgehead. All along the frontier, he said, French troops had been withdrawn, and their places taken by National Guard to deceive the Allies. The entire French army, he told them cheerfully, was gathering in the area between Maubeuge and Beaumont, in preparation for crossing the border into Belgium.

Lucy remembered what Rosamund had told her of René Larosse's interpretation of the Emperor's state of mind. This latest news seemed a vindication of his view. Lucy mentioned it to Danby; Larosse was still in the house and was sent for, and a rapid conversation had resulted in the two of them leaving at once for Headquarters to talk to the Duke again.

The following morning — the fifteenth — Brussels seethed with rumour, and one or two of the more nervous visitors looked to their trunks and horses, wondering if the time hadn't come for them to leave for England and safety. But the Duke was seen walking in the Park with the Duke of Richmond and Lord Fitzroy Somerset, chatting with the greatest of calmness. When pressed to comment on the rumours, he said with a faint smile and a shrug that he believed it was true that the French had crossed the border, but that they were probably only intending to make a feint. There was no cause whatsoever for alarm. The dress-ball was certainly still to be held, and the Duke himself would be there, with the Prince of Orange, who was dining with him that afternoon.

Brussels allowed itself to be calmed. Everyone said that as Boney was known to have been in Paris with the Imperial

Guard on the tenth, he couldn't possibly have got this far already. Besides, the Lennox girls were everywhere in town that day, on errands connected with the ball. They declared that if anything were really afoot, Papa would have been bound to know, and he had said he knew nothing of any movement on the frontier. They thought it was all a hum, just like the other rumours. The ball would definitely go ahead: there was no cause for alarm.

Danby was at Headquarters all day, returning to the Rue Ducale at about five.

'Well?' Lucy asked him at once.

'Lord knows what's going on,' he said, accepting a glass of sherry from her and sitting down. 'The French are over the border — but why and how many we don't know. A report came in this afternoon from Ziethen to say that the Prussians had been engaged since four this morning. There was firing all along the Prussian line, and Thuin had been taken. The Prussians have fallen back in good order on Charleroi. But that was sent off at nine this morning — since then, nothing.'

'Then it looks as though Larosse was right?'

'The Beau doesn't think so. We've also had reports of aggressive movements from the Lille and Dunkirk garrisons, you see, which looks as though they mean to attack Ostend. That would mean this business at Thuin is only a feint, and the real attack will come further to the west — at Mons, probably — with the object of cutting us off from our supplies. The Beau won't do anything until he hears from Mons. We've got Colonel Grant out there — he's a good man. Always knows everything first.'

Lucy studied his face. 'What is it, Danby?' she asked after a moment. 'There's something wrong about this, isn't there?'

He sighed, and frowned. 'It's just that young man — he can be damn' persuasive.'

'Larosse?'

'He was there all afternoon, trying to convince the Beau that Boney means to come up the centre. The road from Charleroi to Brussels lies open, he says — and what's more, half-way up it's crossed by the road from Nivelles to Namur —'

'At Quatre-Bras?'

365

'That's right. It's our only real connection with Blücher's forces. Now if Larosse is right, and Boney marches up that road and takes Quatre-Bras, he cuts us off from the Prussians. The only other way to Namur is through the forest and cross-country through Wavre — and that's a damned bad road. Artillery'd never get through.' He shook his head. 'I don't know. He's got me thinking, damn him.'

'And what did the Beau say to all that?'

'He just listened quietly and then said the Charleroi road was too bad for a full-scale advance, and that he'd wait to hear from Mons before he made up his mind.'

'Well, he can't decide without information, can he?'

'Hmm. But to make it worse, Ziethen's report recommended concentrating the army at Nivelles, which looks as though he's in Larosse's way of thinking. But then he didn't know about Lille and Dunkirk. I just don't know what to think.'

Lucy perched on the arm of the sopha and stroked the fair hair back from his brow. 'Don't think anything for the moment. There's nothing more you can do now. The ball still goes on, I suppose.'

'Lord, yes! It would take more than the French Armée du Nord to stop the Richmonds' ball.'

'Then let's go upstairs,' Lucy said. 'We've time before dinner, and you've been at Headquarters all day. That wasn't why I wanted you to come back to Brussels early.'

He looked at her for a moment with a blank frown, still deep in his troubled thoughts, and then it cleared and he grinned at her. 'Shameless wanton!' he commented with satisfaction.

She caught his hand and laid it over her breast. 'Insults will get you nowhere, my lord,' she said sweetly.

Marcus called at the house at seven, just as the occupants were preparing to retire to dress for the ball.

'I'm on my way home for the same reason,' he said cheerfully. 'I just thought I'd call in and tell you the latest news.'

'Oh, is there more?' said Lucy.

'Have we heard from Grant?' Danby asked, to the point.

'N'ary a whistle! Nothing later than nine this morning. But

the Beau's made a move at last, given out orders for the concentrating of the army. All the cavalry's to collect at Ninove, the Dutch-Belgics at Nivelles, and the other divisions in a semi-circle to the west and south. De Lancey and Lord Fitzroy are hard at it, and all the staff is put on readiness. Lord knows if we'll get to the ball — but as things stand, I don't know that I mind very much.'

'Then — it has come at last?' Lucy said sharply.

Marcus shrugged. 'The official word is that this is just a feint, and there's nothing to worry about. But unofficially, we all think the army will soon be engaged — and it can't be soon enough for some of us! However, the ball goes on — the Beau don't want a panic. And here's some good news for you, Cousin Sophie — Monsieur le Duc's obtained an invitation for Major Larosse, since he's been at Headquarters all afternoon. He was even invited to dine with the Beau and Baron Muffling! Well, I'd better be going — I have to change and get back on duty. But I just wanted to give you the latest, and to ask Rosamund — if I do manage to get to the ball later on, will you save a dance for me?'

Rosamund was deep in thought. It took a moment or two for her to find her voice. 'Yes — yes, of course I will. Gladly,' she said. Soon engaged? How soon? Where? And tonight she must give Tantony his answer, and she still had no idea what it should be.

The ballroom in the Duchess of Richmond's house in the Rue de la Blanchisserie was a mass of candles and flowers — June roses and white lilies, whose heavy, almost sickly, scent vied with the smell of hot wax and hot people on the warm, still air. The french windows onto the garden were open, but no breath came in to ease the suffering of the gentlemen in their high collars and tight stocks, heavy uniform coats, gold lace, epaulettes and sashes. The women were better off, in light silks and muslins, bare-armed and deeply *décolletées*, but everywhere there was the bird-wing flutter of fans vigorously plied to cool a complexion from undesirable rose back to natural lily. Scarlet and gold were the dominant colours, Hussar blue and Rifle green, yellow facings and silver lace: the soft, light colours of the women's gowns disappeared in contrast, like wild flowers overpowered by a hothouse bouquet.

The Theakstons' party arrived at about ten, and Bobbie Chelmsford met them inside the door, eager with news.

'My step-papa arrived about an hour ago from Namur with a despatch from the Prussians, to say that Blücher is moving his men up to Sombreffe on the Nivelles road, and that Charleroi is the French objective. But Marcus says that the Beau won't make a move until he hears from Mons: he's still sure it's a feint. Mama and Papa are coming on later; and Uncle Horace has had to go back to Ninove, so I offered to escort Lady Barbara and Barbarina. I'd better get back to them, if you'll excuse me — I want to make sure Bab's saved me the next waltz! I say, sir, do you think it's really coming?'

'Looks that way,' Lord Theakston said laconically.

'Well, if this is the last ball, at least it's a capital one!' Bobbie said with a grin, and departed.

Sophie, led onto the floor by Larosse, trembled a little as his arm encircled her waist, still unable to believe her happiness. He looked down at her with smiling eyes, reading her thoughts.

'Believe it: it's true! What's more, your excellent Mama has given permission for us to regard ourselves as betrothed, though we have to wait for your father's consent before it is announced; which means we may properly dance together all evening. No more rationing ourselves to two dances! No more watching you circling in another man's arms, racked with jealousy —'

'You were not!' she protested. 'I don't believe it.'

'Oh, but I was — even though you looked so kind and bored that I had no fear that you might like them better! But I don't want any man but me ever to dance with you again, my Sophie. I am a jealous lover, and so I warn you! Thou shalt have no other man but me.'

She was faintly, delightfully shocked at the near-blasphemy. 'I want no other.'

'Then promise me.' He leaned over her exultantly. 'Promise me you will dance with no man but me!'

'I promise,' she said easily. 'But it is in your hands, in any case. You have only to claim me each time the music starts —'

'If I am here,' he said. 'What when I have marched away, my Sophie? What then?'

She looked up at him anxiously. 'Will it be soon, then?'

'Haven't you noticed that I am the only officer here from my division? The rest of my fellow-officers are already on alert.'

She looked around. Everywhere there were young people with laughing faces and bright eyes, whirling to the music in each other's arms. The lights, the music, the flowers, the gaiety: war could not have seemed further away. But it was true: apart from Larosse and the Duc, there were no Dutch-Belgic officers. It laid a shadow over her happiness.

'Do you think I would have the heart for dancing when you were gone away?' she answered, subdued.

'No, not really.' He smiled down at her. 'But I'm not sorry it's come at last. It is better that we get it over with, then we can get on with our lives. Have I told you yet how beautiful you are tonight? Like a star, like a lily —'

'Oh, don't! Lilies make me think of funerals. I hate the smell of them. When Maman's friend Flon died —'

'Foolish thing! Well, then, not like a lily. Like a princess. I'm glad you chose to wear white for tonight. All those colours —' he gestured about him at the other dancers — 'are well enough, but they are commonplace. But you — you are robed in white and gold, and crowned with stars, like a dark princess. How could I ever have deserved you? Oh my Sophie, my own love, I will make you happy, I swear it!'

'Don't swear: there's no need. I am happy.'

'René! Call me by my name, love.'

'I am happy, René,' she said shyly. 'Happier than I ever knew was possible.'

'It's only the beginning. There is so much more to come — being together, living together — have you thought where you would like to live? When all this over, we will be free to choose from the whole world! We'll buy an estate, found a new line. Where will you like to live when you are Madame Larosse?'

She blushed and looked away. 'Oh!' she said. 'How strange it sounds.'

'Not strange,' he corrected. 'Natural.'

369

Rosamund had been besieged from the first moment by members of her court, and having danced with Lord Ponsonby, Lord Farringdon and Sir John Wilmot she was just about to accept the invitation of Harry Pyne when a dashing figure in Jack-a-lantern green interposed itself, and Lieutenant Pyne was politely but firmly routed by Captain Tantony.

'I beg your pardon, Pyne, but this dance has already been promised to me. Lady Rosamund — your hand, if you please!'

'Oh, I say, this is too much! Do you mean to let him bully you, Lady Ros? After all, a ball is for pleasure, not duty. Tell him to go away, the insolent fellow!'

'Oh, Lord! You know we females are all mad for Rifleman green,' Rosamund said, with a fair imitation of languishing. 'I can't resist! Take me away, Captain! The Hyde Park soldiers must wait.'

'Now that,' said Tantony when they were safe on the floor, 'was cruel!'

'War is cruel,' she said, fluttering her eyelashes, and he laughed.

'What are you up to, my lady? You've devilment in your eyes.'

'My lady! I like it when you call me that!'

'I hope that you will be my lady. You haven't forgotten —'

'No, I haven't forgotten that I am to give you my answer tonight. But you must be patient a while longer, Captain Tantony.'

He cocked his head at her. 'You want to torment me? Well, I have been patient for so long — a little while longer won't hurt me.'

She eyed him curiously. 'You're a strange lover, I must say! A little *im*patience would be more flattering.'

He smiled at her tenderly. 'If I have learned one thing, my lady, it is that any man who wishes to win you and keep you must first learn how to handle you.'

'Like a horse? I don't think I care to be *handled*, Captain.'

'Oh, you will, I promise you. You will,' he said softly, and meeting his eyes, she felt a most extraordinary sensation of fluttering and swooping, as though a flock of small birds was trapped inside her stomach. It was unnerving, and exciting, and different from anything she had ever felt before.

'Don't,' she protested, but without much conviction.

'Don't what?'

'You know very well — look at me like that. It makes me feel strange.'

He responded by holding her a little tighter, and whirling her a little faster. For the first time in her life, Rosamund was not completely in control of herself or the situation; and in a tremulous sort of way, she found she liked it.

Marcus arrived at half-past eleven, and was at once surrounded by people wanting to know the latest news.

'Where's the Duke? Doesn't he mean to come?'

'Where's Boney? Where are the French?'

'What news from Mons? Has Grant come through at last?'

Marcus held up his hands. 'Give me room, good people! Yes, we've heard from Mons, but not from Grant. The word was from General Dornberg: no sign of the enemy, but his best intelligence is that they are moving on Charleroi.'

There was a silence, and then the babble broke out louder than ever.

'But what's the Beau doing? Is it orders, Morland?' Ponsonby managed to make himself heard over the top.

'He was still at Headquarters when I left. He said he was coming on with Muffling to the ball very soon. But he was calling for de Lancey as I was leaving, and you know what that means.'

Everyone had their own speculation. Marcus stopped trying to distinguish one voice from another, and looked around him to see who was here; and his roving glance alighted with the inevitability of fate on Lady Annabel Robb, standing a little way off with her fiancé. She was in a gown of *bleu céleste* China silk thickly encrusted with gold embroidery; she wore a Roman-style half-tiara of old gold, and her hair hung from it behind in thick ringlets; and on her finger was a ring with a single sapphire almost the size of a robin's egg.

She looked magnificent. Beside her every other woman

371

paled to insignificance; and the little simian man beside her looked almost as bemused as proud as he chatted to the curious who came up to congratulate him, and every now and then turned to stare at his betrothed as if he thought she might be snatched up to heaven on a cloud at any moment.

Now she had seen Marcus. Their eyes met, and he thought that perhaps she looked a little pale. But she lifted one white hand — not the one weighted with sapphire — and beckoned him over.

'Well, Captain Morland! I didn't think any of you staff-officers would arrive at the ball tonight,' she said lightly. 'My cousin still isn't here.'

'I was sent ahead of the Duke. He will be here at any moment, and I dare say all the rest of the staff will be with him.'

She glanced over her shoulder. 'Damn! Here comes my faithful hound — and that will be the end of our conversation!' She looked directly into Marcus's eyes. 'Won't you ask me to dance, Captain Morland?' she asked pointedly.

He was taken aback, but bowed, and silently offered his arm, and turned with her towards the floor just as de Ladon came scurrying up.

'Thank God! We've shaken him off,' she muttered as they reached the safety of the floor. Marcus felt oddly sorry for the little man; a little reproachful of Bel; confused about his own feelings. They took their place in the set; she looped up the gold-encrusted hem of her gown while he finished buttoning his gloves; and then there was no reason for them to avoid each other's eyes any longer.

'So. You are all moving up tomorrow,' she said at last.

'Are we? That's more than I know,' Marcus said in surprise.

'I spoke to your step-uncle a few minutes ago. He left Headquarters after you, and heard the Duke giving the orders to concentrate on Nivelles and Mont St-Jean.'

Marcus stared beyond her, assimilating the news. 'I see. Then he must believe that Boney is coming up the road from Charleroi after all. Of course, what we had from Dornberg pointed that way, but —'

'Military strategy is a blank to me,' she interrupted him.

'All I know is that this is to be the last ball.' She paused, a queer, bright look in her eyes. 'The last time I shall dance with you — one way or the other. If it is to be battle, you'll take care of yourself, I hope.'

Her words arrested his attention. He looked at her, and suddenly the mask of sophistication was gone; he was the supplicant again, young and bewildered as she always remembered him. 'Oh, Bel, why did you do it? You can't love him!'

She smiled wryly. 'Love him? My dear, what has love to do with marriage?'

'Everything — it ought to have everything to do with it!' he cried passionately.

She shrugged still smiling. 'Impossibly romantic!'

'You don't love him, then?' he pressed. 'I didn't think you could.'

She felt exasperated, and strangely motherly towards him, and neither was a feeling she relished. He had no right to be so young, and make her feel so old. 'Not at all. I am marrying him for his title — everyone knows that. His title and his palace.'

He was fool enough to believe her. She saw it in his eyes, and in the sulky way he asked, 'And did you ever love me? No, I suppose you didn't. Stupid of me to ask.'

'It was stupid, but since you did ask —' She looked at him intently for a long time. 'Yes, I loved you — as much as it's in me to love.'

Now he was confused, not knowing if she were serious, or making fun of him. 'Then why wouldn't you marry me?' he asked at last. 'If we loved each other —'

She laughed, tilting back her head. 'Oh, Marcus — what on earth would you have done with me? A boy like you!'

He blushed with anger. She made him want to put his hands round that taut white throat and squeeze and squeeze ... 'Man enough to hold you in my arms,' he said furiously. 'Man enough to kiss you until you were faint —'

'And then what?' she mocked, her eyes gleaming with the memory of the kisses she had accepted, and the many she had refused. 'Oh, Marcus, Marcus, you're such a child! There's more to marriage than four bare legs in a bed, you know.'

He was shocked by the brutality of her language. 'How can you talk like that?' he cried, and then, goaded by her, low and passionately, 'How can you even think of getting into bed with that *creature?*'

She smiled lightly. 'Shall I tell you a secret? I never shall. I can make him do — or not do — anything I want. He is an ideal companion — faithful, obedient —'

'Like a dog!' Marcus said contemptuously. 'I should have thought you would want a real man —'

'Who would treat *me* like a dog? Let me tell you something, Marcus: when this foolish war is over, Auguste and I will travel Europe, and wherever we go we will be the leaders of Society. We will glitter in every court in Europe, where there is none of that Gothic prudery which makes England so intolerable! I shall be able to do as I please, dress as I please —'

'Is that your ambition? To glitter in the courts of Europe? All those shabby, penniless kings and princes we put back on their thrones?' he said contemptuously. 'You wish to be admired by *them?*'

'And what would you have offered me? A bed in your tent? A share in your horse?'

'I offered you a lifetime of love and devotion —'

'Following the drum?' she jeered.

He put his head up. 'Yes,' he said defiantly.

'Then, my dear,' she said lightly, 'it is as I feared — you are quite, quite mad! I think I will not finish this dance with you — there are a great many of our brave soldiers — *line officers* — with whom I wish to dance tonight. It may be the last ball, after all, before the fighting starts. I should not wish to deprive them of such a sweet memory.'

'Go to the devil!' he cried, losing control completely.

She smiled, her eyes glittering. 'Oh, indubitably I shall — but I will get there my own way, Marcus, I promise you! My own way.'

The Duke arrived at last a little after midnight, wearing his usual calm and inscrutable smile. The tensions of the day, however, had built up to such a point that his appearance caused every conversation to stop, and every head to turn enquiringly towards him. Lucy and Danby happened to be near the door as he entered, and Lucy, with a glance at her husband, went straight up to the Commander-in-Chief and said in a clear voice, 'Come, Duke, let us have the truth of it! Is it orders?'

There seemed a moment of silence, as if everyone in the room had held his breath, and then the Duke smiled and said lightly, 'Oh yes. The French opened hostilities this morning. We shall all be off tomorrow. But there's time first to dance and have supper. No-one need miss this splendid ball!'

His words were passed back rapidly from those nearby to those further away, until the whole ballroom seemed to bend and whisper like a corn-field in a breeze. Gradually the level of conversation rose to a buzz of excitement and consternation. Then the music struck up again — a waltz — and couples began, a little hesitantly, to take to the floor. The Duke moved on, smiling and chatting to the ladies of his acquaintance, and Lucy and Danby were left alone.

'Well,' she said at last, a little shakily, 'it begins.'

'Yes,' said Danby. He tried to sound indifferent, but as he had absently taken possession of her hand and was gripping it hard enough to hurt her, the subterfuge didn't work.

'It's strange,' she said. 'We've known for days — weeks — that it would come. We've waited for it. There was never any doubt. But now it has come, it's different. I'm afraid, Danby!'

'Darling —' he protested gently.

'It's all right, I'm not going to cry or make a spectacle of myself. But I wish you hadn't gone back to your regiment.'

'Hussars don't get killed,' he said lightly. 'We're skirmishers. The worst that may happen is that —' He stopped abruptly, and reddened.

'That you'll get wounded?' she finished for him, meeting his eye wrathfully. And then suddenly she laughed. 'Oh, Danby! How you do manage to say the wrong things!'

He grinned at her ruefully. 'Never was a great courtier.'

'Yes, you were! *Are*! When will you have to leave?'

'Depends where my regiment's being sent. My guess is that they'll be ordered to support Perponcher's at Nivelles. That means I'll have to leave early in the morning to meet up with them.'

She looked down at their linked hands, and then up again. 'Then — can we go home? Now? I don't want to waste our last few hours together at this stupid ball. Please, Danby?'

He glanced around him, as though he would find permission or denial written large on the walls. Then he met her eyes, and they read each other's care, and apprehension, and need.

'Come on, then. We'll slip away. I'll tell Richmond while you get your cloak. Meet you downstairs in ten minutes.'

Rosamund was looking round for Tantony when Marcus appeared at her side and caught up her hand.

'Rosy, you promised me a dance! Come and waltz with me! We've never waltzed together, have we?'

The big, warm, familiar hand was engulfing her fingers, and the old tug at her heart was comforting in this moment of uncertainty and apprehension.

'Yes, all right,' she said.

He laughed, and put his arm round her waist and swung her straight onto the floor. 'You do it very well,' he said after a while. 'You must have had plenty of practice since you came to Brussels.'

'You know I have. I've danced with every eligible officer in the town. Mama ought to be pleased with me.'

'And have you enjoyed your Season?' he asked, detecting the irony in her tone.

She eyed him curiously. 'Yes. Yes, I suppose I have. Why do you ask?'

'Why? What a strange question! Because I hoped you would. Because I care about you, little cousin.'

She grimaced. 'Not so little, Marcus — or hadn't you noticed?'

He smiled automatically, and then the smile faded and he looked at her searchingly for a moment. 'No. No, I suppose I hadn't noticed. Foolish of me! You've grown up, Rosy. You're a grown woman now.'

'Thank you, Captain. Most observant of you.'

'Don't mock me,' he said gravely. 'Too many people are laughing at me already. I've been a fool, I know —'

'You have,' she agreed.

'But I'm paying the price now. Don't rub salt into the wound. Not you, Rosy. You at least never tried to turn me against her. I could always talk to you.'

376

'Oh, Marcus —!'

'She is not what I thought. I was mistaken in her. But if you'd seen her as she was with me, at the beginning —' He sighed. 'Anyone might have been deceived.'

'Many were.'

'She was different with me then — vivacious, charming, but somehow gentle. Perfectly womanly. She was everything that was lovely.' He swallowed painfully. 'But when she spoke to me just now — the brutality of her language shocked me. I suppose she must always have been like that, but it didn't seem so. Not at the beginning.'

They danced, their bodies moving in automatic harmony. She was tall for a woman, but he was strong, with the powerful grace of the cavalryman. They were well matched. Rosamund said nothing. His thoughts were far away, and she was able to look at him without being observed; study the handsome familiar face with pity and affection and something else — a distant and disappointed sense of revelation, perhaps, that Marcus had not been the only one to be deceived.

He came back to her, and almost visibly searched for something to say. 'I like the way you've dressed your head,' he said at last. 'No-one else wears it like that. Is it your own thought?'

'Yes,' she said patiently, sadly. 'I made it myself. Moss was in terrors that I would make a mull of it.'

He smiled. 'My capable little cousin would never make a mull of anything she turned her hand to.' He surveyed her a moment, and a strange look came into his eyes — something like surprise. 'You're grown beautiful lately, did you know that? Has anyone told you that you look very beautiful tonight?'

'Yes, someone has,' she said quietly.

'Tantony? Yes, I saw you dancing with him.' She didn't answer. He looked away. 'Dance all you can, Rosy. Tomorrow we will all be going away. I think we'll be in action soon.'

She pressed his hand suddenly. 'Marcus — you'll take care, won't you?'

He smiled. 'Don't worry, staff-officers don't get killed.'

'That isn't what you told Bobbie,' she said painfully.

377

'And would you mind if I did?'

'Of course I'd mind!' she said angrily.

He went on studying her face, and she felt herself blushing, and felt tears gathering in her eyes, and didn't know whether she was angry or hurt or why she should be either. She felt as though something precious and irreplaceable had been taken away from her. She felt as though she had wakened from a dream to a grey morning.

'Rosy,' he said at last, very softly. 'My little cousin Rosy! How comfortable this is! I wish we'd had more opportunity to dance together. I feel as though we've wasted so much of this Season.'

The music came to an end, and they stopped, and he looked down at her without releasing her, smiling fondly. Suddenly she wanted to get away from him. He no longer felt safe and familiar and homelike.

'I think I'll go and find Captain Tantony,' she said. 'I promised to dance with him again, and it's getting late.'

Marcus let her go without another word.

She found Tantony looking for her.

'It seems that we will definitely be off tomorrow morning,' he said.

'Yes,' she said. 'So I am to give you your answer just in time.'

He smiled, but looked nervous. 'Ah, you mean to answer me, then?' he said foolishly.

'Did you think I would not keep my word?'

'Oh, no! I was sure you would. It's just that —' He surveyed her face a moment, looking for clues. 'If it isn't the answer I want, I think I'd sooner wait.'

She smiled. 'Ask me to dance,' she said. 'They seem to be playing a lot of waltzes tonight.'

'Perhaps the orchestra has heard the news. There are a great many lovers on the floor, all, I suppose, saying goodbye.'

She turned to face him, and he stepped close and put his arm round her waist, and a little shudder ran through her at his touch — the stranger's touch, which was somehow deliciously, dangerously familiar. She was puzzled at the

378

paradox. She had known Marcus all her life, Tantony but a few weeks; but now, which was the stranger? The music with its insistent rhythm tugged at their feet; his arm was firm around her, and she leaned to it with confidence. They whirled away.

'Well then, Captain,' she said.

'Well, my lady?' he smiled.

'I have to give you an answer.'

He cocked his head at her. Her eyes were dark with thought; he could not fathom her feelings. 'Not if you aren't sure,' he said evenly. 'I don't wish to hurry you. I can wait, if you need more time to know your mind.'

She shook her head, not in negation, but to make space between them for the words.

'Tantony, when you were a boy, did you have a hero? A great storybook hero that you admired and dreamed about and loved and longed to emulate?'

Like the satisfying person he was, he did not laugh or protest at her line of conversation. 'Hektor of Troy,' he said at once. 'Tall and handsome and noble, the warrior prince with the tender heart! Mighty in battle, magnanimous in defeat! Hektor was my hero. My father always said that Achilles was the archetypal hero, but I could never see it so. He postured and boasted, and then sulked in his tent, while Hektor got quietly on with the job. I always cried when I got to the bit where he was slain, and Achilles dragged his body behind his chariot round the city walls.'

Rosmund looked up at him, a small smile tucking the corners of her mouth. 'Hektor!' she said. 'Yes, I can see why. Very appropriate!' The smile disappeared. 'But supposing you were suddenly to meet Hektor, the real Hektor, in real life; and he turned out to be two inches shorter than you, and the mighty shoulders were only buckram padding?'

He looked at her searchingly. 'It would rather shatter the illusion, I suppose. But isn't it better to know the truth?'

'Is it? Wouldn't you rather keep your dreams intact?'

He considered. Not fully understanding how her thoughts were running, he could only try to answer honestly, and hope that it would do. 'No,' he said at last. 'I'd sooner know the truth. But even so, knowing the real Hektor wouldn't change my storybook hero. He'd still be there in the story, whenever I took out the book to read.'

'But you'd know he wasn't real.'

'Not so. They'd both be real to me — just different, I suppose.'

She smiled now, a warm, affectionate smile that made his heart lift with hope. 'You are such a *good* man,' she said abruptly.

He raised an eyebrow in protest. 'Oh dear! That sounds rather damning. Virtue is usually considered rather dull.'

'Not to anyone with any sense. Do you still want to marry me?'

'More than ever!'

'Then — I will marry you.'

He stopped dead, causing minor havoc as two couples swerved violently to avoid him and cannoned into each other.

'Do you mean it? Are you sure?'

She looked up at him, studied his face. It was a good firm face, a face whose strength came from the inside, and would never need to prove itself by any show of heroics. She imagined waking up beside him every day for the rest of her life, and knew that it would be all right. More than all right? She didn't know. He was the better man; Marcus has been no more than a dream. This was the right decision, the grown-up decision.

'Yes,' she said. 'I'm sure.'

His slow smile transformed his face. 'I'm glad. Because I love you very, very much.'

'Yes, I know.' She met his eyes, and the strange fluttering sensation assailed her again. Waking up beside him every morning? Oh yes! What a fool she'd been! The real-life adventure was going to be much, much more exciting than the storybook one! 'I think we will be very happy together,' she said with decision.

Larosse saluted and turned away from the Duc, and walked back to where Sophie was waiting for him under one of the sconces by the open french windows. She was standing very still and erect, her hands lightly clasped before her in a way that reminded him of the French sisters in the little white convent at Montherme, which he had known when he was a boy. There had been about them that same air of stillness, as if at the core of them there were a column of radiant crystal that could not be disturbed by the troubles of the world.

He came and stood before her and looked down at her. She was so young! He marvelled again at her youth and absolute innocence, which could co-exist with such extraordinary strength. She was only a little more than half his age, yet she was his equal in everything but worldly knowledge.

She returned his look, her dark eyes enquiring, apprehensive, but trusting. The roses in her hair — ivory and pale-pink — were beginning to droop a little. Their delicacy made the thick dark ringlets look the more vigorous by contrast. He loved her absolutely, and wanted to tell her so, but there were no words powerful enough for such a consuming experience.

'I have to leave,' he said. He saw her take a little breath, but she said nothing, simply waited. He had to touch her! 'Come outside with me for a moment.'

She hesitated no more than a second, then walked with him through the french doors onto the terrace above the garden. Already the short June night was fading towards dawn: it would be light in two hours. The terrace was empty — almost everyone had gone in to supper. He turned to face her, and took her hands, and they rested warm and dry and alive in his, as she attended to him not only with her mind but with every part of her body.

'There's been fresh news — the first since Ziethen's message this morning. You saw the aide speaking to the Prince of Orange?' She nodded. 'He came with a message from Baron Constant, written at half-past ten this evening. Charleroi fell this morning, not two hours after Zeithen's message, and the French marched straight up the Brussels road toward Quatre-Bras.'

'Just as you said they would,' she whispered.

He nodded distractedly. It gave him no pleasure to be right. 'The Duke was furious. "Bonaparte has humbugged me!" he cried. But it is not so serious as it might have been. When the French got to Frasnes — about three miles south of Quatre-Bras — they met up with Prince Bernard and the Nassauers, who held them off after a skirmish. Probably the French didn't realise there was only half a division in front of them: they've dropped back and bivouacked for the night. Constant's taken authority into his own hands and sent my brigade — Bylandt's — from Nivelles to support the Nassauers. We have to hope we can hold the French off until the rest of the army can be moved up. I have to go at once, Sophie.'

'Yes, I understand,' she said. Her eyes burned into his. 'Will — will it be all right?'

He held her hands more tightly. No lies for her, not even social, tactful lies. 'I don't know. But I *believe* it will,' he said. 'God is on our side — Napoleon's time is over. We shall beat him. And when it is over, I shall come back for you, my Sophie, and we shall have a long and happy life together.'

'Yes,' she said.

He drew her hands against his chest. Time was pressing. 'I love you, Sophie. I love you with all my heart, as I've never loved anyone before. Do you believe it?'

'I believe it.' He saw tears gather in her dark eyes, and shine like diamonds against her lashes. 'I love you, René.'

He took her in his arms then, cradled her head with his hand, and her hair was soft and harsh like fire against his cheek. 'Remember, *C'est moi qui t'aime le mieux,*' he whispered, his lips against her ear. 'I'm coming back, Sophie: believe that, too!'

One moment longer; then he put her gently back from him. 'I must go,' he said.

'I want to give you something,' she said desperately. 'I wish there were something I could give you.'

He smiled. 'One of your roses,' he said. 'A white one.' She put her hands eagerly to unpin a flower. He guided her blind fingers, took his rose, tucked it carefully inside his jacket; and now he really must go.

'*Adieu,* my Sophie. Wait for me. Don't be afraid.'

'I'm not afraid,' she said. 'God bless you!'

And then she was alone, staring at the empty doorway, not quite sure what to do with herself from now on.

As the grey light of dawn crept into the streets, the crowing of cockerels was answered by the braying of bugles, and the drums began to beat the assembly. From every house billeted soldiers began to appear, pulling their uniforms straight, putting on their caps, shouldering their kits. Waggons blocked the way, being hastily loaded; there was the sound and smell of excited horses, the endless sound of tramping feet and clattering hooves on the cobbles. The social town had dropped its mask to reveal the warlike face beneath.

It was an orderly chaos: the anthill, broken open, seethed with purpose as the reserve regiments formed up and the waggon-trains assembled. Rosamund and Sophie hung out of the window of their room, too excited to sleep, despite everything that had happened in the long day and night that were just ending.

'You see how right I was to pick this room?' Rosamund said. 'Look, here comes one of the Scots regiments — the 42nd, I think. Don't those pipes make you shiver?'

The swinging tramp-tramp of the marching feet filled the street as they wheeled round the corner and went past on their way to the Namur Gate. The red-and-white cadis stockings above the grey gaiters flashed all together, the kilts swung, the feathered bonnets nodded, all moving as one, a sight threatening in its improbability. Ribbons fluttered from the bagpipes, and the terrible, beautiful music mingled with the martial rattle of the side-drums. An officer's horse skittered delicately sideways, mounting the flagway opposite the house and champing its bit as the spurs in its side drove it back into place. The officer glanced up at the two young women, and raised his hand in a jaunty salute.

The last of the Highlanders went past, and in the lull the distant sounds of the town were heard again. The sun was coming up. Sophie and Rosamund looked at each other, a little heavy-eyed now.

'So we are both engaged,' Rosamund said with satisfaction.

'It seems very strange,' Sophie said.

'Does it? It's what we came here for, after all.'

'Yes, I suppose so. But we have nothing to shew for it. We are engaged to be married, and both our fiancés are going off to war. We've hardly even had the chance to dance with them. At home there would be weeks of going to balls and parties together, and all the wedding plans and congratulations —'

Rosamund made a face. 'You may have those, and welcome. I have a thousand awful relatives on my father's side who would all expect a formal visit — deadly dull! But I know what you mean. I do feel rather empty and let down.'

'Yes. As if something's been forgotten or left undone.'

'Never mind,' Rosamund said briskly. 'We shall have all that and more when they come marching back again, victorious. Think of the celebrations then! Victory and betrothal all in one!'

Sophie smiled. 'I think our husbands will like each other very well. Shall we remain friends after we're married? Let's always be friends, Cousin, whatever happens.'

'Of course we will. Oh, listen! Another regiment's coming!'

The first ranks came round the corner: there were the dark green overalls and silver ball-shaped buttons of the 95th Regiment of Rifles. Rosamund drew a breath, and her hands gripped the sill as she leaned out perilously, straining eyes and ears as they marched past below her.

There he was at last! She picked out his bay horse even before she recognised the face above the black-silk-frogged silver-buttoned jacket, and the glamorous grey-furred pelisse. The handsomest, the most dashing, of the uniforms; and her quiet captain, her Hektor, the best of the officers, riding his horse one-handed, his other hand resting on his sword-hilt. Oh, she was proud of him! She wanted to shout out to everyone that he was hers.

He looked up as he approached, expecting her to be there, and smiled with satisfaction as he saw her. One of the men marching beside him glanced up, following the direction of his eyes, and a nudge and a grin ran along the rank. Suddenly one of the men shouted out, 'First in the field and last out of it — the Bloody, Fighting, Ninety-Fifth!' He was answered by a huge full-throated roar from a hundred marching riflemen, and Tantony's horse went sideways on tiptoe, its eyes wide with shock, as Tantony grinned up at her and touched his hat.

It had been for her benefit, she thought, that shout and roar. She was their captain's woman. Pride and a sense of belonging filled her, and she lifted her hand and waved to them, laughing, waved to all of them, though her eyes were

384

on Tantony. His head turned back as he went past her, to look at her as long as he could. She heard him quite clearly say 'I love you', though his lips didn't move; and she kissed her fingers to him as he was carried inexorably away and out of sight on a moving river of humanity.

At five it was fully light, the sun was rising above the houses, and Danby was dressing to leave. Lucy was sitting on the bed in her wrapper, her knees drawn up and her arms locked around them, looking in that posture and with her tousled hair too young to be Rosamund's mother.

Deacon was standing by with his master's boots as Danby buttoned his magnificently braided jacket: he had cast one look at Lucy, and was now avoiding noticing that she was present. He had always disapproved of her, and his gloomy half-uttered prognostications when Danby had announced that he was to marry her had almost cost him his job. Deacon thought her ladyship was entirely lacking in conduct, as was proved by her being there in the room while his master dressed, which no decent woman would dream of. Danby was a patient man, and understanding that Deacon was devoted to him, allowed him to remain in his services, though every now and then when the dark looks and mutterings grew too overt, he was forced to renew the threat of dismissal until they subsided.

The glossy boots were drawn reverently on, and Deacon knelt at his master's feet to rub away with a soft cloth any ghost of an imprint of fingers on their radiant surface. Lucy watched all this impatiently, and when Deacon rose and picked up the sash, she jumped up off the bed and took it from his mutely protesting fingers.

'I'll put it on, thank you, Deacon!'

'Your ladyship doesn't know how,' he said in a dead voice, hardly concealing his fury.

Danby tired of him. 'Thank you, Deacon, that will be all. Leave us, please.'

Deacon fixed him with a searing look. 'Your hair hasn't been arranged, my lord.'

'I'll do it myself, thank you. I'll ring when I want you.'

Deacon stared a moment longer, then his eyes dropped,

and he backed out, closing the door with reproachful quietness. Lucy stepped up to her husband with the sash, and passed her arms round his waist.

'Thank you. How that old man hates me! But I wanted to be alone with you.'

'So did I,' Danby said, kissing her as she wound the sash round him; and when she had tied the knot, drew her firmly against him.

'I wish you weren't going,' she whispered against his mouth.

'So do I. Damn Boney.'

'You're not looking forward to the battle? You don't relish the thought of being a hero?'

'I'll be careful,' he answered the thought rather than the words. 'No death-or-glory charges for me.' He kissed her again, and then, pulling his head back, saw the tears glinting on her lashes. 'Darling!' he protested. 'I'm coming back, I promise you. All of me!'

'Oh, Danby!' He made her laugh even while her mind protested at the images his last words conjured up. 'I love you so much.'

He pulled her close again, knowing how difficult, even now, it was for her to say the words. 'I love you, too,' he said.

'Are you afraid?' she asked after a moment, her face buried in his hair.

'Of course I am,' he said. 'A soldier's no good if he isn't afraid — gets himself killed straight off. The Beau don't like us to get killed, you know — spoils his plans.'

'Please be careful,' she whispered.

'I'll come back,' he said again, seriously. 'I wouldn't leave you. I wouldn't do that to you.'

There was a scratching at the door, and they drew apart. Deacon came in looking triumphant at having a legitimate excuse to disturb them. 'Trooper Bird, my lord. He says it's urgent.'

Lucy turned away to dry her eyes and give Danby privacy. He stepped outside the door to talk to his servant, and she heard only the mutter of voices, could not distinguish the words. Then he came back into the room, and she turned, feeling something was wrong.

386

He looked at her hesitantly. 'Lucy —'

The fear jumped to her eyes. 'What is it? What's happened?'

'Nothing serious — don't be afraid. But Bird tells me Dancer's dead lame. I have to ask you — will you let me take Magnus?'

'Magnus? Can't you hire a horse?'

He lifted his hands. 'Hire a horse? In Brussels — today?'

She saw the impossibility. But Magnus — her lovely Magnus! Her lip trembled. 'You could take Hotspur?' she said in a small voice.

'He wouldn't carry me. And Dancer's saddle doesn't fit him. Darling, I wouldn't ask if it weren't necessary —'

She was ashamed. 'Of course. I'm being stupid. You can have him; of course you can! You'll — you'll take care of him?'

'He'll take care of me,' he said, taking her hands and kissing them one after the other. 'That's my brave girl,' he murmured, too low for the servants to hear. 'I have to go now.'

She looked up at him with drowned eyes. Every one of her freckles seemed to stand out in the pallor of her face. She couldn't articulate the terror in her heart, that she was seeing him for the last time; nor the anguish, that she had neither time nor words to tell him all that he meant to her — her dear, dear lover and friend! Her lips were too dry even to say goodbye. He smiled at her and pressed her hands, and then he was gone.

By half-past seven the regiments had all marched out, and the sunny streets were empty and silent. Only the Commander-in-Chief and the staff remained, and they were on the point of departure.

In the mews behind the house in the Place de l'Eglise, Bobbie held Marcus's stirrup for him while his cousin mounted, and then fiddled aimlessly with the fringe of the shabraque while Marcus settled himself. Marcus gathered the reins, and then looked down at the bent, bare head with understanding. Bobbie so longed to be riding away with him. It had been his lifelong ambition, and now it seemed that the war was coming to an end at last, and Bobbie would have played no part in it. If it was hard to be a hero, it was harder still not to be.

As for Marcus, his emotions had been in such a turmoil lately that he was looking forward to the approaching battle with something like relief. At least there was no conflict of interest there, no doubt, no hesitation. His part would be to obey orders. He need only hate the French, admire the Beau, and shew no fear before the ranks, all things he knew very well how to do, had done uncounted times before. Love, women, and all those complications could be set aside for a while.

'Well, that's it, then,' he said. Bobbie looked up. 'You'll take care of Mama and Bab, won't you?'

'Of course.' He hesitated. 'You don't think there's any need to leave Brussels, do you? I know Lady Tewkesbury told your mother yesterday she was leaving for Antwerp today; but I'd sooner not leave until — until it's all over.'

Marcus smiled. 'I won't ask you to miss the fun!' he said. 'The Beau says we won't stop the French at Quatre-Bras — we'll have to make a stand further up the road, between Waterloo and Mont St-Jean. That's where it will all happen, Bob — practically close enough to hear the guns! But Boney won't get past us, don't worry. The only thing is, there may be a lot of wounded coming into the city, and that won't be pleasant for the women. I leave it to you to decide what's best. If there seems to be any danger, you'll get them away, won't you?'

'Of course. Trust me,' Bobbie said. He reached up for Marcus's hand. His was cold and small in the soldier's large, hard palm. 'I wish I were coming with you.'

'I wish you were, too. But someone has to mind the shop.'

'This damned earldom!'

'You're the best man for the job,' Marcus said, and then, grinning, 'and I hope my sister will make a fine countess, too! I shall like having you for a brother, Bob!'

Bobbie grinned, too, and pressed the hand before releasing it. 'God bless you, Marcus! Go and give Boney a thrashing! And take care!'

'I will,' Marcus said, and turning his horse, clattered out of the yard into the quiet street.

BOOK THREE

The Heroes

Friend of my bosom, thou more than a brother,
Why wert not thou born in my father's dwelling?
So we might talk of the old familiar faces —

How some they have died, and some they have left me,
And some are taken from me; all are departed —
All, all are gone, the old familiar faces.

Charles Lamb: The Old Familiar Faces

CHAPTER FIFTEEN

When Jasper Hobsbawn returned from the mills to Hobsbawn House it was after eight o'clock, and his hunger had passed from a grumbling to a gnawing, and then to a dull sickness. The gathering of the enormous armies in Belgium had meant overtime working for both clothing factories and cloth-mills: soldiers had to have uniforms, shirts and stockings; horses needed blankets and saddle-cloths; even corpses needed winding-sheets. Hobsbawn Mills had been working full out for weeks, and the mill-families were buying meat as well as bread and potatoes for their evening meals.

Jasper would have been glad of a comfortable wife waiting for him at home with a meal ready on the table, however simple it might be. At Hobsbawn House he never knew what to expect. Mrs Murray was growing very odd these days. Sometimes delicious food would be prepared, and she would appear in a silk dress and a false front, cooing and bridling over him, almost as if she expected to be invited to sit down and eat with him. At other times she would treat him with lofty indifference and tell him she had too much to do to order meals for him; at other times again she would simply absent herself without warning.

He would be glad when the 'infantry' was finished — even more so when the business of the Will was finally decided. One way or the other, it would mean he need never see the housekeeper again. He knew that she expected him to keep her on, if the inheritance fell to him, and for the sake of peace he allowed her to go on thinking so, even though it puzzled him. Granted she was a good housekeeper — or had been until recently — but she must know he didn't like her. Her recent oddness would at least give him the excuse. He wondered if she had started drinking. God knew it would be easy enough for any of the servants to get into the cellars, with the keys hanging on a nail in Bowles's pantry for any passer-by to extract.

On this particular evening he was not to discover whether any sort of dinner had been prepared for him. Bowles met him at the door to say that Mr Whetlore, the attorney, wanted to see him most particular, and was waiting for him in Master's business-room.

Jasper sighed, gave Bowles his hat and gloves, and walked resignedly across the hall. The business-room was still filled with a mountain-chain of heaps of paper, a semblance at least of order which had been achieved by Jasper through unremitting hard work. He was annoyed, therefore, to find Whetlore sitting in his chair with his feet on the desk, sifting through one of the piles casually, and probably putting the papers back in the wrong order.

Just for a moment Jasper longed to be master of the house, so that he could tell Whetlore exactly where to put himself. He contented himself for now with saying sharply, 'I hope your business is important, Whetlore. I've had a very long day.'

Whetlore, unabashed, put down the papers and got leisurely to his feet, only to seat himself on a corner of the desk, swinging one leg nonchalantly. 'Important? Yes, I suppose you might call it so. I say, have you seen the *Chronicle* today? What about all these rumours from Belgium, that Boney's on the move! I've several bets on at the club that we shall have a battle before the month's out.'

'Extremely unlikely, I should have thought,' Jasper snapped. 'Boney's outnumbered two to one at least. He won't attack until he's got the new class out and under arms.'

'Well, yes, perhaps. Unlikely, I suppose — but then you don't get the long odds for a certainty, do you? Sir John Warren's given me five to one on twenty guineas, and there's never any knowing with armies, is there?'

'Is this what you came to speak to me about?' Jasper said wearily.

'Lord, no! Just making conversation.'

'Then I wish you wouldn't. I'm very tired. Please come to the point.'

'Very well. Just as you like,' Whetlore said with a shrug. He

392

drew out a crackling piece of paper from his inside pocket. 'What do you know about *rigor mortis*, Mr Hobsbawn?'

'*Rigor mortis?*' Jasper repeated, mystified. 'The stiffness of death?'

'Your Latin is impeccable,' Whetlore nodded. 'Cadaveric rigidity; another way of saying the same thing. I have here,' he flourished the paper, 'a letter from the good Mr Pobgee of Pobgee, Pobgee and Micklethwaite, acting for the estate of the late Mrs Fitzherbert Hawker, in which he suggests that we might establish the time of death of your late lamented cousin by the extent of rigidity in the poor old gentleman's body when it was discovered.'

'Good God!'

'Just so.' Whetlore nodded. 'He suggests that we interview the priest who was brought to the late Mr Hobsbawn that morning, as his evidence might provide a satisfactory *corroboration* of what the doctor and the manservant told him on the subject.'

Jasper frowned. 'Well — what did they tell him?'

'Apparently, that this cadaveric rigidity had already "set in", as he puts it, by the time the worthy Simon found his master dead in his bed in the morning.'

Jasper sat down. 'But Simon's statement was nothing to the purpose. Why should we want it corroborated? Mrs Murray saw my cousin alive after the time of Mrs Hawker's death — that's all that matters.'

Whetlore smiled. 'I rather think friend Pobgee is intending to cast doubt on Mrs Murray's testimony. He says here: "*While the housekeeper's statement was doubtless made in good faith, I feel that certain elements in that statement are at variance with what may be established as the facts in the case.*" Which means, in plain English to you and me, that he thinks she's lying.'

'But what has that to do with the priest and this *rigor* whatever-it-is? I don't understand. You'd better explain to me what you're talking about.'

Whetlore rubbed his hands together in glee. 'Certainly, at once. Oh, this has all the makings of a first-class case after all, and just when I was thinking it was all cut-and-dried and dull as could be! I take my hat off to Pobgee, I really do! The thing

393

is, Mr Hobsbawn,' he went on hastily as Jasper threatened to explode, 'that Mr Pobgee has a friend who is an eminent surgeon, who is ready to swear that cadaveric rigidity takes approximately eight hours to begin in a corpse, and that as Simon says the late Mr Hobsbawn's jaw was stiff at half-past six in the morning, he must have died no later than half-past ten the night before; and that therefore if Mrs Murray says she saw him alive at two in the morning, she must be lying. Beautiful, isn't it?'

Jasper thought it through. There were many things he could think of to call it, but beautiful did not spring readily to mind. He remembered his uneasiness about Mrs Murray, his puzzlement over why she hadn't spoken up before ... But no, she *wouldn't* lie about such an important matter. It couldn't be right. 'There must be some mistake,' he said at last.

'No mistake,' Whetlore said cheerfully, 'Just a lovely, lovely case! Pobgee's friend is only one eminent medical man, you see. We shall have to find ourselves another who will swear that stiffness comes on in four hours — or, say, three, to be on the safe side.'

'But — but how can we — ? If what he says is true — '

'It's all a matter of opinion, Mr Hobsbawn. There's no proving these matters. I've come across *rigor mortis* in cases before. Its progress is not a constant factor. Many things affect it — temperature, for one. Most physicians agree on eight hours as a general rule — but we've plenty of room to play with it. And the beauty of it is, since Pobgee has shewn us his hand, we can prepare ourselves for anything he might throw at us. Forewarned is forearmed, as they say.'

'Why do you suppose he's done that?' Jasper frowned. 'Isn't that rather an odd thing to do?'

Whetlore positively grinned. 'I rather think friend Pobgee's been finding life in a quiet country town rather dull. I think he's rubbing his hands at the thought of a grand pell-mell battle, just as I am. That's why he's shewn us the lines along which we can draw up our troops! And, I must say, he's got himself a grand champion: Havergill is going to take a lot of matching as a medical witness. But we shall find someone, never fear. These medical men are all as jealous as green wives! They like nothing better than to be at each

394

other's throats, especially in the witness box.'

Jasper sat up. 'Then — you mean you will have to take it to Chancery?'

'Not a doubt in the world. Nothing else for it, now that Pobgee's decided to give us a run for our money! Oh, I like that man, positively I like him!'

Jasper shook his head dazedly. 'This needs thinking about. I must have time to consider.'

'Consider? Well, if you really feel — but there's nothing to consider, in my opinion. Pobgee wants a fight — that's why he sent this letter.'

'Nevertheless, I would like time to reflect. I will speak to you again tomorrow. And now, would you be so kind as to leave me? I am very tired. Oh — and leave the letter, if you please — Mr Pobgee's letter.'

'By all means.' Whetlore put it down on the table, smiled and bowed himself out, his temper unshakeable. Jasper bid him goodbye absently, already deep in thought; and so he sat for the next hour, his chin in his hand, going over and over what had happened and what had been said, and what he had read in Pobgee's letter.

All a matter of opinion. Most physicians agree. Eight hours. Half-past ten the night before. Mrs Murray. Simon. The physician attending. No brandy-glass. Stiffness in the jaw. Eight hours.

Suddenly he sat up and rang for Simon. After a long delay the door opened, and he shuffled in, meek enquiry in his rheumy old eyes. Jasper stared at him in silence for so long that the old man began to feel nervous.

'You rang, Mr Jasper, sir?'

'Yes.' Jasper pulled himself together. 'Yes — Simon, on the morning that you found Mr Hobsbawn dead in bed — '

'God rest his poor soul, sir,' Simon said quaveringly, the eyes growing moister. 'A better master there never was, and not a cross word did he — '

'Yes, quite,' Jasper said impatiently. 'But cast your mind back, if you will to that morning — '

'Gave me such a turn, sir, as I never hope to feel again! I thought he was asleep, you see, until I took the liberty of touching his shoulder, and then I knew how it was. I knew it was all up with him, then, all right — '

'Ah, yes! How did you know?'

'How, sir? Well, I just did. He was cold, sir, cold and stiff. There wasn't no mistaking it, sir, not when you've once had dealings with — '

'Stiff? What was stiff — his shoulder?'

'Not to say his shoulder, sir, exactly. But his face and his neck was stiff. I couldn't close his mouth, you see, Mr Jasper, which he always slept with it open, as many a gentleman does when they gets to his age, and I'm sure it's not to be wondered at, though in a general way his health was excellent, barring that little trouble of his. But I wanted to make him more comfortable, you see, only it wouldn't close, nor his neck wouldn't bend when I tried to lay him down a bit decent. So I left him a-sitting up as he were, and sent for the doctor.'

'I see. Thank you, Simon.' Jasper sank back into thought.

'Was there anything else, sir?' the bewildered Simon asked after a moment.

'No. Yes — you might ask Bowles to bring me a glass of whisky. I've had rather a shock.'

Simon warmed. 'Yes, Mr Jasper — right away, sir. I was thinking you didn't look quite the thing. Should I send for the doctor for you, sir? P'raps you ought to have a lay-down. I could — '

'No, no, I'm all right. Just the whisky, if you please — that will set me right.'

'Very good, sir, if you're sure.'

When he was alone again, Jasper pondered the matter. Half-past two — half-past six. Four hours — only half the time 'most physicians' generally agreed on. All a matter of opinion? But why in that case had Pobgee written the letter? Forewarned, as Whetlore said, they had all the time in the world to prepare their counter-attack.

Because he's honest — because he knows you're honest.

It came to him like a small clear voice. That was it, wasn't it? Everything pointed to Mr Hobsbawn's having died almost as soon as he fell asleep, except for the statement of Mrs Murray. And if it was a choice between believing Mrs Murray or the eminent Doctor Havergill — Pobgee's trusted friend —

which is what it came down to ...

Whetlore thought Pobgee was looking forward to a prolonged, prestigious and expensive fight in the Court of Chancery, but Jasper remembered the genial, gentle, aesthetic old man to whom he had offered hospitality in this house, and knew better. Pobgee was offering Jasper the chance, as a man of honour, to withdraw his claim.

But why would Mrs Murray lie? She would get her pension whichever way the decision went. It could make no difference to her ...

Bowles came shuffling in with the whisky decanter and a glass balancing precariously on a tray.

'Is Mrs Murray in the house, Bowles?' Jasper asked abruptly.

'Why, yes, Mr Jasper, I think so. I think she's in her room.'

'Would you ask her to be so kind as to spare me a few moments of her time?'

'Now, sir?'

'Yes, now. At once. If you please.'

Mrs Murray was a long time in coming, and when she did appear it was plain that she didn't quite know what attitude was expected of her. She looked at him with a mixture of resentment and defensiveness, her hands clasped before her in the classic housekeeper's pose, and her chin at a very unservantlike angle.

'Ah, there you are, Mrs Murray,' Jasper said.

She went straight into the attack. 'I'm entitled to an evening off, Mr Jasper. And if you'd have let me know how late you were expecting to be, I could have given orders accordingly. But with only three in help, I can't keep the kitchen in a state of readiness all hours of the day and night, and that's the fact of it.'

'I didn't send for you to talk about food,' Jasper said. Mrs Murray bristled a little at the idea of being 'sent for', but a certain wariness came over her posture which did not escape Jasper's notice. 'It's my late cousin's death I wanted to discuss with you. And, in particular, your having seen him alive in the middle of the night.'

She looked at him alertly, rather like a blackbird eyeing

something pink in the grass which might or might not be the tip of a worm. 'Yes, Mr Jasper? What about it?'

'You made a statement to me and to Mr Whetlore that you spoke to Mr Hobsbawn after two o'clock. Are you quite sure of that?'

'And why shouldn't I be?'

'Is there anything in that statement you would wish to change on further reflection?'

'Change, Mr Jasper?' She was observing him intelligently, trying to determine what he wanted. 'Change in what way?'

'Well, it was something you remembered at a time of great excitement, when your senses were perhaps disordered with shock. You might easily have made a mistake, or been confused about the time, or even the date. It might have been another night altogether when you spoke to your master at two o'clock.'

She was wary now. 'What are you trying to say?' she demanded. 'There's nothing wrong with my memory. If you're trying to test me — '

He put Pobgee's letter down on the desk in front of him and smoothed it flat with his hand. She glanced at it and then at him, sharply.

'If there's nothing wrong with your memory, Mrs Murray, then I can only conclude that you were deliberately lying,' he said smoothly, watching her face for her reaction.

Her brows drew together, but she did not look afraid. 'What are you talking about?' she said. 'Don't play games with me.'

'I'm not playing games.' He laid his hand over the letter so that she could not read it, even upside-down. 'I have proof here — incontrovertible proof from a medical source — that Mr Hobsbawn died as soon as he lay down in his bed the night before. At two o'clock, when you say you spoke to him, he'd been dead nearly four hours.'

She took a step forward, looking angry now. 'Is this some kind of a joke? What are you up to?'

'No joke, Mrs Murray. This — ' he tapped the letter with a rigid finger, 'is fact. You were lying, weren't you?'

She dropped her fists on the desk and leaned across it, thrusting her face at him belligerently. 'Lying, you call it?

398

Giving you the evidence you wanted? Come on now, Mr Jasper, don't give me that innocent look! What the devil do you think's been going on here? Who's been getting at you? I don't know what you've got on that piece of paper, but if we hold firm there's nothing they can do to shift us. Don't you want to win?'

'Win? You mean that you *were* lying?' he said slowly.

She stared at him, and then drew herself upright, her face hard as a trap, her eyes hostile. 'What's all this about lying? What's your game? You're going to try to drop me, is that it? Because let me warn you — '

'Oh God,' he said, drawing a hand over his face. 'Why did you do it? Why? It could make no difference to you — your pension was secure.'

She laughed shrilly. 'Why? Why? *You* ask *me* that? You wanted proof that the master died after Miss Fanny, and I gave it to you. If it was a lie, it was one *you* bought and paid for — or were willing enough to pay for, when you thought it was going all right. Now someone's put a scare on you, you think you can put all the blame on me and get out of it that way — '

'Mrs Murray — !'

'You white-livered coward! They can't prove anything, don't you see that? No-one was there! If we hold fast, we'll win, and then we'll be living as high as coach-horses for the rest of our lives. All you've got to do is keep mum!'

'Mrs Murray,' Jasper said determinedly, standing up to face her, 'I swear to you that I didn't know you were lying.' A look of contemptuous disbelief came over her face. 'If I had known, I would never have gone along with it. How can you think it for a moment?'

'How? Because there's the whole inheritance at stake, that's how! Do you mean to let that little bitch win? Do you mean to let everything go to her estate, everything you've worked for? And what about me? Years and years I worked on that old man, smarming and smiling and flattering the old goat, and for what? A mean little pension that don't come to a *quarter* of what I made out of this house when he was alive! Well I won't have it, do you hear? I won't let you throw it all away!'

'Oh, stop it!' he moaned. 'I can't bear any more! If I'd known — dear God, what a terrible tangle! And what the deuce is to do now? How am I to get us out of it?'

She fixed him with a hard glare. 'If you try to drop me into it, I'll make sure I take you with me!' she said. 'Do you know what they'll give us? It's transportation for perjury, if it's not the rope! Well I won't go alone — I'll make sure they know you were in on it too!'

'But I wasn't,' he said helplessly, bowed by her venom.

'Do you think they'll believe that, with all you stood to gain?' she said triumphantly. 'You just think about it, Jasper Hobsbawn, before you go accusing people of lying.'

'I — I don't know what to do. I must do what's right. I shall have to think — consider — '

'Well, just you think about the rope, that's all! Just you consider what a noose of rough hemp feels like when they put it round your neck!' she hissed. 'It's easy money, or it's hanging for two — either way, we're in it together, and don't you forget it.' She gave him one last, hard, admonitory look, and then she swept out, and the door clicked closed behind her, leaving Jasper feeling as though he had fought several rounds with the legions of Satan, and not at all sure he had won.

James was walking home over the fields from Ten Thorn Gap with Kithra and Castor at his heels. He was walking slowly, his head bent, his hands thrust into his pockets in a comfortable way that would have made Durban shake his head. It was a sunny day, the grass was green, and in Fellbrook Field the mares were grazing steadily while their new season colts racketed round on their stilty legs with their absurd tails stuck up in the air, like kittens chasing leaves.

James, however, was thinking about death and loss. Fate, or Life, or what you will, was never on his side. Everything he valued was always taken away from him. Whatever he did, he seemed always to be punished — even his good actions were misunderstood. Angelica, for instance. He had never meant her any harm. As if he could! All he had wanted was to give her pleasure — to let her see the open sky and breathe the fresh air of the moors which she longed for. But did people applaud this genial intent? Did her father thank him for his kindness in rescuing the poor child from that gloomy shop for a few hours? Not a bit! Instead he was accused of all sorts of criminal intentions, and reviled as a despoiler of youth, practically a murderer!

And now he could never see her again. She was so sweet, so gentle — oh, the curve of her cheek, and the way the little curls grew round her ears, and the set of her head on her slender neck! And that fool of a father of hers wouldn't even let him provide her with a dowry, so that she could marry a gentleman and live in the comfort she deserved. Instead, she would spend her life drudging in a dark, dusty shop, until her loveliness faded and she dwindled into middle-age.

His sad, confused thoughts halted him, and he stood with his head bent, staring sightlessly at the dusty path, feeling more lost and lonely than ever in his life before. He didn't know where to go or what to do with himself; he didn't know what he was for, or what he was worth. What was the purpose of his life? He felt as aimless as a dead leaf blowing about in the wind: it didn't seem to matter to him or to anyone else what direction he took.

The dogs were waiting for him impatiently, looking over their shoulders, eager to go home, and Castor gave a short bark of encouragement to help him along. Kithra merely swung his tail a little, yellow eyes bright in his grey face. Grey, yes! the old hound was very grey now, and stiff in the mornings — he limped for the first few steps he took every day. Well, he was an incredible age — what was it? — seventeen next month. Born the same month as Sophie. James looked down gloomily into the hound's upturned face. He supposed the old fellow wouldn't last much longer. Seventeen was a good age for a dog. Twenty-five was a good age for a horse — Nez Carré had been twenty-five when he died. But Fanny had been only twenty, and full of health and vigour. Cut down like a strong young tree by a cruel and unheeding axe. Tears filled his eyes. He remembered her sweet young face and those bright, wicked eyes, the dark curls, so full of life, and the curve of her cheek, and the set of her head on that slender neck.

Not fair, not fair! And all he had ever wanted was the best

for her, to make her happy, to give her everything she needed and wanted. Fresh air and sunshine and the freedom to run about; a good marriage, a comfortable home, lovely things to wear and good things to eat. And they had never understood: all the time they had complained and nagged at him and told him he was spoiling her — spoiling her! No-one had ever loved her as he did, and yet they talked as though he were some kind of criminal. They didn't understand. No-one understood. And now she was gone, gone for ever. He would never see her again ...

He reached the top of the rise and there below him was Morland Place. He paused, as he always did at this point when he came home by this track, to look at the house, sitting square and solid in its setting of gardens and orchards and trees and the jumble of outbuildings: warm pink-red of brick, soft honey-grey of stone, gold of lichen on the roof-tiles, all the thousand different greens of growing things, and a glint of silver from the moat and the fish-ponds for a relish. He never tired of looking at it. It all looked so immutable and permanent and *right* that it was impossible to imagine its having been built by the hand of man. Surely it had grown up from the ground, warmed by the sun and watered by the rain, and would go on growing as long as the world turned?

Suddenly he shivered. The blank squares of its windows were like eyes in an inscrutable face, watching him, waiting. Morland Place was not simply a house where his family lived, and had lived for four hundred years: it was more, so much more that it seemed to have an existence of its own entirely separate from them. It sheltered them, produced the wealth which supported them — but did they own it, or did it own them? He thought of his brother, grown grey in its service, having no life outside the demands of the estate. And himself, given by Morland Place in marriage in order to secure a dowry for the estate's improvement. Why, the very children he had sired had been created not for him but for the estate. He had married to produce an heir for Morland Place — *that* was what his life had been for!

Only he and Edward left. His father had died meekly serving, as he had served all his life, without ever having hoped for or expected reward. His mother, the Mistress, died

402

fighting to preserve what she valued with a love that was almost religious: for the *idea* of Morland Place, even more than for its fabric. Of his brothers and sisters, Charlotte had died young, and William, Mary, Harry and Lucy had all escaped to the outside world, the real world. With Edward held in thrall by the fact of his seniority, James might also have escaped: but he was his mother's child, more than any of the others. He belonged to Morland Place as she had. Edward served the estate faithfully, to the exclusion of all other concerns, but he didn't love it, understand it, *feel* it as James did, as his mother had.

He looked down at the house dreamily as he trudged down the short slope towards it. It squatted there below him like some ancient pagan god demanding sacrifice. It must be served — it wanted lives. That was what he, James, was for — to create the new lives for the old monster to consume. Héloïse was Mistress now — she was the High Priestess — but his was the blood that would satisfy the god.

He was almost at the drawbridge when Durban appeared under the barbican, his usually impassive face drawn with anxiety. James felt a momentary spasm of impatience at Durban's apparently insatiable desire to nursemaid him, and then impatience was driven out by a sense of foreboding. Something was wrong. Something had happened. He hurried forward.

'What is it? What's the matter?'

Durban fell in beside him as he strode rapidly through the gate and towards the house. 'It's the children, sir. Something happened this afternoon while you were out. Miss Rosedale wants to see you right away.'

'Are they hurt? Tell me, quickly? Is Nicholas all right?'

'He's had one of his turns, sir — a very bad one. He's all right now, resting, but very poorly. Matty wanted to send for the doctor, but Miss Rosedale stood against it — '

'Did she, by God! We'll see about that!'

'Yes, sir — she said the doctor would frighten him and make him worse. Said he just needs to be quiet now. He's been asking for you, but Miss Rosedale wants you to speak to her first, before you go and see him. She says it's very important, sir.'

403

'But what the devil happened?'

Durban bit his lip. 'I think you'd better let her tell you everything, sir. It'll come better from her. It — it's a bit hard to believe, first time off.'

James stopped and stared at him, saw how pale and anxious he was, and remembered, unbidden, that same look when Durban had discovered the needle under the saddle of Sophie's pony, when it had appeared that someone had tried deliberately to kill her. Had someone tried to kill Nicholas? His heart stood still at the thought. Not Nicholas! Was that to be the next sacrifice? The house had taken Fanny and Fanny's son — was that not enough?

All this passed through his mind in a flash. 'Where is she?' he said tersely.

'In the day-nursery, sir. I'll go with you.'

'No need,' James said, and started forward. Before he reached the main door he was running, and Durban was running with him.

Miss Rosedale must have heard him coming, for she came out into the passage as James appeared at the other end of it, and put her finger to her lips in urgent admonition.

'Shh! Don't make a noise. He's sleeping. It's all right now — nothing to be afraid of. But I must talk to you.'

'How is he?' James asked in a low voice. 'For God's sake — !'

'He'll be all right. I've dressed his hand — '

'His hand?' James cried explosively.

'The dog bit him in its panic. But he's — '

'What dog?'

'The puppy, sir,' Durban said. 'The one you gave to Master Benedict. It bit him — '

'Bit Benedict? But I thought we were talking about Nicholas.'

Miss Rosedale shot a look at Durban and put a steadying hand on James's arm. 'You must let me tell you everything in order. Be assured that the children have come to no physical harm. For the rest, come with me into the Red Room and I'll explain as best I can.'

The Red Room seemed an odd choice. 'Why not the day-nursery?'

'Because Benedict's asleep in there. I gave them both a draught, but I thought it better for them to be separated for the moment. Matty's watching Nicholas, and Jenny's with Benedict. Come, I'll tell you everything.'

In the Red Room, Miss Rosedale sat down on the chair by the dressing-table, and waved to James to sit down on the edge of the bed opposite her. Durban gave her a nod, and left them at the door, closing it behind him. Miss Rosedale faced James squarely, her hands on her knees.

'This may come as a surprise to you,' she said without preamble, 'but there has been serious rivalry between your sons for a long time.'

'But they're only children,' James protested.

'Nevertheless, Nicholas is very jealous of Benedict, because everyone makes a pet of him. Oh, it's understandable. Benedict is a handsome, charming little boy, easy to love. Nicholas is — more difficult.' James stared at her uncomprehendingly. 'He worships *you*,' she said, 'but he thinks you despise him because of his weakness. He thinks you, too, favour Benedict. It makes him very unhappy.'

'Nicholas — a child of seven — told you that?' James said increduously.

She ignored the question. 'The last straw was when you gave Benedict the puppy.'

'I wanted to give it to them both,' James said quickly. 'Nicholas said he didn't want it. He said he hated dogs.'

'Did he? Well, that's understandable. He wanted you to give it to *him*. At any rate, he couldn't bear Benedict to be favoured again. So he called on the Piepowder Man to avenge him.'

James shook his head. 'I think you've gone mad,' he said. 'What the deuce is the Piepowder Man? Is this some kind of fairy story you're telling me?'

'No fairy story,' Miss Rosedale said grimly. 'This is the most unpalatable fact I've ever had to deal with. The Piepowder Man is a character that Nicholas made up. He invents stories about him, and tells them to Benedict when they're in bed together. I don't know why he called him that — I suppose he must have heard the name somewhere and liked the sound of it. Anyway, the Piepowder Man is — well, a

405

sort of hero, a larger-than-life character with miraculous powers. As far as I can gather from the children, his early adventures were largely heroic — like the deeds of Odysseus, perhaps. But lately they've become darker, more sinister — he's become more demon than hero — an avenging demon.'

'Bedtime stories, you say?' James said, trying to make sense of it.

'That's how it started. But he's not a storybook character to them now. Nicholas half believes in him as a real person; Benedict believes in him wholly as a terrifying creature who will come and fetch him away if he does the wrong thing — or fails to do the right one. The creature speaks through Nicholas, of course — but I'm not entirely sure Nicholas is aware of inventing what he says,' she added, as though to herself. 'At any rate, Nicholas tells Benedict that the Piepowder Man will be very angry if Benedict doesn't do such-and-such, and Benedict, poor creature, is too frightened not to do it.'

James stood up. 'This is fantasy — the sheerest fantasy.'

'Sit down!' Miss Rosedale said sharply. 'Listen to me! I'm talking about your children — *your children*, do you hear?'

James sat, bewildered and angry. 'Now, just a minute — !'

'Listen — don't interrupt me! You gave Benedict the puppy. Benedict adored it — Nicholas was hurt and horribly jealous. He referred the matter to the Piepowder Man, who gave the order to Benedict, through Nicholas, that the puppy had to be sacrificed.' James's eyes widened, but he said nothing. Miss Rosedale shook her head unhappily. 'I suppose he got the idea from Greek or Latin stories — even from the Bible, perhaps. Abraham and Isaac — the Roman generals before a battle — the classics are full of the notion of sacrifice. However it was, Benedict was told that the Piepowder Man demanded the offering or he would be very angry, and Benedict was too frightened not to agree.'

'But how — ?' James began, and then stopped, aware that he really didn't want to know how.

'Nicholas was going to help him do it. They retired with the puppy behind the shed in the old orchard. Well, I won't distress you with the details. I don't care to think about them myself. At any rate, the puppy eventually grew frightened

406

enough to struggle, and then bite Benedict. He began to scream, more in mental pain than physical, I imagine, and Nicholas fell into one of his fits. One of the gardeners came to find out what the commotion was; the children were carried up to the house, and I was called for, and — well, things got sorted out eventually. I got half the story from Benedict, who was sobbing with terror because he had failed and thought his fate was upon him, and the rest from Nicholas.'

She stopped speaking, and the silence which followed almost pulsed with frantic thought. James stared down at his feet. Eventually, when it became obvious that he could not speak, she went on, 'I cleaned and bandaged Benedict's wounds, and gave both children a draught. Benedict's asleep now, and Nicholas is drowsy — still a little wheezy, but breathing steadily. He had a bad attack while he was telling me the story — the worst I've seen. I thought we were going to lose him. He stopped breathing altogether at one point.'

James lifted bewildered, agonised eyes to her. 'Is it true? Is all this true? Because I just can't believe that my son — it was just a game, wasn't it? Just a make-believe. They were "playing at sacrifices", that's all. Children play at make-believe all the time.'

She sighed. 'I was afraid you would think that. I can only ask you to believe me when I tell you that is not the way it was. No harm has come of it, no lasting harm, but if it had not been discovered, I don't like to think what would have happened next. Children live by absolutes in a way that we find hard to believe. If things had gone on the way they were, sooner or later the Piepowder Man would have wanted a greater sacrifice than any of Benedict's possessions. It would have wanted Benedict himself.'

He stood up angrily. 'You're telling me that my son would have murdered his own brother? You're mad! These are children we're talking about — little children. *Ordinary* little children! And Nicholas loves his brother. Everyone always says how well they play together.'

'Yes, he loves him! That's why he feels so badly now. He's had a terrible shock: he realises very well what he's done. I don't think there'll be any more stories about the Piepowder Man — but that isn't all you need to worry about. Nicholas is very sensitive, and very unhappy. He needs you, Mr James. He needs you to love him and to tell him so, to tell him you forgive him, to spend time with him and play with him and favour him.'

'And Benedict?'

'Benedict will always know how to get the love he needs. Nicholas is different. He can't ask — that's why he suffers. Now you can ignore what I've told you — you can tell yourself I'm mad, imagining things, dismiss the whole thing from your mind. But he's your son — your responsibility.'

James felt frightened and angry and resentful all at once. His responsibility? Nicholas was only a child — children were the province of women. What did he employ three nursery-maids and a governess for, to say nothing of the chaplain-tutor? It was not his business to do their work for them. And all this — this *nonsense* that she had told him! An overworked imagination, that's what she had. She'd been reading too many novels. Two children played an innocent game, and she blew the whole thing up out of all proportion, and made it into a Gothic horror!

He stood up, feeling himself shaking, and thought it was the anger. He opened his mouth to tell her exactly what he thought of her; and then he met her eyes, and he closed it again. He knew she was right. He remembered Benedict's nightmares when he had started giving the boy riding lessons; yet Benedict wasn't afraid of horses — he loved all animals. He remembered the incident of the cloth dog, and the inexplicable smashing of the automaton. The evidence was there if he cared to consider it.

And it *was* his responsibility — not just because he was Nicholas's father, but because he was capable of understanding. He had been the odd one out in his own childhood, had lived a solitary life of the imagination, without playmates of his own age, and he knew how powerful imagination could be. And he knew the power of love, particularly love which was denied its proper expression.

'I'll go and see him,' he said abruptly. He saw the question in her eye, and shook his head. 'It's all right,' he said. 'I understand.'

He left her there, still doubtful. Out in the corridor, he

passed the hovering Durban with a dozen questions in his eyes. The door to the night-nursery seemed a very long way away. Inside a shaded lamp was burning, and Matty, who had been Nicholas's wet-nurse, was sitting very still beside the bed, watching the small figure under the white counterpane with the intensity of animal love.

Nicholas was not asleep. The heavy, dark-shadowed eyes came round to him as he appeared in the doorway, and the white, pinched face seemed to grow sharper with anxiety, as the breathing grew immediately more laboured. The familiar pang of love and guilt squeezed James's heart. He tried to smile, and walked over to the bed, saying, 'It's all right, Nicholas. I haven't come to scold. How are you feeling, my boy?'

Nicholas could only wheeze. James caught Matty's eye and jerked his head to dismiss her, and she retired unwillingly to the other end of the room. James took the little hard nursery chair she had vacated and looked at his son. Nicholas tried to speak, but he could only manage to gasp in his anxiety.

James reached over and took his hand. It was cold and clammy and limp: all Nicholas's effort was directed towards dragging air into his lungs.

'Be easy, Nicholas,' James said. 'It's all right.'

Nicholas shook his head. The limp hand gripped; the troubled eyes stared. 'Papa — I — didn't — ' he gasped. 'Didn't — mean — '

James squeezed back. 'Don't try to talk. It's all over now. We won't think about it. Everything's going to be all right.'

Nicholas dragged in a crowing breath. 'Papa, I'm sorry!' he cried.

'I know.' James pressed his hand again. 'I understand. Things are going to be different from now on.' He had begun talking at random, simply to sooth the boy, but into his mind now like an inspiration came the image of the brown-rushing river, and the pool under the overhanging willow. 'I was thinking, Nicky,' he went on casually, 'I haven't had my old fishing-rod out for years. I wonder if you'd like to come out fishing with me? I could teach you how to fish. It takes a lot of patience, but you're a patient sort of fellow, aren't you?'

The eyes were eager, but doubtful. He licked his lips.

409

'Really?' he whispered.

'Really,' James smiled. He saw another question in the eyes, unvoiced, and understood. 'Just you and me, I mean,' he added. 'Benedict's too young — fishing's a man's sport.'

The eyes shone with such transparent, fragile joy that James felt happy and ashamed and grateful and guilty all at once. 'Yes, please,' Nicholas whispered.

'Good. Then it's settled,' James said. 'So you'd better rest now and make sure you get well quickly. There's a little pool I want to shew you, where I used to fish when I was about your age — '

He talked, and Nicholas listened, growing comfortably drowsy. James told him about his favourite fishing-places, his best catches, his worst mistakes, and Nicholas lay with his hand in his father's, watching with bright, heavy eyes that could not yet quite believe that all the trouble was over. Finally weariness caught up with him and he drifted off to sleep; but James stayed where he was, holding his son's hand while his thoughts rambled over past and present. He had wanted a purpose, something to put into the emptiness where Fanny had been. This small one — the redemption of Nicholas — was not much: he had never been a man for sons; but it would do to be going on with, perhaps.

CHAPTER SIXTEEN

The little village of Quatre-Bras clustered around the crossing-point of the Charleroi to Brussels road, which ran south to north, and the Namur to Nivelles road, which ran south-east to north-west. The village consisted of little more than a large farmhouse with its outbuildings, surrounded by a stout wall, and a dozen cottages, and stood on a slight elevation, so that the ground fell away, gently undulating, on all sides.

Around the village were gardens and orchards, little rivulets, ponds and trees, and beyond them, the open fields were deep in standing corn and rye, the latter crop growing to an astonishing height, eight feet in some places. There were two large areas of woodland in the immediate vicinity: the Bossu Wood, which ran in a dense band from Quatre-Bras south-westward, on the west side of the Charleroi road, and a little further off, the Cherry Wood, running northwards from the eastern arm of the Namur–Nivelles road. South of Quatre-Bras, on the main road, was a large farmhouse, Gemioncourt, with a walled yard; to the east of it, and a little further south, a smaller farm called Piraumont; and to the west and still further south a third, larger, farm called Grand Pierrepoint, which stood near the southernmost end of the Bossu Wood.

These farmhouses marked the line of the front General Perponcher had chosen to defend, a curving line about two miles long, its concave side towards the enemy. It was a large area to cover with only seven thousand men, a mere sixteen guns and no cavalry. Perponcher had done his best, placing a battery in the centre across the Charleroi road with a strong defence, lightly occupying the two outlying farmhouses, and placing the bulk of his defences between the Charleroi road and the Bossu Wood.

When the Duke and his staff arrived at about ten o'clock,

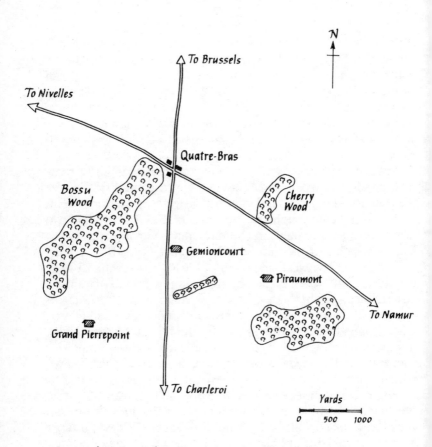

To Brussels

N

To Nivelles

Quatre-Bras

Bossu
Wood

Cherry
Wood

Gemioncourt

Piraumont

Grand Pierrepoint

To Namur

To Charleroi

Yards

0   500   1000

Site of the Battle of Quatre-Bras

everything was quiet. From the high ground of Quatre-Bras they could look down the Charleroi road, which ran quite steeply downhill for a little way, before levelling out into a plain. Here could be seen the rooftops and church spire of a small village — Frasnes — beyond which the ground rose again to a higher plateau where the French had their bivouacs, no more than a mile away.

General Perponcher made his report about the previous day's activities, and the Duke employed a glass and surveyed the scene in silence for some time, before shutting it with a snap.

'No sign of any activity,' he said.

'None at all,' Perponcher agreed. 'We've been watching them all morning, and apart from foraging and cooking, they haven't stirred. You can even see, over to the right there at one of the bivouacs, that the arms are still piled. They don't seem to be proposing any hostile move.'

'Hmm,' Wellington said thoughtfully. 'Well, that's all to the good for us — gives us more time to move our troops up. I shall make an inspection of your lines, General, and then I must ride over to Ligny and consult with General Blücher. Will you lead the way?'

The two great men rode off, and the staff-officers followed behind. It was clear to Marcus that the situation had been much more grave than anyone in Brussels had realised. If it had not been for the initiative of Prince Bernard and Baron Constant, and the intelligent support of Perponcher, there would have been nothing to stop the French from coming straight up the hill and taking control of that vital cross-roads.

The main body of Bylandt's brigade was in the centre of the line at Gemioncourt. Here Wellington and Perponcher stopped to talk to the Duc de Veslne-d'Estienne, and Marcus, seeing Larosse sitting on a straw-bale beside the road a short way off, eating a piece of bread, stepped aside to talk to him.

'Good morning, Major. How's it going?'

Larosse looked up, nodded, and waved his piece of bread briefly, 'Quiet — as you see.'

'We've just heard what happened yesterday,' Marcus went on, a little awkwardly. 'You were right all along about what

Boney would do. It might have been very serious. If it hadn't been for Prince Bernard, and your general — '

Larosse shrugged. 'I am not one to say "I told you so". As it is, it has come out all right. We are here, and the French —' he jabbed his bread in a southerly direction — 'are there, and all's well with the world.'

Marcus stared in the same direction. Presumably there were both Allied and French pickets in forward positions, but the undulations of the country, the roadside hedges and the height of the standing crops made it impossible to see very much. 'Do you know who it is out there?' he asked.

'Maréchal Ney,' Larosse said. 'The Bravest of the Brave. The Prince of Moskova.' He smiled tightly. 'I wish it were not him — I loved that old man. But he's an odd choice on the Emperor's part for such a command.'

'Why so? I've always understood he's a good soldier.'

'He's a soldier's soldier, but he's not a tactician. In fact he never thinks at all — he just acts as the passion takes him. Keeps his brains in his sword-arm.'

'There's also the question of his loyalty, isn't there? He abandoned Boney and went over to the Bourbons, even if he did come back at the first opportunity.'

'I think perhaps it was a political appointment — to shew how the Emperor forgives those who return to his side. *Pour encourager les autres*, you might say.'

'Perhaps,' Marcus agreed. 'So you don't think it was a good choice?'

'Good for us — not for the French. Why did he stop last night, for instance? If the Emperor had been commanding, he would have pushed on and taken Quatre-Bras yesterday. Or at least at first light this morning.'

'Yes, I suppose so,' Marcus said. 'It's very quiet out there. We thought we would find you already engaged.'

'There's been nothing but a little skirmishing in and out of those hedges.'

'Do we know how many of them there are?'

'Fifteen, maybe twenty thousand, I should say.'

Marcus was startled. 'Good God! Then — why don't they attack? They must know how weak we are.'

Larosse smiled. 'Must they? Well, I wonder. One of the

414

pickets reported this morning that he thought he saw General Reille out there, consulting with Ney. As Reille has fought against Wellington before, he will know all about the Duke's habit of hiding the majority of his men from sight until the last minute. Probably they do not know that what they see is all there are.'

'Yes, of course — they're afraid of a "Spanish battle". Just as well for us! Picton's veterans are marching down from Brussels this moment, and some line regiments are on their way from Nivelles. The longer the French delay, the better for us.'

'Amen to that.' Larosse put the last of his bread in his mouth and stood up, brushing the crumbs from his knees. 'How were things in Brussels when you left?'

'Quiet. I don't think anyone's panicking — they all trust the Beau implicitly.'

'They may trust us, too. We have everything to fight for,' Larosse said.

'You more than most,' Marcus said, with a smile. 'You're a lucky man, Major — and you'll be a sort of cousin of mine when it comes off, so I ought to know. Sophie's the dearest creature, and I wouldn't be surprised if you two didn't suit each other down to the ground.'

'Thank you,' Larosse said gravely. He reached into his inside pocket and drew out the ivory-coloured rose, flattened by its journey and rather limp, and glanced up at Marcus. 'There wasn't time to have a miniature painted, you see. This was the nearest thing I could get to her likeness.'

Marcus laughed. 'You're a complete hand, Larosse! Well, for your sake, if for no-one else's, I hope we get this business over with as soon as possible. It's damnable that we had no better intelligence yesterday from the Prussians. We might have settled it already if we'd known what was happening. Oh, the Old Man is moving on — I must go. Good luck to you.'

'And you, Morland. I suppose you may be in Brussels again before me?'

Marcus grinned. 'It's entirely possible. What was the message?'

Larosse smiled too. 'Oh, just my love, you know, and tell

them that I am all right.'

'I'll say all that's necessary, I promise.'

At one o'clock Wellington, with Muffling and a chosen few of his staff, reached Ligny, where things were in a greater state of readiness. Some eighty-four thousand Prussians and over two hundred guns were spread out across a seven-mile front along the marshy banks of the Ligny Brook. The troops were drawn up along the exposed forward slopes of the overlooking hills, which caused the Duke to exclaim with alarm and surprise.

'The French artillery will hardly refuse such an invitation,' he said to Muffling. 'Even if they miss the fighting line, they will hardly miss the reserves and supports.'

Blücher had his headquarters in the mill at Bussy on the hillside overlooking the centre and right of the field. Wellington's party was directed to it, and from the vantage-point of the high ground Marcus could see the French columns down below already advancing to take up positions for battle. Riding behind the chief and the Prussian attaché, he could overhear snatches of their conversation, and was inclined to agree with their view that the business in front of Quatre-Bras was no more than a demonstration, and that the real business was to take place here. From their best intelligence, this was, after all, where Boney himself was.

Inside the mill all was bustle and activity. There was white-haired, white-whiskered old 'Papa Forwards', as blunt and blustery and brave at seventy-two as he had been as a Hussar corporal of sixteen; and smooth-speaking, chubby-faced, subtle Gneisenau, his chief of staff. Between the two was Peter Firth, who hurried forward to greet Wellington as he entered, and to interpret for him.

It was plain even to Marcus that there were various tensions amongst the great men, though least of all perhaps between Blücher and Wellington. They were very different in temperament, but they shared an absolute honesty, and both desired only to see Napoleon beaten. Blücher, indeed, hated the Corsican with a rare and personal fervour, and said several times that he looked forward to hanging Napoleon with his own hands. He was hoping for assistance on the field

416

from Bülow and his Fourth Corps, who were still on their way from Liège, though Firth gave his opinion to Wellington that they wouldn't come up in time.

Muffling then put to Blücher what he and Wellington had already discussed, about this being the real theatre of operations, and Gneisenau agreed eagerly. He thought that what was before them at Ligny was almost the whole French army. The Allies should join up with the Prussians at once, he said. But Wellington said that the French force at Quatre-Bras ought to be destroyed first, and Muffling suggested that, having done that, the Allies should then march round to the south and attack the French at Ligny from the rear.

A brisk discussion broke out between Blücher and Muffling in German, and Wellington took the opportunity to put the point to Gneisenau about the disposition of the Prussian troops on the open hillside. 'They are very exposed — inviting casualties. The French artillery is strong — there could be heavy losses. For myself, I always place my men on the reverse slope, out of the firing-line.'

Firth, translating, murmured, 'He doesn't care for that, my lord. I fear he takes it as a criticism.'

'It was meant as one,' Wellington said, observing the sharp drawing together of the eyebrows. 'Better smooth him down, however. Tell him every man knows his own troops best, of course, but if I placed my own men so, I should expect them to be beaten.'

Gneisenau responded with a brittle smile and a short reply which Firth translated: 'He says that Prussian troops prefer always to have a clear view of the enemy, my lord. And he asks how many men you will bring over to help him.'

'We shall have to see how things fall out,' said the Duke. 'I will come myself with the whole army if we are not attacked at Quatre-Bras. Above all, we must remember that we are not two armies but one, united in a common purpose.'

The words attracted Blücher's attention, who broke off from his discussion with Muffling to agree heartily, and to shake Wellington's hand and pledge himself to that common purpose. Shortly afterwards the Duke and his party left to return to Quatre-Bras. Firth excused himself to Blücher to exchange a few words with Marcus as they walked back to the horses.

417

'And what's your view of the situation at Quatre-Bras?' he asked. 'Since it was I who taught you military theory, I should be able to rely on your interpretation!'

Marcus smiled. 'I should say "Thank you, sir", but that was obviously meant as self-praise. Well, it was an abominably close call! Perponcher has seven thousand men, infantry only, and Ney is camped about a mile off with an army of twenty thousand. When we left they were not even under arms, thank God; but everything depends on how quickly our reinforcements can get there.'

'Yes, I see,' Firth said gravely. 'Thank you, Marcus. Was everything all right in Brussels when you left?'

'Yes, sir. Bobbie's as blue as megrim about not being able to join us. But he's promised to take care of everyone if anything should happen — if there's a retreat, I mean.' He looked at his former tutor anxiously, his youth shewing through for an instant. He was a Peninsula veteran, but he was still only twenty years old. 'Is it going to be all right, sir?'

'I don't know. Boney's played it just right, setting up two separate engagements like this. The Prussians and the Allies must support each other: whichever of us prevails first must send help to the other. But Gneisenau doesn't like us, you know. Still, he's a good tactician — and there's no better leader than Old Forwards.'

'But what if one of us loses? Or both of us?'

'Don't even think it. I must go — and so must you. Good luck, Marcus. And — if anything happens to me — '

'It won't, sir — but yes, I know. I will.'

'Good boy!' And he smiled his genial smile, and went back quickly inside, while Marcus ran for his horse.

The attack at Quatre-Bras began at around two o'clock. Six thousand French infantry and two thousand cavalry advanced under the covering fire of the famous French heavy artillery. The waiting Allies heard the brisk brattle of musketry in the hedgerows, and then the Dutch-Belgian skirmishers came scrambling back from the forward positions to the safety of Gemioncourt's walls, where they were received by their rather nervous compatriots.

Larosse disposed the men in his command to the best

418

advantage to await the French. It was a tense period, and there were one or two very pale faces amongst the Netherlanders. Larosse went up and down the lines, giving quiet words of encouragement where they seemed most needed, giving last orders to the company commanders. One of them, Captain Dietmar, was himself in a green sweat, and accosted Larosse with the familiarity of panic.

'I say, Larosse, is it true we're outnumbered?' he asked, sliding a finger round inside his collar. He craned his neck awkwardly as he tried to catch a glimpse of the situation around the corner of a barn without exposing his body to possible enemy fire. 'How many of 'em do you think there are out there? This isn't much fun, is it?'

'Be quiet, you fool! Your men can hear you,' Larosse said brusquely. 'And you call me "sir". We're not in the ballroom now.'

Dietmar coloured. 'Oh, really — sir,' he added quickly as Larosse frowned. 'But, I say, we've done our bit already. We held 'em off last night. It's about time the British did something. Why should it all fall on us? And I couldn't get a decent bite of food last night, either. Do they expect us to fight on empty stomachs? I think — '

'Don't think,' Larosse snapped. This was the worst of volunteers, he thought. It was bad enough commanding raw troops, but when the officers were also without any experience ... Fortunately not all of them in his battalion were as bad as Dietmar, whose soldiery went no further than a love of smart uniforms. 'I've always known you were a fool; but you are also an officer under orders. Just hold your position, and keep your men firing. That's all you have to do. Leave the thinking to those equipped for it by nature.'

Dietmar opened his mouth and then thought better of a reply that could get him court-martialled. Larosse moved on. From his observation position near the road a few moments later he watched almost with detached interest as four brigades of French infantry emerged one after the other onto the flat plain to his left between Piraumont and the road, and formed themselves into columns. There were two brigades of cavalry, too, trotting out on the flank on the other side of the Charleroi road — they would need watching. Firing was

419

coming from Piraumont almost continuously. Gemioncourt was still silent — the French were not properly within range yet. The numbers, of course, were huge. More troops had been marching up all morning. Ney, he reflected, must have thirty thousand or more at his command by now. There was no possibility they could hold them here. It was a delaying action, that was all.

Time, he had always found, ran differently during battles. It went sometimes very slowly, so that a minute seemed to crawl by, and there was time to notice everything, almost to see the grass growing; and at other times it accelerated absurdly, so that you would suddenly find it was growing dark and that hours had gone by unnoticed. While the French marched up, wheeling their columns to attack Piraumont and Gemioncourt simultaneously, time passed very slowly. Just a delaying action, Larosse thought. His thoughts revolved like a squirrel in a cage. Hold them until the reserves come up. More troops arriving all the time. Delaying action. Won't hold them here.

If only he had managed to convince Wellington sooner that he was right about the Emperor's plan, the Allied army would be in position now and ready to give battle, instead of having to march from miles away — marching against time. Time. Still time to go along his lines again, hearten his men. They were peeking about them like nervous horses, shewing the whites of their eyes. They knew they were absurdly outnumbered, and were already looking for a route of escape. Well, who could blame them? A man could be killed in a delaying action just as well as in the main battle. Shot and shell had no pride or prejudice: they would take a man anywhere — and these troops had never seen action before. When the first one broke, they would all break. He turned his horse and rode back to them.

'Steady, you men,' he called to them. Heads turned, frightened eyes looked towards him hopefully. Used to commanding veterans, he felt saddened by their pathetic trust. What words could he give them that would keep out the musket-ball or the bayonet-point? It was the raw recruit who fell first, everyone knew that. They were fodder to shovel into the maw of the ravenous monster-god, Battle. Sacrifice —

propitiation. They were here to die instead of the veterans, that was all.

No, they were here to delay the French advance until the veterans arrived — he must remember that. And those of them who survived this first encounter would perhaps become veterans. He shook the incipient despair away. They would win because they could not afford to lose.

'Are you all properly loaded, primed and closed? Then make sure of your aim when the time comes. We don't want any wasted shot. And wait for the command. The honour of the first blood falls to us. Stand steady until I give the command.'

There was a brief whining sound, like the drone of a mosquito, and a solid smack which jolted him in the saddle. He looked down curiously, and saw a musket-ball embedded in his saddle-flap just below his thigh. He was surprised: he had not noticed that they were being fired at. The ball had evidently been at the limit of its flight, for it had not penetrated the leather, but merely sunk itself in to half its depth. He dug it out with his fingers. It was hot, and he juggled it in his palm to cool it. Glancing round, he saw that Time had performed one of its tricks: the French were suddenly much nearer.

'Ready, men,' he said. 'Make sure you're rammed down. And make sure you've taken your rammer out, too! Don't fire that at the French, for that's one present they won't send back!'

There was a ripple of laughter — a very slight one, and very nervous laughter, but he saw that the incident had had its use — the men were impressed and heartened by his indifference to the closeness of the ball, and were readying themselves to fire, rather than looking over their shoulders for escape.

There was a band of trees five hundred, six hundred yards away to the south-east. The French who had gone through rather than round emerged suddenly from it. Larosse stared at them hungrily as they trudged towards him against the background of the trees. Black shako, white face, short-waisted blue jacket, baggy white trousers; short-legged, broad-shouldered, tough and handy, tireless marchers, fearless fighters: French veterans, his own men, perhaps, whom he had commanded in another battle, a lifetime ago. Betrayal came hard, even when it was for the best of reasons. He understood why Ney had gone back — oh, only too well! And why, having gone back, he seemed to have been infected with this indecision, this fatal lethargy. A man's spirit so easily sickened and died — much more easily than his body.

The time had come. Larosse gave the command. One hothead beat him to it by a fraction, and the word 'Fire!' was simultaneous with the crack of the first musket. The others followed instantly in a volley close enough together to have satisfied any but a veteran British officer. That first volley, fired at leisure and by properly loaded guns, was always the most telling, and the French soldiery hated and dreaded it. Men had fallen out there; the advancing column wavered for an instant, before coming on.

'Reload! Prime and close! Stand steady, there! Give 'em another, lads!'

The second volley was inevitably ragged, as some men reloaded more quickly than others. One fool had done something stupid with his charges, and his musket exploded in his face, sending him reeling back with a wild shriek — only one, quickly cut off — with most of the side of his head missing.

The end of the third volley joined up with the beginning of the fourth, and firing became raggedly continuous. Now there were casualties amongst his own men, too — French balls were lighter and didn't carry so well, but once the French got close enough they did their job. Larosse shouted encouragement, gave orders, directed men to new positions as casualties left spaces. The sound of firing disappeared as he ceased to take notice of it, and became the neutral background against which other sounds were silhouetted.

Time accelerated again. Now there was no space for more firing: the French were scrambling over the last few yards, and there was hand-to-hand fighting. Men struggled breast to breast like wrestlers, or slashed and jabbed at each other with their bayonets. Some at the last minute lashed out despairingly with their musket-barrel as though it were a big stick picked up in a childhood quarrel.

Larosse's sword was in his hand, though he had no

422

recollection of drawing it. His horse was quivering under him, snorting in fright and shock. The pungent reek of gunpowder smoke overlaid the friendly farmyard smells of hay and manure now — and his horse could probably smell blood, too. A French officer was riding at him, arm upraised. Now there was no more thought, only slash and parry; controlling the horse with knees and spurs and tight left hand, wheeling its muscular panic this way and that; looking about him in quick glances for the situation and his own safety.

Turn — slash — parry; grinding scrape of steel on steel, setting his teeth on edge; yielding of flesh to his steel, sickening, oh yes, even after all these years! There was still firing; and men shouting, hoarse, shapeless shouts which splurged out of their mouths senselessly as they jabbed and struggled.

And men running now. Stem the flood!

'Stand fast, you men! Stand your ground! Keep firing, lads!'

A burning pain in his thigh: he glanced down, and parried at the last second with a frantic jerk the bayonet-blade that was driving upwards at his face. He had to let go the rein to grasp the musket-barrel with one hand, yanking it from the French soldier's grasp, while he slashed backhanded at him. The grim face turned upwards at him was frighteningly young. He looked no more than fifteen. The Emperor must have called out every possible man for this last effort. The blade of his sword buried itself in the Frenchman's neck just above the collar, slicing it half through, coming up with a jolt against the neckbone. Blood fountained from the severed great artery, splashing over his leg, his horse's flank, his shabraque — scarlet on pale blue — warm over his hand and wrist. The man fell without a sound, leaving the musket in Larosse's hand, even as his horse leapt away in panic, terrified by the blood, no longer restrained by the bit.

Larosse swayed frantically, knowing that to lose his seat now, with the enemy all around him, was certain death. He dropped the musket, grabbing for the reins, feeling the Frenchman's blood cool and grow sticky between his fingers and over the left leg of his breeches. The hard surface of the *pavé* was under the clattering hooves now, and his horse slipped on it as he dragged on the reins, digging the spurs in cruelly to turn it against its will. But his men were running now, absurdly outnumbered; running with their muskets held out before them as if in supplication, their mouths wide open in soundless terror; running for their lives — literally so — with the French behind them, one or two pursuing with stumbling eagerness.

Nothing for it but to retreat and form up further up the road. No need to shout orders to his men — they were heading where he would have sent them anyway, for the safety of Quatre-Bras itself, straight up the road. He need only stay with them, rally them, turn their panicking run into an orderly quick march. The French were hanging back, making sure of the farm they had just taken. Larosse rode round his men, chivvying them together like a dog rounding up sheep, slowed them to a steady jog, got them into something like a column. Retreating now, not fleeing. Still under discipline. Still soldiers.

But here was a new menace: the cavalry he had seen out on the flank earlier on had evidently found themselves hampered by the soft going of a marshy field and were returning to the road. God damn them! They had seen his retreating columns now, and were turning to attack them, baying for blood. His men flung terrified glances as the horses plunged through the heavy mud towards them, the riders brandishing their short cavalry swords, levelling hideous horse-pistols. Now they were out of the mud and thundering towards them. There was no hope in the world of making his men stand; no purpose either, since they would never be able to load in time.

For one second the column stopped where it was and wavered like something seen through heat-haze; then it broke, disintegrating like a river-bank under a flood wave, and the men were running like hares in different directions, some up the road, some northwards towards the Bossu Wood, some eastwards across open country. Some of them threw away their arms as they ran, and with them all pretence of wishing to defend their country from the French invader. Those, Larosse knew, would never fight again — they were as much casualties as if they had been shot and killed. But the others, those who by chance or instinct or desire were clinging on to their muskets as they ran — they could be gathered up

424

to fight again. They were still useful. He must preserve them.

A quick glance told him that those heading for the wood had the better chance. Once under cover of the trees, he could turn them and make them fight again. He wheeled his horse in a tight circle and placed himself out to the side of his men, cantering with them, edging them, again like a sheepdog, towards the safety of the trees, cheering them on. There were two more of their own battalions in the woods — they could join with them and make a fresh stand.

Suddenly he lurched in the saddle, losing his right stirrup, and almost came off over his horse's neck. The animal stumbled and then regained its balance; Larosse abandoned pride and grabbed a handful of mane and hung on. For some reason he couldn't get his stirrup back; in fact, he couldn't feel his right foot at all. He glanced briefly down, and saw that the right thigh of his breeches was soaked in blood, and for a moment he couldn't think what was odd about that. Then he remembered that the soldier he had decapitated at the farm had been standing on his left side: it was his left leg which had been soaked with French blood.

It was plain to Marcus, when he arrived back from Ligny, that they were not doing well at Quatre-Bras. Piraumont had fallen to the French, leaving the Namur road perilously open; and shortly after the Netherlanders went scrambling out from Gemioncourt, the French drove the defenders back from Pierrepoint to Bossu Wood. All three chosen positions were now in French hands. Marcus glared through the glass as though he could change things by looking hard enough.

A voice cursed roundly in his ear. 'God damn and blast those cowardly Belgians! All they know how to do is run!'

Marcus lowered his glass to find Billy Cecil beside him. 'They're heavily outnumbered,' he replied.

'They won't stand like British troops. I've always said so.'

'True, but they've never been under fire before. One can't expect too much of them. And they seem to be holding the wood.'

'But for how long? You haven't been watching them as I have,' Cecil snorted. He looked round, and his voice changed. 'Oh, thank God — help is at hand! Look there!'

He jerked his thumb over his shoulder, and Marcus spun round to see the cheering sight of the front rank of a large body of soldiers coming down the road from Brussels. At last! 'It must be Picton's division,' he cried, lifting his glass again. 'Yes! And it's the 95th in the front! It's all Jack-a-lantern green out there! Hurrah for the Rifles! Now we'll see something!'

'Not a moment too soon,' Cecil said. 'I say, Morland, you're wanted! The Beau's beckoning! Better scurry, man!'

A few moments later Marcus was cantering his horse up the road towards the approaching reinforcements with Wellington's orders to General Kempt ringing in his head.

'We must secure the Namur road at all costs,' he had said. 'I propose to set up a counter-attack on Gemioncourt with the Netherlanders, supported by one of the line regiments, to give us more time. Meanwhile I want the 95th to move immediately on Piraumont, to take it if possible, but at all events to secure the Cherry Wood and hold the road open. Tell Sir James I shall dispose the rest of his own and Pack's regiments along the Namur road as they march up — the Rifles will have their support as soon as they're in position. You had better go with the 95th, Morland, as far as Piraumont — they won't know the ground. Then report back to me.'

It was an order exactly to the taste of the Peninsula veterans. As soon as the gist of it filtered back through the ranks, a great roar went up, and the first company yelled their pride as one man: 'First in the field and last out of it! The Bloody, Fighting, Ninety-fifth!'

Marcus placed himself alongside Tantony, who checked his curvetting horse and said, 'The Old Man wastes no time! How bad is it?'

Marcus explained briefly what had happened so far. 'We're just holding them; but now all the farmhouses have fallen, Ney can move his men right up to the wood without challenge, and if he controls the wood he can outflank us on our right. That's the danger — that and the Namur road.'

'Old Ney, is it? Well, he's an enemy to respect, at all events. Who's holding the wood?'

'The Nassauers, and what's left of Bylandt's. But Van Merlen's on its way from Nivelles, so we'll have some cavalry at last.'

426

'Bylandt's were pretty cut up, were they?' Tantony asked mildly, but with a worried frown.

Marcus shrugged. 'They took the brunt of the first attack, but they got scattered when they ran for it. Larosse rallied a couple of companies of the 5th Militia, though, and got them away in good order. He's a good man.'

The frown cleared. 'Ah! You've seen him, then?'

'Only from a distance. I haven't been to the wood yet. But yours is the important business now — we must hold the left wing. The Beau plainly thinks a lot of you riflemen, Tantony, sending you off on your own like this!'

Tantony smiled. 'It's those Bakers of ours — never a wasted shot! One Baker's worth ten muskets. That and the fact that we move so fast!'

Despite their undoubted speed across country, before the 95th had covered half the distance to Piraumont, the French had moved up so powerful a force on the farm that attack by one battalion was plainly useless. Another body of Frenchmen was coming from the same direction, quick-marching towards the Cherry Wood. Orders rang out, and the riflemen moved with astonishing speed to deploy themselves across the road while their reserve took up positions in the wood, and within minutes were firing steadily. Marcus paused for a moment to admire the beautiful rhythm with which the ranks worked together. He knew that in the Rifle regiments each rifleman chose his own companions to be his front- and rear-rank men, and that the three of them bivouacked and messed together, fought together, and were rarely parted except by death, so that they became as close as brothers.

The speed and constancy of their fire were not only checking the French, but driving them backwards, and the 95th was gradually extending its line. Marcus saw the front ranks of the 79th, the next of Kempt's battalions, coming down the road from Quatre-Bras to support the Rifles, and decided it was time for him to report back to Wellington. The 95th seemed to be holding on all right. One could always trust the Light Division, he thought, turning his horse and trotting away.

At the house in the Rue Ducale, Lucy slept at last, and woke

427

feeling confused, tired and too hot. The light was coming in strongly through the curtains. She reached out for her watch, and stared at it dazedly. A quarter past eleven? What was she doing in bed at a quarter past eleven? Why had Docwra not woken her?

And then she remembered. She jumped out of bed, pulled the bell and went over to the window, drawing back the curtains to look out. Everything was still — unnaturally so, after the bustle of military departure last night and this morning. Even the normal daily traffic was stilled. The street lay empty in blinding sunshine and sharp black shadow, the silent heat glaring back from the cobbles and the flagway. The Park was deserted: after weeks of uniformed officers strolling with muslin-gowned beauties, nothing moved there now but the birds, and one grey-striped cat slipping along under the bushes on some secretive feline business.

Past eleven o'clock! Where were they all? Was battle joined? Had the French been stopped in their tracks? News, she must have news! It was intolerable not to know. She left the window and began hastily to dress herself, and only when she was impatiently tugging a brush through her hair did Docwra appear, looking for once in her life dishevelled and gum-eyed.

'Where the deuce have you been? Where is everyone? What's been happening?'

Docwra looked stupid. 'I don't know, my lady. I've only just woken up meself. Everyone's asleep, I think, my lady: it's only half-past eleven.'

'Only — ! Well, never mind. Go down to the kitchen and see what you can find by way of breakfast. I'm starved. And find some boy to send out for Parslow — I want to see him as soon as possible.'

When she got downstairs she gave vent to some of her restlessness by going around drawing all the blinds and curtains, and exclaiming at the clouds of dust the operation produced. When she returned to the morning-room, Héloïse was there, looking wan and drawn.

'Couldn't you sleep?' Lucy greeted her.

'I slept, but it doesn't seem to have helped,' Héloïse said. 'All through the night I kept hearing trumpets and drums and

428

marching feet. And every time I fell asleep, I had the same dream, that I was back in Paris during the Revolution — ' She broke off, the shadows of dreams still drawing down her mouth and darkening her eyes.

'Come and sit down,' Lucy said, more gently. 'I've sent Docwra to the kitchen to try to find some breakfast. Of course, it must be different for you, all this. I always forget what you went through — and when you were just a child.'

'I forget it, too, most of the time. But there are some sounds which bring it back to me. It was — not good.'

'Well, it will soon be over, and this time for ever. When Boney's beaten, they'll make sure he never gets loose again.' She stared sightlessly out of the window for a moment. 'My God, imagine — the end of it all! I can barely remember the time before the war. And so much waste, so many victims!'

This was an unfortunate train of thought. She shook it away, and looked quickly at her sister-in-law, and saw the shine of unshed tears. 'I'm sorry, Héloïse — stupid of me. You don't need reminding, any more than I do — '

Héloïse shook her head. 'It's all right. It isn't that. At least, not entirely.'

Lucy tilted her head. 'There has been something wrong for some time now, hasn't there? Oh, I know I'm not very quick, but I've noticed how quiet you've been lately. Is it Sophie? Don't you approve of her choice?'

'I like Major Larosse very much — and I think he will be a very good husband for Sophie. I hadn't considered it before, but I see now that she will be much happier with an older man. No, it's not that.'

'What, then?' Lucy pressed, and then, with unexpected insight, 'Is it Jamie?'

'Why do you say that?'

Lucy made an impatient gesture. 'I know Jamie very well. He was always my favourite brother, but he's always been, well, difficult. My sister Mary used to get so angry with him! I remember when he announced he was going to marry Mary Ann — ' She broke off abruptly. 'Well, that's another story. But he made Mother cry many and many a time, and it wouldn't surprise me if he didn't do the same to you. He probably,' she added generously, 'doesn't mean to hurt you.'

Héloïse looked down at her hands. 'I had a letter — '

'Oh, he's written to you at last?'

'No, not from James. A letter from Mrs Skelwith.'

'Not Mary Skelwith? Don't tell me she's still intruding in his life?'

Héloïse nodded. 'She said — that James had — been —' It was hard to say the words aloud: '— taking a young woman out riding in the carriage. Alone.'

'Oh, but really — ' Lucy began.

'In my phaeton,' Héloïse finished, looking up. 'The one you and he designed for me.'

'Héloïse, you mustn't pay any attention to stories like that,' Lucy said. 'You know Mary Skelwith is strange in the head. She's just making it up to hurt you, out of jealousy.'

'I don't think she is making it up. I think she is — misinterpreting it.'

'Well, then. You don't think James cares for anyone but you, surely? He's never cared for anyone but you.'

'What about Fanny?'

'But Fanny was his daughter, not his wife,' Lucy said impatiently. Héloïse saw that the ideas were beyond her. Just as she had never understood the true nature of her first husband, so she would never understand what James was really like — only that he was 'difficult'.

'He loved Fanny to the exclusion of everyone else; and I don't know if he will ever get over her death,' Héloïse said. 'And lately — well, I have been wondering if there is any reason for me to go home. I have been thinking that maybe I should stay here, and make a new life for Sophie and me here, in Belgium — or maybe in France, when the war is over.'

'Stay here?' Lucy stared in plain astonishment.

'Charles has asked me — '

'Oh, Charles!' Now Lucy was angry. 'I've never heard such nonsense — wicked nonsense! I don't know what's come over you! Abandon James and run off with that idiot Duc of yours? And when you've just finished saying that James is heartbroken over Fanny's death! And what about your little boys? Do you mean to abandon them, too?'

Héloïse opened her mouth to reply, but Lucy rode over her. 'And what about Morland Place? Mother left it to you — to

430

you! She passed over Edward, who's worked for it all his life. She passed over James and Harry and even me, for the matter of that — all her children. And her grandchildren — and she always had a soft spot for Polly, who after all is the eldest. But no, she put all of us aside and left Morland Place to you, because she thought you'd look after it best. Well, I've never questioned that — Mother always knew what she was doing, and it was hers to leave as she chose. But when I hear you say things like that, I begin to wonder whether she made the right decision after all!'

Héloïse had turned very pale during the tirade, and covered her face with her hands, as if to shield herself from the words. Now when she put her hands down again, she looked bewildered, like a sleepwalker waking in the wrong room. 'You're right,' she said faintly. 'I don't know what's come over me, either. Why didn't I think of those things? I've been so deep in self-pity that I never considered the other aspects.' She bit her lip with remorse. 'What a coward I've been,' she said at last. 'A pitiful, selfish coward. Oh, Lucy, I'm sorry!'

Lucy was uncomfortable. 'No, no, I had no right — you've never been a coward. Look what you've gone through! I spoke too plainly — it's a fault of mine. Mother used to say — '

'You were right to speak as you did,' Héloïse said. 'It needed to be said, and I'm grateful to you. These have been — ' involuntary sigh — 'a hard few months; but what are tests for but to test us?' She sat up straighter, squaring her shoulders, and even the unimaginative Lucy could almost see her girding on her armour to take up the good fight again. 'Thank you for making me see it. I shan't fail again.'

'Lord,' Lucy said, embarrassed, 'I'm not one to give advice! I've been a fool lately, too. And it was always you who told me how to get on with things. When I stayed with you that time, before Thomas was born — '

'If I helped you then, I am repaid now. And I am thinking, Lucy — '

She broke off as the door opened, and Docwra came in with Parslow and a tray which contained, as well as other things, a pot of coffee. The smell of it drifted over to Lucy and brought her eagerly to her feet.

431

'Coffee! Wonderful! Was there someone in the kitchen, then, Docwra? I know you can't make it.'

'I can make it, my lady, but not so's you'd drink it,' Docwra said succinctly. 'And there was no-one but Parslow in the kitchen.'

Lucy looked at her groom, who met her eyes blandly, 'You?'

He nodded. 'I make it for myself, my lady, in my own quarters. And since none of the Belgian servants was about —'

'Parslow, you continually surprise me.' She shook her head. A groom who drank coffee? The idea was extraordinary. 'It's a morning for shocks, it seems. Héloïse, will you pour?'

'You wished to speak to me, my lady?' Parslow prompted her gently.

'Yes, about the horses. I have a fancy that there will be a number of people wanting to leave Brussels today, and if there should be anything like bad news from the front, horses will become valuable merchandise.'

'Yes, my lady. I understand. I shall take every precaution.'

'Is there a boy you can trust to keep an eye on them when you're not there?'

'Yes, my lady. I'll see to it.'

'And how long will it be before Dancer is fit?'

'It was a split hoof, my lady, where she'd cast a shoe. I had her reshod yesterday with special nails, and she'll be all right for light work tomorrow, but the hoof will need watching. She won't be fully fit until it grows out.'

Lucy bit her lip. 'Then if — if the colonel sends for another remount, there's only Hotspur left.'

Parslow looked at her with understanding. 'I'll see what I can do, my lady. There may well be gentlemen leaving who don't want to take their riding-horses with them.'

'Yes. Thank you, Parslow.'

'Shall you be wanting horses today, my lady?'

'No, not today.'

'Then I'll exercise them myself, my lady. It's only about ten miles to Mont St-Jean,' he added casually.

Lucy smiled suddenly. 'Bless you, Parslow! You think of everything.'

432

When the servants had withdrawn, she fell on the bread and cold beef which Docwra had brought from the kitchen. Héloïse sipped coffee gratefully. 'I hope Parslow can bring us some news,' she said. 'Waiting is always the hardest part. If only there were something we could do to help. It's dreadful to sit and do nothing while the men are at such exertions for our sake.'

Lucy's eyebrows rose. 'Do to help? Of course there is, you simpleton! We have to turn this house into a hospital.'

'A hospital?'

'Certainly. We have the space, the servants, and my special skills — Docwra's, too, after all these years of helping me. We must be ready to receive the wounded, whenever they start to arrive.'

Héloïse looked her dismay. 'The wounded,' she echoed bleakly.

'Yes — now don't look so blue! There won't be any of our men amongst 'em! But this lull is exactly what we need to get ourselves organised. There's plenty to do. We have to visit all the ladies who are staying and find out who will help, and collect bandages and splints and sheets and bedding and bowls and kettles and whatever medicines there are in the town. And find out how many surgeons there are, too, and make sure everyone knows what to do when the time comes. There's a whole day's work ahead of us at least,' she finished vigorously.

Héloïse, still looking a little pale, nodded. 'Yes, of course. I will help you. It will keep us occupied.'

'And the girls, too — we'll get Rosamund and Sophie up right away. That will stop them fretting over their fiancés! And Roberta — we must include her! And if we can get Barbarina away from her mother, she can help us too.'

'I imagine Lady Barbara will be one of those leaving Brussels,' Héloïse said.

'Oh no, you're wrong there. Whatever you think of her, she's no coward, and with her husband and her son both in the field — ' She drained her cup and set it down so hurriedly it chattered in the saucer. 'Have you finished breakfast? Because there's really no time to waste, you know. We have a thousand things to do.'

There was no news. Parslow reported back that the Char-leroi road was blocked with waggons and that he could not get through, and no-one seemed to have heard anything. The hot day advanced, with people coming and going, everyone asking the same questions and getting the same negative answers. The Morland women at least kept busy, their numbers increased by the arrival of Roberta and Bobbie, whom Lucy cordially invited to stay for the time being.

'There's no sense in your being all alone at home. News will come here as quickly as there. And we may need your help later on.'

Roberta was a soldier's daughter, and understood the real-ities of war. 'Once they are engaged, we certainly shall. This is an excellent idea of yours, Lucy.'

She shrugged. 'I wish you might convince Dr Brugmans of it. He tells me that it's not only impossible I should know anything of medical matters, it's also indecent.'

Roberta smiled. 'He's quite right, of course. But you shouldn't mind him.'

'I don't, except that I shall need some kind of a physician here when the time comes. I've passed the word amongst our acquaintance — we must just wait and see. There's still a large body of opinion that holds we shan't have a battle at all.'

Roberta looked around the room at the women quietly at work: Héloïse and Sophie tearing bandages, Rosamund supervising the making up of beds by some of the servants. 'I wish I could believe that,' she said, 'for all our sakes.'

'Well, perhaps — ' Lucy began; but the sentence was never to be finished. Her head jerked up, she turned towards the window staring intently at nothing. There it was again — far away, a low, rumbling boom like distant thunder. 'Listen!' she said.

Everyone in the room was suddenly silent, motionless, listening. Sophie stared at her mother across the sheet they were tearing, her eyes dark smudges in her white face. Rosa-mund stood with an empty palliasse drawn taut between her hands, her mouth grim, and she and Lucy exchanged a look of rare sympathy across the distance between them.

'It's the guns,' said Lucy. 'They are engaged.'

The presence of a few more seasoned troops in the Bossu Wood steadied Larosse's men and gave them respite. Larosse himself, not knowing where Count Bylandt was, reported to Prince Frederick.

'Very well — join your men with mine. We shall need all the help we can get — the woods are bound to be an object.' He glanced at Larosse's bloodstained breeches. 'What's happened to you, man? Are you wounded?'

'I think so, sir,' Larosse said with a grimace. 'Not all the blood's my own, but my right leg is numb. I think I may have been hit there.'

'You'd better get it seen to.' He jerked his head over his shoulder. 'My barber's up at the back somewhere with my servant. Get him to take a look at it — he's a good man. But try not to be too long. I need the seasoned officers back here.'

Larosse saluted and turned his horse away. The wood was partly coppiced, and there were cleared paths running all through it, making movement inside the wood easy — easy for them, and easy for the enemy, he thought. He found the Prince's servants at last almost at the end of the wood, in sight of the Nivelles road, sitting on his bivouac-box with the resignation of veteran soldiers, who know that life is made up of long periods of boredom interspersed with short bursts of hideous danger.

'The Prince sent me,' Larosse said. 'Which of you is the barber?'

To his relief, the man who stood up was the most sensible-looking of them, a short, middle-aged man with cropped hair and mild grey eyes, which observed the bloodstained legs before returning to Larosse's face.

'I am, sir. Are you wounded?'

Larosse dismounted awkwardly, slithering out of the saddle and making sure to land on his left leg, since his right might easily collapse under him. When he put it tentatively to the ground, a burning pain was woken in his thigh, which made him gasp.

Moving with unexpected speed for such a stocky man, the barber was instantly at his side, tucking his short body under

Larosse's arm and taking his weight. 'That's right, sir, lean on me. Can you just hop over to the box, sir? Jan there will take your horse. Keep your foot off the ground, sir.'

Larosse sat down on the box, his leg stretched out stiffly, and the surgeon crouched quickly before him.

'I think you've got a ball in there, sir — See how the cloth's burnt as well as torn. It's beginning to swell, too. I think we'll have to cut your breeches, sir.'

Larosse gritted his teeth. The blunt, broad hands were gentle, but though his foot was still numb, the upper part of his leg was well awake now. 'Go ahead — whatever is necessary.'

The barber produced a rolled-up canvas housewife, unfolded it, and took out a pair of scissors with which he snipped a long cross in the bloodsoaked kersey and folded back the cloth. Larosse glanced down and away again: his outer thigh was black and swollen around the ragged, bloody wound. The hands again, and the burning pain.

'It's not so bad, sir,' the barber pronounced. 'The ball's lodged in the muscle — hasn't touched the bone. I'll dig it out for you, sir, and bandage it up, and you'll be as good as new.'

It crossed Larosse's mind to ask if he had done anything like that before, but then he dismissed the question. Those hands knew what they were doing, and the steady grey eyes were calm and confident.

'Get on with it, then, man,' he said shortly.

The barber felt inside the housewife again, and produced a scalpel and a long-handled pair of forceps. Larosse looked away, and fixed his gaze on a hazel-tree above him, tracing with his eyes the line of branch and twig, the veins in a leaf through which the June afternoon light was shining. These woods were very like the woods of home. He would take Sophie there one day, he promised himself. There would be bluebells in the spring, and wood anemones ... He remembered the picnic in the forest of Sognies; Sophie in white muslin, her dark innocent eyes, the curve of her smile ...

A short and bloody interlude followed. Larosse gripped the sides of the bivouac-box, and in those minutes got to know with great and unwelcome intimacy every splinter and notch of the lid's edge. The blood sang in his ears, and the hazel

436

darkened and dissolved ...

'All done now, sir,' came the barber's voice from far away. 'That's the little beggar for you. You're better off without it, sir.'

The barbarous pain eased one notch. Larosse focused his eyes with difficulty. Between the jaws of the forceps was the disgusting and bloody object which had been nestling in his flesh.

'Good man.' His voice sounded very strange to him. 'In my pocket — inside jacket — flask.'

A square hand slid between his uniform coat and his linen, lingering for a moment over his ribs just below his left breast, and then deftly slipped the silver flask out of his pocket.

'Hold on, sir.' Fire flushed the jangling wound in his leg, and he gasped again; and then the neck of the flask was against his lips. Larosse felt it chatter against his teeth and was disgusted with himself, and forced one hand to let go of the box-lid and catch hold of the flask for himself. A gulp, and the fire was healing fire now, searing his throat and hitting his stomach with a hot, happy thump. One more gulp, and he was in control again.

'Thanks,' he said briefly. 'You're a skilled man.'

'Bless you, sir,' the barber said calmly, 'I've taken plenty of metal out of plenty of men before now. His Highness makes pleasant to say I'm a better surgeon than barber any day of the week! I'll just bind you up, sir, and make you decent.'

He placed a pad over the wound, and then bound a bandage skilfully round the thigh over the breeches, so that it held together the cut edges of the material, too. When he was done he helped Larosse to his feet. From knee to groin, his right leg throbbed like a rotten tooth, while below the knee it was completely numb, a most curious sensation. When he put his weight on it, the pain surged — but he only had to get as far as his horse. With the barber's help he remounted, settled himself, grimacing, and felt in his fob for a coin. It came out gold, but it was worth it.

'Thanks again,' he said, turning his horse.

'Thank you, sir,' the barber said. 'I hope that'll be your last wound today.'

'Please God,' said Larosse.

437

Bit by bit, the French pressed forward through the wood, and bit by bit the Nassauers and Dutch-Belgians fell back, outnumbered beyond any hope of defeating the French. Beyond the wood there might be another battle raging, but they knew nothing of it. Tense pauses, bursts of fire, quick repositionings were all they knew. Larosse kept his two companies together with the power of his will. He would not *let* them run away, but he was aware that there were fewer and fewer blue jackets with orange facings in the wood: the Netherlandish Division leaked like an old bucket.

At some point he became aware that they had been reinforced by some Brunswickers — steady, well-disciplined troops who stiffened the line and stopped the backward movement for a while. But the French poured more and more men in from the south end, and the inexorable process continued, and now even the Brunswickers were losing heart. They had been pushed right to the end of the wood: the road to Nivelles lay temptingly within sight.

Larosse looked around vaguely, half expecting to see his rescuing barber still sitting under the hazel-tree. He had no idea how long ago that had been: it seemed like minutes, but it must have been hours, and though his watch was in his fob, it had unaccountably stopped. He didn't know whether it had received a blow of some sort, or whether he had forgotten to wind it. His leg was merely throbbing now, a background pain he no longer noticed; more of a nuisance was a newer scalp wound which dripped blood persistently into his eye.

He wiped it away again, and saw a staff-officer's cockade going by, heading for the road.

'Captain Morland!'

Marcus turned his head, reined his horse, and looked concerned. 'I say, Major, you look a bit cut about. Are you all right?'

'What? Oh, this is nothing. Just a flesh wound,' Larosse said. 'It looks worse than it is. Can you tell me what's happening? We're completely cut off in this wood. Are reinforcements coming?'

'I've just been to tell the Prince that Alten's has arrived.

You're to have three of Colin Halkett's line battalions, and push down and attack the French left.'

Larosse grimaced. Would he ever get out of this wood? He felt as though he had been here since time began. 'And what of the rest of the battle?' he asked.

'There's some pretty fierce fighting on our left,' Marcus said. 'The French are throwing wave after wave of cavalry against Picton's division. We're just about holding on, but the Highlanders and the 44th have had a bad time of it, and the 95th are taking a pounding, though they've done wonderfully well. You know those riflemen.'

'Captain Tantony?' Larosse asked quickly, and Marcus grinned.

'He asked about you in just the same tone of voice. He was still standing, last time I saw him — not even wounded.' The grin faded. 'Would to God we had some cavalry! We've nothing to break the charges of the cuirassiers. Picton's are taking a terrible beating, though they're standing like rocks.' He met Larosse's eyes, and the words hung unspoken between them — *more than you can say for the Netherlanders.* 'I must go — I'll be wanted. We haven't half enough messengers.'

Larosse turned away and went back to rallying his men. Line regiments were coming, he told them. We shall push back the French this time. General Halkett came storming up, exuding from each angry pore his opinion of the Netherlanders and Brunswickians, and rallied all the available troops in a ditch which ran across the narrowest part of the wood. The French were planning something with cavalry and artillery in the centre of the battlefield which involved clearing the Allies from the wood so as to be able to advance from that position as well. The Allies, therefore, must not be cleared from the wood.

Waiting again for the French to attack, the men crouched in the ditch, weary now, having been in arms all day. In the lull, Larosse reached into his pocket for a handkerchief and his fingers encountered something mysterious, something that felt like the stem of a bunch of grapes. He pulled it out and stared at it, mystified for a second, before realising that it was all that remained of Sophie's rose: a bare stem, all the petals having been knocked off by its passage in his pocket. He

439

looked at it blankly, and then restored it absently to his pocket.

The blood had finally dried on his right eyebrow and the dripping nuisance had stopped, and the whole of his right leg had gradually become numb. He was extremely hungry, but there wasn't much he could do about that. Things could have been worse, he thought, much worse. But he wished he knew what the time was.

CHAPTER SEVENTEEN

The distant sound of the guns, which the women had ceased consciously to notice, died away and stopped at about nine o'clock, leaving a silence which was far more nerve-racking. There was nothing to hear, nothing to do, nothing to know, and yet they could not bear to go to bed. They sat in the drawing-room, waiting. Bobbie had gone out after dinner in the hope of finding someone who knew something, and had not returned. Roberta tried to read, but could not manage to get to the end of the page; Héloïse occupied her fingers with sewing, but her stitches were unusually large and uneven; the others didn't even make a pretence of busying themselves.

A battle had been fought. Was it won or lost? Was their army now in perilous retreat, or in triumphant pursuit of the fleeing French? Was Brussels safe, or would they soon be in flight themselves for Antwerp and England? Most of all, who had been wounded? *Who had fallen?*

Lucy got up and walked over to the side-table to pour herself a glass of wine. Rosamund watched her, in her weariness feeling unexpectedly detached, observing her mother as a stranger might see her. A slender figure, she told herself, rather boyish with those flat contours and that long stride; very upright, a straight back and long neck, product of an old-fashioned upbringing; and the young-looking head with the short curly crop, whose hay-coloured fairness was summer-bleached almost to white at the ends. The sun and long hours in the saddle had produced some reprehensible freckles on the short nose and high cheek-bones; the hands reaching for the decanter and glass were brown and strong and capable.

Her mother! For most of Rosamund's life she had been like a character in a story: the stern, quick-moving parent who came and went unpredictably from the house, living a life as private and separate from the nursery as the Queen of England's; sending down decrees to be enacted by Trot and the nursery-maids, who were real people as her mother was not. Mother — Mama — her ladyship — had loved only Thomas. Little Thomas who was now away at school, at Eton. Little Thomas whose origins were shrouded in mystery, or should have been. Rosamund, with the instinct for survival of the odd-one-out, had always made it her business to know things, and she had found out about Thomas: Thomas was Mama's love-child. Yet it was impossible to associate Mama with love; until Papa Danby joined the household, that was.

And now here was Mother pacing about the room with her long, rider's stride, her sun-freckled face all planes and shadows with worrying about her lover, just as if she were a green girl. Rosamund smiled inwardly. She never would have thought it would be possible for her to *like* her mother as a person, as a real person; but these two months had changed many things, and after their efforts today in a common cause ...

Lucy caught Rosamund looking at her, and raised an enquiring eyebrow at her. Rosamund gave her a small and sympathetic smile. 'He'll be all right,' she said.

The voice, coming after so long a silence, made everyone look up, and Lucy felt exposed. She said, 'For Heaven's sake, play something to us. I can't endure this silence.'

Glad of the excuse for movement, Roasmund rose and went to the piano, opened the lid, placed her hands on the keys. She couldn't think of anything to play: all her pieces seemed to have gone out of her head; her mind was a blank. She ran through a couple of keys, hoping something would suggest itself. After a moment she found a tune forming under her fingers, and she let it develop, her mind far away, her hands following the music as a lamb follows a ewe on the open hillside. It was only when she came to the lines of the chorus that she realised it was 'La Bayadère' she was playing; and seeing Sophie looking at her across the room, she stopped in mid-phrase.

In the silence which followed they heard the sound of someone arriving, male voices in the great hall, and footsteps coming up the stairs. A moment later the door opened, and

Marcus stood there on the threshold. His clothes were grimed, his boots dusty, his hair darkened with smoke and sweat. There was no obvious sign of injury to the eyes that devoured him, but he looked almost dazed with weariness.

Rosamund was on her feet first, but it was Roberta who spoke. 'Marcus, my dear boy! Are you hurt?'

'No — no, it's all right. I saw the lights from the road as I was passing, so I knocked, and they said you were still up.' He looked around from face to face. 'Well, here you all are,' he said stupidly. 'Is Bobbie here, too?'

'He's out looking for news. We expect him back at any time. He's been out since dinner, and it's — ' She looked at the clock. 'Good Heaven, it's almost midnight! I didn't realise it was so late.'

Marcus smiled slowly. 'You keep late hours! As soon as we men take our eyes off you — '

He moved his right hand, which had been down by his side, and Lucy saw the bloodstained rag tied round it. 'You are wounded,' she said sharply, hurrying towards him.

'It's nothing,' he said. 'Just a scratch — more of a nuisance than anything.'

'I should think it is, being your right,' Lucy said, catching hold of it as he tried to put it behind his back, and noting his wince of pain. 'Don't be a fool,' she adjured him shortly. 'You'll be more useful with this properly cleaned and bandaged. Rosamund, fetch him a glass of wine, and then pass me my bag. Sit down there, Marcus. No, no, don't crowd round me, the rest of you,' she added quickly, for she had an idea from the state of the rags what kind of sight they concealed. 'Go and sit down; give Marcus some room to breathe. What are you doing here anyway?'

Marcus wrenched his gaze away from what she was doing and said, 'The Beau sent me in with a message for General Hill. Oh, thank you,' he added as Rosamund handed him a glass. He drank gratefully. 'I've got to get back, but when I saw your lights I had to call in. Why are you all sitting up so late?'

Lucy, with her bag beside her now, took up her scissors and began to cut the blood-stiffened rag away from the wound. 'What a stupid question,' she said. 'We couldn't sleep, not

443

knowing what had happened. For Heaven's sake, tell us the news. We heard the guns — there was a battle, then?'

'Yes, at Quatre-Bras, where the French had halted last night.' He flinched, and took another gulp of wine. 'We've had the luckiest escape, I can tell you! When we got there this morning there was a huge French army facing nothing but a handful of Netherlanders, and if they'd attacked at once, it would have been all up with us. But old Ney didn't make a move until two o'clock this afternoon, and our reinforcements started arriving soon afterwards, and went on arriving all afternoon until we outnumbered 'em at last.'

Lucy pulled the last of the rags from the hand and looked with disatisfaction at the inflamed and ragged wound underneath. 'I'd better put a stitch or two in this if you mean to use it. Rosamund, can you fetch me some brandy, and some clean cloths? What the deuce did you do this on, Marcus?'

'Bayonet,' he said vaguely. 'I got tangled up with it and tried to pull myself free.'

'You'll be lucky if you haven't damaged any of the ligaments. Can you wriggle your fingers?'

'They're a bit stiff — but yes. I say, I'm very glad I came here, now. It's good of you to patch me up, ma'am.'

The door burst open to admit not Rosamund with the brandy but Bobbie, out of breath and looking very pale.

'I saw your horse downstairs. I say, Marcus — ' He stopped, staring. 'You're wounded!'

'Nothing! A scratch. Lady Theakston's putting me back in order.'

'Thank God! I say, Marcus, what's happened? We heard the guns. Is it all over?'

'I was just in the middle of telling. No, it's not over. The Prussians have been engaged all day with Boney himself, and we don't know the result of it. We've only had one message from them all day, and that was to say that they did not look for great success, but hoped to stand their ground until nightfall. We've held off Ney and his army, so I suppose you'd call our action a victory, but the French are not destroyed. I don't know what's going to happen next. When the Beau sent me off at nine o'clock the firing had stopped and the French had retired to Frasnes. As far as I know, we were to bivouac for the night at Quatre-Bras. Our men were too done in to move them until the morning.'

'It was a hard-run thing, then?' Bobbie asked.

Marcus nodded. 'I thought, a few times —' He stopped as Rosamund came back in and handed her mother the brandy and the cloths.

Lucy took them and said firmly, 'I'm going to clean this and stitch it for you Marcus, and if you know what's good for you, you'll tell us everything from the beginning, instead of rambling about in this idiotic, piecemeal way. You didn't take a blow on the head, by any chance? Well then, tell us properly, in order, or I might let my mind wander and sew a few buttons on you by mistake.'

It was a way of keeping his mind off the operation — because the edges of the wound were swollen, it would be difficult and painful to stitch. Marcus turned his eyes resolutely from what she was doing, and told them all he knew about the battle at Quatre-Bras.

'About six o'clock I thought all was lost,' he concluded. 'Our men had been driven out of the Bossu Wood, except for some Brunswickers and Netherlanders, who were lost in the undergrowth on the wrong side of the wood and were out of the action. The French there were heading for the Nivelles road, meaning to outflank us on our right. We'd been driven back in the centre, and the French were attacking all out up the Charleroi road; and we were only holding our left wing by the skin of our teeth against the French cavalry. I thought it was all up with us, I can tell you! But then the Guards arrived, and that turned the tide!'

He glanced around at his spellbound audience. 'They were pretty tired after a march of fifteen hours, but they didn't let that trouble them! The Beau set up a three-fold attack. He put the Guards into the Bossu Wood, and down the centre towards Gemioncourt, and sent two Hanoverian battalions to support the Rifles on our left wing. Well, it was pretty hard fighting, I can tell you; but not long after sunset the French cavalry suddenly vanished, and then the firing stopped, and we realised the French had drawn back.'

'They'd called off the action?' Bobbie asked.

'Had enough,' Marcus said triumphantly. 'As it got dark,

the Beau set our picket-line from Piraumont through Gemioncourt to Petit Pierrepoint, which was virtually the same line that wc were occupying in the morning. We'd retaken all the ground we'd lost, so I suppose you could call it a victory. And then I was sent off with my message.'

During the last sentence his voice suddenly faded, and his face seemed to grey with strain and weariness. There was a silence as Lucy finished bandaging the hand. 'There,' she said at last. 'It'll be as stiff as a board for a day or two, but I can't help that.'

'Thank you, ma'am,' Marcus said. He stared at his hand rather dazedly. 'I suppose I ought to be going.'

She sat back, mechanically sorting her instruments. 'You haven't told us the butcher's bill,' she said in a neutral voice.

There was a brief silence, and every eye was on Marcus. 'Can't be sure at this stage,' he said. 'I'd say we probably lost about five thousand or so. We're in pretty good shape, except for the Highlanders and the 44th — and the Rifles took rather a beating. Of course, the Netherlanders took the brunt of it in the beginning, but it's hard to tell how they fared, because so many of 'em ran away.'

'Oh no — ' Sophie protested softly, and he looked at her sympathetically.

'I'm afraid so — I saw them with my own eyes, heading off up the Nivelles road as fast as they could leg. But the 5th Militia held firm — they had a good officer,' he added kindly.

Sophie's attention sharpened. 'Did you see him?'

'Yes, I saw him some time between five and six — still rallying his men. He's a good soldier,' he added in simple praise.

'Was he — all right?'

'He'd been wounded in the leg, but not seriously,' Marcus said, and Sophie was silent, wondering how those two statements could possibly be reconciled. Her palms were damp, she discovered. The thought of his being hurt filled her with helpless rage and fear. Wounded in the leg? What did that mean? Ball, shell, bayonet, sword? Was he in pain? Had anyone taken care of him? An image came unbidden into her mind of red and green, of blood and leaves. Wounded in a wood. Wounded in the leg. René!

446

'And what about the Tenth?' Lucy had asked at last, still in the same colourless voice.

'He's safe as houses,' Marcus answered the unasked question. 'The Tenth arrived too late to be engaged. In fact, none of our cavalry saw action. But the Guards — ' He stopped, realising what he was about to say was not comforting.

'Yes, what about the Guards?'

'They — they fought like heroes, especially when you think they'd just marched twenty-five miles to reach us. But they never forget their reputation.'

'How bad was it?' Lucy asked bluntly, looking at him now.

Marcus met her eyes. 'They lost heavily, men and officers. I don't know how many. But Burnett was killed, and Lichfield, and Freddy Wykeham, and Harry Pyne. And Ponsonby was wounded. I don't know how badly, but I saw them carry him off the field.'

'Oh God,' Lucy said, turning her face away. Rosamund was staring at him blankly, feeling sick. All those young men she had danced with: her court, whom her mother thought might 'do' for her — all dead? She thought of their gaiety and pride, their laughter and courage, all cut short. In her mind's eye she saw tumbled forms in a green field, heard music fading into silence.

Lucy was thinking of Harry Pyne, who had wanted to dance with her, who had flirted and teased her and tried to persuade her to a curricle race. Harry Pyne dead. And Ponsonby, carried off? She knew what that could mean. From her own experience, she knew how frail the human animal was. Warm flesh tore so easily, fragile limbs shattered irreparably, before the impact of flying metal.

'I'm sorry,' Marcus said. 'I shouldn't have said anything.' He swayed in his seat, and Lucy shook herself and reached out a steadying hand to him.

'I asked you,' she said. He was fainting with fatigue now. 'When did you eat? I don't suppose you remember. I'll get you something.'

'No, thank you, ma'am, I must get back. I shall be looked for. But if you can give me something to take with me — ?'

'Of course. Whatever there is in the kitchen, you are more than welcome to. The servants are all in bed, but I'll see — '

447

'Well, perhaps Rosamund could come down with me on my way out?' Marcus said quickly, looking significantly at his cousin.

Lucy interpreted the look, and yielded. 'Very well. Pack the food up for him, Rosamund, so that it will go in a saddle-bag.'

'Yes, Mama.'

Marcus stood up. 'Thank you for my hand, ma'am. I'm really grateful. I'll send word when I can.' He looked around the assembled company. 'I'm glad you're all together like this. I wish Mama and Bab were with you too. I don't like to think of them being alone.'

'I'll send a note round to your mother in the morning, asking if she'd like to come and stay here,' Lucy said with a last access of heroism. 'Take care of yourself.'

'I will. And thank you.'

In the kitchen, Rosamund set briskly about gathering him some food. 'Bread, I suppose you'll want. What else?' She investigated a pantry. 'There's a round of cold beef here will that do; and half a pie — no, that would never last the journey. You'd better eat that now. Here, sit at the table — there's a knife over there, and at my guess there's mustard in that pot. Now, let me see. Ah, some potted shrimps. And here's sausage, and something that looks like a piece of smoked bacon.'

Marcus sat at the scrubbed table and looked at the pie she had placed before him, still in its dish, with no more than a momentary hesitation before hunger overwhelmed him, and he cut into it ravenously. As she had divined, the mustard was exactly what his palate craved after a day of blood and smoke and gunpowder reek. He found himself eating like a starving peasant, and checked himself.

'And what else?' Rosamund murmured, rummaging. 'What about some wine?' Marcus made an indeterminate sound through a mouthful of pie, and she turned to him and smiled suddenly, and he thought how beautiful she looked in the wavering light, tall and golden like a goddess. 'I know where the butler keeps the keys!' she said. 'No, it's all right — eat your pie. I'll be back in a minute.'

She returned as he was scooping up the last crumbs of

pastry, and caught him licking mustard off the knife. He blushed a little at his crudity, but she didn't seem to have noticed. 'I've got you two bottles of claret, and a cloth to stop them clinking. I'll put the rest of this stuff in a bag. Are you sure it's enough?'

'Wonderful, thank you! I shall feast royally on that. But, Rosy,' he went on quickly as she turned away, 'I wanted to talk to you before I left again — '

'Yes, I know you did,' Rosamund said neutrally. 'I suppose it's about Tantony?'

He looked a little surprised. 'How did you guess?'

'How? Why — what else could it be? You said the Rifles had taken a pounding. You'd better tell me the worst straight away. Is he dead?'

'Dead? No, not that I know of. I haven't seen him since about three o'clock, before they had really joined action.'

She stared at him, mystified. 'Then — what did you want to tell me? Why did you want to speak to me alone?'

'Oh, I see, you thought — ?' Enlightenment came to him. 'I'm sorry if I worried you. It isn't that at all.' He looked a little awkward, not knowing quite how to begin, and fidgeted with the edge of his bandage a moment. 'Sit down with me for a moment,' he pleaded. She obeyed in silence, sitting opposite him and resting her hands on the table. He looked at them, avoiding her eyes. 'Ros, I've been such a fool,' he began at last, unpromisingly.

'Yes,' she agreed. 'But what has that to do with me?'

He looked up, searching her face. 'You're really promised to Tantony?'

'He asked me to marry him, and I accepted his offer,' Rosamund said neutrally.

'But it hasn't been announced?'

'No,' she assented.

'Then you might change your mind?' She didn't answer. 'Dearest Rosy, it's sometimes hard to see what's right under your own nose. I've always been fond of you, but I didn't realise how fond. We've always been such good friends, and then I went away, and — I'm not saying this very well, am I?' She waited, neither encouraging nor discouraging. His left hand curled itself into a fist of determination. 'What I mean

449

is, now that I do see things in their proper light at last, I'm afraid I may be too late.'

It was plainly meant as a question, and looking at his handsome, familiar face, Rosamund couldn't quite bring herself to give him the negative her engagement to Tantony demanded. Her feelings for Tantony, still largely undefined, were very new. She had loved Marcus for so long — did love him still — and the old tug at her heart and the old associations were hard to resist. More than anything, she didn't want to hurt him.

'Marcus,' she said gently, 'my mother would never agree to a marriage between us. Never would have and never will.'

'Even if it was what you wanted?'

'She likes you well enough, but you've no title and no fortune — '

'Tantony hasn't — '

'Tantony has sufficient fortune to support me, and for reasons of her own, Mother is prepared to overlook his being a commoner. But she wouldn't accept you, so you might as well put the whole thing out of your head, as I have.'

She knew the last words were a mistake as she said them, but it was too late to bite them back. His eyes took on a look she would sooner not have seen. 'Then — you did think about it?'

She met his eyes steadily. 'I've been in love with you since I was twelve years old. You ought to know that. I suppose all little girls think about marriage, but it's only daydreaming. It's time I put those childish games behind me.'

She stood up, and he stood too, and reached out for her hand, which he carried to his lips. 'It needn't be only daydreaming. Let me hope, that's all I ask.'

She sighed. 'Marcus — ' she began.

'I have to go,' he said. 'Thank you for everything, dear Rosy. When all this is over, when I come back, I may just find the means to give Tantony a run for his money, good man though he is — if you'll permit me?'

He was a soldier, wounded, tired, going back to the front to face God knew what trials and horrors. She didn't have it in her to deny him whatever comfort there might be in that contemplation.

450

'Take care of yourself,' was all she said.

Larosse woke on the morning of the seventeenth to the sound of musket-fire. He opened his eyes, and looked directly up into the grey sky of before-dawn, where a few stars still shone pallidly down on him with the serenity of their detachment from human trouble. He was lying flat on his back, and moving one hand, he encountered cold wet grass and stalks of straw. Despite his cloak and blanket, he was chilly with that particular demoralising cold one feels after sleeping all night on the bare ground.

There was no part of him which did not ache, and he felt more tired than he had ever been in his life before. For a moment even the sound of gunfire was not enough to drive away the desire to sleep a little longer. His eyes closed; he drifted. Then someone nearby groaned, and muttered, 'What's all that firing?' and Larosse was startled into full wakefulness. He opened his eyes and tried to sit up, and for a moment he couldn't move at all. He was stiff — stiff and cold — and when he managed at last to push himself up, the first bending of his leg woke saw-teeth of pain in his right thigh.

Well, that would grow numb again, given time. He stood up and looked about him. The ground was covered in dark shapes — his own men, hunched in sleep, and further off a company of Nassauers, recognisable by the white tops to their shakoes. They were in a field to the north and east of the cross-roads itself, between the Brussels road and the Nivelles road, and a little way north of that damned wood. The field was bound by raised banks, on top of which grew elder-bushes, and away to his right he knew there was a small cottage, though he couldn't see it yet.

The firing was distant, he discovered, and in the grey murk he could see nothing of it, not even the powder-flashes. From the direction, he assumed it was a clash between the French and Allied skirmishers, in the forward positions in front of their respective picket-lines. They had probably started popping away at each other as soon as it grew light enough to pick out the moving shapes. They were down there in the dip between Quatre-Bras and Frasnes — where he and his men had been positioned at dawn yesterday. What a long and

451

deathly day it had been — and here they were, back where they had started!

Well, they had held off the French, that was one thing; and he had managed to keep together two companies of the 5th Militia, although they were much reduced in numbers. That was something of an achievement. He might make soldiers of them yet. It remained to be seen what today would bring. Would the French re-engage? What had happened to the Prussians? If they had been defeated and were even now in retreat, today might be the day the Emperor turned his attention to Wellington's battered army and finished them off. Today might be the day that he died at the hand of one of his own former compatriots. That would be an irony.

He became aware of hunger, and the pressing need to relieve himself. He got his cold feet and stiff legs into motion, and limped away to find a hedge first. And after that, breakfast, he thought. A soldier had a duty to keep himself in fighting trim. His servant was sleeping on his pack nearby. He could come back and rouse him — but it would take time to get a fire going. He might just take a walk about and see if anyone was astir. Perhaps in one of the cottages he might find a peasant woman with a porrage-pot on the go. He would back himself to charm a bowlful out of any woman who walked the earth. In the Peninsula he had never needed to resort to harsh tactics to get himself fed.

But first, the elder-bushes. As he approached, he saw something pale lying underneath them, and a moment later was looking down at a dead and naked man. He was lying on his back, his arms flung out behind his head as though he had been frozen in the act of surrender. He was very young. His skin was unblemished and white, his face hardly more tanned than his body, and his moustache was a very new and experimental affair. He had worn his fair, curly hair rather long. His eyes were half open, a dull shine under the long fair eyelashes; his lips were parted, and there was blood on his teeth and chin.

Larosse stood in silent contemplation. Death must have come to him instantly, for there was a small round hole just under his left breast, and he had hardly bled: only coughed once, and died. Yesterday morning he had been someone's darling son, and, to judge by his fair good looks, probably the beloved of some young woman — maybe more than one. Yesterday he had been warm and alive and full of hope; now he lay naked under a hedge, waiting for corruption and the carrion-eaters to make an end of him.

His clothing and equipment had gone to the last stitch: he lay dead, in the end, without even his name. The fond mother and the tender young woman would never know for sure what had happened to him. They would wait and hope, perhaps for years, that he would make his way back to them at last; they might never believe, indeed, that he was dead, and the betrayal of his absence would become in the end a reproach. He thought of the young Portuguese woman with the baby on her hip. Had she waited for a man to come back to her? Had he ever come? What men do to women, he thought, is very little less bad than what they do to each other.

He turned away and went further down the bank, out of sight of the pale body. After the elder-bushes, he climbed down on to the road, and walked along it towards the cross-roads themselves. A figure was standing there, colourless in the grey light. Hunger and cold and fatigue had made him jumpy, he knew, but for a moment it seemed that the figure had no face, and he paused, his heart crowding up into his throat with superstitious fear. It was Death, that nebulous, blank-faced shape, and it had come for him.

Then it coughed, and he saw that it was only a man in a greatcoat, and that he had seemed faceless because his back was to him. Larosse walked forward again, and the man turned. It was Captain Morland.

'Hullo! I came to see what the firing was,' Marcus said, 'but there's nothing to be seen in this damned murk. How's the leg?'

'Stiff,' Larosse said. 'Wellington spent the night at Genappe, I understand? Is he back now?'

'Yes, and receiving reports. The cavalry has been coming in all night, and we've now got our full complement. Six brigades — forty-five thousand men.'

'Would to God we'd had them yesterday.'

Marcus eyed him with sympathy. 'It's hard to get raw recruits to stand up to cavalry charges. Instinct makes a man

453

run from a herd of galloping horses.'

Larosse shrugged the sympathy away. He glanced at Marcus's bandaged hand, and said, 'That looks like a neat job. You must have had a surgeon at Genappe.'

Marcus smiled. 'Better than that, sir — I had Lady Theakston look at it for me.'

Larosse's attention sharpened. 'You've been to Brussels? You've seen them all?' Marcus nodded, seeing the hunger in the older man's eyes. 'You saw Sophie?'

'I told her you were well — that you had been wounded, but not seriously. They were all sitting up, waiting for news of the battle. At least they are all together,' he added, vaguely comforting. 'Lady Theakston is going to invite my mother and sister to stay with her.'

'Yes,' said Larosse. It was growing lighter, and the fog was beginning to lift. Gradually the scene formed itself around them, the edges of things appearing as though they were being drawn on a blank background by some unseen hand. Buildings took shape — a wall, a roof, a gutter with a sparrow silhouetted black on grey, its feathers fluffed against the dawn chill; then a hedge, each twig rimed with mist-beads, a tree, a sign-post. The road rolled back, extending itself downhill before them, and to the left along the walls of the farm towards the pale luminosity of the rising sun. Somewhere nearby a cockerel crowed and went on crowing; more distantly a horse whinneyed as if in answer, and two troopers suddenly appeared, coming down the road with leather buckets, looking for water — first sign that the cavalry was present. One of them coughed and sniffed, and the sound echoed flatly back off the wall of fog.

Down the hill in the Charleroi direction the growing light and the gradual lifting of the mist was revealing little by little the plain over which the worst of the battle had been fought. It was an unkind hand that would raise that curtain, Larosse thought: across acres of trampled corn lay the discarded bodies of men and horses, humped in the stillness of death, as nameless and useless as the naked boy under the hedge. Close to the cross-roads, not far in front of them, there were so many they lay in heaps, like rags — Highlanders and cuirassiers all dead together, undifferentiated now that their bloody

454

struggle was over. Even as they watched, a crow flew down with a black flutter of wings to land in the road with a bounce. It eyed them with a cautious, bright eye, yarked its raucous cry, and then hopped up lightly on to the curving chestnut flank of a fallen horse.

Larosse turned away. 'I was going to try to find some breakfast,' he said abruptly.

'I've got some food that I brought from Brussels, sir,' Marcus said cordially. 'If you would like to share it, you're very welcome.'

Larosse thought briefly of the peasant woman, the fire and the porrage, and then put the images aside. 'You're very kind,' he said. 'If you can spare it — '

'There's plenty,' Marcus said. A few minutes later they were sitting in the shelter of a wall facing the rising sun, with the food and wine from Lady Theakston's kitchen between them. Marcus paused in the middle of tearing a loaf of bread in half to yawn hugely, and then gave a rueful grin. 'I'm sorry — I haven't slept yet. I only got back from Brussels about half an hour ago.'

'You've been riding all night?'

'I was sent off last night with a message for Daddy Hill, and he sent me straight back with his answer. When I reported to the Beau, he told me to go away and get a couple of hours sleep. I thought I'd gone beyond the stage of being tired — you know how you can — ' Larosse nodded. 'Just now, however — ' He yawned again.

'You had better get some sleep as soon as you've eaten,' Larosse said. 'You never know when you will be called on to exert yourself again; and a soldier's responsibility is always to be ready.'

'I don't think the French will attack this morning,' Marcus said. 'They must be fully as tired as our men.'

'Is there any news of the Prussians yet?'

'There was none when I reported to the Beau. He decided to send someone in the direction of Ligny to try to find out what happened there yesterday. Of course, we don't know where either the Prussians or the French are at the moment, so it's a risky business, but he's sent Colonel Theakston with a troop of the 10th to escort Gordon, so that's all right. Theakston's as wily as a fox — he won't get caught.'

He paused to eat some beef, and Larosse said reflectively, 'I suppose it cannot be good news. If the Prussians had destroyed the French they would have let us know by now, perhaps even joined us.'

'That's what I thought. But it needn't be so bad. If they did as well as us, they might still have the French between them and us. The worst thing is not knowing. I volunteered to go myself — I'm anxious to know whether my old tutor is safe, you know — but the Beau wouldn't hear of it, and sent me away to sleep.'

'Quite right.'

'The main thing is that we still hold the road to Brussels.'

'Yes,' Larosse assented. He knew, as Marcus did, that if the Prussians had lost the previous day and retreated along the expected line, towards Liège, the whole of the French force would soon turn its attention on Wellington's army. Yesterday they had only just managed to hold off Ney's attack; today they might find themselves facing the united French under the Emperor himself — and even with the addition of the English cavalry, what chance was there that they could prevail? It was no comfort to Larosse that he had been right all along. He would sooner have been wrong, victorious and alive, and now on his way back to Sophie and a happy future.

Marcus retired soon afterwards to a sheltered spot to sleep, giving orders to his servant to wake him the moment there was any news, or he was asked for, or the French looked like moving. His servant, being fond of the captain, took a generous view of these orders, and so Marcus slept through all the morning's excitement and activity.

Lord Theakston and his troop arrived back at Quatre-Bras at half-past seven, to report that they had come upon the French picket-line at Marbais, half-way between Quatre-Bras and Ligny. They pursued them a little way and managed to capture one of them, who readily told them that the Prussians were heading northwards on the road to Tilly; and hurrying in that direction themselves, they came upon the Prussian rearguard under the command of General Ziethen. He gave

them news of the previous day's events: after a ferocious
battle lasting eight hours, the Prussian lines had finally been
broken by Napoleon's forces, and the Prussians had been put
to flight.

Wellington listened gravely to this report. The Prussians
had slightly outnumbered Napoleon's force and ought to have
prevailed, but he had seen for himself how badly Gneisenau
had disposed his troops. With the Prussians in flight and the
French still intact, his own army was in even more danger
than on the previous day.

'The worst of it, sir,' Theakston continued, 'is that they've
lost Blücher.' Wellington looked up sharply. 'It seems that at
about eight o'clock he led a charge in person against the
Imperial Guard, to relieve the infantry who were hard
pressed. His horse was shot under him and he disappeared
under the mêlée and never returned.'

'So Gneisenau is in charge now,' Wellington said. That was
bad news, and fully accounted for the Prussian retreat.

'Yes, sir,' Gordon said, taking up the story. 'General
Ziethen said that he called a wayside conference to decide on
a course of action. I'm afraid they elected to retreat to Liège
and onward to the Rhine; but by the light of torches they had
difficulty in reading their maps, and the only town-name they
could find was Wavre, so they're heading that way. I suppose
from there they'll go on to Louvain and then homewards.'

There was a brief silence as Wellington considered the situation. 'We cannot risk being outflanked. We shall have to
withdraw,' he said at last, with decision. His senior officers
were too well schooled to protest, but the protest was palpable
in their silence. He looked round the ring of faces. 'There's
nothing else to be done. I suppose in England they will say we
have been licked, but I can't help it. As the Prussians are gone
back, we must go back too.'

'Will you give the order to move now, sir?' asked de
Lancey.

'Ney's men haven't shewn any sign of moving, have they?'

'No, sir,' said Lord Fitzroy Somerset. 'Apart from the skirmishing between the lines, all's quiet.'

'Then we'll let the men cook their breakfasts first. They'll
march better on full stomachs. See to it, will you, Fitzroy?

And then you'd better ask Lord Uxbridge to come and see me to discuss the covering of the retreat.'

At about noon, Lord Theakston was riding back from Wellington's Headquarters to his battalion, which was stationed out by the Cherry Wood on the left wing. As he left the cross-roads on the Namur road, he saw Marcus sitting on a stone beside the road being shaved by his servant, and called out a greeting to him.

Marcus looked up, recognising Magnus Apollo fractionally before his rider, and stood up with a cheerful, if soapy, grin. Magnus viewed the lathered face and the white towel around Marcus's neck with deep affront, snorted, and walked backwards several steps.

'Good morning, sir! Fine day again!'

'Too hot,' Danby said. 'Oppressive. Storm on the way, I shouldn't wonder. What're you doing shaving at this hour?'

'I was up all night, sir, and my man let me sleep in. Can you tell me what's happening, Colonel? It looks as though we're retreating.'

'Don't look so blue — it's not what it seems,' said Danby. Having persuaded Magnus that shaving-soap was not necessarily lethal to horses, he relaxed a little in the saddle, eyeing the younger man with sympathy. 'You've slept through all the fun — and missed seeing Major Firth, I'm sorry to say.'

'He was here?' Marcus said, disappointed.

'He came in from Blücher at about nine o'clock — tremendous relief all round, I can tell you, because we'd heard Blücher was lost! But it seems when his horse was shot and fell, the old fellow was trapped by the leg underneath it. Most amazing escape! The French and Prussian cavalry charged back and forth over the top of him, and he got kicked and generally trampled until he was only half conscious. But one of his aides stayed nearby, and when it was all over he crept back and dragged Blücher out, and the two of them got away. Firth said he caught up with the Prussian army at Mellery, bruised from head to toe and thoroughly shaken up, but otherwise unharmed. Boney will never know what a prize he missed!'

'No, sir,' Marcus grinned appreciatively. 'So it wasn't

Blücher who ordered the retreat?'

'No, it was Gneisenau. Old Forwards wasn't having any of it. Firth said he dosed himself up with gin and garlic — ' Marcus made a suitable face. 'Kill or cure!' Danby agreed. 'Then he said he'd given his word to Wellington that he'd help him, and he wasn't going back on it. Sent Firth to tell the Beau that they'd regroup at Wavre and wait to hear what he wanted 'em to do.'

'I see, sir. So we're falling back rather than retreating.'

'Precisely. The Beau sent Firth back to say that we'll halt at Mont St-Jean, which is on a level with Wavre, and take on Boney, provided Blücher can send at least one corps. So we've been marching the men off since ten o'clock. The Duke's been sitting by the roadside watching 'em and reading the papers, cool as a melon. When I left him just now, he said, "Well, that's the last of the infantry gone, and I don't care now - Ney may do as he likes." Thing is, Ney's done nothing — not a movement from them. Even the skirmishing stopped about half-past nine, and now they might be asleep, for all we can tell.'

'It's a good day for sleeping, sir,' Marcus said. The midday heat really was oppressive, drying the lather on his face. Magnus was sweating, attracting the maddening little black flies that they had called 'thunder-flies' when they were children, and there wasn't the slightest breeze to disperse them. 'I think you're right about that storm.'

'Know I am,' Danby said, pointing northwards. 'Look at those clouds! But it's my opinion Ney's waiting for orders, and Boney ain't sending 'em. From what we got from the French picket we took this morning, Boney didn't order a pursuit of the Prussians last night. Just settled down for the night in a farmhouse. I'm beginning to believe he's getting too old for this game — losing his grip. If he'd joined up with Ney and attacked us this morning, we'd have had it. As it is — '

'We've had a lucky escape, sir,' Marcus said thoughtfully.

'We have. Well, I'd better get back to my men. We're covering the retreat, of course. Harry Uxbridge is hoping against hope the Frogs come after us — frettin' because we missed the battle yesterday!' He eyed Marcus sympathetically. 'Sorry you missed Firth. He sent you his regards — says he's

459

well and unhurt. Where were you last night, by the by?'

Marcus grinned suddenly. 'I took a message to General Hill, sir, and came back via Brussels.' He lifted his hand. 'Sampled her ladyship's handiwork — half a dozen stitches, as neat as needlework.'

Danby smiled fondly. 'Oh, she's up to her old tricks, is she? Was she well?'

'Anxious, sir, as is natural. I'm afraid she was quite relieved when I told her you hadn't arrived in time to see action!'

'So am I, young Marcus! Saving m'self for the big one — I don't ambition to fight in every paltry scrap you fellows set up!' His smile disappeared abruptly. 'Damned awful thing about the Guards — Ponsonby and Pyne and the rest. Fine young men. Ponsonby was a superb dancer, too. It'll break her ladyship's heart.'

'I saw Ponsonby carried off, sir. Is he — ?'

'Both legs smashed. Surgeon took 'em off last night, but he died this morning. Told Sir William myself about an hour ago.' He stared at Magnus's mane thoughtfully. 'Never thought to see him cry. It was the damnedest thing.' He gathered Magnus's reins, and looked at Marcus meaningfully. 'Don't you get yourself killed. Too many people a good deal too fond of you.'

He rode off, leaving Marcus with plenty to think about, especially that last, enigmatical phrase.

The black clouds on the horizon came up quickly and the skies darkened to twilight, just as the French began to move at last, not only from Frasnes, but from Ligny, too, along the Namur road which the 10th and 18th Hussars were covering. Two guns were drawn up across the road, and they opened fire on the French cavalry just as the first blinding flash of lightning seared across the sky, outlining the trees and rooftops in violet-blue against the plum-dark cloud. There was a thunderclap so violent it made even the stalwart artillery horses start, and then the air stirred with the sweet smell of approaching rain. The French horse were turning northward to outflank the Hussars and the order was shouted to turn about in threes to intercept them. There was another flash and another crash, and then the skies opened. The rain fell

460

vertically in a silver-white torrent, bouncing off the *pavé* with a noise like drumming hooves, filling the ditches in minutes to rushing, gurgling races.

It was impossible to see very far. Every vista was distorted by the refraction of falling water, and the artificial twilight was reinforced by the mist of drifting cloud. The temperature dropped as the rain cooled the air, and underfoot the dust turned to slippery mud, which was soon churned into deep, clogging mire by tramping men and horses. The rain favoured the Allies more than the French, who had to pursue over ground already hopelessly cut up by their quarry as the two armies struggled towards Brussels.

At Genappe the road narrowed almost to single file to cross the river by an old stone bridge, and the delay in crossing allowed the pursuing French to catch up for a while. Uxbridge sent a detachment of the 7th Hussars to hold off the leading French lancers, and there was a brief engagement. The Hussars were repulsed with some losses, but when the lancers pursued, they were met by the massive men and horses of the Life Guards, and were driven back and badly mauled. After that the French did not press their pursuit very hard. The going was, in any case, increasingly bad, and except on the *pavé* the mud was soon hock-deep. Both sides gradually drew their forces up onto the road as the false twilight blended into the real one.

By half-past six the Allies had reached the ridge at Mont St-Jean, wet and cold and weary. Wellington concealed the bulk of the troops on the reverse slope as usual. Evidently unsure of the situation, the French paused about three-quarters of a mile short of the slope, drew up four batteries, and opened fire. The batteries of the Third Division replied briefly, and having established that the Allies were there in force, the French ceased fire.

It was still raining heavily and almost dark. The Allied army set up its bivouacs, and Wellington retired for the night to Waterloo, a village about two miles closer to Brussels; the French were still tramping in to gather at their halting-place, marked by an inn on the road called La Belle Alliance. It was too late and too dark and too wet for there to be any further action that night.

In Brussels, the household at the Rue Ducale had slept more peacefully than most, being in possession of at least some information. But the morning of the seventeenth saw the streets thronging with both Belgians and British in a state of muted panic, as rumour followed rumour of a defeat the day before. The fugitives from the Netherlandish battalions brought the worst tales of woe, perhaps to cover their own shame, galloping through the town crying that the Allied army was in full retreat on Brussels, with the French fiercely pursuing. The Morland ladies did what they could to quash such rumours, and to advise those anxious Britons who enquired that there was no need to flee. All the same, quite a few of the visitors began hastily packing, and by noon there was a procession of carriages and carts making its way out of the northern gate.

The stories of the terrible carnage amongst the Highlanders and the Guards caused more concern; and when certain news came in of the defeat and flight of the Prussians, even the Morland women found it difficult to remain resolute.

'Do you think we will have to leave?' Roberta asked anxiously of no-one in particular. Blücher was missing, and his personal command had been badly cut up: she had the most urgent need for news of her man. 'I suppose the Duke will have to retire now.'

'He said all along he would not stop the French at Quatre-Bras,' Lucy reminded her. 'Don't you remember Danby told me that he said to Richmond at the ball that he would fall back on Mont St-Jean and make a stand there? Nothing has changed, Rob. There's no need to panic.'

'Plainly, many people do not agree with you,' Héloïse said quietly from her place at the window. Below in the street people were loading belongings on to carts, crying to each other in panic, some even walking about aimlessly, dazed with fear.

Lucy shrugged. 'We're better off without them. The Duke will send word if there's any need to evacuate the city. We'll know in plenty of time. You may do as you please, but I shall wait here until I am ordered to leave.'

Héloïse smiled faintly. 'No need to roar at us like a lion, dear Lucy. We won't let you down. I suppose,' she added hesitantly, 'there will be wounded to tend from yesterday's engagement.'

'Yes,' Lucy said briefly. 'They may begin to arrive at any time. There at least I may be useful.'

The hospital carts began to come in around noon, overtaking those wounded who had been stumbling along on their own legs all night. Soon the streets of the town were filled with wounded men, dying men, dead men, and with civilians shocked out of their selfish concern to do what they could to help them. Lucy began as a good general should by directing her troops, setting the least useful, or the most squeamish, to soothing the brows of the dying, writing their last letters to their loved ones at their dictation, and to fetching and carrying and searching out supplies. But soon the worse wounded were arriving at the door, desperately needing her skills.

'I must leave this task to you,' she said to Rosamund, who had been at her side all the time. 'You see how I have been arranging things. You — '

'No, Mama,' Rosamund said. 'I'm going to help you in the house.' She was pale from some of the sights she had witnessed, but she met her mother's eyes steadily. 'You need helpers who won't faint at the sight of blood.'

Lucy looked at her doubtfully. 'You don't know what I shall be called upon to do,' she said.

'Yes, I do,' Rosamund said. 'I know, and I'm not afraid. I mean to be where I can be of the most help.' Still Lucy hesitated, and Rosamund added, 'Lots of these men are from the Guards, Mama.'

'Very well,' Lucy said. 'But someone must direct things, or there'll be muddle and waste.'

'I will,' said Roberta. 'Go on, Lucy, to your work. Bobbie and I will manage things here.'

Héloïse was waiting for Lucy at the house when she returned, and Lucy was brought to recognise, not for the first time, the real value of her sister-in-law. When the wounded had started to arrive at the house, the servants had been overcome with horror and had refused to have anything to do with them, and soon there was a budding mutiny, led by the butler, who proposed to bar the doors and close the shutters, as if it were a seige. Hélöıse had calmed the servants and quelled the mutiny by the force of her personality, and had set the footmen to carrying the wounded men and the maids to fetching hot water and bandages, while she and Sophie and Marie did what they could for the poor sufferers. She had held the staff together through her example of calm, but her relief was overt when Lucy came in.

'Thank Heaven you have come! There is so little I know how to do — only to bandage, and sometimes that seems of little help.'

'It's all right,' Lucy said briskly. 'Rosamund will help you now. I shall start operating with Docwra to help me — she knows my ways. You and Rosamund must decide who needs attention first, and send them in to me, and see that the others are made as comfortable as possible. I wish to God I had more laudanum!'

It was a hideous experience to women unused to dealing with such brutal realities. Even Lucy, whose lifelong interest in things medical had given her more experience than many a physician or surgeon, was sickened by the horrible wounds which came before her, and more than once had to stop and turn her face away, and breathe deeply while she waited for her hands to stop shaking. It was more than twenty years since she had dealt with battle-wounds and she had forgotten the horror of them. No natural accident — no fall from a building or carriage, no kick from a horse or goring from a steer, no scald from an upset pot or burn from a falling brand — could produce such unnatural injuries as the cannon-shell, the musket-ball, the sword, the bayonet or the exploding rocket. She amputated shattered limbs, dug out musket-balls and fragments of metal, and sewed up hideous rents in human flesh which had never been intended to withstand such insult; and only her interest in her work and Docwra's stolid support kept her steady.

But in some ways it was worse for the other women, for they had no experience, no skill, and no interest to blunt the effect of the pain and blood and disgusting wounds. Héloïse, as lifelong mistress of a household, had learnt to deal with

464

everyday minor injuries — the bruise, the scald, the gash, the splinter — but to examine and deal with the wounds of these men bent her out of her nature. Her terrible pity, while it increased her suffering, prevented her from running away — that, and the need to save Sophie and Marie from the worst of the sights.

Rosamund, she soon learned, did not need to be saved. Whatever she thought or felt, Rosamund did not give in to it. Her white face set, her lips rigidly closed, she went unflinchingly about the job. She picked splinters and scraps of cloth and gold lace out of wounds, washed away caked blood, bandaged, splinted, soothed the suffering and comforted the dying. She even managed to smile for one poor soldier delirious with pain who thought she was his mother, and to speak cheerfully to those who needed encouragement.

Going to the kitchen at one time for more water, she found Sophie coming out from one of the sculleries, her face green-white and damp, her hair clinging limply to her forehead. She had plainly just been sick, and she looked at Rosamund with enormous eyes, her lips trembling.

'Oh, Cousin, it's so terrible! The men — their wounds!' She put out her hands shakily, and the tears began to roll helplessly from her eyes. 'And you do so much more than me. How do you bear it?'

Rosamund shook her head. 'I don't know. I think of my mother, and how brave she is, and how she does things no other woman would do. I think of Ponsonby and Pyne and all the other poor boys we danced with. I think of who it *might* have been, Sophie, and isn't.' She caught Sophie's hands, and they clung to each other a moment, while Sophie battled with her tears. 'I must go,' Rosamund said. 'I'm wanted.'

Sophie drew back. 'Yes, of course. I'm all right now,' she said as firmly as she could make herself. 'I shan't cry. I shan't. It isn't René. But, oh, Rosamund,' she blurted out helplessly, 'do you think he's all right?'

Rosamund paused in the act of hurrying away to look at her cousin with quick sympathy, and managed a faint, wry smile. 'Yes, I'm sure he is,' she said kindly.

The sense of unreality caused by the unnatural things they

were doing was increased by the artificial twilight of the rain-clouds, and the violence of the rainstorm that followed. The women lost their sense of time and laboured on, growing more exhausted with their exertions and their strained nerves, until it seemed that they were living in the middle of a strange and hideous dream from which they could not escape.

Roberta came in in the middle of the afternoon to help, and told them that the violence of the rain had slowed the influx of wounded.

'I don't know if they are sheltering somewhere outside the city, or if they are simply dying on the road before they can get here, but at all events I am not needed out there.' She was concerned at the evident weariness of her friends, and particularly of Lucy. 'You must rest — you'll knock yourself up if you go on like this.'

'How can I rest?' Lucy said shortly. 'I'm needed.'

'You must eat to keep up your strength.'

'When there are no more wounded to attend to, I'll rest and eat. Now go away, Rob. You're in my light.'

Roberta felt it wiser to leave her for the time being, and persuaded the others to rest in turn and eat something, for none of them had stopped since before midday. And as it began to grow dark, the wounded finally stopped arriving, and Roberta went into Lucy's room again and obliged her to come out.

'I've got food ready for you in the kitchen, and hot water preparing, and you're to come now and eat, and then I shall see that you have a bath. There's nothing else for you to do at the moment.'

'I must clean my instruments,' Lucy said, but it was only the stubbornness of exhaustion.

'Docwra will do them.'

'Docwra's even more tired than I am.'

'Then I'll do them. For Heaven's sake, Lucy!'

Lucy managed a slow smile, the first in a long while. 'No, it's all right. I'll do them later. Take me away, Rob. I'm so tired I can hardly stand.'

'You've done entirely too much.'

Lucy shook her head. 'I've done what had to be done. There was no-one else to do it.'

466

It sounded calm and sensible, but as Roberta offered her arm for support, she found that Lucy was trembling all over like an exhausted horse at the end of a race, and she frowned. It was too much for a woman, even such a woman as Lucy, she thought — and she had said as much to Bobbie more than once that day.

Fortunately, help was at hand. Bobbie had not been idle, and when Lucy had finished eating, while Roberta was trying to persuade her that she need not check on her patients until after she had bathed, he came into the kitchen, accompanied by a stranger in civilian clothes. It was a young man, rather gangling, with a long neck and a prominent Adam's apple. His clothes were old and rather shabby; but his face was intelligent and sensitive, and he looked about him with alert and eager eyes.

'This is Franz Edler, ma'am,' he said to Lucy. 'I found him at Headquarters, enquiring for Dr Brugmans, so I snatched him away. I'm sure he's just what you need.'

'What are you talking about?' Lucy asked dully.

Edler spoke for himself. 'You are Lady Theakston? I am honoured, madame, to make your acquaintance! I have heard so much about you, and, to be honest, I didn't believe half of it. But from what I've seen and heard since I entered this house, it was less than the truth. You have done miracles; and if I may help you, I shall deem it a privilege.'

'How can you help me? Who are you? Bobbie, if this is some joke of yours — '

'No joke, madame,' said Edler. 'I am a physician — or nearly so. I have finished my study at the university, and I was walking wards when this conflict began, and so I came here to see if I could help. It took me a long time, because I had to walk, but here I am, just in time, you see. You may trust me, madame — I am very good.'

She looked at his face, and then at his hands, and slowly she relaxed.

'I don't know why,' she said, 'but I believe you. You had better walk *my* wards, and acquaint yourself with the problems, Dr Edler, and I hope you know better than me what to do. Meanwhile, Rob,' she finished, dragging herself stiffly to her feet, 'I think I shall go and have that bath you spoke about. It would be nice to smell like a woman again.'

Despite the uncertainty of the situation, everyone was so tired that they anticipated no trouble in sleeping, and retired at a very early hour. With Dr Edler to take over responsibility for the wounded in the house, Lucy felt able to give in to her weariness, and went to her room, where the indefatigable Docwra, who must have been as tired as her mistress, insisted on helping her to undress.

Lucy was submitting to having her hair brushed when there was a scratching at the door. Weary as she was, Lucy at once made to rise. 'That'll be a message from Edler, I suppose.'

'You sit still, my lady. I'll go — and if it's not important, I'll send 'em away with a flea in the ear,' Docwra said firmly. She went and opened the door a forbidding crack, but after one glance flung it welcomingly wide and turned to her mistress with a beaming smile. Lucy was across the room in three steps, and an instant later was locked in a passionate but very damp embrace.

'Danby! Oh, Danby!' was all she managed to say.

Danby, while holding her tightly against him, managed to catch Docwra's eye across his wife's shoulder and said, 'I can't stay long, but I'm devilish hungry. Can you arrange something for me?'

'I'll bring you up a tray, sir,' Docwra said, beaming with delight as she departed.

'Are you hurt?' was the first thing Lucy asked, closely followed by 'Have you got Magnus with you?'

'Not a scratch on either of us,' Danby assured her, revelling in the smell of her skin and her strong arms around his waist. 'He's a wonderful stayer — made nothing of the going, or the long trek.'

After a while Lucy released herself to survey him critically. 'I don't suppose you have a dry stitch on you. You'd better strip off, and I'll see what I can find.'

'It's a wet night out there,' Danby said. 'Wellington weather, you know — the Beau says it always rains before his engagements.'

Lucy turned sharply. 'Then there's to be an engagement?'

'My money's on it. We've halted for the night at Mont St-Jean, and the French are about a mile away. It's the battlefield the Beau picked out months ago, you know. He won't care to let the Frogs get any closer to Brussels.'

'Is there danger?'

Danby looked at her steadily. 'You know there is. If the Prussians send us help, we ought to beat Boney — but no battle's won until it's won. The Beau's word is, be prepared to leave, but don't leave until he says it's necessary. He thinks it will be all right — but if it's not, he'll give you all notice.'

'I've a house full of wounded,' Lucy pointed out.

Danby grinned. 'So I noticed. You are a trump card!'

Her lips trembled. 'I'm not. It had to be done. But — oh, Danby, it was awful!'

She was in his arms again, and he held her close, stroking her rough curly head. 'Here, here, don't make me wetter than I already am. I know, my darling, I know. You've been wonderfully brave, and they must all be so grateful.'

'What shall I do if we have to evacuate?'

'You leave them, of course. Boney's not such a barbarian as that — he'll have them taken care of. But I don't think it will come to that. I think we'll beat them. We've got the better leader, the better officers, and the better men. All Boney has is numbers.'

Lucy's lapse was only momentary. She had control of herself again, and pushed herself away, saying, 'I must find where Deacon keeps your shirts, before you catch pneumonia.'

Danby looked at her wet, spiky eyelashes with affection. 'In the closet, of course. I'm not so badly off as some of our men. They're sleeping on wet ground under the open sky. I don't envy 'em, poor beggars. But it's amazing how the old veterans manage to make themselves comfortable.'

He sat down and began pulling off his boots. 'They've managed to get fires going, and they're sitting round smoking their pipes and bragging about the hardships of the Peninsular campaign to the poor Johnny Raws. The worst of it is, hardly anyone's got anything to eat. The road to Brussels is blocked with abandoned forage-carts — the Belgian drivers ran off when they heard we were retreating, and there's been quite a bit of plundering. But we've got a couple of parties out now clearing the way, and we'll get food down to the men by morning. They're better off than the French, at any rate — they've got nothing at all. You know what Boney's like.'

'Yes — he never feeds his men, and I don't suppose there'll be much in the way of pickings in the vicinity.'

As if on cue, Docwra came in with a tray on which she had hastily assembled various leftovers from supper, together with a fresh bottle of claret. 'It's not elegant, sir, but I guessed you'd be in a hurry.'

'Bless you, Docwra — yes, I am. I have to be back in Waterloo by midnight.'

'I'll put up something to take with you, sir, for your breakfast. Can't have you facing them Frenchies on an empty stomach.'

Docwra left them alone, and Danby wasted no time in tackling the food, while Lucy continued to undress him in between bites, and then fetched a towel to rub him down.

'Not so hard!' he cried jerkily. 'You'll make me bite my tongue.'

'Must get your circulation going. Don't be such a baby! Tell me more about the situation. You covered the retreat, I suppose?'

He talked between mouthfuls. 'Uxbridge has shewn his worth — it was a model exercise, and the losses were trifling. It's given our men confidence in him. The 10th hasn't been engaged at all, apart from an exchange of shots right at the beginning. None of ours was hurt. The French didn't pursue very hard, however. It's all quiet now, except for some firing along the picket-lines.'

Lucy frowned, and he shrugged. 'Oh, I know it isn't the thing. We didn't go in for that sort of nonsense in the Peninsula, but there seems to be quite a bit of bad feeling between the vedettes. The Frogs are cold and wet — they haven't even managed to get any fires going. Hungry, too — and when they pop away at our fellows, we can't stop 'em firing back. It'll be a fierce fight tomorrow, I think.'

She was standing before him, and he read her thoughts easily in her face — fear for the outcome, concern for him, then love, then desire. He had no need to tell her, nor did he

470

wish to conceal from her, how hard it was going to be tomorrow, what a close-run thing it was likely to be. They could not depend on the Prussians sending help, or the help arriving if it were sent; and if the Prussians did not come, the Allies would be outnumbered. Not only that, but large numbers of the non-British troops in the Allied army were unreliable; and the Allied artillery had nothing better than nine-pounder guns, against the massive French artillery with its death-dealing twelve-pounders.

He wouldn't have cared to hear the odds, but there was a very good chance that he would die tomorrow, and that this was the last time he would ever see her. That was why he had ridden in from Waterloo — for the chance of two last hours in her company, not for dry clothes or decent food.

And she knew all of that, of course. Her eyes were very bright, and her lips were trembling. He loved her so very much, and the thought of leaving her made him feel quite hollow and sick. He put the tray aside and held out his hands to her.

'Well, now I've got all my clothes off, it seems a shame to waste it, doesn't it?' he said gently.

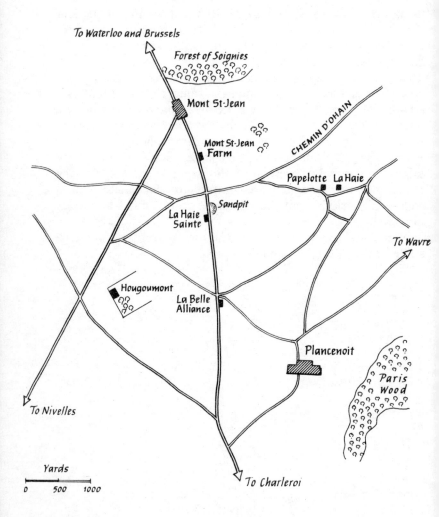

Site of the Battle of Waterloo

CHAPTER EIGHTEEN

The rain stopped at last just as it was beginning to get light, and the men of the Allied army stirred gratefully. They had spent a cold, uncomfortable night on sodden ground, on grass which was so long and lush it held the water as a mattress holds straw. Some of the younger soldiers had dropped off to sleep from sheer exhaustion after the long and gruelling march, but most of the veterans had quickly given up the attempt. They resigned themselves to sitting up, knees drawn up and shoulders hunched to shed the rain, taking what shelter they could from hedges, gun-carriages, horses, or each other, and what comfort they could from smoking their pipes and remembering how much worse it had been in the Peninsula.

When the rain stopped, they managed to get fires going at last, and began to dry their clothes and their arms. The party which had been clearing the Brussels highway and recovering the waggons had finished its work, and there was a welcome distribution of rations — oatmeal, beef, biscuit and spirits. Soon there were camp-kettles of stirabout steaming over fires, and a double issue of gin or rum in the pannikins to warm their chilled stomachs and put heart into them. The sleepers woke and crept miserably to the fires and hunched there like wet birds, yawning and shivering, while the veterans told them cheerfully they were better off than the French, who had to go and search for their breakfast in the inhospitable fields.

Dawn came, pale and muted. The sky was transparent and greenish between watery grey clouds, and the air was damp and cool with the smell of wet leaves; but the veterans snuffed and peered and declared that it would be a fine day. The oppression of the storm had passed away, leaving a drenched and battered but hopeful world. The horses began to whinny and stamp, looking for their troopers and the morning feed, and their simple gladness unconsciously raised everyone's spirits. Someone somewhere whistled the chorus of 'La Bayadère', and from a group around a camp-fire came a burst of raucous laughter; there was a friendly smell of woodsmoke on the air, the sound of muted talk and the clatter of spoons on metal, and the sharp percussion of muskets being fired into the air to clear the damp charges of yesterday.

Some of the young soldiers, between eagerness and apprehension, walked to the edge of the slope to look across the fog-filled valley and see if they could catch a glimpse of old Johnny Crapaud. The ridge of Mont St-Jean was steep on the southward side, facing the enemy, but the reverse slope was shallow — ideal for Wellington's usual tactic of hiding his troops and movements from enemy eyes and artillery. Along the top of the ridge ran an old country lane, the Chemin d'Ohain, lined with thick hedges and sunken in places between banks.

A little to the north the village of Mont St-Jean sat at the junction of the main road to Nivelles with the Brussels–Charleroi highway. The highway therefore ran north and south through the centre of the chosen battlefield. On the road, to the south of the Chemin d'Ohain, was a sandpit, and opposite it a large farmhouse called La Haie Sainte. Then the road ran down into the valley and up again to the second ridge of La Belle Alliance, where the French were beginning to gather. The battleground was mostly open fields, deep in the astonishingly tall rye crop, but the south-western quarter was occupied by a manor house called Hougoumont surrounded with walled gardens and orchards, and sheltered to its south by a small wood.

Now as the sun came up the valley between the ridges was filled with a milky mist, through which the green tops of the dense rye were just beginning to shew. Of the French on the other side there was as yet little to be seen, just the vague mass of dark shapes moving, and occasionally a flash as something metallic — a bayonet-blade, perhaps — caught the rising sun. It was Sunday morning, but there was no sound of bells: just a distant dog barking hollowly from another hillside, and a low murmur, almost below the level of hearing —

474

the indistinguishable, composite sound generated by a great unseen multitude of men.

But now the young soldiers who had come to stare had to scurry back to their companies, for the bugles and drums were sounding the Assembly, and the battalions were forming up under orders to march to their positions. Fires were smoored, camp-kettles hastily emptied, pipes knocked out. Horses caught the excitement from each other and knuckered and stamped and nodded their heads, and there was a squealing and rattling as the artillery companies limbered their guns and harnessed up the teams. The soldiers fell in, buttoning their jackets and straightening their shakoes, some grinning at each other as they dressed the lines, others finding their stomachs suddenly hollow and their palms damp. For more than one, the realisation had come that the June sun strengthening in the pale, damp sky might be the last they ever saw rising.

Between Mont St-Jean and the ridge there was a ruined cottage on the main road where some of the officers of the 95th had spent the night. Now, in the early morning, they lit a fire against the wall and brewed up a huge camp-kettle of tea, sugar and milk. As Wellington came past with his staff on the way to inspect the lines, the colonel offered him some of the sticky, invigorating brew; and when the Duke smilingly accepted, the Rifles officers gathered round delightedly, filling pannikins and handing them out to everyone.

Marcus slipped from his horse and went forward in his turn, to receive his tea from the hand of Captain Tantony.

'How do you do, Morland?' Tantony said pleasantly. 'Did you manage to get any sleep last night?'

'No, I didn't, as a matter of fact — sat up in one of the cottages on the hardest chair ever made, trying to get my clothes dry before a sulky fire of damp birch. I hope you fared better.'

'Hardly — but never mind: have some of our famous brew. And to make it go down the sweeter — how about a little of this in it?' Tantony slid a hand inside his jacket and brought out a small flask.

'What's that? Rum? Stout fellow!'

'Just the thing for a cold morning,' Tantony said, splashing some into the pannikin of tea. 'Hullo! I see you've been injured.'

Marcus sipped the hot, fumy tea gratefully, and glanced at his hand, and shrugged. 'I got mixed up with a bayonet. It's nothing much.' In fact, the hand was giving him a great deal of trouble. As Lucy had warned, it was as stiff as a board, and felt as though it were twice its actual size. Holding the reins with it was both difficult and painful, and he was only too glad that he was able to use his sword left-handed. 'Lady Theakston sewed me up, so all's well,' he concluded.

'You've been in to Brussels, then? You staff-officers are lucky dogs! How was everybody?'

'Very well,' Marcus said. 'You wouldn't expect any despair and panic in that household.'

'Of course not. Have some more tea? You saw Lady Rosamund, I suppose?'

'I did. Thanks.' He accepted the tea, sipped, and looked thoughtfully at Tantony. 'Look here, Tantony,' he said abruptly, 'I like you very much. You're an awfully decent fellow. But the thing is, Lady Rosamund and I grew up together and there was always a sort of notion that we would make a case of it in the end.'

'Was there?' Tantony raised one eyebrow, seeming quite unmoved.

'Well, the thing is,' Marcus went on, a little shaken, 'I understand that the engagement between you and Ros hasn't been announced and — don't take it the wrong way, old fellow, but I think she may change her mind.'

'She told you that?'

Honesty compelled Marcus to take a reef in his enthusiasm. 'Well, no, she didn't exactly *say* — but what I mean is — well, when we get back, after all this is over, I mean to try to take her from you, Tantony, if I can. No offence intended, old fellow.'

Tantony laughed out loud, making one or two heads turn at the sheer good-natured sound of it. 'You are welcome to try, Morland, by any fair means! But you will waste your labour. I'm afraid you have mistaken your hare.'

Marcus eyed him curiously. 'You're monstrous confident, I must say.'

476

'Yes, I am, as it happens. Lady Rosamund will marry me. Her feelings for you, Morland, are just the residue of a childhood fancy — no offence intended, old fellow.'

Marcus handed back the pannikin, a little discomfited. 'Well, we shall see,' he said. 'May the best man win.'

'He will,' Tantony said, his eyes gleaming with amusement. A ray of watery sunshine broke through the soft wet clouds for a moment and wandered across the road. It was the kind of morning which would have been full of birdsong, had it not been for the inhibiting presence in the fields of sixty-five thousand men with their horses and guns. 'It looks as though it's clearing up.'

'Yes, I think we shall have a fine day for it. Do you know yet where you will be stationed?'

'Oh yes — we've been attached to Kempt's. We are to hold the sandpit down by La Haie Sainte. That puts us right in the very centre of the action, just where Boney likes best to attack,' Tantony said cheerfully.

'And just where you like best to be!' Marcus laughed. He glanced over his shoulder, and hastily drained the pannikin and handed it back. 'The Old Man's moving on. I must go. I dare say we shall meet later. Good luck, Tantony!'

'Good luck to you, too — now and afterwards.'

'Thanks — and thanks for the tea! Oh, and I shan't forget to invite you to the wedding.'

'You do that,' Tantony laughed.

By nine o'clock the Allied army was in position, and the Duke rode along the line inspecting and making final adjustments. He was as neat as Brummell, Marcus thought, riding behind him — a subfusc figure in a short cloak over plain blue frock, white buckskins and tasselled Hessians. Beside Lord Uxbridge, glorious in the dazzling braided uniform of the Hussars, he was positively subdued — the only showy thing about him was his choice of a snowy white neckcloth instead of the regulation officer's black. In his cocked hat the Duke wore the black cockade of England, and, for the sake of tact, those of Prussia, Portugal and the Netherlands too. He rode his ugly long-backed chestnut, Copenhagen, who, he said, was neither handsome nor fast, but had not his equal for bottom or endurance; and he carried his glass in his hand, always at the ready.

The far left wing was occupied only by the light cavalry, Vandeleur's and Sir Hussey Vivian's brigades, because that was the direction from which the Prussians would appear when — if — they arrived from Wavre. Lord Theakston accosted Colonel Gordon with an anxious frown as the Duke made his inspection, and said, 'I say, Gordon, what news of the Prussians? Are they coming, or ain't they?'

'The latest news from Blücher was that he would get here or die, with two divisions at least,' said Gordon. 'But you know this rain has ruined the roads, and they weren't all that good to start with. They'll have a job getting through, especially the artillery. God knows how long it will take them! But don't worry; you've only to hold the road open for them. The French won't attack this far over on the wing anyway. You can see from their dispositions Boney means to go straight at the centre as usual.'

'That's exactly what I complain of,' Theakston said indignantly. 'We'll be right out of it up here. I don't want to have to tell my grandchildren that I fought all through the Peninsular campaign only to miss the great battle of Mont St-Jean, when Boney was finally thrashed!'

Gordon roared with laughter, attracting the Duke's attention. 'What's that, Danby? Afraid you'll miss the fun? Don't worry, we'll find you something to do.'

'I hope so, sir, or my wife will have something to say to it!'

'Ah yes — I hear she's been doing great things for our wounded from Quatre-Bras. Morland here has a very pretty example of her needlework about him.' He smiled at Marcus, and then nodded to Danby. 'She's a very remarkable lady.'

'Thank you, sir. I think so. I shouldn't like to let her down.'

Next along the line were Vincke's and Best's Landwehr battalions; and then occupying the left centre, just to the left of the Brussels highway, were Pack's and Kempt's Peninsula veterans, the much-reduced survivors of Sir Thomas Picton's division. Picton himself was still in civilian clothes, his burly body wrapped in a shabby old drab greatcoat, his coarse, square-jowled face shaded by the battered top-hat he had worn all through the battle of Quatre-Bras. The trunks containing his uniforms had been held up somewhere on their way from England and had not yet reached Brussels.

The right centre, across the main road, was held by Sir Charles Alten's division: Ompteda's KGL battalions, Colin Halkett's line regiments and Kielmansegge's Hanoverians. The right wing — the hill to the rear of Hougoumont — was held by the Guards under Maitland and Byng, and seven companies of Coldstreamers were stationed in the manor house itself under Sir James Macdonnell, while Nassauer and Hanoverian skirmishers invested the wood to the south of the manor house. Finally, the Nivelles road was guarded by Mitchell's 4th Brigade, also Peninsula veterans.

The heavy cavalry was massed behind the front line. The Household Brigade — the Blues and the Life Guards under Sir Edward Somerset, huge men on magnificent long-tailed horses — were to the right of the main road to the rear of Ompteda's, while Ponsonby's Union Brigade were across the road to the rear of Picton's. Here Marcus came for the first time in weeks upon his father, who spurred his great grey horse forward to meet him. The grey was called Manchester, a rare attempt at humour on Colonel Morland's part. As Wellington's horse was called Copenhagen, and Napoleon's white stallion was called Marengo, the colonel had said he felt he must name his mount after his own most famous victory — against the machine-smashing Luddites of the north of England.

'Well, my boy!' Horatio said genially. 'This is something like, eh? We shall have a fine day for it, and the Duke has chosen an excellent position! A smashing downhill run against the Frogs, and their poor little horses — hardly bigger than dogs, some of 'em — will have uphill galloping all the way.'

Manchester fretted and danced and snatched sideways at Marcus's bay. Marcus eyed him cautiously. 'He's very fresh, sir.'

'Eager for the fray — we all are,' Horatio said. 'By Jove, it's been a long time coming!' He glanced at Marcus's hand, curved unnaturally upon the rein of his docile mount. 'Wounded?'

'It's nothing, sir. A scratch I picked up at Quatre-Bras.'

'Ah yes, we missed that little party,' Horatio said with keen

479

regret. Manchester dug the ground vigorously, champing his bit so that the curb-chain jangled like small, cold music. 'Completely in the wrong place when it all began. Between you and me, there's been some mis-management about the affair — but hush! We'll see what we shall see today. Harry Uxbridge knows his stuff. And Ponsonby's a grand fellow. Damned shame about that nephew of his — you knew him didn't you?'

'Yes, sir — he was one of Rosamond's admirers.'

'Ah, yes. Well, with her dowry she won't lack for others. Seen your mother and sister at all?'

'Yes, sir — I went into Brussels the night before last. They were well, only anxious, of course. I asked Lady Theakston to invite them to stay — Mrs Firth and Bobbie were already there. I hope Mama will accept the invitation — it is a time when women need to be together.'

'Yes — well,' the colonel said doubtfully. 'Ha-hm! You know what your mother thinks about Lady Theakston. And she won't want to throw Bab and young Chelmsford together more than she must.'

'No, Papa. But I must be going — the Beau's moving on.'

'Very well.' Horatio's eyes filled with sudden sentiment. 'This is a great day for me, you know, Marcus. I'm very proud to be here, and to have my own son fighting alongside me. It will be a thing to talk of for the rest of our lives. I only wish you could be with your regiment.'

'Someone has to carry messages, Papa. I'm happy enough with the arrangement.'

'Well, I dare say. Good luck to you, my boy. I'll share a bottle of champagne with you tonight, after our victory.'

Marcus grinned. 'Thank you, sir. I'll look forward to it.'

It was ten o'clock. The large clouds moved across the sky, giving vent to occasional showers, and in between there were shafts of welcome sunshine. The mist had cleared from the valley, revealing a smiling scene of fertile crops, the dark-green of clover, the pale green of barley and tall bending rye, the oats and wheat beginning to be touched with gold, and here and there the dark, rich brown of a bare plough. Far away to the left there were touches of white and slate-blue where a number of tiny villages crouched amongst their hedges of beech and hornbeam; forward and to the right the solid grey walls of Hougoumont nestled peacefully amongst their ancient orchards and kitchen-gardens.

On the hillside opposite, the dark masses of French infantry were assembling to the sound of drums, and a cacophony of military bands all playing different tunes, of which only the hated 'Marseillaise' was readily distinguishable. The cavalry squadrons trotted here and there, bright splashes of colour, green and gold and white, blue and cherry-red, plumes swinging and penants fluttering: a moving mosaic, flinging back from the fitful sun the flashes of light from bronze and silver breastplates and helmets. The Allied lines stood quietly watching. The distant sounds and movements had a spuriously merry effect, as though it were a country fair getting under way. Now and then they caught a glimpse of a solitary figure on a white horse, and the men would nudge each other and murmur that it was old Boney himself.

At last the assembly was complete, and the music and trumpets died away, and silence fell over the valley. The Duke had taken up his position under an elm-tree at the cross-roads of the Chemin d'Ohain with the Brussels road. He sat with a loose rein, scanning the opposite ridge with his glass from time to time. Everything about him spoke of calm; old Copenhagen cocked one hind foot and dozed, his lower lip trembling, his ears at half-mast.

'What the deuce are they waiting for?' Marcus said after a while, to no-one in particular. 'Why don't they attack?'

'Waiting for the ground to dry out, I shouldn't wonder,' said Assherson, another of the aides. 'Those twelve-pounders of theirs will be stuck fast if they try to move 'em. The delay's all in our favour, at any rate.'

'I expect Boney's still waiting for half his troops to be rounded up,' said Colonel Gordon, overhearing them. 'The men will have been well scattered this morning, looking for food. It will take time to get them together and march them up in any kind of disciplined order. What we can see over there is not his whole army by any means, depend upon it. Hullo! Who's this coming?'

It was a British officer in scarlet, with Peninsula flashes

and the buff facings of the 40th of the line. He came cantering down the *pavé* from the direction of Brussels and rode up to the Duke and saluted smartly.

'Hullo, Dodd, where did you spring from?' the Duke greeted him genially.

'General Lambert sent me ahead, sir. We have just arrived from America — the 4th, the 27th and the 40th, marching from Brussels. Have you any orders, sir?'

'Indeed I have — I shall need every man of you soon! You are just in time. We shall have a hot time of it today. Go back quickly, give my compliments to General Lambert, and ask him to halt his men at the junction of the Nivelles road. I shall send my detailed orders to him soon.'

Dodd saluted and rode away, and the Duke beckoned Colonel Gordon over to discuss the best use that could be made of these welcome reinforcements. Soon afterwards, Gordon rode away to brief General Lambert more fully on the situation, and the rest of the aides settled down again after the brief excitement to watch the opposite hillside again.

'Why doesn't Boney attack?' Marcus said after a while, sighing with impatience. 'What the devil is he waiting for?'

The battle began at a little after eleven o'clock with an attack on Hougoumont. Four French regiments, supported by artillery and cavalry, marched on the manor house and engaged the Nassauer and Hanoverian skirmishers in the wood.

'Here we go,' said Marcus above the din of artillery. 'It begins at last.'

'I don't know,' Assherson bellowed back. 'I think it's just a diversion.'

'Nonsense! Boney's starting by attacking the wings, just as he always does. See, the cavalry's attacking the left wing at Frischermont.'

'But that's just a show,' Assherson said. 'You can see it isn't meant seriously. Look at the way they're circling, just out of range! I think Gordon's right — Boney hasn't had a chance to bring all his men up, so he's passing the time with a little diversion.'

'No, no, no! Boney's attacking the wings in the hope that

the Beau will move men from the centre, where he means the real attack to come,' Marcus said. 'It's what he always does — the same old tactic. Boney's running out of ideas, that's what I think. Haven't you read any military history, Fred?'

'We haven't all had the benefit of a Firth for a tutor,' Assherson retorted. 'Anyway, it looks as though the Nassauers are holding 'em off. Good show!'

The French cavalry on the left wing soon fell back and abandoined the attack on Frischermont, but on Hougoumont the French rallied and attacked again, and gradually the Nassauers and Hanoverians were driven back through the wood from tree to tree. Wellington sent three companies of the Guards to support them, and a brisk battle broke out amongst the trees and the hedges of the back-lanes around the manor house. Whether or not it had originally been meant by Napoleon as a diversion, the battle for Hougoumont gradually heated up, as the French threw more and more men into it. The Allies were forced to retreat behind the walls of the courtyard, abandoning the wood; but since the French, inexplicably, did not bring up heavy artillery to bombard the walls, the Guards and the skirmishers managed to hold out very well, tying up valuable French forces in the useless attempt to take the manor house.

The bulk of Perponcher's Netherlanders, after their poor showing at Quatre-Bras, had been put out on the extreme wings where they were not likely to see much action; all except Bylandt's, the best of them, which had been positioned at the left centre, between the Landwehr battalions and Picton's brigade. The Duc de Veslne-d'Estienne, cantering along the line reconnoitring for his general, looked for them in vain at first; and then discovered to his horror that while the rest of the fighting line had assembled on the reverse slope out of harm's way, Bylandt's brigade was drawn up on the forward slope, on a level with the skirmishers and the Allied artillery, and in full view of the enemy.

Cursing, he turned his horse and cantered down towards them. The 5th Militia were to the right of the mass, and seeing Major Larosse sitting his horse impassively at the front of his men, the Duc reined in hard beside him and cried, 'Larosse! What the deuce are you doing here? Why aren't you drawn up on the reverse like all the others? This isn't Wellington's way.'

As Larosse's hand came down from the salute, he shrugged as only a Frenchman can. 'This is where his excellency has placed us, sir.' He met the Duc's eye with a look as flat as the sole of his boot. 'The orders from the Commander-in-Chief were simply "form up as usual". I daresay that means different things to different people, sir.'

The Duc frowned, inching his horse nearer and lowering his voice. 'It's too late to move back now. But you're badly exposed, you and your men — you'll take the brunt of it when the French attack.'

Larosse gave him a faint, wry smile. 'I wonder whether that might not be the idea, sir. His excellency was gravely concerned about the showing of the Pays Bas soldiers in the last engagement. I know that he thinks honour has been touched: perhaps this is meant as atonement.'

The Duc swore fluently, but softly. 'If it is to be a bloody sacrifice, it will help no-one.'

'Surely not that, sir,' Larosse said flatly.

The Duc looked at him curiously. 'Look here, Larosse, you and I are Frenchmen — and soldiers. It's too late to fall the men back now — it would cause chaos — but for God's sake take care, won't you?'

'I don't mean to die, sir — not yet,' Larosse said, still with that wry smile in his eyes. 'I have — if you remember — a great deal to live for.'

The Duc nodded. 'Good man,' he said briefly. 'I must go and speak to the count. How's the leg?'

'Tolerable, sir, thank you.' It was completely numb, except when he moved it, which indeed made it just tolerable. Worse than the leg was the ache of his heart — a mixture of regret for the Frenchmen he must help kill, and longing for the young woman in Brussels whose society had suddenly become sweeter to him than anything else in the world. It had often been said that soldiers ought to be married, because they fought all the harder for the sake of the women left at home; but Larosse doubted whether the same were true of an officer. For the first time in his life he was afraid of death — not of the dying, but of the thought of having to leave Sophie, perhaps without even saying goodbye. Oh, he would be careful, all right!

For an hour and a half nothing much had happened across the battlefield except the struggle for Hougoumont; but as one o'clock approached, the Allies saw battery after battery of French artillery being drawn up on the ridge opposite, covering the whole centre of the Allied line.

'We shall be for it soon,' Marcus observed. 'There must be eighty or ninety guns there — and big ones, too.'

'Yes — old Boney's "Beautiful Daughters".' Assherson squinted into the fitful sunshine. 'And, I say, Morland, look over there, by the farmhouse — ain't that Boney himself? White horse, green coat — swear it is!'

'I think you're right.'

'Makes you think, doesn't it? If only we had a long-gun and a sharpshooter, we might blow the old devil to Kingdom Come, and be done with the whole nonsense!'

Marcus shook his head. 'The Beau wouldn't have it. He says it's not the business of general officers to fire at each other. Professional standards, you know.'

'I know,' Assherson sighed. 'And I suppose I agree — one must win honourably, or it's no victory. But when I think of my brother at Vimiero, and my uncle at Salamanca, I can't help wishing some assassin had managed to slip a knife between Boney's ribs long ago. All this show is for him, you know. If he weren't here, we could all go home, back to our wives and mothers and dear old England!'

The distant church bell of the village struck one, and as if at that signal, the French guns opened fire, first vomiting orange flame, then black smoke, and an instant later a hellish crash that made everyone jump, even though they had been waiting for it. The first shots fell short, but as the guns warmed up, roundshot came screaming through the air to smash into the ground and plough up long furrows in the mud. Company commanders had ordered the men to lie down, and, protected by the slope of the hill, the battalions suffered little damage. Normally in such a cannonade even the hidden troops suffered some casualties as shots striking the earth ricocheted and leapt right over the ridge; but the earth was so sodden after the rain-storm that most of the roundshot sank harmlessly where they fell.

But there were casualties all the same, and the din was terrifying, particularly to the new recruits, who had not had enough experience to be philosophical about it. They hated the fact that there was nothing they could do to retaliate. It was worst of all for the men of Bylandt's brigade, exposed on the forward slope of the hill, on a line with the Allied artillery, enduring not only the havoc of French roundshot ploughing through them, smashing limbs and spattering them with the blood and brains of their colleagues, but also the maddening, deafening din of the Allied nine-pounders' reply. When Count Bylandt himself was wounded and carried off, the men would probably have fled, except that they were a great deal too frightened to stand up.

After half an hour, the cannonade slackened, and in the comparative quiet which followed the French drums could be heard beating the advance. Larosse looked up, and saw what appeared to be the whole hillside on the move. Four divisions were advancing in columns — about eighteen thousand men, he thought — supported by two brigades of cuirassiers. The French artillery ceased fire as their own men obscured their aim, and the infantry advanced to the eerie sound of drums alone.

Fascinated, Larosse watched the strange caterpillar of the French army moving down the hillside towards him, white legs flickering beneath the composite blue mass of their jackets. He saw that for some unknown reason the two divisions which were going to attack the left wing had been drawn up in the old-fashioned *colonnes de bataillon par division*, which had been proved again and again to be unhandy, dangerous and inflexible. The columns presented a frontage of only two hundred men, while the ranks were twenty-seven deep, which meant that of, say, four thousand men, only about four hundred were able to use their muskets. The massive unwieldy columns were also impossible to manoeuvre, and very slow, which made them ideal targets for the enemy artillery.

Some mistake or failure of command had occurred, he thought, which seemed typical of the way the French army had been commanded in the past few years. He thought of the horrifying, wretched, Russian campaign of 1812, the lack of communication, the hesitations, the wrong orders, the missing orders. The Emperor was losing his grip. Perhaps he had lost the will to fight? There must come a time in every man's life when the effort became sickening to the soul, when all he wanted to do was to stay at home quietly and watch his crops and his children grow. The Emperor, he thought, had missed his moment. There was a time when he had been the victor of Europe, when his nation loved him, when his enemies would have been glad to let him alone. If he had stopped then, made peace, allowed his countrymen to enjoy what they had fought so long for, he might have ruled for ever.

But he would not let Europe rest; and now he had committed himself to eternal warfare, or death. It would be death, Larosse knew in his heart. The Allies would never rest until Napoleon was dead; and it was necessary for the world that he should die. But there was that in him which regretted it, which still, against his judgement, mourned his former master. I will do all in my power to destroy you, he said inwardly, his eyes on that distant, tiny figure taking the salute in the road beside La Belle Alliance; but I will grieve for you when you are gone. That is my punishment.

But now he had work to do. The artillery was firing into those slow-moving columns with shouts of glee. 'Here's for you, Old Trousers!' and 'What a target, lads! Let 'em have it! And another!' He must assemble his men, get ready for action. At the order, the Dutch-Belgians scrambled unwillingly to their feet, ducking in fright at every crash from the guns, peeking about them for the roundshot they expected still to be flying over their heads. An appalling number of them had not risen, and the sight of their fallen comrades did nothing to hearten the survivors. One youngster nearby was weeping, his face beslobbered with tears like a child's. He was wiping his hand, splashed with a comrade's blood, again and again down the front of his jacket as though it would never be clean.

Orders rapped out steadily as the officers strove to appear unmoved by the situation.

'Close the gaps, there! Are you loaded, men? Prime and close! Take careful aim — don't waste your shots. You, Foulard — take your rammer out, man! Wait for the command. Stand steady, you men! You'll be dishing it out soon, lads.'

The great mass of Frenchmen was coming steadily up the hill, and though many of them were falling to artillery- and musket-fire, the advance did not waver. Oh for veterans like those! Larosse watched, waiting for the right moment to open fire, seeing out of the corner of his eye the uncertain movements of his own men. The range was almost right — better let them fire, to give them something to do. They would stand better if they were fighting back.

'Right, lads! Now's your time. Take aim — fire!'

The volley went off raggedly, and most of the shots were wild, having no discernible effect on the advance. 'Reload!' Larosse shouted. Some of the men complied, clumsy in their panicking haste. Some of them tried 'jogging' the ball down the muzzle by banging the stock on the ground, rather than ramming home, because it was quicker. Some forgot to charge their muskets; others simply fired wildly in the air in their anxiety to get their shots off quickly.

'Steady, men! Don't waste your shots. Aim properly. Ram down, there! Reload, prime and close!'

But it was no good. Men in the front ranks were falling now to French musket-fire, and the infection of panic was spreading through them. For the second time Larosse saw that awful wavering and slow crumbling of his lines, and then suddenly they were all in flight, scrambling away up the slope, screaming like children, some of them flinging away their muskets as they ran, clapping their hands over their ears as though to keep out the sound of the shot that might kill them. A terrible derisive howl was set up by the soldiers of Picton's as the Netherlanders rushed through the space between the divisions. The worst of it was that Byleveldt's battery was bowled over and driven back by the wild flight, widening the dangerous gap which had been torn in the front line.

Larosse and the other officers tried desperately to halt the rush; and Larosse, who was well liked by his own company,

488

managed for a moment to hold back about twenty men. By the power of his will, he made them turn and stand, and though they were trembling with fear, they began to reload their muskets. But then his horse screamed and collapsed under him, and as he came crashing down with it, those twenty gave one fearful glance and joined in the rush for safety.

Bruised and breathless, his head ringing, Larosse extricated himself, and crouched beside his horse. It was thrashing in pain, its eyes wild and supplicating, blood gouting from its mouth. Shot in the lungs, he thought dazedly. He could not leave it, poor beast; he dragged out his pistol from his belt, placed the muzzle between the gelding's eyes, and fired.

A spate of oaths smote his ears, and he looked up to see Sir Thomas Picton above him, whirling his maddened horse in circles. 'What the devil are you doing, man? Get your carcass up and get after your men! Form 'em up and bring 'em back here! Blast their eyes! Hi, Swinton! Bring your men over here — double, man, double! Seventy-ninth — keep firing, damn it!'

He was gone. Larosse got to his feet, shook his head to clear it, and went back through the line at a staggering run. A company of Kempt's brigade ran forward to fill the gap left in the line. Pack's Highlanders were firing after the fleeing Netherlanders, though their officers tried to restrain them. Larosse passed the men of Byleveldt's horse-battery, who had managed to separate themselves from the rout and were now re-forming under their officers. One of them shouted to him. 'You'll never get them back! They won't stop this side of Antwerp!'

'Let the bastards go!' shouted a Gordon Highlander, overhearing as he ran in the other direction. 'We're better off without them! Bloody cowards!'

Larosse staggered on, his ears ringing, his right thigh a grinding pain. Did he hear, or imagine, the word 'renegade' shouted after him? He was a French officer, commanding Dutch-Belgic troops, some of whom had fought under the Eagles. What could he expect?

It was a perilous moment. The flight of the Netherlanders had

489

left a gap in the line where it was weakest, and now the three thousand survivors of Picton's were facing a seething mass of bluecoats, ten thousand of them, maybe more. There was no help to be expected from further along the line: the right wing was engaged with the other two French divisions, while around La Haie Sainte there was ferocious fighting, and the 95th were being hard-pressed to hold the sandpit, even with the help of Ross's battery, whose guns were trained on the road.

Picton cast no glance after the Dutch-Belgians. He barked out a volley of rapid orders, re-forming Kempt's brigade from three ranks to two so that their longer line would fill the space. Another order, and Dennis Pack's Highlanders stormed forward, bellowing their battle-cries; from the rear the dreaded wail of bagpipes started up, terrifying to the French. Volleys of musket-shot rattled out, and the bluecoats recoiled a moment, and then came on again, an irresistible weight of men.

Picton whirled his horse on the spot, eyes everywhere, judging the mad struggle of his few men against the mass of French. There was hand-to-hand fighting now; Kempt's were holding firm, but the Camerons were coming under cross-fire as they were outflanked, and the 92nd, first of Pack's to engage, were beginning to waver. They must have cavalry support, or the line would break. Glancing around him he saw one of Lord Uxbridge's aides, a Captain Seymour, behind him.

'Seymour!' he bellowed. 'Rally to the Highlanders! Tell Uxbridge — ' Seymour, who was already turning his horse to obey the instruction, saw to his astonishment that General Picton had three eyes — a third one, round and black, had appeared in the middle of his forehead, above the glaring pale blue pair. Then the General was gone, tumbling from his saddle, shot dead by a musket-ball through the head.

A great groan went up from his own men, and the French, scenting victory, pressed forward again, giving tongue like wolves. The Allied line, fighting desperately, was giving back. All seemed lost. And then there was the thrilling sound of trumpets, and up over the ridge appeared the massive horses and men of the heavy cavalry, the Royals, Inniskillings and the wild white horses of the Scots Greys, like a foaming tidal wave leaping the bank and thundering down on the dumbfounded French. On the other side of the road, the Household Brigade had appeared with equal suddenness, both having been hidden from the French by the reverse slope. It was plain that the French had expected only infantry against them — the appearance of the horses terrified them and they milled in panic, and then broke and ran as, with the slope in their favour, the cavalry pounded down on them, gathering speed.

The hard-pressed Highlanders cheered wildly as the horses thundered through the intervals between their companies, and seeing the French flee, some of them grabbed at the stirrups as the horses passed and were borne forward down the hill, shrieking, 'Hurrah, 92nd! Scotland for ever!' as they leapt over the ground with seven-league strides. They rode down the French columns, the Greys laying about them with their deadly cavalry sabres, while the 92nd jabbed and slashed with their bayonets. Men cried out and died; horses shrieked and fell; and the French began flinging down their arms and crying quarter — those who could not run. Thousands were taken prisoner. The enemy's attack was broken, repulsed, driven back. The near-disaster had turned suddenly to victory.

Carried on by their momentum, the Union Brigade thundered across the plain at a mad gallop. Seeing the French still yielding before them, they charged on up the opposite slope towards the French position, towards old Boney himself, standing impassive as always in the road outside the farmhouse of La Belle Alliance. There were the guns up ahead — what glory to capture them! Colonel Horatio Morland, feeling his strong horse mad with excitement under him, seeing his men drunk with speed all around him, couldn't resist it.

'Charge! Charge the guns!' he screamed. The speed of their charge was irresistible. There was shot all around them, humming and whining through the air, but they rode over the guns, slashing off the heads of the gunners and drivers, cutting the traces, oversetting the guns, putting the horses to flight. Twenty guns — thirty? It was glorious! And two Eagles captured! To his left, Horatio saw one of his men, Sergeant

491

Mitchell, jump his horse right over a French nine-pounder in pursuit of two gun-layers, and swipe off both their screaming heads with one blow. An entire battery was out of action; the effect on French morale would be shattering.

The colonel checked his sweating horse, looking for more.

'To me! To me, Greys! Over here!' he shouted, seeing the central battery under Napoleon's command still untouched. He jabbed his spurs into Manchester's sides, and the big horse squealed and leapt forward again. But the slope was steeper now, and the horses were blown. The Greys were out too far in front of their own men — too far in amongst the French. There were solid masses of infantry in front of them now, firing in volleys. Men and horses were crashing down; and now the French cavalry was moving on the wings, curving columns heading to outflank them.

The troopers slowed, stopped, looked about them like men waking, seeing where their mad charge had brought them, feeling the heaving sides of their blown horses, seeing the cuirassiers riding towards them. The officers who had survived now took alarm and tried to rally their men. 'Royals, form on me!' came a cry. Horatio, whirling Manchester to face the oncoming French, yelled to his own men. 'Greys, rally! To me, to me!'

A fat Frenchman on a weedy bay horse was coming at him. Poor men, poor horses, can't ride, Horatio thought contemptuously, slashing with his sabre. Wouldn't last two minutes in *his* regiment! The man ducked and cried out; but there was another, and another coming at him. Too many of them. Blades glinted in the sunlight, whirling like some deadly machine, come to reap a human harvest, come to reap him! There was a sharp, cold pain, and suddenly his left arm was gone, just gone, and there was only blood and confusion as Manchester, exhausted and afraid, lost the steadying pressure of his rider's hand on the reins; turned, stumbled, his white mane dappled scarlet.

Outflanked — must go back now, or never, Horatio thought vaguely. The horror, the shock, seemed to have thrown him into another dimension, where everything was crystal clear, and yet distant, tiny, almost unimportant. He felt no pain, nothing at all. Perhaps it was a dream. But no, the reins were loose; there was blood everywhere. His arm ...

Gripping Manchester with his knees, turning him with his heels, he croaked, 'Come on, lads! That's the road home!' He picked up the reins with his right hand and stuffed them between his teeth to leave his sword-arm free. He sensed rather than saw the remnant of his troopers closing on him, Sergeant Mitchell there, helmetless, grey overalls red-patched, staring at him open-mouthed, as he kicked Manchester into a heavy canter straight at the French lancers who had closed round behind them, cutting off their retreat.

Speed would do it, only speed. Galloping, they would break through. With one small part of his attention he saw that there was help at hand, the light cavalry of Vandeleur's division was racing across from the left wing to cover their retreat. Good men, Vandeleur's! Here were the French. A swarthy face, gashed with a black moustache, stared at him in horror. No stopping now.

Just as he reached the line of French lancers, a roundshot from the main battery behind him felled Manchester, blowing his legs out from under him. Horatio seemed to fly, carried onward through the air by the sheer momentum. He felt the reins jerked painfully from his teeth, and saw brightness as two cavalry swords caught the light, one either side, raised as he went past between two French troopers.

That was the last thing he saw. He was dead before he hit the ground; his head, struck off, bounced as it landed a yard in front of his body, and two yards in front of his dead horse.

Some of the Netherlanders kept on running, heading for the forest of Soignies where they might hide, or perhaps even for Brussels, home and safety. But others had gone no further than the Chemin d'Ohain, where the high, thick hedges cut out a great deal of the noise of the battle and gave a spurious sense of safety. Here Larosse found plenty of the blue coats with orange facings crouched, pressing themselves against the rough twigs, arms over their heads, trembling like terrified rabbits pursued by hounds.

Some of his officers were there, too, already trying to round up the men. They looked hopefully at Larosse as he came limping through a gap in the hedge into the lane.

'Vivoorde — you go that way; Hastière, to the left. Form 'em up back here, and don't let 'em go. If you can find a trustworthy sergeant or corporal, send 'em back to collect up any muskets that have been dropped. Come on now — no time to waste.'

He glanced at the pitiful creatures shivering in the hedgerow, and pitched his voice to carry to them. 'Come along, you men, you've a job to do. You're soldiers, you know! Form up now, and do as your officers tell you. You won't feel so bad if you stick together.'

A few white eyes rolled towards him, but no-one moved. He picked out the familiar broad back of one of his own men, a fat Belgian called Poisson, who had been a pastrycook until patriotic fervour called him to arms. He was a good-natured man, a willing butt of company humour, and something of a favourite with his comrades. Inwardly blessing Providence for him, Larosse said, 'Come on, Poisson, let's have you on your feet.' The man looked at him, startled. His face was as white as lard, the fat of his jowls trembled. 'Shew these others what you're made of. You can't poison the French with your cooking, you know — you'll have to find some other way of killing 'em.'

There was a cackle of laughter — rather hysterical laughter, but better than nothing — and the man crouched next to the pastrycook poked him hard in the ribs, making him stand up in sheer surprise.

'There's our noble cook! Come on, you others,' Larosse barked. 'Form up on Poisson. Don't be scared. If the Frogs shoot at you, you can throw his pastries at them.'

More laughter. They were moving now, making derisive remarks about each other, some looking a little shamefaced, others plainly so frightened they were willing to take orders from anyone who would reassure them in any way. Dietmar suddenly appeared in the lane, still mounted, thank God.

'Captain Dietmar — come and take charge of these brave soldiers!' Larosse shouted. As Dietmar stopped beside him, Larosse grabbed his sleeve and pulled him towards him, and added *sotto voce*, 'Don't let 'em go, for Christ's sake. I'm going through there to smoke out the rest. When they're formed up, march 'em along there to Vivoorde. I'll have to take your horse.'

494

Through the second hedge. Here, behind the fighting lines, there were servants, surgeons, wounded men, baggage and ammunition carts, and the forward line of the reserve troops of Lambert's division, waiting uneasily for the call to come. A movement called his eye and he looked away towards his right and saw a group of about ten Netherlanders disappearing into a little coppice.

He mounted Dietmar's horse and kicked it into a trot. One of the fleeing men glanced over his shoulder at Larosse and then ducked under the trees, shoving a companion in the back to move him faster. The gesture for some reason incensed Larosse: it had not the look of genuine fear, but of calculation. He hated cowardice. Poor old Poisson was frightened almost to death, but he had stood up and straightened his fat shoulders like a man when Larosse singled him out. He pushed on into a canter, itching to lay the flat of his sword across that man's buttocks.

It was not much of a coppice, not much of a hiding-place: a clump of birch and alder with sparse undergrowth, a few brambles, bracken and soft weeds. Larosse pushed the horse in where the passage of the men had broken some branches, rode forward a little way, and then halted and listened. The sun had gone in, and there was a light pattering of rain on leaves, but otherwise the wood was silent, no birdsong, no rustling of movement — a listening silence. From here the sounds of the battle were distant and indistinguishable. It reminded him of the murmur of adults talking somewhere in the house, when as a child one lies in bed half asleep.

The horse sneezed and rubbed its muzzle on its knee, jingling the bit-rings. He pressed its sides gently and it walked forward a step, two steps, and then suddenly it started, throwing up its head and catching Larosse a painful blow on the nose as one of the fugitives jumped up from the scrub to avoid being trodden on. He turned to flee, but Larosse shot out an arm and caught his collar.

'Oh no, you don't!' he said grimly.

'Lemme go! Lemme go, I say! I ain't going back! I ain't gonner get killed for nobody!' the man squealed like a stuck pig.

'Shut your mouth, you miserable coward,' Larosse said

sharply, 'or we'll see how you like the flat of my sword as a persuader.'

'Lemme go! Jean-Claude, help!' the man shrieked. Suddenly they were not alone. The trees and the undergrowth silently peopled itself with blue jackets, and to Larosse's left appeared the man he had seen look over his shoulder, a grim-faced individual, tall for a Belgian, with a powder-burn down one cheek that marked him for a veteran. He had not been under Larosse's personal command, but he had seen him before. Presumably this was Jean-Claude. Larosse wished he knew his other name — names give power.

'Let him go, Major,' the man said. The others watched, tense but trusting. He had authority — he was a dangerous opponent.

Larosse did not let go his quarry, but he grew alert, his eyes narrowing as he judged the situation.

'Come on, you men — you're going back. The Duke needs you. Your country needs you,' he said evenly. 'You're soldiers —'

'Not any more,' the dark man cut in. 'We quit. We're not fighting the English's battle for them.'

'Don't be a fool,' Larosse sneered. 'Whose country do you think they're defending?'

'Not yours, at any rate, Major,' the dark man said. 'You're French yourself. Why are you killing your own countrymen?'

The man moved a step forward. Larosse let go of his quarry's collar and straightened slowly, his hand mutely judging the distance to his sword-hilt. 'We're not discussing my business,' he said sharply. A stealthy rustle behind him — he was surrounded now. His anger rose, hot and invigorating as brandy. 'Are you going to let Napoleon's army walk into your country unopposed? Are you going to let them plunder your homes and rape your women while you stand by and cheer them on?'

There was a growl from someone, and the dark man said, 'None o'that! I fought under the Eagles, Major. I'm not going to kill my old comrades in arms. We had French rule before, and it wasn't so bad. If you and the British want to fight, that's your business. We're going to light a fire and smoke our pipes and wait and see what happens.' A muted cheer from

496

his companions. 'Go on back, Major. You do your business, and we'll do ours.'

'Cowards' business is what you're doing,' Larosse said. 'Letting other men fight your battles for you, you sneaking dogs! Well it's not going to be that easy.'

The dark man's eyes went beyond Larosse, and there was the stealthy movement behind him again. 'Go back, Major,' he said. 'We don't want to harm you. Go back and leave us alone.'

Larosse felt the hair rise on the back of his neck. He turned just in time as the man behind him broke and ran at him, grabbing the hand that held the knife and turned the blade aside. 'You cowardly, murdering dog!' he hissed as he struggled for possession. The face below glared up, stupid with hate and fear. Dimly he heard the dark man shouting: 'No, you fools, leave him! Leave him!' Then there were two of them, three, and he was being pulled from the saddle. The horse whinneyed in fear, surging this way and that. Larosse let go the reins and reached with his left hand for his pistol. At almost the same instant there was a loud explosion, and a burning pain in his side; the horse surged forward from under him and he fell amongst his assailants.

He thought for an instant he had accidentally shot himself, but realised almost at once that someone else must have had a pistol. There was a smell of bruised bracken and the pungent sweat of fear. The dark man was cursing someone — 'You bloody fool!'; the horse was snorting, its trampling hooves dangerously close to his head. His sword was gone, but his hand was still on his pistol-butt at his belt. He had fallen with his arm under him; his fingers were caught in his belt and he couldn't get it out.

A man stooped over him, darkening the sky, but the dark man's voice came again. 'No, leave him, for God's sake! Take the horse and let's get out.'

Sounds of trampling hooves and feet. Larosse struggled to free his arm. The sound of snapping twigs, heavy bodies crashing through the wood. Then he knew he was alone. He gave one last heave and freed his arm, and cried out at the terrible, disintegrating pain; and then coughed, agonisingly and bloodily. His eyes darkened, and he collapsed onto his

497

back, and the wood surged about him, black and red, swirling.

He didn't quite lose consciousness, was aware that one part of his mind was cursing weakly and continuously — damn, damn, damn! — ludicrously inappropriate to his situation. The darkness cleared slowly from his eyes, and he lay in burning agony, looking up at the canopy of leaves above him: they moved in the light breeze, spattering a few cold drops of rain on his face. The slight shower had passed over, and the moving clouds made the light wax and wane as though behind a curtain of thin, not quite transparent material. It was beautiful, really.

He dragged his mind back. How badly was he hurt? he wondered. The ball had entered his side, just below his armpit, breaking some ribs; missing his heart, obviously, or he'd be dead, but doing God knew what other damage. He could feel the lump of lead, burning like indigestion as it worked inside him: disgusting, a vile, alien thing in his body. He moved slightly, and the pain snatched, and there was a sense of disintegration, of internal wetness, as though something were leaking. He was hurt — oh, yes. He realised with a sudden access of fear that he was badly hurt.

Tears filled his eyes. Not like this! Not in this ridiculous, futile way! Help, he must have help, someone must help him! 'Help me!' he cried out, and the weakness of his own voice shocked him to silence. I'm going to die, he thought, opening his eyes wide and staring upwards in sudden realisation. Even if someone comes, even if they get me to a surgeon, he can't take a musket-ball out of my chest. If I don't die from this bleeding I can feel inside, I'll die anyway, horribly, in a few days, from mortification.

The prospect was so horrifying that he felt faint. He had seen men die that way. Better to die here, now, quickly, decently. He had the means — he could do it. Better that, than to rot to death in continuous agony. Helpless tears again. Oh God, help me! He tried to move his left hand to the pistol-butt, but the pain made him sweat, both sharp and grinding, and he desisted. Don't be such a coward, he adjured himself. Get on with it. Do it. You know what lies ahead if you don't.

And then he thought of Sophie. She came into his mind with the suddenness of revelation, filling him with a new agony. Oh God, Sophie! He didn't want to die. He didn't want to die! He didn't want to leave her. What a stupid, futile, pitiful way for it to happen — not suddenly in battle, but hunting down a bunch of fugitives, shot by one of his own men in a scuffle in a wood. To lose her, and their life together, for so small a reason made him want to scream with frustration and rage. Sophie! Sophie! Not fair!

But here was a reason not to die just yet, after all; to live as long as possible, even if the end were worse, so that he could see her again, just once more. Not to die without having said goodbye, without having told her once more how much he loved her. *C'est moi qui t'aime le mieux!* Oh, Sophie.

He lay very still, listening. How long would it be before anyone found him? To survive now was an object — he must survive. He must stay very still and conserve his strength, breathe shallowly so as not to damage his lungs. Absurdly, hope reasserted itself, the human inability to believe in one's own death. Perhaps they could save him after all. Some of those army surgeons were very clever men. If the ball hadn't damaged any vital organ, it might be possible to remove it. The thought of what it would be like to endure such an operation flitted across his mind and he turned resolutely from it. Sophie. He must survive for Sophie, to see her again. He didn't want to die. He must not die.

He drifted, and then came back to consciousness. The clouds darkened again, and then rain spattered down. Larosse licked the drops from his lips gratefully — he was hideously thirsty. His lips tasted salty, and gritty from powder-smoke. Some men liked the taste, he reflected vaguely. There was a small, very small rustle in the grass near his head, and he rolled his eyes sideways to see the wedge-shaped reddish head, tiny boot-button eyes, and white throat of a weasel, rearing up to look at him before it disappeared into the weeds again. How long had he been lying here? How long before they found him? Surely someone would come soon. Far away the sound of the battle sank below a murmur, and then seemed to stop altogether. Larosse dozed.

CHAPTER NINETEEN

At three o'clock the fighting died away, except for the battle which raged continuously around Hougoumont. The English cavalry charge had driven back the French infantry, and now there was a pause while both sides regrouped and counted the cost.

Marcus was sent back to Mont St-Jean with a message for General Lambert to bring up his troops to reinforce the left centre, where Kempt had been appointed to take over General Picton's command, and it was not until he reported back to the Duke that he learnt that his father had fallen. Lord Uxbridge himself took Marcus aside to tell him the story.

'He was killed rallying his men — none of them would have got back if he hadn't charged straight at the French lancers,' Uxbridge concluded. 'It was a brave act.'

'Yes, sir,' Marcus said blankly. His father dead? He felt nothing, nothing at all. The words didn't seem to mean anything. He couldn't attach them to anything inside his head to make sense of them; but he knew Uxbridge was trying to comfort him. 'Thank you, sir,' he said.

'We've lost Ponsonby, too — Sir William Ponsonby,' Uxbridge went on, and then suddenly his handsome, stern features wavered, and he thudded his fist into his palm in grief and fury. 'It's the devil of a business! I've lost half my men — a thousand men and horses, maybe more! The cream of the English cavalry, all gone in one mad charge! I blame myself, most bitterly. It's the most appalling business!'

'Yes, sir,' was all Marcus could say. He thought irrelevantly that his father's body was still out there somewhere, on the French side. When the battle was over, he would have to go and look for it, to bring it back. Mama would expect it. He wondered if he would be able to recognise it. Perhaps if he looked for the horse? Poor old Manchester must lie somewhere nearby. Find the horse first, then look for his father. When it was all over.

Uxbridge had recovered his poise, and now looked keenly at Marcus. 'This must have been a shock for you. Are you all right, Morland?'

'Yes — yes, sir, thank you,' Marcus said. 'I'd better get back to my duties, if you will excuse me, sir.' Uxbridge nodded, with the suggestion of a shrug. Marcus saluted and turned his horse away. He hoped there was something for him to do. What he needed now was to be kept busy.

There were other losses, too. Frederick Ponsonby, Colonel of the 12th Light Dragoons, had also been killed covering the retreat of the remnant of the heavy cavalry, along with many of his men. Kempt and Pack were both wounded; Bylandt's brigade was to all intents and purposes wiped out; and the 95th Rifles had been badly cut up and forced to evacuate the sandpit. They were saved from annihilation only by the cessation of action following the cavalry charge.

The respite from fighting was useful to allow the wounded to be carried back behind the lines, and for the farriers to go out and despatch the wounded horses that were lying within reach on the battleground. Two thousand French prisoners were formed up under guard and marched away towards Brussels, where no doubt the sight of them would cheer the citizens. Marcus, like the other aides, was kept busy with a multitude of messages about regroupings, troop movements, the care of the wounded and orders for the supply of ammunition. Skirmishers were sent out to collect up the French arms which had been abandoned in the mass surrender, and every battalion set men to work collecting up spent musketballs. The French ball, being smaller than the British, could be used by the Allies in their Brown Besses; the French had no such option.

The respite lasted for about an hour, though it seemed much less. Then significant movements were seen on the French side, and after a few minutes the customary artillery bombardment began as a preliminary to a fresh engagement. The Duke and his staff, once more at the observation post at the cross-roads, watched in amazement as battalion after battalion of cavalry was drawn up at the bottom of the French slope, plainly preparing for attack.

'A cavalry charge — unsupported — on unbroken infantry?' Assherson exclaimed. A flying splinter had torn his forehead, and his brow was now decorated with a handsome bandage. 'What the deuce is old Ney playing at? Has he gone mad?'

'You'd have thought he'd have learned his lesson at Quatre-Bras,' Marcus replied. His own voice surprised him, sounding so distant and so calm. 'Or perhaps he's got something up his sleeve.'

'Nothing more dangerous than his arm, in my view,' said Assherson sternly. 'I think he's deliberately trying to lose this battle. I say, Morland, the Beau wants us again. And they say it's an easy life on the Staff! Come on.'

Moments later they were cantering away down the line to take the order to the infantry commanders to have the men form squares.

'And my compliments to the artillery commanders: their gunners are to fire until the very last minute, and then take refuge in the nearest square, after disabling their guns if possible.'

The infantry regiments were already drawn up in chequerboard fashion, and once formed into squares they presented a formidable defence to cavalry alone. The commanders received the orders with relish. Major McLeod of the 42nd nodded impassively and said, 'Aye, ah-huh, we'll do just that. The poor bodies'll no' stand a chance. But just tell me, Morland, what do you make of that? You've young eyes, laddie — what's that movement over against the wood there, behind the French? Is it reinforcements they're bringing up?'

To the rear of the French right was a dark mass of trees, the edge of the Paris Wood, and straining his eyes obediently in that direction, Marcus saw the tiny movement of troops emerging from the trees. He stared, and then said excitedly, 'No, sir, I don't think so. I think it may be the Prussians at last!'

McLeod looked sour. 'Aye, well, I'll just believe in the Prussians when I'm standing alongside one of them. Thank you, Morland. My compliments to the Duke, and we'll do just as he says, and make a bonny fight of it.'

Over on the far left wing, Marcus finally came up with the pigtailed men of the 10th Hussars, and Colonel Theakston rode up to him, his face grave.

'I heard about your father. I'm so sorry, my boy.'

'Sir,' said Marcus. He looked across the colonel's shoulder. 'I think it's how he would have wanted to go. One of his sergeants — Mitchell — told me about it. Even though Papa was badly wounded, he charged straight at the French and broke through them — otherwise none of them would have got back.'

'Yes, I heard about it.' Something in Lord Theakston's voice told Marcus that whatever either of them said, they both knew that the cavalry charge had been an appalling waste of men and horses, and that it was not so much glorious as bungled. But the dead had their dues. 'It's going to be a dreadful shock to your poor mother,' Theakston went on.

'Yes, sir,' Marcus said. And without Papa's support, he thought, what chance is there for Bab to marry Bobbie? Well, once I'm twenty-one, I shall be head of the household, and we'll see then if I can help matters along. Head of the household? Absurd thing to be thinking in the middle of a battlefield, he rebuked himself sternly.

'You must take care of yourself, my boy,' the colonel said. He thought of the Guards at Quatre-Bras. 'We've lost too many young men already.'

'Yes, sir.' Marcus hesitated. 'A bad business, that, sir — Bylandt's.'

Theakston shrugged. 'Not entirely unexpected, I believe. And they were badly positioned. Do you know what's happened to Sophie's young man?'

'I saw him going back to try to rally them, sir.'

'Ah, so he wasn't hurt. Good. Good. Well, he'll be out of the battle now, I suppose. Our womenfolk would be glad to know at least one of their men is going to come home safely.' He looked across the valley to where the French cavalry was now assembled in a solid mass behind the guns. 'This looks as though it'll be a hot one.'

The customary cannonade was more intense than before, the

heaviest, said many of the veterans, they ever remembered. The silence which followed seemed to ring with after-echoes, and then the battered ears of the Allies distinguished the sound of cavalry trumpets. Company by company the French horse began to move down the hill and across the valley: cuirassiers on the right with their shining helmets and breast-plates; and on the left the lancers with their bright, gaudy uniforms and festive, fluttering pennons, and the chasseurs, magnificent in gold-frogged green, bearskins and swinging fur-trimmed pelisses.

They moved only at a slow trot, for the astonishing Belgian rye was well up to their girths, and the horses shouldered through it as though breasting a strange green sea. Under-neath the ground must already have been badly poached from previous troop movements: the height of the rye had prevented the earth from drying out after the heavy rain. When they reached the slope of the Allied position, their progress became even slower, as the weary horses slipped and stumbled on the wet, greasy turf. Instinctively they turned sideways to the hill and moved up it at a diagonal, presenting an ever-wider target to the Allies.

Then the guns opened fire. The carnage was hideous. Horse after horse fell, whole squadrons being wiped out, and the French wavered as the heaped bodies of dead horses further impeded the advance. The gunners, true to orders, blasted away until the French were almost on top of them, and then scurried back to the nearest square, most of them bowling a wheel from the gun carriage before them, and flung themselves down under the bristling hedge of bayonets with their hands over their ears.

The French were through the batteries now. There was nothing they could do about the guns, having no means of spiking them, and being unable to tow them away; they reformed their disordered front ranks, quickened their pace and charged the squares across the short stretch of level ground. At thirty paces the redcoats opened fire, pouring out musket-shot on the French, the balls rattling on the breast-plates and helmets like hailstones, felling horses and toppling men. The rear ranks reloaded and passed the muskets forward, so that the fire was almost continuous, and the

French cavalry veered aside, only to find themselves under flanking fire from the sides of adjacent squares. This was the great strength of the chequer-board arrangement.

The pressure of the advance compressed the cavalry into the confined spaces, making them ever a better target, and they milled about, suffering heavy loss, seeking for some weak place in the Allied defence and never finding it. One or two bravely rode up to the redcoats and fired their pistols into the ranks, perhaps in the hope of drawing fire and giving their colleagues a chance to charge empty muskets. But the weary horses, now hopelessly crammed together, were unable even to trot. They walked round and round the hedges of bayonets in a helpless mill until they were shot down.

Lord Uxbridge, meanwhile, had gathered together what cavalry he could, and now counter-charged, and the French horse were driven back off the ridge and down into the valley. Immediately the Allied gunners scuttled forward again, bowling their wheels before them, to man the guns for the next attack. As soon as the French cavalry was back behind its own lines, the artillery cannonade began anew, and the Allied soldiers were ordered to lie down again.

Now the Duke, with his staff behind him, road up and down the lines, inspecting the damage and heartening the men. Everyone hated the artillery cannonade, but the sight of the leader, that expressionless face and the cold eyes above the famous hook nose, steadied them. He paid no more attention to shot and shell than if they were summer flies, and old Copenhagen heeded them even less. If he could stand it, the men thought, so could they.

The deafening barrage stopped, and for the second time the masses of French cavalry started up the hill under fire from the Allied artillery and from skirmishers crouching behind the bodies of dead horses. At the order, the redcoats scrambled gratefully to their feet to form squares again. This was infinitely preferable to lying in the mud, helpless and unable to reply, while shells exploded all around and richocheted overhead. Cavalry charges were terrifying to foot-soldiers, but this was nothing like a charge — no whirling cloud of dust bearing down on them, no growing thunder of hooves, no sudden emergence of maddened horses and gleaming blades, no irresistible impetus. Instead, here were very human, tired, exasperated Frenchmen driving their weary, sweating horses in pointless circles, fetlock-deep in mud, swearing like the troopers they were as they tried in vain to find a weak place to thrust in.

It was dangerous all the same. There were so many of them, armed with swords, sabres, pistols and carbines, that it seemed sometimes they would prevail simply by force of numbers. The infantry was hard-pressed: men fell, and the cry of 'Close up!' was heard like the punctuation of musketry. But the squares held firm, firing their devastating volleys; when a man fell, another took his place, keeping the walls intact, while the rear ranks dragged the dead and wounded into the middle of the way; and at last the Allied cavalry appeared again to drive the second failed attack back down the hill.

The hellish cannonade began again, and the men lay down, covered their ears, and prayed. Marcus, cantering along the line to relay a request for ammunition, was suddenly flying through the air, his horse having been blown out from under him by the ricochet of cannon-ball. He rolled over twice, and then sat up cautiously, feeling his undamaged limbs with astonishment.

'That was a close one, laddie,' came a familiar voice, and he looked up through a mask of blood to see Major McLeod, his puce face clashing horribly with his scarlet jacket. 'Are ye all right?'

'I think so, sir,' Marcus said dazedly, putting a hand up to his head. 'I seem to be bleeding a bit.'

'Och, that's a wee bit of a cut, no more. Everything's still in place, dinna worry,' the major said cheerfully. 'I'll get my surgeon to clean you up. Here — McFazdean — have you a wee bit of lint to spare for a staff-officer?'

Marcus got to his feet, looking about him. 'My horse — ' he began, but McLeod laid a huge hand on his shoulder and shook his head. 'There's no' much left of him, the poor beast.' His blue eyes were sympathetic. 'Hard pounding, this — but we'll see who lasts longest! You staff-officers run the gauntlet, don't you?'

The surgeon came up with his bag, parted Marcus's hair

506

with brisk fingers, and said, 'Nothing but a scalp wound — they always bleed like the devil. Clap this to it, while I bind you up. It's only a shirt-sleeve, but I've run out of bandages. The owner doesn't have any need for it now.'

'Wheesht, man,' McLeod said testily, but the surgeon shrugged.

'I'm a doctor, sir, not a soldier. There, you're done. How do you feel? Headache? Double vision?'

'No, I don't think so.'

'Good. Because if you were concussed and I advised you to lie in a darkened room for two days, I don't suppose you'd do it.' And then he was gone, leaving Marcus feeling a little bemused.

'Thank you, sir,' he said, turning to the major. 'I must go and find my spare horse and get back to the Duke.'

'Aye, well,' said McLeod. 'I heard about your father, by the by. It was a bonny charge — you'll be proud of him.'

'I haven't really managed to take it in yet, sir.'

'Aye, I dare say. You'll know it when all this is over. It'll be the women's tears that bring it home to you. I remember when my son was killed at Salamanca, it was just the same way. I never knew it till I went home and told my wife. Away ye go, laddie,' he said dismissingly, and then, 'Ah, Jesus — !' A ricocheting ball had just knocked three of his front-rank men into smash, and the soldiers on either side of them were scrambling instinctively away from the mess. 'Lie still, you beggars! Ye'll get your damn' heads blown off!'

The major strode away to his men, and Marcus wiped the blood out of his eyes with his sleeve, turned his gaze resolutely away from what was left of his horse, and set off towards the cross-roads.

The cannonade stopped again, and the army waited breathlessly and a little disbelievingly for yet another cavalry attack.

'Why don't they send up the infantry?' Assherson exclaimed for the tenth time. 'They've seen what our squares do to their cavalry.'

'They've seen what their cavalry does to our squares. They're getting smaller all the time,' Marcus said, engaged in cleaning his face with spit and a handkerchief. He had taken

507

over his second horse, and his servant, a veteran from the Duke's Sepoy days, had insisted on going back along the line to see if he could retrieve the tack from Marcus's dead first mount.

'All very well for you, sir,' he grumbled when Marcus expostulated. 'You haven't spent the hours what I've spent cleaning that there saddle, to say nothing of the stitching of the brow-band with me own 'ands. And if I leaves it there, some sojer'll 'ave it, and the next thing you know you'll see it in some saddler's window in Brussels, labelled second-'and, one gentleman owner.'

'It's probably damaged beyond repair. I'm afraid there wasn't much left of poor old Fieldfare. You'll get yourself killed for nothing.'

Bates's eyes took on a little moisture. ''E were a good 'orse, sir, poor old bugger,' he gave his feeling epitaph; and then his face hardened. 'All the same, that's a good English 'unting saddle, and I ain't a-going to let no thieving footsojer take it 'ome for a soovy-near, and that's all about it, sir.'

Marcus's mind came back to the present as Assherson said, 'I wonder if it's because of those troops you saw coming out of the Paris Wood? Say they were the Prussians after all? If they were, Boney'd have to send someone against 'em, wouldn't he? Maybe that's what's keeping the infantry busy.'

'You may be right,' Marcus said. 'If so, the Prussians may save the day after all. But we're going to be busy enough without the infantry — see, here they come again.'

'Magnificent beggars, aren't they?' Assherson said, shaking his head. 'Come on, the Beau's on the move. I think the men are going to need him! They're hard-pressed — it's been over an hour, now.'

The third cavalry attack was the heaviest of all: the French mounted more than ten thousand men, and also brought up a horse-artillery battery, which from a range of four hundred yards rained terrible destruction on the Allied lines. The squares contracted, and within their red walls the dead and wounded lay heaped, crying in pain, tortured with thirst from the heat and the smoke, while the army surgeons crawled amongst them doing what little they could to relieve the suffering. The aides galloped frantically up and down, relaying desperate appeals for more ammunition, for new officers, for instructions; and turning back the occasional fugitive when the cuirassiers managed to cut off a few men from the corners of the squares.

But still the squares did not break, and Allied artillery brought up from the rear at last began to tell on the attackers. They wavered and began to fall back, and for the third time the remnant of the Allied cavalry came forward to drive the enemy back down the hill. Marcus caught sight of Colonel Theakston at last seeing the action he had longed for. Whooping like a banshee, whirling his gleaming sabre like a circus juggler, the colonel galloped through the lines with his troop, riding down the fleeing French with every appearance of savage enjoyment.

Marcus grinned to himself, thinking how hard it was to associate this fierce fighting man with the elegant, languid figure which had graced so many a London drawing-room. He checked his horse to allow two soldiers to cross his path, carrying a wounded officer between them to the safety of the area behind the lines. He glanced at them a little suspiciously — it was always possible for cowards to evade action by carrying wounded back and then not returning — and he was about to admonish them not to linger when he realised that the glaring blue eye in the empurpled face belonged to Major McLeod. There was only the one — the other was covered with a bloody handkerchief which stuck here and there in patches to what was left of the face underneath.

The cavalry charges had been repulsed, but the battle was not over, and a new crisis was brewing in the centre. For the first time the French mounted a properly balanced attack of infantry supported by artillery and cavalry, directing it straight up the road on the farmhouse of La Haie Sainte. Major Baring, defending with his men of the KGL, was running out of ammunition. He had sent repeated requests for more ammunition — Marcus had gone back with two of them — but the bullets had never arrived. One waggon had lost its driver to a French sniper and had not reached him; and the one consignment that had arrived had proved to consist of ammunition for the Baker rifles of the 95th, which would not fit their German Lands.

Now under the concerted French attack — the third attack of the day on the farmhouse — the KGL were down to their last few rounds per man. Of the original four hundred defenders, there were now only forty on their feet. Baron Ompteda, noting the situation, led a counter-attack with a battalion of infantry, but the French cuirassiers turned aside and cut them down, killing the Baron himself. The farmhouse had caught fire, and Baring's men had fired their last shot. They had no alternative now but to evacuate, after having held the position all day; and they withdrew, fighting a hand-to-hand rearguard action until they could fall back behind the defence of the riflemen in the sandpit.

Marcus, on his fresh horse, had been sent off beyond the left wing to look for the Prussians, and returned to find the situation as bad as it had yet been. Using their control of the farmhouse, the French were bringing up heavy artillery with the obvious intention of mounting a battery on the road, from which position it could tear the whole centre out of the Allied line. The riflemen, reduced to a handful, were still holding the sandpit, but under increasingly heavy fire from the farmhouse. Behind them Sir John Lambert was holding firm with all that was left of his 10th Brigade, still in a square around the heap of their dead comrades.

Marcus was sent across to the right wing to order Colin Halkett to move his men over to fill the gap left by the destruction of Ompteda's, and passing behind the sandpit heard his name called, and saw Philip Tantony limping towards him.

'Are you hurt?' he asked quickly. Tantony's face was black with the smoke both from the burning farmhouse and the guns, which kept drifting across obscuring the view, but his eye-sockets were pale where he had continually rubbed them. His clothes were mud-spattered and the sleeve of his jacket was torn, and the lace was hanging off his left shoulder where a ball had torn through it. More than all that, however, he looked exhausted.

'No, no, I just twisted my foot,' he said hastily. 'The thing is, we can't hold on much longer. Can you tell the Duke I shall have to fall my men back — '

'Your men?'

'All the senior officers are dead. I'm in command now,' Tantony said. He seemed a little dazed. 'Nearly everyone's dead. We have to fall back, unless he wants us to die where we stand. It's up to him. But we haven't had any orders for hours.'

'Everyone's been asking for orders,' Marcus said. 'The Beau just tells them he hasn't any — his plan is simply to stand ground until the last man falls.'

A salvo from the French battery shook the ground under their feet and shot whistled past on either side of them. Marcus flinched, but Tantony didn't move, only said, 'For God's sake', in a dazed sort of way.

'I must go,' Marcus said. 'Message for Halkett. Do you want me to tell the Duke anything?'

Tantony seemed to shake himself awake. 'I'm falling them back,' he said. 'It would be madness to stay. If someone doesn't knock out that battery, there'll be hell to pay. Tell him that.'

And then he was gone, scrambling through the smoke back to his own position. An irrascible voice shouted, 'Get out of the bloody way! You're masking my fire!' and Marcus kicked Blackbird hastily into a trot and crossed gratefully behind the hedge on the other side of the road.

By half-past six the French battery had wrought terrible damage on the centre of the line, and the Duke sent for almost his last reserves — the Brunswick infantry and Chasse's division from the far right wing — to plug the gap. The Prussians, owing to some confusion in the line of command, had still not arrived on the left wing, though part of the Prussian army — Bülow's troops — had indeed emerged from the Paris Wood and had been engaging Napoleon's attention at Plancenoit.

Alten had fallen; the Prince of Orange had been carried off wounded; Oliver de Lancey had been struck down by a cannonball at the Duke's side, and was dying; Assherson was dead, shot through the head. Marcus was sent to order Vandeleur's and Vivian's from the far left wing to reinforce the infantry at the centre and stop the French from breaking through under the cover of their artillery. Passing behind the line, he hadn't gone very far when he realised that there was a company of light cavalry riding towards him, and that the officer at the head was Colonel Theakston.

'I was just coming to fetch you, sir,' Marcus called out. 'The Duke needs the 4th and the 6th Brigades to reinforce the heavy cavalry at once.'

'Sir Hussey has already given the order on his own initiative,' Theakston called back. 'The Prussian cavalry's starting to arrive at last. Thought we'd be more use in the centre.' He glanced around at the scene of desolation. There were dead and dying men everywhere, and the bleeding wrecks of horses, some still crying out their sad and trusting appeals to their human masters. A pall of smoke hung over everything, darkening the afternoon, and through it guns spoke with orange flashes, and shot came tearing through the twilight to gouge up the earth and fling a hail of stones and mud over the hard-pressed defenders.

'Bit of a mess,' Theakston remarked mildly. 'Where's Lord Edward Somerset? Orders to join up with him.'

Marcus directed his gaze to where the cavalry commander sat with two squadrons of heavy cavalry on the far side of the road. 'Over there.'

'But where's the Household Brigade?' Danby asked.

'That's it,' Marcus said, turning away.

Leaving the light cavalry, he rode back along the line, looking for the Duke, to make his report. He met Billy Cecil, hatless and with the breast of his jacket torn across, riding across from the right wing. 'Do you know where the Duke is?' Marcus called.

'He's bringing the Brunswickers up. Some of them were wavering, and he decided to rally them himself,' said Cecil.

'Thanks,' said Marcus, making to ride on.

Cecil held out a hand to stop him. His mouth was trembling as though he were about to be sick. 'I say, Morland, this is some show, ain't it?' Marcus stopped and eyed him frowningly. 'Did you know Canning's dead? And Gordon's got it — the Beau don't know yet. And de Lancey. And —'

'Shut up!' Marcus said. 'What good does that do? Pull yourself together, for God's sake!'

Cecil's eyes filled with tears. 'I didn't think it would be like

512

this. Thought it would be rather a lark. Bel said she'd dress in men's clothes and come with us. We were going to — ' He broke off suddenly and turned away, and kicked his horse into a trot. Marcus stared after him, and saw him hunch his shoulders, his hand pressed over his mouth.

Marcus shrugged and rode on. He was coming up to the centre where the line was being swept by artillery fire, and since he didn't want to be killed uselessly, he swung north to pass behind the heavy cavalry and cross the road further up. It was comparatively quiet back here, and a large number of wounded men were lying on the grass, being tended to by army surgeons and, he noted, by a number of women. Soldiers' wives were astonishingly tough and brave, he thought. They might have stayed well back with the baggage, where it was safe, but most of them seemed to prefer being near their men and making themselves useful. They were a practical breed, who would mend and cook for their men, barber them, tend their wounds, clean their arms and, when their husband fell in battle, would bury him and marry someone else from his company, so as to remain on the ration-strength. There was seldom any shortage of applicants, for only five women per company were allowed, though there was a certain amount of winking at irregularities.

Marcus remembered one tough little woman, like an iron-clad fieldmouse, who had gone through the whole Peninsular campaign with the same company, being married by the regimental chaplain to six men in succession. When her second-last husband had fallen at Salamanca, she had searched the battlefield for him, and finding him mortally wounded, had carried him back to camp on her back, though he was twice the size of her.

Thinking these thoughts he had almost reached the road when a wounded man nearby raised a hand, and glancing down, Marcus saw that it was Philip Tantony. The realisation hit him like a wave of icy water, and he pulled Blackbird up and slithered clumsily down from the saddle to kneel beside the rifleman.

'Morland — damn' glad to see you,' Tantony whispered. Someone had rolled up his jacket and propped it under his head; his shirt was red and wet.

513

'Tantony — are you badly hurt? Has someone seen you?' Marcus said. He was ashamed to find his voice shaking. Tantony's mild brown eyes were clouded, his face was so drawn that Marcus thought Rosamund would probably not have recognised him. 'I'll get a surgeon to you, old fellow — '

'Don't.' The word was hardly more than a sigh, but accompanied by an urgent movement of the hand that must have cost a great deal. Marcus caught the hand in his, and it gripped surprisingly fiercely. It was very cold, and clammy. 'No use. I've had it.'

Marcus felt his lip trembling, felt helpless tears hot behind his eyes. 'No, don't say that, you'll be all right. You'll be — I'll get someone. They'll patch you up.' He was babbling, he knew, and stopped himself. Tantony held on to his hand and waited, and when Marcus fell silent, he smiled slightly, and closed his eyes.

'Glad you're here,' he whispered. 'Wanted to say — ' A long pause; Marcus had the sense to wait this time. Beside, he was afraid if he spoke he would sob. The unshed tears were making his throat ache. 'Best man won after all!'

'No — ' Marcus said, and in speaking, sobbed. All around him men were dying, but he wept for Tantony, bitter, bitter tears.

'When you see her — tell her — goodbye from me. Wish you well.'

Marcus bent his head, and his tears fell hot and painful on his cheeks.

'Make her happy.' Tantony's voice was a faint whisper now. After a while his hand grew slack, and Marcus thought he had gone. He laid it down on Tantony's chest, but as he tried to release it, he felt the slightest pressure. Tantony's eyes opened again.

'Glad I saw you,' he whispered. 'Lonely - dying.'

'I won't go,' Marcus said. 'I'll stay with you. I'll stay until someone comes.'

But Tantony's gaze was fixed on the sky. Marcus knelt in the wet grass, and his tears made clean tracks down his grimy face.

It was seven o'clock. Heavy smoke hung over the centre of the

514

Allied line, and over the battered walls of Hougoumont, which still had not fallen to the French. On the far left wing the Prussian skirmishers and some cavalry were keeping the French occupied; and from beyond the French right flank could be heard the dull booming of Bülow's guns. In the centre the French battery was still causing trouble, but the light cavalry, reinforcing the remnants of the two heavy brigades, still held the Brussels road, refusing to move out of range for fear of leaving it open to the French. To everyone's surprise, a company of the Dutch-Belgian 5th Militia marched up under their junior officers to make a stand. Colonel Theakston looked for Major Larosse but couldn't see him; recognising Captain Dietmar, he called him over and asked where the major was.

'I haven't seen him, sir, since the first attack. He went after some deserters and didn't come back.'

'Didn't come back? What are you saying, man?' Theakston frowned.

Dietmar shrugged. 'I don't know what happened to him, sir,' he said neutrally. 'I've been over on the right wing, guarding the Nivelles road, ever since then. Now we've been ordered up to reinforce you.'

There was no time — and no point — in questioning further, but Danby was disturbed by the story and the inference. He would have staked his reputation that Larosse was sound, but it was always possible that he could have been mistaken. If it were so — if Larosse had taken to his heels, either from cowardice, or from the sudden realisation that he had not the stomach to kill his own countrymen — it would be a damned hard thing for poor little Sophie. And for her mother — Héloïse had taken to Larosse. Well, damnit, they all had. No, it wasn't possible. He'd stake his life that Larosse was sound. He was somewhere around — or else he had rejoined the fight somewhere and been wounded.

An aide — one of the few remaining — came galloping up to warn that the new attack that could be seen massing all along the line was to be led by Napoleon himself. 'A French deserter warned the Duke, sir: it's the Imperial Guard this time. Boney's down to the last shot in his locker.'

The aide was about to go on, but Danby stopped him.

515

'What does the Duke say?' he asked.

The aide shrugged. 'He says we'll stand to the last man, sir He says it's either nightfall or Blücher.'

Danby laughed. 'Ha! That's like him! Very well — le Boney come. The Tenth will know what to do with him.'

Larosse was even at that moment with Sophie. They were in a farm cart, lying back in the soft, fragrant hay as the stolid horses clopped peacefully home from the fields. The road ran through the woods — one of those old, old lanes which had sunk over the years, so that the trees grew up above them on banks twisted into caves by the exposed roots. There was a delicious smell of damp earth, moss, beech-mast, leaves, and the sharp-sweet odour of vetch and cow-parsley. Lying back, they looked up at the leaves, a green-gold cave arching above them where the branches grew right across the road. The sun was going down. It had been a long day filled with pleasant labour, and they were sun-dazed and langorous with sweet weariness.

Sophie leaned over him, smiling. Her teeth were very white and sharp. Her dark hair fell forward over one shoulder. It smelled of hay and sunshine; her skin smelled of warm apples. She was laughing. He loved her, and they were going home together, to his home — their home. She tickled his face with a wisp of hay, and he laughed too, because it prickled, and made him want to sneeze. He laughed protestingly: he wanted to push it away, but he was too weary. For some reason he could not move his arm ...

He woke suddenly with a cry of fear. The savage little wedge-shaped head drew back, the whiskers which had touched his face twitched, and the weasel was gone, leaving only its stink behind. It was dark in the wood. Larosse strained his eyes upwards at the leaf canopy, not knowing if it were really growing dark, or if it was the darkness of death on his eyes. He was very cold — probably that was what had emboldened the weasel. He shuddered inwardly at the thought of the beastly thing nibbling at him, eating him while he was still alive.

He was abominably thirsty. That was the worst thing — far worse than any pain, for pain one could shut one's mind

516

to, but thirst nagged and nagged, an ever-present trouble. No-one had come. He had no idea how long he had been drifting. Consciousness seemed to have come and gone, but he was no longer sure what he really remembered and what he had imagined. He had dreamed often of Sophie — they were good dreams. He had dreamed, too, of rescue, and the waking from those dreams was doubly painful. Twice he had wept, helpless to prevent himself, in grief at the realisation that they had only been dreams.

And what about the battle? He heard its voice in the distance, sometimes louder, sometimes seeming further away. It was still going on, that was all he could say for sure. There seemed to be more artillery fire now — someone was getting pounded, but whether it was the Allies or the French he had no way of telling. Suddenly, savagely, he wished for a round-shot for the Emperor himself, a flying mass of hot metal to smash Napoleon into red syrup, to annihilate him, to release the world from his hateful grip, to give them all peace, so that they need never fight again, never again.

'Die!' he cried out, his voice cracking; and he sobbed, bitterly, like a child: dry sobs — no tears, for he had no moisture to spare.

'Hulloo!' a voice came back, distant, mocking. Go away, dreams, Larosse sobbed inside his head. You've fooled me before. Let me die in peace. 'Hulloo! Anyone there?'

It was a woman's voice. Oh, that was cruel! The mind could develop such refinements of torture: a wicked mockery of a voice. Not like Sophie's voice at all, but still a woman's — a soft, fleshly woman, with warm breasts to pillow one's head, soft hands to caress one's cheek — dark hair that smelled of fresh moss, and dark eyes, and soft lips parted, speaking his name — 'René — I love you, René — '

'Sophie,' he croaked. He reached for her, but she dislimned, like all the other times. 'Sophie, don't go!'

'Hulloo!' The voice was nearer now, and there was a sound of a body moving through the undergrowth, a snapping of twigs, a rustling. He hadn't dreamed those before. And then someone was beside him, and the voice said, 'Ah, there you are. You give me such a fright. Hullo, Major — what's come of you then?'

517

She knelt beside him. He smelled her before he saw her - rank female sweat, and the sourish smell of dirty clothes. Then his eyes focused, and through the gloom he saw that it was a soldier's wife, a shortish, stoutish woman, her hair dressed behind in a larded pigtail in the old style. A veteran army wife, then. She might have been any age from forty to sixty; her face was as hard and red as a rose-hip, her eyes bright and black like the weasel's and her smile revealed teeth stained brown from chewing tobacco. She had probably been following the drum all her life. She must be tough as mule-hide to have survived it, he thought vaguely.

The contrast between her and the Sophie he had been imagining was so ludicrous it made him want to laugh, but to his shame he could only cry helplessly. She stroked his hair off his forehead with a hand as hard as ration beef, and said kindly, 'There, sir, don't you fret. I nearly went away, thinking I 'magined it, till you called again. Give me such a fright, you did! I thought my last hour'd come, for Sophy's my name — I thought it was the ghost of my second come back to 'aunt me! But there, I reckon it must a' been your wife or your sweetheart you was calling, eh? Sophy's a common enough name, ain't it?'

While she was talking she had drawn out from some recess of her clothing a small flask, which she now put to his lips, sliding her hand under his head to raise it a little. Larosse's parched lips and tongue came forward, dreaming of water — cool water — lakes and rivers and waterfalls of water — but it was the fumes of gin that rose to his nostrils.

She must have read his eyes, for she said, 'Thirsty? Well, I got no water on me. Take a drop o' this, anyway. Give you strength. I'll have to try and carry you, and by what I see of you, sir, it'll hurt.' He drank. It was soldier's gin, cheap and rank and harsh, but the fire in his stomach made him feel much less like crying, for which he was glad. His mind was largely rational, but there were bits of it which seemed beyond his control.

She repocketed the flask and ran her tough hands swiftly over him. 'Broken ribs,' she said. 'You should be dead by all the rules. I'll have to bind your arms to your sides, or you'll spring something. It'll have to be my petticoat,' she cackled,

518

making to rise to her feet, 'so don't you look, or my old man'll have the hide off you!'

'Wait!' he said urgently. She stopped in surprise, and then knelt down again, bending over him. 'Bullet inside me,' he said. 'When you move me — may die.'

Her eyes were intelligent. 'Can't leave you here, sir, or you'll die anyway.'

'I know — but listen.' He gathered his resources. 'If — I do — want you — tell — '

'Your wife — your Sophy,' she finished for him. He closed his eyes in assent. 'Fair enough — what's your name, Major?'

'Larosse.'

'Sophy La-ross,' she repeated, nodding.

'No — Morland.'

'Not your wife? I see. English girl, is she? In Brussels? All right, sir, don't you fret. I'll tell her — alive or dead, I'll get your message to her.'

'Tell her — I love her — best. Take — pocket — '

It took a few attempts for her to locate the right thing. She looked in astonishment at the rose-stalk, shook her head, muttered a little, but at last said, 'Whatever you say, Major. You're the guv-nor. And now, I'd better get on with shifting you. There's a mort o' wounded coming back all the time, and now they say there's another attack a-coming — ole Boney hisself and his blinking ole Guard, curse his hide! I'd like to take my belt to him, that I should! I'd whip him till he fell over, and then I'd beat his brains out with a spade — that's what *I'd* do.'

The Emperor of the Franks — the Old Guard — those magical words! The splendour of France! The might of the Empire! And this common soldier's wife would like to whip him with her belt. Larosse closed his eyes, smiling at the delicious incongruity, and chuckled. It was only the faintest chuckle, but the soldier's wife heard it and nodded approvingly.

'That's right, Major — keep your spirits up. Won't be long now, sir, and we'll have you back in the village, and a surgeon to you. You'll be right as ninepence in no time.'

★

It was half-past seven. The setting sun broke through the clouds at last and lay its red-gold rays horizontally over the bloody field. The Imperial Guard — four or five thousand veterans, the cream of Napoleon's army — was advancing on the Allied right centre and right wing, led by Maréchal Ney, old Michel Ney, the Bravest of the Brave. Nearest to La Haie Sainte, Colin Halkett's brigade was the first to engage. Halkett himself fell, wounded, but his men held firm, winning time until General Chasse could bring up the reserves and the guns. A volley of fire shook the attackers; the Duke himself galloped over on the tireless Copenhagen to rally the Brunswickers. The 33rd cheered, pressed forward, and the Guard fell back.

The other two columns of the Guard had swung further to the west and were advancing on the Allied right wing. Here Bolton's battery was still firing in front of the position occupied by Maitland's Guards, who were down out of sight of the French in the sunken Ohain road. From rallying Halkett's, the Duke had ridden on down the line and was sitting his horse behind them, with General Maitland beside him, and General Adam, whose division was to the right of the Guards.

The Duke had his glass to his eye, and seeing the other two columns fall back before Halkett's and the Brunswickers, he lowered it to say cheerfully to his two generals. 'By God, you know, I think we shall do it! We'll beat them yet. Tell your men to hold their fire, Maitland. I want every man to keep out of sight until I give the word.'

The Imperial Guard advanced as steadily under the battery fire as if they were on manoeuvre. They were in column, about two hundred men across, and when they finally halted about twenty paces away in order to deploy into line, the Duke whipped off his hat and waving it in the air, shouted, 'Now, Maitland! Now's your time!'

The Guards rose to their feet, a long, long line of redcoated giants, muskets at the present, bayonets glittering redly in the rays of the setting sun. The French stopped dead, utterly dumbfounded, and the next instant the muskets spoke, sprewing a volley of death at point-blank range into the packed ranks of the Imperial Grenadiers. Fourteen hundred muskets fired volley after volley, and able to reply only with their two hundred, the Imperial Guard was forced to fall back. As soon as they wavered, the Guards sprang forward with an irresistible bayonet charge; and when the Imperial Guard tried to rally, Adam's division completed the rout. The Fighting 52nd suddenly sprang up from behind the standing corn on the far right wing, and subjected the French to a volley of stinging crossfire.

The two divisions of Imperial Guard wavered, turning this way and that, tried to rally and only fell into confusion, masking each other's fire and welding themselves into an unwieldy mass. Another volley of British fire, and another bayonet charge, and suddenly it was over. The unbelievable was happening. 'The Guard is fleeing!' someone shouted.

Not for nothing were they called the cream of the Armée du Nord. They did not retreat lightly, but turned and rallied again and again, and there was heavy loss on both sides; but still they were driven back. Wellington had ridden back to his outlook post at the cross-roads, and from there saw a glorious sight. The Prussians had arrived at last, in force, pouring on to the field from the left wing, throwing the French there into utter confusion. Muffling came galloping up, grinning with glee.

'What do you think, sir? The French saw the Prussians coming, but thought they were French reinforcements, Grouchy's army! When the Prussians started firing on them, they thought it was a plot. Now they're all crying "Treason!" and "*Sauve qui peut!*" We've done it, sir! We've done it!'

Wellington rode forward to the edge of the ridge, stood in his stirrups, and waved his hat forward towards the French. A cheer went up from the nearest troops, spreading like flickering heath-fire down the line in both directions, for this was the pre-arranged signal for the General Advance. Down from the ridge they had held all day the battered remnant of the Allied forces ran, bayonets forward, cheering with all the might of their parched lungs. The Hussars and Light Dragoons drew their sabres and spurred to a gallop, passing the running foot-soldiers and bearing down on the French, who were now fleeing wildly, running for La Belle Alliance, while more and more Prussians poured on to the field from the east.

The Old Guard, mindful of their reputation and their Emperor, tried desperately to form square to protect him, but the press of the fugitives battering against them like waves broke their formations and they had to retire. Fighting a rearguard action, they retreated from the field in the direction of Genappe, while the Young Guard at last yielded Plancenoit to the growing Prussian bombardment.

The Prussians, marching down the side-road from Plancenoit, came up with the Allied army at the junction with the Brussels road, where stood the inn called La Belle Alliance. The Prussians, looking encumbered and hot in their greatcoats, were chanting a German hymn as they marched along, but they fell abruptly silent at the sight of the grimed and battered Allies; and then the military band marching with them struck up a very tactful 'God Save the King', and a muted cheer went up from the grinning victors.

It was growing dark, and after having routed some show of resistance from the last of the French cavalry, Colonel Theakston ordered his men to form up beside the road and went looking for further orders. He found Sir Hussey Vivian a little further down the road.

'Ah, Theakston — your men all accounted for?' said Vivian, recognising Magnus Apollo, who was noticeably too big for a Hussar horse.

'Yes, sir — I've got 'em penned up over behind the inn. Are we to go after the French, sir?' he asked. 'I'm afraid of losing half my regiment in the dark.'

'I'm waiting for orders myself. Colborne says the Duke's on his way to shake hands with Blücher — ah, there's Vandeleur! Over here, Sir John!'

Vandeleur rode up from the Brussels direction and halted his sweating horse beside them. 'Uxbridge has got it at last — stopped one in the knee just as we charged for the last time!'

'No! What infernal luck!' cried Sir Hussey. 'And he'd come right through the day without a scratch.'

'Missed the Beau by that much — ball passed right over old Copenhagen's withers, Colin Campbell said. He carried

Uxbridge off. I suppose he'll lose the leg — damn' bad show.'

'So you're in command now,' Vivian said. 'You're the senior. Are we to pursue the French?'

'We'd better wait and ask the Beau — he's on his way here now. The first thing will be to order the cease-fire — our men and the Prusskies are shooting each other in the dark.'

'If we are to pursue, I'll need my other horse. This fellow's all but done in — and yours doesn't look in better case,' said Sir Hussey.

They both looked at Magnus, who arched his neck and scraped the *pavé* with a forefoot in acknowledgement of the compliment. Vandeleur laughed. 'I think that beast of yours might out-kick old Copenhagen himself!'

Theakston smiled. 'He'd try, sir — he's as game as pie; but I'll take my old Bell if we're going after the French. Her ladyship will want this fellow back.'

'What ho — look, there's Old Forwards! And here's the Beau. A pretty sight this will be,' Sir Hussey stage-whispered. 'A guinea says Blücher manages to kiss our Duke!'

'What, on horseback? You're on!' said Vandeleur.

Wellington with the remainder of his staff, and Baron Muffling, rode up to the road outside the inn, where he came face to face with Field-Marshal Blücher and his staff. Theakston saw Peter Firth amongst them, and nodded to him in pleasure and relief, and Firth gave him a swift grin as he rode forward with Blücher to translate. Wellington rode forward with Muffling and the two generals met in the pool of light falling from the lamp someone had lit in the inn window.

Blücher's face was red with suppressed excitement, his white moustache bristled, his eyes were bright with admiration. '*Mein lieber Kamarad!*' he cried, and in spite of being on horseback, he leaned forward, grasped Wellington's bony shoulders, and kissed him heartily on both cheeks.

'That's worth two guineas,' Vivian murmured to his companions.

'The Beau don't even flinch,' Vandeleur whispered in pretended admiration. 'And think of the stink of garlic! The man's a hero!'

Blücher now whipped off his hat, and his thick white hair seemed to quiver like a lion's mane in the wavering light. He waved his hat eloquently around him and said, '*Quelle affaire!*'

'And that,' said Sir John, 'accounts for his entire knowledge of French. I must go and get my orders.'

The three cavalrymen rode up closer. The Marshal Prince had dropped into German now, which Peter Firth translated, while Muffling translated Wellington's replies. Blücher first expressed his admiration for the Allied troops, their gallantry, their endurance, and for the skill and generalship of his dear friend and ally the Duke. Wellington replied with his customary brevity, thanking Blücher for being true to his promise and bringing his army to the battle. 'If you hadn't arrived when you did, we should not have prevailed.'

Next the cease-fire was agreed upon, and the order despatched, and then Vandeleur, with a polite cough, introduced the subject of the pursuit. Blücher intervened with a flood of German, waving his hand over his staff and his army, invisible in the dark, and Firth translated: 'His excellency begs to be allowed the honour of pursuing the fugitives. His men are fresh, and yours are very tired.'

'But, sir,' Vivian broke in hastily, 'my brigade at least is quite fresh. We have had an easy time of it over on the left wing. Let us take up the pursuit, sir, please!'

Even as Muffling was translating this, Wellington shook his head. 'No, no, Sir Hussey, your men have done a hard day's work. You must put them into bivouac.'

And Firth translated for Blücher, who bent a kindly eye on the cavalry commander: 'His Highness says that General Gneisenau had four thousand horse who have not yet been engaged, and who will pursue the French with all the vigour you could wish.'

Wellington nodded. 'Be it so. I'll speak to you later at Headquarters, at Waterloo.'

Another flood of German drew his attention courteously back to the Prince, who spread both arms wide, looking about him and nodding significantly as he spoke. This time Baron Muffling translated before Firth could begin.

'The Field-Marshal says he will call this battle La Belle Alliance, which is very appropriate and symbolic, you will agree.'

The three cavalry commanders looked expectantly at their leader, and Theakston had to bite the inside of his cheeks to stop himself laughing. They all knew what Wellington's invariable custom was, and the frosty look the Duke bent on the eager old Prussian was really very comical.

'I shall write and sign my battle-despatch to Lord Bathurst tonight at my Headquarters at Waterloo,' said Wellington coldly. 'That is what *I* shall call the battle.'

Around ten o'clock Lord Theakston rode back across the battlefield towards Mont St-Jean, having put his men into bivouac, to report to the Duke at Waterloo. The moon was up, silvery bright between the occasional small, wispy clouds: it was a serene and beautiful night, the kind of June night when you might expect nightingales in the wood and the smell of summer jasmine rich on the air.

There were neither nightingales nor jasmine on the plain across which Danby now rode. The moonlight sparkled in a thousand winking points, reflecting from steel caps and breastplates, and shone on pale, still faces turned up expressionlessly to the sky. Those who watched the tranquil sky so quietly were perhaps the lucky ones, for everywhere amongst the uncounted dead were those who still bled and suffered, sometimes half-rising with a groan, only to fall back again. And there were horses, too, lying in their own blood and entrails, their mild eyes puzzled but patient, waiting for relief; and others who struggled again and again to rise, whinneying their sad appeals to masters who no longer heard them. Magnus, despite his day-long weariness, was much upset by it, and flicked his ears this way and that, sometimes shuddering at some particularly piercing cry of pain.

Away to the left, the battered remains of Hougoumont still sent up a thin column of black smoke, and there the corpses lay thickest, heaped upon each other, tumbled into the ditches, piled against the walls. The battle there had gone on all day, for possession of what no-one wanted to keep or care for.

In this small area, perhaps three square miles, there must be forty thousand dead, and God knew how many horses, lying amongst the trampled and blood-soaked crops of what

525

had once been a sweet and fertile valley. Around the horizon the little villages slept, their spires touching the sky, looking as they had looked for a hundred years. So much suffering, Danby thought; so much slaughter — and for what?

Magnus shied and snorted, and stopped dead, ears going back and forth with distress. Danby, who had been sinking into a daze of weariness, jerked upright in the saddle and saw a little ahead and just beside the road a horse sitting up on its rump like a dog, turning its head this way and that, whinneying again and again in pitiful appeal. Magnus whickered, not so much in reply but in anguish, and the horse turned its head to stare at Danby with great troubled eyes. He stopped Magnus, feeling his stomach knot with nausea and an almost unbearable pity. Both the creature's hind legs had been shot away.

It cried out to him again, and now Danby reached the end of his tether. Amongst all the suffering there was around him, amongst all the horrors he had witnessed that day, this was one too many. He felt for his pistol, drew it out, examined it. It was still loaded — the habit of many years was always to reload when it had been discharged. With hands that trembled almost uncontrollably he primed it, and then slowly dismounted. Magnus might not stand, he thought, when he fired the pistol. He looked around and saw the shaft of a gun-carriage poking up towards the sky, and hung the reins over it, and with reluctant feet walked towards the wounded horse.

He reached out a hand to its head, and when he touched its cheek, it knuckered softly, and nudged at him, grateful for kindness after such long suffering. He caressed its cold ears, and then placed the muzzle of his pistol to the white star on the broad forehead. The horse whickered again, and he found that he was sobbing, but quite tearlessly. He wanted to speak reassuringly to it, but he was unable to, and so he pulled the trigger.

The shot sounded horribly loud, and seemed to echo back off the bright sky. Magnus jerked his head back, but stood quietly. The wounded horse collapsed to the ground, twitched once, and was still. Danby managed to control the spasms of his throat, found himself automatically beginning to reload his pistol, and cursing himself softly, put it away. And then he heard a human voice somewhere nearby, weak but desperate.

'*Moi aussi! Ah, m'sieur, moi aussi!*'

He turned, unable to judge the direction from which it came; turned right round on the spot, and then saw, just beyond the now-dead horse, a man pushing himself up feebly with one arm, his pale, fair head glittering in the moonlight as he gazed urgently at Danby. Unwillingly, Danby took a step forward and then stopped. There were so many wounded on the field — he could not help them. He must get back and report.

As if he had read his thoughts, the Frenchman extended his hand. '*Tuez-moi!*' he cried in a hoarse whisper. '*Pour l'amour de Dieu, tuez-moi aussi!*'

Danby could not wrench his eyes away, and yet he was shaking with the horror of it all. 'I can't,' he whispered. To kill in the heat of battle was one thing, but he could not, he could not shoot this man where he lay, even at his own request. '*Peux pas,*' he said. 'My poor fellow, I can't.'

The Frenchman sank back down to the earth without a sound. Danby turned away, stumbled back towards Magnus, almost broke into a run. He had seen battlefields before — many of them; he had viewed the horrors, and though never quite reconciling himself to them, he had learned to endure them. But this — this — ! He wanted to get away. He could not bear it. He seized Magnus's rein, swung into the saddle, clapped his heels to his sides, and Magnus broke into a weary canter. The *pavé* clattered beneath his iron-shod hooves, and man and beast fled up the road towards Waterloo as though pursued by devils.

In the comparative sanity of Headquarters, he found what remained of the staff assembling reports. Colin Campbell met him as he came in.

'You came through — I'm glad. By God, we could have done with you towards the end! We damn' near ran out of staff.' He shook his head as though with disbelief. 'The Old Man said to Fitzroy — "I've never fought such a battle," he said, "and I trust I shall never fight such another."'

'How is Fitzroy?'

'The sawbones has taken off his arm, but he thinks he'll

live. It was his right, more's the pity — bad luck for a military secretary — but he says he'll soon learn to write with his left. He's through there, sleeping. Gordon's there, too, but — ' He shook his head.

'Gordon, too?' said Danby bleakly.

'He won't live the night,' said Campbell harshly, to cover his own feelings.

'How many more?' Danby made himself ask.

'Canning. De Lancey. Barnes and Elley. Billy Cecil. Young Assherson — '

'Morland?'

Campbell shook his head. 'We don't know. He went over to Papelotte with a message and didn't come back. No-one's seen him, so we have to assume — '

'I see.'

Campbell laid a hand on his shoulder. 'You don't want to hear any more. Better go in and get it over with.'

'Yes. Thank you.' Danby pulled himself together, straightened his shoulders, and knocked on the door of Wellington's room.

The Duke was sitting before the fire at the ugly little table, a pen in his hand, his report before him, and papers all around. Danby could see at a glance that they were casualty lists, and that they were hideously long. The Duke looked up as he came in, and Danby thought he had never seen a man so tired.

'I've brought the casualty list for my regiment, sir,' Danby said, saluting, 'the farrier's report, and the returns.' Wellington nodded expressionlessly. Danby placed the papers on the table, and went on hesitantly, 'I wanted to offer my congratulations, sir. It was a remarkable victory — '

'Oh, don't congratulate me!' the Duke cried out. 'I've lost all my friends! Canning — Gordon — ! Dear God! There's nothing more horrible than a battle won, except a battle lost.'

'But you did win, sir. It's all down to your account — every last man in the army knows that,' Danby said gently.

'It was the closest run thing I ever saw,' the Duke said reflectively, staring at the wall with a frown, turning the pen back and forth in his fingers. 'I don't mind telling you, Danby, I thought myself at times we shouldn't do it. And, by

God, I don't think it would have done if I hadn't been there. But at what a cost!'

'The French are thoroughly trounced, sir.'

'Yes. Every company Boney had was engaged — he has no reserves. I think we have him this time. There's nothing left for him to do but hang himself.'

He sighed wearily, and Danby reminded himself that his General still had a whole night's work to do before he could hope to rest. He mustn't take up his time. He drew himself up.

'Any orders, sir?'

'Your men are in bivouac?'

'Yes, sir, at La Belle Alliance.'

'We will move all the able troops to Nivelles tomorrow — there are supplies there, and ammunition. The Prussians have the start on us, but we must pursue Boney back to Paris. A clearing-up operation, I should call it. I don't anticipate any organised resistance.'

'Very good, sir. Then, may I have permission to go to Brussels?'

'Now? Aren't you tired?'

'I've a fresh horse, sir. I can be back by morning.'

'Very well. You can take some messages for me, then. I shall be there myself tomorrow, but I must let Sir Charles Stuart know what's happened and what I intend.'

'Yes, sir.'

Wellington twirled the pen again. 'I have vacancies on the staff, you know. Wouldn't you like to rejoin us? Anyone can command your regiment in the only sort of action it's likely to see now.'

Danby hesitated, a little embarrassed, and the Duke went on without waiting for an answer. 'Well, think about it, at all events, will you? I'll have the letter for Stuart ready for you in ten minutes. Just wait outside — Campbell will keep you company. And you needn't come back tonight. Report to me at Headquarters tomorrow morning.'

'Yes, sir. Thank you.'

CHAPTER TWENTY

The day had seemed very long to those in Brussels — a long Sunday without news. Bobbie had gone early in the morning to Sir Charles Stuart's, the Ambassador's house. He learned that a despatch had come in from the Duke, written at three in the morning, to say that he expected to give battle that day at Mont St-Jean, but after that nothing more was heard.

The wind had gone round in the night, and it seemed unlikely that any gunfire would be heard, though it did not prevent everyone from straining their ears all day long at any and every sound from without. The day was fresher, less oppressive, and the streets had a Sunday calm about them. Indeed, many of the natives of Brussels went about their usual business as if nothing was happening — going to church, strolling in the Park, sitting at the café tables in the sunshine and drinking the Flemish beer that had so impressed Colonel Morland.

For the women at the house in the Rue Ducale, the day passed like the previous one in the care of the wounded. Dr Edler had proved his worth many times over, and had greatly relieved Lucy's mind by arranging with Dr Brugmans for the removal of the dead to the designated place outside the city walls to the north. He had also organised the less seriously wounded men into teams of sickroom attendants – Lucy referred to them as the loblolly boys — to perform some of the basic daily nursing tasks. It was out of the question, Edler said, for such things to be done by ladies of quality, and the house servants were on the brink of rebellion. Everything ran more smoothly after that, though Lucy complained that she had been left nothing to do but bathe fevered brows with lavender-water.

Bobbie spent the day migrating restlessly between the house, Headquarters, and Sir Charles Stuart's, bringing bulletins back to the ladies every now and then.

'You never saw such a crowd as there is around Headquarters! Everyman and his wife are clamouring for passports: they seem to think that Mont St-Jean is altogether too close, and that if the army has run away once, it can't be trusted not to do so again.'

'Gross calumny!' Rosamund exclaimed. 'They didn't run away — it was a tactical withdrawal, wasn't it, Mama?'

'So I'm told,' said Lucy vaguely. She was worried about a young boy from the 7th Hussars who had lost a leg, and was running a high fever. He didn't understand that his leg was missing — he could still feel it, of course — and he kept asking again and again if he was going to be able to ride to hounds next season. She did her best to quiet and reassure him, but she was afraid of what the shock might do to him when eventually he found out.

The very fact that he was a Hussar brought her husband's danger frequently to mind. There was nothing she could do to prevent what she so desperately feared; she was superstitiously afraid that imagining it might make it happen; but her tired nerves continually ambushed her with images of death and mutilation. Sometimes, as she re-bandaged stumps, she thought that outright death would be preferable to such a fate. She remembered what it was like to lie in his arms, her body stretched out against his, whole and smooth and delightful; and then she imagined life without the comfort of his society, the calm joy of their companionship, and knew that to lose him would be far, far worse.

'Of course we're going to win,' Bobbie was saying. 'So I told everyone I spoke to, but they're all clucking like chickens smelling a fox. You never saw such sights! The passage-boats to Antwerp are so loaded it's a wonder they don't sink, and the northern gates are choked with carriages and waggons. I met Parslow walking poor Dancer, and he told me that three people had begged him to sell her — even though he told them she wasn't sound. Well, I'm glad to be able to say to anyone who asks that none of *my* people is leaving!'

'Have you spoken to Lady Barbara today?' Roberta asked.

Bobbie shrugged. 'I asked her again to come and stay with us here, but she wouldn't. She says news of Uncle Horace and

Marcus will reach her more quickly there. Do you know, I believe she *expects* there to be bad news!'

'Some people are like that, my love,' Roberta said. 'It's in their nature.'

'Yes, but she upsets poor Bab, and that isn't fair, I wish I could take her out for a walk or a drive or something. She hasn't been outside the house for two days now, and she looks so pale.'

Roberta smiled inwardly. Bobbie had always been the kind of boy to like taking care of helpless creatures, and she was glad that he had found someone on whom to lavish his tenderness, who really deserved it. 'She always looks pale, darling,' she said. 'But don't worry — I believe she's quite strong.'

'Well, I've told her that there's not the slightest chance in the world of Marcus getting hurt, and she believes *me* all right,' said Bobbie triumphantly.

Rosamund snorted. 'If your word is all that's needed, perhaps you'd like to say the same of all our men? Fling the mantle of your protection over them, by all means!'

During the afternoon, there was a surprise visitor to the house: Lady Annabel Robb called, and was shewn into the Green Parlour, where Lucy came to her after a brief delay.

'Lady Annabel,' Lucy said unenthusiastically. 'I must ask you to forgive me for receiving you in this way — I am, as you may understand, rather preoccupied.'

Lady Annabel shook her head impatiently, and her glossy ringlets trembled under her smart hat. 'I haven't come to do the pretty, Lady Theakston, but to see if I could help. I heard what you were doing here for our men, and I think it's splendid. When I think of all those poor Guards officers — ' She bit her lip, and her heavenly eyes glinted with tears. 'Farringdon at least has been spared, but Harry Pyne and Burnett and the rest — it's too horrible!'

Lucy was surprised, and allowed it to shew. 'I would have expected you to be on your way to Antwerp by now,' she said, and then, thinking that was a little too rude, she added, 'Does not your fiancé fear for your safety?'

Lady Annabel lifted her chin a little. 'You forget, ma'am, that de Ladon lives here. This will be my home. It is not for us to flee, like visitors.'

Lucy nodded. 'Well, I'm sure your sentiments do you credit, but there is nothing for you to do here. Nursing is not a woman's job — '

'But there must be something I can do! I've seen them in the streets! Young men, handsome men, men I have danced with, so horribly wounded, dying! I can't bear it!'

Lucy considered her with interest. It was an intriguing mixture of sentiment, compassion, fear and regret. She would not have liked to give odds on the marriage with de Ladon coming off, if any of Lady Bel's former suitors survived. Even Marcus might not be safe if he came back from the battle with all his limbs intact.

'If you really want to help, the best thing you could do would be to collect supplies for us from around the town. We need more bandages — as many as you can get — and sheets, and any medical supplies anyone still has hidden. There must be ladies who have kept their laudanum drops. Did you come in your carriage?'

'Yes, it's outside.' Lady Annabel nodded with a mixture of relief and doubt. 'If that is really all you want me to do — ?'

'It will be of the greatest help,' Lucy said gravely. 'And now, if you will excuse me — '

'Of course.' Lady Annabel looked as though she meant to say something else, and then with an abrupt nod of the head, she turned and left.

The arrival in the early evening of the French prisoners taken at the time of the great cavalry charge sent everyone's spirits soaring; but that was the last good news to arrive. Soon the wounded were beginning to come in, and each told the tale of a ferocious battle, the worst they had ever seen or heard of: desperate fighting, hellish noise, smoke and slaughter, and the French coming on after each repulse as hard as before. The Prussians had not come, and there was no knowing if they ever would. Without them, the Allies were outnumbered. The two great cavalry brigades had been all but destroyed — only a handful of men and officers had survived. What could save Brussels now?

Bobbie went at once to Lady Barbara's house, then to

Headquarters, and then came back to the Rue Ducale to say that he was going to ride out towards the battlefield to see if he could learn anything more certain. Before he had returned, however, a wounded trooper from the Greys had been brought in, and he told the whole story of the great charge, and of Colonel Morland's death.

'We wouldn't have got out, none of us, ma'am, but for him,' he told Lucy as she bandaged his thigh. 'He was a brave man, our colonel, and as good as a Scotsman any day, and so I'd be proud to tell anyone.'

When Bobbie came back and heard the story, it was a great shock to him. In spite of everything Lady Barbara could do, he and his uncle had grown quite fond of each other of latter years. After discussing it with his mother, he determined that it would be best for him to take the trooper at once to Lady Barbara's house and break the news to her, and let her hear the story at first hand. 'I will stay there for a while, ma'am, if you can spare me. It will be a great shock for them both.'

'Of course,' Lucy said. 'Everything here is in a way to be done.' And so it was indeed, for an army surgeon had joined them, sent by Colonel Jones, the military commander in the Duke's absence, and he would not hear of Lucy's performing anything but nursing duties. As the numbers of the wounded arriving increased, there was still plenty to be done, but some of the horrors and the responsibility she had faced alone after Quatre-Bras were spared her.

She had time now to reflect on her cousin's death. She had liked him much better of late than when he was a young man and courting her sister; or just after his marriage, when he had been always grubbing for money and wheedling for invitations to live at someone else's expense. While his marriage to Lady Barbara had brought out all the worst of his faults, making the army his career had brought out the best in him. He had died gallantly, and she was glad to be able to reflect on that. It was Barbarina she felt most sorry for: there would now be no-one to counteract her mother's parsimony.

By ten o'clock the wounded were arriving in a steady stream, and once again the streets were filled with dead and dying men for whom no provision had yet been made. Lucy had

Parslow harness her horses to a common cart, and those wounded who could be moved from her house were taken to be billeted around the town in the burghers' houses, to make room for the new influx. They came, some on their own feet, others in carts, sent on from the tents at the Namur Gate when too many arrived at once to be cared for immediately.

Major Sinclair, the military surgeon, came upon Lucy kneeling beside a young Highlander, engaged in digging out a musket-ball from the muscle behind his knee.

'Don't!' the major cried hoarsely, profoundly shocked at the sight. There was blood on her hands and her skirt, a scalpel in one hand and forceps in the other. 'Don't do that!'

Lucy looked up impatiently. 'Don't waste your breath, Major. I will do what needs to be done. I assure you a simple operation like this is within my capabilities.'

'But you're a woman,' the major said, pale with the outrage of it. 'You must not do such things.'

The Highlander turned his grey, sweating face towards the officer. 'She's a lady, sir,' he said between clenched teeth, 'but I reckon she knows what she's doing. Leave her help me, sir — please.'

From the other end of the saloon Edler called urgently, 'Major Sinclair! I need your help, sir!' Sinclair hesitated. 'If you please, sir!' He sighed angrily, and turned away. The Highlander smiled weakly at Lucy, who had already gone back to the business in hand.

'I reckon he's right, ma'am — it's no thing for a lady to be doing. But I'm right grateful to you.'

'Shut your mouth,' Lucy said, not unkindly. 'I'm going to probe now.'

A few bloody, writhing moments later, she said, 'There. That's done. It hasn't broken the bone or damaged the ligaments. If it doesn't mortify, you'll be as good as new. You're lucky you've so much muscle there.'

'I'm a Scotsman,' he joked feebly. A little of the colour began to return to his cheeks now the probing was over. Lucy bandaged the limb tightly, and was about to stand up when he caught her hand in a fierce grip and carried it to his lips, and then laid his cheek against it. She paused, startled. 'God bless you, ma'am,' he said. 'Where did you learn to do such a thing?'

She smiled. 'From a drunken old horse-doctor called Morgan Proom,' she said. 'When I was a little child I wanted to run away with him and travel the world in his caravan. He told me that if you can doctor animals, humans come easy — they at least can tell you where it hurts!'

The Highlander chuckled. 'Horse-doctor, eh? That'll make a good story to tell the lads when I get back. As it says in the Good Book, ma'am, angels come in many guises.'

'I'm sure he'd be flattered to be called an angel,' Lucy said.

'You go on doing what you're doing, ma'am, and never mind the major,' the Highlander said seriously. 'It's wrong, but it's right.'

There was little chance that anyone would get to bed that night, but though they were all tired, they were too anxious to have slept anyway. Thus, when the Duc de Veslne-d'Estienne came by at midnight, he saw the front door open and torches flaring to light the steps, and walked in to find everyone up and fully occupied.

Lucy received him, with Héloïse and Sophie, eager for news of how the battle was going.

'I'm afraid my news is not the latest – I left the battlefield at around seven o'clock. I have been to Hal, and then to report to the Baron — the Secretary of State, you know.'

'Well, but what was the situation when you left?' Lucy asked impatiently. 'We have had nothing but partial views — every soldier sees a different battle, so the saying is. Has it gone as badly as the men seem to think?'

The Duc looked grave. 'It is not well, ma'am, that I must admit. The fighting has been the fiercest I have ever seen, and our men have fallen in terrible numbers. When I left the field, the Duke was calling up his last reserves against an expected attack by the Imperial Guard themselves. We had lost control of the centre of the field to a French battery, and the heavy cavalry was all but destroyed. But the Duke is amazingly calm, you know. He never shews any fear, and still goes on saying we shall win.' He shook his head. 'I don't know. I cannot be sanguine.'

'Well, but what of our own people?' Lucy said impatiently. 'Can you give us news of our men?'

'I'm afraid not. I've heard nothing.'

'The Netherland regiments, Charles,' Héloïse interpolated quickly. 'What of them? You must know how things have gone with them?'

He hesitated. 'We have lost many men. Count Bylandt was wounded in the first cannonade, and the Prince of Orange was carried off shortly before I left with a ball through the shoulder. But I'm afraid — I'm sorry to say that the Netherlanders disgraced themselves.'

'They ran?'

He nodded unwillingly. 'There was some excuse, I suppose. By some mistake, Bylandt's brigade was drawn up in the wrong position, in full view of the enemy, and they took the brunt of the bombardment. They were badly cut up, and when the French infantry advanced, they broke and ran.'

'Ah' said Héloïse, a soft sound of distress.

'It was a great deal to expect of raw troops, I suppose,' the Duc said. 'And some of them — a few — formed up again afterwards and rejoined the battle, but they were not enough to redeem the name.'

Sophie could bear it no longer. 'But, sir, what of Major Larosse? Please — what of him?'

Charles faced her unwillingly. 'His men broke and ran,' he said slowly. 'He tried to stop them, but they went back behind the line, out of the firing. He went after them — one of his captains saw him go after them — but since then — ' He shrugged. 'When the remnant of the 5th Militia formed up again, Major Larosse was not with them.'

Sophie's eyes opened wide. 'What are you saying? I don't understand.'

Charles's look was of reluctant sympathy. 'He left the field on his own feet, unharmed, and he did not return. One can only assume that for some reason he did not wish to rejoin the battle. I suppose he took shelter somewhere, or perhaps he just kept going — '

'No!' Sophie said.

'It happens sometimes. A man can get sick of battle, and simply be unable to face — '

'No! I don't believe it!'

'Sophie, *ma chère* — '

She turned. 'No, Maman, you don't believe it, do you? René was not a coward, you know that!'

'I would not have thought him a coward,' Héloïse began, but the Duc interrupted.

'He was in a very difficult position, you know. He was a Frenchman, he had fought under Napoleon. It must have been very difficult for him to face having to kill his own countrymen, perhaps the very soldiers he had once commanded —'

'No! You're wrong! You're wrong! He would not have run away! Something happened to him, I know it did! Maman, something's happened — tell him! Tell him René's not like that!'

She was growing hysterical. Lucy intervened, taking her niece firmly by the shoulder and escorting her to the door. 'That's enough, Sophie. You're not helping matters, you know. Come with me now, and we'll find something to make you feel better.'

Alone with the Duc, Héloïse said gravely, 'You believe it, then — that he is a coward?'

He looked uncomfortable. 'I wouldn't say exactly a coward. But we know that Napoleon inspires great loyalty in those who serve him. Look at Maréchal Ney. I think perhaps Larosse underestimated the strength of his feelings towards the Emperor, and when the time came, he just could not fight against him.'

Héloïse shook her head gravely. 'Poor man! If that is the way it was, he must be suffering dreadfully. Shall we see him again, I wonder?'

'He'll hardly dare to shew his face here after that,' Charles said, startled.

Héloïse gave him a clear look. 'He would not leave Sophie without a word. He would not do that.'

'You can't — you wouldn't let her marry him now, after that?'

She frowned in thought for a moment, and then said, 'If he has done what you think, he would not ask to marry her. But he would at least tell her — explain to her. He loves her very much, you know.'

'As I love you.' He stepped near, reaching for her hand. 'Héloïse —'

'Oh, no Charles. My dear, you must not.'

'Must not?'

She looked at him steadily. 'Charles, I have made my decision. When all this is over, I am going home. Yes! Please don't say anything. My dear friend, you have been so kind to me, and I am very grateful to you. But my duty lies at home.'

'Your duty,' he said. 'But what of your pleasure, your comfort? I can't bear to think of your being sacrificed to duty, leading a cheerless, loveless life —'

'No, Charles, my dear, you're wrong. It is not just my duty, but my pleasure, too. I belong there. It is home. And I love James. That has become very clear to me. I love him, and he needs me, and I should never have left him to come here. It was foolish and wrong of me. I have been weak, and I am very sorry if I have made you unhappy.'

She had hurt him, she could see. He held himself rather stiffly, avoiding her eyes. 'It is I who have been foolish,' he said. 'I have thrust myself upon you —'

'No, not that! You have been everything that is kind.'

He bowed his head slightly. 'I am glad to have been of service. And now, if you will forgive me, I had better be on my way. Duty calls me, and I must not linger.'

She let him go without another word. He will never forgive me, she thought. And I will never forgive myself.

It was a little over an hour later when one of the footmen came into the Long Saloon, where the ladies were tending the seriously wounded, and said that there was a person below asking for Miss Sophie.

Sophie straightened from wiping the feverish sweat from a soldier's face, and turned towards him, hope springing up painfully.

'For me?'

'What sort of a person?' Héloïse asked in French.

The footman turned to her gratefully and became voluble in his own language. A very strange sort of person, milady, he thought — a woman of a certain age, not a peasant woman, but more like a gypsy. Poor and very coarse. She was English, he thought; and she was asking for Miss Sophie by name, and very insistent about it.

'It is a message from René,' Sophie said. 'He has sent her with a message. Oh, Maman, I must see her!'

'We shall both see her. Take this person to the Green Parlour, Alphonse.'

Lucy gave an enquiring look, having followed only half of it. 'Is it something about Major Larosse?'

'I think so,' Héloïse said. 'Do come with us, please. We may need your advice.'

The visitor looked very out of place even against the shabby elegance of the Green Parlour. Sophie wrinkled her nose involuntarily at the smell of her, and her heart sank a little. Such a person could not have come from René.

The solidier's woman looked warily from one face to another. 'Well, now, 'ere's a welcome party and no mistake!' she muttered.

Lucy, hearing the accent and seeing the pigtail, knew at once what she was dealing with. 'Name and regiment?' she asked sharply.

The woman turned to her. 'I'm Mrs Buckfast, ma'am, and my man's in the 32nd, Captain Riley's company. Would you be in the military way, ma'am?'

'I'm Mrs Colonel Theakston of the 10th Hussars,' Lucy said briefly.

Mrs Buckfast looked suddenly respectful. 'Oh yes, ma'am. I knowed the colonel in the Peninsula — Major Wiske as he was then, ma'am. A very well-liked gentleman 'e was, I'm sure.'

'Yes, yes. Now what's all this about? Have you a message for me?'

Mrs Buckfast bared her brown teeth. 'Not unless you're Miss Sophy, ma'am, which I know well enough you ain't. No, it's with the young lady my business lies — persooming I got the right young lady. Are you acquaint of a major in the 5th Militia, miss? Name of La-something? Which I ferget exactly.'

'Major Larosse.' Sophie stepped forward eagerly. 'You've seen him? He sent you to me? Where is he? Is he all right?'

'La-ross, that was it. I knowed it. I knowed it was La-some-thing. Yes, miss, I seed him all right. It was me what carried

540

him back and got him put on a cart, and stayed with him all the way to Waterloo.'

'Carried him? Is he hurt?' Sophie cried.

'Waterloo?' Héloïse said at the same moment.

Lucy intervened, giving them both a quelling look. 'Hush, please. Buckfast, tell us what you know, and be quick about it.'

'Yes, ma'am. Well, I was behind the lines helping with the wounded and such, and I went off into this bit of wood to relieve meself, and I heard of the major crying. Calling my name, I thought he was, which it startled me considerable, only o' course it was another Sophy he was thinking about. Then I found him, ma'am, lying wounded —' She turned her head, distracted, at Sophie's cry, and then carried on. ' — lying wounded. So I carried him back to Monson John, and got him onto a cart what was taking the wounded back. But when we got to Waterloo, surgeon says this here major mustn't be moved. So I stops with him, and then I comes on here, which he give me a message for Miss Sophy.'

'Oh, please, what was it?' Sophie's lips were white.

'To tell you he loved you, miss, and to give you this.' Mrs Buckfast produced it reluctantly, and handed it over with an air of dissociating herself from it. 'He was very insistent I give it you, miss. I dunno what it is.'

Sophie took it with trembling fingers, and raised frightened eyes to the soldier's woman. 'How badly is he hurt?' she asked, hardly above a whisper.

Mrs Buckfast eyed her uncomfortably. 'Well, miss —'

'Oh, please tell me! Tell me the truth!'

'He was very bad, miss, when I found him. He'd been shot in the chest. I dunno how he came to be so far back behind the line, or how long he'd been a-lying there. He must have been strong to've lived so long.'

The tears overflowed Sophie's eyes, but she seemed to have no awareness that she was crying. 'Shot — in the chest?'

'The surgeon said he had other wounds too, but they was old ones. I stayed with him, miss, but he never said nothing else. I don't think he knew where he was at the end.'

'He's dead?' Sophie turned the flower-stem round and round in her fingers, staring at the woman sightlessly. 'Not dead?'

541

'He died at the inn, just about the time they called the cease-fire. He knew he wasn't going to make it back, miss. That's why he give me the message to give to you. Just tell her, he says, that I love her best —'

'Oh God!' The song. *C'est moi qui t'aime le mieux.* Sophie stared around her as though the room were revolving. Everything was pain — there was no escaping. 'I knew it,' she cried in a strange voice. 'I knew he didn't run away.' She turned blindly. He wasn't coming back. He had left her. The pain was so bad she wanted to die. She stretched out her hands. 'Maman — !'

Héloïse caught her. 'I'm here, my Sophie.'

Lucy woke from a dreadful nightmare to the awareness of someone hanging over her. She tried to scream, but all that came out was a whimper; she thrust out her hand to push the danger away, and then her vision cleared, and she saw it was Danby, outlined in the grey light of dawn.

'Oh, Danby — Danby! I was dreaming! The wounded — crows — it was horrible!'

He sat on the edge of the bed and took her in his arms, and he was real, solid, whole. He smelled of smoke and sweat; his cheek was cool from the dawn air, and very bristly. She clung to him, and the next sound she made was very like a sob.

'My darling!' he said with enormous tenderness. He laid his face on her hair, and felt a terrible upsurge of tears, and he was grateful to be able to remain still and silent until they were under control again. Her hands were spread over his back so as to touch as much of him at once as possible; all her senses were exploring him, for reassurance that he was unharmed.

At last she released him, and they looked at each other for some time. 'I knew you'd come back,' she said, and he almost laughed, except that it had been so terrible. Then the inevitable question. 'How long have you got?'

'A few hours. I brought a despatch in from the Duke. I'll have to report later this morning, but I expect I'll be sent off to get some sleep, since I've been up all night. You don't mind my wakin' you up at such an unearthly hour? It's only five o'clock.'

'Fool! You're not hurt?'

'Not a scratch. I was one of the lucky ones, though. It was a victory, Lucy — but at what a cost!'

'I've seen,' she said. 'They've been coming in all night. Oh, Danby!'

'I know. It's too much for a woman.'

'Yes — but if I hadn't done it —'

'I think that's how the Beau feels — there was a job to be done, and he did it. But it was no triumph to him. At Waterloo, afterwards, he was crying over the lists of the wounded.'

'And is it really over?'

'I think so. The Prussians are pursuing. We'll have to go, too. But the French army is destroyed. I don't think Boney can put it together again.'

He pulled her close again, wanting to feel the warm reality of her, to drive away those horrible images from the moonlit field. 'The horses are all right,' he offered her at last. 'Magnus carried me all day. He was magnificent. I brought him back safe and sound, as I promised.'

She nodded in silent thanks. Then, 'Tell me,' she said quietly.

He gave a shuddering sigh. 'We lost Ponsonby, Gordon, Canning, de Lancey — so many old friends. Harry Uxbridge was wounded, and Fitzroy. Horace Morland was killed —'

'Yes, we heard about that. One of his troopers came in. He said it was a magnificent charge.' Danby didn't refute it. 'Go on.'

'We lost young Farringdon, Lucy. I'm sorry. The fighting was very fierce in that quarter. The Guards put up a tremendous show.'

Her face was hidden against his chest. 'Who else?' she said, after a while.

'Philip Tantony.'

'Ah, no!' She pulled herself up, staring at him in distress.

'I saw his name on the list at Headquarters at Waterloo. The first battalion of the 95th was fearfully cut up. Every one of their senior officers was killed – altogether they lost thirty officers.'

'There's only one I cared about. I liked him, Danby! I

looked forward to having him for a son-in-law.'

'I know. I honoured you for it — for liking him for himself. He died bravely —'

'I don't care! He's dead, and what does it matter how?' She bit her lip. 'How shall we tell Rosamund?'

'We'll just tell her,' he said wearily. 'It's —'

'Oh, Danby, you probably don't know — Larosse, too! A woman came to tell us — she found him lying in a wood behind the line, shot in the chest.'

'What's that? Where?' She told him the story, and he pondered it. 'It's very strange. Could he have been wounded in the line, and not known it, or concealed it? I suppose it's possible. Strange things happen in the heat of battle. Dear God, our young women have had the worst of luck!'

She scanned his face. 'What else? There's something else, isn't there? Marcus? Is it Marcus?'

'Yes, I'm afraid so.'

'Ah, Danby!' She began to cry.

'Lucy, darling!'

'That wicked, evil man! All for his own ambition! My poor daughter — and Sophie! It isn't fair!' She became incoherent, and he let her cry for a while, holding her quietly. The storm was soon over. She wiped her eyes with the back of her hand and drew an unsteady breath. 'And Bobbie — it will break his heart — he loved Marcus so! Oh, Danby, how do we bear it?'

'I don't know. No-one wins a war. And this one has been such a long struggle. I'm tired — we're all tired. I just thank God it's over.'

Lucy heard the strain in his voice, and took a firm hold of herself. He was grey with weariness; she must not impose her weakness on him.

'You need to sleep,' she said. 'Come, I'll help you get your things off.'

'I must wash,' he said vaguely. 'Not fit for your bed.'

'Nonsense! Just you sit there while I get your boots off.' She undressed him as far as his shirt and stockings, and when she turned back from hanging up his jacket, she saw that he had fallen back on the bed, and was already fast asleep. He didn't wake as she hauled his legs up onto the bed and covered him over, and when she got in beside him, he only murmured and turned towards her. She rested her face against his shoulder, and thanked God she had him back safely.

In stories and songs, Rosamund thought, battles end with the victors in possession of the field and the enemy in flight — glorious, victorious; cheering, singing; trumpets, drums and banners; maidens lining the streets and throwing flowers to the smiling soldiers as they march by.

It wasn't a bit like that in real life. The songs and stories didn't tell about the waking day after day to the realisation of grief — your own, and other people's: Sophie's silent suffering — her pinched, pale face; Bobbie trying not to cry — far worse than if he had broken down and sobbed. They didn't tell about the white-faced women hanging around Headquarters waiting for the lists, the lists; the Belgians tugging at every returning soldier's sleeve, asking for news: Did you know my husband, my son? Have you seen him? Did you see him fall?

The stories didn't tell about the wounded, more and more of them coming in every day, and the dead going out on the carts to the war graves; and the convalescents, hobbling round the streets, sitting on steps, staring at you with their haunted eyes; bandaged stumps and bandaged heads, torn faces, missing eyes, missing noses, missing ears. You never heard, either, of the deserters and stragglers who thronged the town, looting and drinking and destroying property, robbing even the wounded, who were too weak to cry out or to offer resistance.

No-one ever mentioned the battleground, either, after the proud moment of victory. But it existed — oh yes! Rosamund, naturally, had not seen it, but there were plenty who had — Bobbie amongst them. He went out there every day, and came back sick to his soul, and Rosamund, seeing how bad it was for him, made a point of making him talk to her, to get it out of him, for she guessed it would fester in his mind if he didn't tell about it.

He had refused to believe from the beginning that Marcus was dead. He had asked everyone he could find, but no-one had actually seen him fall, and therefore, in Bobbie's eyes, his friend and cousin must still be alive.

'But where, Bobbie? How?' Rosamund had asked him, trying to make him think logically. 'If he were alive, he'd have come back, wouldn't he? Or someone would have brought him back. He must be dead.'

But, 'He's not dead,' was all that Bobbie would say. It was his way of enduring what was otherwise unendurable. Rosamund hardly knew what she felt about Marcus. His loss had not yet touched her in any way: she did not think of him in relationship to herself. Ironically, everyone who knew her well was sure she must mind far more about Marcus than about Philip Tantony: she had known Tantony for such a short while, and accepted his offer, as it were, in lieu. She received only formal sympathies on the loss of her betrothed: everyone's compassion was reserved for the way they believed she must be grieving for Marcus.

Yet it was Tantony who had left a great hole in her life. She would not have expected to mind so much: she had thought very little about their future life together, but now it had been snatched away from her, she regretted it bitterly. His companionship — his understanding — his love and esteem. She had lost a man who truly cared for her, who would have devoted himself to seeing that she was happy, comfortable, contented; who would have held her honour as dear as his own. The world was a very fine man the poorer; and as for her — her loss was incalculable.

At night in bed she lay on her side, staring at the wall, remembering everything about him, her throat aching with the tears that would not come. She missed him, and the fact that no-one expected her to weep for him — that she was, in that sense, not entitled to weep for him — made her sorrow the more painful. It was her punishment, she thought, for her folly in clinging to her childhood dreams about Marcus, for not recognising sooner that Tantony was immeasurably the better man. If only she could have the time over again! If only she could tell Philip how she felt! If only she could have him back again! Oh vain, helpless, hopeless wishes! The irrevocability of death fell like a guillotine-blade, severing her present from the bright, hopeful future she had learned too late to appreciate.

She remembered how she and Sophie had hung out of the

window, watching the men march away in the early morning light; saw again Tantony's face turned up to her as he passed below. Still it was impossible to believe that it was her last sight of him, that she would never see him again. She would never marry now. Sophie, grieving openly for her acknowledged loss, would get over it one day and fall in love again; but Rosamund had lost the one man she could truly esteem, and there was not such another in the world.

Bobbie had more than his own grief to bear. Lady Barbara had come at last to the house when she had heard the news of Marcus's presumed death, to accuse everyone of everything, shrieking out all her pain and anger at the loss of the son who was dearer to her than her husband. It was Bobbie's fault for encouraging Marcus to be a solider, Roberta's for buying his commission, Lucy's for marrying Danby Wiske, Rosamund's for wanting to marry him, Barbarina's for wanting to marry Bobbie, Bobbie's again and most of all for admiring Marcus and so encouraging him to risk his life in trying to be a hero. It was anyone's fault, for any reason you liked, but she had lost everything she held dear, and someone, somehow must pay.

Bobbie had borne it all, pale and resolute; and on him the responsibility had fallen, the most unpleasant task, of bringing back the dead. Peter Firth was still with the Prussians; Lord Theakston after a few hours in Brussels had been sent off to Nivelles. Bobbie was the only man of the family around, and with the help of his old friend Parslow, he had driven out first to Waterloo to fetch back the body of René Larosse, who had no-one else to give him a decent burial; then to La Belle Alliance to find and fetch back the body of Colonel Morland; and then, every successive day, to search for Marcus.

The battlefield! It wasn't even, he told Rosamund, so much the dead, though it was impossible to walk without treading on them. The dead one could get used to. After a while, even the most hideously mangled corpse was just a corpse, a strangely irrelevant addition to the landscape. Seen *en masse*, all those tumbled bodies, all that bare flesh, made him think somehow of bread: the valley was a vast bread-basket full of broken bread and torn loaves.

Were they naked, then? Rosamund had asked.

Why yes, Bobbie said, his mouth wry. The scavengers were all over the field, rifling the bodies. One was forever seeing them staggering up the road, weighted down with armfuls of clothes.

But it wasn't so much the dead one minded as the living. Amongst the corpses there were so many who clung to life with an astonishing tenacity, despite the most frightful wounds. Mostly French by now — the British soldiers had largely been found and carried away for treatment, but the French lay there, waiting either to be helped or robbed and murdered by the pillagers. Patiently, so patiently, they lay amongst the corpses, so courteous and grateful for anything that was done for them. There was little he could do but give them water. The eyes followed you, he said — you could feel them, even when you couldn't see them. You'd turn round, and there would be those dark eyes fixed on you imploringly. It was horrible.

And then there were the horses — but he wouldn't tell her about the horses. Parslow took a pistol and a box of ammunition with him every day now, to despatch them when they came across them.

The Duke left Brussels on the twentieth to rejoin the army in pursuit of the French. He had asked Lord Theakston again to rejoin the staff: his services were desperately needed now that so many of the senior aides were dead.

'Do you mind, my darling, if I go?' Danby asked Lucy. 'I promise you there's no more danger. There'll be nothing like a pitched battle — only a little skirmishing, if that. I shan't get killed, I promise you.'

Lucy eyed him sadly. 'You want to go, don't you?'

He was uncomfortable. 'Yes. I can't help it, I do. I've been through so much with Old Hookey, the Peninsula and now this. Damnit, we've been at war with Boney for twenty years — I want to be there at the finish! Can't you understand that?'

'Oh, I understand it all right.'

'But you don't want me to go?'

She stepped up close to him. 'I wish you didn't want to go.

548

But since you do — I won't try to stop you. Only be careful, won't you?'

'Of course I will. I told you I wouldn't get hurt at the battle, didn't I? And I wasn't. Just a few weeks more, just till I've actually seen old Boney lie down and roll over, and then I'll sell out and come home, I promise.' He put his arms round her. 'Why don't you go home with Héloïse and Sophie? And take Rosamund with you. Wait for me there.'

She looked at him with a bright, mocking eye. 'How can I go home, fool? I have a houseful of wounded here.'

'They're not your responsibility.'

'Oh yes they are. Besides, Rosamund won't go until Bobbie finds Marcus's body. She thinks he needs her support.'

'I wish she'd persuade him to give it up. It ain't healthy to go poking around a battlefield day after day.'

'It's the not knowing, you see. That's the worst part of being the one to stay at home. You soldiers have your hardships to bear, but those who wait behind have others. Poor Bobbie feels it very much that he didn't go and fight. He feels to blame in some absurd way for Marcus's death, and he's told himself he must find the body and bring it back for burial before he can be forgiven.'

He eyed her. 'How do you understand so much about him all of a sudden?'

She smiled. 'Actually, it was Rosamund who told me that.'

'You and Rosamund — you're almost coming to be friends, aren't you?'

'She's a good girl, and a great help to me. There's a lot of me in her, you know.'

'There is,' Danby agreed, 'but I hardly expected you to approve.'

Héloïse and Sophie went home on the twenty-first, the day after René Larosse was laid to rest in the little burial-ground at Langeveld. The Duc arranged it all, the ceremony according to the rites of the Old Church, the plot, and the headstone, which was to be put in place as soon as the grave had settled. He accompanied the women to the ceremony, supported them gravely and kindly throughout, and then took his farewell. He had nothing to take him away from

549

Brussels, but he had nothing to keep him there now, either. He said goodbye without great ceremony to the woman he loved, knowing it was better that she should have nothing to remember afterwards.

'Where will you go?' she asked.

'To Ghent, I suppose. To His Majesty. He may have use for me.'

'Oh, Charles — I'm sorry.'

He smiled down at her, his hat in his hand, the breeze lifting the hair on his forehead. It was a warm, damp, grey day, and the rooks were wheeling and cawing about the tall elms that sheltered the graveyard.

'No — it's all right,' he said. 'Thank you for everything. God bless you, Héloïse.'

'And you, Charles. Be happy!'

But he only smiled and walked away.

CHAPTER TWENTY-ONE

Ottershaw, the butler at Morland Place, was extremely proud of his position. Being a local man, he had a proper sense of the importance of the Morland family — which, as far as anything that mattered was concerned, came directly after God, the King and the Prince of Wales, and not too far below them. And being a house-servant from a long line of house-servants, he knew that the butler's standing reflected the family's standing, and that everything — comfort, convenience, reputation and honour — all depended on the king and master of the backstairs.

He was inclined therefore to view the man at the door with disfavour. There were those, in Ottershaw's view, who presented themselves at the great door, and those who did not, and each man who walked the earth ought to know which he was. The great door was for family and for visitors — gentlefolk and, at a pinch, professionals — doctors, lawyers and clergy. Everyone else went to the side.

There was a certain ambiguity about this man, which annoyed the butler, who liked things to be plain and simple. It was hard to place him. His clothes were shabby and hard-worn, he was dusty and dishevelled from travelling, and he had arrived — telling point! — on his feet rather than on horseback or in a carriage. On the other hand there was a certain authority in his bearing, and his voice and manner, though strange and not precisely those of a gentleman, did not mark him down as a labourer or tradesman.

On the whole, Ottershaw was inclined to take a cautious view, and instead of sending him away with a flea in his ear, merely fixed him with his most withering look and remarked icily, 'Her ladyship is from home at present.'

The visitor made a restless movement. 'Well, where is she? When will she be back?'

Ottershaw permitted himself a lift of an eyebrow. 'I am not at liberty to say. Her ladyship is in Brussels,' he said quellingly.

The visitor was not quelled. 'Brussels? Good God!' The brows drew together sharply as he absorbed the information. 'I had better see Mr Morland, then. I suppose he is not from home as well?' Ottershaw hesitated, and he added impatiently, 'Come, man, I have business with your master. My name is Hobsbawn — I suppose that name is not unknown to you?'

Ottershaw's features wavered. 'Mr Jasper Hobsbawn?' That was very awkward indeed. As a cousin of the late Miss Fanny, he was Family and must therefore be treated with respect; on the other hand, it was no secret in the servants' hall that Jasper Hobsbawn was in the process of trying to rob her ladyship of Miss Fanny's rightful inheritance. Ottershaw, for once in his career, was completely at a loss. 'I — er — I cannot say — sir — if the master is at liberty,' he stammered. 'It — er — you —'

Jasper felt a brief sympathy for him, and gave his a grim smile. 'I'm sure your master will see me. My business is of the greatest importance, and I have come a very long way to conduct it. Come, man, do you mean me to discuss it on the doorstep, for every groom and stable-boy to hear?'

At which reminder, Ottershaw saw that there were indeed a number of outdoor servants gawping in the background, and he stood back hastily and admitted Mr Hobsbawn to the great hall.

Jasper looked around him with interest. He had hardly known what to expect when he embarked on what was for him the longest journey he had ever undertaken. He had imagined, if anything, that Morland Place would be a grander version of Hobsbawn House — larger, more elaborately decorated, and even fuller of expensive furniture, vases, clocks, statues and ornaments.

He had not expected to find himself crossing the moat of what seemed to be an infant castle. He had no taste for the old, crooked and picturesque — he liked things to be new, straight, clean and airy. He was surprised that a family like the Morlands should not have pulled down this place and built anew; and even more surprised that the inside of the house was so bare. In the great hall there was a large fireplace with a dog sleeping before it, a side-table covered in gloves and whips and hats and spurs, several small, hard and inhospitable chairs, a number of dim old portraits. There wasn't even a carpet on the floor.

Ottershaw hurried away to find his master, and the dog, with the grey muzzle and pale eyes of extreme age, came up and inspected Jasper before returning to its place before the unlit fire. A moment or two later the butler returned to conduct him across the hall, across another hall containing nothing but a staircase, and into a long drawing-room which struck him as being again surprisingly empty of the accoutrements of wealth, and, equally surprisingly, full of people. Apart from Mr Edward Morland, whom Jasper knew by sight from his visits to the mills, there was another man whose slight family resemblance marked him out as Mr James Morland, a tall man in a priest's cassock, a plain, middle-aged woman in a brown dress, two small male children and three dogs.

Edward came forward. 'Mr Hobsbawn,' he said gravely, without offering his hand. 'I'm sorry you should have been kept waiting. We are rather at sixes and sevens this morning, with the news from Brussels.'

Jasper glanced from him to James. 'News? Not bad news, I hope? I trust her ladyship is well?'

James looked at him sharply. 'Haven't you heard, then?'

'I've been in a coach for the best part of two days. I've heard nothing.'

'There's been a battle at a place near Brussels called Quatre-Bras,' Edward said. 'It's hard to separate rumour from fact, but it seems that Boney took the Duke by surprise, and there was a pell-mell battle. They say our army is in retreat —'

'It's a tactical withdrawal,' the priest interpolated firmly. 'I've said it before and I'll —'

'But we don't *know*, that's the long and short of it,' James said impatiently. His face seemed to Jasper very drawn, as if he had been ill for a long time. Of course, as his blacks indicated, he was in mourning for his daughter, and Jasper was quite willing to believe *someone* had been fond of Fanny Morland. 'It's the not knowing that's so intolerable.'

'I'm sure her ladyship is all right,' said the plain woman. 'You know rumours always exaggerate, and the Duke would surely have made everyone leave Brussels if there were any danger.'

'But he was taken by surprise,' James cried in frustration. 'That's the whole point!'

'The whole point,' Edward said, 'is that they're with Lucy. I can understand your anxiety — I'm anxious too — but Lucy knows what's what. She's very practical, you know, Jamie. She'll take care of everything.'

The plain woman seemed to remember what they had evidently forgotten, that a vile interloper was present and listening. 'I had better take the boys away and leave you to talk to Mr Hobsbawn in private,' she said warningly.

Jasper smiled inwardly, but said only, 'Thank you, ma'am. My business is with her ladyship, but since she is not here, I suppose either Mr Morland or Mr James will wish to hear what I have to say.'

The priest took the hint and excused himself likewise, and in a moment Jasper was alone in the drawing-room with the two brothers, and the watching eyes of a dozen dead Morlands looking out from their gilded frames around the walls.

Edward said, 'Well, Jamie, I suppose this is really your affair.' Jasper looked at him sharply, gathering from his tone of voice that there was some hostility between the brothers on this subject.

James gave his brother a rueful smile, and said, 'Don't go, Ned. I don't feel up to much at the moment, after this news.'

'Perhaps Pobgee ought to deal with it,' Edward said. 'If there's some question of —'

'You needn't worry,' Jasper interrupted. 'I haven't come to quarrel with you — quite the reverse. I've come to apologise, and to put matters to rights. I think, Mr Morland, you will probably want to hear what I have to say, too.'

They looked at him with interest now, and Edward, belatedly hospitable, said, 'Won't you sit down, Mr Hobsbawn?'

'Thank you, but I've been sitting too long already. I'll

stand, if you don't mind.' The brothers had preforce to stand. There was a brief silence as they waited for him to begin, Edward looking at him neutrally, a little warily, perhaps; James with guarded hostility, though he was plainly more preoccupied — and naturally so — with the safety of his wife in Belgium. Jasper wondered briefly what she was doing there — it seemed odd — but obviously no-one was going to tell him.

'I expect you've guessed I've come about the Will, and you'll be wondering why I've come here instead of dealing with Mr Pobgee,' Jasper began. 'The fact is, I'm a plain man, and I like plain dealing. It's the only way in business, and business is all I know. I was born and brought up in the mills; I've worked in 'em and for 'em all my life, and I won't hesitate to tell you I was not best pleased when my cousin left everything to his grand-daughter. She and I,' he said, with a glance at James, 'didn't see eye to eye. I didn't like her, sir, and I didn't believe she had the best interests of Hobsbawn Mills at heart.' James stared. 'I tell you this not to hurt your feelings, but to explain why I acted as I did.'

'Go on, sir,' Edward said. 'You intrigue us.'

'Very well. I was angry when the Will was read, and the mills I had spent my life building up were left to Mrs Hawker. So when new evidence came to light which would mean the mills would come to me instead, it seemed to me that justice was being served. I offer it not as justification, but explanation. I was, perhaps, not as critical of the evidence as I ought to have been.'

Edward was looking puzzled. James, more frank, or perhaps merely less sympathetic, said, 'I don't understand a word you're saying. I thought you said you liked plain dealing?'

'The long and the short of it is, I have discovered that the housekeeper's evidence concerning the time of death of Mr Hobsbawn was a lie. She invented the whole thing in order that the inheritance should come to me, in the belief that I would be grateful to her and reward her financially. I think —'

James was growing red. 'Why, you scheming, treacherous —'

555

'Be quiet, Jamie. Let him finish.'

Jasper shot Edward a look of gratitude. 'I think Mrs Murray may even have hoped I would marry her,' he went on. 'She had been hoping for some time that my late cousin would elevate her from housekeeper to wife, and she was very bitter that she'd been cheated — as she saw it — of what was rightfully hers. She didn't like Mrs Hawker either. But I ask you to believe, gentlemen, that I knew nothing of her schemes. I did not connive at the lie. My fault is only that I accepted her evidence without examining it more carefully. I was uncritical, as I have said — and for the reason I have stated.'

'How did you find out that it was a lie?' Edward asked after a pause.

'Mr Pobgee planted the seed of doubt in my mind, and when I questioned Mrs Murray more closely, she broke down and admitted it.'

'So — when did Mr Hobsbawn die?' James asked, to the point.

Jasper shrugged. 'I have no way of knowing for sure.'

'Then we're back where we started,' said James angrily.

'Not quite,' Jasper said. 'It seems likely that Mr Hobsbawn died almost as soon as he got into bed, which would mean that Mrs Hawker survived him.'

'Then why —' James began.

'Please let me finish. I have to tell you that I am here against the advice of my man of business. He assures me that there is no evidence which would satisfy the Court of Chancery over the time of Mr Hobsbawn's death, and that if I insist on a court hearing, the most likely result is that the estate will be divided between me and Mrs Hawker's heir — who I believe is her ladyship. The next most likely result is that I will be awarded substantially more than half the estate.'

'Then why the devil are you here?' James asked explosively.

'To tell you that I don't mean to fight you,' Jasper said. 'To tell you that I mean to give up any claim to the estate. It is her ladyship's for the taking.'

'But why?' Edward asked. 'Why should you do that?'

'Because it was Mr Hobsbawn's wish that Mrs Hawker

should inherit. Because I am angry and ashamed at having been taken in by Mrs Murray. But most of all,' Jasper looked down at his hands, 'most of all because if I do fight you, if the case does go to Chancery, the costs will be so enormous that the estate will likely be swallowed up. The mills will be ruined, the business destroyed.' He looked up again, his eyes burning in his pallid face. 'I've worked all my life to build them up, and I won't see them destroyed if I can help it. I would sooner you had them, than that. So I give the mills to you, freely and completely. All I ask is that you take care of them. Don't let it all be for nothing.'

There was a silence, broken only by the ticking of the huge marble clock on the chimney-piece, and the faint snoring of the spaniel curled up in the chair by the fireplace. Edward looked at James, but James turned his head away, biting his lip.

'Mr Hobsbawn,' Edward said at last, when it was clear that James was not going to reply, 'I hardly know what to say. This is such a surprise. We need time to think about it —'

'What's to think about?' Jasper said harshly. 'I give up my claim. The Hobsbawn inheritance is yours. That's all.'

'No, it's not! It's not all by a long chance,' Edward said. 'You've behaved most generously — honourably — and I've been churlish. Good God, man, you've travelled all this way, and I haven't even had the common courtesy to offer you refreshment!'

'Oh, come — I didn't expect —' Jasper began, taken aback.

Edward held out his hand. 'Forgive me, please. We are related by marriage, though distantly. Allow me to make you welcome to this house, in the absence of her ladyship.' Jasper gave his hand, and Edward shook it, smiled, and then pulled the bell-rope by the chimney. 'At the very least you will stay to dinner?'

'Dinner. Well, I don't know —'

'You can't be meaning to travel back today? If you came by mail —'

'Stage.'

'Then you certainly can't go back today, for there isn't another until tomorrow. Have you your luggage with you?'

'I left my bag at the Hare and Heather.'

'I'll have it brought over. You'll stay here, of course,' said Edward. The door opened, and Ottershaw appeared. 'Have William go down to the Hare and fetch up Mr Hobsbawn's traps, Ottershaw, and ask Mrs Thomson to make up a room for him. And bring us some wine and biscuits.' He turned back to Jasper. 'We keep early hours, Mr Hobsbawn, so you won't have to wait too long for your dinner. We dine at four.'

Things had moved too fast for Jasper. 'Mr Morland, I'm much obliged, but there's no need for —'

'There's every need,' Edward said. 'We've a great deal to discuss.'

'But I'm afraid my presence isn't welcome to your brother,' Jasper said, glancing at James's averted profile.

'Nonsense,' Edward said stoutly. 'James is —'

'Deeply ashamed,' James exclaimed, turned to look at Jasper with bright eyes. 'I have been behaving like a fool, and I'm mortified! Your generosity, Mr Hobsbawn, has made me see myself in a very unflattering light. Please, you must stay, or I shan't be able to live with myself. As Ned says, there will be a great deal to discuss. We ought to have Pobgee in on it, too.'

'We'll get him up tomorrow. There's no need to worry about that now,' Edward said. 'Today you are our guest, and we must do our best to make you comfortable and entertain you agreeably. Tomorrow is soon enough for business.'

Jasper swallowed this near-heresy meekly. He had found the long journey very wearisome, and his nerves had been at a stretch for many weeks past. The idea of taking a holiday from his cares was very tempting. What lay ahead of him he could not begin to imagine. In giving up his claim to the mills, he was giving up the only life he knew — his work, his home, his security. He would be adrift upon the world, alone and friendless, and tomorrow was certainly soon enough to worry about that.

'Do you ride, Mr Hobsbawn?' Edward was asking hospitably. 'If it would interest you, I'd like to shew you round the estate.'

'It would interest me very much,' said Jasper.

'I wish you would speak to Bobbie,' Roberta said to Lucy.

'Me?' Lucy looked up from the bandage she was rolling. 'What can I do? You're his mother — if he won't listen to you, he'll hardly listen to me.'

'But he admires you. Anything I say he just dismisses as a mother's worrying, but he respects your opinion.' Lucy shrugged. 'It isn't right for him to go on and on searching like this, day after day. Even Lady Barbara doesn't believe Marcus is still alive. It isn't reasonable that Bobbie should.'

'Bobbie didn't fight in the battle: this is his way of atoning,' Lucy said briefly.

'You blame me for preventing him from taking part?'

'Not the least bit, Rob,' said Lucy patiently. 'I understand your reasons, and so does Bobbie. He just can't help himself. You can't argue with love, you know.'

Roberta sighed and looked away. 'I'd give anything if Marcus could be brought back alive! You know how fond I was of him, Lucy.'

'You almost brought him up,' Lucy said obediently. 'I know.'

'But there's no possibility he's still alive.' She frowned. 'I wish I could make Bobbie admit it. He must know in his heart — why won't he give up?'

'He'll give up when he finds Marcus's body. Lady Barbara at least agrees about that. She wants her only son to have a decent burial.'

'Poor Lady Barbara — her husband and her son! What a hideous thing.'

'Yes.' Even Lucy could feel some sympathy in this case.

'But at least,' Roberta went on, 'you could forbid Parslow to go out with Bobbie to the battlefield again.'

Lucy gave an exasperated smile. 'That wouldn't stop him. He'd go without Parslow if he had to — don't you understand that? And wouldn't you rather he had someone to keep an eye on him? That's why I let Bobbie use Parslow. I'd far sooner have my groom to myself, I assure you.'

'Oh, Lucy — I'm sorry. It's just that I'm so worried about him.'

'I know. But you'll have to let him find his own way. I think he's beginning to come to terms with it. He's an intelligent young man — he'll work it out for himself.'

Rosamund saw the cart draw up outside the house, and ran out into the blue air of dusk and down the steps to meet it.

'No luck, I suppose?' she said. Parslow, holding the reins, exchanged a quick look with her, and Bobbie, his shoulders slumped with weariness and depression, shook his head.

'No,' he said. 'No luck. I'm beginning to think ... But he must be somewhere! He can't have disappeared into thin air.'

'Bobbie, I don't think you're going to find him,' Rosamund said. 'I think you ought to resign yourself to that.'

He looked up fiercely. 'Not you, too! I'm not going to give up, so there's no use your telling me to!'

'I wasn't going to tell you to give up — only to be prepared for the worst. I don't want you to go on hoping, only to be disappointed.'

'I'd have thought you of all people would be on my side,' Bobbie said bitterly. 'What with Mama and your mother — and even Lady Barbara doesn't believe any more. If it weren't for Bab — and Parslow —' He threw a glance of burning gratitude at the groom. 'The same time tomorrow, Parslow?'

'Yes, sir, if you wish,' said Parslow. Bobbie jumped down from the cart and walked past Rosamund into the house.

Rosamund watched him go and then turned to Parslow, but the groom's attention was directed elsewhere. Following the line of his gaze, Rosamund saw a soldier in a tattered Dutch-Belgic uniform, a dirty bandage round his head, clinging to the railings of the Park across the road. As she looked, he slumped down and sat on the flagway, his shoulders hunched, his head hanging.

'Oh, Lord, another of them,' Rosamund exclaimed, and started across the road.

'No, miss!' The command was so sharp, she paused and looked back. 'I'll go. You hold the horses.'

She opened her mouth to protest, and then came back and took hold of the bit-rings. Parslow wound the reins and jumped down, and crossed the road quickly to crouch down by the soldier. Even from there Rosamund could see the man was shivering violently. After a moment Parlsow straightened up and came across the road to her. His face was so grim that

Rosamund felt a chill of foreboding.

'What is it? What's the matter?'

He took the reins from her. 'Go inside and fetch your mother to me. And send one of the footmen out to take the horses. Go on — lively now!'

He had no right to give her orders, but she had no inclination to disobey. A few minutes later she was back, following in her mother's wake. A footman had led the horses away; Parslow was crouched by the wounded soldier again. He looked up as Lucy came across to him.

'What is it?' she asked quietly.

'Take a look, my lady.'

Lucy stooped, and looking across her shoulder, Rosamund saw that the man's face was flushed and strangely dusky. His eyes were closed and he was shivering, evidently feverish. As she watched, his lips parted and he attempted to wet them with a dry swollen tongue. Her mother did not touch him. She looked, and then she sniffed, and then she stood up, and her eyes sought the groom's.

'Putrid fever?' she said.

'That's what I thought, my lady,' said Parslow.

'We can't leave him here. We'll have to set up an isolation ward.'

'What is it, Mama?' Rosamund asked. 'What's putrid fever?'

Her mother wasn't listening. 'It would be better to find an empty house somewhere. There are bound to be others.'

'What about the summerhouse, my lady? It's not exactly weather-proof, but at this time of year —'

'Excellent! It's away from the house, and there's room in there for ten or a dozen. It may come to that, before we can set up a proper plague-house elsewhere.'

'Dr Brugmans ought to be told at once, my lady.'

Rosamund paled. 'Plague-house? Mama, what is it?

'Yes. You can go as soon as we've moved this man.'

'*Mama!*'

Lucy turned to her at last, distracted. 'Putrid fever. Jail fever. Hospital fever. Different names for the same thing. I should have been expecting it. I suppose I simply hoped it wouldn't shew up; but with the battlefield so close, and so many corpses unburied —'

'*Typhus?*' Rosamund said.

'Typhus,' Lucy agreed grimly. 'To the victor the spoils, so they say.'

Bobbie was only positively missed when he didn't appear at dinner the next day. It wasn't hard to guess what had happened.

'I suppose he must have hired a horse and cart and gone on his own. I told you it wouldn't help if I took Parslow away,' Lucy said to Roberta.

'I know you did,' Roberta said unhappily, 'Oh, I wish Peter were here!'

'Will he be all right, Mama?' Rosamund asked.

'Of course he will,' Lucy said briskly. She had far more urgent worries on her mind. Brugmans had confirmed her diagnosis of typhus, and there were now three men in the summer-house, and more appearing in the streets all the time. Brugmans had decreed that Lucy was not to nurse the fever-cases, and she had no inclination to argue with him. A fever nurse had been sent along, and a plague-house was to be set up as soon as a suitable building could be prepared.

But Lucy was anxious about the wounded still under her care. They were convalescent now, but most of them were weak from loss of blood, which made them vulnerable to the infection. Moreover, they were her sole responsibility now — Sinclair and Edler had both been moved to military hospitals where their services were more urgently needed. If the fever were not contained, Brussels would become a dangerous place to be, and it would be her duty to persuade Roberta and Bobbie to leave, and to take Rosamund with them. She could guess what resistance she would encounter.

For the moment, however, Roberta was obviously more anxious about her son, out searching the battlefield alone. 'I hope he comes home before it gets dark,' she said. 'He'll probably forget all about the time, and never even notice he's hungry. He gets so exhausted — and it's been so hot today.'

'I'll send Parslow out to find him,' Lucy said resignedly, standing up to ring the bell. Then she paused, her head tilted, listening.

'A cart,' Rosamund said. 'It's stopping — do you think it's Bobbie?'

Lucy was at the window, looking down into the street. 'Good God,' she said softly.

'What is it?' Roberta asked. Lucy didn't speak or turn. She rose to her feet anxiously. 'Lucy, what is it? Is that Bobbie?'

Lucy turned at last, a strange expression on her face. 'Yes, it's Bobbie. In a hired gig - most unsuitable.' She shook her head slightly in disbelief. 'He's got Marcus with him.'

All was confusion, voices, exclamations. Two of the footmen carried Marcus in, and Lucy directed them to put him in Bobbie's bed for the time being. He was barely conscious; thin, pale, extremely dirty, with a grimy bandage round his head and another round his torso under his shirt. His boots and frock-coat were missing, and he smelled to High Heaven, but, Lucy was glad to note, not of mortification. Her first quick examination suggested he was suffering from exposure and loss of blood, but she was naturally concerned about the head-wound.

Bobbie stood in the hall, beseiged by questions, looking bemused, relieved, and exhausted.

'Well, Bobbie, you were right all along! I must admit I didn't believe it,' Lucy said. 'I want to hear the whole story, but the first thing is to see to Marcus. Roberta, will you give me a hand?'

'Yes, of course. Bobbie, you must be starving. You won't have eaten all day.'

'I'm not hungry, Mama,' Bobbie said wearily. 'My head aches, rather — it was so hot out there today.'

'Rosamund, take Bobbie into the saloon and pour him a glass of wine, and don't bother him with questions until I come back,' said Lucy. 'He looks all in.'

Half an hour later the two women returned to the saloon. Bobbie was sitting in a high-backed chair, his eyes closed, while Rosamund sat opposite watching him, chin in hand, deep in thought.

'The skull isn't fractured, that's one thing,' Lucy said as she came in, and both young people started and sat up. 'It's a nasty wound, though. It looks to me as though a musket-

563

bullet creased his scalp, making him fall from his horse, and then in falling he hit his head on something. Probably he would have been unconscious for some hours. Then there's the other wound — a sword-gash in his side. He must have lost a lot of blood from it.'

'Did he speak? Did he know you?' Bobbie asked.

'He hasn't regained consciousness,' Lucy said. 'He seems to be very weak, which is hardly surprising, since he's been without food or water all this time. The wonder is he survived at all. Was he conscious when you found him?'

'Yes, just about. He knew who I was, anyway,' said Bobbie. He grimaced. 'He was damned glad to see me, too. It was the rummest thing, though. I can hardly believe it myself.'

'And where did you find him?' Lucy asked. 'On the battle-field, I suppose? How had he come to be missed?'

'No, ma'am, he wasn't on the battlefield,' Bobbie said. 'That's what's so strange.'

'Where was he, then?'

'I'll tell you the story,' said Bobbie.

His daily visits had not gone unnoticed, it seemed. There were various working parties on the battlefield, peasants performing the disagreeable but necessary task of digging pits and burying the unclaimed dead. When Bobbie had arrived in the gig to search the last area he had not yet combed — the corner near the village of Papelotte — one of the workers had accosted him and asked if he were looking for anyone in particular.

'His French was so awful it was hard to understand him. But I told him I was looking for my cousin, an officer, fair-haired, about my age, in a blue coat. I can tell you, Mama, I was glad I'd had a good tutor, who made me learn to speak French as well as read it.'

The man had grown excited, and Bobbie at last understood that there was a wounded officer in one of the houses nearby who fitted the description. He had offered, in exchange for money to take Bobbie there, and Bobbie had had no hesita-tion in agreeing.

'He took me to a cottage — well, just a hovel, really — up on the hillside. It was separate from the village, a dreadful, low sort of place. I got a bit suspicious — thought he was gammoning me, or meaning to rob me, but Marcus was there all right.' He stopped, looking a little dazed.

'Go on,' Rosamund prompted. 'What did you do?'

'I went in — the man stayed outside. He seemed nervous. He'd told me there was something strange about the woman who lived there — I suppose he thought she was a witch or something. It was hard to understand him. I expected it to be an old woman, but she was quite young, only I think — quite mad.'

'Mad? What can you mean?' Roberta asked.

'She was keeping Marcus there — not quite a prisoner, not that exactly, but she didn't mean to let him go. She'd bandaged his wounds and put him into her bed — it was the only piece of furniture in the room, apart from a table and a wooden stool — and she was sort of brooding over him, like a cat with a kitten. She'd given him water when he asked for it, but nothing else. I don't think she understood he needed to be fed. He would have died if I hadn't found him. He was so relieved when he saw me —' He had to stop and swallow. 'He was almost too weak to speak, but he clutched my hand and stared at me, as if he thought I might go away and leave him there.'

'But why would she do such a thing?' Roberta asked at last. 'Why would she keep him there?'

Bobbie looked at her dazedly. 'As I said, I think she was mad. The man helped me carry Marcus out and put him in the gig. She didn't try to stop us, only stood there wringing her hands and weeping. I tell you it was — I hated it! He told me, the man told me, that she'd lost her husband and three children all at the same time — some kind of fever, I suppose — I couldn't understand what. Since then she'd become, well, strange. I think perhaps she wanted Marcus to replace them, like a child, or even a pet.' He rubbed his eyes. 'I gave him all the money I had about me, and drove back here. And that's all.'

There was a silence. Then Roberta said, 'How horrible! My poor darling, it must have been dreadful for you.'

Lucy pondered. 'She may have saved his life, all the same. The wound in his side — he might have bled to death if it hadn't been bound up. What I'd like to know is how she got hold of him in the first place. Did she go down there and drag him up the hill? Did someone take him to her? Or perhaps he wandered there in his confusion. I suppose we'll never know.'

'Will he survive?' Rosamund asked, raising her eyes unwillingly to her mother's.

'There's every chance,' Lucy said. 'He's young and strong, and his wounds are not grave. He's been sheltered and given water — rest and good food should restore him to health. My only worry is whether the blow on the head might have disordered his senses — but he seems to have recognised Bobbie, which is a good sign. I suppose, Roberta, you ought to send a note to Lady Barbara. I don't really want her coming here and disturbing him, but she is his mother — it's only fair.'

'Yes, I suppose so,' Roberta said. She looked with concern at her son. 'Bobbie, you look so tired! I think perhaps you ought to go to bed.'

'Yes, I think so too,' he said rather thickly. He stood up, swayed, and had to catch hold of the chair-back.

Lucy went across to him and steadied him unobtrusively. 'I'll walk up with you. I want to check on Marcus again.'

Outside in the passageway she stopped him and laid a hand over his brow. 'Let me see your tongue,' she commanded. 'Hmm. I think you are a little feverish, young man.'

'It was very hot out there today,' he said defensively; then, 'I don't want Mama to worry.'

'All right,' said Lucy. 'I won't say anything. Straight to bed with you, and we'll see how you feel in the morning. It's been quite a strain on you, all this searching.'

'Yes,' he admitted. 'But I'm glad now. I almost gave up, you know. If I had —' He shuddered. They began to climb the stairs. 'I didn't tell you the worst thing. Well, I couldn't say it in front of Mama and Rosamund. But — in the cottage — there was only the one bed. Marcus wasn't lying in the middle of it.' He stopped and looked at Lucy, his eyes shadowed with horror. 'He was lying to one side. I couldn't get it out of my mind that she'd been sleeping in the bed with him all this time. And I thought — I thought — if he'd died — if I hadn't found him —' He swallowed. 'I wondered if she'd have gone on —'

'Don't,' Lucy said quickly. 'Your imagination is a little fevered, too. No more thinking, Bobbie — just sleep.'

'Yes, ma'am. Let me just look in at Marcus once more, though.'

Docwra was sitting by the bed, and the candle-light flowed back and forth across the thin face on the pillow as they came in and disturbed the air.

'He's awake,' Docwra said softly. Her eyes met Lucy's reassuringly. 'He's all right, I think, my lady.'

Lucy went across to the bed, and Marcus opened his eyes and looked up at her. 'Do you know who I am?' she said. After a moment he nodded slightly, and she smiled. 'Good. You're safe now. And you're going to be all right.' She placed a hand over his. 'You've lost a lot of blood and you're very weak, but rest and quiet and good food will soon bring you back to strength.' He looked as though he wanted to speak, and she pressed his hand. 'No questions now,' she said. 'Tomorrow you can talk all you like. Now you must sleep.'

He closed his eyes obediently, but then opened them, looking agitated. 'Bobbie?' he whispered.

Bobbie came forward, and Lucy moved back to let him take her place. 'I'm here, Marcus. Don't worry, you'll be all right now.'

Marcus's hand moved, and Bobbie took hold of it. Marcus fixed him with an urgent look. 'Knew you'd find me,' he said. 'Thanks — for not — giving up.'

Bobbie's eyes filled with tears. 'You'd have done the same for me.'

Marcus closed his eyes, faintly smiling. 'Best —' he began; then he was asleep.

The improvement in Marcus was astonishingly rapid: proper nursing, nourishing food and the elimination of anxiety restored him almost to normality, apart from a natural weakness and langour. He slept a great deal, waking to take regular nourishment, and seeming happy just to look at the familiar walls around him. Rosamund sat with him a good deal of the time, as being the person most easily spared.

The second day, he told her his side of the story. 'I don't remember being wounded, or falling. I suppose the head-

wound caused that. I don't remember anything about it a
all.'

'Concussion,' Rosamund said. 'Mama says you'd have been
unconscious for some time.'

'I suppose so. I simply don't remember. The first thing I
knew, I was in that bed in that damned little shack, feeling as
weak as a newborn kitten, with a headache like a volley from
the entire French artillery. And there *she* was, looking at me.'
He shuddered.

'Don't think about it,' Rosamund said.

'She cared for me, you know,' he went on. 'That was the
strange thing. And yet I was getting weaker and weaker. If
Bobbie hadn't found me, I'd be dead by now.' He shook his
head.

'Well he did find you, and you're safe now. It's over. All
you have to do now is get your strength back.'

'Yes — though as soon as I'm strong enough, Mama will
want to take me away,' he said ruefully. 'Perhaps even
before.' It had only been Lucy's intervention which had
rescued him from his mother's joy that first morning. Lady
Barbara had wanted to get Marcus out of Brussels and away
from the increasing danger of typhus, and Lucy had needed
all her powers of persuasion to convince her that he must not
be moved for several days yet. Lady Barbara had evidently
suspected some kind of plot, but the sight of Marcus had
finally convinced her.

'As soon as you're strong enough, I suppose you'll want to
go after the Duke and be in at the kill, like Papa Danby,'
Rosamund said cheerfully, to give his mind another direction.

'I'd like it, but Mama would never stand for it. I'm to sell
out and go home with her. Now that Papa's dead, she'll need
me.'

He brooded a little, and Rosamund kept a tactful silence.
Then he moved his hand across the counterpane and
captured hers from her lap. She started and looked at him
warily.

'Ros,' he said, 'I want to tell you how sorry I am about
Tantony. He was a fine man, and he fought bravely. He's a
great loss to us all.'

Rosamund looked away. 'Don't,' she said.

He kept her hand fast. 'I'm your oldest friend,' he said. 'I care about you. I want you to know I'm here, if ever you need me. I would give my life to serve you.'

'There's nothing I need,' she said.

He persisted. 'I know it's not the moment to say it, Ros, but one day, when you've recovered from the shock — well, I'll still be here. I love you, and I want to marry you, and in time, when you're ready to start again —'

'Marcus, I've told you,' she said with gentle exasperation, 'Mother would never give permission for us to marry. Nothing's changed.'

'I think it has,' he said. 'The battle — what we've all been through — it has changed things. I don't think your mother would refuse now, if it was what you wanted.'

She drew back her hand. This was not the time. He was too weak and vulnerable for her to tell him it was not what she wanted. She evaded his eyes and hurried on, 'It would be the height of folly for us to marry without money. We could never be happy. You may think me mercenary, but I wasn't made to live in poverty. It would wear me down, and we should quarrel, and everything would be horrid. It's out of the question, Marcus. Please don't speak of it again.'

He sighed a little. 'All right, we won't talk about it now. I shouldn't have mentioned it — I'm sorry. It's too soon. There's plenty of time. We have all our lives ahead of us.' Rosamund said nothing. He studied her profile for a moment, and then said, 'Where's Bobbie? I thought he would have been in to see me.'

'Mama says you aren't to be excited, and if your mother's coming later, you mustn't have any more visitors. In fact,' she added quickly, standing up, 'I ought to leave you now to rest. You'll need to build up your strength, for I'm sure your Mama will cry over you again.'

He was not distracted. 'Bobbie wouldn't excite me. That's nonsense. Why hasn't he been in to see me? Is something wrong?' She didn't answer, and he grew alarmed. 'Are you keeping something from me?'

She hesitated. 'Of course not. Why should I?'

She was a bad liar. He struggled to sit up. 'What's happened to him? Ros, you must tell me. Where is he? For

God's sake, I'm not a child — I don't need protecting.'

Rosamund pushed him back down. 'All right, but don't te
Mama I told you. Bobbie's sick.'

'Sick? What do you mean, sick?'

'They thought it was just being out in the sun all da
without food,' she said unwillingly. 'But it seems — well, he'
got typhus fever.'

Marcus's face seemed to grow more gaunt. 'Typhus! Oh m
God!'

'He's in one of the attic rooms, to keep him away from
everyone. Mama's with him, and Aunt Roberta.'

'How bad is he?' Marcus clutched her hand. 'Tell me th
truth.'

'Mama says he's got a good chance. He's young and strong
It's all in the nursing, she says.'

'It's my fault,' he said, staring at the wall. 'It's all my
fault.'

'Don't be stupid!'

'I know how he got it — wandering about the battlefiel
amongst all the corpses, looking for me. Oh my God! And I
was safe in that cottage, while he was risking his life —'

'It wasn't your fault. There was nothing you could do
about it. And in any case, he's going to be all right.'

'I should have known, when he didn't come and see me.
And Aunt Roberta hasn't been in either. Oh, Bobbie, Bobbie!'

'Stop it, Marcus! You'll work yourself into a fever, and that
won't help anyone. I shouldn't have told you —'

'Yes you should. Ros, promise me you'll keep telling me. I
want to know how he is. Find out, and tell me everything —
please!'

'All right, but only if you'll promise to keep quiet and not
fret. Mama will get him through it, you'll see.'

Mr Pobgee was much less surprised at Jasper's presence, his
story and his decision than the Morland brothers had
expected him to be. All the same, he would not have been an
attorney if caution had not run in his veins.

'Have you consulted your man of business?' he asked
Jasper. 'My dear young man, you must do nothing without
advice.'

Jasper almost smiled. 'How you men of the law stick together! I have consulted Mr Whetlore, sir, and he disagrees with me profoundly. I am here expressly against his advice.'

'But in that case —'

'Mr Whetlore *wants* the case to go to Chancery,' Jasper continued, 'and I have already explained why I cannot allow that to happen.'

'I think you are very wise,' Pobgee said, nodding. 'I advised against it myself. These Chancery cases are not the thing at all. Have I not said so to you, James, from the very beginning?'

'Well, what's to be done, then?' Edward said restlessly. 'How is it to be resolved?'

'I've told you,' Jasper said, 'that I give up all claim. I'll sign a paper, if that's what you want.'

Edward looked at Pobgee.

'A legal document could be drawn up to that effect,' Pobgee said slowly. 'The Will will still have to be proved, but if no counter-evidence is presented, our medical witness's opinion as to the time of death will be accepted, and Mrs Hawker will be deemed to have inherited before her demise.'

'Well, then,' Jasper said, turning his head away, 'be it so. I'm sick of it.'

Pobgee smiled. 'You are an impatient young man, if you will forgive me! But impatience and the law do not go well in harness. I must consult her ladyship in the matter, before taking any final action.'

'But she's in Brussels,' Edward objected.

'I shall write to her,' Pobgee said. 'Be assured, I shall not waste any time.'

'Then I had better go back to Manchester,' Jasper said, standing up.

That made James laugh. 'What, this minute? Do you mean to walk? There's no coach until the morning. You must stay another night, at least.'

'Oh, longer than that,' Edward said quickly. 'Will you not spend a few days with us? It's so long since we had any company — and you're a better whist-player than Miss Rosedale. Do stay — a week, at the very least.'

Jasper looked at him, bemused. 'You are very kind, sir —'

'Not kind at all. We are kin, of a sort, are we not? Well, hastily, 'no need to work out the heres and theres of it. Jamie tell Mr Hobsbawn he must stay.'

James complied gravely. 'You will be doing us a grea service. I'm damnable bad company for Ned, fretful as I am And I'm sure there are a thousand things Pobgee will want t discuss with you.'

Pobgee bowed his head. 'I cannot undertake to advise you myself, placed as I am, but you ought, indeed you ought, sir to take legal advice. If you will not think it impertinent, I can recommend a colleague of mine to you.'

Jasper yielded. 'I still say there is nothing to discuss. But I shall be happy to stay a few days. It must not be longer, for I don't like to be away from the mills. I've good foremen, but there are things they cannot decide for themselves.'

'Then that's settled,' said Ned, pleased. 'Thank you, Mr Hobsbawn.'

'Nay, it's for me to thank you,' Jasper said. 'I have little company at home, and little comfort. It will be a great pleasure to me.'

For the rest of that day, Edward enjoyed himself shewing Jasper over the estate, and then over the house, until James remarked to Father Aislaby that it looked as though Ned meant to sell the place by the trouble he was taking to make Hobsbawn in love with it. Father Aislaby replied a little sharply that Edward was enjoying the company of an intelligent, sensible man, and what was surprising about that?

James only shrugged. For himself, he was glad that Hobsbawn had come to the right decision, and that Fanny's inheritance was to be hers after all. He couldn't see why there should be any delay — let Pobgee write out some form and have Hobsbawn sign it before he changed his mind — that was how he would like to see the cards played.

But Fanny's inheritance was of secondary importance to him at the moment. First and foremost he wanted news of Héloïse and Sophie. He missed Héloïse so much! He hated turning over in the night and finding the other half of the bed cold and empty. He missed talking to her. He missed her company, her love, her perfect understanding. And Sophie — dear little Sophie — his only daughter now! Why had he ever allowed them to go to Brussels? He must have been mad — literally mad.

The image of Angelica came before him, and then that of her father, grave and reproachful. He writhed inwardly at the memory of that episode. And then there had been his boys — he had not been a careful guardian in Héloïse's absence. His mind shied away from recollection — things he had said and done: he wanted to forget, wanted things to be the way they were before. He had lost Fanny, and that loss would be with him for the rest of his life; but he had the sense to realise now that there was yet so much more to lose.

If only she came back safely — if only *they* came back safely — he would conduct matters differently. He would shew he knew how to appreciate what he had. He would be a model husband and father, revel in his family, and be content with them and nothing more for the rest of his life. And he would never, ever, let Héloïse out of his sight again.

On the following day, the 22nd of June, the news of the battle of Waterloo reached York from London. The city erupted in relief and jubilation, mingled with anxiety to see the lists of the killed and wounded. Everyone knew someone who had been in the battle, if they hadn't a husband, son, uncle, brother, nephew or cousin directly involved. No-one could talk about anything else; little work was done anywhere in the city that day, except by club-servants and innkeepers and tapsters and waiters.

The Duke of Wellington had his health drunk many a thousand time, and Boney was proclaimed no match for him. Everyone had always known how it would be, and everyone was scornful of everyone else, who had thought it was all up after Quatre-Bras. Everyone else hotly denied it, and declared that, on the contrary, it was everyone who had been quaking in his shoes; everyone else had never doubted for an instant that the Dook would prevail. Thus many a brisk fight broke out, to be dampened down a few minutes later with another round and another toast to Old Hookey — God bless him! There never was his equal!

James's immediate fears were relieved by the knowledge that the French had not got closer than ten miles to Brussels, and were even now posting away as fast as they could in the opposite direction. But no sooner were his anxieties for his family's physical welfare relieved than he began to worry how the shock and strain must have affected their minds and sensibilities.

'Why don't they come home? They must come home!' he said over and over again. He thought of the horrors they might witness in the aftermath of the battle, and moaned. 'Perhaps I should go and fetch them? I should never have let them go in the first place! Oh why don't they come home?'

'They're probably on their way this very minute,' Ned said, trying to keep his patience. 'There's nothing you can do, Jamie. If you go, you'll probably cross with them, and miss them altogether.'

But intense as his sufferings were, they were correspondingly short. The evening of the next day brought the excited sounds of arrival in the great hall, and James erupted from the drawing-room to find the two travellers, swaying with weariness, being divested of their travelling-cloaks and bonnets by the eager servants.

James stood still and stared. Héloïse looked smaller and thinner than he remembered her, her face drawn with weariness and anxiety, though she smiled patiently at the greetings from the servants, and automatically caressed the frantic Kithra, who was doing his best to knock her down, the better to be able to lick her from head to foot. She looked as though her attention were frayed to the very snapping-point, and that if one more thing were demanded of her, she would simply break into small pieces.

Then she saw him and her eyes widened, and her lips began to curve into a smile of joy; only to stop as she remembered the terms on which they had parted. The very dearness of her overcame him; took him like a twig snatched away by a flood. He crossed the hall without any knowledge of having done it, and then she was in his arms, and he was crushing her against him, his cheek pressed against the top of her head, and hot tears burning his eyelids.

At last he let her go just enough to tilt her head back so that he could see her face. Her smile was troubled, her eyes longing and doubting.

'I've missed you,' he said. 'Please, never go away again.'

It was enough. 'Oh, my James,' she said.

The way she said his name made him tremble with old and lovely associations. He kissed her. People were crowding around, others were going to demand her attention, he and she were going to have to wait for hours to be alone to say everything they wanted to say. But some things could not wait.

'Are you all right?' he demanded. 'I've missed you so —'

'Yes. We're all right. But, James,' in a low voice, 'Sophie's young man was killed.'

'Her young man?'

'Didn't you get my letter about him?' He shook his head quickly. 'I'll tell you all about it later. Be gentle with her now. She's very unhappy.'

'I will.' He pressed his mouth to her ear. 'I love you, Marmoset.'

A warm, breathy whisper. 'I love you too, my James.'

And now he must release her, let the others have their turn. Here were the little boys clamouring to be kissed, Miss Rosedale smiling, glad, and all the servants pressing into the hall, with Barnard to the fore, almost weeping in his pleasure.

And here was Sophie, pale and sorrowing, waiting for her father's greeting. He went to her, took her cold hands in his, looked down at her. Her face had grown thinner, but not just with grief. He saw that something else had happened to her before the tragedy had quenched her smiles.

'My little Sophie,' he said gently. 'You've grown up.'

'Papa,' she said. She didn't smile; her eyes were bleak; but her hands grew warm in his. He pulled her to him, and she returned his hug.

'I'm glad you're back, Sophie. I've missed you. We must spend more time together now. We'll have a long talk tomorrow.'

Ned was there, kissing Héloïse. 'I'm glad you're back. The house is not the same without you.'

Then Héloïse said, 'Where's Father Aislaby?'

'In the drawing-room with our guest,' said Ned, looking towards James.

'Guest?' said Héloïse.

'It's Jasper Hobsbawn,' James said, and briefly explained the reason for his presence. 'I'll tell you more later, when we have time. For now, I suppose we must go and be polite to him.'

'Of course we must,' Héloïse said at once. 'Poor man, how sad he must have been, and worried. And how good and brave of him to do what he has done. We must assure him that we don't want to take his mills from him.'

Ned and James both spoke at once.

'Oh Lord, don't say that — !'

'For Heaven's sake, don't mention anything of the sort —!'

Ned took it up. 'Just don't say anything yet, Héloïse, please. Wait until you've spoken to Pobgee about it.'

Héloïse looked tired and distracted. 'Oh, very well. But I must say something to reassure him, and I shall. Come, James, let us go through.' She held out her hand. 'Sophie, my love!'

Jasper Hobsbawn was on his feet, waiting for the first glimpse of the woman who was to have everything he had worked for all his life. She was not what he expected. A small, thin woman, hardly bigger than a child, with a long, dark face that would have been ugly if it weren't for the beauty of the eyes and of the gentle smile. She came forward, her hand outstretched in welcome.

'Mr Hobsbawn, I am so glad to see you. It is very good of you to come so far, and on such a mission,' She glanced sideways at her husband and brother-in-law. 'They tell me I must not say anything to you until I have seen Mr Pobgee; but I cannot help it. I must say this much — that if the mills *are* to belong to me, you shall have a share in them. I wish justice to be done.'

'Thank you,' said Jasper, blinking, a little bemused. 'But —'

'We shall talk more about it tomorrow,' Héloïse said with decision.'I hope you are making a long stay with us now? Here is our daughter, by the way — Fanny's half-sister. Sophie, this is Mr Hobsbawn, Fanny's cousin.'

Sophie came forward obediently to shake hands. Jasper looked, and looked again, and forgot to release her hand. The gentle, sad, lovely face aroused in him a strange desire both to weep, and to rush out and kill anyone who ever threatened this tender creature's happiness. Her dark eyes lifted to his, and he saw a faint, fleeting resemblance to Fanny — too elusive to be pinned to any particular feature. She had something of a look of Fanny, that was all. But where Fanny had been hard, glittering, fierce, predatory — a beautiful and untamed animal — her half-sister was all womanliness, all gentleness. Sophie, he thought, looked as Fanny might have done if she had been as God intended women to be.

'I'm honoured to make your acquaintance, Miss Morland,' he said, gazing down at her; and the words seemed entirely inadequate to the occasion.

The evening seemed endless. Outside the windows the life of Brussels went on unheeding in the long summer twilight. Roberta sat as if she had been turned to stone. Lucy pretended to read. Rosamund sewed, hardly aware of what she was doing — every stitch would have to be unpicked again later. There was nothing anyone wanted to say, and yet they all hated the silence, for it was peopled with unwelcome thoughts.

'If only we could go home,' Lucy said at last. 'If only our men would come back. Now Boney's abdicated again, surely it can't be long?'

'What will happen to him?' Rosamund asked, glad to have something to talk about. 'When they catch him, will they kill him?'

Lucy shook her head. 'I don't think so. The world would be a safer place if he were dead, but I don't believe our government can be his executioner. Probably they will lock him up somewhere. Another island — smaller and more remote this time — and with gaolers to keep him in. Unless his own people kill him. Fouché might do it — he's capable of anything.'

The silence fell again. Lucy looked at Roberta and wondered what she would do now. Peter Firth would surely come back at once when he heard. His job might be important, but Bobbie had been her only son: she had nothing left now but her husband. Perhaps, though, it would be better if she didn't go home to England, if the Firths made

577

a new life for themselves in the new Europe that was going to be fashioned from the broken pieces of the old. In England there would be too much to remind her. In England — in London — she would have to witness every day the progress of the young man who had taken her son's title, and whose rescue had claimed her son's life.

Lucy thought how ironic the whole thing was — how one might laugh if one weren't so intimately involved with the victims of the drama. Marcus, who had always loved Bobbie like a brother, had never wanted the title his mother so longed to see bestowed on him; had wanted nothing more than to be a soldier and follow the drum without responsibilities. Well, he would have to sell out now. Lucy remembered how he had cried when she told him; how he had railed against fate, and wished he had died instead. It was partly his weakness, of course — though he had made an astonishing recovery — but she thought, too, that he and Bobbie had known their own natures very well. Bobbie had been well suited to the burden he had been called to; Marcus would bear it very ill. And of the two, in a strange way, the quiet Bobbie had been the stronger: Marcus would find it hard to go on without Bobbie's support.

Ironic, too, to think about Colonel Morland — Cousin Horace, who had always wanted to be earl, who had believed himself cheated of what was rightfully his when his childless brother married again and Bobbie was born. He had missed succeeding to the title by a matter of days. He had only to have survived the battle, and he would now be 8th Earl of Chelmsford, with a joyful wife, and a son to succeed him.

How ironic that it was Bobbie who had died while Marcus survived! It was an irony she feared Roberta would never learn to accept. She had refused to allow Bobbie to go to war, because she did not want him to risk his life; Marcus, of course, might do as he pleased. And Marcus had come back almost unscathed from dreadful peril while Bobbie — she didn't like to think of how Bobbie had died. Typhus didn't take its victims gently. He had raved, at the end, before the soaring fever had burned him out like a piece of paper. He had thought he was still searching for Marcus amongst the corpses.

There had been little anyone could do. There was no treatment for typhus but nursing: the victims either got better or died, and most of them died. Bobbie had been exhausting himself day after day with his searching, and with his anxiety, guilt and grief. When it came to it, he had not had the strength left to fight the illness. His struggle had been brief — he had sunk rapidly.

Well, Lady Barbara had what she wanted now. She had taken Marcus away, and would by now be on her way to Antwerp and thence to England with the new earl and her bewildered, weeping daughter. Barbarina had loved Bobbie almost as much as Marcus. Lucy remembered with bitter humour how her ladyship had admonished her daughter not to be selfish, not to regret Bobbie's death. It's better this way, she had said. Before, even if you had married Bobbie, Marcus would have been unprovided for. Now your brother's an earl, you can marry anyone you please. Strange as it seemed, Barbarina hadn't seemed to find any comfort in the thought.

Lucy glanced at her daughter, and there found the only glimmer of relief in the darkness that Bobbie's death had spread all around those who had loved him. There was at least no longer any reason why Rosamund should not marry Marcus. He had title and fortune now, and even his mother would no longer object to the match, especially since it was what Marcus wanted. It was hard to fathom what Rosamund's feelings were. She must regret Tantony's death — she had certainly been fond of him — but Marcus was now by far the better match. Lucy had always had doubts that Tantony's fortune was sufficient, and that Rosamund would settle to a quiet life out of the public eye.

She would be able now to be a countess, and live a full and stimulating life. And Marcus had always been her hero — the first love of her childhood. Of course, she had grown up in the last few months, and changed a great deal, but she and Marcus knew each other very well, and now that there was equality of rank and fortune, they would make a very pretty pair and probably deal excellently together. It would be a match to satisfy everyone, Lucy thought. They might marry as soon as a decent period of mourning had passed.

Rosamund felt the eyes on her, and looked up, and in an

unwelcome access of sympathy knew exactly what her mother
was thinking. The knowledge sank through her mind like a
stone. She saw how it would be: there would be no escaping it.
Everyone would expect her to marry Marcus, and the expectation would have its way, especially as it was what Marcus
himself now wanted. It was ironic, she thought, to consider
that Bobbie would have been pleased that this good had come
out of his death. Bobbie would have been glad that she was to
marry his hero. It was enough, she thought, to make one
laugh; except that she felt a great deal more like crying.